What readers are saying about The Song of the River series

"A new historical series has readers ty
Mississippi with memorable charac
themselves and their families. These e a
long-ago era of riverboat adventures he
story line. They work very well toget

—*Romantic Times*

"Diane Ashley and Aaron McCarver have written a beautiful story of the South right before the Civil War. You will feel immersed in the Southern culture and setting."

—Margaret Daley, author of *From This Day Forward*

"I loved this book. Well-developed characters I really cared about, authentically detailed setting, and a story line that kept me riveted through the pages."

—Lena Nelson Dooley, author of *Mary's Blessing*, *Maggie's Journey*, and *Love Finds You in Golden, New Mexico*—a Will Rogers Medallion Award winner

"Soft as a Southern breeze, the compelling characters wrap round your heart and won't let go."

—Laura Frantz, author of *The Colonel's Lady*

"The collaboration of Diane Ashley and Aaron McCarver brings a tale as steeped in the flavor of the South as a frosty glass of sweet tea."

—Marcia Gruver, author of the Backwoods Brides and Texas Fortune series

"Ashley and McCarver have created a lasting tale as poignant and deep as the river upon which it's set."

—Elizabeth Ludwig, author and creator of The Borrowed Book

"With the skillful use of rich and well-researched setting description, vivid scenes, and realistic dialogue authors Diane Ashley and Aaron McCarver have crafted a riveting historical romance that is sure to leave fans swooning."

—Debby Mayne, author of the Class Reunion series

"This charming tale. . .is sure to capture your heart and leave you smiling at the end."

—Vickie McDonough, award-winning author of the Texas Boardinghouse Brides series

"With brilliant style, the team of Ashley and McCarver has perfectly blended Mississippi gentility and steamboat adventure. You will enter the characters' world and experience the excitement and dangers they endure in this gripping tale."

—Janelle Mowery, author of the Colorado Runaway series

"I have a special fondness for Southern literature and if the same is true for you, I think you're going to find *Lily* to be a pleasurable gem."

—Tracie Peterson, award-winning, bestselling author of over ninety-five books, including the Striking a Match series and *House of Secrets*

"Diane Ashley and Aaron McCarver have created a compelling tapestry of characters who live their lives, loves, and faith in a fascinating era of American history in an enchanting location along the Mississippi. Their attention to detail helps frame the story and tempts the reader to forget the armchair in which she's sitting."

—Cynthia Ruchti, past president of American Christian Fiction Writers and author of the 2011 Carol Finalist *They Almost Always Come Home*

"Ashley and McCarver have woven a tale as gentle as a summer breeze and as treacherous as a shifting sandbar."

—Erica Vetsch, author of *A Bride's Portrait of Dodge City, Kansas*

"*Gone with the Wind* meets *The African Queen*. This book has all the action and adventure of the grand riverboat days, coupled with all the romance and grandeur of a pre-Civil-War South."

—Lenora Worth, *New York Times* bestselling author

Diane T. Ashley &
Aaron McCarver

Print ISBN 978-1-63058-455-9

eBook Editions:
Adobe Digital Edition (.epub) 978-1-63409-253-1
Kindle and MobiPocket Edition (.prc) 978-1-63409-254-8

All scripture quotations are taken from the King James Version of the Bible.

This book is a work of fiction. Names, characters, places, and incidents are either products of the author's imagination or used fictitiously. Any similarity to actual people, organizations, and/or events is purely coincidental.

Cover Photo: Johner Images/GettyImages

For more information about Diane T. Ashley and Aaron McCarver, please access the author's website at the following Internet address: www.dianeashleybooks.com

Published by Shiloh Run Press, an imprint of Barbour Publishing, Inc., P.O. Box 719, Uhrichsville, Ohio 44683, www.shilohrunpress.com.

Our mission is to publish and distribute inspirational products offering exceptional value and biblical encouragement to the masses.

Printed in the United States of America.

Lily

Dedication

Aaron: I dedicate this book to my best friend, William D. Devore, Jr. It is hard to put into words how much you mean to me. The closest of friends for over twenty years, God has used you in so many ways in my life. I have learned so many things from you: how to be more patient, how to not allow life to stress me out, and how to be a true friend, to only name a few. Like David and Jonathan, God has knit us together as true brothers. You are indeed a special gift from God to me, one that I will always treasure. "As iron sharpens iron. . ."

Diane: For Deborah and the "Walleen" sisters: Good memories with great friends. Thanks for your supportive words, caring hearts, and wise advice. The true measure of our friendship is that it remains strong even when our pathways diverge. All three of you are precious to me, and I treasure the times when we are together. May God continue to bless you as you have blessed me.

We, of all people, know what a collaborative effort a book truly is. We would like to thank the many people who helped us with our newest endeavor:

Our agent, Steve Laube, who tirelessly works on our behalf and muddles through legalese and other languages foreign to us.

Our editors, Becky Germany and Becky Fish, and the wonderful team at Barbour. May God bless our work beyond what we can possibly imagine to bring about His will.

And a special thank-you to Dr. Don Hubele and his Bibliography and Research class of Spring 2011 for your invaluable research assistance: Naomi Ahern, Amanda Barber, Christopher Bonner, Kirsten Callahan, Salina Cervantes, Alexander Crowson, Samantha Edwards, Ebony Epps, Kathleen Hennessy, Erin Hoover, Evan Jones, Allison Kalehoff, Krista Kliewer, Bonnie McCoy, Angela Morgan, Mary Morris, Aubry Myers, Chelsea Randle, Karisa Rowlands, Mark Samsel, Megan Timbs, Isaiah Tolo, Deanna Vanderver, Phillip Williams.

Chapter One

Natchez, Mississippi
Spring 1859

Lily Anderson watched the passing scenery from the comfort of her uncle's carriage. Stately mansions with manicured grounds gave way to the smaller, sturdy homes of local merchants as they traveled toward the Mississippi River. They passed a busy mercantile and several shops before the carriage took a sharp leftward downturn toward the raucous, bustling dock that lay far beneath the genteel residences of Natchez's wealthy plantation owners and merchants.

Natchez Under-the-Hill. She sniffed the air appreciatively as she disembarked, picking up the scents of fresh coffee, burning wood, and fish. How she loved the river. She barely noticed the disreputable, rickety inns and saloons that sprouted like weeds on either side of the winding road called Silver Street.

Roustabouts slumbered in the scant shade of ramshackle buildings while a pair of glassy-eyed Indians staggered down the street, each clutching a brown bottle close to his chest. Lily's eyes widened at their blatant drunkenness, but their presence did not deter her eagerness to absorb every detail of her surroundings as she followed Aunt Dahlia.

Voices shouted in an exciting mix of languages. . .English, French, German, and even lilting Norwegian dialects. The latter brought disturbing memories, but Lily pushed them away, determined to enjoy her outing on the river.

As she and her aunt picked their way past bales of cotton and barrels of tobacco, her gaze absorbed the myriad boats lining the banks. Rugged keelboats and waterlogged rafts butted up against lofty steamboats, each awaiting cargo or passengers to be transported downriver to the port of New Orleans.

"Don't dawdle, Lily." Aunt Dahlia's annoyed tone drew her forward.

Lily would have liked more time to soak in the energy and color of the busy landing area. If she had her way, she would spend every afternoon down here. Sometimes she dreamed she would even have her own riverboat, *Water Lily*, and ply the crowded waters of the wide river. If not for the accident that took her parents, she would not have to dream. She would already live on the river.

A snap of her aunt's fingers brought Lily back to the present. "Come along, girl. Quit gawking like a simpleton." Aunt Dahlia shook her head. "One would think you had not grown up in Natchez."

Lily glanced toward her aunt, comparing her to the memory of her mother, the sweet and gentle woman whom God had called home far too quickly. Her aunt could never match the beauty and spirit that flowed from Mama. Aunt Dahlia was more. . .commanding. At a height of five foot eight, she towered over the other ladies and most of the gentlemen in Natchez society. Mama had been much shorter and more genteel. Even though her mother had died nearly a decade ago, if Lily closed her eyes, she could see Mama's shiny blond hair and laughing blue eyes. Aunt Dahlia, however, had inherited her father's coloring, her hair and eyes as brown as the river flowing along the nearby bank. When she was vexed, her upper lip thinned out and nearly disappeared. It was hard to imagine that Mama, so happy and carefree, was Aunt Dahlia's sister or that the two women had shared a common upbringing.

"I'm coming, Aunt Dahlia."

"I've never seen you move so slowly, girl. What's the matter with you?" Her aunt sniffed and reached for the handkerchief in her reticule. "One would think you don't appreciate your good fortune in being able to attend the Champneys' party. The invitation indicated we should arrive prior to three or risk being left at the dock."

Sunlight beamed down on them, warming Lily's shoulders. "It cannot be—"

A young boy barreled into Lily, nearly knocking her over. "Oof." Sharp pain distracted her as her teeth stabbed her tongue. A sudden tug separated her reticule from her forearm, and the child raced off, triumphantly escaping with her belongings clutched to his dirty chest.

Forgetting that she was not chasing one of her sisters in the gardens at home, Lily grabbed her skirts and dashed after him. "Stop, thief!"

Heads turned, but no one seemed to absorb the meaning of her words, or perhaps no one wanted to help.

Lily couldn't let him get away with her reticule. It held too many valuables, like the handkerchief her sister had embroidered for her last year. Was the distance between them narrowing? It seemed so. She pushed her legs to their limit. He would have to stop running at the bank. There was nowhere for him to go.

But she underestimated her quarry. He glanced back, and she caught a glimpse of his wide green eyes. She bunched her skirt with one hand and reached out with the other, nearly catching hold of his skinny arm.

The boy avoided her grasp by inches and sprinted up the muddy bank. He hesitated a bare instant before leaping across a narrow stretch of stagnant water to land like a cat on the deck of a barge laden with wooden casks.

Lily stood panting, her gaze clashing with the young thief's. "Come back here with my bag!" Forming the words made her tongue sting, but she ignored the pain.

An impish grin split the boy's freckled face. "Come take it from me." He made a face before turning away.

Frustration boiled through her. Lily measured the distance to the boat. She would have to leap across nearly two feet of water. She would never make it.

The boy walked to the front end of the barge and jumped from it to a side-wheeler, one of the steamboats whose giant paddle wheel was mounted along its center instead of its back end.

She paralleled his progress on the bank, hoping to find a way to reach him. Squinting against the sunlight, she thought she could see a gangplank ahead that had been extended to the bank. Perhaps she could catch up with him there and wrest her property from his thieving hands.

A steamboat whistle blew its mournful tones, and a nearby paddle wheel began to thrash the water. The sound must have distracted the boy as he jumped once more because he misjudged the distance. Lily watched in horror as his feet teetered on the edge of the steamboat deck he was trying to reach. Then he fell backward into the river and disappeared.

"Help!" She croaked the word, her throat dry from her exertions. Lily took a deep breath and tried again. "Help—man—overboard!" Her shout was louder and garnered more attention from the nearby deckhands.

The many boats vying for space near the bank made the water appear paved with decks. Lily pointed a shaking hand to the place where the towheaded boy had disappeared. Time stretched endlessly as she waited to see if he would resurface. Had he drowned?

Her heart faltered. She should not have chased him. A prayer of supplication slipped from her lips as guilt pressed down on her.

"What's going on out here?" A tall, dark-haired man strode onto the deck of the steamboat where the child had fallen. His eyes, as blue as a summer sky, sharpened as he glared at her. "Are you responsible for all the noise?"

She gulped in air and nodded. "Child. . .overboard. . .chasing." The steamboat rocked gently in the water, and she gasped. If they started the huge paddle at the back of the boat, the child might be dragged into it and killed.

His gaze left hers and swept the water. A gurgle alerted him, and he ran to the edge of his steamboat, dropping to one knee in a fluid movement and reaching into the water. When his hand lifted up, she could see the child's wet blond hair and waxen face. The stranger heaved mightily and lifted the boy onto the deck.

A roustabout appeared from the darkened recesses of the steamship. He looked over to her before swinging a narrow plank toward the bank.

Lily ran across as soon as it touched the ground.

"You ought to keep a closer eye on your child." The tall man knelt over the boy, but his gaze speared her.

She could feel her cheeks warming under his intense stare. How rude. Did he really think she was old enough to be the boy's mother? Her mouth opened and closed, reminding her once again of her aching tongue.

The boy coughed and pushed himself to a sitting position, relieving her concern that he had drowned.

The stranger slapped him on the back. "You're going to be okay, son."

The boy nodded and coughed again.

"Don't you have anything to say for yourself?" A lock of coal-black hair fell across the rescuer's forehead, making her want to reach out and push it back. Shocked at the errant thought, she dragged her mind back to the subject at hand.

"I'm. . .he's not—"

"He's not dead, no thanks to you." The man stood up and pushed back the lock of hair with an impatient hand. His eyes were hard and cold.

Before Lily could order her thoughts, the discharge of a gun made her jump.

The stranger took two steps forward, placing his body between her and the dock. "Get back." He pulled his own weapon free of his holster, holding it easily.

Lily's heart thumped in time with the paddle wheel on the boat next to them. She sidled up closer to the tall stranger and peeked around his shoulder. "What's going on?"

The man did not answer. All she could see was a knot of men standing on the dock. One of them was pointing back the way she had come, and Lily suddenly thought of Aunt Dahlia. Had she been hurt? Robbed? Had the cutpurse who had gotten her own reticule been a distraction to separate the two of them?

Unseen hands shoved rudely against the small of her back, unbalancing Lily. She tried to stop her headlong sprawl, but it was no use. She fell hard against the stranger, and he tumbled toward the deck, too. Squeezing her eyes shut, Lily waited for what seemed an eternity for the impact.

Crash. The deck wasn't as hard as she had thought it would be. She opened one eye and looked into his startled blue gaze. The stranger's body had cushioned her fall. Somehow he had landed on his backside, so now she was lying on top of him, her nose squashed up against the brass buttons of his brocade vest. "Oh!"

"Are you hurt?" His hands grabbed her shoulders.

"No." The sound was so soft she couldn't hear it herself. She'd never had so much trouble with her voice. Lily swallowed. "I'm fine." Much better. She pushed against his chest but somehow felt bereft when his hands let go of her. It must be relief she was feeling at being freed. It couldn't be disappointment. . . .

"This is what I get for being a Good Samaritan." The irony in his voice stung like a wasp.

Lily slid off him and sat up, one hand checking to see if her hat, a small white cap edged with the same blue lace as her dress, had been knocked awry. It was still firmly affixed. Probably due to Tamar's careful work of securing it this morning.

The stranger stood up, holstered his gun, and brushed dirt from his clothing, taking an inordinate amount of time. He reached out a hand to help her stand.

She would have liked to refuse it, but she didn't want any of the strangers on the dock to witness her efforts to stand on her own, so she grimaced and put her hand in his.

He pulled her up with ease, nearly jerking her arm out of its socket. "Don't expect me to continue rescuing your rambunctious son, madam." Again with that thick irony.

How dare he? She was not some wayward female. She was the victim. "He's not my son!" There, she'd finally gotten the words out.

"Well, whoever he is, he's not staying around to thank his rescuer."

Lily swung around to see the thief disappearing around a bend in the road. "He took my reticule."

"I see. Well, I doubt your reticule survived the dunking in the river. I suppose now you expect me to chase after him, but you'll have to look elsewhere for a knight-errant." He turned on his heel and stomped toward the interior of the steamboat.

Lily looked after him for a moment before collecting herself. She wondered about the gunshot that had distracted her and the stranger but shrugged. No telling in this part of town. It could have been an argument over words, goods, or even a loose woman.

She made her way to the bank and plodded tiredly back to her aunt. Lily sighed, steeling herself for the lecture she was sure awaited her arrival. At least Aunt Dahlia seemed unharmed, if not happy.

Chapter Two

"Where have you been?" Snapping brown eyes inspected Lily's appearance. Aunt Dahlia's exaggerated sigh reminded her of the woman's penchant for blowing every incident out of proportion. "Do you have to act the hoyden?"

"He took my reticule." Lily dropped her gaze to her feet, unable to bear her aunt's look of censure. She wished she were anywhere but standing in front of her angry chaperone. She was a grown woman. Hadn't she been mistaken for the mother of the young boy who had stolen her purse? Not that she wasn't a bit miffed at being connected to the raggedy youngster. But she was old enough to avoid being treated like a child no older than nine-year-old Jasmine, her youngest sister.

"This is a lawless, wild area. Even in the daylight it's not safe for women to travel unaccompanied." Aunt Dahlia raised her ruffled parasol and opened it with a click. "Let's get to the boat. Hopefully there will be adequate protection amongst our own kind."

Lily didn't argue, but she didn't much feel like the guests at the party were "her own kind." She felt more kinship with the stevedores and sailors walking up and down Silver Street. They loved the river as much as she did, and she envied them their ability to make their living on the river. With all its hazards, the Mississippi called to her like Homer's mythological sirens.

"You look as flushed as a washerwoman, Lily Catherine Anderson. I declare I don't know what to do with you." Aunt Dahlia shook her head and looked to the cloudless sky. "Your uncle and I have tried to raise you three girls to take your rightful place in society."

"Yes, ma'am, I'm sorry." Long experience had taught Lily it was the best answer to give. Silently she listened as her aunt bemoaned all the trials she had endured because of Lily and her sisters.

She followed a step behind her aunt to the boarding platform of the *Hattie Belle*, grateful because arriving at the party would end her aunt's harangue.

A line of finely dressed matrons were attended by their equally well-dressed spouses. A group of young ladies about Lily's age were standing in a tight circle, whispering behind their fans and watching the antics of the young men vying for their attention.

Why had she asked permission to attend this soiree? Although the invitation sent by the newly arrived Champney family had intrigued her, she should have known it would be a disaster. Maybe she could salvage a tiny bit of the expectation that had led to her attendance.

She and the other guests were to enjoy a leisurely float down the river to the Champney plantation, where they would disembark and enjoy a light luncheon on the grounds overlooking the river. Then they would return to the steamboat and chug back up to Natchez Under-the-Hill. She supposed it would have been easier and less expensive to go to the Champney mansion by coach, but she was glad their hosts had decided to transport their guests by boat, where there would be dancing—a different kind of ballroom to be sure.

A warm breeze teased at the ladies' skirts and the men's hats as the Champneys' guests waited to cross the gangplank and board the beribboned steamboat. There were three levels on the boat, with the bottom floor almost completely taken up by two forty-foot-long cylinders. Lily knew these were the boilers that would push the long pistons back and forth. The movement of the pistons turned the paddle wheel at the back, which propelled the boat through the water.

Her father had always known by its sound if a boiler was building up too much pressure and might explode. He'd said it was the first thing a sailor should learn about his boat. She could remember spending hours listening to the *hiss* and *whoosh* of his boat's engine. Being on board this afternoon brought back feelings she thought were long buried—memories of grief and betrayal caused by the death of her mother and her father's subsequent desertion of his three daughters.

She shook off the dismal thoughts and concentrated on the present. Her interested gaze took in the graceful curves of a wide staircase that led to the second floor, probably the level on which they would dance. The third-level hurricane deck was open to the sky, limited only by the pilothouse and a pair of tall, black smokestacks that would soon belch smoke, ash, and red-hot cinders.

Mr. Dashiell Champney, a tall, handsome man with dark hair shot through with white, stood next to a much shorter and rounder woman who must be his wife, Gabrielle. Lily waited behind her aunt while she exchanged greetings with their hosts. Then her aunt introduced her. Hoping her skirts showed no tears or dirt from her recent adventure, Lily curtsied deeply. She comforted herself with the thought that Aunt Dahlia's keen eyes would have spotted any problem. Her exacting aunt would not have hesitated to point out any shortcomings.

"What a charming young woman." Mr. Champney bowed over her hand. "You look more like your mother than your father."

Her shocked gaze met his. "You knew my parents?"

Mr. Champney frowned and glanced toward her aunt.

Aunt Dahlia tittered. "Oh, you misunderstand, Monsieur Champney. Phillip and I are not Lily's parents. Her mother, my sister, died some years ago, and Lily and her two sisters were left with my parents." She laughed as though her words were humorous. "Of course we consider the girls as dear to us as our own children."

Lily clenched her jaw to keep it from falling open. What an exaggeration. Aunt Dahlia and Uncle Phillip tolerated her and her sisters because they had no choice.

Aunt Dahlia put a hand on her shoulder, and Lily schooled her features into a polite expression. "Monsieur Champney is doing some business with your uncle, dearest. I suppose he was talking about his concern for your future." She turned back to their host. "I'm certain that's how the misunderstanding occurred."

"Our English is a little. . ." Mrs. Champney glanced toward her husband.

He patted her hand. "Shhh, Gabrielle, we will learn."

Lily's soft heart was touched. She put aside her shock and reached out toward their embarrassed hostess. "My papa also struggled with accents."

"You are sweet, *enfant*." Mrs. Champney smiled at her. "Such a kind heart you have. Go on inside and enjoy yourself."

"Thank you." Lily could feel her face flush. Expectation made her stomach clench. When her grandparents had introduced her to local society two years ago, it had been the same—terrifying and exhilarating all at once as she entered any ballroom.

Mr. Champney passed a white handkerchief across his forehead before turning to greet the next guest.

Lily moved down the line behind her aunt and came face-to-face with the Champneys' son, the young man who, according to rumor, was the real reason for today's party. He was said to be a bachelor on the lookout for a compliant wife. Her heart sped as she wondered which lady he would find interesting.

He bowed and kissed the air above her hand. "It is a pleasure to meet you."

"Thank you, Monsieur Champney."

His smile was wide and inviting, transforming his face from pleasant to handsome. Two dimples bracketed his mouth, and his dark eyebrows rose in the center. "My father is Monsieur Champney. You must call me Jean Luc."

For once Lily's face didn't flame. But a dozen butterflies seemed to have awoken in her stomach.

"And I hope you will save a dance for me."

Was he teasing her? She searched but could find no hint of mischief in his expression. "I. . .I would be gl—"

"Come along, Lily. You must not monopolize our host." Aunt Dahlia's voice seemed to come from a distance.

Jean Luc's impudent grin drew an answering smile from her. He squeezed her hand briefly. "I will find you later."

"I—" Her voice came out in a squeak, betraying her once again. Lily pulled back and took a deep breath to steady her nerves. "Thank you, monsieur." That was better. She sounded more confident, less terrified. "I look forward to having you partner me."

Then her aunt whisked her away. Lily didn't know whether to be relieved or disappointed. Was Jean Luc Champney flirting with her? What an odd feeling. And one she could easily grow accustomed to.

As she followed her aunt to the second level of the steamboat, Lily realized how glad she was that she had worn her new dress, a tailored suit with a fitted top and wide flounced skirt. Jaunty blue ribbon outlined each flounce and fluttered with every step she took. The sleeves were soft and generous, with blue-edged cuffs. A line of pearl buttons decorated the bodice from the edge of her beribboned collar to the wide blue grosgrain ribbon at her waist. The outfit was perfect for this party. Even though she would never be as beautiful as her middle sister, Camellia, Lily's fashionable attire and Jean Luc's obvious admiration made her feel pretty.

She held her skirt aloft with one hand so she wouldn't trip while her other hand traced a bronze handrail rubbed to a rich sheen. A welcome breeze brushed by as she reached the main landing.

The stateroom was a large, open area with floor-to-ceiling windows that provided light and a view of the Natchez bluffs. At one end, a full orchestra awaited the arrival of the guests while a wide, arched doorway dominated the other end, its leaded-glass doors thrown open to coax river breezes into the room.

The boat whistle sounded. Several guests hurried outside to watch the ropes loosened and the gangplank lifted away from the wharf. Some young ladies covered their ears because of the clanging boilers and hissing stacks. The boat shuddered as the long pistons began to move back and forth, slowly at first but with increasing speed and thrust.

Lily rushed outside to see the stern-wheeler begin churning the brown river water. The busy dock receded quickly as the *Hattie Belle* slipped into the strong current. Someone joined her at the rail, and Lily turned to see Jean Luc standing next to her. Unable to contain her exhilaration, she smiled widely. "Isn't it glorious?"

"Yes." But his gaze was fastened on her.

Unable to think of anything to say, she gazed at the green banks slipping past. Silence fell between them, almost like they were in their own private bubble that none of the other guests could inhabit. Her shoulders tensed with each second that ticked by.

Jean Luc moved a tiny bit closer. "Is this your first time on a steamboat?"

The romance of the moment fled. Lily shook her head. "My. . .my parents had a steamboat." She swallowed hard. "My mother d–died in an accident."

"How terrible for you." He put a hand on the one she had rested on the guardrail. "I didn't know."

Lily appreciated the kindly tone, but she pulled her hand from underneath his. "It was a long time ago. I was only a child."

The orchestra began playing a lively tune, and Lily pushed away from the rail.

"Wait, Miss Anderson. I didn't mean to pry." He offered his arm to her. "Please forgive me."

She hesitated before resting her hand on the crook of his elbow. "It's not your fault. Being here has brought old memories to the surface."

"Do you want me to have the captain turn the boat around?" His features were drawn in a frown of concern. "We can reschedule the picnic for another day."

Lily was touched by the offer but shook her head. "I wouldn't dream of depriving your guests for such a selfish reason." She pasted a wobbly smile on her face. "I'm just being overly sensitive."

"Good afternoon, Monsieur Champney." Grace Johnson, the beautiful, tawny-haired daughter of one of Natchez's wealthiest tobacco merchants, floated toward them, her movements as elegant as a swan's on a moonlit lake. She opened a fan and fluttered it in front of eyes as blue as chicory blossoms. "What an exceptional idea your family has conceived to host a floating gala. I predict they will become all the rage."

A hard look from Grace made Lily realize she should not monopolize their host's attention. She wanted to protest that he had followed her, not the other way around. Yet she felt guilty, so she started to remove her hand from his arm. She was stalled when he placed his hand over hers and applied a slight pressure.

"Thank you, Miss Johnson." Jean Luc's dimples appeared as he smiled. "Please excuse us. Miss Anderson has just agreed to let me partner her on the dance floor."

Lily's heart tripped. Dance? She couldn't dance with him. They would be the focus of everyone's attention. She would trip over her dress or step on his feet. . .or somehow make a fool of herself. Her mind screamed warnings even as he led her into the ballroom. She barely heard Grace's huff of irritation over the cacophony in her head.

Then they were in the center of the room. Jean Luc placed one arm around her waist, leading her into a waltz. She concentrated on following his lead for the first few bars but relaxed when she realized she was not going to make a fool of herself. The lessons she had complained about were paying off. She was thankful Grandmother had been so insistent.

"I'm glad you and your aunt were able to come this afternoon. Especially since I now know about your aversion to the river."

"Oh no, Monsieur Champney, I am not averse to the river." She could feel his fingers tighten around her waist. "On the contrary, I love the river. It is so alive! So full of intriguing characters and beautiful scenery. I deeply regret that my mother lost her life while boating, but I fault my father's lack of foresight rather than the river itself."

His midnight-dark gaze speared her. Lily could feel her heart flutter at the intense scrutiny. A blush heated her cheeks.

"Mademoiselle, you are an intriguing young woman. As fascinating as the ladies of Paris."

"You have been to Paris?" Lily jumped at the chance to change the subject. "Please tell me all about it."

He swept her into a complicated series of turns. She could feel the material of her gown swirling out and hoped the movement was not so energetic that her ankles were exposed.

"Paris is a very sophisticated city. There are endless things to do—balls every night, the opera house, the zoo, and of course Versailles."

"You have been to the Palace of Versailles?"

"Oh yes. It is *magnifique*, though the emperor, Napoleon III, does not reside there, of course. It is too much the symbol of Bourbon imperialism, and Napoleon and his wife are populists."

Lily nodded and tried to think of some dazzling remark. Like why a populist had become emperor. Hadn't he been elected president of France? She was not sure enough of the facts to question him. "I suppose they would avoid it."

"But a pretty girl like you does not want to hear about dreary politics." Chagrin deepened his voice. His mouth turned up on one corner. "I should be telling you how lovely your dress is and how your eyes sparkle. How light you are on your feet and how much I want to spend the rest of the evening at your side."

A blush heated her cheeks. Did he really think she was pretty? "N–not at all. I find your descriptions fascinating. You have seen so much more of the world than most of the men from Natchez. And you understand so much more than they."

Their dance came to an end before he responded, and Lily wondered if her compliments had been too gushing. Perhaps he had interpreted her enthusiasm as an attempt to flatter him, but she had been sincere in her sentiments.

He returned her to her aunt, who was visiting with some of her cronies in a corner of the room. Jean Luc bowed to them and chatted for a moment before excusing himself.

Aunt Dahlia drew Lily away. "Where did you disappear to, Lily? I was about to introduce you to a special friend of your uncle's, but I could not find you anywhere."

"I went outside to watch as the captain steered the ship away from the docks."

Her aunt shook her head and sighed. "I should have known. One would think you had no thought for your future. Are you content to always be a burden to your poor grandparents?"

"I danced with the Champneys' son," Lily defended herself. She had imagined her aunt would be pleased. Why was she so disgruntled?

"I'm sure he was just being polite. The Champneys have exquisite refinement, and surely their son has been schooled to spread his attention equally among his guests." She nodded to the other side of the room where Jean Luc stood talking to a group of young ladies.

Lily noticed Grace Johnson among their number. Her heart dropped like a heavy stone to her toes. How had she let herself be swept away by Jean Luc's easy charm? Plainly, her aunt was right. He was nothing more than a kindly host doing his duty. She dropped her gaze to the floor.

"I declare, I don't know why I keep trying to instruct you. It seems you will never learn the basic rules governing our little corner of society." Aunt Dahlia opened her fan and fluttered it.

Lily could feel the fan moving air against her warm cheeks. How could she have so easily forgotten herself? She was not beautiful or artistic or even witty. Her talent lay in her practicality, her ability to watch out over others and steer them from trouble. A girl like her would never be able to secure the interest of someone as debonair, charming, and cultured as Jean Luc Champney, the heir apparent to his father's vast shipping interests.

The first indication Lily had of trouble floated toward her in a cloud of strong cologne. She opened her own fan and used it to disperse the overpowering smell.

Aunt Dahlia's overly bright tones were the second indication. "Oh, good. Mr. Marvin has returned. I know you're going to be delighted by his interest."

Lily glanced at the man who approached. Her heart sank. He was old! As old as Uncle Phillip and Aunt Dahlia. Surely this was not the man her aunt wished her to meet. Casting one last, longing glance toward the lively group of young women surrounding Jean Luc, she sighed and waited for her aunt's introduction.

Mr. Marvin asked Lily to dance, and Aunt Dahlia practically shoved her at him. But Mr. Marvin did not seem to notice. They exchanged the usual pleasantries as they moved about the room in time to the musicians.

When the music ended, he returned her to Aunt Dahlia with aplomb. From that point on, she was handed from one partner to another, some more skillful with their steps than others. Even though she had not attended many balls, she knew most of the guests, as they were from local families.

She was dancing with Louis Roget when a disturbance at the ballroom door drew their attention. "What do you suppose is happening?"

His hazel eyes narrowed. "It looks like a message is being delivered by someone's slave." Roget halted as the orchestra's notes died away.

Lily recognized the black man who was making his way toward Aunt Dahlia. It was Amos, Grandfather's personal slave. Her heart began to hammer. She pushed her way past the couples still standing on the dance floor and reached her aunt just as Amos straightened, his message apparently delivered.

She glanced at her aunt, surprised to see that the color had washed from her face. "What is it?"

"We have to go. Something has happened to Father, and Mother wants us to come immediately."

Lily helped her aunt stand and followed her out of the room, all thoughts of the river, her dance partners, and the attractive Jean Luc Champney fading like mist under the concern blazing through her.

Chapter Three

Jean Luc Champney yawned and glanced toward his papa, who was writing a letter to *Grandmère*. What could he find to write about this boring town? How did his parents expect him to find a proper wife in this backwater?

They had invited everyone from the area to the party a few weeks earlier, and he hadn't found a single girl worth remembering. Well, maybe one or two. The tall blond had been interesting until she laughed. He couldn't remember a more horrible sound. What was her name? Grace somebody-or-other. And then there had been the quiet girl who he thought might be interesting to pursue. Her eyes had sparkled with interest and intelligence when he'd talked about his travels. She'd even been able to ask questions to show her interest. But then she'd left the party early.

He lifted his crystal snifter to his mouth and took a long drink, savoring the thick liquid before letting it slide down his throat. Realizing he had emptied his glass, Jean Luc pushed himself up from the leather chair and sauntered to his father's desk. He unstoppered the leaded decanter and splashed a generous amount of the liqueur into his heavy goblet.

"You'd better slow down, Son." His father looked up from his correspondence. "It's not gentlemanly to drink yourself into a stupor."

Jean Luc put down the decanter with a thump. "What else is there to entertain a gentleman in this mud hole?"

A sigh answered him. "Natchez is a bustling port city."

"What does that matter when you won't let me take part in your business?" Jean Luc could feel the old resentment building in his chest. What kind of father didn't trust his own son? The situation made Jean Luc furious. How was he supposed to learn the shipping business if his father refused to include him?

"Your mama and I have been discussing that very thing." The older man put down his fountain pen and folded the stationery with deliberate movements.

Silence built in the room. Was his father serious? Or leading him on? Jean Luc wanted to say something, but he didn't want to jeopardize his chances, so he returned to his chair and sipped from his snifter.

His father unlocked one of the drawers in his desk and pulled out several sheets of parchment. "We think it's time to give you some responsibility, so I'm deeding one-half interest in the *Hattie Belle* to you."

Shock made Jean Luc gulp down too much of the alcohol. He put the glass down on a table at his elbow and coughed. And coughed.

"Are you okay, Jean Luc?" His father rose from his seat.

Jean Luc nodded, but his thoughts darted back and forth like startled minnows. He could not believe it. His father did trust him. The *Hattie Belle* might not be the newest or grandest in his father's fleet, and he was receiving only partial interest, but she did move a great deal of cargo up and down the river. Once he got his coughing under control, Jean Luc stood and held out a hand. "Thank you, Papa."

His father shook his hand, clapped him on the back, and handed him the parchment. "This makes it official. In a year or so if everything goes well, I will turn over the controlling interest, and the *Hattie Belle* will belong to you. Be sure to keep your deed in a safe place."

His mother entered the room, and Jean Luc greeted her with an enthusiastic hug.

"It's good to see you happy, Son." She kissed his cheek. "Dare I hope it's because you have found a young lady who meets with your approbation?"

Papa cleared his throat. "I gave him the deed."

"*Eh, bien.*" Mama nodded. "We love you, Jean Luc, and we want you to be happy." She crossed the room and settled in the padded armchair next to Papa's desk. "A large part of that happiness will stem from your settling down with a local young woman and starting a family."

Jean Luc wasn't sure his mother's idea of future happiness mirrored his own, but this evening he would be amenable. "I met a few likely candidates at the party."

"I should think so." His father's right eyebrow rose. "We only invited the best families."

His mother nodded her agreement. "What about the young Anderson girl? She seemed like a sweet young woman."

"I did dance with her, but then she and her chaperone were called away."

"A pity." Mama patted a pocket in her skirt. "I received a note of apology from her aunt. It seems the girl's grandfather had a seizure."

"I'm sorry to hear that." The words came easily, although Jean Luc had no real feelings on the matter.

Papa trimmed the nib of his quill with a small knife. "Perhaps you should pay a visit to the young lady."

"I will consider doing that tomorrow." Jean Luc would have promised his parents anything. He would even have agreed to propose to the girl. Not that they would suggest such a thing. Even they wouldn't expect him to marry someone he'd only shared one dance with.

After the conversation turned to more general topics, Jean Luc excused himself and retired to his bedroom, his deed clutched in one hand. He looked around for a safe place and finally settled on the ornate box his parents had given him years earlier. He smoothed the pages and perused the document one last time before placing it in the box, which he locked with a key he wore around his neck. That should keep it safe.

His personal slave, Meshach, slipped into the room. "Do you need help with yo' boots, Master?"

He shook his head. "I'm too excited to retire. Do you know anything about the *Lucky Lucy*?"

Meshach shook his head and looked down.

"I've heard she boasts an honest game of an evening."

When no answer was forthcoming, Jean Luc sighed. "No, I don't guess you would know about that. Tell them to saddle my stallion. I will come out to the stable to get him." Feeling expansive, he waved a hand at the slave. "After that, take the rest of the evening off. I'll undress myself when I return."

"Yes, sir." The door closed behind Meshach with a quiet click.

Why hadn't he asked his papa for a gun while he was in such a giving mood? Jean Luc sighed and picked up the long knife he'd bought off a trader earlier this week, sliding it into the top of his boot. He hoped he wouldn't need a weapon, but Natchez Under-the-Hill had an unsavory reputation. Not that he was worried. He was young and strong, and his father had made sure he was accomplished with swords and had received training in pugilism.

Slipping quietly downstairs, he avoided his parents, who still sat in the parlor. They wouldn't understand his restlessness. He crept to the stables, mounted his horse, and galloped toward the distant yellow lantern glow at the river's edge.

It didn't take him long to find the *Lucky Lucy*. She was a smaller, older boat, but she seemed to be drawing quite a crowd.

His eyes widened when he entered the main cabin. He'd imagined it would look like the gambling salons he'd visited in Paris, but the layout was much simpler. Half a dozen straight-backed chairs surrounded a large round table covered with a piece of oilcloth. Most of the guests were filling plates from a pair of long, narrow tables laden with steaming dishes of food, while others stood in small groups talking and enjoying liquid refreshment. It looked like he had stumbled into his mother's drawing room rather than a gambling establishment.

"Welcome." A tall man with dark hair and blue eyes walked over to him. "We've plenty of food and drink." His eyes narrowed as he looked at Jean Luc closely. "But you look to me like a man who wants to match wits at a card table."

Jean Luc hadn't realized how tense he was until his shoulders relaxed. He smiled and extended his right hand. "Jean Luc Champney."

"Well, Mr. Champney, I'm Blake Matthews." The man had a firm handshake. "If you're looking for an honest game, you've come to the right place."

Another man joined them, a rueful smile on his face. "That's right. No cheating allowed." He turned his pockets inside out. "That will not guarantee you a win, but you stand a better chance here than at any other place under the hill." All three of them laughed.

Jean Luc was so glad he'd decided not to stay home. This Matthews fellow was quite likable. For a moment, he envied Blake's lifestyle. How exciting to sleep all day and entertain all night. From the looks of the lavish spread, the man had plenty of money to spend in making his guests comfortable. The fancy pastries, fresh vegetables, and huge platters of roasted meat reminded Jean Luc of the party his family had hosted to introduce him to the local planters. "What type of game do you offer, Mr. Matthews?"

"Poker." The other man's smile warmed. "Would you care to join us?"

"I'd be delighted." He jangled the coins in his pocket. "But I don't know if I brought enough money with me."

"I understand." Mr. Matthews waved a hand toward the buffet tables. "It was a pleasure to meet you. Please help yourself to food and libation. And don't forget where we're moored if you decide to come back another day."

Jean Luc was impressed when the man didn't try to coerce him into playing. He was not a cardsharp looking for easy prey. A servant offered him a glass of champagne. Jean Luc accepted and stood sipping the bubbly liquid as he watched several cardplayers take seats at the round table.

Mr. Matthews sat on the far side, allowing him to have his back to the wall. Many a gambler had met an untimely end from a bullet in the back. At least Mr. Matthews's position meant he stood a better chance of not being caught off guard.

Jean Luc watched the card game progress. Finally deciding he could gamble as well as most of the men playing and better than others, Jean Luc sidled up to the table. "Is it too late for me to join?"

Mr. Matthews looked up and nodded toward an empty seat. "Not at all." He introduced Jean Luc to the other players. "Sit down, and I'll deal you in."

Chapter Four

Blake Matthews reached for a boot and tugged it on. As he pushed his left foot into the other boot, his eyes lit on his soiled clothing piled in a corner. He would have to make the trek up to Natchez today to drop them off at the washerwoman's shop. He didn't trust the women in Natchez Under-the-Hill to do a proper job, and he had learned early on that appearance and personality were as important as his skill with cards. His subsequent addiction to cleanliness had paid off nicely, drawing in fastidious, rich customers who were ready to wager large sums at his table.

A pleasant feeling brought a smile to his lips. Thanks to a particularly generous client last night, he was no longer a nameless gambler eking out a living between port cities. He supposed he ought to feel a little guilty for fleecing the young man of his property.

But he wasn't in the business of raising youngsters. All of them had an equal chance at winning or losing. The only edge he held was an ability to read his opponents from their gestures and expressions—and that he remained sober when most of the men were at least half-lit. But he neither dragged them onto the *Lucky Lucy* nor poured liquor down their throats. And he ran an honest game.

Still, he shuddered to think about the scene that had likely occurred in the Champney household when Jean Luc had confessed his loss to his parents. Blake shrugged. He'd probably done the young man a favor—he wouldn't soon forget the dangers of drinking and gambling.

Blake drew on his brocade vest and thought about how his life was about to change. He was a businessman now. He was the owner of a boat. A picture of his father flashed in his mind. The old man couldn't accuse him of being a ne'er-do-well anymore. How he would enjoy informing the stodgy puritan of his success. Perhaps one day he would chug his steamboat upriver and make a visit.

A sigh escaped. Probably not. Even if he did, Blake had the feeling reality wouldn't be as fulfilling as his imagination. Besides, he had left that life long ago. There would be no going back for him. Not that he wanted to. No, he and his father would never see eye to eye. It was better for them to be as separated by distance as they were by belief.

Blake shook his head as he sauntered across his stateroom to the bureau that held all his belongings. His holster and gun were draped across the top. He checked the gun carefully. Natchez Under-the-Hill was far too rowdy a town for him to wander about unarmed.

Satisfied the weapon would fire if needed, he laid it down and picked up his leather gun belt, securing it around his waist and letting the holster dangle against his upper thigh. He tied the strips of rawhide around his leg and dropped his gun into the holster. He hoped he wouldn't have to use it. He'd never yet shot a man, but there was always the first time. The danger surrounding his occupation was part of its attraction.

He opened the top drawer and pulled out two blades—a genuine Bowie knife, made famous right here in Natchez, and his sword cane, his weapon of last resort. He slid the knife into the inside top of his left boot, where he could reach it quickly. He leaned the cane against the wall and shook out his frock coat before putting it on.

A deck of cards slid into a pocket. A new purchase, they had proven to be worthy of the money he'd spent. He dumped his soiled clothing into a gunnysack and tossed it over one shoulder, grabbed his cane, and made for the door. Blake glanced in the mirror at the smile curving his lips. It was going to be a wonderful day.

Summer was quickly approaching. Warm air slapped him in the face like a wet facecloth when he stepped outside. Amazing. It was hardly past the middle of May. Blake hoped his neckcloth would stand up to the humidity.

"Good afternoon, Mr. Blake. We sure had a good crowd last night."

Blake turned back to the corridor where the boat's cook/steward stood. Jensen Moreau was not a handsome man, but his thick shoulders and brawny arms had brought him a fair share of respectful glances from those who visited the *Lucky Lucy*. An inch or two shorter than Blake, Jensen had swarthy skin and dark features that hinted at mixed ancestry. He also sported a thick scar over his left eye. Apparently whatever had caused the scar had severed a muscle, making him appear to squint all the time.

"It's good to see you, Jensen." Blake held out his right hand. "Yes, we did have a crowd. I don't doubt it's your food that draws them in for a visit."

The shorter man's smile was as wide as the river. "Mr. Blake, you're a real jokester. Everyone knows they come here to play an honest game or two of cards. So many would cheat and steal to take their money. Word's gotten out you run a straight game. That's why we fills up the boat every night."

"Even if that's true, your wonderful meals keep their bellies full." Blake smiled at the ruddy color filling Jensen's cheeks. "Which puts me in mind of a matter I wanted to discuss."

Jensen straightened his shoulders and brushed off his apron. "Yes, sir?"

A chuckle rumbled through Blake. "I'm not going to shoot you, man. I want to offer you a job."

"A job?" A frown brought Jensen's left brow down. "What kind of job?"

"Were you paying attention to the game last night? Especially a certain young man who had more money than sense?" Blake glanced to see if Jensen remembered.

He looked confused, so Blake continued. "This young man holds the title to some rather valuable property. Or I should say he used to hold the title. It has come into my own hand."

"Wow! You're a landowner?" Jensen's right eyebrow crept up, making Blake think of a caterpillar.

"Not a landowner. Something much more suited to folks like you and me." Blake tossed a smile at Jensen. "You're looking at the proud owner of the *Hattie Belle*."

"You don't say." Jensen's smile lit up his face. "That's amazing. And it happened last night? I didn't realize what high stakes you was playing."

"Yes, and I'm on my way to pick up the papers in a little while. I don't know exactly when I'll take possession, but I'd love to have you come on board with me. If you agree to work for a percentage of the table, you'd be my very first crew member."

"I'd be honored, sir. You'd be a good man to work for."

Blake slapped him on the back. "I'll get with you once I know more details. It's always been my dream to have a floating palace for gambling. Then if the locals get puritanical on us, we can shove off and go where we're more welcome."

"Exactly right. And we can always look at moving some cargo, too. A big ol' steamboat like the *Hattie Belle* has plenty of decks to accommodate a few barrels of whiskey or bales of cotton."

"We'll see." Blake wasn't sure he wanted to be a trader. He did much better when he was seated at a card table. But a wise man always kept his options open. "I'd better get out of here before my appointment gets the idea I'm not interested in claiming my winnings." He stepped back into the warm afternoon sun and crossed the deck of the *Lucky Lucy*. He would talk to the captain later, once he found out exactly when he'd be leaving.

The gunnysack thumped against his back with each step. No matter that Blake shifted its weight from shoulder to shoulder, by the time he reached the top of the bluff, he was ready to toss the irritating bundle into a ravine. Eventually he reached the shanty where the washerwoman lived and worked.

He dropped off his clothing and dickered with the old woman, whose back was bowed from years of bending over hot tubs and scrub boards. Normally she would have delivered the clean clothes in a few days, but since Blake wasn't sure where he'd be living, he told her he'd come back to collect them in three days. By the time he left, both of them were satisfied with their arrangement.

The trip down the hill was easier and cooler. He could see a boat chugging its way upstream, loaded with immigrants. It was a common sight. Dozens of families crowded onto steamboats. The lucky ones could afford to rent rooms in the interior of the boats while the poorer immigrants had to eat, live, and sleep on the upper decks, exposed to all weather conditions.

As he made his way back to the river, the boat docked, and her passengers flowed onto the muddy banks like ants from an overturned mound. Some of them headed uphill while others stayed in the lower town, probably wanting to remain closer to their boat. He hoped they would stay away from the trapdoor saloons, a row of buildings clinging to the river south of the docks. They were perched on tall stilts to avoid damage from frequent floods, but they housed the most dangerous inhabitants of Natchez Under-the-Hill: hardened criminals who were on the lookout for easy prey. Unwary travelers were sometimes clubbed to death inside the saloons and stripped of their valuables. Then the hapless bodies were tossed through trapdoors into the river below. Most of them ended up caught in the eddies of a wide curve just south of the city, aptly named Dead Man's Bend.

Blake nodded to several men who had gambled at his table the past few weeks. Natchez had been good to him, giving him enough money for food and shelter. Now it had also given him his dream.

His musings were brought short by a shout from a nearby brothel. The front door flung open, and two men stumbled onto the wooden sidewalk. Judging from the angry words being exchanged, the argument had begun when the two conceived a desire for the same woman.

One of the men, a short, broad-shouldered Cajun who sported a red rooster's feather in his black slouch hat, backed into Blake and nearly fell. "Watchit!" His snarl was as threatening as a mad dog's. "Whaddaya doin' here?"

Part of Blake's mind registered the smell of alcohol on the short man's breath even as his hand clamped down on his sword cane. Should he back away from the combatants? Or would that be perceived as cowardice and end with his receiving a bullet between his shoulder blades? Should he try to be a calming voice in the quarrel between the two men? Or would they then join forces and attack him?

The irony of the situation did not escape him. He was finally beginning to see his dream come true. Would he die this afternoon, the accidental victim of chance?

"Excuse me, gentlemen. I was wondering if either of you knows the way to the Silver Nickel? I'm meeting a client there in a few minutes." He hoped his bogus question would take the attention off him. As far as he knew, there was no such place in Natchez.

The taller combatant dropped his fists and scowled. "What? Silver Nickel? I ain't never heard of it. How 'bout you, Pierre?"

Pierre's shoulders lowered slightly. He looked from one man to the other and scratched at his head, almost dislodging his hat. "Never heared of it neither."

"Oh well, thank you, gentlemen." Blake took a step past them, watching for any sudden movements toward a gun or knife. "I guess I'll continue my search."

The two men resumed their argument. Blake reached a corner, breathing a sigh of relief when he knew he was out of their line of sight. They were too drunk and belligerent to come looking for him. All he had to do was make sure he didn't bump into them again. Even though his current route would take a few extra minutes, the safety it brought was worth it.

He arrived at the saloon and stopped a minute to check for an ambush. When a big prize was at stake, it was prudent to be extra careful. Seeing nothing suspicious, he stepped inside and looked around for Jean Luc Champney. Several patrons perched at the bar, but he didn't see any sign of the man he was supposed to meet. Deciding it was too early to be concerned, he sat at an empty table and ordered a cup of coffee from a frowsy-headed waitress.

She put one hand on her hip. "Don't ya want anything stronger?"

Blake used his most winning smile. "No, thanks. Coffee will be fine. Tell me, have you seen a young gentleman in here this afternoon?"

"Well of course, honey. I seen lots of men in here. That's why they call it a saloon."

"I'm looking for one in particular. A little shorter than me. Good looking with expensive clothes."

She wrinkled her nose. "No. But give it a few minutes. I'm sure he'll be right in." She flounced off, her long skirt dragging across the dirty floor.

The saloon grew more crowded as time wore on, but still Blake saw no sign of Jean Luc. If he didn't show up soon, Blake was going to have to go in search of him. At least he knew the young man's last name. It shouldn't be too hard to discover his whereabouts.

The next time the waitress came to check on him, Blake showed her a gold coin. "I need some information."

Her eyes watched the coin as she nodded. "I'll be glad to help ya."

"I need to know where the Champney family lives."

She wrinkled her nose before answering him. "I don't rightly know, but I can ask my boss."

He nodded, but when she reached a hand out to take the coin, Blake shook his head. "Information first."

She huffed and walked away. He watched as she talked to the

bartender. He nodded and pointed toward the roof. Then more gestures as he apparently described the exact location of the Champney home.

Blake had the coin ready when she came back. "Well?"

She repeated the instructions, although she didn't use as many gestures as the bartender had.

Blake asked a couple of questions to make sure he understood before handing her the money.

She placed it in a tiny pocket in her skirt. "Thanks."

Blake stood up. "Have a good evening."

Her pout was supposed to be attractive, but Blake was unmoved. She was more pitiful than voluptuous. He wished he could tell her to go home and find a husband.

Instead he picked up his hat and settled it on his head. He had more important things to see to. . .like claiming his boat and the new future that awaited him.

When he met his mother's concerned gaze, Jean Luc realized he should have gone out instead of taking a meal with his parents.

"You've hardly touched your dinner, enfant. Are you ill?"

He shook his head. "I'm fine."

"But it's not like you—"

Papa interrupted. "Leave the boy alone, Gabrielle. He doesn't have to stuff himself at every meal."

Jean Luc shared a sympathetic gaze with his papa.

Mama pushed her chair back. "I will leave you gentlemen alone, then. Will you join me in the parlor later?"

"We won't be long." Papa's voice lost some of its irritation.

A slave moved to open the door, and Mama sailed through. "We'll need a tray in the front parlor." The slave nodded and left to do her bidding.

Papa tossed his napkin on the table. "I was surprised you didn't come to the office today."

Grasping his goblet, Jean Luc drained the wine in one gulp. "I was busy."

Silence filled the room. He could almost feel his father's piercing gaze burn straight through him, but he refused to look up. Papa would see the truth. Another thought made his heart stutter. Did Papa already know? Against his will, Jean Luc's gaze rose and smashed into his father's.

Feeling like a youngster, Jean Luc gulped. He tried to marshal his thoughts, but his mind wouldn't function properly. He opened his mouth to confess when a knock on the door interrupted them.

"I wonder who that can be?" Papa rose from his chair and opened the door.

"Good evening. You must be Mr. Champney."

It could not be. Jean Luc started at the sound of the voice that had dogged him through every waking minute today. He coughed in an attempt to ease the dryness in his throat.

"I'm afraid you have me at a disadvantage, Monsieur. . ."

"Matthews. Blake Matthews."

Papa waited, a look of mild curiosity on his face.

"I need to speak with your son, sir."

Papa's gaze raked Jean Luc before turning back to Matthews. "Come in. You've arrived too late to join us for dinner, but perhaps you would care for a glass of brandy." He moved back to the table.

Matthews followed. "I don't believe so, sir. I don't wish to disturb you. I was only coming by to make sure Jean Luc was not ill. He missed our appointment today."

Papa raised an eyebrow. "With all this concern over his health, I'm beginning to wonder if I should send for a doctor."

"Before you do, sir, could I have a few moments alone with your son?"

"Whatever you have to say to Jean Luc can be said while I'm here."

Jean Luc pushed back his chair, indignation and horror fighting inside him. Had he stumbled into a nightmare? Surely Blake Matthews hadn't dared to come here to demand payment. But he could not ignore the evidence. "Shouldn't you be on your boat?"

A tight smile appeared on the man's face. "I would be, but I cannot gain access."

"I'm sorry to hear that." Jean Luc tried for an imperious stare. All he needed to do was imitate his father's expression. "But I don't understand what I have to do with that unfortunate circumstance."

"I'm not talking about the *Lucky Lucy.*" His eyes glittered like shards of glass. "I'm referring to the boat I won from you last evening, the *Hattie Belle.*"

"What?" Jean Luc's father looked from Matthews to his son. "What is he talking about, Jean Luc?"

"I'm sure I haven't the slightest idea." Jean Luc dropped back into his dining chair. "Mr. Matthews must have me confused with someone else."

The genial host he vaguely remembered from the night before had disappeared. In his place stood an angry volcano. Mr. Matthews took two long strides toward the table, his hand reaching for something in the inside pocket of his coat. Was he going to shoot him here in his family's home?

The gambler pulled out a sheet of paper and held it in front of Jean Luc. "Are you going to deny this IOU?"

Jean Luc opened his mouth, but no sound came out.

His father stalked over and grabbed the piece of paper. "What is this?" His eyes perused the short statement. "It says that you have sworn to turn over the deed to the *Hattie Belle* in lieu of the debt you owe Mr. Matthews." He balled up the paper and tossed it on the table.

All three men watched as it bounced off the edge of Jean Luc's dinner plate and rolled toward a pair of lit candles in the center of the table.

"That paper has your son's signature on it. And I have half a dozen witnesses who will verify he signed without any duress. He was certain he held the winning hand, but alas, the cards were against him."

"You were against me, you mean." Jean Luc could hear the note of panic in his voice. He cleared his throat and looked at his father. Papa's face had aged ten years in ten minutes. A stabbing pain of remorse shot through him. But it was too late for remorse. He would bluff his way through this. Surely his father would believe his word over that of some stranger. "I don't owe this man anything."

"Did you go to his gambling hall last night?"

"Yes, but—"

His father pointed a finger toward the note. "Did someone else sign that or force you to?"

Reluctantly, Jean Luc shook his head.

More color drained from his father's face. "Go upstairs and get the deed."

"But Papa, the game was fixed."

A sound from Mr. Matthews indicated he was ready to defend himself. Jean Luc's father turned toward him. "I apologize for my son. He has no excuse for his words or his behavior."

"You don't have to apologize for him. Jean Luc is a grown man."

"Apparently he's more immature than I had hoped." Papa turned back to him. "Get—the—deed. Now!"

The last word propelled Jean Luc from his chair. He practically ran from the room, his humiliation complete. How could he have been so stupid? How could he have gambled away the first thing his father had entrusted to him? How would he ever make up for his colossal error?

The questions chased him upstairs and circled in his mind as he unlocked the box. Hot tears blurred the words on the deed. He wiped them away with an angry hand before they could fall on the paper. He would be a man about this.

Jean Luc considered several scenarios. Could he claim the deed had disappeared or been stolen? No one would believe such a coincidence. Besides, since Blake had the IOU, he could force Jean Luc to have an attorney draft a new deed.

He had to give the deed over to the nefarious gambler tonight, but he would find a way to get it back. He had been cheated. None of the provincials in this backwater town could have defeated him honestly. He had played in some of the best gaming halls in France, and he'd never had such ill luck.

He had hoped to have a few days to find out how he'd been cheated, but that was not to be. He had to temporarily admit defeat. But one day he would prove his suspicions and wrest his property back from Blake Matthews. He would do whatever was necessary, no matter how difficult. He would once again bask in the glory of his father's approval. On the day he succeeded, he would make Mr. Matthews pay for his humiliation. On that day, he would put his boot on Mr. Matthew's neck and make him scream for mercy. On that day, everything would be right again.

Halting steps brought him back to the dining room. It was galling to have to look up at the man as he handed him the deed. Before his father could prompt him, Jean Luc bowed. "I hope you will forgive me for what I said earlier. I was overset."

The other man's shoulders relaxed a tiny bit. "It is hard to admit one's mistakes."

"Yes." He watched as Matthews took his leave, studying each movement the man made. He needed every advantage if he was going to defeat his adversary.

Chapter Six

Birds chirped in the warm air, undisturbed by grief or other human concerns. Lily wanted to shoo them away. Perhaps if they weren't singing, she could summon tears like those that washed the cheeks of her grandmother and her sister Camellia.

But her heart had turned to stone. It was as though her emotions had left when Grandfather's soul departed his mortal remains. She moved through the days like a shadow, drifting from room to room as she considered what life had become without him.

His strength had seemed indomitable. But in the end, he had succumbed to death as any other man. In the end, he had left her alone to fend for herself in much the same way her father had all those years ago. Of course, her father had chosen to leave her; Grandfather had remained until his health failed.

Lily picked at the heavy black material of her wide skirt as Camellia placed a bouquet of fresh flowers on Grandfather's grave. She was worried about her sister. Camellia had always been Grandfather's favorite, his perfect little lady.

Golden ringlets moved with Camellia as she traced the marble headstone with a gloved hand. "I miss him so much."

"As do we all, Camellia." Grandmother's voice was choked with tears but still managed to convey warmth. "It is hard to say good-bye to our loved ones, but it is given to man to die."

"Grandfather would be pleased with the flowers." Lily forced her lips to curve upward as she met Camellia's blue gaze. The smile became more natural as she considered how beautiful her fair sister looked in her mourning clothes. Not that Camellia ever looked less than lovely.

"Do you think so?" Camellia's hopeful words wrung her heart.

"I think Grandfather is flying around heaven with his new wings." Jasmine flapped her arms and ran around a nearby tree, her black dress making her look more like a crow than an angel.

Laughter threatened to bubble up as Lily thought they probably looked like a flock of crows in their black dresses.

"Jasmine, get back here." Aunt Dahlia clapped her hands. She turned to Lily, a frown on her face. "I don't know where she gets her manners. Can you not do anything to control her?"

Lily felt the stab of her relative's disapproving gaze. "Jasmine, please come here."

With a whooshing sound, the young girl complied, letting her arms drop to her sides.

"You must learn to act like a lady." Aunt Dahlia clipped her words as though her tongue were a pair of scissors. "You should try to emulate your sister Camellia."

Lily wanted to contradict her. One prissy girl was enough for any family. She loved Camellia, but she had none of Jasmine's playful exuberance. Lily put a protective arm around her youngest sister and squeezed.

Jasmine looked up at her, her violet-hued eyes wide. "I'm sorry."

"I know you are, Jasmine, but you need to think before you act."

"I won't do it again." The young girl's lower lip trembled. Tears threatened.

Lily wanted to comfort her, but she could feel her aunt watching them so she sighed and nodded.

"Tamar, come take the girls back to the house." Aunt Dahlia beckoned to the middle-aged black woman standing a little apart from them. "We need to talk a bit before we rejoin Phillip for afternoon tea."

Lily supposed she should be flattered to be included as an adult, but she had an idea she was not going to enjoy the talk her aunt had in mind.

Her bonnet ribbon fluttered in a light breeze, tickling her cheek. Lily caught it between her fingers and pleated it with restless fingers.

"Quit fidgeting, child." Aunt Dahlia's frown deepened. "It's no wonder Jasmine is so restive."

Grandmother closed her eyes. "That's enough, Dahlia."

Aunt Dahlia's mouth dropped open. She was not used to anyone challenging her opinions. She unfurled her fan, whipping up a breeze to cool her reddened cheeks. "I suppose I should not be surprised, Mother. You never have exercised enough control over your granddaughters. If you are not careful, Lily will become a spinster and rely on you to provide for her the rest of her life."

Grandmother stepped closer to Lily and took her hand. "You're being ridiculous, Dahlia. Lily is barely eighteen years old. She has plenty of time to choose a husband."

"That might be true if we were speaking of Camellia. But Lily is no raving beauty."

If she had not been so numb, Lily supposed the cruel words would have hurt.

"Lily has a great deal to offer any man lucky enough to win her affection." Grandmother's defense had the same effect as Aunt Dahlia's attack.

"Win her affection?" Aunt Dahlia blew out a harsh breath. "It's not as though the whole town is lined up at my niece's door. As far as I know, she doesn't have a single suitor."

Lily wasn't surprised at her aunt's remarks. It was true. No perspective beaus were knocking down her door. And why should they? Although she expected to inherit a respectable dowry from her grandfather, the bulk of his money and his entire estate would go to Aunt Dahlia and Uncle Phillip.

And Lily had never been under any misapprehension about her looks. She was too short to be considered fashionable, and her waist was several inches thicker than her middle sister's. Instead of Camellia's changeable blue gaze or Jasmine's exotic violet irises, she boasted dull brown eyes that refused to sparkle no matter the number of candles in a room. Her hair was lifeless, too. No long, fat ringlets for her. Instead, Lily had to be satisfied with a sensible bun at the base of her neck.

Aunt Dahlia snapped her fan shut. "Luckily for you and Lily, Phillip and I have not been sitting idly by. I believe we have found a suitable candidate who is interested in courting Lily. He met her at the Champneys' party, and even though we had to leave unexpectedly, he has assured Phillip he finds my niece acceptable."

Clarity struck Lily with the suddenness of a lightning bolt. Her stomach clenched. The man from the party. The old man. She could stomach her aunt's unflattering assessment of her chances to find a husband, but she refused to consider linking herself to a man who was at least twice her age.

Grandmother drew her shoulders back. "You ought to be ashamed of yourself, Dahlia Leigh. We are still grieving. All but you. You and your husband are both too busy trying to take over the estate."

"That's not it—"

"Stop right there, Dahlia." Grandmother pointed her fan at Lily's aunt. "I have listened to you, and now you will pay me the same courtesy." When Aunt Dahlia said nothing, she continued. "Have you forgotten that you told me the Champneys' son danced with Lily? She lacks none of the social graces, and while she may not be a raving beauty, she has many admirable qualities."

Lily was thankful for her grandmother's defense, but part of her wished she were as beautiful as either of her sisters. Why did she have to be the one with admirable qualities? As young as Camellia was, men were already drawn to her whenever she was in public. Ashamed of the envy trying to take root in her heart, Lily tamped down her thoughts and concentrated on her relatives.

"Even if you were right, Dahlia, which I do not for one moment believe, Lily will always have a place of honor in my home."

"Surely you'll not reject this man before you meet him." Expecting an explosion of rage from her volatile aunt, Lily was surprised at the reasonable tone of her words.

A sigh came from Grandmother. "I suppose you may invite him to visit my home, but that is all."

"Of course, Mother." Aunt Dahlia kissed Grandmother on the cheek and turned to retrace her steps back to the porch, her strides long and purposeful.

"That must be the attorney arriving." Grandmother's voice drew Lily's attention to a carriage that had arrived at the front steps just ahead of Aunt Dahlia. "I suppose we should go in and hear what he has to tell us about your grandfather's will."

After a few steps, however, she turned back to Lily. "I don't want you to worry about your aunt's plans. She has no say in the running of the household. I promise you she will not force you into a loveless marriage."

Lily nodded, but a new worry took root as she watched her grandmother's unsteady steps across the front lawn. She might always be welcome in Grandmother's home, but one day Grandmother would join Grandfather in heaven. While she prayed that day would be far in the future, what would happen to her then? Would her aunt and uncle be as loving toward her? Would they allow her to live with them, or would they expect her to find another home?

And what about her little sisters? What if they had not yet found men they wished to marry? Would they have to accept the first offers that came their way?

She would not—could not—allow that to happen. Her sisters had to be protected. . .no matter what.

Chapter Seven

Blake looked up at the fancy sign boasting a picture of a sternwheeler with the words Champney Shipping emblazoned below it. It hung on the facade of an equally fancy building and seemed to fit with the self-assured owner he had met so recently. A much more shrewd businessman than the son, Jean Luc. But he was ready for this meeting, ready to describe his plans to his new business partner.

Funny how things turned out. When he had finally received the deed, he had been disappointed to learn that it represented only half ownership of the *Hattie Belle*—49 percent to be precise. He wondered if it galled Monsieur Champney to be in business with a gambler as much as it galled him to find he was not the sole owner.

After some time angrily pacing the contours of his room, Blake had realized the situation could be salvaged. Partial ownership was better than nothing. From that thought came an idea to present a plan to Mr. Champney. The man would be a fool to turn down easy profits. With his knowledge of the gaming world, all his partner had to do was sit back and reap the profits.

Blake twisted the polished brass knob sharply, entering the main room of Champney Shipping with a firm step. His gaze rested on a narrow-shouldered clerk sitting behind a polished oak counter. "Good morning."

The man looked up and adjusted his spectacles. "May I help you, sir?"

"I'm here to see Mr. Champney."

The man frowned and glanced over his shoulder toward the door that must lead to the owner's office. "Do you have an appointment, Mr. . . ?"

"Yes." Blake tapped the rolled papers into his open palm. "He's expecting me to come by with this proposal."

"If you'll wait here a moment." The clerk slid off his stool and knocked on the door to Mr. Champney's office. After a moment, he opened it a few inches and spoke to someone inside. When he turned back to Blake, his face held a warmer expression. "You may come in, sir."

Blake stepped around the end of the counter and entered the room, his heart beating hard. Was it excitement or dread? Probably both.

A thick carpet cushioned his footsteps, its rich burgundy and navy colors a pleasing contrast to the oak-paneled walls of Mr. Champney's office, walls that were interspersed with tall mahogany bookshelves. This was luxury. His gaze wandered over the books and ledgers stored inside the office before finally resting on Mr. Champney's desk. Ornately carved and larger than a formal dining table, the desk was situated between two floor-to-ceiling windows that commanded a spectacular view of the river below.

"I didn't understand your note exactly, Mr. Matthews, but I have a little time to listen to your proposal." Mr. Champney's cultured voice focused his thoughts.

He could be impressed by the man's property later. For now he needed to impress Mr. Champney with his plans for the *Hattie Belle*. Blake cleared his throat. "I'm sorry if I was cryptic." He moved forward and placed his roll of papers on one polished corner of the desk. "I have some ideas I think will interest you."

"Captain Steenberg mentioned you had visited the *Hattie Belle* several times this week."

"I don't plan to be a silent partner." Blake unrolled his plans with a flourish. "I know you are much more familiar with the shipping business than I, but I have some knowledge of other areas you may be lacking. I am hoping to combine our strengths and make the *Hattie Belle* more profitable than you ever dreamed."

"You have my complete attention." Mr. Champney leaned forward. "What do you have in mind?"

"Most of your expenses with the *Hattie Belle* come from moving her up and down the river with heavy loads of goods?"

"Yes, but that's what shipping is all about."

"What if you didn't have to move her at all? What if you could make just as much money from her here in Natchez, maybe even more?"

A frown creased the older man's brow. "I don't understand."

"For the past six months, I've been running a profitable business from the main deck of the *Lucky Lucy*. My proposal is to create a luxurious, floating casino that would rival the gambling houses of Europe. We could reserve a couple of staterooms for those who come a distance to play at our tables, but the rest of the boat would be dedicated to games of chance." His words came faster. "I have always run fair games, so our reputation would spread like wildfire. Everyone would be welcome—planters, farmers, traders, anyone who has a little money to spend on entertainment. We'd fill every floor of that boat with people who want a chance to leave with more than they had."

"You certainly seem passionate about this." Mr. Champney sat back.

Blake wanted to press the point, but he had learned early in his career not to push someone too hard. Allowing a man to make up his own mind generally yielded the same result without any hard feelings. So he waited.

"I find your proposal interesting if unusual, Mr. Matthews." Mr. Champney steepled his hands. "But I don't know if I want to be associated with the dubious world of gambling."

"That's where I come in. I run a clean ship as I mentioned before. You can check with anyone who has gambled on the *Lucky Lucy* since I came to town at the beginning of the year. Except for one or two who may be sore about losing at my table, you will find nothing but good reports. I have sent a host of men away winners."

"Then how do you make a profit?"

Blake leaned forward. "There's a saying in my world, sir. Gambling money always makes its way back home. And when you own the house where it lives, you cannot help but profit."

Silence slipped into the room as Blake waited, his confidence building with each second that passed. He was good at reading what a man was thinking. It was one of the reasons he was successful in his chosen profession. He was sure Mr. Champney wanted to throw in with him.

Champney nodded. "What will it take to put your plan into action?"

Trying to keep his jaw from dropping, Blake flipped through his paperwork. He might need to work on his divining skills more. Although he had seen the other man's desire to partner in his venture, he hadn't expected his wholehearted support. But he might as well take advantage of it. With Champney's financial backing, he could make the *Hattie Belle* even more spectacular. She would be a showplace! "I can have you a list by the end of the day."

Mr. Champney rose from his desk and held out his right hand. "Ask my clerk for a list of businesses in town with whom we trade. He'll make sure they extend you credit." His eyes narrowed, and his grip on Blake's hand tightened. "But if I have any suspicion you are not being honest with me, our deal will be off."

"You won't be disappointed."

"I had better not be. I am not a good man to cross, Mr. Matthews. Although it would pain me, I would rather sink that boat than let you take me for a ride." He released Blake's hand.

"I understand, sir." Blake wanted to stretch his hand but refused to show any weakness. He slowly rolled up his papers and tapped them into a neat cylinder. Let Mr. Champney threaten all he wanted. Soon his new business partner would learn to trust him. Soon the money would begin rolling in. This was going to be a profitable venture for both of them. He was certain of it.

Chapter Eight

"Aren't you excited to meet your suitor?" Camellia stood at the window, keeping watch for their dinner guest.

Lily rolled her eyes and turned slightly, forgetting for a moment the curling iron Tamar was applying to her hair. "I am not."

"Hold still, Miss Lily, or you'll get burned."

Lily obediently turned back toward the mirror and made a face at her reflection. "It might be worth it if it kept me upstairs during dinner."

Camellia came to stand beside the dressing table. "I wish I could go in your place. I'd adore having a handsome man gazing at me and telling me how beautiful I am."

"Oh, Camellia, you have no idea what you're talking about."

Her sister put her nose in the air. "I know Aunt Dahlia said you'll have to marry Mr. Marvin, or you'll be a burden to her forever."

"Now you be quiet, Miss Camellia. You shouldn't be repeating gossip, especially hurtful things like that." Tamar's fingers twisted the curling rod, pulling it from Lily's hair. "I'm sure you misunderstood your aunt. She only wants the best for all her nieces."

Lily shook her head now that it was free of the hot iron. "I think she's more worried about her comfort than our futures."

"I think it's romantic." Camellia sighed. "Do you think he'll propose tonight?"

"I hope not." Lily shuddered. The tight coils Tamar had so painstakingly fashioned began to sag and droop. She felt like doing the same.

Tamar tsked and reached for the iron once more.

"Just pull it back like always. No sense in torturing either of us any longer. I still have to put on my hoops and that dress."

Camellia reached for one of the hairpins on Lily's dresser. "Don't you want to get married?"

"Of course I do, but marriage is a serious decision, an oath that cannot be broken. When you marry someone, you should be certain he is the right one according to the dictates of the Lord."

Tamar put the finishing touches on Lily's hairstyle and moved across the room to retrieve the hoops that would be fastened over her chemise. "You should listen to your sister, Miss Camellia. She's very levelheaded. She'll never let herself be carried away by a gentleman's looks."

Lily wondered if she was as levelheaded as Tamar thought. Her mind went back to the party on the Champneys' steamboat. Dancing with Jean Luc Champney had been much more thrilling than her dance with Mr. Marvin. She closed her eyes to conjure up memories of that night, surprised when Jean Luc's dark gaze was supplanted by eyes as azure as a summer sky. Now why had she thought of the stranger who had accosted her before the party? He might have been handsome, but he had also been rude, judgmental, and uncouth.

Her unruly thoughts were interrupted as the door to Lily's bedroom burst open and a dark-haired windstorm swept in. "Jasmine." She stood up and held her arms out in welcome, unwilling to chastise her youngest sister for her lack of decorum. Jasmine was such a happy young lady, taking joy in every moment. As the oldest sister, Lily had a duty to make sure both of her sisters behaved, but she couldn't bring herself to dampen Jasmine's pleasure. She was only nine years old, after all.

Jasmine threw her arms around Lily. "I love you, Sissy."

Who could resist such warmth? Lily placed a kiss on Jasmine's forehead. "I love you, too."

Camellia crossed her arms. "Aunt Dahlia said you need to stop calling her sissy. It makes you sound like a baby."

Jasmine stuck out her lower lip. "It does not."

"Tell her, Lily."

Lily shook her head. "As long as it's just us, I don't see the harm."

"You always take her side." Camellia plopped down at Lily's dressing table. "I think you love Jasmine more than me."

"Don't you be saying such things about your sister." Tamar shook out the folds of Lily's skirt as she spoke. "You should be ashamed of yourself. Miss Lily loves both of you more than anything else in this wide world."

Lily held up her arms so Tamar could lift the skirt over her head. "It's all right, Tamar. I know she doesn't mean it. Camellia is disappointed because she has to stay up here and entertain Mr. Marvin's children."

"What do you suppose his children are like?" Jasmine had a dreamy look in her eyes. She was probably hoping to meet children her own age.

Lily often worried that Jasmine had no one to play with. Her youngest sister had been a toddler when Lily lowered her skirts and put up her hair, and Camellia had not been far behind.

With only three years between them, she and Camellia had shared both their lessons and their dolls. They'd had plenty of skirmishes over the years, but they had also spent hours together pretending and exploring.

Jasmine had been too young to romp with them. Camellia was six years older than their youngest sister and could have played with her, but she was too fastidious. Sometimes Lily thought Camellia was growing up faster than she was.

Her heart turned over as she watched them perusing her hairpins. She might get outdone with one or the other at times, but Lily's sisters were so precious to her. Sometimes she felt as protective as a mother would be. No one else could love them more than she did.

"Here's your fan." Tamar's words snapped Lily out of her pensiveness.

Jasmine turned from the dressing table, her mouth forming a perfect O. "You look beautiful, Si—Lily."

"Thank you." Lily took a deep breath. "I suppose it's time for me to go face the music."

"There's going to be dancing, too?" Camellia's voice was full of envy.

A nervous giggle bubbled up and escaped Lily's throat. "It's just a saying. Think about it. Have you seen any musicians coming to the house?" She pointed to the black material of Camellia's dress. "You know dancing wouldn't be proper while we're in mourning."

Camellia hunched a shoulder, but Lily ignored her ill temper. She hugged both of her sisters tightly. "I wish you could come downstairs with me."

Jasmine threw her arms around Lily's neck and hugged her with enthusiasm. After a brief hesitation, Camellia returned her hug, too. Lily's heart throbbed. She wished the moment of total accord could last forever, but the sound of a carriage announced the arrival of Mr. Marvin's children. Lily straightened and headed for the door, a smile pasted to her lips and a prayer in her heart.

❧

"You need to move away from that window, young lady. What if your guests saw you spying on them?" Tamar tried hard to hold on to her frown. She understood Miss Jasmine's curiosity, but if Miss Dahlia caught one of her nieces staring out the window, she would scold Tamar. "Come over and sit beside Camellia."

Jasmine turned, a pronounced pout evident. "But I won't be able to see Mr. Marvin's sons."

"They'll be up here with us soon enough. In the meantime, you should work on your sampler."

"I don't want to."

"Young ladies must learn how to make neat stitches, or you'll never get married." Camellia's voice was a perfect imitation of her aunt Dahlia's.

Tamar shook her head. "Miss Jasmine is much too young to be thinking on such things."

"Aunt Dahlia says one is never too young to be a lady."

"I'm sure she's right, Miss Camellia, but that doesn't mean your little sister should be worrying about marrying." But that day would come. Miss Lily was likely to be wed before the year was out, and no one could doubt Miss Camellia would be snapped up before she was eighteen.

It seemed like only yesterday when the three girls had come to live with their grandpa and grandma. So sad they'd been to lose their ma in that terrible storm. Tamar's heart had been torn by their tears, even though she'd never rightly known her own ma. That was to be expected for a slave. But not for the privileged white children of a wealthy family. Then they'd lost their pa, too. She'd heard the others slaves say Master Isaiah had made him promise to stay away. Such a sad thing—

Her thoughts were interrupted when the door to the nursery burst open, and two young men stepped inside. One sported a thatch of straight red hair while the other had a head of dark, curly hair. But their relationship was obvious in their facial features and stocky, square bodies.

The older one sketched a bow and advanced to the sofa where Camellia and Jasmine sat. "I'm Adolphus Marvin Jr., and this is my little brother, Samuel. It's a pleasure to meet you." A smile of assurance turned up the corners of his mouth.

A handful that one would be. Tamar shook her head and picked up Miss Jasmine's porcelain doll, placing it carefully on a shelf. He was the type who would catch a girl in the shadows and steal a kiss or even more, if possible. She might be a slave, but she could recognize trouble when it walked into the room.

The younger boy wore an expression of admiration as he watched Adolphus Jr. talking to the two girls. It seemed Samuel was likely to follow in his older brother's footsteps.

Tamar continued to move around the room, straightening the books and toys that had not been put away as she listened to the children getting acquainted. They talked about whether they would become related and how odd it would be if the two girls were to become their aunts. A smile touched her lips at the idea.

"I brought my marbles." The younger Marvin boy held out a hand to show off four shiny orbs. "Do you want to play?"

"Of course they don't want to play, Samuel." The older boy rolled his eyes. "They're girls. They can't sit on the ground to play."

"I can." Jasmine put down her sampler and slid from the sofa to the wooden floor. "See?"

Tamar stepped toward her. "Now, Miss Jasmine, you're going to get your dress all dirty."

Adolphus Jr. sneered. "Leave her alone, slave. It's not up to you to tell your betters how to act."

Tamar stepped back as though she'd been slapped. She might be a slave, but as the maid to the beloved granddaughters of the Blackstone home, she had earned a place of respect. Miss Dahlia might scold her for some perceived infraction, but no one ordered her around like one of the field hands.

Both Marvin boys laughed. Camellia giggled, but Jasmine stood up. "You don't talk that way to Tamar. She's my friend."

Camellia's face went slack with surprise. She glanced from her little sister to the two boys, who were laughing. "Stop laughing."

Samuel made a rude noise. "You can't tell me what to do."

Tamar knew it was her duty to maintain order in the nursery, but she *was* only a slave. She didn't need to make any enemies, especially if these boys were going to visit often. She had heard below stairs how much Miss Dahlia and her husband wanted Lily to marry Mr. Marvin. They might not react well if she defied the man's children and the boys complained.

All four children were glaring at each other. Jasmine made a fist and shook it at them. "You're dreadful, mean boys."

"I can do whatever I want." The younger Marvin boy took a step toward Jasmine, but the dark-haired girl stood her ground.

"Leave my sister alone." Camellia put a hand on his arm.

Tamar gathered her courage. "The good Lord must be shaking His head at you boys. What are you going to do? Have a fistfight with girls?" She hoped her words would ease the tension in the room.

The redhead looked at her, his gaze inscrutable. Then his shoulders relaxed. He cuffed his brother on the shoulder. "Put your marbles away. We'll find something else to play with."

Tamar's heart sank at his calculating expression. What was he planning to do? The younger one, whose dark curls had made her think he might have a sweet temperament, birthed a smile of pure evil.

"Maybe over here." Adolphus went for the shelf of dolls, pushing them onto the floor. When the shelf was empty, he looked around for another target.

His brother mimicked him, attacking the books on the other side of the room. Soon they were in a heap on the floor.

"Stop that!" Camellia ran after Adolphus, swatting the boy around the head and neck. He shrugged off her blows and kept up his destructive actions.

Jasmine took a step toward them, but Samuel grabbed her arms in his chubby hands. "What do you think you're going to do?"

"Let me go!" Jasmine struggled to get free. "Let go."

Another crash sounded as Adolphus jerked a drawer loose and emptied its contents on the floor.

Tamar's instinct took over. She stepped forward to pull Jasmine free of the younger guest's grasp. Jasmine must have decided to take matters into her own hands. She kicked the boy holding her. He howled and bent over Jasmine, his mouth locking onto her arm. Jasmine screamed and began crying, falling to the ground when Samuel released her.

"Let me see your arm." Tamar cuffed the boy before scooping Miss Jasmine into her arms. She didn't care if she got in trouble. No one was going to hurt one of her girls.

Startled by Jasmine's cries, Adolphus had stopped strewing the girls' belongings and watched, his eyes traveling from Tamar to Samuel to Jasmine. "Quit being such a baby."

Camellia picked up a parasol from one of the heaps on the floor and used it to attack him. "You're a boorish oaf." She landed several blows on his head before he wrested her weapon out of her hands. Undaunted, she pointed at him. "I hope my sister never marries your pa. Get out of my house."

Tamar was proud of her. Camellia was finally showing her true mettle. She watched as the two boys slunk away. "What should we do now?" She stroked Jasmine's shoulder and whispered comforting phrases in the little girl's ear. But Jasmine would not be comforted.

"Do you want me to go get Aunt Dahlia and Uncle Phillip?" Camellia fell onto the sofa as though exhausted.

Tamar shuddered at the thought of breaking up the dinner party downstairs. "No, I don't think that's a good idea. Maybe I can draw Lily away without too much commotion. She always knows how to calm Jasmine, and she can make certain the others know exactly what happened."

Camellia nodded. "Come here, Jasmine. Let Tamar go downstairs and get your sissy."

Tamar left the two of them leaning against each other on the sofa and went in search of Lily. This night could not end fast enough.

And that's the way I found him almost two hours later."

Everyone seated at the dinner table laughed at the humorous story Mr. Marvin told about his oldest son, Joshua. Lily had to admit he was a gifted storyteller who had kept them enthralled with tales of his travels and his sons. He had a self-deprecating air, as though he was grateful for whatever attention he received.

Lily realized she liked Mr. Marvin. If only he weren't so old.

"Adolphus, I don't know when I've laughed so much." Grandmother took a sip of water before returning her goblet to the table. "When Dahlia told me she wanted you to come over for dinner, I had my doubts. But after what we've been through recently, genuine laughter is a welcome diversion."

"Thank you." Mr. Marvin captured Grandmother's hand in his own. "I was so sorry to hear of your loss. If I've helped in even a small way, I will consider the evening a momentous success."

Was that a blush on Grandmother's cheeks? Lily's heart pounded when Grandmother looked toward Aunt Dahlia and nodded. Was she trying to signal her approval of Mr. Marvin as a suitor for Lily? What a frightening turn of events. No matter that Mr. Marvin seemed to be a nice man. She had no interest whatsoever in marrying him. Ever.

Grandmother pulled her hand from Mr. Marvin's. "That's very kind of you, Adolphus. We must have you over again soon."

Uncle Phillip nodded his agreement. "I concur, Adolphus. You should consider yourself a member of the family." Lily's heart sank further as she glimpsed the determination on her uncle's features. She had always thought of him as a weak man, controlled by Aunt Dahlia's whims, but recently she had seen him in a different light. He was the man of the family now that Grandfather was dead, and he seemed eager to embrace the role. That would not have bothered her except that his primary objective seemed to be arranging a marriage between her and Mr. Marvin.

Mr. Marvin glanced at Lily. "I would like that very much."

"Shall we retire in the parlor while the men gather in the study?" Satisfaction had settled on Aunt Dahlia's face.

Lily slid her chair out quickly, ready to escape the dining room. How had this happened? Grandmother was supposed to be on her side. It was bad enough she had to worry about Aunt Dahlia and Uncle Phillip trying to hurry her off into a loveless marriage. Now Mr. Marvin had managed to turn her only ally against her.

"Are you enjoying your evening, Lily?" Grandmother sat down on the black horsehair sofa and patted the place next to her. "I found Mr. Marvin engaging, didn't you?"

"She ought to fix his interest." Aunt Dahlia took a seat in the red brocade chair on the opposite side of the sofa table and reached for her sewing bag. "You could do a lot worse than marry him, you know."

Feeling besieged, Lily tried to come up with an answer that would satisfy them. A knock at the door followed by Tamar's familiar face seemed like a reprieve. "What's wrong?"

Tamar stepped inside the room. "It's Miss Jasmine. She's crying for you."

Lily stood.

"Where do you think you're going?" Her aunt's voice halted her escape.

"I'm going to see about my sister, of course."

"I don't think that's a good idea." Aunt Dahlia stabbed at the sampler with her needle. "I doubt there's anything terribly wrong with her, but if there is, Tamar or another of the girls can see to her."

"Let her go, Dahlia." Grandmother smiled. "Don't you remember what it was like to look to your older sister?"

Aunt Dahlia sighed. "Well, be quick about it, Lily. We don't want

Mr. Marvin thinking you are trying to avoid him."

Lily made her escape and hurried up to the nursery. The normally tidy room had been turned upside down. Toys lay scattered about, and several pieces of furniture were upturned. "Did an army invade while I was eating?"

"Near enough." Tamar righted a chair. "It's those imps whose father is courting you. I don't know what he's taught them, but it wasn't company manners. They fair terrorized your sisters before Camellia told them to leave."

Lily could hear faint sobbing coming from the bedroom attached to the nursery and hurried inside to find Camellia sitting next to her younger sister's bed. Jasmine lay facedown across the bed, her pillow muffling her sobs.

Lily sat on the edge of the bed and ran a hand through Jasmine's thick hair. "What happened?"

Jasmine sat up and threw herself into Lily's arms.

"Master Samuel Marvin bit her." Camellia took Jasmine's hand in her own and held it so Lily could see the circle of teeth marks.

"How barbaric." She rocked back and forth, whispering words of love and sympathy.

Jasmine's tears slowly abated, and she hiccuped.

Lily put her hand under Jasmine's chin and tilted her face upward. Dark eyes ringed by darker lashes stared at her. "I'm sorry, Jasmine. Do you think we should bandage it?"

Jasmine's eyes grew larger. She nodded.

"Tamar, go see if Alice has any bandages in the housekeeping supplies." Tamar turned to do her bidding. "And check with Mary about the strawberry-rhubarb tarts she fixed for tea yesterday. If she has any left, bring them back with you. I know how much better I feel when I eat one of her fruit tarts."

Camellia hovered around them, alternately patting Jasmine's shoulder and fussing with the bows on her own dress. "Those boys ought to be whipped. They were nasty to Tamar, and they rushed around the nursery, pulling all our things onto the floor."

"I don't like the way they acted." Lily got up and dipped a cloth in the washbasin next to Jasmine's bed. She handed it to Jasmine before turning her attention to Camellia. "But perhaps they have some excuse since they have no mother to care for them."

"We have no mother," Camellia declared. "But do you see us tearing up our rooms or terrorizing little children?"

Was this a foretaste of what her life would be if she allowed her family to coerce her into marrying Mr. Marvin? Lily wondered. Her resolve hardened. She would not bend, no matter the cost. But for now, she needed to calm her sisters. "We are blessed to have Grandmother and Aunt Dahlia to teach us how to behave."

"Lily, I know why they're so bad." Jasmine's voice was dreamy, like she was about to fall asleep.

"Why is that, little one?"

"Cuz they're made of 'snips and snails and puppy dogs' tails.'"

Laughter bubbled up. "That's right." Lily hugged her sister close. She glanced up at Camellia and saw her lower lip protruding. She no longer looked like she was on the cusp of becoming a woman—she looked like a little girl who needed comforting. "Come over here, Camellia. You're too old for cuddling, but I think Jasmine would appreciate an extra hug, and I know I would."

For once Camellia forgot her dignity. She crowded onto Jasmine's bed.

Silence filled the room, and contentment spread through Lily as she put an arm around her middle sister. She wanted to save this tender moment for future remembrances. It had been far too long since the three of them had sat together with their arms wrapped around each other. Although Lily was sorry for the trouble that had arisen, she would much rather be up here than downstairs with the adults.

Tamar bustled in with a tray laden with treats and bandages. "Those boys are in the kitchen running around like a couple of heathens."

"I hope they're not causing Mary too much trouble."

"She has plenty of help down there. More than your sisters and I had when they attacked the nursery." Tamar set her tray down on a piecrust table and handed the roll of bandaging to Lily.

Jasmine lay back against her pillows while Lily and Camellia cleaned the wound and wrapped it in soft cotton.

"Can I have a tart?" Jasmine's eyelids looked heavy, as though she would fall asleep at any moment.

"Of course, dearest." Lily nodded to Tamar, who took a plate from the tray and put a tart on it. "If you can stay awake long enough, that is."

Camellia rolled up the bandaging while Jasmine took a few bites from one of the treats.

"Thank you, Sissy." Jasmine handed the plate to Lily before settling back against her pillows once more.

Lily pulled her coverlet up to Jasmine's chin, relieved to see the returning color in her cheeks. Putting a finger to her lips, she signaled Tamar and Camellia toward the nursery. They spent the next half hour discussing the day, ending with the earlier disaster.

Camellia wiped her mouth after finishing one of the delicious tarts and folded her hands in her lap. "I couldn't believe it when that boy bit Jasmine." She looked toward Lily, tears welling up in her blue eyes. "I was trying to get the other one to stop tearing up our things, but I should have been protecting Jasmine."

"It wasn't your fault, dearest. You did what you could. And you had Jasmine mostly calmed down before I got here. I'm sure that's why she fell asleep so quickly."

Looking pleased, Camellia stood up. "I suppose I shall go to bed, too. Is your dinner party over?"

Horror overcame Lily. "I forgot. As soon as I help you straighten up in here, Tamar, I'll go back down and see if Mr. Marvin is still here. I hope he is. I have some hard words for him about his children."

"You go on down, Miss Lily." Tamar returned their dishes to her tray. "I can clean up this mess in no time."

Camellia added her voice to Tamar's. "I can help her, Lily."

"Are you sure?"

Both of them nodded, so Lily shook out her skirts. Checking to make sure there was no rhubarb on her skirt, she left them working and went downstairs.

On her way to the parlor, Lily noticed the door to Grandpa's study was open. Certain the men had joined the women in the parlor by now, she stopped to pull it closed. But with her hand on the doorknob, she heard a voice. Someone was inside! Who could it be? The terrible Marvin boys? She leaned closer to make sure before going in to confront them.

"I tell you steamboats are what you should be investing in." She recognized Uncle Phillip's voice and realized the men were still discussing business. "They are the easiest, fastest, safest way to transport people and goods. If you've never seen the inside of a steamship, you should do yourself the favor of taking a trip, say to New Orleans or Memphis. You will be amazed at the luxury to be had. The quarters are comfortable, the food is as good as our cook prepares, and the scenery is astounding."

Knowing she should turn away, Lily couldn't. Would Mr. Marvin be interested in purchasing a steamboat and raising a family on the river? She might change her mind about the man if she could be assured of living on the Mississippi River.

"I don't know, Phillip. I'm not a man to take risks."

"I tell you there is no risk, no risk at all. Everyone connected to a riverboat makes money—from the shipwright to the crew, not to mention the planters, farmers, and shipping tycoons who rely on the river to deliver their goods."

Lily closed her eyes as she imagined the scene in the study. Her uncle would be sitting in Grandfather's leather chair, a cigar in one hand and a glass of brandy in the other. Mr. Marvin would be sitting on the other side of the desk, leaning forward with eagerness to learn more of her uncle's ideas.

"I'm not saying I'm ready to take the plunge, but if I was, how would I proceed?"

Lily leaned closer.

"I normally wouldn't tell anyone this, but since you are so close to becoming a member of the family, you should go to Dashiell Champney." Her uncle's voice was quiet, confidential, like he was sharing a deep secret. "He owns several boats and would likely have one or more for sale. It's better than having money in the bank. I don't know how your finances are, Adolphus, but it never hurts to have a goose to lay a few golden eggs, eh?"

"I don't know if you should be so hasty to consider me a part of your family." Mr. Marvin coughed. "Your niece is less than receptive to my overtures. She seems more concerned about her sisters than finding a husband."

"You let me worry about that. As long as you would like to have her as your bride, all you have to do is propose." Uncle Phillip chuckled. "I'll make certain Lily says yes."

Mr. Marvin's laughter joined her uncle's, creating a revolting noise. Uncle Phillip was supposed to be her protector, not someone willing to pawn her off on the first man who approached. Or had Uncle Phillip approached Mr. Marvin? Either way, she would not stand for it.

All thought of rejoining the dinner party evaporated. She could not abide the idea of being polite to either Uncle Phillip or Mr. Marvin. Lily picked up her skirts and fled to her bedroom. Shutting the door with a firm click, she flung herself across her bed. Hot tears flooded her down pillow as she fell victim to despair.

What would she do? What could she do? She was only a girl, a girl who had inherited nothing more than an adequate dowry. The same amount of money each of her sisters had inherited. If there was some way to put all their money together, she might be able to come up with a solution. What she needed was a way to take care of all three of them.

Inspiration struck. Mr. Champney was Jean Luc's father. He had seemed interested in her when they danced. He could use his influence with his father to allow her to purchase one of his steamships. All she had to do was convince Grandmother to let her have her dowry now. It might be sufficient to buy a boat, but if it wasn't, perhaps Mr. Champney would sell her the boat if she promised him a large percentage of the riches she would earn transporting goods along the river.

Lily sat up in bed, her tears drying as she considered the idea. She would take Camellia and Jasmine with her. They could make a home for themselves on the river. It would be unconventional, but it would also be free of the restrictions they faced here. No one would be able to tell them what to do or whom to marry.

The more she thought about her idea, the more excited Lily got. When Tamar entered to help her get ready for bed, she could hardly contain her emotions.

Tamar combed out her long hair and braided it. "It seems someone has stars in her eyes. Are they stars of romance?"

Lily rolled her eyes. "I don't know what you're talking about." Her plans were far too vague to share with Tamar. Perhaps in the days to come, but tonight she would keep the information secret. "I didn't speak to him after I left you and Camellia. The idea of being polite to him after seeing what his child did to Jasmine was too much to bear. I hope he understands I'm not at all interested in him."

Tamar cocked an eyebrow. "Maybe the child needs a mother to teach him how to act."

"Maybe so, but I don't plan to take on that job, and I pity the woman who does."

"I thought your aunt and uncle were in favor of a match." Tamar pulled back the covers and waited for Lily to climb into bed.

“They may be, but Grandmother assured me I do not have to marry anyone I don’t wish to.”

Lily thought she would be too excited to sleep, but her eyelids grew heavy as soon as Tamar blew out the last lamp. Schemes and dreams blended, and she barely had the energy to bid Tamar good night before sleep claimed her.

Chapter Ten

Blake wiped his forehead with a grimy sleeve. "I'm not used to this kind of work anymore."

Jensen grunted. "I thought you never worked with your hands."

A laugh burned his throat. "There was a time all I knew was physical labor. Every bite of food I put in my mouth came from hard work."

"I never heard you talk about your past." Jensen gave a final tug to the drapes he'd spent the past hour hanging. "You were a farmer's son?"

How he wished the days of his youth were so easily described. Blake shook his head. "Ma taught us how to plant a garden, or we'd have perished from starvation."

He leaned over the wood he'd been sawing and started work again. His mind, however, had been primed like a pump. Memories flooded through—cold nights, empty stomachs, his baby sister crying for milk. No longer able to bear her pitiful sobs, he'd stolen out of the house after dark, climbed a fence to get into Farmer Weems's pasture, and squeezed nearly a quart of fresh milk from one of his cows. Of course his father caught him feeding Ada and had rained down the punishment prescribed in the Bible for spoiled children.

Blake had taken the whipping without a sound, focusing his attention on the way Ada had looked when her hunger was satisfied. Afterward, his father had tried to comfort him. Blake still remembered the hatred and shame he'd felt. Not because of what he'd done, but because his father insisted on relying on God to feed his family. What kind of God demanded starvation and poverty? Not the kind of God he wanted to worship. Blake hadn't darkened the door of a church since he'd left home. And he was much happier for it.

"You sure can make that saw sing." Jensen's shout interrupted his thoughts.

Blake pushed down once more, surprised when his saw met little resistance. He'd nearly sawed the plank in two without realizing it. With another quick pull and thrust, he finished. Standing up, he rubbed his back and grinned at Jensen. "It's funny you say that."

"Why?" Jensen's unscarred eyebrow rose. "You was working harder than a lumberjack trying to meet his boss's tally."

"Back home, some people use saws like this to make music." He held the tool to his chest and pretended to drag a bow across its back. "They can make a saw sing with a voice as clear as an angel."

Jensen's face was a mixture of curiosity and doubt. "Are you trying to humbug me? I know I don't have much learning, but I'm not a daft old coot."

"Not at all. When you can't afford to buy fancy violins or pianos, you look around for alternate ways to entertain during a long winter's night."

"Well, if that don't beat the Dutch." Jensen scratched his head. "I heard of blowing into a bottle, and I've seen men beating out a rhythm on an upturned washbasin, but I've never seen nobody making music with a saw."

The floor shifted under Blake's feet. "I wonder who that could be. Maybe the captain has decided to return." He set his saw down and strode outside. "Lars, is that you?" Only silence answered his call.

From his vantage point on the second floor of his boat, Blake had a wide view of the dock and the first-floor decks. As far as he could see, no one had come aboard. He looked out toward the river, wondering if they'd been jostled by a passing boat, but saw no sign of recent activity. He shrugged. Maybe a gator had nudged them.

He looked around at the curtain of trees separating them from civilization. As soon as he'd taken possession of his boat, Blake had decided to move it away from the bustling dock at Natchez Under-the-Hill. He would need to make major renovations to *Hattie Belle* to meet his needs, and he wanted peace and quiet while he worked. Shaking his head, he walked back inside.

"Who was it?"

"No one as far as I could see."

Jensen's face whitened. "There's spirits living in some of these backwaters."

Blake would have laughed, but he could see his friend was serious. "I imagine it was more likely an alligator. You'll find a lot more wildlife than ghosts out here. Besides, it's not even noon. No self-respecting ghost would be out in broad daylight."

"Go ahead and make fun of me, but I've seen things on this river that would make you stop and think." Jensen nodded in emphasis. "Many a unsuspecting traveler's been attacked on the Natchez Trace, robbed and killed and left without a proper burial. What's to stop them from rising up and wandering around out there in the woods?"

"Death would do it, I'd think." Blake stacked the planks he'd sawed and grabbed another.

Jensen shook his head. "One of these days you're gonna see something that'll make you stop and scratch your head."

"Maybe so, but until then I prefer to put my faith in the natural world." Blake sent Jensen downstairs to fix some lunch and got back to work on his final project. As soon as he had his bar finished, the gaming room would be complete. Then he'd move back to Natchez and open up the most amazing gambling hall this part of the world had seen. He hoped it would become so famous they'd hear about it upriver, all the way up in Hannibal. A tight smile twisted his lips as he imagined the reaction of one man in particular—the Reverend William Matthews.

Chapter Eleven

"I don't know if this is a good idea, Lily." Grandmother pulled out a stack of golden coins, each valued at fifty dollars, from the safe Grandfather had installed in his study years earlier.

"The money will be safe in the bank and earn interest." For the past half hour, Lily had been trying to convince her grandmother to let her deposit her dowry at Britton's Bank.

"And what if the bank has to close its doors before you are ready to collect your dowry?"

Lily understood her grandparent's distrust. In the past, banks had closed, and people's banknotes had become nothing more than worthless paper. She remembered hearing of two such disasters from Grandfather.

If she had been planning on depositing her dowry with Mr. Britton, she might have had second thoughts, too. But she intended to spend the money as soon as she could. On a steamship. Telling her grandmother her real plans, however, would result in a bigger argument if not an outright refusal.

Wishing she could be honest with her grandmother, Lily sighed. "Things are different now, Grandmother. My money will be safe."

"It is your money, even though your grandfather intended it for your dowry." Grandmother closed and secured the safe. "I only hope nothing happens to it before you wed. Once you are safely married, your husband will be the one to decide how to keep it safe."

"Yes, ma'am."

"Speaking of husbands, what did you think of Mr. Marvin?" Grandmother opened the top drawer of Grandfather's desk and pulled out a leather pouch.

Lily shrugged. The last thing she wanted to discuss was Adolphus Marvin. He'd become a veritable nuisance in the last few days, sending notes or dropping by to pay a call. It had taken all her ingenuity to avoid him, and she had the feeling her efforts would soon be curtailed by her uncle. "He seems to have many virtues."

Grandmother nodded. "But?"

Another shrug. "I don't know, Grandmother. I've always dreamed of meeting a special man." She chose her words with care. "The Bible says God made Eve from one of Adam's ribs—that He designed her as Adam's mate, a woman he would love above all others."

"And that's what you hope to find?" Grandmother sighed. "That's your youth speaking. Once you have met a few more eligible bachelors, you will realize any one of a number of men can love you and care for you."

"Yes, ma'am." Lily folded her lips together. Even if her grandmother was right about there being more than one man she could love, there had to be someone much better suited to her who would allow her to follow her dreams. She would wait for him to find her. . .even if it took the rest of her life.

Grandmother scraped the money into the leather bag and handed it to Lily. "Is Dahlia going with you to town?"

"No, ma'am." Lily's attention was on the heavy pouch. Her future—and her sisters' futures—were represented in its contents.

"I hope you are not planning to go alone." Grandmother pointed a finger. "It's not safe for a young girl to gad about alone, especially with all that money."

"Tamar will be going with me." Lily leaned over to kiss her grandmother's cheek. "Thank you so much."

"I don't know what your uncle is going to say."

"He won't say anything if you don't tell him." Lily adopted the most innocent expression she could manage. "It's not like I'm stealing something that belongs to him, after all."

"I suppose you're right."

As she left the room, Lily felt a pang of guilt. Grandmother had always been accommodating. But since Grandfather's death, she had become as easily swayed as a rudderless boat in a hurricane.

Hardening her heart, Lily told herself it was necessary to use her grandmother's kindness to achieve her goals. Aunt Dahlia and Uncle Phillip were influencing Grandmother with their ideas—ideas that would ensure a bleak, loveless future for Lily. She had a different future in mind. One that would include hard work and sacrifice, but that would come with many rewards such as pride, wealth, and freedom.

Lily took a moment to dream about one day landing at Natchez Under-the-Hill, happy and successful. She would smile patronizingly at her uncle when he looked with envy on her beautiful boat. Everyone would heap praise on her for her daring. Her sisters would be happy with their exciting lives on the river. Her breath caught as she imagined a man standing beside her. Her husband—tall, handsome, and kind—a man who made women swoon, a modern-day David with a heart for the Lord.

Yes, once she bought a steamship and moved her sisters aboard, no one would be able to force her to do anything she didn't want to do. Until then, she had to keep her plans hidden. She had no doubt Uncle Phillip would put a stop to them if he found out.

A shiver of dismay whispered down her spine. What would God think of her deceit? But she wasn't deceiving anyone. Lily was going to tell them the truth. . .later. The Bible didn't say it was wrong to choose one's timing. She truly believed buying the steamboat was God's will for her and her sisters, to give them freedom from society's dictates. She would have to tell her grandmother as soon as she could.

Feeling better, Lily asked one of the footmen to call for the carriage and hurried upstairs to get her bonnet and gloves. Her sisters were in the classroom, working hard on their lessons. She peeked in but didn't want to break their concentration, so she put a finger to her lips and shook her head at the tutor.

Grandfather had been insistent all three of them learn to read and write, as well as have a strong grounding in literature and history. He had always told her to study the past or be prepared to repeat its mistakes. Once they moved onto their steamship, she would never be able to afford to pay the fussy little man who was currently teaching her siblings, so Lily would have to teach them what they needed to know.

Tying a large bow under her chin and pulling on her gloves, Lily checked her appearance in the reflection of her bedroom window. She needed to present a professional image and impress Mr. Champney.

Lucretia Mott would be her model. The Quaker woman had been so outspoken in her views about women's rights, the abolition of slavery, and other important issues. She could be as strong as that lady. These were modern times, after all, even if things changed more slowly in the South. Lily would not be hindered by others' views of a woman's proper duties. She would bring change to Natchez and the other ports along the river. Perhaps one day people would read about her crusades in the newspaper. Perhaps other young women would strive to be like Lily Anderson—strong, fearless riverboat captain.

She could almost hear the mournful sound of her steamship's whistle as they rounded the bend and sailed majestically into Natchez. The cannons announcing their arrival would boom like thunder. All the people of the town would stand along the bluffs and wave at her. It would be wonderful. All she had to do was persevere, and one day her dreams would come true.

Lily's thoughts occupied her all the way to town. She could tell Tamar was curious, but she didn't want to reveal her plans just yet. Plenty of time would be available once she had bought her boat. By then it would be too late for anyone to interfere.

She directed the coachman through the streets until they reached the large building of Champney Shipping.

"What business could you possibly have here, Miss Lily?"

"Nothing much." Lily waited until the coachman let down the step before disembarking. "Only the future of my family."

She stepped to the door and twisted the doorknob, taking a deep breath. The clerk's shocked expression did nothing to bolster her courage, but Lily knew she could not allow herself to retreat. She lifted her chin and marched forward. "I would like to see Monsieur Champney."

The man gulped, apparently as frightened as she felt. He nodded and stood. "Who should I say is calling?"

Divulging her name might jeopardize her plans if word got out of this office. "I'm a friend of the family."

His Adam's apple worked once more before he opened a large oak door and disappeared behind it. When he reappeared a few moments later, Monsieur Champney was with him.

The older man's dark eyes twinkled with recognition as he swept his arm in a welcoming gesture. "Bonjour, mademoiselle. Please come into my office."

Lily entered the sumptuous room and perched on the edge of a large chair.

"How may I be of assistance?" The shipping magnate settled into his even larger chair on the far side of his gigantic desk, a polite expression on his face.

She couldn't think of any way to ease into the subject. "Do you have any steamboats available for purchase?"

"I, uh. . ." Monsieur Champney cleared his throat. "The short answer is yes, but—"

"Excellent. Then all we need to concern ourselves with is the asking price." Lily wondered where her newfound courage sprang from. Fear of failure? She squeezed her hands together and prayed for guidance. She had to succeed. If she didn't, she and her sisters would be separated forever. She wouldn't be able to care for them, guide them, or watch them grow into the self-assured young women she dreamed they would become.

Her host studied her, his dark eyes reminding her of his handsome son. What would Jean Luc think if he knew she was doing business with his father? Would he admire her pluckiness or decry her boldness? And why did she care? She would soon be captain of a steamboat, plying the muddy waters of the great Mississippi River. She might never see him again.

"I have an idea." Monsieur Champney's words grabbed her wandering attention. "You are familiar with the *Hattie Belle*, no?"

"Yes, sir." Excitement zipped through her. The *Hattie Belle* was a beautiful boat. And huge. Far larger than she had hoped to be able to purchase. If only she could afford it, she and her sisters would be certain to succeed. "But I don't know if I have enough—"

He waved away her words with one hand. "I have been thinking for some time that I should sell her, but I didn't want to let that beautiful boat be ruined by the wrong owner." He smiled broadly. "I can see what a determined young woman you are, the perfect owner for *Hattie*. There is, however, one small consideration."

Lily nodded. "I have my money with me." She could hardly contain herself. Never before had God been so quick to answer her prayer. She thanked Him mentally and made a promise to spend time on her knees that evening in gratitude and praise. But for now she needed to close this deal.

His eyebrows rose. "You do not want to take a tour of the boat before making your purchase?"

"No, sir. I've been on board, remember? My aunt and I attended your party."

"Of course you did." Monsieur Champney looked through the various stacks of paper on his desk before pulling out a leather-bound portfolio. He focused his attention on the papers he held. "Here we are. I thought I had the proper paperwork on my desk. I'll need your signature here so the transfer will be properly recorded."

She barely heard his explanation, nodding as he talked about deeds and rights and filing. She signed where he indicated and handed over the money she had received from Grandmother, her mind occupied with thoughts of the river.

Her dream was coming true. She could see herself standing in the pilothouse, looking for the next port to load or unload her lucrative cargo. Her sisters would be at her side, watching the water for hidden dangers. It would be a glorious way to spend their days. Of course, the *Hattie Belle* was large enough to take on passengers as well as freight, an unexpected development for their first boat.

Wouldn't her parents have been proud to see their children following in their footsteps? Her eyes burned with unexpected tears. Sadness for Mother's death battled against the anger she felt at their father's abandonment.

Determined to turn her thoughts from the past, Lily concentrated on the idea of sifting through the backgrounds of prospective passengers before selling them berths. It would be awful to expose her little sisters to the riffraff. She would only accept the most unexceptionable people—parents with children of their own or aristocratic couples. Perhaps President Buchanan would one day petition them for passage.

"And I believe we have completed all the necessary paperwork." Monsieur Champney held out a hand. "Congratulations, you are now the proud owner of the *Hattie Belle*."

Lily's emotions nearly overwhelmed her as they shook hands to seal their arrangement. She had really done it! Her future and her sisters' futures were secure. They would make their fortunes on the river. She could hardly wait to break the good news to them.

☙

Foreboding made Tamar's heart thud as the carriage made its way back to the plantation. What had happened to the quiet girl she had cared for all these years? Lily had bloomed into a determined young woman who would not blindly follow the wishes of her elders. Yet had there really been a change? Or was Lily's decision a natural outcome of her love for her sisters?

While Tamar envied her charge the freedom she had to control her own future, she also was unsettled by Lily's ability to enter into a man's business and make a shocking, unheard-of purchase. "Tell me again exactly what you've done."

Color rode high in Lily's cheeks. "I've bought a boat—a beautiful, glorious boat called the *Hattie Belle*. It's going to be our home. I'm going to give Camellia and Jasmine a taste of life on the river. What better place for them to learn about life as they become young ladies?"

Tamar shuddered. She could think of several places.

"And we want you to come live with us, Tamar. I'm going to ask Grandmother to let you come. Won't it be wonderful?"

"I don't know." The words came out slowly. Tamar's mind went back to the first time she'd ever seen Lily—a tall, thin, towheaded child with skin as brown as a nut. A heartbroken little girl who had lost her mother and was about to lose her father. A girl determined to protect her baby sisters. That had been eight. . .no, nine years ago. In the intervening years, things had changed—Lily's skin was white and her hair had grown darker. But she was still as fiercely protective of her sisters. "Won't it be dangerous to live on a boat?"

Lily's eyebrows drew together. "I suppose you are referring to the accident that took Mother's life." Sadness invaded the carriage, an echo of the grief that had once been a part of Lily's daily life.

Tamar summoned a shaky smile. "I'm sorry, Lily dear. I didn't mean to dredge up old memories. All I meant is we're always hearing about boats catching on fire or getting sunk or attacked by pirates. Living in your family's home seems a safer choice."

It took Lily a moment to respond. Tamar wished she could find the words to bring Lily some comfort.

"I don't care." Lily's raised chin was an indication of her strong will. "It might have been safer at one time, but since Grandfather died, things have changed. I'm afraid that Aunt Dahlia and Uncle Phillip will convince Grandmother to make me marry Adolphus Marvin. She's already half-certain it would be the right thing to do."

"Your grandmother loves you, Lily. She wouldn't force you to do anything you don't want to do."

"You're probably right, but I cannot take the chance." Lily sighed. "I have to grab this opportunity. Uncle Phillip says it's a sure way to make a fortune. Besides"—a smile lit her face—"I have river water in my veins. Father always said so."

Tamar wanted to argue with Lily, but she didn't know what else to say. "I'm sure everything is going to be all right." Where had those words come from? It seemed highly unlikely that anything would be all right if Lily stuck to her plan. The list of things that could go wrong was longer than Tamar's arm.

As the carriage turned into the drive leading to Les Fleurs plantation, peace spread over her like a familiar quilt. It was the Lord. He was whispering that He was in control. It was the same voice that had brought her comfort throughout her life. The voice that had strengthened her when she needed it, reassured her whenever she took the time to listen.

Tamar smiled. "Everything is going to be all right." This time when she said the words, she knew they were the truth.

Chapter Twelve

Jean Luc strolled down the boardwalk, swinging his walking cane. Even though his world had crumbled. . .again. . .he would not wear his problems on his sleeve. The *Hattie Belle* was lost to him for now, but he would recover. He must recover.

Last night he had taken a few dollars and returned to the *Lucky Lucy*, only to find his nemesis had left the day before. He sat down and played a few hands of poker, retaining enough sense to get up and leave the table when he doubled his stake. If only he'd had that much sense a week ago.

The money jangling in his pocket was evidence that he was too good a gambler to stay behind forever. Too bad his father didn't see it his way. Every gambler knew all he had to do was to keep gambling. Eventually everything would flow his way.

A carriage pulled away as he turned the corner of Canal Street. A common occurrence at Champney Shipping. His father dealt with most of the prominent businessmen in town.

Jean Luc raised his cane in greeting as the carriage drew even with him, but his hand froze in mid-salute when his gaze discovered a large pair of sparkling brown eyes. A lady! She didn't seem familiar to him, although he found something arresting about her expression. Something that teased at his mind.

She couldn't be one of the young women he'd met at the round of social gatherings, could she? There were so many beautiful Southern belles. Blonds, brunettes, redheads. He'd met every marriageable daughter in town and most of the ones from the outlying communities. A shame they all blended together into a single image—empty, vacant, subservient. He wished he could find one who had some spirit.

Her cheeks colored, but the young lady did not look away from him. A slight smile turned up the corners of her mouth, again striking some chord in his mind. Jean Luc could not place her, so he looked to see if he recognized those she traveled with.

A female slave sat beside her, a middle-aged woman with a stern look on her honey-colored face. No brother, father, or other male accompanied them. That fact alone piqued his interest.

Was the mystery woman a young widow? No, she looked far too innocent for that role. Maybe she had dropped off some family member at his father's office and would pick him up when she finished shopping. Deciding this must be the case, Jean Luc bowed as her carriage picked up speed and passed him.

It would be interesting to meet her relative and find out more about her. So far, all the young women paraded in front of him had left him yawning at the least, horrified at the worst. He wished his parents were not so anxious for him to find a bride. At least not here. If they would allow him to travel to New Orleans, he had no doubt he could find an acceptable candidate, but sophistication could not be found at the back of beyond.

A derisive smile curled his lips. The newspapers proclaimed the Mississippi River the gateway to the West, the muddy divide between civilization and wilderness. To his mind, Natchez should be on the far side of the river. The whole state of Mississippi, as far as that went, should be moved to the wilderness. It seemed to be composed of nothing but impenetrable forest and provincial settlers.

With a sigh, he opened the front door and strode past the clerk, entering his father's sanctum after a brief knock with the silver head of his cane.

His father reached for his pocket watch and grunted. "It's about time you arrived, Son."

Jean Luc yawned and flopped into one of the chairs opposite his father. "Mama didn't mention a time when she told me you wanted to see me."

His father's lips folded into a straight line. He leaned back in his chair, causing the wood to creak ominously. Jean Luc refused to be intimidated by his father's tactics. He'd already heard plenty about his stupidity at the gaming tables. But Papa would soon find out who knew more about that.

He lifted his cane and studied the snarling panther's face. He felt a kinship with the predator. Jean Luc might have to lie in wait until the time was right, but one day he would pounce. On that day, everyone who had ever bested him would be sorry.

"I've managed to take care of the problem we have with the *Hattie Belle*."

Jean Luc glanced up at his father. "What do you mean?" A vision of Blake Matthews floating lifelessly in the eddies of the river came to mind.

"I had an interesting interview with a young lady you may remember, Miss Lily Anderson, whose grandfather, Isaiah Blackstone, recently died."

Jean Luc cocked his head to one side. A collage of images took form in his mind—a distraught young lady at the launch of the *Hattie Belle*, that same young lady eyeing him with admiration as he twirled her about on the dance floor of his boat, a concerned girl who left behind an air of mystery, and the young woman he had just seen in the carriage. Lily Anderson.

"It seems Miss Anderson will not inherit her grandfather's estate, at least not yet. But she did receive a generous settlement, a dowry of sorts."

"How generous?"

His father cocked an eyebrow. "Not enough to support your habits."

Jean Luc sat back, a flash of anger passing through him. He was tired of being gigged about how he spent his leisure time. Why could his father not forgive and move forward? Deciding that to ignore the pointed comments was the best response, Jean Luc composed his features into a mask of nonchalance and waited.

"It is, however, enough for her to purchase my portion of the *Hattie Belle*."

The cane clattered to the floor. "You sold controlling interest to a girl?"

"That's right. Imagine the surprise Blake Matthews will receive when he discovers I am no longer his partner." A bark of laughter came from Papa. "I almost wish I could be there."

Jean Luc's mind whirled. Lily Anderson had managed to possess the thing he wanted most to get his hands on. Why hadn't his father offered it to him? Or had he? It suddenly occurred to Jean Luc that selling to Miss Anderson might be his father's way of offering the boat to him. An attempt to kill two birds with one stone. Ownership of the *Hattie Belle* was a prize for which Jean Luc might pursue a marriage in earnest.

He picked up his cane and stood.

"Where are you going?" Papa's voice was dark with emotion. "I'm not through talking to you, Jean Luc."

"I have a lady to meet." He threw the answer over his shoulder as he headed out the door. He had absolute confidence in his skill with the ladies. Miss Anderson would be like putty in his hands. He would woo her and win her affection. Then he would force Blake Matthews to sell his interest in the *Hattie Belle*.

Even if it meant playing into his father's hands, Jean Luc had to take advantage of this situation. Papa might have won this skirmish, but Jean Luc was determined to win the war.

Chapter Thirteen

"Someone's driving up to the house." Jasmine struggled against Camellia to retain her place at the window.

"Move, Jasmine. I can't see who it is."

Lily held her breath, waiting to hear her sisters' pronouncement. She prayed it would not be Mr. Marvin. She had no desire to spend half an hour in the parlor ignoring her aunt's pointed looks and thinly veiled suggestions. "Serve Mr. Marvin his tea, Lily. Show Mr. Marvin what an excellent needlewoman you are. Walk Mr. Marvin to the door, Lily." The incessant directions came each time he visited. Could her aunt make her plans any more obvious? It was humiliating enough to think her relatives wanted to throw her at the first man who came courting. But they could wait until the period of mourning for Grandfather was over, or at least until a few months had passed.

"I don't recognize the carriage, but the driver is quite distinguished." Camellia glanced over one shoulder toward Lily. "Do you think it's another suitor?"

With a shrug, Lily traced the monogrammed initial in her handkerchief. Camellia had been kind enough to sew one to replace the handkerchief lost to the cutpurse in Natchez Under-the-Hill. "I doubt it. More likely a business acquaintance of Uncle Phillip's."

Camellia made a face and wandered away from the window. "I wish someone would come visit me."

"Are you going to marry Mr. Marvin?" Jasmine stood next to Lily's chair. Her lower lip trembled slightly.

Lily gave her youngest sister a reassuring hug. "No." She considered telling her sisters about their steamboat, but she had decided to wait until she could show them the *Hattie Belle*. She hadn't yet found a way to tell Grandmother, either. "I don't plan to marry anyone right now. Especially if it means leaving you here with Aunt Dahlia and Uncle Phillip." She reached out, taking one of each sister's hands. "I have a different idea for my future and yours."

A knock at the door preceded Tamar's entrance. "You are wanted in the parlor, Miss Lily."

Her fearful glance met Camellia's. Was it Mr. Marvin after all?

Camellia shook her head, her golden ringlets brushing her cheeks. "It's not Mr. Marvin. His coach is not nearly as fine."

"I wonder who it can be." Lily released her sisters' hands and stood.

Tamar frowned. "You have a spot on your collar." She hurried over to Lily's bureau. After a moment of searching, she pulled a length of black-dyed cotton from the top drawer with a satisfied sound. "Here's a fresh one. Let's get that one off."

Lily removed the offending collar. "I don't know why you must make a fuss."

"You are my responsibility, Miss Lily. I'd never let you appear to guests looking less than your best." Tamar smiled as she tweaked a lock of hair into place. "Your grandmother would have a fit if you showed up in her parlor looking like a ragamuffin."

Knowing it was useless to protest, Lily allowed Tamar to fluff the ribbon around her waist and fuss with her skirt. Finally Tamar stepped back and nodded. "Go on down, now, before your grandmother sends someone to find you."

A giggle threatened to escape. Lily swallowed it as her gaze once more met Camellia's. "I'll be back before long and tell you all about it."

Camellia shrugged as if she did not care, but Lily knew better. Both girls would be antsy until she returned.

Lily descended the stairs, her heart tripping as she considered who might be awaiting her arrival. Although they had received many visitors since Grandfather's death, most of them had been older. Perhaps this was another visitor of the same ilk. But why the summons to the parlor?

She stood outside the door and took a deep breath. Pinning a smile on her shaky lips, Lily pushed open the door and stepped inside. The man who rose from the couch made her mouth drop open. It was Mr. Champney, Jean Luc Champney, the son of the man she'd bought the *Hattie Belle* from. Had he come to tell her family of her purchase? Or perhaps he was coming to tell her the sale was invalid.

"Good morning, Miss Anderson." He bowed over her hand.

She sank into a curtsy, acting on instinct as her mind considered half a dozen reasons their guest might be here. "It's a pleasure to see you, Mr. Champney."

His smile was as attractive as she remembered from the afternoon they had danced on the upper deck of the boat she now owned. "I am honored you remember me."

Lily took a seat on the sofa and nodded toward her grandmother.

He sat down on the sofa, too, but on the far end as was proper. "The weather is so nice today. I hoped you might be interested in a leisurely drive this morning."

This was better than she'd imagined. He was interested in getting to know her better. Perhaps he was considering a courtship. Lily's cheeks warmed at the idea of being alone with him. She glanced at her grandmother for permission and received an encouraging nod. "I would greatly enjoy that, Mr. Champney." Perhaps he would be amenable to taking her to the river so she could tour the *Hattie Belle*. Her boat. The words thrilled her. Did he know she had purchased the boat?

Grandmother sent Tamar for Lily's cape before giving Mr. Champney strict instructions on their outing. She was to be returned home by the time lunch was served. He was to keep his carriage on the main roads, and they were to take Tamar with them for propriety's sake.

Once she and Tamar were ready, Mr. Champney helped Lily into the front seat of his fancy cabriolet. His footman assisted Tamar into the backseat located on the outside of the fancy carriage. As Mr. Champney climbed into the front seat and settled himself beside her, Lily hid a grin. Tamar was muttering under her breath about the dangers of traveling. Something about breakneck speed and her desire to use her own God-given limbs.

Mr. Champney raised his riding whip to encourage the pair of horses, and they set off. "Do you have any place in particular you would like to go?"

How nice of him to consider her wishes. Lily couldn't help comparing the man beside her to the one her aunt and uncle were trying to foist on her. If they had chosen Mr. Champney, she would not have been forced to find her dire solution. Of course, she would also not be about to realize her dream of living on a riverboat like her mother. "I'd love to go to the waterfront."

He nodded. "I suppose you want to visit your boat."

Lily could feel her cheeks heating. "Please don't mention it to my family."

"They don't know you purchased the *Hattie Belle*?"

Lily shook her head. "I don't want them to stop me. As soon as I make sure everything is ready, I plan to move my sisters and myself aboard. We're going to live on the *Hattie Belle*."

His hands jerked on the reins, and his horses swerved. For a moment he had to concentrate on the horses, but as soon as he had them under control, he turned to stare at Lily. "You can't live on a riverboat."

Lily stared at him. Wasn't his family involved in shipping? "Why not? My parents did. My father was the captain of his own boat, and he and my mother often took trips together before th–the accident."

"That's precisely why you should abandon this idea. It's far too dangerous for a lady."

A wagon trundled toward them, its bed empty. Lily wondered what it had carried to the river. Cotton? Sugarcane? Corn? Or maybe some handmade goods? Whatever the cargo, it had likely been loaded onto a steamship destined for sale in some distant city. Her heartbeat accelerated. Maybe it was even now sitting on the *Hattie Belle*, waiting for her arrival before sailing off.

"You can't say anything to change my mind." Lily looked away. "I'm going to make a home for myself and my sisters. A place where we can make our own choices and live our lives the way we wish."

Silence fell between them as they entered Natchez. The traffic was heavy, and Mr. Champney had to pay attention to their route. She could feel his disapproval like a wall between them, but it only made her more determined. No obstacle would stop her. Living on the *Hattie Belle* was a dream come true.

"Very well, I'll take you to your boat." His voice held a note of something she could not name. Amusement or resignation? "I only hope you won't be too disappointed."

He guided the carriage through town but did not take the road to Natchez Under-the-Hill.

"Where are we going?" Lily could not keep the suspicion out of her voice.

"To see your boat."

"But I thought—"

"Miss Anderson, I have only your best interests at heart. I hope you will one day learn to trust me."

His tone made her feel guilty. Abashed, she watched the road silently. Soon they came to a bend, and she caught sight of the brown water of the Mississippi River. She caught her breath as a pair of white smokestacks appeared. She turned to Mr. Champney and had to fight the impulse to hug him.

His dark gaze seemed to read her mind. His smile widened, giving it a wolfish quality she had not noticed before. Before she could react, a banging sound turned her attention back to the *Hattie Belle*. "What is that?"

"I would imagine that is Blake Matthews." He brought the carriage to a standstill and waited for his footman to come to the horses' heads. "My father said he was making some alterations to the boat."

"Is he the captain?"

"Not exactly."

Lily was beginning to lose her patience with Mr. Champney. What kind of game did he think this was? "Is he one of the crew?"

"I suppose you could say that." Mr. Champney climbed down and came around to help her disembark, his hand outstretched.

Lily put her hand in his and leaned forward, trusting him to balance her weight until her feet could touch the ground. To her shock she found herself caught in his embrace. "What are you doing? Put me down!" She pushed at his chest to no avail.

"Hold still, Miss Anderson. The ground here is quite muddy." With several long-legged strides he reached the boat and stepped aboard before setting her gently on her feet.

Not sure if she should be angry or thankful, Lily straightened her bonnet and stepped back. "You might have warned me." His teasing look brought a smile as Lily realized how silly her complaint was. "Thank you." She glanced back toward his carriage.

"Shall we begin our tour?"

"Tamar is still in the carriage awaiting help."

The teasing look disappeared from his coal-black eyes. "You want me to assist a slave? She can make her own way to the boat."

The disdain on his face brought her up short. Tamar was more than a slave. She had mothered Lily and her two sisters from the time they first came to live with their grandparents. She had wiped away their grief-stricken tears and bandaged their scrapes. "Tamar may be a slave, but she's part of my family. She is also my chaperone, and I refuse to take one more step until she is standing beside me."

His lips tightened, and he gave her the briefest of bows before returning to the carriage. He carried Tamar as though he held an armful of firewood. His attitude might not be uncommon in this part of the world, but he should have some consideration for Lily's feelings.

"Who's out there?" The gruff voice sounded vaguely familiar to her.

"It's Jean Luc Champney. I've brought the new owner of the *Hattie Belle*."

She liked the sound of that. The new owner. Before she could fully savor the introduction, her thoughts were cut short.

The man responded with a crude epithet.

Who did he think he was to speak so before checking to see if a lady was present? Lily's ears burned. "Please mind your tongue. I am not accustomed. . ." Her words trailed off as he stepped onto the deck above them. The man who had accused her of being the mother of a thief. The man who had already given her the rough side of his tongue, although he had refrained from curses that day. The man whose strong arms had encircled her and held her protectively close when it had seemed someone might be shooting at them. Hot blood flushed her neck and cheeks as she remembered the feel of his muscular chest cushioning her fall.

"And I'm not used to idlers who interrupt my work with foolishness." He stared down at them.

Lily's gaze made note of his leather shoes before traveling up the length of his dark trousers. They might have been black, but she couldn't tell because of the liberal coating of dirt or dust. His shirt, which she supposed had once been white, was now a dingy yellow from the same dusty substance. Her gaze halted for a brief instant on the open collar of his shirt, as it allowed more of his chest to show than she was accustomed to seeing. Raising her eyes to meet his gaze, Lily was mesmerized by the blue fire in them, a fire that set free a host of butterflies in her stomach.

She gulped in some air to quiet the tickling sensation and reached for Mr. Champney's arm, her fingers gripping with the strength of an eagle's talons. "I don't know what work you could possibly have on *my* boat."

His jaw dropped. He disappeared inside, and she heard his heavy footsteps descending stairs before he reappeared, his broad shoulders filling the main entrance. "What on earth are you talking about?"

Mr. Champney coughed, and she thought she saw him hide a smile.

Letting go of her escort's arm, Lily opened the strings of her reticule to pull forth her deed to the *Hattie Belle*, glad a last-minute impulse had made her bring it along. "I recently purchased this boat, and you are to vacate it immediately." She waved the vellum sheet toward him for emphasis.

He grabbed the deed and unfolded it.

Lily didn't see why he should be so interested in reading about her purchase, but she supposed it wouldn't hurt for him to see the proof in black and white.

"What kind of trickery is this?" The man ignored her and directed his question to Mr. Champney. "Or have you been gambling again?"

Her breath caught as Mr. Champney's face turned bright red. Was he about to demand satisfaction for the insolent words?

The butterflies in her stomach turned into a hardened lump. "I don't know what you're talking about, sir."

"He's no 'sir.' His name is Blake Matthews." Mr. Champney's voice had an edge she had not heard before. "He's nothing but a gambler—a man who relies on Lady Luck to make his living."

The anger she had sensed in Mr. Matthews dissipated suddenly. He folded the deed and handed it to Lily. "Yes, I'm a gambler, and I depend on my wits to survive. I like to think of my lifestyle as being free of the strictures of modern society." His gaze speared the man beside her. "It's better than being the wastrel son of a conniving businessman."

Mr. Champney's brows lowered once more. "Be very careful who you slander."

"What slander? Your father decided to bail out of our business deal by selling his interest to a naive young girl who ought to be home, batting her eyes for an adoring husband."

The air seemed to thicken. How dare this man—a gambler—patronize her! She drew herself up to her full height of five foot three. "I don't know what you're doing here, Mr. Blake Matthews, but I suppose it is an arrangement you had with Mr. Champney when he was the owner of the *Hattie Belle*. Since that is no longer the case, I would greatly appreciate it if you would gather your belongings and remove yourself from the boat."

"And if I don't?" The look in his blue eyes reminded her of a stalking cat—predatory, dangerous.

Lily lifted her chin. "Then I will call on the sheriff to remove you."

"That will be hard to do, my dear." His lips curled into a triumphant smile. "You see, barely a week ago the upstanding young man next to you lost to me in a card game. And he gave me his deed to the *Hattie Belle* as payment."

"But I own—"

"If you read your paper carefully, you'll find you own a portion of the boat we're standing on."

Lily unfolded the deed once more and saw the language he meant. "Controlling interest?" She skipped the legal wording that made no sense to her and found that she owned exactly 51 percent of the *Hattie Belle*. Her mind spun. She didn't own the boat outright? After all the money she had spent, she had to share her boat with someone else? Tears sprang to her eyes as her dreams collapsed.

She had been duped. Tricked by Jean Luc's father. The sunlight dimmed, and the sounds of the river seemed far away. What was she going to do? What could she do? Beg her uncle for help straightening out this mess? Unthinkable. She would have to make the best of it. Hadn't she planned to face down any obstacles to her plans? She would not give up at the first challenge.

Her mind raced. She could still make this work. Surely a few trips delivering cargo would give her enough money to buy the rest of the boat. She nodded and lifted her gaze to meet the blue eyes of the man standing in front of her. Her partner. Her temporary partner. "As soon as I have sufficient money, I will buy you out."

His eyebrows rose. "You're going to buy me out? I don't think so. I have my own plans for the *Hattie Belle*."

"And that will be fine as long as they meet with my approval."

"Your approval? You're only a girl."

That might be so, but Lily had been raised on a thriving plantation, and she had seen her grandfather handle myriad problems through the years. She drew on that experience for her reply. "Nevertheless, I am the one in charge."

Mr. Champney coughed. Was he amused? She didn't have time to be affronted, so Lily ignored him, concentrating instead on Mr. Matthews. "I would like a tour of our boat."

His face looked as if chiseled from a block of stone. She could read disapproval in every line of his body.

Part of Lily wanted to run back to Les Fleurs plantation. But that was her old life. Her new life was in front of her, if only she could summon the courage to embrace it. She would do this, for herself and for her sisters.

Mr. Matthews apparently recognized her determination. He bowed and swept his hand toward the inside of the boat. "Right this way."

Chapter Fourteen

Blake watched the little spitfire as he took her through the boat—their boat. Grudging admiration filled him for her spirit, but she needed to learn this was no place for a lady.

Maybe explaining the physical labor involved would convince her to be a silent partner. Instead of being bought out, he could likely put together enough money in a month or less after opening his casino to pay her off and forget she existed.

"We have constructed several tables for poker, and I am looking for a roulette wheel to purchase." His chest expanded as he detailed his plans. The *Hattie Belle* was going to be gorgeous when he finished. "I'll hang ruby-red curtains on the windows to keep the customers from realizing what time of day it is. That way we can run the games constantly. This boat will earn more money in a week than it could earn from six months of running cargo up and down the river."

"Delivering cargo will not strip wealth from people." Her disapproving tone matched the look on her face.

What had he expected? She was no doubt too puritanical to immediately agree. But if he could make her see the profits at stake, surely she would change her mind. "We'll have food and libations available at all times. I already have an excellent chef who will take care of the meals."

Jensen stepped from the doorway of one of the staterooms, and Blake heard a soft sound from the spitfire. He expected to see an expression of horror on her face, but instead sympathy filled her large brown eyes. Her gaze met his, and he was instantly wrapped in her warmth. "This is Jensen Moreau, my steward and chef and handyman rolled into one."

Jensen seemed to be lost in a trance. He was looking at someone behind Blake, a silly expression on his weathered face. If Blake wasn't mistaken, adoration filled every inch of Jensen's face.

Blake turned to see what had caused such a response. Miss Anderson's chaperone? Curiosity kept his attention centered on the woman. She had to be a few years older than Jensen, and if he judged correctly, a necessary ability of a gambler, she was devoted to her mistress and would have no time for a romance.

"Good morning, Mr. Moreau." Miss Anderson stepped forward and curtsied.

Jensen came out of his trance, but the gentle smile that looked so odd on his face remained. He bowed, exhibiting more grace than Blake would have thought possible. "Welcome aboard the *Hattie Belle*."

"You may not realize it, Jensen, but you are welcoming your new employer." He shot a tight smile at Jensen's shocked face. At least he had managed to refocus the man's attention to important matters. "Miss Anderson has purchased interest—"

"Controlling interest."

Her interruption made him grind his teeth. He consciously loosened his jaw before continuing. "*Controlling* interest in the *Hattie Belle*, and intends for us to get the boat in shape to run cargo."

"I don't rightly understand." The man looked from Blake to the spitfire, but his gaze moved back to the slave and settled there. It appeared Jensen had been struck by Cupid's arrow.

Jean Luc made a disgusted sound. "Can we get this over with? I promised I would have Miss Anderson home in time for luncheon." He pulled a watch from his waistcoat. "We need to leave before much longer if I am to keep my word."

She tilted her chin upward in a gesture of defiance, showing she intended to stay as long as she pleased.

If Blake didn't want the lot of them here all day, he needed to come up with a distraction. "I do have a problem you could help me with, Miss Anderson."

Her chin came down a notch. Her brown eyes gleamed with

triumph. "What is that, Mr. Matthews?"

"Jensen here needs to concentrate on getting the kitchens ready, but I cannot do all the carpentry by myself, much less the cleaning." He nodded to the scattered bits of wood and sawdust where he'd been working. "Perhaps you could hire some help."

She nodded, and her bright smile moved her face from the realm of pleasing to attractive. "Do you have a captain?"

Blake gathered his wandering thoughts. "I don't think we'll need a captain since the boat won't be leaving the bank."

"I see." She ran a finger across her chin. Miss Lily Anderson's frown was rather cute.

Blake steeled his heart. He couldn't afford to let her puppyish eagerness get under his skin. He would give her tasks to keep her busy until he could put together enough money to buy the boat outright. Then he would send her home where she belonged.

"You've given me much to think about, Mr. Matthews."

He bowed to the three of them and swept his hand outward. "This way to the stairs."

Jensen came up beside Blake as he watched Jean Luc help the women pick their way around muddy patches on the way back to the carriage.

"That's one mighty pretty girl."

Blake frowned. Was Jensen talking about Miss Anderson? He followed his friend's gaze to where the slave, Tamar, was climbing to her seat.

"I thought she turned your head, but I have to warn you, I doubt she'll leave her little chick. She'll probably want to stay with Miss Anderson until she marries, and perhaps even after."

Jensen sighed. "She'd never look at the likes of me."

"Don't be ridiculous, man. You're a fine fellow with a steady job and a good heart. Any woman would be lucky to be the object of your affection." Blake hid his doubts from the other man. Jensen would probably forget all about his attraction after a few days. As much as Jensen prized his freedom, Blake could not see the man settling into matrimony. But if his friend decided he did want to win Tamar's heart, Blake would do everything in his power to help him realize his dream.

❧

Jean Luc whipped up his horses on the ride back to Lily's home. He needed to figure a way to turn the obvious enmity between Lily and Blake to his advantage.

Sliding a glance to the young woman perched beside him, Jean Luc wondered what had happened to her determination to use the *Hattie Belle* for ferrying cargo. She had seemed so certain of her plans. Had she been overwhelmed by the enormity of the work to be done? Or had she simply knuckled under the pressure applied by Blake?

Of course she was only a woman. Truth to tell, he was a bit relieved Lily wouldn't be joining the world of business. Women had no place in that sphere. He might not have put it as crudely as the gambler had, but ladies should concentrate on their families and households.

He stole another glance at Lily. What was she thinking? He couldn't tell from her expression, but it must be engrossing as she had not said a word for the last mile. "Is everything okay?"

She started as if awakened. Her brown eyes were full of apology as she turned to him. "I'm afraid I was caught up in my plans. Thank you so much for taking me to the *Hattie Belle*. I don't know when I could have gotten there on my own."

"It is my pleasure. When Papa told me what Blake intended to do with the boat, I thought you would want to know about it."

"Yes. And you knew right where it was docked. I doubt I could have found it on my own."

He basked in her approving words. At least she admired him. He could grow accustomed to her smile and the glow in her large brown eyes. It was a welcome relief after the vitriol he'd recently gotten from his parents. "I could not believe Matthews wanted you to hire help. I doubt you'll want to ask your uncle for assistance since you said you wanted to keep him from learning about your purchase, so I'd be glad to take on the task of interviewing some of the local workmen and sending them to the boat."

"Thank you, Mr. Champney. It is sweet of you to offer, but I won't be hiring anyone."

Jean Luc frowned. "Do you plan to leave Matthews and his servant to do the work?"

"Not at all." She beamed. "I plan to do the work myself."

Her words blasted him like a winter gale. "You plan what?" He was shocked to the core of his being. She must be teasing him. One glance at the determined set of her chin, however, told him she was serious. "But your reputation—"

"Oh, I will have plenty of chaperones." The look she shot him was full of mischief. "I'm going to take Tamar and my two sisters. We can do the cleaning and arranging in the kitchen and leave the men to work on the upper decks."

Jean Luc's shoulders shook with laughter.

"I don't see what you find so amusing, sir." The mischief was gone from her expression, replaced by cool disdain. "I assure you we are quite capable."

He sobered immediately. "You misunderstand, Miss Anderson. I wasn't laughing at the idea of you and your sisters working." He swallowed his laughter and slowed the horses some so he could concentrate on explaining himself. "I was just thinking of Matthews' expression when you tell him you are moving aboard."

A giggle answered him. "It won't be what he's expecting, but Mr. Matthews is going to find I am not some biddable female who will allow him to ruin the *Hattie Belle*. She is going to be my home whether he likes it or not."

It was an unconventional solution, to say the least. Jean Luc doubted even his father, the quintessential opportunist, could have foreseen this turn of events. But the more he considered her idea, the better he liked it.

All he had to do was lead her on. Lily was already showing signs of being bowled over by his knowledge and abilities. With a little work, he had no doubt he could make her fall in love with him. He might even marry her.

As her husband, he would control the day-to-day operations of the *Hattie Belle*. If Matthews could offer him enough incentive, he might let the man continue turning the boat into a casino.

Even if he didn't marry Lily, he could make sure she depended on him. Then when she tired of her foolishness, she would come to him for help. He would offer to take over. No matter which way he went, Jean Luc would end up controlling the *Hattie Belle* without having to spend a dime. And his father would have to admit he'd been wrong.

They were nearly back at the Blackstone plantation before another idea came to him. "You're going to need a captain."

She nodded. "I can put an advertisement in the *Courier* or *Free Trader*. There are probably many good captains in Natchez. I'll simply choose amongst them."

"You might find that more difficult than you think." Not wanting to offend her, Jean Luc chose his words carefully. "Although I don't agree with them, some men will be reluctant to work for a woman."

Her face puckered in a frown. "They would care more about that than about earning a good salary?"

"I'm afraid so." He let the horses slow to a walk. "But since my family owned the *Hattie Belle* until a few days ago, I know the man who captained her for us. I could talk to him privately and assure him of your ability."

"You would do that for me?" A slow smile appeared on her face. "I'd be very much in your debt."

"Think nothing of it." He leaned toward her, happy when she did not move away as she had earlier. "I want to be of service in any way."

Her cheeks suffused with blood. "Thank you, Mr. Champney."

"I have only one request." He felt her body tense, so he rushed on. "I'd like for you to call me Jean Luc."

"Is that all?" She relaxed and looked down at her hands. "I would be most happy to grant your request, Jean Luc."

He smiled as he turned the horses into the drive. He'd make sure Lars Steenberg reported to him daily on the activities aboard the *Hattie Belle*. And all he had to do to romance the girl sitting next to him was be patient and attentive. Miss Lily Anderson would soon give him everything he wanted.

Chapter Fifteen

"It's a good match." Aunt Dahlia added her voice to her husband's. "You ought to be thankful your uncle has arranged your future for you."

"Maybe I want to plan my own future." Lily glanced at her grandmother, whose hands twisted in her lap as she listened to the argument. Grandmother understood her reluctance to marry a man she did not love. They had spoken of it on more than one occasion. But it seemed Grandmother was not going to support her now.

Uncle Phillip pushed away from the mantel and took up a position behind his wife's chair. "And what type of future do you think you can arrange for yourself, young lady?"

"I suppose she could be a governess." Aunt Dahlia sniffed. "Mother and Father have certainly paid enough to educate her over the years."

Lily shuddered. The idea of being cooped up with someone else's children held about as much appeal as marrying Mr. Marvin. "I want freedom. Freedom for myself and for my sisters."

Uncle Phillip's frown darkened.

She wished he would not be so angry, but she would not bow to his wishes. Lily was determined to stand up for herself. She closed her eyes and prayed for the words to convince her relatives her way was best.

"And exactly how do you propose to get that freedom?"

Her heart thudded in anticipation of the response her answer was going to bring. "I have purchased a steamboat."

"You've what?" Her aunt's screech made Lily wince.

Grandmother gasped, and Uncle Phillip's jaw dropped.

Lily had the sudden urge to tell him to be careful or he was likely to swallow a few flies. She stifled a giggle. Nothing about this discussion was funny. She had to keep her head. . .for her sake as well as Camellia's and Jasmine's. She had to be strong. "I took the money my sisters and I inherited from Grandfather and bought the *Hattie Belle*. Mr. Champney sold it to me on Monday, and I went to see it this morning. It is in need of some repairs, but I expect to be able to load cargo on it within the month and take it on the river."

"Preposterous." Her uncle sputtered the single word. "You're a girl. What do you know about running a boat? At best you'll end up losing every dime you've invested. At worst you'll end up as dead as your mother."

Lily could not believe the callous words. Tears stung her eyes. She wanted to lash out, to turn her back on her family. They obviously didn't love her.

"That's enough." Grandmother stood, ignoring her needlework that fell to the floor. "I will not have you casting aspersions on either my daughter or my granddaughter."

"But—"

"Not another word, Phillip. Lily has made her decision. She has already purchased a boat, and though I might have wished she had consulted me before taking such a drastic step, what's done is done."

"Surely you cannot support her in this madness," Aunt Dahlia challenged Grandmother.

"Lily is eighteen, and no longer a child. She should have the right to spend her inheritance in whatever way she sees fit." Grandmother sat next to Lily on the sofa and put an arm around her shoulders. "I love you, darling. I don't want to see you miserable."

"Thank you, Grandmother."

Uncle Phillip snorted. "Both of you have lost your minds. Lily's reputation will be in tatters if you allow her to go off on a riverboat."

"It may be unconventional," Grandmother said, "but the Blackstone family has never bowed to convention. Lily will be following in the footsteps of many of her forebears—men and women who risked everything to follow their dreams."

He turned his attention to Lily. "I don't know what bee has gotten into your bonnet, young lady, but I wash my hands of you. Don't think you can come back here and beg me to introduce you to any of my acquaintances."

"I'll keep that in mind." Relief flooded Lily. Did Uncle Phillip think his words were threatening? On the contrary, she ought to thank him for his promise.

"You ought to be ashamed of yourself, Lily." Aunt Dahlia shook her head. "Do you know how much effort your uncle has put into this match? And now he's going to have to tell Adolphus you are not interested in his suit."

Uncle Phillip put a hand on his wife's shoulder. "Can't you see that your words are falling on deaf ears? Your niece is determined to bite the hand that feeds her."

"That's enough," Grandmother interjected. "If you cannot keep a civil tongue in your head, Phillip, you can leave."

He closed his mouth with an audible snap, but the look he threw Lily promised more repercussions.

She lifted her chin and glared back at him. She refused to be intimidated. And thanks to Grandmother's championship, she didn't have to worry about her aunt and uncle's disapproval.

"How soon do you plan to leave, dear?" Grandmother's voice broke the staring match.

Lily turned her attention to her grandparent. "Tomorrow morning."

Sadness crept into her grandmother's violet eyes, eyes that reminded Lily of her youngest sister. "So soon?"

"There's so much to be done." Lily hesitated, hating to ask her grandmother for a favor at this time, but she couldn't see any way around it. "May we take Tamar with us?"

Aunt Dahlia's mouth dropped open. But Grandmother stopped her words with a raised hand. "Of course. I'll feel much better knowing you have her to watch out for you and your sisters."

Relief and anticipation filled Lily. She hugged her grandmother before standing. "I promise to take good care of Camellia and Jasmine."

"I'll hold you to that." Grandmother smiled through tears. "And I expect all of you to visit as often as you can."

"We will." Lily left the parlor, her mind already consumed with the things she needed to gather for all of them. She could hardly wait to tell Tamar and her sisters about the changes coming to all of them.

Chapter Sixteen

"Will we be back in time for my piano lesson on Tuesday?" Camellia's pout had not lightened all morning as Lily and Tamar rushed about to get everything ready for their departure.

"I'm not sure how long it will be before we can return for a visit." Lily knew Camellia was going to have a difficult time adjusting to life on the river. She loved the comforts that went along with being the pampered grandchild of a wealthy planter.

"Is there a piano on the boat?"

Lily closed the trunk she had just finished packing and sat on the lid. She tilted her head at her forlorn sister as she tried to remember whether the boat had the desired instrument. "They had one during the ball I attended several months ago, but I didn't see any sign of one yesterday." She patted her sister's knee. "Everything is going to be all right, Camellia. I'm only trying to do what I think is best for all of us."

When Camellia didn't respond, Lily directed, "We'd better finish packing. The morning is slipping away quickly."

A little before noon, the three sisters and Tamar finally climbed into the carriage. The family's largest wagon—usually reserved for carrying baled cotton to market—followed them, its bed piled high with clothing, trunks, and household items.

"Whooo." Jasmine leaned against the side of the carriage, looking out the window at the passing scenery. Jasmine would embrace this adventure, and Lily would have to keep a close eye on her.

Camellia's frustration boiled over as Jasmine continued making strange noises. "What are you doing?"

"Making the sound of a riverboat." Unperturbed, Jasmine turned from the window and smiled at Lily. "Have you heard the *Hattie Belle*'s whistle?"

Lily ignored Camellia's disgusted sigh. "Yes, it's quite distinctive. You'll love it."

"Could be none of us will hear it for a while." Tamar joined the conversation. "From the look of things yesterday, a great deal of work remains to be done before your boat will be ready to leave."

Tamar's observation had merit, but Lily hoped to be done with the cleaning and repairs in a couple of days. She made a mental note to ask the captain about securing profitable cargo to load. Excitement zipped through her. She could hardly wait until they pushed the *Hattie Belle* away from the bank and headed out on their first adventure.

"I see it! I see it!" Jasmine bounced up and down. "There it is!"

Tamar put a quieting hand on the little girl's arm. "Yes, it is, but you must not hop about like a grasshopper. Once we are on the water, you are liable to fall overboard."

An awful vision of Jasmine flailing about as the river swept her away formed in Lily's mind. Had she made a terrible mistake to bring her sisters? But she could not stand the idea of leaving them behind. She would simply have to be vigilant.

The carriage came to a halt, and Lily gathered her skirts. "Be careful where you step. The ground is very damp. I don't want either of you to fall into a mud hole."

Camellia shuddered and closed her eyes. "Perfect." Sarcasm dripped from the two syllables.

"I'll be careful, Lily." Jasmine mimicked Lily's motions as they waited for the coachman to let down the steps and open the door.

Lily stepped from the carriage, relieved to see the sun had dried the ground some since her earlier visit. "Tamar, will you direct the loading of our things while I introduce the girls to Mr. Matthews and Mr. Moreau?"

Lily picked her way across the fern-strewn bank and stepped onto the boat before turning to help her sisters. Her unseen partner must be still abed. No doubt that was why he had not accomplished much work. Well, he would soon learn better habits. "Mr. Matthews, I have returned with my best labor force."

Nothing answered her but the loud song of a bird along the riverbank. Finally the stomp of boots on the staircase heralded his approach, and she took a deep breath. She fully expected a battle with Mr. Matthews when he learned of her plans.

"What on earth are you doing back here?" His voice reached them before he did. When his large frame appeared, Camellia gasped. Jasmine made no sound, but her hand tightened around Lily's fingers. "And what are you doing with a gaggle of children? You were supposed to bring me workmen."

"You will find that my sisters and I are hard workers. We've spent many hours putting up vegetables and fruits. We can clean better than most men. And we won't charge an exorbitant fee for our services." Lily was proud of her calm voice. The sentences tripped off her tongue just as she had practiced as she lay in bed last night. No hint of trepidation betrayed her true feelings.

Blake Matthews quirked an eyebrow and stared at all three girls, his blue gaze finally coming to rest on her face. "I suppose Jensen and I can do the heavy work if we leave the cleaning and organizing to you ladies."

Lily's pent-up breath whooshed out. Where was the battle royal she had expected?

"Let me show you to the kitchen." He moved out onto the deck. Lily and her sisters fell back a step to let him pass, but he froze, his attention caught by something on the bank. "What is that—that stuff they are bringing aboard?"

Turning her head, Lily saw the men from home approaching, their arms full of burdens. "Those are our belongings."

His gaze swiveled back to her, and his face paled. "Your belongings? You and your sisters are going to live aboard the boat with Jensen and me?"

Lily nodded.

"You don't mind being exposed to gambling and drinking?" His voice was incredulous.

"Of course I would, but no gambling or drinking will occur aboard the *Hattie Belle*."

He raked a hand through his dark hair. Several locks fell across his forehead, giving him a mysterious, slightly dangerous appearance.

Lily could feel her heartbeat accelerate. Blake Matthews was very handsome and probably used to getting his way with women as a result.

Well, he would find she was impervious to his charms. That was one thing for which she could thank her worthless father—she would never fall in love with any man. Never again would she put herself in the position of being abandoned. Even Grandfather had failed her when he died—

A tug on her hand interrupted her thoughts. Camellia pulled free of her grasp and executed a graceful curtsy, her blond hair gleaming in the midday sun. "Please excuse my sister's lack of manners, sir. I am Camellia Anderson, and this is my little sister, Jasmine."

The brooding air lifted from Mr. Matthews's face, replaced by a look of bewilderment.

Camellia rose and stretched out a white-gloved hand for him to place a salutatory kiss. "I'm sorry, but I didn't catch your name."

Lily sighed. Trust Camellia to attempt a flirtation with the man. She was not nearly as concerned with guarding her heart. But then she didn't know about their father's true perfidy. She and Jasmine had been told that he had died. Their grandparents had decided that would be the best way to handle the situation. Only Lily knew the truth—Papa had not loved them enough to stay with them. "His name is Mr. Matthews, Camellia, and as soon as he shows us the way to the kitchens, you and Jasmine will don your aprons and begin working."

"Right this way." He walked stiffly down the right side of the riverboat.

Lily followed his lead. "Be careful," she instructed Camellia and Jasmine. "The wood looks damp where it's in the shade." She was relieved when their guide opened a door in the approximate center of the boat.

"This way, ladies." He bowed, irritation obvious in the stiff movement of his arm. "I trust you won't be overwhelmed."

The dark room felt like a cave. Lily waited for her eyes to adjust to the gloom. "Aren't there any windows?"

Mr. Matthews sighed and walked outside.

"Where did he go?" Although she couldn't see, Lily recognized Jasmine's fearless voice.

A clunking sound came from outside, and sunlight blasted into the room. Mr. Matthews must have removed a shutter.

Something skittered into the shadows, eliciting a tiny shriek from Camellia.

"It's only a mouse." Mr. Matthews stood in the doorway once more, a half grin on his face.

Lily supposed he was trying to frighten them. "Once we get this place cleaned up, no vermin"—she tossed a meaningful glance at him—"will dare make their home here."

His grin widened. "I'm sure you're right. No mouse would dare remain near a shrew."

Lily turned from the irritating man. "Hang up your cloaks on those pegs, girls."

Tamar appeared, her arms full of linens. "I've brought the aprons."

"Good." Lily looked around for a clean surface, gave up, and pointed to a counter under the window. "If you'll help the girls get started, Mr. Matthews and I have a few things to discuss."

Blake watched in fascination as Miss Anderson took over. How had it come to this? They had been invaded by a marauding army. An army of females. The enemy forces had taken over the *Hattie Belle* without firing a single shot.

He'd never met such a managing female. She had more backbone than many of the men he'd met in his travels. She reminded him of the women in his family—as innocent as Ada, as determined as his mother.

Not that Ma had ever been pushy. She always let Pa take the lead. He couldn't imagine Ma owning property, but if she had, she would have insisted on keeping it clean enough to serve dinner on the floor. And she never would countenance serving alcohol or gambling.

But that didn't mean he should let Miss Anderson get her way without a challenge. She headed toward the paddle wheel, chin high, skirts swaying back and forth.

He caught her elbow with one hand. "Where are you going?"

"I want to explore every inch of my boat. I need to start a list of repairs we'll have to make." She tried to shake him off, but her foot slipped.

To stop her from falling overboard, Blake grabbed the girl around the waist and pulled her close against his side. She clung to him for a brief moment. Her curves felt so comfortable against him—so right—like she was made to fit against him.

The thought shook him, challenging everything he held dear. To mask his confusion, Blake adopted a cynical tone. "Careful there, honey. If you're going to move onto *our* boat, you've got to learn to keep your feet under you."

"I am not your honey."

That was better. She was as stiff as a piece of plywood in his arms. He let go of her but remained ready to grab her again if she was still unsteady. "I didn't mean anything by it."

She sniffed. "Does the paddle wheel need any repairs?"

"Right to business. I like that in a partner." At her dark look, he assumed a more serious expression. "The Champneys had it repaired after the *Hattie Belle*'s last run from St. Louis."

"Good." She turned back and eased her way past him. "The deck looks like it's in good shape. How many staterooms?"

"Six. Jensen and I are using two of them, but that leaves plenty of room for your family."

She shook her head. "That will never do. We'll have to take on passengers as well as cargo. You and Mr. Moreau will have to share a stateroom. We'll share another one, which will leave room for four paying passengers."

"If you want to make money fast, you need to give up your plan to carry cargo or passengers. I can make you more money in a week without leaving the bank. I've been making tables for the ballroom upstairs. All I need is a little time—"

"Mr. Matthews, I want to get one thing straight—I am a respectable woman from a God-fearing home. I will not countenance games of chance on this boat. We can make a comfortable living moving cargo and passengers on the river."

"What if I don't want just a comfortable living? If we follow my plan, we'll both be rich beyond our wildest dreams. Then you can buy all the reputation you want. You can afford a big house in town where you can have tea and introduce your sisters to the best society."

"If you want to spend your time taking money from unsuspecting clients, pack up your things immediately and go back to where you came from." She lifted her nose in the air.

He wasn't about to leave. This was his dream as much as it was hers.

He studied her features objectively as she began enumerating all the reasons he would bow to her wishes. Miss Anderson would never be considered a beauty, but something in her face, something in her whole attitude, filled him with longing. What was it about her? She had some indefinable quality that he admired. She was very cute, too, standing up to him even though he was at least a foot taller and could toss her over the side of the boat without much effort.

"So you must see my point." She looked at him, her chocolate-brown eyes shining.

He gathered his wandering thoughts. "Just because you own a measly two percent more of this boat than I do doesn't mean I'm going to allow you to turn the *Hattie Belle* into a charitable concern."

"I don't expect you to." Her voice was earnest. She put her hand on his arm, making his muscles tense in response. "I'm sure we're going to work well together as soon as we establish a few basic rules."

He pulled his arm free and held up a different finger for each point he made. "So we can't have any gaming; I have to move in with my hired help; we won't have any workmen to help with the repairs; and we have to hire a captain."

"That's right, except for hiring a captain. I've taken care of that." She smiled broadly. "I'm glad we've got that all straightened out. After yesterday, I was worried we would have a problem. I had no idea you would be so reasonable."

"What do you mean you've hired a captain?"

"Yesterday on the ride home, Jean Luc Champney offered, on my behalf, to approach the man they used to employ."

A feeling of foreboding settled on his shoulders. "Not Lars Steenberg. . ."

She shrugged. "If he was the captain before you took over. Please don't tell me you disapprove of him, too."

Blake leaned against the wall. "I was not overly impressed with his abilities, but at least he has some experience on the river and with our boat."

"Good, that's settled, then." She dusted her hands and turned to go back to the kitchen.

Blake decided it would be better to bide his time than wrestle with Miss Anderson right now. Life on the river was difficult. She and her sisters would be ready to go back home after the first week of snags and tree islands. He would gamble his part of the *Hattie Belle* on it.

He climbed the stairs slowly as he thought about it. Yes, that was exactly what would happen. As soon as she saw how hard it was to move cargo, the determined Miss Lily Anderson would change her mind. Then he and Jensen could go back to their original plans.

Chapter Seventeen

"We've been cleaning for days." Jasmine's lip protruded. With her hair wrapped in a white cloth, she looked more like a servant than a young lady.

Lily withdrew her list from one of her apron pockets. "Sometimes we have to work hard to accomplish our dreams."

"But this is not my dream." Camellia perched on the edge of the bed they shared and wrapped a second cloth around her head. They had learned the importance of covering their hair after rubbing the brass fittings in the engine room. Their activities had raised a storm of dust that had settled on them like a quilt.

"I need to go into town this morning for some supplies Mr. Matthews needs."

"We're supposed to call him Blake, remember?" Camellia sighed.

"Would the two of you like to go with me?" Lily pinned a bright smile on her face. She was not happy about the way Camellia mooned over the gambler, but she had to admit he always treated the girl like a younger sister. In the past week, all of them had spent a great deal of time in close quarters as they polished, dusted, and scrubbed their way from aft to stern. And Blake had a knack for getting more work out of Camellia than anyone else. Lily wrestled with a touch of jealousy at the easy camaraderie he shared with her sisters. Why couldn't he be as charming to her?

"I do!" Jasmine executed a twirl in the center of the room, managing to bang her hand against the table holding their bowl and pitcher.

Lily grabbed the table before it could overturn, so relieved to have a new focus for her unruly thoughts that she didn't chastise Jasmine.

Camellia walked over to the mirror and leaned against one wall of their bedroom. "I don't want anyone to see me looking like this."

"Suit yourself, Camellia. You can stay in the carriage and wait for us." Lily ignored the exaggerated sigh and left the room to get Tamar.

Walking the length of the second floor, she had to admit to a feeling of accomplishment. The tables Blake had made for his gambling salon had become dining tables, lined up with military precision along one side of the former ballroom. Sparkling crystal chandeliers would illuminate the room during meals. A wood-burning stove in the far corner would offer warmth during cool, damp evenings. If she closed her eyes, she could almost see well-dressed passengers sitting around the stove as they discussed their comfortable travel. Maybe they could find a piano. That would please Camellia. It was the thing she bemoaned most often.

Blake's deep voice interrupted her daydreaming. "Jensen is waiting outside."

Lily could feel her cheeks heating. The man had a talent for making her feel inadequate. She tried to quiet her heart as she turned to face him. "Did he have any trouble finding a carriage?"

As usual, Blake wore only dark trousers and a flowing white shirt with sleeves rolled up above his elbows. His dress should have made him look like a greengrocer or laborer, but he carried himself with the assurance of a planter. From the set of his shoulders to his wide stance, Blake was a man one could not ignore. "I doubt it. Jensen has a way of acquiring whatever we need."

Had he stolen the equipage? She hesitated to voice the question. What if he confirmed her fear?

"I sent him to the livery stable." The lift of his right eyebrow and the half smile on Blake's lips indicated he'd read her thoughts.

More hot blood rushed to her face. She glanced down at the floor. "Have you seen Tamar?"

"She's already outside." He stepped closer and lifted her chin with a finger. "Unless I am mistaken, there is romance in the air."

Her brain sizzled. What did he mean? Had he formed an attachment for her? Impossible. They barely spoke.

"I only hope Tamar will not break his heart."

Her heartbeat slowed its frantic pace, and Lily pulled away from his hand. "Tamar would not be so foolish. She is here because of her love for us, not because she wants to find a husband."

He just raised that eyebrow again.

Camellia and Jasmine exited the bedroom and stood beside Lily. "We will be back before too long."

"Are you sure you don't need me to accompany you?"

She shook her head.

"You have the list I made out?" His question chased her down the stairs.

Lily shooed her sisters ahead of her. The sooner they left him behind, the better. She breathed deeply as they hopped off the deck and picked their way to the road.

She cast a furtive glance back toward the boat as she settled on the seat of the rented carriage, but Blake was not standing on the deck. The feeling that pierced her chest could not be disappointment. It had to be relief. Didn't it?

❧

"What do you think of this material?" Tamar held a length of navy-blue broadcloth. "Would it look good on the dining tables?"

Lily's eyes widened. "It's perfect. All it needs is lace edging." She looked around for a bolt of the lace she envisioned.

A bell tinkled at the front of the mercantile, and she looked up to see if it was one of her sisters. They had begged her to let them go to the park. Camellia wanted to stroll; Jasmine wanted to explore. Lily agreed to let them go after making them promise not to talk to strangers.

But instead of seeing one of her sisters, her gaze met the dark eyes of the intriguing Jean Luc Champney. "What a happy coincidence." She moved forward with her hand outstretched.

Jean Luc took it in his and placed a warm kiss on her skin.

The gesture should have made her heart race, so why didn't it? Why didn't blood rush to her cheeks the way it did every time Blake Matthews talked to her? Maybe because Jean Luc was not abrasive and challenging like Blake always was. Yes, that had to be the answer.

"I thought I saw you and your slave entering." He squeezed her hand before releasing it. "How are things going on the boat? Has Captain

Steenberg moved aboard? I trust he meets with your approval."

"Yes, thank you for sending him." She paused, choosing her words with care. Truth to tell she had not been overly impressed with the man. He was loud and did not practice the best hygiene. "He is quite a colorful character."

"Yes, well, he is an excellent captain. You will come to no harm while he guides the boat. He can probably supply you with an engineer and several crewmen."

"Thank you, but that won't be necessary." Lily could not imagine more of the same type of men on her boat. They would not impress the passengers she hoped to draw. "We've already hired a new crewman, and Mr. Moreau is going to act as our engineer for now."

He shrugged. "Whatever you—"

"Lily! Lily!" Jasmine barreled into the mercantile like a cannonball. She ran past Jean Luc, grabbed Lily's hand, and tugged her toward the door.

"Wait a minute, Jasmine. What's wrong?"

"Come quick. They're going to kill him."

Thinking someone must have attacked Jensen, Lily tossed a glance at Jean Luc. "Pardon me."

"Hurry, Lily! Please hurry." Jasmine pulled harder. As soon as they were outside, her little sister picked up her skirts and dashed across the street, disappearing into an alley between two buildings.

Lily plunged into the alley, following her sister and praying for their safety as sounds of a scuffle reached her ears.

"Leave him alone!" Her sister's voice carried to her from a shadowy corner.

Dazzled by the change from light to dark, Lily willed her vision to clear. Several boys stood in a semicircle looking down while one of them kicked whatever lay on the ground. It looked like a pile of rags, but from the solid impact made by each kick, someone was under the rags. "Stop what you're doing." Lily put all the authority she could muster into her voice.

The largest boy, who was doing the kicking, laughed. "We already took care of your friend. Do you want us to do the same to you?"

Lily's first concern was for her sisters. She pointed toward the street without taking her eyes off the bullies. "Jasmine, you and Camellia go find Jensen."

"But—"

"Go. Now." She listened for the sound of their retreat before raising her parasol in a threatening manner. "If you leave now, I won't have you arrested."

One of the other boys grabbed the leader's arm. "He's learned his lesson. He won't be filching our fish no more."

The other accomplice added his voice. "Let's get out of here."

After one more vicious kick, the third boy looked at her, a snarl twisting his face. "I oughta teach you a lesson, too."

Lily had never been so frightened, but she couldn't let him see her fear. She raised her chin and narrowed her eyes. "It won't take long for my sisters to find our coachman. He'd probably like to teach you a thing or two himself."

They took to their heels, leaving her alone with their groaning victim. Lily was about to go to him when Jensen, followed by her sisters, dashed into the alley.

"What's going on here?" His growl reassured her, slowing the rapid thump of her heart. He looked around for the miscreants. "I don't see no one here."

"They ran off." Was that weak sound her voice?

"Are you all right, Miss Lily?"

"Yes, Jensen."

Jasmine dashed past them and sat down in the alley, ignoring everything else as she lifted a young boy's head into her lap. "We have to take him back to the *Hattie Belle*."

Lily understood her sister's impulse to help the stranger, but they already had enough challenges to face. "I don't know if that's a very good idea."

Camellia pushed her out of the way and sat next to Jasmine, her hands gently prodding the boy's arms and legs. "We can't leave him here."

Lily sighed and looked from her sisters to Jensen.

"Don't you remember the story of the Good Samaritan?" Jasmine's voice held a hint of desperation.

Closing her eyes, Lily remembered the prayer she'd whispered as they'd entered the alley. The Lord had kept them safe. How then could she refuse to do her Christian duty? "I think it would be better to find his parents. They must be worried about him."

Camellia leaned back on her heels. "What if he's a foundling?"

"Then we'll leave him at the foundling home." Lily realized this was a losing battle. She knelt next to Jasmine and Camellia, bending to get a closer look at their victim. He flinched as she reached a hand toward his bruised face, an awful mat of gashes and bruises. It was the boy who had stolen her reticule. Her heart melted, and she looked over her shoulder toward Jensen. "Go get the carriage."

Chapter Eighteen

Jean Luc hung around the mercantile for another half hour, waiting for Lily Anderson. He pulled out his pocket watch and flipped it open.

"Are you sure I can't help you, Mr. Champney?" The storekeeper had already asked him the question twice before.

He shook his head and walked to the plate-glass window, staring at tall white clouds that were starting to pile up in the southern sky. How much longer could she be?

"Are you waiting for someone?" The man was at his elbow, as annoying as a mosquito.

Jean Luc sighed. "If you must know, I'm waiting to speak to Miss Anderson."

"She's not coming back." The man smiled as though conferring a gift. "Her man loaded her supplies in the carriage and left a quarter hour ago."

Anger burned in the pit of his stomach. How dared she ignore him? First she rushed off to see about some child instead of talking to him, and then she didn't bother to come back. His jaw tightened. Lily Anderson would rue the day she ignored him. He stormed out of the mercantile and headed toward his father's office.

"Good day, Mr. Champney."

Jean Luc almost bypassed the man. But then he realized he could begin to settle the score right away. He smiled at the man who owned one of the largest shipping companies in town. "Hello, Sweeney. I trust business is going well."

Sweeney nodded. "I heard your father sold the *Hattie Belle*."

"Yes." Jean Luc tapped his cane against his chin. "I was as surprised as anyone. Especially when I learned who the new owners are." He shook his head and put an arm around the other man. "Just between you and me, he must have gotten a really good price."

"Is that so?"

"Why else would he sell to a woman?" Jean Luc shook his head. "I hate to say it, but he may be slipping. Selling the *Hattie Belle* to someone who will likely run it aground on her first run? What sense is there in that?"

The older man looked pensive. Then he chuckled. "Maybe your father is wilier than you think. He's probably expecting this woman to come running back to him. Then he'll offer to take the boat off her hands, and he'll make a tidy profit in the deal."

Jean Luc raised his eyebrows. "You may be right." He stood as though considering the other man's suggestion then shook his head slowly. "Still, I worry about any shipper who lets her take his cargo out. He'll lose the whole load, and she certainly doesn't have deep enough pockets to repay the cost."

"But I thought she was Isaiah Blackstone's granddaughter. Surely they wouldn't hang her out to dry."

"Do you really think they approve of her going into business? They've probably washed their hands of her."

Sweeney looked thoughtful. "You may be right."

"No, no. Don't rely on what I've said." Jean Luc shook his head. "It's only speculation on my part."

"Of course not, my boy. Of course not. But I couldn't forgive myself if I didn't spread the word to my colleagues."

Jean Luc shrugged. "I can't speak to that, Mr. Sweeney. You must do as you think best."

The older man was shaking his head as they parted.

A sudden wind pushed Jean Luc along the street. Thunder rumbled, and lightning split the sky, matching his mood perfectly.

If Miss Anderson wanted to be his enemy, she would find herself in deep water. His smile widened. In very deep water indeed.

❧

It was far too quiet. Blake held a peg as he brought his hammer down. He was an idiot. He actually missed the chatter and giggles of the Anderson girls.

In the distance a cannon boomed, announcing the arrival of a steamboat. It was such a common occurrence these days he was surprised the city of Natchez didn't run out of ammunition. Another reason Lily's daft idea was doomed to failure. With so much river traffic, who would want to take a chance on a boat full of females to ship their goods?

He missed the peg, and pain exploded in his left thumb. Harsh curses rose to his lips, but a week of choking them back had become a habit. "Owww!"

Blake checked his thumb. No blood. He would live. With a shake of his head, he went back to work. Lily wanted benches, so she would have benches. He was almost finished attaching them on the starboard side of the main room—the room she had turned into a dining hall, even though he would rather see it a gambling parlor. But she wouldn't budge.

He'd tried to wheedle her into allowing one corner of the room for friendly games of poker, but she would have none of it. It was a shame, really. All this work that he would have to tear apart when Lily quit. At least he could reuse this wood—it would make a good buffet table when he finally opened his casino.

Somehow his dream had gotten tarnished since the Anderson girls had moved aboard. They brought sunshine to every corner of the *Hattie Belle*, even the engine room.

Footsteps brought his head around. Were they back already?

The uneven rhythm of his heart settled when Captain Steenberg appeared, chewing on the stubby end of a cigar. Blake had never seen him light it, not that Lily would allow smoking on *her* boat. Steenberg removed the cigar, holding it between his thumb and finger. "It's kinda quiet around here."

"The ladies went to Natchez to do a little shopping."

The captain nodded. He planted his feet wide apart and stared at Blake.

Blake drilled a hole for the next peg, blowing it free of sawdust when he withdrew the bit.

The captain remained.

"Did you need me for something?"

"I was thinking about going to town myself. I hear there's a new saloon in town. I thought I'd try my luck."

"I see." Blake felt a tug to join the man. He'd been working hard. No one could say he didn't deserve a night off. He looked at the unfinished bench. Maybe later. "Try not to lose money you haven't earned yet."

"I was wondering about that." The captain studied his cigar. "I know we ain't gone on a voyage yet, but my time is valuable." He put emphasis on the last word. "I was thinking mebbe I could get a little advance for my first trip."

"I doubt it." Blake pounded a new peg into the hole he'd just created. "Money's going to be tight until we make our first delivery." He sank the peg and reached for the drill, falling back into a rhythm as he worked.

After a while he realized he was alone. Again. His heart clenched. He'd always been a loner. Well, not always. But for a very long time. And, he reminded himself, he liked it that way.

The sound of hoofbeats brought his head up. They were back. He was up and halfway down the stairs before he realized his intention. He halted; then with a shrug he decided he might as well see what Lily had managed to purchase. He stepped outside as Jensen jumped to the ground and tied off the horses.

Lily opened the door and waved at him. "We could use your help."

He didn't like the frown on her face. "What's wrong? Is it your sisters?"

She shook her head and disappeared back inside the carriage.

He strode to the door and looked inside. Lily and Camellia occupied one seat while Jasmine cradled someone in her lap. "Who's that?"

"He was attacked." Jasmine looked up, tears giving her eyes the velvety look of dew-sprinkled violets. "We're going to tend to his wounds."

"Really?" His gaze met Lily's. What was she thinking?

She lifted her shoulders. "We could hardly leave him bleeding on the street."

Thunder rumbled in the distance. "Let's get him inside." Blake picked him up and carried him to the *Hattie Belle*. "I suppose you want him to bunk in my room."

They decided to use the ladies' parlor for the time being. It was on the floor above the staterooms, a pleasant room with the most comfortable furniture, including a fainting couch, which they turned into a makeshift bed.

Camellia took control, directing the others to boil water, make bandages, and bring fresh clothing to replace the boy's filthy rags.

An afternoon thunderstorm rocked the boat. Rain made rivulets on the windows, chilling Blake despite the fact it was summer. Gloom seemed to have invaded the *Hattie Belle*. He had been assigned the task of watching over Miss Jasmine. After she told him about finding the patient, they stared at each other.

"I have an idea." Blake went to his bedroom and retrieved his deck of cards and an old bowler hat. Jasmine was sitting on one of the new benches when he got back, her pert little nose glued to a window. "Let's play a game." He riffled the cards in one hand.

Jasmine's eyes grew as wide as saucers. "I don't think Lily wants me to gamble."

"I'll keep that in mind." Blake set the hat upside down about ten feet away and moved to the bench where Jasmine sat. "How good is your aim?"

She regarded him with curiosity. "I once knocked the bloom off one of Grandmother's roses with a rock."

"Pretty impressive." He held a card between the first two fingers of his hand and flipped it toward the hat, watching as it turned over and over before landing several inches short of the target. "Do you think you can get closer than that?"

She took a card and studied it. He showed her how to bend her wrist to get the most action from the card. Her first attempt didn't make it to the table. "Can I try another?"

"Of course." He gave her half the deck while he retained the other half. "One at a time, now."

Soon the gloom had disappeared, and they were laughing as the cards flew all over the room like crazed butterflies.

"What's going on in here?" The laughter stopped. Lily stood in the doorway, arms crossed. "Are you teaching my sister card games?"

"Of course not. We were just—"

"I think I can trust my eyes more than your words, Mr. Matthews. You don't have to add lying to your list of sins." She pointed a finger at Jasmine. "It's time for you to eat some supper and get to bed."

"Yes, ma'am." Jasmine handed him the rest of her cards and exited the room, her head down.

Blake was speechless. How dare she condemn him without giving him a chance to explain. It was ridiculous. All this time spent acceding to her every wish, and still Lily didn't trust him to watch over her sisters. Then again, he hadn't thought to prepare food for Jasmine.

A fist wrapped around his heart. Maybe Lily was right. Maybe he didn't deserve her trust.

Chapter Nineteen

"Have you lost your mind?" Blake paced the main room, stopping when he drew even with Lily. "Keeping that boy on the boat is sure to lead to trouble. We're liable to wake up one morning to find him gone and all our valuables with him."

"I don't care what you say. My mind is made up." Her voice was calm, but bolts of lightning flew from her brown eyes.

Blake took a deep breath. He should have learned by now that anger was not the right approach with this young woman. "You're about as contrary as a mule."

"Look, I don't like the idea any better than you—"

"Then why are we having this discussion? Send that cutpurse on his way."

"And leave him to the tender mercies of the thugs who were beating him yesterday?" She crossed her arms and tapped one foot.

"Then Jensen and I will take him to the foundling home."

Lily shook her head. "I sent Jensen to make inquiries earlier. The foundling home is overcrowded. They cannot take him in."

"I understand you're tenderhearted, but we cannot be picking up every waif we come across or we'll find ourselves without room for paying passengers. I've yet to see a city that doesn't support at least a dozen just like the one upstairs."

The fire in her eyes faded. "I cannot abandon David Foster now."

"David Foster!" He blew out an exasperated breath. "I doubt that's his real name. He was probably born out of wedlock to a mother who tossed him on the street as soon as he could walk."

"All the more reason to let him stay with us."

"You're not making any sense, Lily. He may be an object of pity, but it doesn't follow that we should take him in."

"It may not make sense to you, but I have very sound reasons for keeping him aboard."

"Then explain them."

She cocked her head. "If I throw him off the boat, my sisters will hate me."

Surprise made him take a step back. She couldn't believe such a silly thing. But she was a female, and females often got odd ideas—just one of the reasons they should content themselves with being mothers and wives. "That's utterly ridiculous, girl."

"How many times do I have to tell you I am not a girl?"

He ignored her interruption. "Your sisters adore you. They watch your every move. If you don't care for mussels, they won't touch them, either. They walk the same way you do, imitate your laugh and even the tilt of your chin when you feel challenged. That's the way it is with younger siblings."

"I don't know about all that, but I do know I cannot disappoint them on this matter. Besides, they have both promised to keep a close eye on him. For now David is recuperating, but once we are under way and he is better, I'll make sure he stays too busy to get into any trouble." She paused and looked over Blake's right shoulder. "Did you need me for something, Jensen?"

Blake turned around, surprised to see the sheepish look on his friend's scarred face. "Is something wrong?"

"No, sir." Jensen twisted his hands. "I was just going to offer to help with the boy. He reminds me a bit of myself at that age. I know how different my life woulda been had someone taken me in and cared for me."

"Am I the only one on this boat with a lick of sense?" Blake expelled a harsh breath. "All right then, I suppose I'll have to bow to your insanity. You do have controlling interest. But don't come running to me when your jewelry disappears."

He strode out, brushing past Jensen. "Traitor." Knowing Lily couldn't see his face, he added a wink to soften the accusation. "You're going to be the death of me yet."

"Where are you going?" Lily's question brought him up short.

Blake turned on his heel and smiled slowly. "I didn't know you cared."

Her cheeks darkened, and her gaze shifted away from him.

He shook his head. From conquering Amazon to shy maiden in the blink of an eye. It drove him crazy. "I have an appointment in town."

Blake didn't wait to hear her answer. He stopped by his room to grab his coat then left the boat. What was it about Lily Anderson?

She had begun their discussion this morning with an apology for jumping to the wrong conclusion last night, explaining her misunderstanding of the situation and thanking him prettily for keeping Jasmine occupied. Then she had told him about the boy, and they had gone right back to sparring mode.

He really shouldn't tease her, but the temptation was sometimes impossible to resist. Especially since it ended whatever argument they were having. He loved seeing that startled look in her eyes, as well as the ready color that flushed her cheeks. Besides, it was about the only way he could get the last word.

Whistling as he walked, Blake smiled at the green canopy above his head. He wondered what her reaction would be if he kissed her. . . .

❧

"I'm not taking you, Camellia, because I'm not going shopping." Lily ignored the pout on her sister's face. "You would have to stay in the wagon all day. You'd be redder than the sunset by the time we got back."

"But I could help you—"

She put a hand on her sister's arm. "You can help me most by staying here and keeping an eye on Jasmine and David. Blake and I will be back as soon as we arrange for a paying cargo. Just think of it. We could be leaving for New Orleans as early as tomorrow."

"I don't want to go to New Orleans. I want to go home." A solitary tear traced a path down Camellia's cheek.

Lily sighed. "This is our home now."

"This is not a home." Camellia stomped her foot for emphasis. "It's a boat. A nasty, ugly boat. I hate it. I hate the way it rocks and creaks. I want to go back to Grandmother's house and sleep in my own bed. I'm tired of sharing a bedroom with you and the others."

Pulling on her gloves, Lily wondered what Blake would think if he could hear her sister now. Contrary to his belief, Camellia didn't admire anything about her older sister. "I am sorry for that, but it doesn't change anything. You are to stay here with Jasmine and the boy you begged me to keep. If anything goes missing, I am holding you personally responsible."

Camellia sniffed. "I can't wait until I'm older. I'm going to find a husband who'll take me to his home. It'll be larger than Grandmother's house. We'll have parties and balls and eat grapes every day."

"I'm sure I wish you the best in your search, but until then you will do as I say. Now go find your sister. We'll be back before you know it."

She watched as Camellia flounced off, her nose high. Lily sincerely hoped she hadn't taught her younger sister that particular attitude.

With a shake of her head Lily joined Blake, who was waiting in the wagon. They had decided to rent it rather than a carriage in case they needed to bring cargo back with them.

Blake reached down a hand to help her climb up. "Where do you want to go first?"

"I've been thinking about that." Lily was proud to show she had a head for business. "I think the market would be a good place to start. Tamar says they have all sorts of stalls selling goods. Perhaps we can offer to move—"

Her words were cut off by laughter.

Miffed, she frowned up at Blake. "What's so funny?"

"You are. You couldn't find your way out of a feed sack without directions." He laughed again. "Those people only sell their goods locally."

Lily tilted her chin up, thought of Camellia's flounce, and lowered it again. "That may be true, but they can probably direct me."

He shook his head. "You should have stayed back at the boat with the others and let me do this alone."

"I suppose you're an expert at shipping?"

"No, but I know a great deal more about business than you do."

No one had the ability to make her feel like an imbecile more than the man sitting beside her. With a gesture he could reduce her to the level of a dim-witted schoolgirl. "Where would you go, then?" Anger made her voice sharp.

A horseman careened around the corner. Blake pulled back on the reins, the muscles in his arms straining to stop the wagon. As though time had slowed, Lily saw his jaw clench, saw the horseman's shocked expression. She scrunched her eyes together, certain they would crash into the horseman, but somehow Blake managed to avoid a collision.

After a moment she remembered to breathe.

He pulled the wagon to a standstill and grazed her cheek with a hand. "Are you all right?"

"I'm fine." As she gazed into his eyes, Lily forgot about their near miss. She forgot her irritation with him, forgot everything except his mesmerizing blue eyes. How had she ever thought they were cold? They were as warm as a summer day. Up close they looked like flower petals with black centers.

His lids lowered, and for some reason her heart increased its speed. She should pull away, but it was all she could do not to lean toward him. His breath fanned her face. His pupils dilated. He blinked and pulled back. Then turned away from her.

Lily's heart pounded. She was breathing like she'd run all the way to Natchez. What had just happened? Had he almost kissed her? She put a hand to her chest, certain her heart was about to jump free. "I. . . I'm not hurt."

"That's good." At least he sounded as winded as she did.

Lily watched as he jumped down and went to the horse's head. He spoke quietly to the animal and checked to make sure it was unharmed. "You were amazing."

He glanced back toward her, his gaze unreadable, and nodded. "I would suggest you start with either Sweeney's or LeGrand's. They are two of the largest shippers in Natchez."

So they would ignore what had just happened? She supposed that was as good an answer as any. It wasn't as if they could develop any romantic feelings about each other. Neither of them wanted the same things from life. He saw the *Hattie Belle* as a means to achieve riches. She considered their boat her home, a place to raise her sisters and to live free from the strictures of local society. They had absolutely nothing in common.

Besides, she knew his type. Like Father, he would desert her. He'd get bored, or earn enough money, or find some other excuse. Then he would disappear. And leave her to pick up the pieces.

"Did you fall asleep?" His voice brought her back to the present.

Lily gathered her skirts in one hand and climbed down. “I’ll go to Sweeney’s since it’s the closest.”

“Fine. I’ll just wait here.”

She walked away from him without a backward glance—not to assert her independence but rather because she knew the less she looked into his blue eyes, the better off she would be.

Chapter Twenty

Lily tapped her foot. A wall clock told her she'd been waiting half an hour. What could be keeping Mr. Sweeney? Why had he left her in his office?

The door opened. "I'm sorry to keep you waiting, Miss Anderson."

"I understand you are a busy man, Mr. Sweeney." She pasted a smile on her face. "I hope you have found a load for the *Hattie Belle*."

"Who is your captain?" He walked to the large window overlooking the street.

"Lars Steenberg. He recently worked for the Champney family."

"I see." He turned to her. "Miss Anderson, I'm afraid I do not have good news for you."

"You couldn't find anything for us to transport?"

He shook his head. "Not so much as a bale of cotton."

"Yet I have seen any number of wagons unloading their goods at your warehouse across the street."

"Yes, but those clients are particular about the boats I hire."

"Exactly what are you saying, Mr. Sweeney?"

The older man cleared his throat. "They don't feel comfortable with a boat that has a female on it."

"I see." Lily thought hard. Suddenly she wished she'd invited Blake to join her. He would know how to broker the deal. Inspiration dawned. "What if I offer to charge half of what others are getting?"

"Miss Anderson, may I be blunt?"

She answered with a nod.

"Then let me encourage you to go back home to your parents and leave the dangers of river travel to men."

"My parents are dead."

"I'm sorry for your loss." His sympathetic words left her cold. "Isn't there any family you can turn to?"

"Mr. Sweeney, my personal life is none of your concern." She stood up and pulled her gloves over shaking fingers. "If you don't have any cargo for me, I suppose I will have to take my leave. Perhaps those at LeGrand Shipping will be interested in making a profitable deal." She swept out of the room on a righteous tide.

One day Mr. Sweeney would be sorry he had not given her a chance. One day the *Hattie Belle* would be so much in demand the shipping companies would be fighting over her.

Lily deflated when she reached the wagon. Where was Blake? Had he given up on her? She looked around as people passed, hoping she wouldn't see anyone she knew. She didn't feel like making small talk.

"Did you have any success?" His voice came from directly behind her.

She jumped. "You scared me." His half grin made her blush. "Where did you come from?"

"I ran into some old acquaintances, and I have good news." His grin widened, making him look years younger.

With a little imagination she could see the boy he'd once been. Her heart turned over. "You found some cargo?"

The gleam in his eyes confirmed it.

Lily squealed. "What is it? Tell me all about it. Is the pay good? Tell me, tell me."

He tweaked her nose. "It's a full gross of whiskey barrels. Not a full load, mind you, but if we pick up a few other items, we should be able to make a profit."

Her joy evaporated. "Whiskey?"

"That's right." His smile wavered. "Please don't tell me. . ."

"We can't transport alcohol."

He groaned. "I can't believe you. We cannot afford to be picky about our first load. We need to make money."

Lily wanted to agree, but she knew it was wrong. She shook her head. "It's impossible."

"I should have known. You're such a little puritan. Always have to hold yourself to a higher standard. What kind of sanctimonious, self-righteous, judgmental girl are you?"

His words were sharper than a razor blade. But Lily knew she had to stand up for her beliefs. Anything less would doom her to the future she'd been trying to escape. "You'll have to cancel the deal. I'll go to LeGrand Shipping and see if I can find a respectable load."

❧

Jean Luc retraced his path through the park and climbed back into his carriage, a smile of triumph on his face. He could not believe how well things were going. It looked like the time was growing ripe to offer Lily a deal for her portion of the *Hattie Belle*.

He'd thought at first that Blake was going to bring everything to ruin, but Lily had rejected the whiskey on moral grounds. Perfect. After a few more setbacks, she should be ready to grasp at whatever solution he offered.

Of course, returning to her old life would not be possible. The gossip at parties, behind fluttering fans, was that Lily Anderson had ruined her reputation by moving aboard the boat with a man. He doubted she would ever be received again in polite society unless she married someone who could face down the talebearers. Perhaps he would do that—take pity on her, offer to marry her in exchange for the deed. Or maybe he would just set her up in a little house along the bluff and visit her from time to time.

He reached in his pocket and pulled out a coin. Too bad he'd wasted money bribing Captain Steenberg. Stopping to look back over his shoulder, Jean Luc pursed his lips. He had an idea. If it worked out, he could tell the captain his services were no longer needed.

❧

At least the couple at LeGrand Shipping had not made her wait for their bad news. Lily kicked at a clod of dirt. She got back to the wagon ahead of Blake and climbed onto the bench to wait. Maybe she should give up. Had she been wrong to turn down Blake's client?

"What a beautiful afternoon this has turned out to be."

Lily blinked and looked down. "Jean Luc?"

"I stopped by your house a few days ago, but I was told you were away from home." His dark eyes devoured her face. "I haven't offended you, have I?"

"No, no, not at all." She summoned a smile. "I have moved onto the boat I bought from your father."

"You're living on the *Hattie Belle*?"

"Yes, that's right."

"What about the gambler? Did you send him off with a flea in his ear?"

Lily shook her head. "He's still on the boat, too."

"I see." His mouth turned down.

A blush heated her cheeks. "I assure you everything is proper. My sisters and I have a chaperone."

"I see." He paused as though considering her explanation. "I was disappointed when you didn't return to the mercantile the other day."

"I am sorry for that. My sister encountered some trouble, and we had to go back to the boat straightaway. I'm sorry if our departure worried you."

"I don't know how to answer that. . .Lily." He put his hand over hers where it rested on the side of the wagon. When she didn't say anything, he continued. "If I say I was not worried, you will think I don't care; if I say I was worried, you will claim I am being difficult."

A giggle slipped out. She pulled her hand from under his.

"Please say you'll have dinner with me this evening."

"I don't know—"

His pitiful look stopped her.

Why not? Perhaps he or even his father could put in a good word with the local shipping companies. "I am very flattered, Jean Luc."

"I will come out to the boat around sunset to collect you." He touched his cane to the brim of his hat and stepped back. "Until then."

As she watched him walk away, the wagon rocked. She turned to greet Blake, but the words stopped when she saw his frown. Lily folded her lips together and stared straight ahead. It was going to be a long ride back to the boat.

Chapter Twenty-one

Lily had never been inside this dining establishment. The main entrance opened into a room large enough for a ball. Candles burned from the chandeliers, casting a golden glow over the dozen or so tables scattered about. "This is lovely."

Jean Luc held a chair for her. "I'm glad you approve. The food is remarkable."

She nodded. If the pleasing aromas were any indication, the same would be true this evening.

A waiter spoke briefly with Jean Luc while Lily stared at the other diners. Although she recognized one or two from the balls Aunt Dahlia had made her attend, no one acknowledged her. Starting to feel a little uncomfortable, she touched the loose hairs at the nape of her neck. Had Tamar's arrangement come undone? No. Her gaze settled on the unrelieved black material of her gown. Was she being judged for dining with Mr. Champney while she was in mourning?

Jean Luc's words interrupted her fretful thoughts. "Tell me about your sister."

Lily let her hand drop to her lap. "Actually, I have two sisters. Camellia and Jasmine."

"What interesting names."

"All the women in my grandmother's family are named for flowers. Her given name is Violet. She and Grandfather named their daughters

Dahlia and Rose. Rose, my mother, continued the tradition."

Jean Luc placed a linen napkin on his lap. "A lovely tradition."

"Yes, Grandfather even named the plantation he built Les Fleurs, which as you know means 'the flowers,' to honor his new bride's family."

"Obviously he really loved your grandmother." He leaned forward. "Now which sister came running into the mercantile, and what calamity overtook her?"

Where to begin? Jean Luc was a pleasant companion, but she doubted he would understand why she allowed David to remain aboard the *Hattie Belle*. "You will appreciate this story. It goes back to the party you and your family hosted on the *Hattie Belle* several weeks ago."

"The first time I met you." His voice was husky, intimate.

It brought a flush to her cheeks. "Yes, that's right. . .but before we arrived at the party there was a boy. . . . He took my reticule."

"I'm so sorry. Were you hurt?"

Lily shook her head. "Only my pride. I couldn't believe I'd been so unaware. Anyway, he snatched my reticule and ran away." She decided the chase and David's subsequent dunking in the river were irrelevant. Besides, she didn't care to describe her first meeting with Blake to Jean Luc. The two men didn't have a very good relationship. She sipped from her glass of water as she considered what to say.

"What does this have to do with the mercantile?"

"My sister Jasmine is a curious little girl. She heard a noise coming from one of the alleys and went to investigate. She found a group of bullies beating a young boy. That's when she came to get me. The older boys ran away, and we managed to get their victim to the carriage. I recognized him and thought we would take him to the doctor's office, but Camellia insisted she wanted to nurse him." She glanced up and waited for Jean Luc to get the point of her story.

He frowned for a moment before understanding dawned. "The pickpocket."

Lily nodded, and Jean Luc laughed out loud. It was a nice moment, but her heart plodded steadily on as if she were making biscuits or dusting furniture. Why didn't this debonair man make her heart trip? She took another sip of water.

"Where is he now?" Jean Luc chuckled again.

"Still aboard the *Hattie Belle*."

His face grew serious. "You have taken him in? He may take

advantage of your kindness while making plans to murder you in your sleep."

Irritation filled her. "Why does every man in my life think he has the right to dictate my actions?"

Jean Luc leaned toward her. "Surely you can understand how dangerous it is to open your home to a criminal?"

Lily studied his face. He was debonair. Earnest, kind, and thoughtful. And he seemed truly interested in her welfare. So why did her heart remain so stubbornly calm? Why didn't her cheeks flush with awareness and excitement? "I understand your concern, Jean Luc, but you must allow me to decide how to conduct my life."

He reached for her hand. "Please forgive me if I've offended. I can't help worrying about you."

Her heart fluttered as he squeezed her hand. "Thank you, Jean Luc. It makes me happy to count you as a friend. If I'm going to support myself and my sisters, I will need all the friends I can muster."

He raised her hand to his lips and pressed a warm kiss on it.

Lily should have enjoyed the sensation and the admiring glance in his eyes, but she felt uncomfortable. She pulled her hand away. "Please, Jean Luc. That may be acceptable behavior in Paris, but here in Mississippi, too much familiarity is frowned upon."

His cheeks turned red, and a look of exasperation crossed his face.

Before he could respond, a familiar lady's voice interrupted their conversation. "Hello, Miss Anderson."

Lily turned. An older, attractively dressed couple stood beside her. It took her a moment to recognize the owners of LeGrand Shipping, whom she had met that afternoon. "Good evening, Mr. and Mrs. Hughes."

"I am so excited to find you here this evening." Susannah Hughes turned to the man at her elbow. "I believe God's hand is in this, Judah."

He put a hand on her shoulder. "You make an excellent point, my dear." He turned to Lily. "After you left this afternoon, we received an unexpected shipment that must be in New Orleans before week's end. Our normal ships have already departed Natchez or have no room for additional cargo."

Mrs. Hughes took up the conversation. "I know you said you are doing some work on your boat, so you may not be able to do this, but we wanted to give you the opportunity if you think you can be ready to sail tomorrow."

Lily looked from one to the other, her excitement building with each word. She wanted to dance a jig or turn a somersault. Since those reactions were forbidden, she smiled widely. "Oh yes, we can be ready as soon as we get your cargo loaded." She paused as her earlier conversation with Blake came to mind. "What type of goods would we be transporting?"

"A hundred hogshead of milled corn," Mr. Hughes answered. "Our daughter and her husband run our New Orleans office. They moved there to take over after Monsieur LeGrand, the original owner, fell ill. I don't have fond memories of that area—it's where I lost my leg—but they love it. We'll give you directions to their office when you're getting your load stored away."

"You will love our daughter, Charlotte. She is a bit older than you, but I have a feeling you will become close friends." Mrs. Hughes had a twinkle in her eye.

Unable to remain in her chair a moment longer, Lily jumped up and hugged the older lady. "If she is half as charming as her mother, I'm sure we will. Thank you both so very much. I can hardly wait until tomorrow."

"Is this your co-owner?" Mr. Hughes gestured to Jean Luc, whom Lily had almost forgotten in her excitement.

"No, please excuse my lack of manners. This is Jean Luc Champney, a dear friend who has gone out of his way to help me." She could feel her cheeks burning. Grandmother and Aunt Dahlia would be horrified. "I thought you were acquainted since Mr. Champney's family is also involved in the shipping business."

Jean Luc stood and greeted the Hugheses with more reserve than she expected. Was he upset because their dinner had been interrupted? His behavior seemed out of character.

"We'll leave you to your dinner, then." Mr. Hughes bowed and took his wife's arm.

Lily smiled at them. "You have made me so happy. Thank you."

The handsome couple smiled before making their way to a table on the other side of the room.

After Jean Luc and Lily returned to their seats, he said, "I can hardly believe it's true."

Was there an edge to his voice? Lily could read nothing other than support in his dark gaze. She must be imaging things. "I can hardly believe it, either. Mrs. Hughes was right about God's involvement. When I spoke to them this afternoon, they had nothing, and now they have a shipment and no ship to deliver it. What else could explain such a happy string of coincidences?"

"What indeed?"

Perhaps Jean Luc was put out because he felt ignored. Lily reached across the table for his hand. "And you must be His instrument, too, in bringing me to this place where we would run into each other."

She thought his smile faltered, but before she could ask him what was wrong, he squeezed her fingers. "I am very excited for you."

His smile was back in place. Perhaps she had imagined his irritation. He pulled his hand away and began eating again.

Lily picked up her fork but put it down without eating another bite. She was too excited to concentrate on anything as dull as food. She sipped at her lime soda and began to dream of the coming day. Her life on the river was about to begin.

Chapter Twenty-two

Lily was partly terrified, partly elated as she watched the bank sliding past. The trip from their quiet cove to the bustling port of Natchez had gone without a hitch so far.

Jasmine darted from side to side of the pilothouse, looking like a ruffled dragonfly. "When will we see Natchez Under-the-Hill?"

Captain Lars rolled his eyes. "The pilothouse is no place for young girls."

Lily frowned at him. "Just because Monsieur Champney recommended you does not give you the right to dictate how *my* boat will be run."

Jasmine turned away from the scenery, her violet eyes wide as she looked from Lily to the captain. "I'm sorry."

"You have nothing to apologize for, dearest. We are all excited about our first voyage." Lily pulled Jasmine close for a reassuring hug. Jasmine's arms went around her waist. Lily basked in the moment. Was there anything sweeter than the love expressed by a child?

Captain Lars grunted and reached for a leather cord to his right. A low moan filled the air.

Tears stung Lily's eyes as she listened to the first long blast, followed by two short toots and another long whistle. "Mother would be so happy if she could see us."

Jasmine pulled away from her embrace and clapped her hands in excitement. "I want to learn how to do that."

Blake appeared at the doorway, his blue eyes reflecting the bright sunlit morning. "Don't you think we should head down to the main level? We'll want to make sure we get the right cargo."

Lily and Jasmine followed him, passing through the spotless parlor and on to the first floor where Tamar and Camellia were already positioned at the rail. They waved at the people watching their arrival. Their very first landing. Lily wanted to hug the whole world.

The boat churned the brown water slowly as they approached the wharf. Blake uncoiled a rope nearly as thick as her arm and fashioned a loop at its end that reminded her of a hangman's noose. As the *Hattie Belle* nudged against the wet, gray wood of the dock, he tossed the rope over one of the posts and pulled it tight, his muscles rippling with the effort. As soon as it caught, he strode past them to the back of the boat, grabbed a second rope, and repeated the process.

Lily could not help but be impressed. She had so much to learn. As soon as they were under way again, she would ask him to show her how to make that loop so she could help the next time they landed.

Jensen appeared from the engine room, wiping his hands on a handkerchief. "The engine seems in good shape." He took a position next to Tamar, his elbow almost touching her arm.

Tamar moved away and frowned before turning her attention to Lily's sisters. "Jasmine, you and Camellia come with me. It's time to check on your patient. We'll leave the cargo to your sister and the men."

A chorus of moans answered, but the girls obediently followed her to the aft cabin.

Lily spotted Mr. Hughes waiting beside a mountain of barrels. He doffed his hat in greeting.

Their crewman, Jack Brown, swung the landing platform over the dark water, and it contacted the wharf with a loud clap. As soon as it was down, Mr. Hughes crossed over and handed her two pieces of paper, one signed, one not. "This is the bill of lading. It specifies exactly how many barrels are being loaded on your boat and the value of each."

Lily glanced at the paper, frowned, and looked toward Mr. Hughes. This could not be right. "I don't understand. I cannot afford to pay you this amount of money."

He shook his head. "That amount will be paid to our New Orleans office once the goods are delivered. In turn they will pay you a percentage of their profit for bringing the shipment to them safely."

A burden seemed to slide off her shoulders. "I see."

"You should carefully count the items delivered, however." He patted her arm and chuckled. "Not all businessmen can be relied upon to be honest."

Another question occurred to Lily. "What happens if I don't deliver all the barrels listed here?"

"Unless you can afford to purchase insurance, you would have to pay the difference."

A lump formed in her throat. Lily swallowed hard. "Then I'll have to make certain every barrel arrives safely."

"I'll be praying for you the whole time."

A snort behind her made Lily turn. Blake leaned against one of the posts, a sour look on his face.

"You don't believe in the power of prayer?" Mr. Hughes voiced the question in her mind.

"I wouldn't go so far as to say that, sir." Blake sauntered toward them. He held out a hand toward Mr. Hughes and introduced himself before continuing. "Asking God for favor cannot harm us, but I'm not certain it will do us good, either. I'd rather purchase insurance and remove all worry."

Lily drew herself up. "I will not throw away money on insurance for such a short trip in good weather. By this time tomorrow, we'll be in New Orleans safe and sound."

"Insurance is quite expensive," Mr. Hughes added. "It would eat up a large portion of your profit."

Blake's half smile curled up one side of his mouth. "I'll bow to your superior knowledge."

His reply was obviously directed toward Mr. Hughes. She had less actual experience than anyone else on the boat except for Tamar and her sisters.

Lily folded her lips into a tight smile as Mr. Hughes glanced at both of them. He probably wondered what position Blake held on her boat, but she had no desire to explain.

Mr. Hughes cleared his throat. "I have signed this copy of the bill for you to keep. It also has directions on how to reach our New Orleans office. You need to sign the second copy and return it to me."

While Mr. Hughes directed loading operations, Lily retreated to the small office just ahead of the engine room. It took her a little while to locate pen and ink before she signed her name with a flourish.

By the time she returned to the loading area, Blake had disappeared, and all the barrels were stowed in neat rows. Oilcloth lashed across them would protect them from rain and spray. She smiled at the sight before turning to the wharf, where Mr. Hughes waited. She leaned against the rail to hand him his copy, noticing that the loading dock seemed higher.

A memory returned from the worst day of her life. She and her father were standing on Grandmother's front porch, watching an overladen steamboat struggle to make its way against the river currents.

"Filling your boat so full that the river washes across the deck is a sign of a foolish captain." Her father's gravelly voice spoke to her. "Always remember to balance your profit against your risks, Water Lily. All the money in the world cannot return loved ones to us once they're gone."

That was the last advice her father had given her before he'd walked out of her life. Before he'd abandoned them without a backward glance.

Mr. Hughes's kind voice brought her back to the present. "I wish you a safe journey." He tucked his copy of their agreement into a coat pocket and bowed.

Lily waved good-bye as the dockworkers released their ropes and tossed them onto the deck. The giant paddle wheel began moving, and a single, long, steady blast from the captain indicated they were on the move.

Their first voyage had begun.

Chapter Twenty-three

Tamar searched the dining parlor but found no sign of her youngest charges. It seemed she'd spent all her waking hours chasing after Jasmine and David since he'd been allowed to leave his sickbed the day before. She had a feeling the friendship between those two was going to give her a head of gray hair.

Where could they be? She hurried down to the first floor, but she saw no sign of Jasmine's dark curls or David's wheat-colored thatch of hair—just cargo and empty deck. A sense of foreboding filled her. She could almost see Jasmine leaning over the rail and falling into the brown water. Tamar put a hand over her chest and turned away from the rail.

"And the steam makes the pistons go back and forth—"

"What's a piston?"

At the youthful voice, Tamar sighed with relief. She pushed open the door to the engine room to find both young people standing next to Jensen Moreau, the one man she'd rather avoid. Whenever they were in the same room, she could feel his dark gaze on her. And he liked to sidle up close to her, like he was interested in courting her. It made her uncomfortable.

She had no time for romance, and even if she did, she wouldn't encourage someone like him. Jensen Moreau was younger than she and a man of the world. Beyond that, he was a freeman, and she was a slave. Any relationship between them was doomed to failure.

She tried to ignore him, concentrating on Jasmine and David instead. "I've been looking all over this boat for you, Miss Jasmine, and you, too, Master David. Not being able to find you has nearly scared me out of ten years of my life."

Jasmine jumped and twisted around. "Tamar! What are you doing here?"

"I was halfway convinced you'd fallen overboard and drowned."

Jasmine flipped her hair over one shoulder. "I wouldn't drown. I know how to swim."

"I wouldn't let her come to any harm." David's soulful green gaze was centered on Jasmine.

"They wasn't doing no harm, Miss Tamar." Mr. Moreau wiped his hands on a rag. "Just wanting to see how this old engine works."

Tamar put her hands on her hips. She should have known Jasmine would charm the gruff man like she did everyone else. The girl was going to be a handful when she became a woman, leading her older sister on a merry chase until some man took her off Lily's hands. "She can learn about her home after she studies history and arithmetic."

Mr. Moreau's eyes widened. "You teach the children?"

A reluctant smile turned her lips upward. "I don't hardly know how to spell out my name. I wouldn't be any good trying to teach them."

"Tamar is very good at other things." Jasmine moved to her side and put an arm around her waist. "She's an excellent seamstress, and she knows all the stories from the Bible."

Warmth filled Tamar at the way Jasmine rushed to her defense. She had once dreamed of having little girls of her own, but as the years passed, she had come to realize she would never marry. Her heart had never been touched by any man, and now she was too old to be thinking about such things. But the good Lord knew best. And He'd seen fit to give her the joy of raising the motherless Anderson girls. It was enough to satisfy her most times.

Jensen's unscarred eyebrow lifted. "I have the feeling Miss Tamar can do most anything she puts her mind to."

The engine room suddenly felt uncomfortably warm. The boiler hissed and popped. No wonder Jensen. . .Mr. Moreau. . .only wore a white shirt and loose-fitting trousers. He looked like a bloodthirsty pirate with his swarthy skin and scarred face. All he needed was a neckerchief and a broadsword to complete the picture. "Th–thank you." What was the matter with her? She was acting like a love-struck girl.

"We need to leave Mr. Moreau to his important work." Tamar shooed the children out of the room. She ignored the urge to look back. She was a grown woman, an old woman. And she was a godly woman, not one given to carrying on with men—no matter whether one set her heart to fluttering. She would keep her mind where it belonged, regardless of how hard that might be.

Midafternoon heat made it impossible for Lily to nap with her sisters. She tossed for half an hour before getting up and returning to the kitchen to see if she could help Tamar. The older woman was sitting at the table, her hands folded together, her eyes closed.

Tamar was praying. It made Lily think of how little time she'd spent lately talking to God. She needed to do better. Unearth her Bible and get back to reading to her sisters and Tamar. Perhaps she could invite the men to a nightly devotional time. Happy with the idea, she carefully picked up a chair and carried it out onto the deck.

The bank slid silently past, and Lily considered how uneventful their voyage had been. No storms, no pirates.

They had caught up with a smaller steamer, the *Daniel Boone*, right after resuming their journey at dawn. Captain Lars had wanted to race the steamer, but Lily vetoed the idea. She had no desire to collide with a snag or stray out of the channel in such a frivolous pursuit. She wanted to get safely to New Orleans, collect their payment, and pick up their next load. They still managed to leave the smaller boat in their wake, not surprising since their paddle wheel was nearly twice as large.

Tamar's voice interrupted her musings. "I thought you were taking a nap."

"I'm sorry. I didn't mean to disturb you."

"You didn't disturb me, honey. I was just thanking the good Lord for protecting us."

"You're such a good example for us, Tamar."

The older woman looked down at her hands. "I don't know about that."

Lily stood and hugged Tamar. "I do." She pushed Tamar down into her chair. "Why don't you sit here and relax a bit? I'm feeling too restless to sit still."

Lily wandered toward the main staircase. Maybe she could talk to Blake about taking on passengers for their return trip to Natchez. Although they would have to hire more crew to help take care of the passengers' needs, they could still realize a profit.

She entered the shadowy room and ran a hand across the edge of the main dining room. They'd eaten in here last night, all nine of them. Blake had sat at the head of the table while she'd taken the spot at the foot, like they were a real family.

A smile teased her lips. An odd family indeed. From David, their rescued foundling, to Jensen, the reformed pirate, they made a motley crew. And she enjoyed all of them—Captain Steenberg and the tongue-tied crewman, Jack. They had become the heart and soul of the *Hattie Belle*.

A staccato sound made Lily catch her breath. Her warm feelings melted away. Blake Matthews had better not be playing cards. She would not allow gambling on this boat.

Anger carried her through the empty dining hall and into the gentlemen's parlor. Blake and their new crewman, Jack, were sitting on opposite sides of a small table. Her arrival apparently went unheard as neither looked up. Lily took a moment to size up the situation. Blake had his back to her, but a pile of coins at his elbow told the story. She had caught the man red-handed. "What are you doing?"

Jack gasped and stood, his movements almost oversetting the stack of coins.

After a brief hesitation, Blake continued to deal the cards. "We're enjoying a friendly game of cards."

"I thought you understood my feelings about gambling on the *Hattie Belle*." Lily walked to where he sat, acting as though her desires were of no interest or validity. "I won't have it."

"Don't get so upset. Haven't we earned a little relaxation?"

Just as she reached the table, the floor bucked upward. She screamed and grabbed the table with both hands. The boat lurched again, and a horrendous scraping sound filled the air. Blake stood and grabbed her around the waist, holding her close as the world shook and shuddered.

"What's happening?" she asked.

"I'd guess we've run aground." His deep voice tickled her ear.

How had she ended up in his arms again? Confusing emotions clamored for attention—fear, anger, pleasure. . . . Why was she clinging to him like some weak debutante? Lily made fists of her hands and pushed against his chest. "Let go of me."

When he complied, she staggered back but compensated by windmilling her arms. He was almost out of the parlor by the time she recovered, never having looked back to see whether she had fallen.

Lily swallowed her exasperation and followed him to the pilothouse. Coming out onto the hurricane deck made her realize how bad the situation was. From the sounds of it, the *Hattie Belle* was tearing apart at the seams. Lily could see the bank some distance away on both sides of them. What had happened?

She stepped into the pilothouse right behind Blake and groaned. Ahead of the boat was a wide expanse of sand. The captain had run them onto a sandbar. "Where is he?"

"Hey, there." The captain appeared at the door to the pilothouse. "We had an acci. . .ac. . .acshident."

"You're drunk." The disgust in Blake's voice was as deep as the main river channel. The channel their drunken captain had taken them out of.

"No, I'm not." The captain hiccuped and grinned. "Only had a nip." He held up a thumb and finger as a measurement.

Lily closed her eyes. She wanted to toss the man onto the sandbar and leave him.

"Take our gallant captain downstairs and get some coffee into him." Blake bit out the words as though he was angry with her. As if the whole fiasco was her fault.

She wanted to take exception to his tone, but this was not the time. They needed to get their boat back into the river. Besides, her sisters, Tamar, and David would be terrified. She needed to reassure them.

Guilt speared her at the thought of the trouble they were facing. She should have listened to Blake. He was right about the captain, and he was also right about purchasing insurance. A tiny sob escaped her as she realized her dreams might collapse. Why hadn't she let Blake convince her? Why was she always so determined to ignore his advice?

She was going to have to apologize to him, admit that he had been right. And she would. . .if she got out of this mess.

Chapter Twenty-Four

He had to fix this mess, get them out of the disaster *her* choice of captain had caused while she gave him grief over an innocent card game. Blake pushed away the memory of Lily's stricken expression. He didn't have time to worry about her tender feelings.

A pang of guilt shot through him. If he'd been in the pilothouse instead of gambling downstairs, the accident might not have happened. But didn't he deserve a little relaxation? Was he supposed to shoulder all the responsibility for this venture? It hadn't been his idea, after all. He'd gone along with Lily Anderson because he had no choice.

Jensen appeared at the door to the pilothouse. "I've turned off the boiler."

Blake nodded. "Good. Can you tell how bad it is?"

"Bad enough," Jensen admitted, shaking his head. "I'm not sure if we'll be able to get free before the current turns us broadside."

Blake shuddered. They'd lose the boat for sure if that happened. The *Hattie Belle* couldn't compete against the force of the mighty Mississippi. "Can we dig our way out?"

Jensen shrugged. "We can give it a try."

"Good. I'll be downstairs as quick as I can to help. You go ahead and get started with Jack."

❧

Lily headed back toward the parlor, her ears stretched in hopes she would hear the churn of the paddle wheel. She had left the captain in the kitchen with a pot of black coffee. She needed to check on David and her sisters, warn Tamar to be ready to get them out safely, and then get outside to see how bad the damage was and what she could do to help.

"Lily." Blake's voice stopped her. "How is the captain?"

She turned to answer his question. The expression on his face deepened her foreboding. "He's nursing a mug of coffee, but I'm not sure how long it's going to take him to sober up. How bad is it?"

"I've checked on the cargo, and it's fine. . .for the time being." The corners of Blake's mouth turned down. "But half the boat is up on the sand. If we can't dig around it enough to get it floating again, the *Hattie Belle* may break apart."

Lily closed her eyes. *Please, God.* All her yearning went into the plea.

"We're doing everything we can, but you need to make sure the children are ready to abandon ship if necessary."

She swallowed hard, opened her eyes, and nodded.

The floor lurched. "I've got to get back out there." He turned sharply and ran down the passageway.

Lily wanted to follow him, but she knew she had to check on her sisters. David was the first one she saw in the parlor, his back to her as he peered through the window. She glanced around and found Tamar sitting on the sofa, hugging both Jasmine and Camellia close. Her sisters' faces were pale, their eyes large. They jumped up and ran to her.

"What's wrong, Sissy?" Jasmine barreled into her.

Camellia wasn't far behind her. "Did we hit another boat?"

Lily held both of them. "No, we scraped up on a sandbar. It's going to take us a while to dig out."

David moved toward them. "Can I help the men?"

Lily shook her head. "I need you to stay here and keep my sisters calm." She gave both of them a little shove. "Why don't you get out the checkerboard and enjoy a few games while we wait?"

As they got out the checkers, she pulled Tamar aside. "I don't want to alarm the children, but we are in trouble."

"What can I do?" Tamar asked.

"Stay here with the children. Be ready to get them out quickly if something happens."

"What are you going to do?"

Lily patted her arm. "I'm going to change clothes and help."

"Won't you be in the way?" Tamar's voice was pitched low, but it conveyed her concern.

"Not as soon as I get a shovel in my hand." Lily slipped out of the parlor and ran to her room. Putting on her oldest skirt, she prayed for deliverance. They needed God's intervention to survive this disaster.

❧

The sun beat against Blake's shoulders through his shirt. It seemed he'd been digging forever.

"I need a shovel."

Lily's voice brought his head up. "What are you doing here?"

"I can't sit inside and wait for our dreams to be lost." She crossed her arms. "I may not be able to dig as fast as you, but every grain of sand I move is one you won't have to."

Part of him wanted to send her inside to safety, but Blake understood her frustration. He inclined his head. "If we have any more, they'll be in that bucket."

She nodded and marched away, her shoulders as straight as a sergeant's.

As he redoubled his efforts, Blake thought about Lily's temerity. He had to admire her spunk. He didn't know a single other woman who would volunteer to shovel sand. He only hoped it wasn't too little, too late.

"You look like you could use a helping hand."

Blake straightened and looked out at the river. A boat had pulled even with them, a boat he recognized. It was the *Daniel Boone*, the boat they'd passed earlier. He climbed out of his trench. "We sure could." For the first time since they'd landed on the sandbar, Blake felt his shoulders relax.

The captain shouted an order, and one of his crew tossed a towline out across the water. Blake and Jack secured it to the bow while Jensen and Lily picked up the shovels. As soon as they had all climbed back onto the *Hattie Belle*, the smaller boat's paddle wheel started churning. At first Blake thought it would not be able to pull them free of the grasping sand, but with a lurch, their boat began to move.

Jensen fired up the boiler while Blake loosened the grappling hook and tossed it back to the captain of the *Daniel Boone*.

Lily was standing next to him, her skirt covered in sand and muddy water but a wide smile on her face. "I can't thank you enough. I was beginning to think our first voyage was going to be our last."

The broad-chested captain tugged on his cap. "It's a harsh river we're riding. We have to help each other or we all lose."

Blake was humbled by the man's attitude. If nothing else positive came from this disaster, he would always remember the captain's actions and never forget to extend a helping hand to those in need.

They limped into New Orleans before the last ray of sun had slipped from the sky. By the time the *Hattie Belle* was secured, the shadows were running together into dusk. He was filthy, exhausted, and sore. And quite certain he didn't want to earn a living running cargo.

He was more suited to the life of a gambler. Tonight he couldn't remember why he hadn't walked away from the *Hattie Belle* when Lily first showed up and claimed majority ownership. As soon as he got paid for this trip, he would disappear. New Orleans was as good a place to start over as any other.

He felt rather than saw Lily join him at the rail. "We made it."

She put a hand over his. "Thank you. I know we wouldn't have made it without your hard work."

Blake liked the feeling of her cool skin on his. He wanted to turn his palm over and run the tips of his fingers across her soft skin, but he didn't want her to pull away. So he remained still and basked in her appreciation. Their differences sank beneath the surface of his tumbling thoughts, taking his frustration and weariness with them.

They stood close together like kindred spirits and looked toward the other boats in the harbor. Many of them were lashed together, and he made out the figures of men leaping from one deck to another with the nimbleness of experience.

The slap of water against wooden hulls was punctuated by greetings, shouts, and laughter, all melting together to create the unique sound of a floating city. The warm yellow flames of cooking fires glowed, and the air was heavy with the exotic fragrances of unfamiliar spices. He could have remained standing there for the rest of the evening.

Lily squeezed his hand and pulled away. "I suppose we need to get moving if we're going to find LeGrand's this evening."

Blake turned toward her, his gaze following the outline of her graceful neck up to the determined chin and pert nose he could barely make out in the growing darkness. "I doubt it'll be open."

"It will be. It has to be." Her chin rose a notch.

He sighed. He should have known she would insist on finding the business tonight. "Do you have the directions?"

It was for the best. Hadn't he just been thinking about cutting his losses and walking away? He needed the reminder that Lily was always going to want to call the shots.

She would never be a conformable female. If he ever decided to marry, it would not be to a woman so bossy and self-righteous. He would choose someone quiet, someone who adored him and would be a good role model for their children. Not a woman who strode about on the deck of a steamship and expected everyone to fall in with her plans.

A stab of regret pierced his heart, but Blake ignored it. After a nice long soak in a warm bath and a good night's sleep, the pains he had earned today would fade away. Including the ache beginning to lay claim to part of his heart.

Chapter Twenty-five

As they approached, Blake saw a lamp gleaming in the front window of LeGrand Shipping. Even though Lily had to be as exhausted as he was, she practically leaped from the wagon he had hired.

"If you'll wait a moment, I'll help you get down." He tossed the reins to a child who came running forward, then jumped down, holding back a groan with some effort. The sooner they concluded their business, the sooner he could rest.

He walked to the far side of the wagon and held out a hand. As soon as Lily's feet touched the ground, she let go of him and straightened her skirts. He moved up the two steps and opened the door to the shipping company, setting off a tinkling bell and causing the man at the counter to look up.

As a gambler, Blake had learned to size up people quickly. Thinning hair on the man's head was compensated for by a neatly trimmed beard and mustache. Probably about two decades older than he, the man smiled readily, a sign of an honest merchant. As the man removed his spectacles, Blake recognized the intelligence in his hazel gaze. "May I help you?" he asked as Lily and Blake entered the orderly office space.

Lily consulted the paper in her hand. "I'm looking for Lloyd Thornton."

The man's smile widened, and he put down his pen. "You've found me. What can I do for you?"

Before Lily could answer, the curtain covering a doorway behind Mr. Thornton moved, and a woman stepped into the room. She was short, even shorter than Lily, and her blond hair looked almost colorless in the lamplight. Her light-brown eyes contained the same combination of friendliness and canniness as the man she stood beside. "Well, I see we have some late business, or is this handsome couple seeking directions to the French Quarter?"

"I was about to find out their errand when you entered, dearest. They seem to be seeking us, however, since this lovely young lady has my name."

"*Quel charme*. It's charming to meet you." The woman's gaze was as bright and interested as a bird's. "I'm Mrs. Thornton."

Although both Thorntons looked to Blake, he glanced at Lily. She held out her paper to Mr. Thornton. "We have brought cargo from Natchez."

Mr. Thornton took the paper and returned his spectacles to his face. After a moment he looked at his wife. "This is the cornmeal we were hoping to send to Barbados. I wasn't sure your parents would be able to get it to us in time."

Mrs. Thornton nodded and turned to them with her attractive smile. "Did you and your husband have a pleasant voyage to New Orleans?"

"He's not my husband." The words flew out of Lily's mouth.

At the same time, Blake spoke forcefully. "We're not married."

"Oh." Mrs. Thornton looked toward her husband who answered with a shrug.

"I suppose their situation must be entirely proper or your parents wouldn't have trusted them with the cargo."

"My sisters and I own a majority share of the *Hattie Belle*. Mr. Matthews owns a smaller portion." Color had darkened Lily's cheeks. "A chaperone travels with us."

"I assure you our relationship is purely business." Blake picked up the explanation. "Miss Anderson convinced me we should try our hand at shipping, and here we are with our first delivery."

"I see." Mr. and Mrs. Thornton exchanged a glance before Mrs. Thornton continued. "Then I trust you and your business partner had a pleasant first voyage."

Blake nodded but saw Lily shaking her head. "We had the ill fortune of running our boat on a sandbar. Although we were blessed to be towed back into the channel by a passing steamship, I'm afraid we sustained some damage."

"Praise the Lord you made it to New Orleans." Mrs. Thornton put a hand to her chest. She stepped around the end of the counter. "But what do you plan to do until your beautiful boat is repaired?"

Blake cleared his throat. "We haven't gotten that far. We arrived only a little while ago."

Mrs. Thornton looked at her husband, an unspoken question in her gaze. Mr. Thornton removed his spectacles and nodded.

These two seemed able to read each other's thoughts. Past sermons from Blake's childhood came to mind. Could two people really become one? Or did one simply find a pretty, compatible female and marry her?

"All of you will come to our house and stay until your boat is fixed."

Mrs. Thornton's words made Blake's jaw drop.

"We couldn't do that. It would be too much of an imposition." Lily's words had a wistful tone. "There are seven of us not counting the crew."

"Our town house seems so empty now that Eli and Sarah are gone. Tell them, Lloyd."

"Charlotte is right." Mr. Thornton cleaned his spectacles with his handkerchief as he spoke. "You would be doing us a favor. You can tell us about her parents and what's happening in Natchez."

"We do need somewhere to stay." Blake added his support to the Thorntons' suggestion.

Lily looked at him as though he had betrayed her. "I thought we'd stay in the *Hattie Belle*. Make sure the repairs are carried out properly."

He raised an eyebrow. "I doubt workers will appreciate having women and children running underfoot. Jensen and I can stay on board and supervise the work."

"That makes no sense." Lily frowned at him. "You're more exhausted than I. You deserve a chance to recoup your strength."

That was true enough. Blake would pay a large sum for a bed as long as his frame. "But—"

"I won't hear of it." Mrs. Thornton overrode both of them. "We may have to ask the gentlemen to share a bedroom, but we can manage things. Now go on back to your berth, gather your belongings, and come back here. Lloyd will wait for you while I make sure everything is ready."

Lily opened her mouth, but Mrs. Thornton raised a finger. "You're coming to stay with us. That's the end of it."

Mr. Thornton joined his wife, putting an arm around her waist. "I learned long ago when to let Charlotte win an argument. Besides, she will enjoy having you to fuss over. So you may as well give in gracefully and let us coddle you a bit."

Blake could tell the moment Lily decided to stay with the Thorntons. He breathed a sigh of relief. The Thorntons' generosity was like being dealt a royal flush—a stroke of good luck no gambler would ignore.

"Thank you so much." Lily smiled at the couple. "We would be happy to pay—"

Mrs. Thornton laughed. "Don't be silly, child. I won't hear of such folly. We can afford twice as many guests. Besides, you will be doing me a favor. Since my daughter, Sarah, got married, I have had no girls to discuss fashion and shopping with. We'll have such fun together."

"I can also arrange for a reputable company to do your repairs." Mr. Thornton moved back to the counter and began searching through some papers. "I'll have all the information together by the time you return."

Blake led Lily back to the wagon by the light of a gas lantern. On the ride to the boat, she was uncharacteristically silent. Did she regret agreeing to stay with the Thorntons? "I think you made a good decision. Who knows how long it will take to complete the repairs on our boat?"

She turned her face up to him. "Please promise you will come with us."

Warmth filled him, traveling outward from his chest in a flood of emotion. Was she worried about him? Or maybe she wanted his company. He really liked that idea. She was growing fond of him in spite of their differences. He patted her hand. "I won't desert you."

As soon as the words escaped, Blake wanted to call them back. Wasn't he ready to wash his hands of Miss Anderson and her troublesome troupe? Then why had he given his word to stay at her side? The question had no answer, or at least no answer he wanted to consider.

❧

Early the next morning, Blake rolled his shoulders as he waited for the repair crew Mr. Thornton was sending over. He hadn't seen Captain Steenberg yet. Maybe the man had decided to disappear. Good riddance. It would save Blake the trouble of telling him his services were no longer required. The sound of footsteps on the back stairway drew his attention.

"I feel like a herd of buffalo's running through my head." The captain winced as a shaft of sunlight landed on his face.

Stale waves of alcohol washed over Blake. Was Steenberg still drunk? Or drunk again? "You should be glad we didn't leave your sorry carcass on that sandbar."

"For making a mistake?" the man said, his face showing surprise. "Don't I deserve a little relaxation?"

Guilt speared Blake as the man used the same excuse he'd given Lily when she'd discovered him playing cards. Had he been negligent in expecting the captain to shoulder all the responsibility of piloting? He shook his head. "You ran us aground. We could still be stuck out there on the river or trying to walk our way through the swamp to New Orleans."

The captain shrugged. "But we're not."

How could the man be so dense? So careless? And how could Blake have been so wrongheaded as to ignore his intuition about Steenberg? It was time to take action. Time to stop letting Lily Anderson call the shots.

"No thanks to you. Clear off this boat."

The man's jaw went slack. "What do you mean?"

Blake remained silent.

The captain's face hardened. "You didn't hire me. You don't have the right to tell me to leave."

"I most certainly do have the right. I can assure you Miss Anderson and I are of one mind on this matter." Blake winced inside as he made the statement. Surely Lily would agree once he explained the situation. "Get your things."

Fear and regret replaced the captain's rebellion. "Please give me another chance. I promise I'll do a better job. Besides, you need a licensed captain."

Blake shook his head. "Don't worry. We'll find someone."

"Lots of luck." The captain spat and took a step forward. He shook a finger under Blake's nose. "Where do you think you'll find someone to replace me? Do you think anyone else is going to take a chance on this doomed boat?"

He knew he ought to remain stoic, but curiosity overcame Blake. "What do you mean?"

"Everybody knows having a woman run a boat is bad luck. And I'm sure word has gotten out about her running aground. No one's going to want a berth, much less a job, on the *Hattie Belle*. You might as well change her name to the *Flying Dutchman*."

Blake laughed. Superstition? Ludicrous. He'd seen a lot of men blame luck and superstition for their own shortcomings. It seemed the captain was ready to take it one step further. "You're trying to blame your mistake on Miss Anderson?" Laughter bubbled up again. "Go ahead. Any man with sense will be able to see the truth."

A sound turned Blake's attention to the wharf. The repair crew. He wondered how much they had heard of the argument. At least no one was running away. "I'll be right with you." He turned back to the captain. "You have five minutes to gather your gear and get off this boat."

"You'll be sorry." Steenberg's bravado faded as he hissed the threat. "Everyone's going to hear about the way you've treated me. I'll make sure you and all those Anderson girls pay for this."

Blake shouldn't have been surprised at the threat. They were the weapons of a coward. "That's enough." He advanced two steps and pointed a finger of warning at the man. "Believe me, if anything *ever* happens to this ship or to any of the Andersons, I will find you, and you'll wish you'd never been born."

The captain backed away, stumbled over the bottom step, and then practically ran to his quarters.

Blake hoped he'd convinced the troublemaker to leave them alone. He turned back to the repair crew. "I'm glad to see you."

The burly man who boarded first nodded. "We'll just take a look at your paddle wheel and let you know how long it'll be."

The minutes dragged by, and Blake paced the deck, torn between his desire to oversee the repair crew and his need to make sure Steenberg wasn't packing any more than he'd brought. Loud footsteps took the decision out of his hands. The irate captain reappeared, a black leather bag slung over his back. Shouldering his way past Blake, the man stepped onto the wharf. "You'll be sorry for this."

"Are you threatening me?" Blake clenched his fists.

Captain Lars held his gaze then looked down. "No. I'm just saying captains aren't standing on every corner, waiting to find a boat."

"That's my problem, not yours." Blake strode to the rear of the boat to check with the workers.

He found the burly foreman taking measurements and recording them in a small book. "It's going to take at least two weeks to get your boat ready."

Blake took a deep breath. "Are you sure?"

A nod answered his question. "You're lucky to have made it to New Orleans. I'm not sure how you did without breaking up. You must have had an angel riding with you."

His lips turned up in a grin. He wouldn't exactly describe her as an angel. Lily was a little too forceful to spend her time strumming a harp. He dreaded telling her how bad the damage was. She was probably planning to get back on the river this afternoon or tomorrow at the latest. If she did have a halo hidden away somewhere, it was going to get a little bent.

Blake gave the order to proceed and left to check with Mr. Thornton on available captains. At least he had plenty of time to conduct interviews and find a suitable candidate. That should please Lily if nothing else did.

Chapter Twenty-six

Lily left Tamar helping her sisters get dressed and hurried downstairs, wondering how long it would take her to get back to the boat. She exited their bedroom on the third floor, surprised to realize she was eye level with a beautiful crystal chandelier that held dozens of candles. She reached out one hand for the wooden railing as she began descending the U-shaped stairwell.

Last night she had not noticed the intricate woodwork on the posts or the number of doorways in the Thorntons' town house. The craftsmanship signaled the luxury in which their new acquaintances resided.

Reaching the end of the stairs, she had a choice of direction. The door through which they had entered the home stood in front of her. She remembered the parlor was to her left, so perhaps she would find the dining room to her right.

Lily bypassed the first door since it was closed. She doubted their hosts would close the entryway into their dining room. Light spilled from the second doorway, and when she reached it, she found a spacious room with a large table at its center. The dining room.

Lily entered, surprised to find the only other occupant was Mrs. Thornton. "What a beautiful home you and Mr. Thornton have."

"Thank you, dear. I am glad to see you are looking less bedraggled this morning." She smiled. "Did you sleep well?"

"Yes, ma'am." Lily slid into the seat her hostess indicated.

Mrs. Thornton rang a bell. "Someone will be here with your food in a moment. We normally eat croissants with marmalade or fresh fruit for breakfast, but I can instruct our cook to fix something else if you prefer."

Lily picked up a snowy-white napkin and placed it on her lap. "Oh no, thank you. Your breakfast sounds wonderful."

A round-faced girl in a plain dress appeared and served Lily a plate with two rolls that had been twisted in a spiral and bent into a half-moon shape.

Lily thanked her and picked one up, breaking it open to see steam rising from the flaky interior. She placed a dab of butter on her croissant and bit into it, her eyes closing as the bread melted in her mouth.

Mrs. Thornton smiled. "Our cook is an artist with food."

Lily nodded. "I'm rather surprised Blake and your husband are not here. Have they already left for the office? I was hoping to talk to Blake before they departed."

"I'm sorry, dear." Mrs. Thornton picked up her fork and speared a fresh strawberry. "Mr. Matthews must have decided to stay on the boat last night. He never made it to the town house. But don't worry. I'm sure he simply decided to guard your cargo since it could not be unloaded last night. Lloyd was going to check on him this morning, make certain he has all the help he needs to get your riverboat repaired."

"I see." Lily's appetite fled. While she had been sleeping in luxury, Blake had been guarding the boat. They had worked hard to get the boat free from the sandbar yesterday. They all deserved to sleep well.

"If you're worried about Mr. Matthews, I can send one of the servants to check on him."

"Thank you, but that's not necessary. I'm sure he's fine." Lily pinched the end of one of her croissants. She still wasn't hungry, but her hands needed something to do. Besides, she did not want to offend her hostess by not eating the sumptuous meal.

As she continued to pick at her food, her mind was consumed with plans. She had thought they might have time to tour the fabled city of New Orleans, but that would have to wait for a future trip. As soon as her sisters ate breakfast, they would all have to go to the boat to help out with the repairs. Even if they couldn't do the heavy work, they could at least prepare meals and keep the rest of the boat clean. Maybe they could make up nice flyers to advertise for passengers.

Camellia and Jasmine made an appearance then. Lily was thankful for their nonstop chatter as it allowed her to concentrate on the proper wording of the advertisements, as well as the apology she owed Blake.

When her sisters had finished breakfast, Lily rose from her place at the table and turned to tell Camellia and Jasmine to come upstairs with her. All of them needed to change into their working clothes. The outfits they were wearing were more suited to a day of sightseeing.

Before she could issue her instructions, however, a commotion in the foyer diverted her attention.

Mrs. Thornton checked the watch suspended on her fleur-de-lis chatelaine pin. "I cannot believe we have visitors this early."

A familiar voice made Lily's heart race. "I believe it may be my business partner. He's probably come to tell me how much our repairs are going to cost and how long they will take." She ignored the wide smile on Mrs. Thornton's face and walked out into the hall.

Blake was striding toward the dining room but checked himself when she appeared.

Lily thought he looked a bit haggard and wondered if he'd spent the whole night standing watch at their boat. A wave of shame swamped her. She remembered how ugly she'd been to him right before the accident. Again. Was she turning into a shrew? Pushing the thought aside, she composed herself and produced a welcoming smile. "I'm so glad to see you. We have many things we need to discuss."

No answering smile turned up the corners of his lips. "I suppose we can make use of the Thorntons' parlor."

Lily's heart stuttered. Blake must have bad news. Her smile slipped away. What could be wrong now?

❧

Blake followed Lily down a black-and-white-tiled hallway and entered a well-appointed parlor. She sat on the upholstered sofa and fluffed her black skirts around her, fussing with the material as though it was imperative to have it just right. "Mr. Matthews, this is difficult for me—"

Blake held up a hand to stop her. "I want to apologize, Lily. You were right. I should not have been playing cards. If I had been in the pilothouse, I could have stopped the captain from overimbibing." He didn't realize that he'd been staring at his feet as he delivered his apology until Lily's skirts appeared before his gaze. He looked up, his gaze meeting her wide eyes, eyes that seemed filled with remorse. What was this?

"You're not at fault as much as I am, Blake. I seem to remember your trying to warn me Steenberg might not be a good captain. Because I refused to listen to you, I share a large portion of the responsibility. Please forgive me for placing the blame on you yesterday."

Surprise rippled through him. He who prided himself on being able to understand others was always caught off guard by Lily's behavior. Where was the puritanical firebrand who had condemned him? "You had every right, Lily. But please believe me when I say I'll make it up to you."

"I know you will, Blake. I've learned that you're a man I can depend on."

Was she manipulating him? No. A glance in those deep brown eyes told him she was being honest. He wanted to enfold her in his arms, dance about the room. She had faith in him. In that moment he knew he would do whatever it took to get their boat running again. He would make sure her dreams came true, even if he had to swim the Mississippi from end to end to find cargo for the *Hattie Belle*.

"How long will it take to complete the repairs?" Her question brought him back to reality.

Blake paced in front of the fireplace. He wished he could give her better news, but he couldn't lie to her. "At least two weeks."

"Two weeks!" She croaked out the words. "I thought you said it would be one week. We can't afford to be off the river for two whole weeks."

"Jensen and I will do what we can, but some of the supplies are in high demand because of a break in the levee system at the Bell plantation. The people on the other side of the levee are trying to shore things up, and they keep buying up everything available." He paused before continuing. "Since there's such high demand, the lumber is more expensive."

"Isn't there something my sisters and I can do to speed things up?"

"No. In fact, I don't want any of you out there as long as the repairs are ongoing. It's dangerous with all the strangers around, and there's nothing for you to do until we're ready to leave for Natchez."

Blake was ready to comfort Lily when she broke down and began to cry. He hoped she had a handkerchief, because the one in his pocket was not as pristine as he might have liked. He lowered himself onto the sofa next to her and reached for one of her hands, pressing it between his palms and rubbing as he waited. "Everything is going to work out."

No tears flowed. Instead she straightened her spine and lifted her chin. "Of course you realize the good Lord knew we'd be facing this problem. Since the day you and I were born, He knew we'd end up sitting on this very sofa in this town house discussing this problem."

Not seeing why she wanted to bring God into the discussion, he waited.

Lily turned to him. "He already had things worked out, Blake. Don't you see? He'll help us through this trouble. I'm sure of it."

"If you say so, Lily." She might want to rely on God, but he was more a man of action than of prayer. That was why he'd considered their predicament from every angle. He had a solution, but would she accept it? Could she let go of her strict moral code long enough to allow him to put his plan into action? He doubted it but felt he needed to try anyway. "There's another way around this."

The look she gave him was full of hope. It brightened her eyes and her smile. "What is that?"

"I can host a quiet evening or two of cards on *Hattie Belle* during the evenings once the repairmen leave. It shouldn't take me long to earn enough to pay for the repairs and whatever additional expenses we run up."

"I can't believe you'd suggest such a thing. You know my stance on gambling and drinking. They're immoral and wicked, and they lead to absolute debauchery. I will not countenance them on my boat."

He should have known she wouldn't listen to reason. "Don't you think it's about time you got off your high horse, Lily? I've gone along with your self-righteous rules and pretentions. Where has that gotten us? We're stranded in New Orleans with little cash and no prospects. Dependent on the kindness of strangers for a safe place for you and your sisters to stay. Isn't it about time you let go of your highfalutin morals and embraced a little common sense?"

"Banning your dissolute habits is common sense, and as long as I own controlling interest in the *Hattie Belle*, you'll have to live with my highfalutin morals." She pointed a finger at him. "So get used to it, or get yourself another boat."

He raked a hand through his hair. Why couldn't she see reason? "I'd like to do that very thing, but I've sunk all my assets and not a little bit of my time into *our* boat. I'm not about to walk away."

"Fine." Lily walked to the door, opening it a few inches. "I'll go meet with Captain Steenberg and see if he can find someone more capable than the repairmen you hired."

"You won't find him aboard *Hattie Belle*."

His words stopped her. Her knuckles whitened around the doorknob she still clenched. "Why won't I?"

"I fired him."

She slammed the door shut. "You what?"

"You heard me." He crossed his arms and leaned back. "I told him to clear his gear out and be gone before I got back. I don't expect you'll find him anytime soon. He's probably gone to a saloon to drown his sorrows."

"You had no right to do that."

"Why not? The man's a drunkard. He nearly got us killed."

Lily shook her head. "I could have controlled that by removing his alcohol from the boat and keeping him under tight scrutiny."

"You're lying to yourself. No one can stop a drunkard who is intent on his drink. Steenberg would have hidden a bottle in his boot, in his shirt pocket, even in his breeches if he needed to. And the minute your back was turned, he would have taken a little nip. And another and another. Until he was as drunk as he was yesterday."

"You should have kept him until we found someone to take his place. What if we have to hire someone without experience? How will we be any better off?" She paced the floor.

"At least there'll be a better chance to arrive in Natchez with an undamaged boat."

"But we know Steenberg's weakness. We won't know anything about the man who replaces him. He could murder us while we sleep."

"I don't understand you, Lily." He sat forward. "You'd have thrown me overboard if I did what Steenberg did. And he's not your business partner. Why is it you want to forgive him for something much more heinous than anything I've ever done? You say you know I'm trustworthy, but when it comes time to put your words to the test, to put your faith in me, you can't do it."

Lily stopped pacing and looked at him. A frown of confusion marred her face. "I. . .you don't have the right to fire someone I hired."

"You mean someone Jean Luc Champney hired. Is that it? Are you concerned about upsetting your friend?"

"Don't try to bring him into this argument. Jean Luc is a fine gentleman. A kind man who considers my wishes. He's been very considerate toward me and my family."

Blake couldn't stop his grimace. "That's because he's trying to romance you."

"It's not like that." Her words rushed out with force, but her cheeks reddened. "Besides, my relationship with Monsieur Champney is none of your concern."

"I see." He raised an eyebrow. "We'll get away from such an uncomfortable subject since my point has already been proven. You're very quick to defend everyone except me."

She took a turn about the room, her skirts swishing and swaying. When she stopped in front of him, her eyes were as frosty as a January morning.

Something inside him hurt like he'd been punched in the stomach. How had they gotten here? Why did they always seem to end up on opposite sides? He opened his mouth to apologize for firing Lars without consulting her, but she held up a hand.

"We'll have to hire another captain. You fired Captain Steenberg, so it's your responsibility to find his replacement. Fix it."

Anger swept through him. His desire to apologize was swept away by her demand. How dare she order him around like a hired hand? He started to challenge her but decided it might be better to take a different tack. "If that's the way you want it, that's the way it will be."

"Good."

He pointed a finger at her. "And you can't second-guess my choice, either. The man I hire will captain our boat."

"That's fine by me. But if I don't like him, don't expect me to keep him aboard after we reach Natchez."

Blake watched as she jerked open the door and swept through it. With a weary sigh, he pushed himself up from the sofa and trod to the door.

Arguing with Lily was as exhausting as anything he'd done in the past week. Part of him wanted to please her, wanted her to be as forgiving toward him as she was toward everyone else. But that seemed impossible. He supposed they would continue bickering until they dissolved their partnership and went their separate ways.

Chapter Twenty-seven

Lily trudged up to her bedroom on the third floor, her heart heavy. Would she and Blake ever see eye to eye? It didn't seem so.

Why had he gotten so upset when she suggested keeping Lars Steenberg? She understood what the man had done. But they could have controlled him while getting back to Natchez, back to a part of the world she was more familiar with. Back to an area where she knew people who could help them locate the right candidate.

If only Blake had consulted her, she would not have been so taken aback. Why couldn't he seem to remember they were joint owners of the *Hattie Belle* or that she owned more of their venture than he? Maybe she should have a flyer printed up for him—one he could hang in his room and read every night before he fell asleep: LILY CATHERINE ANDERSON OWNS 51 PERCENT INTEREST OF THE *HATTIE BELLE.*

Feeling a tiny bit better, she entered her bedroom. "Camellia? Jasmine?"

No one answered. Where were her sisters? Lily sighed. At least they would appreciate not having to work so hard over the next few days. When she'd first brought them on board the *Hattie Belle*, she'd promised exciting adventures in cities like New Orleans. Perhaps she could begin making good on her words today. If Mrs. Thornton agreed, they would take a tour of the city and maybe do a little shopping—as long as they didn't spend too much money, of course.

She opened the bedroom door and leaned out into the hall. Her sisters were not hiding on the landing. Where could they be? Faint music made her tilt her head. The tune sounded familiar. Was it a hymn?

She followed the sound down the stairs and found herself outside the conservatory, on the first floor opposite the staircase from the parlor. She pushed the door open.

Camellia was sitting on a piano bench, her fingers moving across the keys with sure movements. Jasmine sat beside her sister, facing the room. She was singing "O for a Thousand Tongues to Sing." The notes issuing from her were clear, strong, and sure.

Lily caught her breath. When had Jasmine developed that wonderful voice? She sounded like an angel. She knew how much Camellia liked playing the piano, so she was not surprised at the way her middle sister's hands coaxed such wonderful harmonies from the Thorntons' instrument. But Lily had never heard her youngest sister sing except during church services. And her voice had sounded breathy and scratchy then. Nothing like the pure tones Jasmine was producing this morning.

Jasmine held the final note for an extra beat as Camellia ended the song with a flourish.

Mrs. Thornton, ensconced in a leather wingback chair, applauded. "That was lovely. Both of you have so much talent."

Lily clapped, too. "I am proud to call you my sisters, as I always am."

"You should be." Mrs. Thornton nodded her agreement. "They're as talented as they are beautiful."

"Yes, they are." Lily hugged them both.

"Did you finish your business with Mr. Matthews?" asked Mrs. Thornton.

Jasmine reached up to tug on her arm. "Can we go to town now, Lily?"

"I don't. . . I'm not sure."

Her sisters groaned.

"I knew it." Camellia pushed away from the piano bench. "We're in the biggest, most exciting city on the Mississippi River, and we're going to be stuck inside the whole time."

Mrs. Thornton laughed. "I doubt that. Not with so much to see and enjoy."

"But we don't have enough money to do much." Lily hated to throw a damper on them, but someone had to be practical.

"Could we at least walk to Canal Street?" Camellia's blue eyes implored her to say yes. "It won't cost a thing to look in the store windows."

"Don't be silly." Mrs. Thornton clucked her tongue. "You made a great deal on the cargo you brought to New Orleans. And even though your *Hattie Belle* was damaged, you did not lose a single barrel. I'm certain you will be able to repair your riverboat and still have enough to enjoy a few distractions."

"But you don't know the worst of it." Lily squared her shoulders. She would rather have kept their financial circumstances to herself, but the others would not be satisfied until she explained her reluctance to fritter away their earnings. "Blake says the repairs will take nearly two weeks and the material is going to be more expensive than normal. We'll be fortunate to avoid going into debt."

Mrs. Thornton rose from her chair and enveloped Lily in a fragrant hug. "Don't worry. It's not as bad as you imagine. My husband, Lloyd, can work miracles. You wait and see. We will talk to him. And poof! All your troubles will be gone."

A hint of hope returned to Lily. "But we cannot—"

The older lady stopped Lily's word with a shake of her head. "Not another word. You will stay with us for as long as it takes. Lloyd and I have many rooms and would enjoy having you and your charming sisters as our guests for as long as you stay. We will send a note to my daughter, Sarah. You will love my Sarah. She is quite the popular hostess. Together we will have a wonderful time."

Feeling a bit like a leaf caught in a thunderstorm, Lily let herself be carried along with their hostess's plans. Doing anything else would be like taking on an army she could never defeat.

Chapter Twenty-eight

If Lily compared Mrs. Thornton to a thunderstorm, the next few days taught her that Sarah, Mr. and Mrs. Thornton's only daughter, was more akin to a hurricane.

A short, stylish hurricane, to be sure. Sarah Cartier, *née* Thornton, was barely five feet tall. But what she lacked in height, she more than made up for in energy. Married to an eminent surgeon, she had a generous nature and a caring heart. It didn't take long for Lily to realize that her hostess's daughter was a strong Christian who was always looking for opportunities to spread the Gospel.

All of Sarah's conversations were liberally sprinkled with references to the Bible. But she not only knew the Word, she lived it—spending her mornings at the hospital where her husband worked, praying with those who were sick and in pain, healing their spirits as her husband healed their bodies. The vivacious young matron also devoted one afternoon each week to meet with some of the ladies in her church. *Les Femmes du Patre*—the Women of the Shepherd—studied together, supported each other, and aided families from all walks of life.

Sarah also found time to host balls, soirees, and all manner of social events. One such was coming up at the end of the week. She and her mother had been trying to convince Lily to attend and bring Camellia. Sarah had come to the town house with the latest copy of *Godey's Lady's Book*.

Soon they were oohing and aahing over the dresses modeled by and for stylish young ladies. If fashion dictated that skirts grow much wider, Lily wondered whether she would be able to negotiate the passageways on the *Hattie Belle.*

"Look at this receipt for royal crumpets." Mrs. Thornton pointed to the next page. "They sound so dainty and scrumptious. I wonder if you could make those to serve with tea for passengers on your boat."

Lily glanced at the list of ingredients. "I have no idea. We rely on Jensen to plan our meals. He has a wide knowledge of many dishes."

"I can copy it down for Jensen." Jasmine made the offer from her position on a footstool in front of the sofa.

Camellia frowned at her younger sister. "I don't see why you should bother. We never have formal meals on the boat."

Lily shook her head. "That may have to change since we'll be taking on passengers for our next voyage." Blake had informed her last night that several people had inquired about passage. At least one thing was progressing as planned. Not like the repairs, which seemed to be taking forever.

"Can we have parties on the boat, too?"

Camellia's question turned Lily's mind from her unpleasant thoughts. "I don't know." Lily smiled to soften her words. "We'll probably be very busy preparing food and helping Tamar keep everything clean."

Jasmine, who had looked up at Camellia's question, made a face and went back to copying the receipt.

"I declare. You are the most glum group of ladies I have ever been around." Sarah jumped up and struck a pose. "I have it!"

Camellia focused on the animated young woman. "What do you have?"

"The answer." She clapped her hands. "We'll go shopping. No matter the problem, a little shopping always puts one in a better frame of mind."

Lily sighed and shook her head. "I don't think that's a good idea."

"Nonsense." Mrs. Thornton smiled at her daughter. "I agree with Sarah. The reason we are so melancholy is because we are surrounded by a river of mourning attire."

"Mama, you are a genius!" Sarah returned to the sofa and flipped the pages to a style they had all found attractive. "We will have this dress made in dove gray for Lily."

Lily shook her head. "It's too soon."

"Grandfather has been dead forever." Camellia drew out the last word to emphasize it.

"Look at this one, Camellia." Sarah pointed out another fashion plate. "If we choose a muted blue, it would be perfect for you to wear to my ball."

"But—"

Lily's words were cut off as Jasmine interrupted. "Which dress can I have?"

Sarah put a finger on her chin and tilted her head. "Lavender is the perfect color for you, little one. But it must be a simpler design."

Lily was relieved when Sarah pointed out a dress appropriate for a young lady instead of another debutante dress. Jasmine didn't even pout when she saw it.

The idea of spending money on three dresses made Lily feel a bit faint, but she could not ignore the hopeful look on her sisters' faces. Still, she had to try one more time to make them see reason. "We have no need for new dresses."

"*Mais oui.*" Sarah frowned at her mother. "Did you not tell them of my party on Saturday?"

Mrs. Thornton shook her head. "I thought I would need your support to convince Lily that she and Camellia should attend."

"Impossible." Lily's gaze shifted from mother to daughter. "We cannot afford such an extravagance."

"Jesus said nothing is impossible for those who have faith." Sarah crossed her arms.

Sarah's reference to scripture reminded Lily how often she had ignored her Bible of late. Her glance met the beseeching looks from both Camellia and Jasmine. She had a duty to provide shelter and sustenance for them. She squirmed in her seat. Was she providing them the spiritual guidance they needed? *Lord, forgive me. Show me how to be a better model for Camellia and Jasmine. Help me teach them Your ways.*

"Lily, you and your sisters are as dear to me as my own children." Mrs. Thornton reached for Lily's hand. "It would be a kindness if you would let me pay for these dresses."

"I couldn't—"

"Please, Lily." Camellia's blue eyes were bright with unshed tears. "I would love to have a new dress."

How could she resist? Lily squeezed Mrs. Thornton's hand. "I suppose I could accept a loan."

"Perfect!" Sarah clapped her hands. "Let's go right now before Lily changes her mind."

Although she still wasn't sure it was a good idea, Lily let herself be swept up by the combined efforts of her sisters, Sarah, and Mrs. Thornton. Soon all five of them were crowded into the carriage, headed for the fabled shops on Canal Street.

❧

Jean Luc slapped at an insect buzzing around his head. They seemed to be everywhere these days. Some said they were the carriers of disease, but while he found them irritating, he could not believe they were the reason for sickness. He never got sick. Avoiding the night air made more sense to him. Evil deeds and evil-minded people used darkness as a cover. Why not illness as well?

Plucking a bloom from the flower arrangement in the foyer, he tucked it into the lapel of his coat. He'd told his mother he was going to town. Anything to get away from the oppressive, disappointed glances she still directed at him. Would he never live down his mistake?

Jean Luc mounted his horse and headed to town, passing cotton fields being worked by dozens of slaves. They were planting seed, a job he did not envy as it required hour after backbreaking hour laboring in the sweltering heat. Papa had mentioned something about purchasing a few extra slaves before harvest. Jean Luc shuddered. He didn't like going to the slave market. It was foul smelling and filthy. No place for a gentleman to spend time.

Not like his current destination—his tailor. He was in need of a new dress coat and several shirts. The streets were crowded. Farmers with loaded wagons of fresh-picked melons and peaches trundled past immigrants in rough-spun work clothes. Fashionable ladies in bright-colored finery hung on the arms of their dark-coated escorts, eager to purchase everything from hats to shoes. Street vendors hawked fruit, vegetables, and meat pies.

Jean Luc wove his horse back and forth down the street, his teeth clenching as his progress was repeatedly halted. When he finally reached the storefront of Preston and Sons, Jean Luc dismounted with a relieved sigh and tied his horse to the hitching rail. Before he could enter the establishment, however, he was stopped by someone calling his name.

"I'm so glad to find you, Mr. Champney."

Jean Luc turned to see Lars Steenberg. "Is *Hattie Belle* back from New Orleans?" He shaded his eyes and looked toward the river.

Steenberg shuffled his feet. "No, sir. We ran into a bit of trouble."

Dread filled Jean Luc. "Is she sunk?" Most steamships did not last long. They either ran up on a snag and tore a hole in the keel, or the boiler exploded and set the deck on fire. If nature was not dangerous enough, pirates often lurked along the shore and attacked vulnerable boats. A paddle wheeler with a gaggle of females would fit that description pretty well.

"No, she made it to New Orleans."

"Then why isn't she here? And why are you here without her?"

Steenberg shrugged. "We ran aground north of the city and had to be pulled free."

"You what!" Jean Luc was horrified. "Didn't those idiots know not to travel in the dark? Were they in such a hurry to reach port that they risked my boat?"

"Not exactly. It was daylight."

Jean Luc stared at the older man. "Who was captaining the boat when it happened?"

"I was." Steenberg glanced at him, his expression rebellious. "You said you didn't want Lily Anderson to succeed."

"I didn't mean for you to put the *Hattie Belle* at risk." Noticing his angry tones had attracted the attention of some passersby, Jean Luc lowered his voice. "I only wanted you to keep an eye on things and report back. I didn't want you to sink the boat. If the *Hattie Belle* is lost, I won't have any chance to prove myself to my father."

"She's holed up for repairs, but they'll probably be sailing her back to Natchez in a few days."

"How bad was the damage?"

"Not too bad." The other man shrugged. "A little problem with the paddle wheel and a bit of shattered glass. Probably be as good as new."

"You'd better hope that's true." Jean Luc leaned closer to the captain. "Because if she's not, I'm holding you responsible."

Steenberg cringed. "I can't help it if they don't get her repaired proper."

"She wouldn't have to be repaired if not for your idiocy." Jean Luc started to turn on his heel, but a thought occurred to him. "Do you want to make it up to me?"

"Yes, sir. They let me go, and there's not many boats needing captains." His eyes shifted to the left. "I'd be glad to work for you."

Jean Luc nodded. "Then you watch for my boat to get back in, and let me know the minute it appears around Dead Man's Bend. I want to be on the docks waiting to greet Miss Anderson before her dainty foot touches dry land." He jangled the coins in his pocket. Pulling out a handful, he selected one and tossed it in the air.

"Yes, sir. Thank you, sir." Steenberg caught the coin before it hit the ground. "I'll be on the lookout, Mr. Champney."

"Good, because if you fail me this time, it will be your last." Jean Luc walked away, certain the man had gotten the point.

Now he needed to concentrate on the business at hand. If he was going to convince Lily to allow him to take over the management of the *Hattie Belle*, he needed to look his best.

Chapter Twenty-nine

Conflicting desires pulled at Tamar. She could barely concentrate on getting the two older girls ready for the ball because of wondering whether Jensen would come to visit while the others were out dancing. He'd come to the Thorntons' home several times over the past week, but that didn't mean he would come tonight, not after she'd told him to leave her alone.

She regretted her words even if they were sensible. He was too nice a man to get tangled up with the likes of her. She would be happy if he didn't come, wouldn't she?

The answer was simple. She wouldn't be happy at all. There were so many reasons to push him away. A thousand obstacles stood between her and Jensen, not the least of which was that she had no right to marry. She was too old, too plain, too dark, and too sensible to listen to his suggestions.

"I think you've pulled my corset too tight." Lily reached back to tug on her hands.

Tamar released some of the pressure on the laces. "I'm sorry. I don't know where my mind is tonight."

"I wish I could go." Jasmine sat pouting in a corner of the girls' bedroom. "I'm going to be all alone."

"No, you won't." Camellia stood in front of the mirror, admiring her new blue gown. "David and Tamar will be here."

"I'm practically grown up." The whine in Jasmine's voice contradicted her words. "Besides, you and Lily can't dance. You're still in mourning."

Tamar knew her girls well enough to know that Camellia would probably be on the dance floor before the beginning of the second song. Here in New Orleans no one knew about her grandfather's death, so she would see no reason to deny herself. Lily would probably remain seated with the matrons and old maids, content to watch the younger girls dip and swirl in the arms of their suitors. If she didn't watch out, she would find herself alone as her sisters married and began families.

"I hope both of your sisters will dance, Miss Jasmine." She reached for the hooped crinoline that would make Lily's skirt stand out in a bell shape. "I'm sure your grandfather wouldn't disapprove. He'd like to see his girls having a wonderful evening."

Jasmine crossed her hands over her chest. "I'm not so sure about that. He'll probably be upset to see me staying here with you and David."

"Don't be so anxious to grow up, Jasmine." Lily stood still while Tamar lifted her new skirt over her head and settled it around her waist. "You need to learn the trick of finding enjoyment no matter your age, or you'll always be so busy looking ahead that you'll miss a lot of grand adventures."

"But you and Camellia are wearing your new clothes. Why did you get a dress for me if I can't wear it?"

Tamar frowned at Jasmine. "You'll wear it tomorrow when you go to church."

Jasmine turned her face to the window.

Tamar tweaked the gray material of Lily's skirt, making sure every fold was perfect. Not many women could wear this color without looking like they were ready for a grave marker, but the soft color reflected on Lily's face, muting the line of her stubborn chin and bringing a special glow into her sweet brown eyes. She looked as young and fresh as Camellia, who came to stand next to her. Seeing them made Tamar feel old and worn out, like a well-used rag.

Camellia's golden curls were fastened on top of her head with three white camellia blossoms. A matching blossom was pinned to the front of her bodice, its delicate bloom standing out against the dark moiré silk of her gown. Her milky-white skin also contrasted against the material, glowing in the candlelight. She was sure to be sought after by all the young men at the ball.

Smothering the desire to wear something flattering instead of her shapeless brown gown, Tamar concentrated on her charges—collecting fans, smoothing gloves, and settling cotton lace shawls around their shoulders. She had no reason for the tears that sprang to her eyes as the two young ladies left the bedroom. Wishing for the impossible only made a body miserable. She was going to have to spend extra time on her knees this evening, asking God to root out the envy in her heart. She needed to concentrate on the blessing of having kind owners and a chance to see something of the world beyond the boundaries of Natchez and Les Fleurs plantation.

As soon as the bedroom was straightened up, Tamar went down the back stairs toward the kitchen, which was separated from the main house by a courtyard. She tarried in the cooler air, her fingers trailing across the wide leaves of a palm tree. Her gaze went to the sky, wonder filling her as she gazed at thousands of stars and the bright round globe of the moon.

" 'Tis a lovely evening."

She jerked in surprise. Her gaze traveled around the courtyard, searching for the person who'd spoken. "Jensen." She recognized his voice, of course. It was the voice that entered her dreams, whispering of things she shouldn't consider. Tempting her to reach out for a future that didn't belong to her.

He stepped from the far corner of the courtyard, nearest the stable. "Stay a moment and talk to me."

"I told you yesterday we don't have a thing to talk about."

"Of course we do, only you don't want to listen." Jensen moved closer.

Tamar's heart beat so hard she thought he could probably hear it. She knew she should turn her back on him, but her legs wouldn't move. "I'm listening." Was that her trembling voice?

He reached out slowly, his hand traveling toward her face. Tamar's breath caught, and her heart stopped beating altogether. His fingers gently smoothed her hair against her temple where it had escaped her cap. They left a trail of fire in their wake. She felt like she might die right there, right then. Then his whole hand cupped her cheek, warm and a little rough. She couldn't speak, couldn't step back, couldn't do anything but look into his eyes. What she saw made her knees shake. Fierce emotion burned inside this man. But rather than frighten her, it kindled a flame inside of her.

His lids drooped and the corners of his mouth turned up. "I want to steal a kiss from you, Tamar. I want it more than I want to draw my next breath." He moved even closer, his shoulders blocking out the rest of the world. "Please say yes."

Tamar lifted her hands. She had to put a stop to this now or be lost forever. "No." Forming fists with her hands, she pushed at his chest.

Pain entered his face as though she had struck him, but Jensen moved back. She felt like she had thrust a knife into the man's heart. Or was it her own heart she had wounded? Tamar wasn't sure. She wasn't sure of anything except that she needed distance from the feelings Jensen stirred in her.

With a sound of equal parts pain, fear, and frustration, Tamar ran to the kitchen. She jerked open the heavy wooden door and slipped inside. Slamming the door behind her, she leaned against it and gasped for breath. The other slaves looked up in surprise but didn't ask any questions. That was a good thing. She had no answers.

The Cartiers lived in a huge mansion in Lafayette Square, several miles south of the Thorntons' town house. Lily enjoyed the carriage ride but wished Blake and Mr. Thornton could have joined them inside instead of riding alongside on horseback. But she and Camellia could barely fit their skirts on one bench of the carriage, so wide were their crinolines, and Mrs. Thornton had instructed the men to take horses rather than crowd them.

"Don't leave the ballroom with any strangers, Camellia." Lily had a list of instructions for her sister. "Don't eat too much at the midnight supper. Don't accept any invitations to dance; we are still in mourning. Keep your fan attached to your wrist or you will lose it."

Mrs. Thornton leaned forward and patted her wrist. "It will be all right, Lily. Don't be so worried. Your sister is a sensible young lady."

"I know, but—"

"You're giving me a headache." Camellia touched her gloved hand to her forehead.

Lily sat back with a sigh. "Then perhaps we should turn the carriage around and go home."

"No!" Both Camellia and Mrs. Thornton chorused their disagreement.

"This is my very first ball, Lily. Please don't take away my pleasure."

"I know the feelings you're experiencing, Lily, my dear." Mrs. Thornton's voice hinted at amusement. "I felt the same way the first time I took Sarah to a party. But don't worry. We will all look out for Camellia. As to dancing, I don't see the harm since this is a family party. No one here knows you. They will assume you are my family, and they'll be confused if I am not also in mourning."

Lily found it difficult to argue with Mrs. Thornton's pragmatic view. Besides, this was Camellia's first dance. It should be a memory to treasure. If Camellia had to sit on the wall next to her sister and the other old maids, she would not enjoy herself very much. Pinning a smile on her face to cover her misgivings, Lily turned to Camellia. "If you promise to be circumspect—"

Camellia reached past the material of their skirts and hugged Lily close. "I promise to do whatever you say. I won't lose my fan or my gloves. I won't leave the ballroom with anyone, male or female. And I promise not to eat too much at supper."

Lily returned her embrace and sent a prayer heavenward that she was making the right decision.

The carriage stopped, and they disembarked. Mr. Thornton offered his arm to his wife, while Blake escorted both Lily and Camellia up the shallow steps to the main entrance.

Dr. Cartier, a man some ten years older than Sarah, was fashionably dressed in white from chin to toe. He was much quieter than Sarah, but the love they felt for each other was obvious in the way their gazes locked and the little touches they managed to exchange while receiving their guests.

"Good evening, Mother, Father." Sarah was resplendent in a pale-yellow gown, her dark hair upswept and held in place with a diamond tiara. "I have a surprise for you."

She turned around and grabbed a young man who'd been lurking in the shadows. "Look who got into town this afternoon."

The first thing Lily noticed was the thatch of thick auburn hair on his head. Below that was a pair of eyes as green as grass. Something about him looked familiar, but she did not place him until Mrs. Thornton stepped forward with a glad cry.

"Jonah, why didn't you come to the house to tell your mother you had arrived safely?"

So this was the youngest Thornton child. She glanced at Mr. Thornton and realized why Jonah looked familiar. He was a younger version of his father.

"I'm sorry, Mother. Sarah wanted to surprise you." He hugged her close before turning to shake hands with his father. "I'm glad to see both of you looking so well. We have many things to talk about."

"Yes, yes." Sarah stepped between them. "But for tonight you are to forget all that and enjoy yourself."

He shrugged and turned back to the receiving line. He smiled at Lily as they were introduced, but he couldn't take his eyes off Camellia. She blushed and nodded when he asked for the first dance.

Lily's glance met Blake's, and they shared a moment. It was as if they didn't need words to communicate. Her little sister was going to be a big hit in New Orleans.

Lily and Camellia, followed by a grinning Blake, trailed the Thorntons into the crowded ballroom. Over the next half hour they were introduced to so many of New Orleans' elite that Lily soon lost count.

The musicians began playing, and couples started walking to the center of the room. Jonah came to claim Camellia for the promised dance. He was soon replaced by others, as many of the young men vied for her attention.

One or two of them turned to Lily as a second choice if Camellia was not available, but she refused them all, preferring her role as chaperone.

Between the crush of people and the candles all around the room, Lily grew rather warm and wished she could escape through some french doors that had been flung open in the hope of coaxing some of the cooler night air into the room. She was about to seek out a chair along the wall when a hand on her arm stopped her.

"Would you like to dance?" Blake's drawl in her ear made gooseflesh pop up along her arms.

Lily shook her head resolutely. "I'm here as a chaperone for Camellia. This is her evening to dance."

"It looks to me as though she's had no shortage of partners." Blake stepped in front of her. He looked every inch the gentleman. Her gaze wandered from the high points of his shirt collar to the intricate folds of his necktie. His broad shoulders were razor straight in his black frock coat, and his striped silk waistcoat, blood red in color, gleamed richly in the light of the Cartiers' ballroom.

Lily realized something in that instant. He was as much a gentleman as Jean Luc Champney. More handsome in some respects than the polished Mr. Champney, although perhaps not as well traveled.

That thought led to another. Where was Blake from? Had he grown up in the lap of luxury? He certainly looked comfortable in the trappings of the privileged. But he'd never spoken of his home or childhood. She'd never really thought about it. She knew absolutely nothing about her business partner beyond his current lifestyle.

Perhaps if she accepted his invitation she could ask him about his past. "I believe you are right, Mr. Matthews."

His smile rewarded her acquiescence. Blake held out a white-gloved hand, and she placed her own in it. As soon as they reached the edge of the dancers, he swept her into his arms and swung her into the rhythm of a waltz. "You look lovely this evening."

"I'm afraid I owe Mrs. Thornton a substantial portion of our money in payment for the new dresses we bought for Jasmine, Camellia, and me."

"The expenditure is well worth it."

Had he actually complimented her? What a novel feeling. Lily's hand tightened on his shoulder as she and Blake moved around the room. The other dancers disappeared from her consciousness until all that remained was the music and the look in his deep blue eyes. She felt as though she were floating away on a melody as seductive as the song of the river.

Forgotten were the questions about his background. Forgotten were the warnings she had given her sister. Lily allowed him to pull her a tiny bit closer until only inches separated them. Until his mouth was so close he could lean forward to brush his lips against hers.

Panic struck her. She pulled away to a more discreet distance, racking her brain for some subject to introduce. Anything to avoid falling under his hypnotic gaze again. "How is the work going on our boat?"

His smile widened, as though he knew the real reason for her question. "Don't fret, Lily. We should be able to leave no later than Tuesday or Wednesday."

"Have you found a captain yet?" She pursued the subject of business doggedly.

"I think I have."

Didn't he think she would want to know more about the man who would take them back to Natchez? "Tell me about him."

"I haven't quite decided which one to hire, but Mr. Thornton has sent me a couple of excellent candidates. As soon as I check out a few more things and make my final decision, you'll be able to meet him." He hesitated a moment. "But remember your promise. The man I choose will be the man we hire."

She stiffened. "I haven't forgotten."

"Good."

Blake executed two more intricate turns, each in the opposite direction, a move that had her head spinning. Lily had to focus on her feet to avoid tripping. She was so overbalanced that she hardly noticed when he swept her through one of the open french doors and out onto the veranda. The sound of the music faded, and his steps slowed, winding down until they were standing still.

Lily pulled away from him and turned to face the manicured lawn. She took two steps forward, standing next to the low wall that ran along the outside of the dimly lit area. He didn't follow her, and Lily was thankful he gave her time to catch her breath. She opened her fan and used it to cool her face. When she finally turned to face him, her breathing had returned to normal.

Blake was leaning against the wall next to the french doors, watching her like a panther stalking its prey.

Another sprinkle of gooseflesh erupted. Lily pulled her shawl over her arms to counteract the effect. "Where did you learn to dance like that?"

"Along the river."

She moved a step closer to him. "That's an evasive answer."

"Maybe I don't like it when curious women pry into my past."

"When have I ever pried?"

He pushed away from the wall. "I have to admit, you've managed to avoid it. . .up until tonight, that is."

Lily decided a softer approach was needed. "I don't know anything about you, Blake, except that you're a hard worker and a dependable partner. Oh, and that you like to play cards."

Blake looked over her shoulder at something in the distance. She began to think he wouldn't say anything at all, but then he cleared his throat. "I left home after a disagreement with my father, and I haven't been back since. It was tough making my way for the first couple of years. One of my earliest jobs was in Oakdale, a little town in Missouri. The owner of the Oakdale Inn hired me to muck out the stables, cut timber for firewood, and do whatever jobs he didn't want to do."

Blake stopped and sighed, his gaze refocusing on her face. "It was a friendly little town without much to do on long winter days once the river froze up. The innkeeper and his wife opened up their dining room a couple of times a week and invited the locals to come for a party. They'd charge everyone a nickel to attend, even the men who brought their instruments and played for the rest. We'd sing and dance and have a good time." He shrugged. "I may not know the right steps to every song, but I can move with the music."

Something about his attitude made Lily melt. Blake Matthews was vulnerable. Uncertain of his skills. She wanted to reassure him. In all their weeks of squabbling and bickering, he'd never seemed to be anything less than supremely sure of himself. Of course she'd had to mount her own defenses to keep him from riding roughshod over her principles. Had she missed other evidence of his real nature? She looked at him with new eyes. "You're an excellent dancer."

He smiled, a slow, dangerous smile that set her pulse jumping. What he might have said was lost as another couple walked out onto the veranda. It was probably a good thing.

Lily gathered her skirts and moved toward the french doors. "We should return to the ballroom. I really do need to keep an eye on Camellia." She rushed back into the ballroom without glancing back, even though she thought she heard him chuckling.

Blake didn't dance with anyone else that evening, nor did she. But Lily found herself wondering what might have happened if they had not been interrupted. And wondering if she was glad or sorry that it had not.

Chapter Thirty

Blake awoke with a start and looked around at his unfamiliar surroundings. It took him a minute to remember he'd stayed in the Thorntons' *garçonièrre*, the apartment their sons used when in town, which boasted a separate entrance from the main town house. The opulence of this family made him wonder if Lily was right. Maybe they could make more money shipping goods than gambling.

He dressed in the change of clothes Jensen had insisted he bring. Smart man. He would have to tell him so when he returned to the *Hattie Belle*. He was eager to get some work done before the weather got too hot. A twinge of guilt reminded him his father would not approve of his working on the Sabbath. But he was no longer living under his father's roof. He could decide for himself what to do with his Sundays.

A knock on his door made Blake shake his head. So much for a quick exit.

"Are you awake, Mr. Matthews?" The voice belonged to Jonah Thornton, the young man he'd met at the ball.

He went to the door and wrenched it open. "Yes, I'm awake."

Jonah blinked at him. He wore more casual garb this morning, making him look younger than ever. "Good. Mother sent a note saying we are expected for breakfast."

Wishing he'd awakened half an hour earlier and made his escape, Blake nodded. "I'll be right down."

"We usually eat in the courtyard on Sundays." Jonah tossed this information over his shoulder as he clattered down the stairs. "Don't be late or you'll miss the croissants."

Blake grimaced as he combed his hair. How was he to avoid attending church with the Thorntons without raising a ruckus?

He was the last one to arrive for breakfast, and the only place left was between Jasmine and David. He greeted everyone as he slipped into the chair.

Lily was no longer dressed in the finery she had worn the evening before, but she looked lovely. Ethereal. She glanced his way and smiled. Her gesture warmed his belly. He could grow used to sharing breakfast in a family group like this one. If only his childhood home had been as warm, his life might have turned out very differently.

A basket of croissants occupied the center of the table. Next to it was a crock of butter and a large platter of scrambled eggs. He started to reach for the basket but halted when Lily shook her head at him.

Mr. Thornton had been reading a copy of the *Picayune*, but he folded it and set it next to his coffee cup. "Good morning. I trust you slept well, Mr. Matthews."

"Yes, sir."

"Excellent." Mr. Thornton bowed his head, and the others followed his lead. "Father God, we thank You for the bountiful food and many blessings You provide. Please keep us ever mindful of Your grace and help us to live more fruitful lives because of Your example. Amen."

David reached for the croissants, took one, and handed the basket to Blake, who followed suit and handed it off to Jasmine.

"It's wonderful to have you back with us, Jonah." Mrs. Thornton beamed at her son who sat next to Mr. Thornton. "I don't know when I've been more surprised than when you appeared at Sarah's party last night."

Jonah ducked his head. "Thank you."

Mr. Thornton stirred cream into his coffee. "Did you stop and visit with Eli on your way back down?"

"Yes."

Silence fell at the table as everyone waited to see if Jonah would add to his brief answer.

Lily's gaze clashed with Blake's. Did she want him to do something? What could he do short of kicking Jonah under the table?

She sighed and broke eye contact before turning to Mrs. Thornton. "Is Eli your oldest son?"

"Yes, he runs the Memphis branch of our business." Mrs. Thornton's eyelids fluttered as though she was holding back tears. "We don't get to see him and his wife, Renée, as much as we would like."

Their host cleared his throat. "I hope he's come to his senses and stopped spouting that abolitionist nonsense."

Blake could see Jonah's irritation in the reddening of his ears. He hoped they were not about to be treated to a family disagreement. Positions on abolition, slavery, and states' rights divided many families these days. The whole country, for that matter.

Mrs. Thornton stepped into the uneasy breach. "We correspond regularly, but I still miss them."

"They are fine, Mother. They send their love." Jonah's shoulders relaxed as he smiled at her.

Blake could feel the tension dissipating. Relieved, he glanced around the table, the hair on his arms rising when he caught the look of intense yearning on Camellia's face. Did she fancy herself smitten with young Thornton? Of course she did. He was not fawning over her as the other young men had done last night. A girl like Camellia would find his disinterest irresistible. Blake wanted to groan out loud. They didn't need any broken hearts on the *Hattie Belle*.

Galvanized by his thoughts, he pushed himself away from the table. The sooner they could get back on the river and put physical distance between Camellia and Jonah, the better for all of them. "Thank you for your hospitality, Mr. and Mrs. Thornton."

"Don't forget it's Sunday." Mrs. Thornton's voice stopped him from leaving. "We'll be meeting in the foyer as soon as everyone has a chance to put on their coats and hats."

"I'm afraid I won't be joining you." He looked away from Lily's shocked expression. "I need to get back to work on the *Hattie Belle*."

Lily got up and moved toward him, putting a hand on his arm. "Please come with us. You've been working too hard as it is. And you may find you have more energy after you spend your morning at church."

What was it about her eyes that made him want to agree with everything she suggested? Before he could summon the strength to turn her down, Camellia and Jasmine added their pleas. It was less trouble to give in.

He would go this one time. But as soon as the service was over, he would explain to Lily why he was so reluctant to darken the doorway of any church. She was a smart girl. She would understand once he explained it to her. And even if she didn't, he was determined to refuse the next time, no matter what tactic she used.

❧

"I hope you girls will like our preacher." Mrs. Thornton nodded to a lady in a puce dress and matching hat. "He is rather young, but what he lacks in age he makes up for in delivery."

"I'll say he does." Mr. Thornton winked at them. "Some of our female members have swooned when he gets caught up in his sermon."

"Father, don't tell them such things." Sarah walked over to them, resplendent in a gold-and-white-striped dress. A dainty matching fan dangled from her right hand. "If Pastor Nolan hears you, we'll be asked to leave the church."

Lily's smile widened at the look on Sarah's face. "It would be the church's loss."

"I concur." A well-dressed little man walked toward them. He had a gentle smile topped by a thin mustache, hazel eyes under thick brown eyebrows, and carefully combed hair that was several shades darker than Camellia's. "We couldn't bear to lose our most dedicated families, no matter their opinion of the preacher."

Sarah and her parents laughed easily.

The man bowed. "Silas Nolan, at your service."

"I'm sorry, Pastor Nolan." Mr. Thornton stepped forward, still chuckling. "Allow me to present our guests, Mr. Blake Matthews, Miss Lily Anderson, and her sisters, Camellia and Jasmine."

"It's a pleasure to meet you." His warm glance touched each of their faces. "And I promise to control my. . .energy. If the Holy Spirit allows, of course."

They all laughed at his self-deprecating humor. Lily liked him immediately. She turned to look at Blake and was surprised to see him looking so stiff. He was usually comfortable in any situation. Why should the friendly pastor disturb him so? Or was something else wrong? Was he hiding something from her about their boat? Had they run out of money? Had he not been able to find a captain?

The questions continued distracting her as the Thorntons and the

Cartiers introduced them to friends who had not been at the ball the previous evening. She tried to concentrate on remembering names and faces, but it was impossible with the nagging questions.

As they entered the church, Jasmine grabbed her hand. "Are you okay, Sissy?"

"Of course I am." Lily glanced around to see if anyone else was listening. "I'm sorry, Jasmine. I guess I'm a little distracted." She took a deep breath. Whatever might be wrong, she would find a way around it. For now she would concentrate on the present. She would enjoy the service and let God take care of the future.

The sanctuary was a large rectangle with two rows of pews that were mostly filled. Abraham, Noah and his ark, and Joseph in his coat of many colors were depicted in stained-glass windows on one side of the room. Jesus in various stages of His life from the cradle in Bethlehem to the Resurrection was the subject of the opposite windows.

Tints of blue, green, and red painted Blake's face as he walked stiff legged beside her. The feeling of unrest tried to grasp her once again until Lily directed her attention toward the large cross that hung on the paneled wall behind the pulpit. Peace settled on her shoulders as she slid onto a pew next to Camellia. A peace she'd almost forgotten, a peace she needed as much as she needed air to breathe.

The murmur of voices died away as the pastor strode down the aisle and bounded onto the dais in two quick steps. He led the congregation in several hymns, familiar songs that brought Lily a great deal of comfort, especially when she heard Jasmine's talented soprano and Camellia's softer contralto joining the others.

How blessed they were to have each other. She smiled toward her sisters and thanked God for keeping them together. No matter what the future held, Camellia and Jasmine would always know how much she loved them. As long as she was their sister, she would find a way to provide for them.

The pastor read to them from the sixty-eighth psalm, one of Lily's favorites. After the death of her mother and the desertion of her father, she had often turned to verse five. She traced the words in her Bible as he read them to the congregation: " 'A father of the fatherless, and a judge of the widows, is God in his holy habitation.' "

When the pastor spoke of singing praises to God and rejoicing in His presence, a desire welled up in her to set aside more time for the

Lord than she had been doing lately. As Pastor Nolan began the closing prayer, she concentrated on praising God to the best of her ability. She would start as soon as they got back on the boat. She would organize a Bible study. It would be good for everyone on board—crew and passengers alike.

Feeling better about the future, she raised her head and gathered her things. It was so rewarding to attend church. She would make a point to be in port on Sundays as they continued traveling the river. It was the best way to fulfill her most sacred duty to her sisters and ensure they were rooted in the faith necessary to sustain them throughout their lives.

Chapter Thirty-one

Blake intended to make a quick exit as soon as they got back to the Thorntons' town house. He had endured enough for one day.

The sermon had been unnerving—especially the part about God being Father to the fatherless. He wasn't fatherless. But sometimes he thought that might be better than having a father who ignored the needs of his family. What about children who had to escape their fathers in order to thrive? If God condoned that type of fatherhood, he wanted no part of it.

Nor did he want any part of the discussion sure to come about how wonderful the pastor was and how inspiring his sermon had been. Eager to escape the cloying atmosphere, he tapped a foot as the others chatted together in the front yard of the church.

The sun was beginning to warm the air. Prickles of sweat trickled down his back, making him long for the deck of the *Hattie Belle*. Would their infernal talking never end? Blake's jaw was so tight it ached.

Finally Lily walked over to him. "Is something wrong?"

He rolled his eyes. "Nothing much."

A frown appeared on her brow. "Why am I not convinced?"

"I have no idea." He nodded toward the Thorntons. "How much longer do you think they'll be?"

She shrugged. "I don't know. Why? Do you have a pressing engagement?"

"Do you have to control every aspect of my life?" He kept his voice low to avoid drawing attention. "Can I not have some tiny corner of my life that is safe from your prying questions?"

Her face paled, and Blake wanted to kick himself. When had he become the kind of man who attacked women?

"I–I'm sorry, Blake. I didn't realize. . . ."

"No, I'm the one who's sorry." Reaching for her hand, he tucked it into the crook of his arm. "I'm hot and hungry, and I'm taking it out on you. It's not your fault."

Sorrowful brown eyes stared at him, looking into his very soul. "Apparently it is."

"No." He took a deep breath. "As soon as we get back to the house, I'll tell you about it. You and I have very different backgrounds. Perhaps it's time for us to sit down and talk. Maybe if I explain a little of my past, you'll understand better why we don't always see eye to eye."

"I'd like that very much." The color had returned to Lily's cheeks. She looked around for Camellia, Jasmine, and David. The Thorntons appeared to have finished their conversations. "Let's start back."

As they walked, Blake tried to organize his thoughts. He wanted Lily to understand enough to leave him alone about certain things. He didn't want to risk repeating this day. Nor did he want her nagging him about going to church. He was never going to be a churchgoing man. Once he explained why he was so reluctant to attend, he hoped she would acquiesce and leave him out of her religious nonsense. It wasn't too much to ask. He'd given way in so many things since they became business partners, surely she would yield once she knew the truth.

When they returned to the Thorntons' town house, Camellia, Jasmine, and David went to their rooms to change clothes before lunch, but Blake and Lily hung back, explaining that they had business to discuss.

"Business?" The lilt in Mrs. Thornton's voice made Blake want to groan. She was raising questions he'd rather avoid. He and Lily did not have any romantic feelings for each other, but if he protested, those in the foyer would begin to share her suspicions. The way Lily's cheeks reddened, they might anyway.

He raised one eyebrow. "Yes, the repairs are winding down, so we need to prepare for our voyage back to Natchez."

"I see." Mr. Thornton looked from his wife to Blake before shrugging and turning to the staircase. "We'll see you shortly."

Blake opened the parlor door and motioned for Lily to precede him.

She sat down on the sofa, removed her hat, and waited for him to begin.

Unable to sit, he swung his arms back and forth a few times. Where to start? "I told you I left home years ago, and I've never been back."

She nodded.

"What I didn't tell you is that my father is the reason I left." He hesitated. "My father, Reverend William Matthews."

Her eyes widened. "Your father is a minister?"

"Yes, that's right." He could hear the bitterness creeping into his voice. "And he's a cold, uncaring man who thinks the word *Christian* is a synonym for *tyrant*."

"I don't understand."

Blake considered what he should tell her. The back of his throat burned in reaction to the memories. How could he share such things with anyone, even Lily? "I don't want to drag you through all the sad occurrences from my childhood, but suffice it to say that my sister and I had to sacrifice every comfort for the sake of my father's religion."

"What did your mother say about your father's treatment?" Her voice was a blend of sympathy and caring.

Lily's question touched on another sore point. "Not much. She was a 'good Christian,' the perfect submissive wife as defined by Paul."

She said nothing, apparently digesting his statements. "Was there no one you could turn to? Grandparents? Cousins? People in the church?"

"None of our relatives lived close enough to know what was going on." He shoved his hands into his pants pockets. "As for the church, who wants to challenge a preacher? A man called by God to lead the flock? They must have felt it would be blasphemy. At any rate, no one crossed my father. No one but me, that is."

"Is that why you don't like going to church?"

Relieved at her quick understanding, he nodded. "I went this morning because it seemed so important to you, but I was not at all comfortable."

"I'm sorry for whatever pain your father caused you, but perhaps you should forgive him for his past deeds. To hold on to your bitterness only hurts you."

"You think I should forgive him?"

Her nod felt like a betrayal.

Would anyone stand up against his father other than himself? Could no one else understand what he and his sister had gone through? He turned from her, not wanting her to see how much her suggestion hurt him.

"You should not condemn all pastors or all churches because of your experiences." Her voice was gentle, but her words struck his heart with the explosive impact of a bullet.

Lily didn't understand what it had been like. Why was that? She was intelligent and caring. Why could she not understand the pain and anguish he'd been through?

Pushing back his pain and anger, Blake took a turn around the room. Perhaps logic would appeal to her. "I've been doing fine without going to church for all these years."

"You may think you're fine, but that's only because you believe you can rely on your own strength. It's not enough, you know."

He stopped pacing to look at her, his jaw slack. "What an odd opinion coming from one of the most self-reliant ladies I've ever met."

Her head dipped in acknowledgment. "I thank you for the compliment."

Blake wondered if it occurred to her that he might not have meant his statement as a compliment. Some men—most men—thought self-reliance was not necessary for a lady. Women were supposed to depend on the strength of their husbands, fathers, or brothers. Lily had none of those to rely on, but it didn't make much difference.

"You should know that God is the source for my strength."

"I see." He raised an eyebrow. "So that's why you spend every Sunday in church?"

A hint of color appeared in her cheeks. "Whenever possible. I know my sisters and I have not been as faithful in our Bible studies or prayer life as we should be, but we've been rather busy."

Heat began to rise in his chest. "So you should attend church and read your Bible only when it's convenient?"

"At least I don't spend my leisure time at gambling halls and cabarets."

How dare she judge him? "No, you spend your leisure time spending money on clothing and dragging your family and friends to parties. If you were truly moved by the Spirit, wouldn't you be spreading the Gospel instead?"

"I certainly am not perfect—"

"That's one thing we agree upon." He couldn't resist the chance to bait her. If he kept her on the defensive, she'd have no time to attack him.

Her chin wobbled. Was she going to cry?

Remorse overcame him. "I'm sorry, Lily. I was only teasing."

She turned her head. When she faced him again, her expression was composed. "At least I don't fidget and fuss the whole time I'm listening to a sermon."

"I agree that I'm not a good Christian, Lily. So why don't we leave it at that? All I'm asking is that you consider my feelings. Show me the courtesy of letting me decide how and where I spend my time."

"If the only reason for attending church was to sing hymns and listen to a sermon, I might be able to do that." She stood and crossed the room, stopping directly in front of him. "But the reason is to draw closer to the One who made you, the One who loves you, the One who wants you to turn your life over to Him."

She looked so lovely standing in the light from the parlor window, her gaze earnest. Something inside him wanted to agree with her. Then sanity returned. Lily didn't know what she was talking about. She'd been raised in the lap of luxury. Buying a boat was the action of a spoiled child who was determined to live her life in opposition to the wishes of her family.

Lily was typical of the type of women he usually steered clear of—the reformers who wanted to save the world. She would never understand how someone could twist religion to suit his own needs. She had never seen the harsh realities he had experienced. Not that he would wish that on anyone, but he wanted to get his point across to her. She needed to stop trying to reform him.

He steeled his heart. He had to put a barrier between them or she would never give him any peace. "You can dress it up any way you wish, Lily, but this is really just another attempt to direct my life."

She stepped back, a frown crossing her face.

Realizing he was finally getting through to her, Blake continued. "I've never met a woman who was so determined to control every action and thought of everyone around her. You may own fifty-one percent of our boat, but you don't own any part of my private life, and I'll thank you to stay out of it."

Blake left her standing there. He knew he had to get out of the room before he recanted every word he'd just said.

Chapter Thirty-two

Jasmine stuck out her tongue at Camellia, who promptly glared back.

"Please don't argue. We don't have time for it." Lily folded her nightclothes and placed them in the trunk. She had allowed the younger girls and David to sleep while Tamar helped her dress. After making sure Camellia was packed, they made short work of getting David and Jasmine ready for their departure, which was slated for noon.

Blake had sent a note the evening before, the only contact she'd had from him since their argument two days earlier. The message had been brief and businesslike.

> *We have four first-class passengers, eight deck passengers, two new crewmen, and a captain. Will leave dock at noon sharp.*

He hadn't signed the note, apparently in too much of a hurry to waste time with niceties.

"I don't want to go." Camellia's steps dragged as they descended the staircase. "Can't I stay with the Thorntons?"

"Of course not." Lily frowned at her. "We're sisters. We belong together until the day you fall in love and get married."

Camellia made a face and continued her slow progress toward the dining room. Jasmine seemed more eager to face the day's adventures.

She bounded down the stairs like a rubber ball. By the time Camellia and Lily made it to the breakfast table, Jasmine was already seated and had filled her plate with preserves and a flaky croissant.

"I cannot believe it's your final morning with me." Mrs. Thornton offered a sad little smile. "I'm going to miss all the energy and excitement you've brought to our home."

"Yes, we will." Mr. Thornton folded his newspaper and reached for his coffee.

"I could—"

"We'll miss you, too." Lily interrupted Camellia's statement, kicking her under the table in warning.

Camellia sent her an injured look but subsided.

The rest of their breakfast was uneventful. David joined them, as did Jonah. When they had eaten their fill, Mr. and Mrs. Thornton called for their carriage.

David rode up front next to the driver. Lily and her sisters settled on the comfortable seats inside the carriage and waved at their hosts until they could no longer see them.

"Where is Tamar?" Jasmine asked.

"She went ahead with our trunks and some food the Thorntons sent." Lily's explanation eased the concern on her youngest sister's face.

Camellia slumped back against the velvet carriage cushions. "I wish we didn't always have to leave."

"Would you rather stay here without me and Jasmine?"

Camellia shrugged. "You could stay, too. Mrs. Thornton said she wished we would."

"She is a dear friend, Camellia, but she is not our mother. We cannot impose on her."

Lily tried to keep the hurt out of her voice. She knew the desire to accept Mrs. Thornton's unconditional love, to revel in the warmth of their home. But it wasn't the *Hattie Belle*. It wasn't home.

Blake's accusation came to the forefront of her memory, and she lifted her chin. She wasn't determined to control everything and everyone. She just wanted her sisters to be happy.

When they arrived at the boat, pleasure filled Lily's heart at the sight of white decks, black smokestacks, and the red-edged paddle wheel. The mighty river rushed beneath their feet as they crossed the gangplank.

Lily wondered where Blake was. She dreaded seeing him, but there was no way around it. They were partners and likely to remain together for quite some time.

David, Jasmine, and Camellia went inside, but Lily lingered on the first-floor deck. She wanted to see the repairs, check for herself that everything was shipshape.

Smiling a little at the pun, she heard footsteps on the deck above her and looked up to see Tamar and Jensen strolling together. Deep in conversation, they didn't see her. Lily was about to greet them when Jensen leaned forward and brushed a finger across Tamar's cheek. Was a romance blooming between them? Was Tamar falling in love? How wonderful that would be. The two of them could be married on the *Hattie Belle*. They would have a pastor come aboard and perform the ceremony. She couldn't think of a more beautiful setting.

Smiling, Lily crept away to give them privacy. She was about to search for Blake when she heard his voice coming from the boiler room. Following the sound, she discovered him talking to someone, probably a new crewman. He wore a red shirt reminiscent of the clothing captains used to wear in the wild days when flatboats and canoes were the only vessels on the Mississippi. Her father had often talked of the red shirts, the larger-than-life characters who carved out livelihoods before steam-powered engines made them obsolete.

Pushing away the memory, she bent her lips into a welcoming smile. "Good morning, gentlemen."

Blake jerked as though he'd been shot and turned toward her. Circles darkened the skin under his blue eyes. "Hello, Lily." He looked tired, and she got an impression of vulnerability.

A gasp from the other man drew her attention. She looked toward the stranger and noticed his face had gone pale. Was he ill? She took a step forward, ready to catch him if he fell over. "Are you all right, sir?"

His mouth opened and closed twice before he managed to make a sound. "Water Lily? Is it really you?"

She gasped and grew faint. "Father?" The two syllables spun out from her mouth for what seemed forever. To stop herself from fainting, Lily took several deep breaths. Then she balled her hands into fists and turned back to Blake. "What have you done?"

Blake looked from Lily to the man he'd recently hired. "What's going on here?"

"I can't believe you did this," Lily hissed. Her brown eyes blazed.

"Calm down, Water Lily." The captain held up both hands. "You don't have to fly off the handle. We'll figure everything out."

"Don't you call me that." She pointed a finger at Captain Henrick. "You may be my father, but you don't have any right to call me that."

Realizing he needed to defuse the situation before something went terribly wrong, Blake stepped between Lily and the older man. "I don't understand. I thought your father was dead. Didn't you tell me you and your sisters were orphans?"

His words seemed to hit her like a bucket of cold water. The fiery sparks in her eyes dimmed. Her cheeks reddened. She seemed unable to look at him. Her gaze focused on the floor. "It doesn't matter what you thought. I won't allow him to remain on board for another minute."

"Oh no, you don't. We have an agreement. I spent a great deal of time and energy finding someone we can depend on. Captain Henrick is the best of the lot. No matter what you say, he's taking us to Natchez."

Lily shook her head. Her face hardened into a look of belligerence. Blake wondered if he'd ever met a more stubborn woman.

"I can leave." The quiet voice reminded Blake that he and Lily were not alone.

"You stay put." He didn't bother to look at the man. The real problem was the persnickety, demanding, unforgiving woman in front of him. "I don't care if he's the first cousin of President Buchanan, he's staying on this boat."

When she looked back up at him, fire had returned to her brown eyes. "This is the man who deserted me and my sisters. We couldn't depend on him then, and we can't depend on him now. If you think we had a bad captain before, I can't wait to see your reaction when he jumps ship because a better offer has come along. And then we won't see him for another decade."

"I don't want to cause trouble, Wa—Lily." The captain pushed his way past Blake's shoulder. "I didn't realize this was your boat when I agreed to take over. I can understand your reluctance to have me here."

Lily crossed her arms over her chest and raised her chin.

Before she could reiterate her position, Blake needed to point out a few things to his business partner. "If he leaves now, we won't have anyone to take us to Natchez. Our paying customers are going to demand a refund so they can purchase tickets on a boat that will leave the dock as advertised. Be reasonable, Lily. There's not much chance he's going to desert us between here and Natchez."

"Camellia and Jasmine think he's dead." She talked past her father as if he wasn't there.

It was the one argument he could understand—the desire to protect her siblings. But there might be a way around this problem. "We don't have to tell them the truth."

He could see the family resemblance in their identical stares of disbelief, even though Lily's features were much softer than those of her father.

"Don't you think someone will notice that we have the same last name?" The question came from Lily. "Or do you think no one will ask who the captain is?"

Blake snapped his fingers. The solution was easy. "We'll introduce him by the name he gave me, Captain Henrick. No one will ever connect the two of you."

A look of yearning filled the older man's eyes as he listened to their conversation.

Lily's chin lifted another notch as she considered Blake's suggestion. She turned to her father. "Do you promise you'll not tell Camellia and Jasmine who you really are?"

Captain Henrick nodded, his expression grave. "I promise."

Uncrossing her arms, Lily sighed. "I suppose you can stay then, but only until we find a suitable replacement."

"Thank you. Thank you so much." Captain Henrick brushed his eye with one hand. "I promise you won't regret it. I'll make sure you and your sisters get to Natchez safely."

Lily sniffed and turned on her heel. "If I find you've broken your promise, I'll throw you overboard myself."

Her threat seemed to linger in the small room. Blake started to apologize for Lily's acerbic words, but then he saw the wide smile on her father's face. Was the man actually proud of his daughter's reaction? He could not imagine how his own father would have reacted in a similar situation. Given a choice, he'd take Lily's father any day.

Chapter Thirty-three

Jensen surprised them all by bringing a milk cow to the boat right before they cast off. Their new captain and crew built a small corral, filling it with hay and a bucket of water for the placid animal. His idea was to offer fresh milk to their first-class passengers since one of the most common complaints about riverboat travel was the lack of fresh dairy.

Tamar thought the idea inspired, but someone had to milk the cow, and they had to use the milk and cream before it curdled. So before the sun was up the next day, she searched out two buckets, one of which she scrubbed thoroughly. Fog swirled around her feet as she headed toward the corral with a bucket in each hand—one to sit on, the clean one to hold milk.

Others were moving about the boat already, stoking the boilers and releasing the vessel from its overnight mooring. The girls would be up soon, too, and she wanted to be back in the galley making biscuits and frying sausage for the passengers in the dining room.

"Good morning."

The unexpected voice behind her startled Tamar. Squinting, she looked back over her shoulder. Lily stood at the foot of the staircase. "Good morning to you, too."

"You already look busy."

"No sense wasting time." Years of rising early and working hard in

Les Fleurs plantation had made it second nature to her. "I'm going to milk our new cow."

"Are you sure you don't want me to do that?"

A laugh escaped Tamar. "I doubt you know how."

"You're right." Lily sighed. "But I'm sure I could learn."

"Why don't you watch me? Then you can try after a bit." Tamar held back the wire fence for both of them to enter the corral. "The cow will have to be milked every day, or she'll stop giving milk."

Lily's nose wrinkled. "The smell out here is rather strong. I'm not sure it was a good idea to bring that animal on board."

"She'll be nice to have for milk."

"That's true. Especially now that we've taken on passengers. Not many of the steamboats offer fresh milk for drinking and cream to put on biscuits and desserts."

Tamar sat on the upturned bucket. She placed the clean bucket under the cow's udder. "You have to get a good hold up here and then you press and pull as you move your hand down." She demonstrated the proper movements, gratified at the sound of milk hitting the bottom of the bucket.

After a few minutes, she traded places with Lily, laughing at the face her charge was making. It took several tries, but finally Lily managed to get some milk into the bucket. She turned and grinned, her pride evident.

The cow continued munching on hay, unconcerned with the efforts of the two women.

Tamar pulled a cloth from the pocket of her skirt and reached for the bucket as the liquid nearly topped its edges. "That's enough for one day. You did very well."

Lily stood up and reached for the second bucket. "Thanks. You're a good teacher."

Tamar held out one arm to balance herself as they walked toward the galley. The riverbank sliding past was green and beautiful. Who would have thought she'd like living on a boat?

Lily's voice drew her away from her daydreaming. "Tamar, can I ask you a personal question?"

"Of course."

"Are you falling in love with Jensen?"

The question was like one of those hidden snags in the river—

appearing without warning and threatening the peace of everyone around. Her thoughts ran in circles. Why did the galley seem so far away? She picked up her pace. "Why do you ask?"

Lily kept pace with her. "I saw the two of you talking yesterday when we got to the boat. You seemed. . .taken."

"Don't go getting any silly ideas. Mr. Jensen is a good man."

"Yes, he is. I think the two of you would make a wonderful couple."

Tamar wished Lily would drop this subject. She didn't want to examine her feelings for Jensen. "You don't know what you're talking about, Lily."

Lily halted, her face showing her surprise at Tamar's harsh tone.

Tamar plunked the bucket of milk down and put her hands on her hips. "I'm sorry, Miss Lily."

"No, I'm the one who's sorry." Lily no longer looked like the self-confident owner of a successful business; instead she looked like the little girl she'd once been—a little girl who needed someone to hold her. "It's none of my business."

Tamar sighed. "I didn't mean to be so abrupt. There's just some things you can't understand." Some things that were better left alone.

The vulnerability in Lily's expression changed to confusion. "Why not?"

How could she explain? The answer was simple. She couldn't. "You may be a woman, but that doesn't mean you're mature enough to understand everything about how the world works."

Lily turned toward the bank.

Tamar started to put a comforting hand around her shoulders but decided they would both be better off if she ended this conversation now. So she picked up her bucket and continued toward the galley, her head shaking as she considered the difference in Lily's and her own life.

How could a girl born to luxury and freedom ever understand the problems of a slave? As much as she loved Lily and knew she was loved by her, Tamar could see the unbridgeable gulf between them. Almost as wide a gulf as the one between her and Jensen.

❧

Lily held her breath as Camellia served the tea for the guests who'd gathered in the ladies' parlor. It wasn't that her sister was unpracticed at pouring tea, but doing so on board a boat that was likely to rock to one side or the other without notice could challenge the most experienced lady.

"I don't know how you do it."

Turning to the tall, spare woman next to her, Lily summoned a smile. "What is that, Mrs. Carlyle?"

"How a young thing like you can manage a large boat like this."

She glanced around the cozy room, furnished with three sofas and a scattering of Queen Anne chairs Sarah had donated, insisting they were gathering dust in her attic. Then she turned to the lady who reminded her rather forcefully of Aunt Dahlia. She'd spent most of the evening before arguing with the crew and other passengers and complaining about the rustic accommodations. Lily wondered if she would ever make the woman happy. *God loves her, too.*

The words in Lily's heart shamed her. She breathed slowly and widened her smile with an effort. "It's quite similar to running a household. Most everyone knows what must be done, and they don't need much more than my encouragement and an occasional pat on the back to keep things on an even keel. And you must remember that Mr. Matthews is my partner. I rely on him greatly, of course."

The words hardly stuck in her throat. She did owe Blake a lot. He had been essential in repairing the boat and finding passengers such as Mrs. Carlyle while she and her sisters shopped and socialized with the Thornton family. If only he had not hired her father.

The conversation turned general, and Lily's gaze wandered toward the other occupants of the room. Mrs. Abernathy, a kindly woman with iron-gray hair and deep-set brown eyes, traveled with her daughter, Karen. Karen was a dark-haired, younger version of her mother.

Lily sipped her tea and nibbled at one of the royal crumpets Jensen, David, and Jasmine had baked earlier this morning. They were an elegant addition to their tea service. She needed to remember to tell all three of them what a success their creation was. It looked a little like a pancake topped with a sprinkling of blackberry preserves and sifted sugar. Even Mrs. Carlyle seemed to be enjoying them.

Camellia engaged Miss Abernathy in a discussion of the latest fashions while Mrs. Carlyle and Mrs. Abernathy talked about the exorbitant price of fabric and the rising cost of most goods.

Given a moment to herself, Lily's thoughts returned to her business partner. She had not sought Blake out after their argument, preferring to concentrate on the welfare of the passengers while he oversaw the crew. It was a workable solution that seemed beneficial for all. Except that every time their paths crossed, she prayed for him to acknowledge her, smile at her, even argue with her. But he didn't. He simply nodded and moved away, apparently unwilling to heal the breach between them. Perhaps if she sought him out and apologized. . . But she couldn't. Not while her father was on board the *Hattie Belle*.

"Please excuse me, ladies." Lily could no longer sit in the parlor. She had to be up and doing something. "I need to check on my youngest sister, but I'll leave you in Camellia's capable hands."

Mrs. Carlyle frowned even as Mrs. Abernathy gave her an encouraging wink. "It must be quite a job keeping up with that young lady."

Nodding her head, Lily made her escape. She walked out onto the second-floor deck and stood at the rail, her gaze taking in the dense forest lining the banks of the muddy river. She ought to be checking the galley to make sure Jensen and Tamar didn't need any help, but after the disturbing conversation with Tamar this morning, she hesitated to interrupt them.

What had Tamar meant? She was no longer a child. Tamar had to have been talking about her status as a slave. But didn't she know Lily considered her an equal? Didn't she have the same freedoms as everyone else aboard the *Hattie Belle*? She worked hard, it was true, but so did the rest of them. Even Jasmine and David had chores.

Lily felt battered by the emotional upheavals of the past few days. She wished she had someone she could talk to, someone who would be on her side no matter what. But that was impossible. Seeing her father again after all these years had reminded her of one thing: no one was dependable. No one could be relied on. She had only herself.

It was all too much. More than she could bear. Then something touched her, light as the breeze, quiet as a whisper. Almost a voice, a reassurance. And she knew there was another she could count on: God. He was her eternal Father. Even if everyone else walked out of her life or this great wide river dried up to a bare trickle—no matter what happened, God would never desert her.

Tears burned her eyes. How could she have forgotten Him even for an instant? God was the only constant. He was the beginning of everything. Yet He was concerned about her. The words of the New

Orleans pastor came back to her. She should rejoice in the Lord. He was her Father, her Lord. He had made her, and He was always ready to embrace her.

Lily didn't know how long she stood watching the bank slip by, but when she turned to go, she felt much better. She would be able to handle whatever lay ahead as long as she depended on God to lead her.

She still wished her earthly father wasn't so close to hand, but she didn't see any way around that until they made landfall in Natchez. Wondering how soon that might be, she headed up to the hurricane deck to ask Captain Henrick. At least she could make use of the man's experience.

"That snag up yonder is what we call a sawyer." The voice she remembered so clearly from childhood wafted across the upper deck as she made her way to the pilothouse.

"I see." Was that Jasmine's excited voice? "Because it looks like a saw going back and forth."

"That's right. You sure are a bright young lady. You remind me of my own little girls—"

"That's enough." Lily raised her voice enough to cut off his words. "Jasmine, you have some reading to do in your room."

The child groaned. "Please don't make me go inside, Lily. I'm learning all about the river from Captain Henrick."

"It's an awful pretty day for a young'un to be cooped up inside."

Lily frowned. "I suppose you're an expert on parenting."

A look of pain deepened the lines on her father's weathered face. Her anger dissipated, but Lily reminded herself that she had good reason to keep this man separated from her sisters. She didn't want them to be hurt as she'd been all those years ago. They didn't deserve that kind of pain. No one did.

Jasmine slid past her without another word.

Lily waited until her sister's dark head had disappeared before turning her gaze back to the captain. "I don't know what you think gives you the right to embroil my innocent little sister in your schemes."

"I am not scheming or embroiling anyone, Lily." He turned back to the wheel. "I just answered a few of her questions."

All Lily could see of him was the drooping line of his shoulders under the ridiculous red shirt he wore. Choosing to concentrate on the shirt instead of his posture, she wondered if her father thought they were still living in the days of the keelboats. She wanted to lash out at him. She wanted to tell him how ridiculous he looked. She wanted to remind him he was only needed to steer the boat, not to teach her sister anything. But she couldn't quite force the words past her lips. So she watched him while he watched the river.

Why did you stay on this boat? Lily wanted to ask, but she didn't dare open up that topic. It was too dangerous.

Shoring up her defenses, she lifted her chin. Perhaps if she kept him isolated from her sisters, up here in the pilothouse where the pilot belonged. . .

"I don't want you talking to Jasmine anymore." She turned on her heel and practically ran toward the staircase as though some monster was chasing her.

Chapter Thirty-four

"Why can't David go with us?" Jasmine's plaintive voice interrupted the instructions Lily was giving Jensen.

"Because he's going to stay here with the other men."

Jasmine's lower lip protruded. "He stayed with us in New Orleans."

"And you spent most of your time bickering," Camellia reminded her. She looked toward Lily. "When can we leave?"

"In just a moment." Lily focused on Jensen. "If you need anything, we'll be at my grandmother's home. Blake knows where it is."

"We'll be fine, ma'am." Jensen rested a hand on David's shoulder.

David looked longingly toward the carriage where Lily's sisters and Tamar waited. Should she let him come home with them? But no, Lily reminded herself, there would be enough controversy at Les Fleurs without bringing a foundling. "Trust me, David, you're better off here. Just stay close to Jensen or Blake, and you shouldn't have any trouble with those bullies in town."

He gave a slow nod. "Yes'm."

Lily gave him an encouraging smile before climbing into the carriage. She hadn't seen Blake since the cargo was off-loaded. Their passengers had disembarked as soon as they made landfall. Blake and Jensen had taken charge of the cargo while the women cleaned the staterooms and made a list of supplies they would need for their next trip. Some of the crew had dismantled the pen on the main deck and scrubbed it with lye soap. She and Tamar had decided to ask Jensen to sell the cow, who had turned out to be a bit too pungent for their passengers. Blake hadn't needed to point out the advantages of keeping the captain. His experience and concern were proof enough that he should remain. . . as long as he didn't reveal his identity.

Camellia adjusted her hat to better protect her complexion from the sunlight. "Are they expecting us at home?"

Lily nodded. "I sent a messenger to Grandmother asking if we could visit. He returned with a sweet note saying that she couldn't wait to see us."

"Everything looks different." Jasmine's head swiveled as they ascended the hill leading away from the docks.

"Don't be silly." Camellia maintained her pose while managing to frown at her sister. "We haven't been gone that long."

Lily agreed with Jasmine. The city did look different. Under-the-Hill had been the same with its ramshackle buildings and throngs of steamboats, but new buildings seemed to have sprung up overnight On-the-Hill. Business was booming, a sure sign they would succeed in their shipping business.

"I want the two of you to be on your best behavior while we're at Les Fleurs." Lily broke into the discussion before it could escalate into an all-out fight. "I don't want Aunt Dahlia or Uncle Phillip saying I have turned you into hoydens."

Camellia elevated her nose and looked away.

Jasmine reached out for Lily's hand. "Of course we will, Sissy."

Lily sent a quick prayer heavenward. Her gaze met Tamar's sympathetic one. Lily couldn't wait to get back on the river. Even dealing with Captain Henrick and the likes of Mrs. Carlyle would be pleasant in comparison to her relatives' homilies.

As they topped the hill, she spied a man on horseback, waving in their direction.

It was Jean Luc Champney. A smile teased the edges of her mouth. She reached forward and tapped on the shoulder of the hired driver to get him to stop.

"Hello," Jean Luc said as he pulled his horse up next to the carriage. He swept a bow. "How wonderful to see you."

"It's nice to see you, too." She could feel the weight of her sisters' gazes on her. Were they shocked that someone so handsome had sought her out?

Camellia peeped at him from under the brim of her hat, but Jasmine was more open in her perusal.

"I trust your first voyage was successful." His dark eyes never strayed toward Lily's more handsome sisters.

"Yes, it was." Lily's cheeks heated under his intense scrutiny.

"Excellent. Perhaps you will have dinner with me so I can hear all about it."

She nodded. "I would like that."

"I'll call on you this afternoon." With a second bow, he resettled his hat and cantered away.

"I think you have a beau." Camellia's voice sounded petulant.

Lily supposed she was not used to having anyone ignore her. It was a novel experience for Lily, too. "Monsieur Champney has been very kind to me. I bought our boat from his father, you know. I think he just wants to help us succeed."

Why did all three of them look at her with varying degrees of surprise or pity? Lily stared at the countryside as the carriage began moving forward. Once again she felt she was being told she didn't understand the world around her. Maybe they were the ones who didn't understand things. They had not been at the dinner she and Jean Luc had shared. Nor had they been with them when he took her out to the boat—well, at least Camellia and Jasmine had not.

"How long will we be staying at Grandmother's home?" Camellia asked.

"No matter how long our visit is, it will be too long for me." Jasmine crossed her arms.

"That's no way to talk about your relatives." Lily frowned, and Jasmine sat back against the seat cushion with a thump. Lily turned her attention to Camellia. "I doubt we'll spend more than a day or two."

"A day or two?" Dismay colored both sisters' words.

"Can't we stay a little longer?" asked Camellia.

Jasmine shook her head in disagreement. "I don't want to spend the night there. It's so much fun on the *Hattie Belle* where we're not cooped up inside all the time."

"We'll be off as soon as we get another shipment. I am hoping to head north this time, toward Memphis." Lily tucked several loose strands of hair behind her ear.

"Really?" Jasmine bounced to the edge of her seat.

Tamar put out a hand to stop her from tumbling to the floor. "Settle down, Miss Jasmine, before you hurt yourself."

"Yes, do settle down." Camellia aimed a disdainful look at her.

Lily sighed. Was she being fair to her middle sister? While Jasmine thrived with the easygoing lifestyle aboard their boat, Camellia was eager to abandon it. Every time they landed, she wanted to disembark immediately and delayed going back until Lily forced her to return. Yet what else could Lily do? She was determined not to let her sister grow too self-absorbed.

The carriage turned into the drive leading to Grandmother's house. Lily should feel excited, but she couldn't summon much enthusiasm. Like Jasmine, she wished she were back on the *Hattie Belle*, floating on beloved muddy waters.

Blake glanced at the floating island of boats lashed together for the night. Men moved from deck to deck, cooking, laughing, playing cards. He wanted to join them, but that wasn't possible. Not tonight. He had more important duties.

Blake turned to the interior of the boat. It was far too quiet aboard the *Hattie Belle*, as though the departure of Lily and her sisters had removed all the joy and laughter.

He wondered how she was faring with her family. Were they welcoming or rebuking her? Of course she would be able to handle herself no matter how her relatives treated her.

He loved the way she was so optimistic, so eager to embrace life on the river. It no longer mattered to him that her vision of that life was so different from the gambling salon he had imagined. He was rather enjoying himself. He might even try a little fishing during their next cruise.

He opened the door of the cabin he shared with David. The boy was lying on his back in bed, his textbook spread across his chest. A warm feeling filled Blake's chest. It didn't seem too long ago that he was the one falling asleep at his lessons. Affection wrapped itself around his heart. Who would have thought he would so much enjoy the role of older brother? He was glad Lily had insisted on letting David stay on board. Another of her policies that had proven to be right. Blake shook the boy's shoulder. "David?"

A grumble answered him.

"Wake up. You need to get out of those clothes."

David rubbed his eyes and pushed himself up.

Blake rescued the textbook before it could slide off to the floor. "I suppose you were absorbing the information in here straight through your chest?"

"I didn't mean to fall asleep."

Blake loosed a smile. "That's all right, David. We'll work on your studies together tomorrow." His smile disappeared. His father had said the same thing to him once upon a time. And had helped him the next day as promised. Why hadn't he remembered that before? Had he only clung to the unhappy memories? Unable to deal with the emotion his thoughts stirred, Blake shut them out and concentrated on helping the younger boy find his nightshirt and climb under the covers.

The light in the room was fading quickly now that the sun had set. He bid David good night and stepped back into the passageway. He wished Jensen had not gone into town. He needed a distraction this evening, something to keep his memories at bay.

"Where are you going?"

Blake stopped in midstride and turned to face Captain Henrick. "I thought you went to Natchez with the rest of the crew."

"No." The older man shook his head, a smile wrinkling his weathered face. "I'm a bit old and staid to enjoy the kind of. . .ah. . . distractions that interest the others."

"With all the storytelling going on out there?" Blake pointed his head toward the deck. "I'm sure you could keep a group well entertained with stories of Mike Fink or some of your own adventures. A man who's seen as much of the river as you must have a host of stories in his knapsack."

"Maybe so, but it's not the same as spinning yarns for the little ones."

Blake raised an eyebrow. "You sound more like a father than a river captain."

"I am, son. Or at least I want to be. But it seems the good Lord hasn't removed all the obstacles in my path even though He had to be responsible for leading me back to my girls."

The man's statement raised several questions in Blake's mind. "Are you interested in explaining what you mean?"

Captain Henrick shrugged. "I suppose. Seems you have the time to listen."

Instead of returning to the deck, Blake nodded toward the dining room. He'd never heard Lily tell the story of why she and her sisters had been raised by their grandparents rather than their father. He assumed her mother was dead. Surely no woman would desert her beautiful daughters voluntarily. But how had this man made the decision to walk away from his children?

Blake had grown to care deeply about all three of the Anderson girls. He couldn't imagine abandoning them. . .and he was not their father.

They sat at one of the empty tables. Captain Henrick leaned forward, placing his forearms on the tabletop. "What do you want to know?"

"Everything."

"That's a tall order."

Blake sighed and leaned back against his chair. "Okay, why don't you start with what happened between you and Lily?"

"There's a tale." Captain Henrick's brown eyes darkened. "It's not an easy story to tell." He sighed, seeming to steel himself to face something unpleasant. "I fell in love with Rose Blackstone. She was such a lovely, delicate, cultured young lady, but somehow I still managed to secure her affection. We married even though her parents never approved of me. Rose joined me on my boat. What a wonderful life we had."

He stopped as if reliving the early days of his marriage. "Then we had our first daughter, my Water Lily. She was a little sailor from the time she could walk. Her mother and I always took her with us on our trips. Then came pretty-as-a-picture Camellia. If you wonder what the girls' mother looked like, gaze on my second-born child." He sighed. "I have no doubt she'll lead some poor man on a merry chase. She never took to living on the river like Water Lily. She was scared of everything—the noises, the smells, the strangers. Traveling as a family grew harder, and her grandparents offered to keep her for us. It seemed like the right thing to do back then, but I'm not as sure now."

Blake nodded. He knew how much perspective was gained when one looked back. He would change several of his choices if he could. "It's better to concentrate on the present and plan for the future instead of spending too much time reliving the past."

"That's true. But it's also important to remember the past, or we run the risk of making the same mistakes over and over. I only wish I'd had more wisdom back then."

They sat in silence. Blake didn't want to push the man. He'd learned that patience often yielded better results. He crossed one leg over the other and waited.

The captain finally continued. "When my sweet Rose told me she was in the family way a second time, I knew we'd outgrown our boat. But we had managed to put some money aside, and we used that to purchase a bigger boat. One that would accommodate our children and hopefully bring us more income. After a few more years, our little Jasmine came. Violet eyes and a fluff of hair as dark as midnight. She looked just like a miniature I once saw of her grandmother, Miss Violet."

A faraway look and wistful smile softened his features. "I could hardly believe we had three girls who were so different in looks and temperament. You must have seen the differences—my headstrong Lily, my comfort-loving Camellia, and joyful, exuberant Jasmine. I'm truly blessed to have three such wonderful daughters."

"Then why did you leave them?" Blake's question blurted out as though shot from a cannon.

"I had no choice." Captain Henrick's eyes were moist. His face showed pain. "The summer after Jasmine was born, Rose and I decided to leave the children with her parents while we traveled upriver. We didn't know a flood was bearing down on us. It hit during the middle of the night, the river rose twenty feet in minutes. Our boat didn't stand a chance. It was ripped free of its mooring and thrown into the main current."

The man halted, untying the scarf from his neck and using it to dry his eyes. He cleared his throat. "We broke up on something—a rock or snag. I never saw it. We were dumped into the water and tossed around like bits of flotsam. At first Rose and I clung to each other, but the water ripped us apart. My sweet wife drowned—" His voice broke.

Captain Henrick shook his head. "When I found her body, I wanted to die. And when I got back to Natchez and told her parents what had happened, they wanted me dead, too." His gaze lifted.

The pain in his eyes made Blake's gut twist. "I'm so sorry."

"Me too, son. That was the darkest time of my life. I didn't understand why God would allow such a terrible thing to happen. Why would He take Rose from her husband and daughters? Why didn't He take me instead? Rose and the girls would have been much better off. Mr. and Mrs. Blackstone would've made sure they never had to worry about finances. Rose probably would have married again. Everything would have been better. If He thought it necessary to take one of us, He made a mistake in taking Rose and leaving me."

Blake nodded. He could understand questioning God. He'd done enough of that himself.

"Old Mr. Blackstone told me that he and his wife would raise my daughters, give them every luxury, every opportunity. At first I refused to consider his offer, but finally I agreed. Then he told me he thought the children would adapt better to their new lives if I stayed away. What was I supposed to do? I was a riverboat captain without a boat. I couldn't take three children with me. We'd starve. It seemed the final proof that God cared nothing about us."

Blake looked away from the captain, suddenly wishing he'd never asked the man about his past. He sensed he was not going to enjoy the rest of the story.

"Over the next few years I wandered from port to port. I did things that bring me shame now. I was lost and angry. I picked fights with men who'd done me no wrong, anything to exorcise my rage. Strangely enough, that's what may have saved my life. . .and my soul."

Exactly as Blake had feared. And from an unexpected source. He might have been prepared for a sermon from a preacher, but not from this old gentleman whom he'd considered kindly and harmless. Blake wanted to push back from the table, but something held him still. Some macabre impulse. Rather like not being able to resist looking toward a dead body caught in a river snag.

"One night more than a year ago, I met a man who stabbed me during a fight and left me for dead. A preacher got me to a doctor. Between them they kept me alive. The preacher shared his rooms with me. While I was recovering, he had a captive audience. I'll never forget the afternoon when he asked me why I wanted to die."

"I'm certain you had an answer." Blake shoved his chair back. "And I'm sure it was a good one. But I don't have time to listen tonight."

Captain Henrick sat back. The look that crossed his face was not condemning. It wasn't even sad. The expression was one of understanding. He nodded at Blake. "I see."

"I doubt that." He stood and stalked to the door. "You don't know a thing about me, so don't go acting like you do."

Blake stomped onto the deck. A group of men sat around a small fire on a nearby boat. Close enough so he could keep a watch on the boat and be ready if David needed something. He headed toward them, eager to drown out Captain Henrick's words.

Chapter Thirty-five

Ashamed of his response to the captain's story, Blake got up early the next morning and fixed breakfast. Soon the aromas of fresh coffee and bacon filled the air. As the sun made its first appearance over the horizon, Jensen, Captain Henrick, and David showed up. Blake scrambled a small mountain of eggs and sat at the table with the others.

Silence reigned as they dug into their food.

Blake washed down his food with a gulp of hot coffee and turned to face the captain. He was determined to clear the air. "Look, I'm sorry for interrupting you last night."

Captain Henrick waved away his apology. "When the time is right, you'll listen. There's no doubt God is whispering in your ear. He wants you to come to Him."

David's eyes widened. "Did you have a fight?"

Blake brushed a hand through the boy's blond curls. "Nothing to worry about. Captain Henrick and I get along fine, don't we?" He shot a glance at the captain.

"That's right." Captain Henrick smiled. "In fact, I'm hoping we're going to be very close."

Nodding, Blake forced a smile to his face. He bent a look at the captain that he hoped spoke to his desire to talk to the man alone. They still had a few things that needed to be straightened out. Things that had nothing to do with religion.

"Let's get this food put away, and then you and I need to spend some time checking how much of that textbook you managed to absorb last night."

Jensen began gathering the dirty dishes and moved to the galley. Captain Henrick headed upstairs to the hurricane deck. Blake and David went to the dining hall to study. Blake hoped he remembered enough about arithmetic to help the boy.

David seemed a bit lost, so Blake pulled out his deck of cards, hoping Lily would not catch him again and accuse him of teaching the children to gamble. He thought by now she should have a better idea of his moral code, but he'd just as soon not test that theory.

"A deck has fifty-two cards." He shuffled the cards and dealt them facedown on the table. "I've dealt four hands on this table. Without counting, can you tell me how many cards should be in each hand?"

David's brow gathered as he tried to reason out the answer.

"If I had dealt two hands, how many cards would be in each hand?"

"Thirty?"

Blake shook his head. "You're guessing. What is half of fifty-two?"

David scrunched up his face, his mouth moving as he divided the number. "Twenty-six?"

"Are you guessing or telling me?"

"I. . .I'm telling you."

Blake nodded. "You're right."

The smile on David's face was a joy to see.

"That's good." He tapped a finger on the table. "So how many cards are in each hand here?"

Another frown from his pupil. "Thirteen?"

"I think you're beginning to understand." He picked up one of the hands and fanned the cards before laying them down. "Now if there are four suits in this deck, how many cards will be in each suit?"

"Thirteen." David's answer was more confident.

"You may have found a new way of studying." He picked up the cards and shuffled them once more. "I'm removing twelve cards from the deck, so how many cards will be left?"

They continued drilling—adding, subtracting, multiplying, and dividing. When Blake felt his student had grasped the subject, he sent David for the slate he and Jasmine shared. "Write your name."

He watched as David meticulously copied out the five letters of his first name, hesitated, and looked up. "I don't know how to spell Foster."

Blake pressed his upper teeth against his lower lip and pushed air through them. "What letter makes that sound?"

And so they continued. He wondered if Lily would be proud of the progress David had made. She might not even notice. "You've seen the name of our boat, right?"

David nodded.

"Good. Then write *Hattie Belle* on your slate."

David wiped his name off the slate with his sleeve and began concentrating once more.

The bond Blake had felt the night before returned in full force. This boy was bright. He would make sure David had a chance to make something of himself. Perhaps one day they would find the boy's father and reunite them. Or maybe he'd be better off staying on the *Hattie Belle*. Between Lily and him, they could see to it that the boy recognized his worth and learned to rely on his talents.

He gave David a series of tasks and left him for a while. Blake wanted to set Captain Henrick straight.

The captain was studying a map in the pilothouse but looked up when Blake entered. "Are you through tutoring that towheaded scamp?"

"For the time being."

Captain Henrick put down his map. "I don't suppose you came all the way up here to enjoy the sunshine."

Blake looked around. The view from the highest deck of the *Hattie Belle* never failed to amaze. Perhaps he should find time to come up here more often. The morning sunshine gleamed on the surface of the water. Most of the boats that had formed the floating island last night were already gone, but there would be more tonight. It was a daily ritual. The old adage of "safety in numbers" was true on the Mississippi. Brigands and pirates could target a lone boat unless it was well hidden.

"No." Blake turned his attention to the captain. "Now that I know Lily can't overhear us, I wanted to talk about what happened when I first brought you aboard. I can't say I didn't get a little enjoyment from taking your side."

"I do appreciate it. Otherwise I wouldn't have gotten the chance to see her or my other daughters."

Blake smothered a smile. "Yes, well, be that as it may be, I won't stand for seeing Lily or her sisters hurt by anyone. If you ever cause them pain, I'll put you off this boat. Whether we're in Natchez, New Orleans, or Timbuktu, I'll make sure you don't get a second chance."

"If I hurt them and you didn't run me away, I would lose respect for you, Blake. I have to live with what I did all those years ago, no matter what my reasons. But I would never, ever do that to them again. I am their father, even if Lily doesn't want me to acknowledge that. I'd never walk away from my family again." The fervor in Captain Henrick's words was obvious.

Blake gave him a curt nod and turned on his heel.

"If you want to talk again, Blake, you know where to find me."

Ignoring the man, he headed for the staircase. Why did it feel like he was retreating? He had nothing to feel guilty about. Then what was the sharp pain in his chest? He hadn't done the same thing to his family. What had happened between him and his father was altogether different. Wasn't it?

❧

"I have come to ask for your granddaughter's company for a sedate ride." Jean Luc smiled widely. He'd found that charming a young lady's chaperone was a fruitful effort.

His gaze followed Mrs. Blackstone's to the sofa where Lily sat, her hands folded demurely in her lap. Her brown eyes sparkled with anticipation. "I don't see why not, Monsieur Champney." Mrs. Blackstone returned his smile. "The weather outside is perfect for a carriage ride."

"Thank you, Grandmother." Lily rose from the sofa. "I'll just get my shawl and hat."

Jean Luc stood when she did and bowed. "I await your pleasure, Miss Anderson."

He appreciated the pink tint to her cheeks as she exited the room. At least she was still an innocent. He'd had his doubts after she'd spent so much time in New Orleans. He knew firsthand about the opportunities to stray in that city.

"Do you follow politics at all, Monsieur Champney?" Mrs. Blackstone's voice captured his attention.

"I'm afraid I keep busy with other pursuits. While I was in Europe, I was plunged into the political world of the king and found it to be sordid and dangerous. My father, however, is well versed in political matters." Jean Luc resumed his seat to the old lady's right. "I suppose he needs to since he's a businessman."

"I'm sure you're right." Mrs. Blackstone sipped from her teacup. "I don't get out much these days, so the newspaper is how I stay abreast of the world. I was reading this morning of a race for the Illinois senate."

Jean Luc adopted an interested expression. "I'm surprised such a race is covered in the local newspaper."

"Perhaps you haven't yet realized how interested we are here in national developments concerning slavery and abolition." Mrs. Blackstone put down her teacup. "I read all I can about national policies."

He could not imagine spending that much time perusing anything. He preferred more athletic pursuits and the excitement to be found in gambling salons, although he limited his time there to avoid more disasters.

"You must be quite the scholar." Jean Luc tried to infuse admiration into his voice while glancing at her hands to see if her fingertips had been blackened from all the newsprint she perused. He hoped her penchant for reading had not rubbed off on Lily. While he appreciated a sensible woman, he had no desire to woo a girl who knew more about every subject than he.

Before Mrs. Blackstone could answer, Lily returned. She was tying the ribbon on a pretty straw hat and had a lacy shawl draped over one arm.

Jean Luc stood and offered his arm. "I am so glad you can join me."

"It's sweet of you to invite me."

Mrs. Blackstone waved them out of the room. "Enjoy your outing, Lily, but don't be late for dinner."

A frisson of irritation passed through Jean Luc. Did the woman think he was untrustworthy? Stifling the feeling, he smiled and bowed toward her before leading Lily out to his carriage.

After getting her settled, Jean Luc took the reins and set their vehicle in motion. "Before we get onto another subject, please let me apologize for the antics of the man I recommended to you."

"You don't need to apologize." Lily put a hand on his arm.

Jean Luc tightened his muscles in response, hoping she would be impressed with his strength. "Yes, I do. You are very kind to forgive me, but I need to tell you how devastated I was when he reappeared here in Natchez."

She removed her hand. "I really wish you would not persist, Monsieur Champney."

He pulled the carriage to the side of the road under the spreading branches of a live oak so he could concentrate on his passenger rather than his driving. "But I must. I must make you believe I had no idea what kind of man Captain Steenberg is." He placed a hand over his chest. "I would never have put you or your family in harm's way. I was so relieved to see the *Hattie Belle* sailing into port yesterday."

"You have convinced me of your innocence." She tilted her head back. "Please don't waste any more time. I never blamed you for his actions. You have been a good friend to me since the first time we met."

"*Merci.*" He took one of her hands, noticing that she was wearing gloves, a barrier to his intentions. Jean Luc used his thumb to slide the white cotton away from the back of her wrist and pressed a fervent kiss against her skin. "I would like to be more than your friend."

She gasped and tugged at her hand. Reluctantly, Jean Luc allowed her to pull away. Color rode high in her cheeks, and the tenderness he had seen in her expression had disappeared. Lily looked uncertain.

Should he take the opportunity to embrace her? He needed to secure her affection. He didn't want her to leave town again without making her aware of his intentions.

"*Monsieur* Champney—"

He could tell from the tone of her voice that she was not as entranced as she should be by his attentions. He groaned, the sound stopping her words. "Please don't tell me I have overstepped."

"No, you're not the problem. I find your sentiments flattering. How could I not? You're a fine gentleman." She sighed and looked down at her lap. "I have so many things to worry about these days, I really don't have time to accept a courtship."

At least she hadn't demurred because she had no feelings for him. Jean Luc would capitalize on this scant encouragement. "I can see the burdens you carry, Miss Anderson. I hate to watch you work so hard. I want to be someone you can lean upon." He could tell his words had hit the mark by the returning tenderness in her expression.

"Jean Luc, you are very kind. But I cannot impose upon you any more than I already have."

"At least let me find someone to replace Captain Steenberg."

"That's not necessary. We found someone in New Orleans. The

crew and even my sisters seem to be taken with him, so I suppose we will keep him in our employ unless something drastic happens."

"Then what can I do for you, Lily?" He reached for her hand, massaging it gently, trying to project unthreatening support. "There must be something you need."

She shook her head. "I think Blake and I have things under control. He hired our current crew and oversaw the repairs."

"I'm glad Matthews is treating you well, but I must admit to reservations about him." He pulled her hand to his chest. "Please promise me you will not lower your guard with him. He may be trying to lull you into a vulnerable position before taking advantage of your trusting nature."

She stiffened. "I know you mean well, Jean Luc, but you must allow me some credit. I am not as naive as you might think."

Jean Luc released her and let his shoulders droop. "Now I've offended you."

"You haven't offended me, Jean Luc. I appreciate your concern. It's just that no one seems to have any faith in me. I am not a helpless debutante." She sat up straight, turning slightly away. "Please take me home."

He had to be satisfied with that. Jean Luc turned the carriage around and started the trip back to her family's home.

Why did Lily have to be so prickly? He had never met a young lady so difficult to please. He only hoped she was worth the effort. And she was, he reminded himself. She was the way to regain everything—his father's approval, his boat, his self-esteem. Lily was the key to his future.

Chapter Thirty-six

"Please, please let me stay, Lily." Camellia's expression was filled with hope, yearning, and optimism.

Lily sighed and touched her sister's pretty curls with a finger. Her heart was tearing in half. Camellia had not thrived on the river like she and Jasmine had. Where they had enjoyed searching for the next adventure around the bend, Camellia had been happiest when they were staying with the Thorntons in New Orleans. But to separate the three of them? And would Camellia be truly happy here, or would she find herself in a situation similar to the one that had made Lily purchase the *Hattie Belle* in the first place? "What about Aunt Dahlia?"

Camellia's face sparkled like sunshine hitting the surface of the river. "She's promised me an exciting season now that I'm old enough to be a debutante. I may even find a husband by Christmas."

Concern flashed through Lily. Camellia was not mature enough to be responsible for a household and children. "You're only fifteen. Don't be in such a hurry to grow up."

"I won't." Camellia walked to the tall window that graced one side of the fireplace, covered for the summer with a hand-painted screen.

Lily followed her to the window and put an arm around her younger sister's waist.

Camellia leaned against her and sighed. "I'm sorry, Lily. I know you want to live on a boat, but I'm more suited to ballrooms. Please say you'll let me stay. I can continue my piano lessons. Uncle Phillip knows an art teacher who can improve my drawing."

Words choked Lily's throat. Was everything changing? Again? Feeling like she'd been stabbed in the chest, she nodded. "I suppose you can stay."

A squeal of excitement was followed by a big hug from Camellia. "Thank you so much, Lily. I promise I'll be good. So good you'll be amazed the next time you come home."

She returned Camellia's hug, hoping she'd made the right decision. It didn't feel right, but how could she force her sister to return to a life that didn't suit her? Perhaps if there were no other option, she would insist that Camellia come back to the *Hattie Belle*.

A thought came to her, an odd echo. Had their father faced a similar decision? She pushed the thought away. Their father had not offered them a choice. He had simply walked away. Perhaps if he'd come to visit them over the years, if he'd made any attempt at communication, she might understand. But none of them had seen him until the day Blake hired him to captain their boat.

Camellia kissed her cheek then danced around the room as if waltzing with a partner. "I hope Grandmother will let me take dancing lessons."

A laugh gurgled up from Lily's throat. "You certainly will be busy with all these lessons. Perhaps instead of remaining here, you should go to a good finishing school."

Camellia stopped abruptly, her blue eyes opening wide. "You would let me go to school?"

"Of course I would." Lily wondered if she could bribe her sister. "We'll be taking our next load to Memphis, but I imagine we'll head back to New Orleans after that. I'm sure either the Thorntons or Sarah Cartier could recommend several good schools. Of course if you're not with us, what good would that do?"

Her sister considered Lily's words. "Will you let me stay here while you go to Memphis? You could pick me up before you return to New Orleans."

Lily nodded slowly. Camellia had never had the problems with Aunt Dahlia that Lily had. But she didn't want to see her sister pushed into a loveless marriage, and minimizing the contact between the two was the best way to make sure Camellia was safe from manipulation.

The door to the parlor opened, and the subject of her thoughts walked into the room. Aunt Dahlia's black skirts swished as she crossed the room and settled on the sofa. "Have you gotten everything settled?"

The pain stabbed Lily again, caused by a sense of betrayal. She looked toward Camellia, who would not return her gaze.

"I hope you'll one day come to your senses, Lily." Aunt Dahlia's voice drew her attention from her traitorous sibling. "But whether you do or not, there's no reason to destroy Camellia's and Jasmine's chances of making advantageous marriages."

"I don't believe seeing a little of the world is a bad thing for a young woman."

"What more could they learn than can be taught here in Natchez? You may turn up your nose at the local society, but I can promise you that the best and brightest young men are to be found right outside our door."

Lily realized she shouldn't give her aunt the satisfaction of an argument, but she couldn't keep silent. "Not every woman thinks marriage is the only future for her. I want to make sure my sisters have choices."

"I want to thank you for giving me a choice." Camellia moved to the sofa and sat next to Aunt Dahlia. "And for accepting that my decision is different from your own."

Lily's mouth opened to refute her sister, but she snapped it shut. Nothing was to be gained by continuing this discussion. As Camellia had pointed out, she did believe in choices. It was the very reason she'd first embarked on her quest to make a home for them on the river. She just wished it didn't hurt so badly to contemplate the schism that seemed to be forming between her and Camellia.

She nodded and left the parlor, feeling like she was leaving part of her heart behind.

Chapter Thirty-seven

Lily took a moment to sit in the shade on the upper deck before beginning her next chore. They missed Camellia, but with the increased number of passengers, no one had much time to dwell on such matters. She had no free time at all. She rose at daybreak, dressed, and headed to the kitchen to help prepare breakfast. Then she scrubbed dishes, washed floors, took care of the needs of the women passengers. No matter how badly she wanted to, it seemed she could never find enough time to read her Bible and pray.

Maybe she should take her Bible to the afternoon tea in the ladies' parlor. Or would that be too pretentious? Would the passengers appreciate a daily Bible study? She could read a few verses and then ask everyone's opinion. Uncertain of exactly where to start, Lily wondered who might advise her. She wished her friend Sarah was with them. She would have bushels of ideas, and the energetic matron would infect all the ladies.

With a sigh, Lily picked up the bowl of butter beans she'd shelled to help Jensen. He was peeling potatoes to go along with his planned lunch of ham and redeye gravy. Her mouth watered as she imagined the delicious—

"Oof." Lily barreled into someone, her momentum causing him to rock back. Her nose was firmly buried in his chest. His hands caught her shoulders and held on as they teetered. In the moment it took him to recover his balance, she knew who held her. Blake's cologne was unmistakable, a heady mix of spice and leather. Why did it have to be him? She pushed at Blake's hard chest and took a step back. "Let go of me."

When he immediately complied, Lily was overcome by a feeling of loss. What was the matter with her? She glanced up at his face.

His gaze met hers, his blue eyes twinkling. A smile softened his face and set her heart thumping. "You've got to start watching your step, or you're going to fall overboard."

"I'm sorry." She forced the words out, her gaze falling to the deck. "I wasn't paying attention."

His hand caught her chin, lifting it with a gentleness that made her breath catch. When their gazes met, she felt it all the way to her toes. Everything in her trembled. Her fingers clung to the bowl of shelled beans as to a life preserver.

"You're working much too hard. We have several new crew members aboard. Let some of them ease your burden." His hand still held her chin, his large fingers cupping her face with disconcerting warmth.

Lily willed herself to take another step back, but her legs refused to obey. She didn't know what to say. Where was the disdainful glint she expected from him? If she didn't know better, Lily would think he was truly concerned about her well-being.

Butterflies fluttered against the walls of her stomach, their wings shutting off her breath. His eyelids lowered, and his head dropped a couple of inches. She swayed toward him, pulled by the gentle tug of his hand.

"Excuse me." The sound of her father's voice was like a bucket of cold river water drenching her. "What's going on here?"

Lily pulled away from Blake's hand with a jerk. Her face flamed as she met Captain Henrick's thunderous scowl. Was her father passing judgment? The man who'd had nothing to do with her upbringing could not think he had any right to dictate her behavior.

"I need to get to the galley." She held her head high and pushed past Blake. All the way down the corridor she felt their eyes on her, but Lily refused to give them the satisfaction of looking back.

As she turned the corner, she thought she heard her father's voice again. Was he angry? And why did she care? With a huff, she thumped her bowl onto an empty counter. "What else can I do?"

Jensen looked at her. "Why don't you go to the ladies' parlor? I served some refreshments awhile back. You look a little. . .upset. A nice cup of tea would calm your nerves."

Lily glared at the man's back, but Jensen focused on his skillet and pots. After a moment she gave up and followed his advice.

As she walked to the parlor, her thoughts drifted back to Blake. What had come over them? He probably couldn't help himself. He was a handsome man, most likely used to women throwing themselves at him. Perhaps he thought she had been making overtures when they collided. Her face burned.

Lily spent the next half hour chatting with the ladies in the parlor. She sipped at her tea and found it did settle her nerves. But she couldn't remain for long. Too much work remained to be done. She placed her porcelain cup on the silver service and excused herself to check on the lunch preparations.

Entering the dining room, she was surprised to find the tables still bare of cloths and plates. Where were Jasmine and David? She was about to look for them in the storage closet they used for a classroom when Tamar entered the dining hall, her arms full of linens. "Where are the children?" Lily took several of the bleached cloths and set them on an empty table.

"They went to the pilothouse to visit the captain." Tamar unfolded a tablecloth with a snap and settled it on another table. "They're not bothering him. I overheard him telling Mr. Blake he loves spinning stories about the river."

"How dare he!" Lily was marching toward the staircase before Tamar could say another word. She moved up the two flights of the boat so quickly it was as though she'd grown a pair of wings and flown. She couldn't wait to give Captain Henrick a piece of her mind.

"And he always claimed he'd been chewed up and swallowed by that ol' alligator."

Blake laughed out loud as much at the round eyes of Jasmine and David as at the outrageous ending of Captain Henrick's tall tale.

"What do you think you're doing?"

Lily's wrathful question wiped Blake's smile off his face. He turned to face her. "What's wrong now?"

"It's nothing to concern you. This is between Captain Henrick and me."

Blake put himself between her and the pilothouse. "What concerns our employees concerns me."

"Let me pass." She tried to push him out of the way.

He put his hands on her shoulders. "Not until you calm down."

Lily redirected her ire at him, but Blake simply returned her stare. She might be able to cow old men and children, but she would find herself at a loss if she tried to intimidate him.

The staring contest continued a moment or two before the fire died out of her eyes.

He felt someone standing next to him and looked down to see Jasmine peeking at her oldest sister, a look of contrition on her face. "I'm sorry, Lily. Is it already time for lunch? David and I'll go downstairs right away."

"I'm not angry at you, Jasmine." Lily's voice had calmed. "But you do need to help Tamar."

"Yes, ma'am." Jasmine and David scurried past, their footsteps clanging as they rushed down the stairs.

Blake waited to make sure they were out of earshot before speaking again. "Now what's this all about, Lily?"

She glared past Blake's shoulder at the captain. "He broke his word."

"I have not."

Blake let her pass and turned toward the pilothouse. "Why don't you explain what's wrong instead of making accusations?"

Lily pointed a finger at Captain Henrick. "He promised he would not try to win the affections of my sisters, but he wants to make them love him. I'm not going to stand for that. I don't want to see their hearts broken like mine was when he deserted us."

Captain Henrick looked like he'd been slapped. Although Blake could understand why Lily was so protective of her sisters, he thought she had gone overboard. "I was here with Jasmine and David. All the captain was doing was telling them a story about Mike Fink."

Her expression didn't change. "I don't care what he was doing. I don't want him to influence my sisters in any way."

"So you want him to be unkind to them?" Blake shook his head. "That sounds like an odd request."

He glanced toward Captain Henrick in time to see the man hiding a grin.

"Of course I don't want him to be unkind. But he can maintain some distance."

Captain Henrick's face smoothed out. "Lily, I hate to contradict you, but I never promised I wouldn't talk to my daughters. I haven't seen Jasmine since she was a baby—"

"And whose fault is that?" Lily's accusation cut off his words.

Blake put a calming hand on her arm. He didn't want her to say something she would regret later.

The captain nodded. "I take full responsibility for that, but Lily, you don't know all the circumstances. You don't know how much I've changed since those dark days."

Blake could feel the tension in Lily's body. Like a taut bowstring, she was ready to unleash a hailstorm of arrows to pierce her father's heart. He could remember feeling the same way toward his father. And he knew from experience that the path she and her father were on would lead to loneliness, remorse, and grief.

"Although I think you and Lily should sit down together and talk about those days, this is not the right time." Blake squeezed Lily's arm to make sure he had her attention. "You need to do it when neither of you is this upset."

"I am more than willing to talk to my daughter about the past." Captain Henrick looked at him first before turning his gaze toward Lily. "I pray that one day she will find a way to forgive me. And I promise to continue loving her no matter how she feels about me."

Lily rolled her eyes. "And in the meantime you'll try to steal my sisters from me."

Understanding flashed through Blake. "Is that why you let Camellia stay with an aunt and uncle you cannot abide? Are you afraid you'll lose her love?"

"Of course not. I let Camellia remain with *my grandmother* because she begged me to let her stay and take part in the Natchez social whirl. It had absolutely nothing to do with him. I acceded to her wishes because I want her to be happy. It's what I want for both of my sisters. And I happen to know they won't be if they discover that our father is alive and then have to mourn him once again when he deserts us—them."

"I'm not sure you're being completely honest with yourself." Blake hoped his words would penetrate the wall of distrust she'd built. "You need to spend some time thinking about your actions and decisions."

"Lily is being very sensible given my history." Captain Henrick shoved his hands into his pants pockets. "I won't tell them who I am unless you say I can, Lily. That's what I promised in New Orleans, and you can count on me to keep that promise. But you can't expect me to be this close to Jasmine and not try to spend time with her."

Blake nodded his agreement. "The captain's not doing anything more than Jensen in keeping them entertained while you and Tamar are busy. You don't have a problem with that, do you?"

"Of course not, but Jensen—"

"Is no different in Jasmine's eyes than Captain Henrick." Blake let his gaze rest on a lock of Lily's hair that had come loose. It gleamed in the bright sunlight, and he found himself wanting to touch it to see if it felt as silky as it looked.

Lily's gaze met his, and her brown eyes widened as if she could read his thoughts. He needed to focus on the conversation, not her hair. Blake cleared his throat. "If you continue to object to her spending time up here, Jasmine is going to wonder why there's a difference. First she'll ask questions that you don't want to answer. Then she'll turn to the captain. She's an intelligent little girl. She will see through your pretense. And you'll have no one to blame but yourself when both of your sisters turn their backs on you."

He could see the pain in her eyes and the sudden paleness of her cheeks. Blake wanted to cut out his tongue. He hadn't meant to hurt her. He'd only wanted to get through to her. "I'm sorry."

"No." Her voice cracked a little. She cleared her throat. "I'm the one who should apologize. You're right, Blake. Both of you are right. I shouldn't have gotten so upset. It's just that I'm so worried they'll be hurt."

"You can stop worrying about that, Water Lily." Captain Henrick smiled at her, a wealth of sorrow in his eyes. "No matter what happens, I'll make sure I never hurt any of you again."

She nodded, the color returning to her face. "I'm trying to believe you."

Blake squeezed her arm to show his appreciation for her words. When she turned her gaze to him, his breath stopped. He'd never before seen so much depth or heart in a woman. A fierce desire rose in him to wrap his arms around her and protect her from whatever or whoever might try to harm her.

His hand moved up and tucked the loose lock of hair behind her ear. Her mouth parted, and her gaze dropped to his lips. If Captain Henrick had not cleared his throat, Blake had no idea what might have happened. But she pulled away and ducked her head.

"I have to get downstairs." She murmured the words and slipped out of the pilothouse, not glancing at either of them.

Chapter Thirty-eight

Tamar shook her head. She was worried about Lily. The poor thing was working herself to death. If she didn't slow down, she was likely to collapse. Then what would they do?

She covered the remaining tables and dusted her hands off. The plates and silverware were needed next. Heading to the galley, she breathed a sigh of relief to find it empty. With David and Jasmine otherwise occupied, she didn't have time for Jensen's tomfoolery. She grabbed a couple of the baskets they used for transporting dinnerware and begin filling them.

"What are you doing in my galley, woman?"

Jensen's voice made her gasp and spin around. "I thought you were busy doing something else."

"I see." He tapped a wooden spoon against one hand. "I guess you forgot I'm the one in charge of the cooking."

"Of course not." His presence made the galley shrink and grow much, much warmer. She tried to slow her pounding heart. What was it about this man?

"Why won't you be kind to a poor, heartsore man?" His gravelly voice held a plaintive note. "I'm only trying to win a smile from the woman I love."

Tamar pointed a finger at him. "If you don't quit talking such nonsense and leave me alone to do my chores, I'm going to take that spoon and use it on your head."

He chuckled. “It might improve my looks.”

Tamar tried to keep from smiling, but it was a losing struggle. She turned to the baskets in an attempt to ignore him. Another impossibility. When the room behind her grew quiet, she sighed. He must've decided to take her at her word. Had she finally convinced him she wasn't interested in him? “Silly man.”

“And here I thought you were the one being silly.”

She jumped a foot and managed to overturn the laden baskets. Everything would have to be washed again. Tamar rounded on him. “Now look at what you've done.”

Jensen stood next to the stove, his arms crossed over his chest. “Me? All I'm doing is trying to catch the attention of the purtiest girl on this boat.” He lifted one of the lids and sniffed the contents. “You see, she's taken my heart, and I want hers in a sort of bartering deal.”

Charmed in spite of herself, Tamar picked up the tableware that had fallen and moved to the large sink on the far side of Jensen. “I've told you before it won't work. You shouldn't be so stubborn.”

He shook his head, one hand going to his scar. “Why won't it work, *cher*? Is it because I'm so ugly?”

“Of course not.” She put the dishes in the sink and reached for a dishcloth. “I'm too old for you.”

“Age don't matter to me.” He sidled up next to her and put a hand on her arm, stilling her movements. “You'll have to do better than that.”

Tamar looked down at the soapy water, tears burning her eyes. She would've thought he was smart enough to figure out the real reason she had to deny him. But apparently she was going to have to be brutally honest. Once he understood, Jensen would have to stop pursuing her. One hot tear leaked out and landed on his hand.

“What is it, Tamar?” His voice no longer teased. “Do you think I want anything less than marriage with you? Is that the reason you're crying?”

“No, Jensen.” She pulled away and wiped her tears. “I know you're an honorable man. That's not the problem.”

“What is it? Please tell me.”

She closed her eyes. “I–it won't work because you're a freeman.” There, she'd said the words. Tamar wished expressing them made her feel better. She felt like she'd aged at least a hundred years.

“Is that what's been worrying you so, woman?” He stepped back a pace, his laughter filling the air.

Shocked at his response, Tamar turned to face him. She had to make him understand. Jensen was a warm, caring man who deserved better than a worn-out old slave for a wife. "You cannot tie yourself to me. Don't you see, Jensen? I work for Lily and her sisters. I don't have time or the right to be a wife and mother."

A noise at the door warned her they were no longer alone. Tamar looked past Jensen's shoulder and saw Lily, a look of dismay on her face. Tamar dropped her rag and moved to the girl. "I don't know what you heard. We were just talking. You have so much to deal with, please don't make this your concern."

"But it is. How can it not be when I'm the one coming between you and Jensen?"

Tamar recognized the determined look on Lily's face. It was the same look she'd worn when she'd decided to rebel against her relatives and set up housekeeping on a riverboat. But this problem could not be solved by determination.

She opened her mouth, but Lily shook her head. "You needn't try convincing me otherwise, Tamar. I'm going to set you free so you can live your life in a way you choose."

"You don't know what you're saying, Miss Lily." She pointed a finger at the younger woman. "You don't own me. Your grandmother does. And when she dies, I'll become the property of whoever she wills me to. I was born a slave, and that's what I'll be until they lay my body in its grave."

Tamar had been so focused on convincing Lily of the folly of her words that she'd forgotten Jensen was still there. He cleared his throat. "I think I have the answer for both of you."

Lily lowered her chin a smidgen, but a frown still marred her face. "What's that?"

"I'll pay the purchase price to your relatives and set Tamar free."

"You can afford that?"

A confident smile accompanied Jensen's nod. "I've managed to put some money aside over the years."

"I can help, too. We made a small profit from our first voyage, and we're going to make even more once we dock in Memphis this evening." Lily's chin moved to its normal level. "We can make this work."

"Wait a minute." Tamar couldn't believe they were talking about her and her future as if she wasn't in the room. "What if I don't—" She stopped. What could she say? That she didn't want to be free? Tamar sent a pleading look toward Jensen. "I can't let you spend that kind of money."

Jensen snorted. "You can't stop me. I'm free, remember?"

Tamar looked from one to the other. A whole new world seemed to be opening for her. It was an exhilarating, absolutely terrifying idea. She'd always known what was expected of her. She'd even had the added benefit of loving all three of her charges as if they were her daughters.

If she let Jensen and Lily do this, everything would change. Lily and her sisters would replace her with another slave. Then what would she do? Tamar had never considered a different future, and she didn't know if she could do so now.

With a wordless cry, she tossed the rag down and ran from the room. Why did life have to be so difficult?

Lily recognized Eli Thornton the minute she saw him. He had his father's good looks and his mother's wise gaze. As soon as he found out who she was, he welcomed her with open arms, offering to let Jasmine, David, and her, along with Tamar, sleep in their home for the duration of their stay. David had asked to remain on board the *Hattie Belle* with the other men, and she had agreed.

They would be leaving in two days, and Eli assured her they would be fully loaded with cargo. One thing was certain—Uncle Phillip had been right about the money available in the shipping business. They were already making more money than she had imagined. Their profit margin was good enough that she would soon be able to buy out Blake's interest in the *Hattie Belle*. He could purchase another boat and fleece innocent victims.

Dinner that evening was a lively affair. Lily took an instant liking to Eli's wife, Renée, a perky beauty with dark hair and hazel eyes. With all three of Eli and Renée's boys joining them, there was scarcely a lull in the conversation. They peppered their guests with questions about current events in New Orleans and the rest of the Thornton clan.

As soon as the meal was over, Lily pled exhaustion and escorted her yawning sister to their bedroom. So tired were they that she didn't even notice the locations of the other bedrooms. She almost fell asleep while Tamar brushed and plaited her hair, her head nodding like a snag in the river. Even Jasmine's animation was muted as they said their prayers and climbed into their shared bed.

Her youngest sister was asleep as soon as her head settled on the pillow, but Lily was so exhausted she was unable to rest. Scattered images spun in her head. Had Blake been about to kiss her? A shiver passed through her. He was not the right man for her, even if he was devastatingly handsome. Good looks had nothing to do with what was in a man's heart. No, she would be better off with someone like Jean Luc, someone she could count on to support her.

She wondered why no shiver erupted as she considered being kissed by him. Probably because he was such a fine gentleman. He would never take advantage of her. Not that Blake had taken advantage. But he had wanted to. She'd seen it in his expression. Or was that her imagination?

Lily sighed and redirected her thoughts to Camellia, wondering if she missed them. Probably not. Jasmine twisted in the bed and punched her with a bony knee. Lily smiled. Camellia certainly would not have enjoyed sharing the bed. If Jasmine kept moving, she was not likely to enjoy a restful slumber herself. . . .

"Wake up." A small hand shook Lily's shoulder. "Wake up, Sissy. Something's wrong."

Lily rolled over and blinked at the unfamiliar room. "Wha—" A hand covered her mouth, pulling her into wakefulness with a start. Her heartbeat slowed as she realized it belonged to Jasmine.

"I think someone is breaking into the house," Jasmine whispered close to her ear. "What should we do?"

Holding her breath, Lily stretched her hearing to its limit. At first she heard nothing but silence. Then a thump, bump, bump. She could feel her eyes widening.

"Did you hear that?" Jasmine's whisper was fearful.

In the dim light, she could barely make out her sister's face. She nodded and pushed back the sheet. "Stay here."

Lily tiptoed to the door and opened it an inch. Crash! Her heartbeat ratcheted up another few notches. She glanced around the room for a weapon and picked up her parasol. It was not much better than her bare hands, but the sharp point at the end of the spine might make an effective threat. Looking over her shoulder, she summoned a smile for Jasmine, who was sitting up, her knees drawn to her chin.

Should she knock on Eli and Renée Thornton's bedroom door? Lily took a moment to look at the other three doors that faced the second-floor landing. Which one belonged to the parents? She didn't want to wake the children, so Lily crept to the top of the stairs, her parasol held high.

Yellow light made a pool in the hallway leading toward the back of the house. A dark figure must be the burglar. He stumbled into a wall. Then another figure appeared. How many burglars were in the house? Praying for courage and protection, she crept down the stairs.

"Halt!" Her voice came out in a squeak. Both figures stopped. She couldn't see their features because of the light behind them, but she brandished her parasol, holding it like a sword in front of her.

"Miss Anderson? What are you doing down here?"

Lily lowered her parasol as she recognized Eli Thornton's voice. "What's going on?"

She could barely make out his features. And who was standing next to him? A servant? Was he being forced to help a burglar?

"Everything is fine, Miss Anderson. You need to go back to bed." Eli spoke as both he and the other man stepped into the light. The staid butler? Why were the two of them creeping about the house in the middle of the night?

"Not until you tell me what you're doing up at this hour."

Eli's sleeves were rolled up to his elbows, and he held a bowl in his hands. His expression was tense, much more drawn than earlier in the evening. Before he could answer her, a door opened farther down the corridor. "Where's that warm water?"

The butler took the bowl from Eli and moved toward the voice.

When Lily tried to follow him, Eli stepped into her path. She brandished her parasol even though the action felt a bit silly. "Whatever is going on must be serious. Perhaps I can help."

"It would be much easier if you returned to your bedroom, but if you'll promise not to tell anyone about what you see. . ."

Lily nodded, and they entered the Thorntons' library.

Several of the Thorntons' slaves were in the room, most of them focused on a figure propped against the edge of Eli's desk. The poor fellow looked a mess, his clothing in tatters, his feet bare. The coppery scent of blood filled the air. She glanced at Eli. "Is he a fugitive?"

Eli nodded. "He escaped from a plantation a few miles south of here because his master whipped him nearly to death for answering too loudly."

Lily's mouth dropped open. She'd heard whispers of mistreatment by slave owners, but at Les Fleurs, no slave ever suffered. "That's inexcusable."

Everyone had been watching her with fear, but apparently reassured by her reaction, they went back to their tasks, some offering food and water while others cleaned the poor man's back.

Eli removed a vial from his shirt pocket and shook it vigorously. "Would you pour some water into one of those glasses?"

Looking about, Lily spied a serving tray on Eli's desk. It held two glasses and a pitcher of water. "How much?"

"Half full."

Lily complied and held the glass while Eli poured his concoction into it. "What's that?"

"Laudanum. It will help him sleep." Eli grabbed a spoon from the tray and stirred. "Then perhaps he can continue on his way tomorrow night."

"The Underground Railroad?" Lily whispered the words. She'd heard of the escape route but never dreamed she would be privy to one of the way stations.

Eli nodded. "Now you know what a dangerous secret we're keeping."

"I's sorry." The fugitive groaned out the words. "I didn't mean to. . ."

A rounded woman who might be the housekeeper patted his hand. "Don't worry. We're doing nothing more than our Christian duty."

The man subsided and let Lily hold the glass of water to his lips.

"Lily?" Jasmine's whisper drifted down the hall. "Where are you?"

"You need to go back upstairs." Eli's gaze met hers. "We can't have the whole household waking up and catching us."

Conflicting desires warred within her, but Lily could not ignore the needs of the frightened, desperate man. "I'll reassure Jasmine, but then I'll be back to help."

Before anyone could argue, she retraced her steps. Jasmine was leaning over the balustrade. "It's okay, Jasmine. It's only a late-night guest." She helped Jasmine return to bed. "Go to sleep."

"Where are you going?"

"Back to help."

"Can't I help?" Jasmine's voice was plaintive.

Lily kissed her cheek. "You need your sleep."

Jasmine's lower lip protruded as Lily left her, but she must have fallen back asleep quickly, as the only sounds emanating from her were the deep breaths of restful slumber. Lily was relieved. Although Jasmine's tender heart would have been touched, she was still a child. Helping an escaped slave was a hanging offense. She might risk her own neck, but she would not risk Jasmine's.

The next hour passed quickly as Lily helped bandage the man's wounds. While she worked alongside the others, the fugitive described his ordeal. He spoke of the girl he'd married by jumping the broom, as slaves couldn't legally marry, and how he'd probably never see her again because she'd been sold to another plantation. He talked about the daily quota of cotton expected of every able-bodied slave. He even spoke about other punishments he'd endured. His back, crisscrossed by a web of gashes, bore mute testimony to the truth of his story.

Thinking of his pain made Lily sick. No human should be so cruel to another. The events of this night had been seared into her memory with the force of a brand. She would never forget.

The sun was turning the sky a pale pink as she trudged upstairs and fell into bed. Sleep overtook her as soon as her head hit the pillow, but Lily's dreams were filled with fractured images of being chased through swamps, her parasol in one hand as the muddy water dragged at her skirts.

Chapter Thirty-nine

Walking past the storeroom filled with crates and barrels, Lily realized the nightmares had begun to fade. Over the past weeks, they had repeated the run between Natchez and Memphis, making regular stops in Port Gibson, Vicksburg, and Greenville. Business was thriving.

If only Camellia had not been adamant about staying with Grandmother and Aunt Dahlia until they took the promised trip to New Orleans. But every load seemed slated for delivery to Memphis. Feeling torn between business and family obligations, Lily had reluctantly yielded to her younger sister's wishes. She wanted to avoid the type of coercion that had sent her fleeing after Grandfather's death. It wasn't the easiest option, but she prayed it was the best one.

Lily sighed as she turned toward the ladies' parlor. At least the Lord had blessed her idea of using afternoon tea as an opportunity for Bible study. No matter how diverse the women passengers were, they seemed to enjoy discussing how to apply the Bible to their daily problems. Today she would suggest reading John 7 about the rivers of living water, the Holy Spirit, which flowed inside all believers.

The afternoon was far advanced when Blake called her out of the ladies' parlor. "Captain Henrick says we'll need to stop and purchase more firewood."

Stopping at wood yards was a normal occurrence, so Lily wondered why Blake thought it necessary to let her know. Did he have another reason to seek her out? Her heart turned over, rushing blood to her cheeks. "That doesn't sound like much of a problem."

His brow furrowed. "It will stop us from reaching Natchez this evening unless you want to risk the boat by continuing after dark."

Comprehension brought a sense of irritation. "Why didn't we stop at an earlier yard? The captain must have known this would happen. We've been up and down this stretch of river several times."

"Lily, can't you let go of your distrust a little?"

His question speared her conscience. Was she being too hard on her father? No. He was supposed to be a seasoned captain. "I would expect the same thing from any captain. By making a mistake like this, he's put the *Hattie Belle* at risk. Why can't you see that?"

The furrow deepened. "What I see is that you are as quick to condemn Captain Henrick as you have been me. I don't understand, Lily. No one on this boat wants to fail, least of all your father. Can't you see how he's trying to win your approval? Last month when we were in New Orleans, you were full of advice about how I should reestablish a link with my family. Maybe it's time for you to listen to your own counsel."

Not wanting Blake to see how his words had affected her, she turned away. A tear trickled down her cheek. Lily refused to be the type of woman who used tears to blackmail a man into doing what she wanted. She was stronger than that. Brushing the tear away with an impatient finger, she took a deep breath and tried to understand why Blake was championing Captain Henrick. What possible reason could the man have for failing to have enough wood on board? If he was as good a captain as he'd claimed, he would not put them in peril. She slammed the door on her emotions and took a deep, cleansing breath.

Blake's hands came down on her shoulders and pressed gently to turn her around.

Lily didn't want to look up. "He's supposed to be captaining this ship. That's the only thing I need from him."

"Lily, both of us know what it's like to make mistakes. You can be so warm and accepting toward others. You are a gracious hostess and a capable manager. Why can't you yield just a little to the captain?"

She glanced up. His eyes drew her in. Their blue depths promised understanding and comfort. Then his lids drooped a bit, and the blue fire in his gaze singed her. Whatever she'd been about to say slipped from her mind. No wonder all their lady passengers—all ladies in general—found him so attractive.

"No matter how hard you try to ignore it, he is your father." Blake's voice was as tempting as a soft pillow.

Lily could feel herself yielding. She pulled away, and as soon as he let go, her mind began working again. She needed to focus on their current problem. "Can we spend the night at the wood yard?"

"I suppose so. According to Captain Henrick, Sanderson Wood Yard is only a few miles away. But stopping now means we'll lose several hours of travel."

She chewed at her lower lip. "Whether we stay here or stop somewhere else, we won't make it home in time to attend church in Natchez."

He shrugged. "Maybe you could have a service on the boat."

Was Blake actually suggesting a church service? She considered the idea then shook her head. "We don't have a preacher on board."

"Captain Henrick could lead a service."

Her jaw clenched to hold back the flood of emotions that once again threatened. "He's not a preacher."

His shoulders lowered a notch. Was he disappointed? "He may not be a preacher, but he has a great deal of insight on matters of faith. If you spent a little more time with him, you might change your mind."

Lily wanted to shout a denial. She had to protect herself. Otherwise— She reined in her thoughts once more. For now she would concentrate on the original problem. She needed to answer the question of what to do after purchasing wood. "There aren't any other ports between here and Vicksburg, so if we continue, we'd be alone when we docked." Lily shuddered. "We'd be vulnerable to pirates."

"That's true, but there've been no reports of pirates operating on this part of the river for years."

Lily spread her hands, palms upward. "We have several children on board—passengers as well as David and Jasmine. I can't take a chance that someone might be hurt. At the most we'll lose a day."

"Do we have enough food?"

She gave an emphatic nod. "I think we have enough for an extra week."

"That's fine then. I'll notify Captain Henrick and the crew."

Lily reached for the doorknob to the ladies' parlor. "I'll tell our passengers." But before entering the room, she watched Blake's retreating back, her mind replaying his words. She didn't like admitting it, but he had a point. She didn't want to be the type of hypocrite who dispensed advice but refused to follow it. Yet she couldn't reach out to her father—not unless she asked for God's help.

Which led to a concern at the heart of the matter. How would she respond if God did smooth out a path toward reconciliation?

❧

Blake slid into the empty seat next to Lily, nodding to David and Jasmine on her far side. The dining hall looked very different this morning. The tables had been pushed to one side, and all the chairs had been placed in rows for the Sunday service.

Tamar and Jensen stood with the passengers' slaves at the back of the room. Jensen's face was clean shaven, and he wore a recently pressed suit. Tamar was in a uniform but looked different—younger and more relaxed. Blake thought perhaps her hair had a new style, or maybe it was the half smile on her lips. Whatever the change, he approved.

His gaze came back to Lily, so prim and proper. He wondered what she thought of his presence.

When Henrick told him Lily had invited him to preach, Blake had been shocked. The captain had seemed pleased about the opportunity although aware his daughter was not ready to seek reconciliation. Blake had reminded him that Lily's actions were a good sign and might be the beginning of a real relationship between father and daughter.

Blake wondered if his conversation with Lily had gotten through her stubbornness. It was a sobering thought. For her to listen to his advice meant she valued his opinion. Was that why he found himself attending this morning? A response to her willingness to change? Or was he just curious?

He would rather believe he was here because of his admiration for Captain Henrick. At least the man was trying to make amends for his past misdeeds. The captain had told Blake how he'd plunged into despair after his wife died. But the man had managed to pull himself out of the hole he'd dug. He'd created a new life for himself. He was even trying to reconcile his past.

Captain Henrick gave all the credit for his transformation to God, but Blake thought he should accept a measure of recognition himself.

It took a lot of determination to turn one's life around. The river towns were full of men like the captain had once been—men who eked out a miserable existence, slogging through life with a minimum of effort, looking for handouts or opportunities to prey on others.

After the passengers stopped entering the dining hall, Captain Henrick stood to get their attention. Dressed in his trademark red shirt and dark pants, the man still managed to look very natural standing before a group of people. His smile was wide and infectious. "Good morning. What a beautiful Lord's Day we are enjoying. This morning I thought I would talk to you about a passage from Isaiah."

He stopped and looked at the floor. Blake wondered if he'd been stricken by fear. He could certainly understand an attack of nerves. He wished he could reassure the captain. Shuffling his feet, he wondered if he should do something to ease the building tension in the quiet room.

Captain Henrick looked up, a serious expression on his weathered face. "Before I get started, I think you should know how proud I am to stand up here. When my. . .employer asked me to talk to you this morning, I thought she was joking." Several chuckles came from the audience. "I'm not a preacher, but the Good Book says you don't have to be to talk to others about God. You only have to be willing. I thought about that and how I want to serve God. Then I thought you might like to hear about how an angry old sinner like me came to be a believer. So I went back to the passage that the Lord used to get my attention."

He opened his Bible and began reading. " 'To appoint unto them that mourn in Zion, to give unto them beauty for ashes, the oil of joy for mourning, the garment of praise for the spirit of heaviness; that they might be called trees of righteousness, the planting of the Lord, that he might be glorified.' "

He bowed his head. "Dearest Lord, we come to You today with hearts full of thankfulness, hearts full of love and devotion. And for those among us who are struggling or grieving or lost, I ask that You fulfill Your promise to give them 'beauty for ashes.' Thank You, Lord, for listening. Please pour out Your Spirit on us today. Amen."

A rustling swept the room as the listeners settled in for the sermon, but to Blake's ears it sounded different. The hair at the back of his neck stood up. He had heard of the Holy Spirit, of course, but he'd never put much stock in such things. He wanted to look around, see if some ghostly mist floated in the air behind him, but he resisted the impulse.

"I remember the first time I read this scripture." Captain Henrick's face was relaxed. "I was in a deep, dark hole. I had done a terrible thing, for which I could not seek forgiveness." He looked over the crowd. "Some of you may be feeling the same way this morning. Some of you may think you can never seek the Lord."

Captain Henrick's gaze settled on Blake. What did the man think he'd done that was so awful? Blake thought back over the years since he'd left home. He hadn't been so bad. He'd never killed anyone or stolen anything. He squared his shoulders and stared back at Lily's father, his sympathy gone. What did Captain Henrick know about anything?

"I was lying in the ashes of despair. I mourned for things from my past. The heaviness described by the prophet Isaiah weighed heavily on my spirit. But God reached out to me. And I stand here today as a testament to His power. I am a different man. I have the peace promised by Jesus. My life is filled with beauty, with the oil of joy, and the garment of praise." Captain Henrick stopped speaking. He closed his Bible.

"Now you may be tempted to seek His blessings just as I was. And I encourage you to do so. But be warned. It doesn't stop there. Your life will become something beautiful and glorious, but that's not the end of it." He opened the Bible again and flipped a couple of pages before continuing. "Listen to the second part of this verse. 'That they might be called trees of righteousness, the planting of the Lord, that he might be glorified.'"

The captain lifted his face up toward the ceiling. "We're not on earth to make a decent living, or to marry and start a happy family. Those aren't bad things, but they are things of this world. They are things we should never see as our goals. We're here to glorify our Maker. He has planted us here for His purpose."

Captain Henrick's lips turned up in a smile of the purest joy Blake had ever witnessed. "Think of it. The Master of all, the glorious Creator, the mysterious I Am. He created you and me to glorify Him through our righteousness. What more wonderful task can we have?"

Blake felt himself caught up in the joy of the captain's sermon. He almost felt the touch of God. He glanced at Lily. Her face was also lit as though from within. She had it, too. Intense yearning swept him. He wanted to feel what they felt. He wanted the joy of knowing God, of living for a higher purpose. The need was so deep and consuming that it nearly brought him to his knees.

But reality seeped in. He couldn't do that. He didn't deserve such a future. It was probably a sham anyway. His own father had been a preacher. Blake knew better than to fall for the empty promises of religion. He would be better off if he'd never given in to the impulse to listen to Lily's father this morning. It would have been a better use of his time to have stayed in bed.

The voice in Blake's head drowned out the rest of Captain Henrick's testimony. He had no need of the emotional flood the man's words could cause. He needed to keep his feet on the ground. Keep working hard.

He and Lily were making a lot of money. Soon one of them would be able to buy out the other. Then they could go their separate ways. He wouldn't have to worry about her prickly morals, and she wouldn't have to fret about his talent with games of chance. All he had to do was keep his focus on the real world, the one he knew so well.

He bowed his head when the others did, his gaze trained on the floor. The yawning jaws of a trap seemed to open at his feet, a snare to deceive those who felt unable to rely on themselves. He refused to fall for it.

Ignoring the dull ache in his chest, Blake followed the others out of the dining hall after the closing prayer. He promised himself he would never submit to another church service.

He ignored Lily's glance and headed toward the engine room. He could not afford to be swept away by pretty words and fake sentiments. Someone on board this boat needed to keep a cool head.

Chapter Forty

Lily stood at the rail as Captain Henrick skillfully navigated them into the dock at Natchez, her mind full of all they needed to do. If the temperature continued to drop, she'd have to ask Tamar to pack warmer clothes for their next trip. Maybe she should learn to pack for herself. Maybe it was time to stop relying on a slave.

After the cargo and passengers had been off-loaded, she went to find Blake. A fruitless search around the lower floors led her to the hurricane deck. She heard his voice before she saw him. He and the captain were talking.

Not wanting to be accused of eavesdropping, she raised her hand. "Hello there."

Both men turned toward her.

"Do you need something?" Blake asked. "I thought you would have gone to your family's home by now."

"I had an idea I wanted to discuss." She hugged herself. It was even colder on the hurricane deck due to the wind. "It's about David."

Blake excused himself from her father and stepped toward her. "Is he causing a problem?"

They walked down the stairs side by side. What would it feel like to walk hand in hand? Suppressing the image, Lily cleared her throat. "No, of course not. David couldn't cause a ruckus if he tried. But he seems more withdrawn lately. Do you have any idea what's bothering him?"

Blake shook his head. "Have you talked to him?"

"I thought I'd ask you to. He seems to look up to you."

"That's just because I'm a foot taller than he is."

A laugh gurgled up Lily's throat. "Stop teasing. You're like a big brother to him. Jasmine told me his father left to search for gold in California. She said he's certain his father is going to return for him someday."

They reached the third floor, empty except for the crewman cleaning the guest rooms. Although the port was as busy as ever, a hush seemed to envelop them.

Blake's expression had grown serious. "I'll talk to him."

Lily put a hand on his arm. "Thank you. I appreciate this, especially since you never wanted to take him aboard in the first place."

"He's been a good companion for Jasmine." He stopped and cleared his throat. "And I have to admit I've grown fond of him, too."

Was it her imagination, or had Blake's cheeks darkened? She squeezed his arm. "Thanks."

❧

Whenever they returned to Les Fleurs, it seemed to have grown smaller. Perhaps it was because Lily had rediscovered how huge the world really was. She smiled at Tamar, who seemed a bit distracted. "I think your mind must still be back on the *Hattie Belle*."

Tamar grimaced. "The longer I'm away from that man, the better."

"What man?" Jasmine's gaze moved from Lily to Tamar and back.

Lily shook her head. "I'll not tell any tales. If you want to find out, you'll have to ask Tamar."

Jasmine's eyes widened. "Who is it, Tamar? Is someone courting you?"

Tamar groaned. "Now why would you say such a thing to Jasmine? You know she'll badger me day and night."

"Jasmine, you are not to bother Tamar with her private business." Lily hoped her command would control her youngest sister's curiosity. Attempting to distract her, she broached a different subject. "Do you think Camellia has a suitor?"

Jasmine moved next to her sister. "She may have a whole line of them."

"I hope not." Lily chuckled at the picture Jasmine's words conjured. Wouldn't the butler be amazed if he answered the door to find not one or two, but a dozen suitors? She would brook no argument from Camellia this time. All three of them would go on the next trip.

Grandmother was sitting on the front porch when the carriage pulled up. As soon as she recognized them, she gave a glad cry, stood, and hurried toward them with widespread arms. "I'm so happy to see you. We were worried something might have happened when you didn't return yesterday as planned."

Lily emerged from the embrace and smiled at the older woman. "You shouldn't worry so. You know we cannot always adhere to a schedule."

"I know, but I will always be concerned for your safety."

Jasmine dashed inside and ran upstairs as Lily and Grandmother followed more sedately. Their happy reunion turned bittersweet as Lily realized Grandmother was probably thinking of the daughter she'd lost to the river.

As soon as she settled her grandmother in her usual chair, Lily sat on the sofa and arranged her skirts. "Is Camellia home this afternoon?"

Grandmother shook her head. "She's out riding with a few young people. That girl has turned into a social butterfly."

The door opened, and Aunt Dahlia entered the room, her head high, a sour look on her face. "I see the wanderers have come home."

Lily decided to ignore her aunt's bad mood. "It's nice to see you looking so well this afternoon." She supposed a lukewarm welcome was all she would ever receive from this woman. And why? Because she had not been interested in the one suitor they had presented? Or was it because she was afraid they would drag the family into scandal? Whatever, it didn't excuse her catty behavior.

Grandmother intervened. "Lily was just telling me about her wonderful crew, giving me a most marvelous idea."

Lily's stomach twisted in a knot.

"How long are you planning to stay with us, dear?"

"Several days, maybe as long as a week." Lily didn't go into all the details. Besides work on the boiler and pistons the captain wanted to see to, Blake wanted to help David find information about his parents, and she wanted to give David every chance to reconnect with his father.

"Oh good, then we'll have time to plan a casual evening."

"Whatever are you talking about?" asked Aunt Dahlia.

Grandmother looked more animated than Lily had seen her since Grandfather's death. "Not a party, mind you. We don't need music or dancing, but we would all enjoy a nice dinner." She paused, beaming a smile toward Lily. "We'll invite Mr. Matthews and your new captain and any other of your business associates. It will be a chance for your family to meet the people who have helped make your venture successful."

Lily blinked several times as her mind spun.

"Well, what do you think?" Grandmother's question was directed at her. "Would you rather schedule it for Thursday or Friday evening?"

"I'm not sure it's a good idea." Lily shuddered as she imagined her family's reaction if Captain Henrick Anderson showed up at their front door. Grandmother would probably faint dead away, Uncle Phillip would throw him out on his ear, and Aunt Dahlia would use him as an excuse to keep Camellia and Jasmine from returning to the *Hattie Belle*.

"I agree with Lily." Aunt Dahlia frowned. "We don't need to advertise the fact that your granddaughters and my nieces are living on a riverboat instead of attending finishing schools."

Although she was much too old for finishing school, Lily did not argue with her unexpected ally. Part of her wanted to defend their lifestyle, the experience they gained by visiting other ports and being exposed to the world of business. Lily hoped she was giving her sisters knowledge they would need to make their own way in the world, but she stopped short of expressing her thoughts. Stopping her grandmother's plans was more important.

"You're being absurd, Dahlia. Everyone knows what Lily and her sisters are doing. We live in much too close a society for something as big as their life on the river to be kept secret." She turned back to Lily. "I think it would be a delightful evening."

"I appreciate the offer, Grandmother, but I doubt whether Captain—" She bit off the word as she realized using even his first name could raise questions she didn't want to answer. "Whether the captain or Mr. Matthews would enjoy themselves."

"I don't see why not."

Breathing a sigh of relief that no one seemed to catch her gaffe, Lily twisted her hands together. She had never foreseen the problems she would face in hiding the captain's identity. The desire to be done with the subterfuge warred with her wish to avoid further confrontations with her family. She had never been—and did not want to become—good at lying.

Grandmother continued to make suggestions. "Why don't you ask them, Lily? If they say no, I'll drop my idea. But they would probably love to meet your family and spend time with us."

Knowing how impossible it would be to convince her grandmother that her plan was an invitation to disaster, Lily decided to avoid further discussion by simply putting her off. "I'll ask them the next time I'm down at the dock."

Her grandmother's eyes lost their luster, and for a moment Lily almost relented. But she needed to keep her heart from misleading her. Delaying a confrontation was the only course to take. Eventually Grandmother would forget her impulse to meet the men.

"I can send them a message if you're not going tomorrow." Grandmother glanced toward her writing desk. "It wouldn't take but a moment. And you can stand over my shoulder to make sure I don't say something that would offend them."

Another crack formed in Lily's heart. "Don't go to any trouble. I'm sure I'll see both of them in a day or two."

"I want the whole world to know how proud I am of you, Lily. You've done something remarkable. You've made your own way in the world. That's an accomplishment we can all appreciate, can't we?" She glanced past Lily to Aunt Dahlia.

"Of course." Aunt Dahlia's confirmation lacked the ring of truth.

Lily wasn't surprised by her aunt's lackluster response. She raised her chin a bit. "Thank you, Grandmother. I'll let you know what they say."

If the captain was any other man, this moment would be filled with unalloyed joy. The acceptance of her family—her grandmother at least—meant a great deal to Lily. But the truth about her father threatened to leech all the pleasure from her grandmother's accolades. She could never let her relatives meet him. Not if she wanted to avoid a disaster that could completely shatter her relationship with her family.

Chapter Forty-one

Jean Luc regarded himself in the mirror, noting with satisfaction the way his hair had been combed toward his face. Combined with the close fit of his coat and the expert twists of his cravat, his appearance epitomized a fashionable gentleman of means. He practiced a wide smile. What female could resist such a handsome fellow?

Lily Anderson. His dimples disappeared. Why did the single woman he needed to woo seem impervious to his charm? At least when he'd called on her at Les Fleurs, she had agreed to dine with him this evening.

He pulled on a pair of gloves and left his bedroom, his mind still chewing on the problem of how to win Lily's affections. Nothing he'd done so far had been very successful. Steenberg had been an absolute disaster, and she and that Matthews fellow had hired a full crew complement before he could suggest someone who would report to him.

Jean Luc considered his plans for their evening. He would take her to the same dining establishment they'd visited before. But this time he had secured a quiet table in a secluded corner. Candles and a fresh flower arrangement would decorate the table, a romantic touch that should impress Lily.

It was a pity she eschewed alcohol, as a glass or two of bubbly champagne would probably put her in a more convivial mood. But perhaps the bottle of effervescent springwater he'd secured would be equally salutary.

He climbed into the family carriage, the conveyance he'd chosen so he wouldn't be distracted by the traffic, and planned what he would say to Miss Anderson on the way to town. He would need to compliment her looks, of course, tell her she was the most charming, witty companion, that he felt honored by her agreement to spend an evening with him. All the things ladies yearned to hear.

His arrival at Les Fleurs was enthusiastic. He sat and chatted with Lily's grandmother, aunt, and uncle while he waited for her appearance. She entered the room, and he stood, allowing his smile to widen as he caressed her with his eyes. He moved toward her, bowed, and kissed her hand. "You look especially beautiful this evening."

As he straightened, Jean Luc saw that Lily's cheeks had reddened. It was a pity she was not a beauty. There was nothing really wrong with her looks, but her face was a little too plain. Her hair was a nondescript brown, and her eyes were about as lovely as a mud puddle.

Perhaps if she wore a color other than black. He recalled the first time they'd met, when she'd been dressed in something white and frilly. Perhaps when she emerged from mourning, she would look better.

"You are very debonair this evening, Monsieur Champney."

He bowed again. "I am honored to please you."

The aunt simpered as though he'd directed his compliments at her.

Jean Luc tucked Lily's hand into the crook of his arm and faced the rest of her family. "Thank you for trusting your treasure to my care."

The grandmother waved a hand at them. "Save your suave compliments for my granddaughter. Now go on, you two, and enjoy your evening."

They climbed into the carriage with a minimum of fuss. As soon as they were settled on opposite benches, Jean Luc rapped on the roof of the carriage with his cane.

"Where are we going this evening?"

"I hope you don't mind, but I wanted to return to the place where we first enjoyed a meal together."

"That will be delightful. I'm sure you remember that I secured my very first cargo that evening."

Jean Luc's jaw clamped. If not for that coincidence, Lily would probably have returned ownership of the *Hattie Belle* to him months ago. "Yes, that's right."

She chattered about her trips to Memphis and yet another branch of the shipping family who had befriended her. He sat back and nodded, biding his time.

They arrived at the hotel, and he escorted her to the dining room. The host caught sight of them and hurried over. "Welcome, welcome. We have your table ready, Monsieur Champney." Bowing repeatedly, he escorted them to the linen-covered table.

Jean Luc hoped Lily noticed how eager the man was to please him. She needed to understand how influential his family was.

After he helped Lily into her seat, Jean Luc slipped an extra coin into the man's palm, which earned him yet another bow. Sliding into his seat on the opposite side of the table, Jean Luc frowned. Although the flower arrangement was lovely, it hid his dining partner from his view. Reaching out, he moved a silver candelabrum closer to the edge of the table and scooted the crystal vase over so he could see Lily's face. "That's better."

If the smile on her face was any indication, he had managed to impress her. She opened her napkin and placed it on her lap. "You must have gone to a great deal of trouble."

"Once you accepted my invitation to dinner, I wanted to make sure this would be a memorable night."

"How could it be otherwise? I always enjoy our time together."

"Then you have forgiven me for offending you the last time we met?"

A fleeting frown crossed her expression. "I could never be truly offended by you, Jean Luc. I value your friendship too much."

That was a start. Jean Luc led their conversation in a different direction as their meal was delivered. Lily ate hers with a bit more gusto than he found attractive, being more used to ladies who picked at their food and abandoned whole plates after only managing to swallow a bite or two. But for now that habit could be overlooked. Once he secured her affection, she would want to please him enough to adopt more genteel habits.

He signaled for their dessert, a chocolate custard accompanied by steaming cups of dark, rich coffee. "I trust you approve of my choices for our dinner."

"Yes." She picked up a spoon and dredged out a mouthful of chocolate. "I'm flattered by your thoughtfulness. You make me feel like a princess."

Jean Luc summoned a burning stare to convince her of his desire. "I would like to do more."

The words fell between them, stilling her spoon halfway between plate and mouth. Her eyes widened. She put down the bite of dessert. "But you've already done so much. I owe you a debt of gratitude."

Leaning forward, he took her hand in his. "Let there be no discussion of debts between us. It is not appropriate when I have such feelings about you. My heart is troubled when you are away. I worry about your safety and think of you almost without ceasing. I wish we were not so often separated by distance."

"But it is delightful to see you whenever I am in Natchez." Her hand fluttered in his hold like a frightened bird.

Jean Luc hid his irritation. "I pine for your smiles when you are not close."

"Your sentiments are very flattering, Jean Luc. I put so much stock in our friendship. You must know how much I rely on your advice and expertise." Her hand stopped fluttering.

"And I will be most happy to advise you, but please tell me that our friendship could evolve into a warmer relationship." He summoned his most devastating smile, one that had won him many favors in the past.

"I don't know. . . ."

He tightened his grasp on her hand. "Has someone stolen your heart from me?"

"Of course not." She tugged her hand free. "I've been much too busy to think of romance. Running a business commands my full attention."

"You must feel overwhelmed by the responsibility." Jean Luc drummed his fingers on the tablecloth. He hoped this was the right time to broach the subject that had been on his mind for several days. "In fact, I have an idea that may help."

"Really?"

He watched her face for a hint of how to proceed. Her features smoothed out so quickly it was like looking at a mask. Was her mind open or closed?

She glanced at the table, and he realized he was still drumming his fingers. He clenched his hand and brought it to his lap. "How would you feel about letting someone else, someone you trust, someone who has your best interests in mind. . ." Jean Luc paused and took a slow breath. "What if such a person offered to take over the day-to-day decisions of your shipping operations?"

"What are you suggesting?"

"I am offering to run the *Hattie Belle*." There. He'd said it. Now he must convince her that his idea was the perfect solution.

"Why would I want to burden you with such a task?"

"Lily, you have seen the river up close. You must know that you are the only woman trying to run her own boat. By your own admission, it is a terrible burden." He reached for his coffee cup. "I think it is admirable that you've given so much to your endeavors. You have proven what you can accomplish, but now it is time for you to come back home. . .settle down. . .perhaps even marry."

"I am quite happy on the *Hattie Belle*."

Jean Luc sipped some of the dark liquid from his cup and set it back on the table. "But you are working much too hard. Don't you see? You should be treated like a princess. If you were here more often, I could court you properly."

She pushed her chair back from the table. "I am not a princess, nor do I aspire to become one."

Jean Luc rose when she did. Was she going to storm out of the hotel? "I meant to compliment you, Lily. I only want you to lead the life to which you were bred."

Her brown eyes filled with flashes of hot emotion. "The life to which I was bred? My father and mother spent many years together on the river. They thought it was a good place to raise a family. I'd say that remaining in Natchez and allowing you or some other man to fawn over me would be contrary to the life my parents imagined for me, wouldn't you?"

He raised his shoulders in a gesture of agreement, but inside he was seething. How dare she spurn his offer? How dare this little nobody—a girl who'd never even seen Europe—look down her nose at him?

Like a volcanic eruption, he felt the anger gathering force. She may have been raised at Les Fleurs plantation, but she was proving a great deal of common blood ran in her veins. "I'm sorry, I must have been mistaken. I suppose you're right. I should have realized that your head has been filled with nonsense from the likes of Blake Matthews and the other wharf rats you've been rubbing shoulders with."

Her mouth open and closed several times, but no words came.

Good. Maybe she was beginning to regret her earlier disdain. But he would be slow to accept her apology. He gestured for their cloaks. "I should take you home."

The ride back was quiet and uncomfortable. Jean Luc got out first and offered her a hand.

She ignored his gesture, climbing out with one hand on the carriage frame and the other lifting her skirts. "Thank you for the meal." Her voice was as cold as winter rain.

Jean Luc bowed and watched as she ascended the stairs and disappeared through the front doors. The minute she was out of sight, he wanted to kick himself. Why had he let himself get so angry? Why hadn't he apologized instead of waiting for her to come to him? He knew how stubborn she was. He would have to demean himself tomorrow and send her a note of apology, maybe a bouquet of flowers. He had to get back in her good graces.

He climbed back into the carriage, his mind on possible solutions. As the coachman headed back to his parents' home, an idea occurred to him. He rapped on the roof of the carriage and shouted new instructions before settling back to contemplate his situation. Maybe he wouldn't need to grovel in front of Lily Anderson after all.

Chapter Forty-two

The housekeeper, Alice, bustled into the crowded kitchen and snapped her fingers at Tamar. "Go see Mrs. Blackstone. She's in the front parlor."

Tamar put down the ear of corn she'd been shelling. "What's wrong?"

Alice settled her hands on her hips. "Can't be Miss Lily or Missy Jasmine. They gone to town to see about that boat y'all been living on."

"Mebbe she's got something special for you to do," suggested the cook.

Mrs. Blackstone's personal maid pursed her lips. "Seems like she'd a-called me for that."

Tamar shrugged as she moved to the pump. "It's probably some rumpus Miss Camellia's caused." She worked the handle and washed her hands in the stream of cool water. After drying her hands on her apron, she removed it and smoothed the skirt of her dress.

"Don't forget your cap." Alice nodded toward the white cloth hanging from a hook on the wall.

"You sure you're not in trouble?" Mary shook her head. "You ain't done nothing wrong, have you?"

"No." Tamar retrieved the cap, shook it out, and settled it on her head. But as she stepped out of the warm kitchen and crossed to the back of the big house, she wondered. Could Mrs. Blackstone have found out about Jensen wanting to court her?

Her heart clenched as she moved from the narrow hallway in the back of the house to the wider corridors the family used. By the time she reached the front parlor, however, her good sense righted itself. No one at Les Fleurs knew Jensen, so she had nothing to fear. She knocked on the door and waited for Mrs. Blackstone's command.

Lily's grandmother was sitting in her chair next to the fireplace. She didn't look angry. "There you are, Tamar." Mrs. Blackstone waved at her to enter. "I need your help with a little project."

"Yes, ma'am." Tamar curtsied and waited.

"I'm sure you know I'm planning a dinner party for tonight as my granddaughters are about to depart once again."

Tamar nodded. It was the reason she'd been helping in the kitchen.

"I can't get Lily to give me a straight answer about her business partner and boat captain. She was supposed to deliver an invitation, but neither of the gentlemen has responded. I would think they would be flattered and even eager to meet Lily's family and friends."

Wondering why Mrs. Blackstone was telling her this, Tamar shifted her weight from one foot to the other.

"I hate to suspect my granddaughter, but I have decided something must have happened to the invitations and she is loath to confess the problem." She sighed and held up two white envelopes. "So I have written out new invitations. Now I need someone to hand deliver these and wait for a response. Of course I could send one of the footmen, but since you know both of the men and they will know you, I thought I would send you instead."

Tamar's heart tripped. She would see Jensen. He had not attempted to contact her since she came back to Les Fleurs more than a week ago. She ought to be glad that he'd stayed away. She'd told him to do just that many times. But now that he'd taken her at her word, she found herself missing his teasing compliments, his easy smile, and the gleam in his coffee-brown eyes.

The door to the parlor opened and Miss Dahlia breezed in with Camellia following a couple of steps behind. "Mama, it's the worst disaster ever."

Mrs. Blackstone turned to her daughter. "What's wrong, Dahlia?"

Her daughter sighed as she sank into a chair. "It's Camellia's dress, the one she is supposed to wear to the dinner party tonight."

"I'm so sorry, Grandmother, but it was an accident." Camellia's eyes were red rimmed. "I was upstairs painting a still life of bananas and apples, and I upset the paints with disastrous results."

"There is a bright spatter down the front of Camellia's new dress." Miss Dahlia took up the tale. "We must take it to the dressmaker to see what may be done to repair it."

Tamar put a hand over her mouth. A disaster indeed. If it had been Miss Lily's dress, she would have shrugged and chosen an older one, but Miss Camellia put much more emphasis on her appearance.

"That's a shame, Camellia." Mrs. Blackstone's calm tone quieted the other two women. "Of course you must take the carriage. I was about to send Tamar to town, so she can ride with you."

Miss Dahlia looked surprised that someone else was in the room. "Of course we can take Tamar."

"That's settled, then." Mrs. Blackstone handed the envelopes to Tamar. "The top one is for the captain."

"Where are you sending her, Mama?"

"To the *Hattie Belle*. I have not heard from either Mr. Matthews or the captain, and it would be a shame if they did not attend because their invitations were not properly delivered."

A spark of interest entered her daughter's eyes. "I was a guest on the boat before Lily purchased it. I've been wondering what changes she's made."

"But I don't want to go back to the river until I have to." Camellia's forehead crinkled.

Tamar edged out of the room as Miss Dahlia warned Camellia to stop frowning or risk premature wrinkles. The joy she'd felt earlier faded as she realized the addition of the two ladies meant she would have no chance of seeing Jensen alone. She might not even be able to leave the carriage if Miss Dahlia decided she wanted to deliver the invitations herself. What had looked to be a delightful outing had become nothing more than another chore.

What else should she expect? She was a slave, not a free woman who could go wherever she chose. For one of the first times in her life, Tamar found herself resenting her lack of freedom.

❧

Lily was more than ready to leave for New Orleans. It seemed so long since she'd seen her friends there. They would have so much catching up to do.

"We should be ready to leave as soon as you get here Monday morning." Captain Henrick glanced toward Blake for confirmation.

"Good. I'll have the girls in the carriage by first light." She was relieved she wouldn't have to continue trying to sidestep Grandmother's plan to have the two men at her dinner party.

Jasmine, followed closely by a laughing David, brushed past Lily's skirts.

"Don't knock any of the crates over," Lily admonished.

David skidded to a halt and looked back at her. "We'll be careful." She would have to be satisfied with his promise, although Lily doubted he could control her youngest sister's exuberance.

"We've come to see where you girls have been living for all these weeks."

Recognizing the voice, Lily whirled toward the gangplank, her mouth falling open as she came face-to-face with Aunt Dahlia and Camellia.

"What on earth are you doing here?" Aunt Dahlia's gaze was fixed on someone standing behind Lily. Then she turned back to Lily. "Why is your father on board your boat?"

"Father?" Camellia gasped out the two syllables. Her shocked face turned toward Lily. "That can't be right. Our father is dead."

"I'm sorry." Lily reached toward her. "I didn't wa—"

"What?" Camellia's shriek rivaled the clamor of a steamship whistle. "You didn't want us to know our father was right here with us?"

"Camellia." Their father stepped toward her. "Don't blame your sister. This is not her fault."

"Of course it is. She knew." Camellia looked past him to Lily. "How long have you known? Why didn't you tell us?"

Lily didn't know what to say. Her sister was right. She should have told them. Even though she'd been only a child when her grandparents decided to tell everyone, including Camellia and Jasmine, that their father was dead, she could have let her sisters know the truth when each grew old enough to understand. She put a hand to her forehead.

"How could you deceive us so?" Camellia's voice broke. She picked up her skirts and ran back to the dock.

"Isn't anyone going to answer me?" Aunt Dahlia's querulous voice drew Lily's attention.

"No." Lily faced down her relative. She wanted to get to Camellia but had the feeling her sister would not listen to her at the moment.

"Not right now. Not while my sister is sitting in that carriage crying her eyes out. She trusts you. Please go comfort her and get her back home. I'll be there soon to sort everything out."

The shock on Aunt Dahlia's face should have been amusing, but Lily couldn't find any humor in this situation. "Please go, Aunt Dahlia. Go take care of my sister."

Her father added his voice to Lily's. "You cannot wish the whole town to know our family business, Dahlia. Your father would be mortified."

"Papa is past worrying about such earthly matters." Aunt Dahlia gathered her skirts. "But I suppose you're right." She glared at Lily. "See that you are home soon."

"What is all the shouting about?" Jasmine and David appeared as Aunt Dahlia marched off the boat. "Where's Aunt Dahlia going?"

Lily looked toward Blake. His sympathetic gaze nearly wrecked her control. Tears burned at the corners of her eyes. She tried to hold the tears at bay.

Apparently their aunt heard her name. She turned back to the boat and pointed at Jasmine. "You need to come with me now."

Jasmine glanced toward Lily for confirmation. Although Lily didn't want her youngest sister to hear about their father from Aunt Dahlia, it couldn't be helped. She needed to figure out how to handle this situation, and she couldn't do that until she talked to her father. Why had she ever let him remain on the *Hattie Belle*?

"Why don't you come up to the hurricane deck with me?" Their father put a gentle hand on David's shoulder. "I've been wanting to show you how to whittle a turtle, and I think now would be a good time." His shoulders drooped as he led the boy away.

Wondering what to do, Lily jumped when someone touched her arm. "Tamar."

"I'm so sorry. I didn't mean to startle you." She held out two envelopes. "Your grandmother wanted me to deliver these to Mr. Blake and Captain Henrick."

"Captain Anderson." She took the envelopes and sighed. "We need to start calling him by his full name. I suppose that's as good a place to start unraveling this knot as any."

"Yes, ma'am."

Blake stepped closer. "I know a certain fellow who's been ornery as a bear since a certain hardhearted female told him to stay away from her."

Tamar's head dropped toward her chest. Were her cheeks darkening? Lily almost smiled at her friend's response to Blake's teasing. But then her problems came crashing down on her once again. What was she going to do? Where could she turn?

She fought a strong desire to loose the *Hattie Belle* from her moorings and float away. But where could she escape her bad decisions? By the time she realized no place would be far enough away, Tamar had disappeared.

"What's going through that head of yours?" Blake's voice was warm, containing none of the condemnation she deserved.

Lily shook her head. She wouldn't—couldn't—cry in front of him.

His hands cupped her elbows, pulled her closer. "It's not that bad, honey."

His reassurance crashed through Lily's defenses. She needed to rest, to lean on his strength. Melting into him, Lily sobbed against his shoulder. After a moment he reached an arm under her knees and picked her up, cradling her against his chest as the hot tears continued unabated. On some level she knew he had moved her out of the way of prying eyes and ears. But mostly she simply released all the worry and dread that had been building inside for so long.

How had everything gone so wrong? Where had the first misstep happened? Was it when she bought the *Hattie Belle*? Or even earlier, when she'd refused to bow to her aunt and uncle's bidding? Perhaps she should have married Mr. Marvin in spite of her misgivings. Or maybe everything would have been different if she'd sent her father away the moment she discovered that Blake had hired him.

Finally the tears ran out. Drained by the storm of emotion, Lily lay against Blake's chest and breathed unsteadily. Little by little she noticed several things. She was sitting in his lap at one of the dining-room tables. His hand was rubbing gentle circles on her back. His shirt was wet under her cheek. She wanted to push away from him but didn't know if she would ever gather the nerve to look him in the eye.

"Feeling better?" His low voice eased some of her embarrassment.

Lily sniffed and lifted her head, her gaze not quite reaching his face. "I'm sorry."

"You don't have to apologize."

She pushed back and reached for the floor with her feet.

"Be careful." He released his hold on her.

"I don't know what's wrong with me." Her voice still sounded shaky, but Lily stood up anyway. "I'm not usually so overcome."

He thrust something under her nose. A handkerchief.

Lily used it to wipe her face.

When she tried to hand it back to him, Blake caught her hand. "Keep it for now."

She shrugged and tucked the damp square into the waist of her skirt. "I don't know what I'll do."

"I'd suggest a cool, wet cloth to wash your face."

A giggle bubbled into her throat. Finally she looked at him. "That's not what I meant."

"Are you asking for my advice?" His eyes, as clear and blue as a summer sky, considered her. For a moment they stood, watching each other. How did he manage to look so handsome, so capable?

"Yes." Lily felt an almost overwhelming urge to place all her burdens on his shoulders, but for now she would only ask for his advice.

"You're going to have to be truthful with your family—every one of them, your sisters, even the aunt and uncle you don't agree with."

She thought she had emptied the reservoir of tears on his shirtfront, but suddenly she could feel the burning of a fresh supply. "I'm afraid they won't forgive me, especially Camellia. She was so hurt and angry when she left."

"Of course she will, Lily. She's your sister. She may be angry with you for a day or two, but she'll come around. She loves you. Both of your sisters adore you. They will forgive you."

The tears receded a bit as his words gave her hope. But another thought intruded. "How can they when I cannot forgive my father for what he did all those years ago?"

A light entered his eyes. "You once told me to make peace with the past and with my father. I'm telling you the same thing today. You have to forgive your father."

She gulped, remembering how easily she had dispensed that advice. Odd how her words had come back to haunt her. Could she let go of the fact that her father had abandoned them when they needed him the most?

Backing away from Blake, she moved toward the bedroom she shared with Camellia and Jasmine. "I'll think about it." She turned and fled before he could extract a promise from her. She needed to do some praying before she decided what to do next.

Chapter Forty-three

The room was as tidy as they'd left it. Lily moved toward her trunk and opened it. She dug through the clothes inside until her fingers closed over the solid edges of the item she sought. Her Bible. Pulling it free, she perched on the edge of her bed.

Clasping the leather volume to her chest, she knelt next to her bed, closed her eyes, and began to pray. The words came slowly at first, but then they began sliding across her mind as she felt His presence beside her.

Lord, You know what's wrong. Please help me figure out how to fix it. I've gotten so far from Your Word, and I'm sorry. Please don't hold that against me. I come to You with my head hung low. I know better than to let my faith grow weak and forgotten in the press of days. I ask for Your forgiveness and patience. Help me to do better. Show me how to lead my sisters so that they will continue to embrace You no matter what our futures may hold. Thank You, Lord, for being so faithful. Amen.

Getting up to sit on the bed, Lily opened her Bible to the New Testament. She flipped a few pages of Matthew's Gospel, her eyes sliding across the familiar verses and stopping when she reached the Lord's Prayer. The words soothed her, bringing peace. Then her breath caught. The warning contained in verse 15 jumped out at her: " 'If ye forgive not men their trespasses, neither will your Father forgive your trespasses.' "

This was the answer she'd been searching for. If she wanted God to forgive her for ignoring Him and trying to do things her own way, she would have to forgive her father. She glimpsed the seriousness of her sin—how she had turned from her Creator, how she had considered herself better than others, how she had relied on her own understanding.

The look of betrayal on Camellia's face haunted her. Yet hadn't she nurtured her own feeling of betrayal? Why had she never told her sisters that their earthly father was alive? Why had she gone along with the lies her relatives had fabricated? Her arrogance had stopped her from telling them, even making him promise to hide the truth. She had thought it would be best for Camellia and Jasmine. Best for everyone. But when had Jesus ever taught that lies were better?

She had to forgive her father for walking away from them. No matter the reasons, no matter the circumstances. Lily looked up at the ceiling. "I want to forgive him, God. I don't want to hold on to the anger and blame any longer. Please help me see him through Your eyes." Warmth spread throughout her body. The pain of betrayal slipped away. Freedom filled with love took its place.

Lily closed her Bible and stood. She couldn't let any more time pass without telling him. She left the room and hurried down the passageway toward the stairs. He would most likely be in the pilothouse. Her feet took wing. She felt like a prisoner seeing the sunshine for the first time in years. She hadn't realized how dark her life had been, overshadowed by anger and distrust.

He stood on the upper deck, looking out at the sea of boats surrounding the *Hattie Belle*, but turned as she walked toward him. "Lily, are you all right?"

Shaking her head, Lily stopped in front of him. "You're not to blame. I'm the one who insisted we hide the truth from my sisters. I want you to come back to Les Fleurs with me. I don't want any more lies between us."

"You don't know what you're saying. You don't know why I left."

"It doesn't matter." She took a deep breath. "What matters is that you want to be near us now. I should have seen that earlier. Please say you'll forgive me. I want things to be different from now on."

His eyes filled with tears. "Lily, you don't have to ask for my forgiveness."

"Yes, I do. . .Papa."

He gasped, and his face crumpled. He opened his arms wide.

Without any hesitation, Lily stepped into his embrace. "I love you, Papa, and I'm glad God brought us back together."

"I'm just so happy to have my Water Lily back." His voice choked with emotion. "You've given me a gift beyond belief, second only to that moment when He entered my heart and changed it forever. I love you so much, my little Water Lily."

Lily hugged him hard, closing her eyes and thanking God for setting them both free. It had taken her far too long to get to this point, but thankfully she was no longer holding on to her bitterness. She only hoped Camellia would forgive her more easily.

❧

The sun was setting as the rented carriage pulled to a stop in front of her grandmother's door. Lily's gaze met her father's as he helped her down from the carriage. He was dressed in borrowed finery loaned to him from Blake's wardrobe. The fit of the blue coat was not perfect, since it would not quite button over her father's midsection, but it looked much better than his usual attire. For this occasion his hat, also borrowed from Blake, had the taller crown and narrow brim befitting a gentleman.

"I still don't think this is a good idea." His face mirrored his uncertainty.

Lily smiled at him. "It's going to be fine. It's about time Mama's family acknowledged you." She swept up the steps and pushed open the door.

Before she took more than three steps, Uncle Phillip emerged from his study. His expression changed from curiosity to outrage. "What is he doing here?"

"He's here at Grandmother's express invitation." Lily lifted her chin and faced her uncle, daring him to continue.

"I don't believe it. Your grandmother would never go against your grandfather's wishes."

Now it was Lily's turn for confusion. Her grandfather, the man who had treated her sisters and her like princesses, had forbidden their father's presence? She turned to Papa. He was studying the marbled floor. "Is it true? Is that why you never contacted us?"

His nod was all the confirmation she needed. If Lily had held any doubts about forgiving this man, they vanished completely. What had that forced separation cost him? "Why would Grandfather do such a thing?"

Her father looked up and met her gaze. "He loved your mother so much. I think it drove him a little crazy when she died. He blamed me, and I agreed with him that I bore the responsibility for her death. He was determined to protect you girls from a similar fate."

"And as his heir, I feel obligated to continue his wishes." Uncle Phillip cleared his throat. "Besides, he's the reason your aunt nearly collapsed from shock. Both of your sisters are in their rooms. I understand Camellia is inconsolable."

Her uncle moved as though to step past Lily, but she stopped him with an angry glare. "All of that is my fault, not his. I'm the one who demanded he keep his identity hidden. When Aunt Dahlia came to the boat, she recognized Papa." Lily shrugged. "I don't see why she should be so overcome, but she is a practical woman. This is a matter between me, my siblings, and our father."

Her uncle sputtered. "I still—"

Lily cut off his words. It was time to remind him that he was far from blameless. "In reality, you have only yourself to blame for Papa's appearance here tonight. If you hadn't tried to force me into marriage with a man I did not love, I would never have gathered the courage to buy a riverboat, and I would not have met my father in New Orleans."

Uncle Phillip's response was drowned out by Grandmother's voice as she opened the parlor door. "Whatever is going on out here?"

Aunt Dahlia was close on her heels. "I can't believe your effrontery."

It seemed her aunt had recovered. It wasn't clear if Aunt Dahlia was addressing her or Papa, but Lily didn't care. She lifted her chin and squared her shoulders. "What effrontery? All I've done is bring my new captain to dinner as Grandmother requested."

"You should know he's not welcome in this house." Aunt Dahlia's voice was heavy with spite. "But trust you to flout the wishes of your family. You have always thought you knew better than anyone else."

Her words struck at Lily's heart. Hadn't she promised God she would not be so rebellious? Did He mean for her to meekly follow her relative's directives, even when they were wrong?

Grandmother clapped her hands and waited until everyone had turned to her. "That's enough melodrama for one evening." She nodded toward Lily's father. "You are looking well, Henrick."

Aunt Dahlia's mouth dropped open. "But—"

"Calm down, Dahlia, and close your mouth before you swallow a fly."

Uncle Phillip put an arm around Aunt Dahlia. "I don't see—"

"Although I dearly loved my husband and would never have countermanded his dictates, I don't believe Isaiah was right to keep my granddaughters separated from their only living parent." She turned to Lily's father and offered him her hand. "I hated seeing them so lost, but I didn't want to oppose my husband. Perhaps now we can bury the past along with poor Rose."

Lily's father bowed over her hand before straightening. "If I could have traded my life for hers, I would have."

Grandmother tucked her hand in the crook of his arm. "I know that feeling well. It is difficult to bury one's spouse."

Grandmother turned to Lily. "Why don't you go talk to your sisters? It's about time for them to celebrate instead of experiencing all these histrionics that Dahlia has encouraged."

"Camellia is overwrought, Mother." Aunt Dahlia pulled away from her husband. "I don't think it's a good idea for Lily to bother her."

"While I am the first to admit that I've made a lot of mistakes, Aunt Dahlia, I am not going to allow you to come between me and Camellia."

"Why do you always imagine I am your enemy, Lily?" Aunt Dahlia put a hand to her forehead. "The good Lord knows I only want what's best for you and your sisters."

Lily could feel her eyes widening. "What's best for—"

"Lily." Her grandmother's voice interrupted her scathing response. She turned to her daughter. "Dahlia, you will not interfere with Camellia further. I believe we can allow Lily to handle the situation in the way she thinks best. And you will smile and converse politely with your brother-in-law tonight and in the future."

Lily escaped to the upstairs bedrooms before anyone else could stop her. Leaning her head against Camellia's door, she took a deep breath and said a prayer for wisdom. Then she knocked and entered.

"What do you want?" Camellia was sitting on the window seat in her dressing gown.

Lily closed the door behind her. "I need to explain why I didn't tell you about Father. I realize now how bad a mistake that was. I'm so sorry. Please say you'll forgive me."

"Do you think it's that easy?" Camellia hunched her shoulders. "Do you think you can waltz in here and tell me you're sorry and I'll say it's okay?"

"No, but I want to explain why I did it."

"Maybe I don't want to listen."

Lily sat beside Camellia and touched one of her sister's ringlets. "I've made a lot of mistakes in my life."

Camellia's eyes opened wide in a perfect imitation of Aunt Dahlia. "Do tell."

Disliking the influence she saw in her sister's behavior, Lily sighed. She had to get her sister away from this world. But for now she needed to concentrate on the current problem. "I know. But please believe me when I say my intention was only to protect you and Jasmine."

"By hiding the truth from us?"

"You're right. It was a terrible idea. But honey, I was afraid our father would burrow his way into our hearts and then disappear like he did when you were barely more than a baby. It was only after I started listening to him that I realized how much he's changed. He asked Jesus into his heart, and it's made him a new man. I no longer think he'll desert us." She hesitated, but now was not the time to hide anything. "And if he does, God will see us through it."

Camellia stood up and walked to her dressing table. She fingered the pearl-handled brush and moved a couple of hairpins around. "I wish you'd let us make the decision to accept Papa or not." Camellia looked toward her, her pale-blue eyes wet with unshed tears. Her bow-shaped mouth was pursed as she considered Lily. "You shouldn't try to keep such things from us, especially me. You're not my mother, you know. And I'm no longer a child."

"I am reminded of that every time I look at you."

"Then why do you treat me like a baby?" Camellia tugged at the sash on her dressing gown. "Why won't you let me take real responsibility? I could help you, Lily. I could do more things on the boat. I am fifteen years old, after all. You can trust me."

Understanding dawned on Lily. Although their father was the ostensible reason for Camellia's anger, the real problem went far deeper. "I'm so sorry. I didn't realize what I was doing."

A tear fell on Camellia's cheek, but it didn't diminish her beauty. Her nose didn't redden like Lily's did when she cried. "That's one reason I like to stay here with Aunt Dahlia. She treats me like I'm grown up."

The comparison was hard to accept, but Lily would have to change if she wanted to remain close to Camellia. "I promise to do better."

A sniff came from Camellia. She managed a wobbly smile. "Thanks."

Lily stood and opened her arms wide. "I love you, Camellia. I can't stand to think I've made you so unhappy."

"I love you, too." Camellia ran into her embrace. "And I haven't been that unhappy. I just want to go to parties and enjoy life."

They hugged each other, and Lily closed her eyes, thanking God for giving her another chance with Camellia. *Please help me do better, Lord.* "Let's get you dressed so we can go downstairs and introduce you properly to our father."

This time Camellia's smile was much steadier. "What about Jasmine?"

Lily nodded. "While you're getting ready, I'll explain things to her. Then we'll go downstairs together and spend some time with Papa."

❧

Jasmine entered the parlor and ran toward their father. She hugged him with enthusiasm. "I'm so glad you're here."

"Me, too." His voice choked with emotion. "Me, too."

At least her youngest sister wasn't going to have trouble adjusting to Papa's reappearance. Lily envied her. How liberating to be young, without all the responsibility of adulthood. She wanted to warn Camellia to stay young as long as she could. But Lily knew that would be a waste of breath. She could well remember when she'd been as eager as Camellia to embrace adulthood.

"Hello, Camellia. . .Lily." Papa nodded in their direction. With one arm still around his youngest daughter, he stepped forward.

Camellia curtsied, her skirts wide, her face downcast. "Good evening… sir. I am happy to welcome you to Les Fleurs."

So that was how her younger sister was going to react? She was hiding behind etiquette. Lily couldn't blame her. Who knew better than she how hard it was to trust a man who had deserted them. Perhaps if she showed that she had forgiven their father, Camellia would follow her example.

She moved toward her father and gave him a quick kiss on the cheek. "Would you prefer we call you Father or Papa?"

While he considered his answer, Lily sat and motioned for Camellia to join her. Jasmine left her father's embrace to perch on the tufted footstool in front of Grandmother's chair.

After they were seated, Papa sat in a wooden chair near the fireplace. "Whichever you prefer."

Lily cocked her head. "I think Papa suits you best."

He nodded, a thankful smile lighting up his features. "Papa it is, then."

Jasmine sprang from the stool. "Papa, I'm so glad you found us."

His smile widened. "I am, too, little one. God is very good to me."

"Will you be continuing to captain Lily's boat. . .sir?" Camellia's hands were clenched in her lap. She let out a brittle laugh. "Or will you be chaperoning us here in Natchez?"

Like an anxious parent, Lily watched the emotions flitting across her sister's face. Anyone else might have thought Camellia poised and self-confident. They might not have caught the slight hesitation before she decided not to call him Papa. But Lily was her sister. She knew Camellia well. She recognized the uncertainty in her blue eyes. And she had the advantage of knowing firsthand the distrust her sister was experiencing. Until she had turned back to God, Lily had felt the same way.

Camellia needed to return to the *Hattie Belle*. Once she was around Papa more, she would accept him. He might not be perfect, but the love he had for them was plain to see. He had respected Lily's wish that he remain anonymous, showing a patience and understanding that she realized now could be likened to Jesus' love for mankind.

Now that she and Camellia had a better understanding, maybe Camellia wouldn't resist coming back to the boat. Lily hoped she wasn't trying to manage her sister. But regardless of what Camellia might think, she would be much better off aboard the *Hattie Belle*.

Lily put her arm around Camellia's waist. "Shall we join Grandmother for dinner? I'm sure they are wondering where we are."

"May I come, too?" Jasmine asked with a hopeful expression.

Lily shook her head. "I thought you already ate your supper before I got back to the house."

Jasmine's face fell. "I don't get to do anything fun. I wish I was back on the *Hattie Belle*."

"Don't worry." Their father stood and placed a comforting arm around her shoulders. "We'll be leaving in a few days, and you and I will have plenty of time to become close friends."

After Jasmine climbed the staircase, the others entered the library. Lily wished Blake were here to offer support, but he had declined, saying that her family needed time to themselves. At least they didn't have to contend with other guests. She could not imagine trying to make polite conversation with some vapid planter's wife after the emotional upheaval they had been through.

Why was Camellia so eager to join the gossip-filled, narrow-minded world of the Natchez debutante? Lily would much rather spend the evening with Jasmine in the nursery or on the deck of the *Hattie Belle*. She had promised to treat her sister as an adult who could make her own judicious choices, but it was going to be a difficult task.

Perhaps by the time Camellia was eighteen, she would understand how empty and unfulfilling the trappings of wealth could be. Lily could only pray she would come to her senses before she found herself bound by her eagerness to embrace luxury and privilege.

Chapter Forty-four

Women don't belong on the river.

Jean Luc studied the note he'd written to make sure his handwriting was disguised. Satisfied, he folded it and handed it to the man standing in front of him. "Make sure you leave this where they can find it."

Lars Steenberg licked his lips. "I got it. When do you want me to do it?"

Did he have to explain everything? "Wait until everyone's off the boat. They don't take many precautions, so I'm sure you'll be able to get on board without much trouble."

A snarl twisted his features. "I'll need some money to pay for helpers if you want this job done right."

Of course the man wanted money. Didn't he always? Jean Luc removed his pocketbook and withdrew a few bills. Irritated to see how little cash was left, he realized it was time to ask his mother for another loan. "Make sure no one's hurt. Remember, I only want to frighten the women, not do any lasting damage. My goal is to recover my boat. And when I do, you'll be able to captain her again."

"I got it." Steenberg pocketed the money and the note.

Jean Luc wished he was not forced to work with someone so shady. But sometimes it was necessary to make compromises to reach a goal. Especially since Lily Anderson was not going to be reasonable. Dealing with Steenberg was better than pleading with her to come to her senses.

No matter what it took, Jean Luc had to regain control of the *Hattie Belle*. He would use whatever tools were available, spend whatever money he could lay his hands on, do whatever he needed to. One day the boat would belong to him again.

"Keep close watch on the *Hattie Belle*. If you mess up again, you won't see any more money from me."

Steenberg's laugh gnawed at Jean Luc's patience. "It's not like you're making me wealthy."

"I've told you I won't have much until the *Hattie Belle* is mine again. When that happens, I'll see you're rewarded." Jean Luc tamped down his anger. He needed Steenberg for now. Once he got his boat back, he'd decide if he wanted to keep Steenberg on. Trusting him wouldn't be easy. "Just remember my instructions."

"Don't worry. That woman will be ready to sign the *Hattie Belle* over to you when she sees what can happen to an unguarded boat." He slinked down Silver Street, disappearing into the mist rolling up from the river, quickly blending in with the other shadowy figures in Natchez Under-the-Hill.

❧

Lily couldn't remember enjoying an evening as much in a very long time. She shared a glance with Blake, wondering if he knew how much she appreciated his advice to forgive her father.

"I'm so excited about finding a school in New Orleans." Camellia's pleasure shone through her expression.

While Lily wasn't looking forward to the eventual separation, it was better than letting Camellia remain in Natchez or forcing her to accompany them to New Orleans against her will.

"What do you think they'll be able to teach you that you can't learn on the river?" Papa propped his elbows on the table and leaned forward.

Camellia frowned. "To sit with my hands in my lap, for one thing."

The volume of Papa's laugh drew the attention of several other restaurant patrons.

"Camellia." Lily shook her head. Another thing they should teach her sister was to show respect for her elders.

Camellia's cheeks grew pink as she focused on the food on her plate.

Lily turned to Blake. "Did you have any success with your search for David's parents?"

Blake shook his head. "His mother lives in a shack next to one of the saloons. No one has seen his father in more than a year. He hasn't returned from California or sent word for his family to join him. I suspect he may be dead."

A pall fell over the group as they absorbed his words. Lily's heart sank. She had been so hopeful Blake would be able to uncover better news. "What about the orphanage?"

"I spoke with the manager. She says they can take him in."

"Why can't we let the boy stay with us?" Papa's question turned everyone's attention back to her.

Lily tucked her napkin under the edge of her plate as she considered how to voice her concerns. "David is a sweet boy, and I appreciate the affection he lavishes on Jasmine." She glanced toward Blake, buoyed by his encouraging smile. "But adoption is not a responsibility I'm ready to shoulder. I don't know the first thing about raising a boy. I hope his father will return, and David needs to be where he can be found, not traipsing up and down the river."

Blake continued the explanation. "David doesn't want to be adopted, either. He loves his father and believes he will come back one day to rescue him. He wants to stay in Natchez so he'll be here when his father returns."

"Blake and I didn't want him living on the streets, so we told David he could stay here if he would agree to remain at the orphanage and apply himself to his studies." Lily finished the story. It was odd how well their minds worked together. As though they were an old, married couple. She supposed it came from their business partnership.

"Does Jasmine know?" Camellia had recovered her equilibrium enough to reenter the conversation. "She'll miss him terribly."

"I haven't told her yet." Lily dreaded that moment. Jasmine was with Tamar at Les Fleurs this evening. While she had spent almost all her waking hours with David since they'd rescued him, Jasmine would have her family to support her. Lily sent a thankful prayer to the Lord for that blessing.

A servant removed their dinner plates before serving small bowls of chilled quince pudding, one of Lily's favorites. "I wonder if we could serve this during our next trip."

"I imagine so." Blake spooned a bite of the fluffy pink dessert, his face registering pleasure. "I don't think I've ever tasted it before. What is it?"

"Quince pudding." Papa answered. He turned to Lily. "I saw an island covered in quince trees a few months back. Unless someone else has harvested the fruit, we can plan on stopping there on our way to New Orleans next week."

She smiled. "Perfect."

Blake settled their account while Papa escorted them to the waiting carriage. "We'll walk back to the boat."

Lily shook her head. She wanted to extend the pleasant evening. "We'll take you. I wanted to ask Jensen about our linens. He mentioned something about new ones the other day, and I haven't had the chance to get back with him."

Blake walked up as she spoke. "What time will we see you on Monday?"

"She wants to go to the boat right now."

The two men exchanged glances. Blake turned to her. "I don't like the idea of you and Camellia riding through that area at night."

"We'll be perfectly safe inside the carriage." She indicated the empty seat opposite her. "Now get in and stop being contrary."

Blake shrugged. "I suppose we'd better do as she says."

The men climbed in, and the carriage began the steep descent. The streets were dark, as was the waterfront. Only the saloons showed activity. The saloons and one of the steamboats.

Lily's heart plunged. She hoped it was not a fire. As they drew closer, she realized the light was coming from lamps, not a fire. Her heart resumed its normal position until she looked more closely and realized the boat was hers. "Something is wrong."

The carriage came to a halt, and Blake pushed the door open. "Stay here while I see what's going on."

Lily ignored his command, climbing down before anyone could stop her. Whatever was going on, she did not want to remain in the dark. Her livelihood was at risk.

She crossed the gangplank on Blake's heels and saw the destruction firsthand. Barrels had been overturned. The door to the staterooms hung at an angle. Her heart thudded. She dreaded seeing her room, but that would have to wait.

Blake was bent over someone propped against the outside rail. A group of strangers, many of whom carried lanterns, stood in a loose circle around him. Jensen! She hurried forward until she could see

Jensen's face. "Are you all right?"

Jensen held a handkerchief to his head. A stain—looking like blood—covered part of his shirt. "Yes, ma'am. The varmints surprised me. Gave me a bit of a headache. I'll be fine, but the rooms are pretty bad."

Blake frowned at her. "I thought I told you to wait."

"You are neither my father nor my husband." She turned to go toward their quarters, but a strong grip on her arm held her still.

"Lily, listen to reason. I don't want you going anywhere on this boat until we're sure the thieves are no longer on board."

Papa and Camellia appeared at her elbow before Lily could respond. Blake's words had given her pause. Especially since Camellia was here.

"I think they've gone." Jensen lowered his hand and pointed to one of the strangers. "He's the one saw what was going on and called for help. Them cowards went running when they realized they might get caught."

Papa dragged out a chair for Jensen from the dining room. "Did you recognize any of them?"

"I never got a chance." Jensen took the offered chair. "They come up behind me and tapped my head with a cudgel. I didn't see nothing until this fellow here helped me sit up."

"Don't worry." Blake's mouth tightened. "We'll catch them."

Camellia leaned toward Jensen. "Do you feel woozy?"

He grinned. "Nah. It'll take a lot worse to break this head of mine. But I am a bit worried about my handsome face."

Comforted by his quip, Lily turned her attention to the boat. Papa was questioning the other men about what they'd seen, but Blake had disappeared. Anger carried her into the passageway. How dare he sneak off while she was distracted?

She headed for the room she shared with her sisters. The paintings they had hung to enliven the passageways had been torn down or sliced to ribbons. So much hard work undone in a matter of minutes. She supposed she should be thankful. It could have been much worse.

The light faded as she got farther from the main deck. Why hadn't she asked to borrow a lantern? A movement ahead made Lily's breath catch. Had Jensen been wrong?

A door opened—her stateroom—and flickering light outlined a familiar shape. She breathed a sigh of relief when she recognized Blake. "I thought I told you to remain with the others." He folded a piece of paper and tucked it into his shirt pocket.

"How bad is it?"

He shrugged. "They didn't do as much damage here as on the main deck."

She considered his face. Did the lamplight make him look so distressed? "What are you hiding from me?"

Blake shook his head. "Nothing. Let's go check on Jensen." He put an arm around her shoulders. "I'll get all of this cleaned up, Lily. Don't worry. It's not as bad as it looks."

She wanted to believe him, but it was difficult. Lily remembered her earlier assurance that she and Camellia would be safe driving through Under-the-Hill. How could she have been so naive?

Chapter Forty-five

New Orleans seemed even busier than during their first visit. It took nearly two hours to secure a decent berth for unloading their cargo, and they would have to move to another location for the duration of their stay. Blake wondered how long it would be. Lily had mentioned finding a finishing school for Camellia. She'd probably want to interview several before making her decision.

"There you are." Lily's voice pulled Blake from his reverie.

As she walked toward him, her footsteps sure and fast, he could not but admire this woman. Ever since the day she'd broken down in front of him, something had changed in the way he viewed her. Although she appeared self-confident, he knew firsthand the fears she hid from the rest of the world. She might be autocratic and jump to the wrong conclusion from time to time, but no one was perfect. And she had shown him a flawless picture of forgiveness.

During the voyage to New Orleans, Lily had been unfailingly warm and loving toward Captain Henrick, introducing him as her father to their guests and spending her afternoons visiting him in the pilothouse. They had delayed their voyage one day when they stopped at the island that held quince trees. Jensen cooked the fruit, and they enjoyed a quince pudding that put to shame the one they'd enjoyed at the restaurant.

Lily seemed happier, as if letting go of her resentment had healed her in some way. He wondered if the resentment he felt toward his father was weighing him down. But how could a person let go of resentment when he'd been wronged?

"I've arranged for a carriage to take you and Tamar and your sisters to the Thorntons' home." His fingers itched to touch the strand of hair that blew across her face. "I will also hire some guards to remain on the ship."

She looked troubled. "Do you think we will be targeted again?"

"Not really, but I don't want to take any chances." He still hadn't mentioned the note he'd found in her room because he didn't want to add to her concerns. But he was determined to find the culprit who had engineered the attack. When he found him, the man would wish he had left them alone.

"You look so solemn. I'm beginning to be worried. Are you hiding something from me?"

"I don't want to have any trouble." She was too perceptive. To distract her attention, he changed the subject. "How is Camellia doing?"

Her brows drew together in a frown. "I'm not sure. She is still so stiff with Papa. I wish she could let go of her anger. I worry that she is still upset with me, too."

"I don't think so, Lily. I imagine she's preoccupied with that finishing school you promised her."

"It worked as a bribe, but I'm beginning to have second thoughts. Camellia sometimes seems to be hiding behind a mask." Lily pushed the strand behind her ear, but it escaped and blew back across her face. "What if the school we choose reinforces that tendency? She is at the very cusp of adulthood. What if I make the wrong choice, and she is ruined for life?"

Blake smiled. "I'm sure Mrs. Thornton and her daughter can help you avoid making a mistake."

"Thank you for knowing exactly the right thing to say." She tucked the errant strand back once more. Once more it blew free.

"Turn around."

She looked up at him, a question in her gaze.

"Trust me, Lily."

"I do." She turned to face the dock. Blake stepped behind her and pulled one of her hair clips out. He used his hand to smooth back her hair, especially the strands that had broken free. Then he refastened the hair clip and stepped back to the rail.

She shot him a glance. "I don't want to know how you learned to do that."

Laughter rumbled through him. "I have a younger sister."

"Really?" She looked up at him. "I didn't realize that."

Silence fell between them, a companionable silence. His thoughts wandered back to the burglary. "I wonder where Captain Steenberg is working."

"Do you think he attacked the boat?"

Why had he spoken out loud? "I don't know, but he did threaten me when I told him to leave."

She turned at his admission. "I didn't know that."

"I didn't want to tell you because I knew he was recommended by your friend Monsieur Champney."

Her sheepish look brought a smile to his face. "I'm so sorry. But believe me. Jean Luc Champney is not exactly my friend. I have discovered we do not see eye to eye."

His smile deepened. He looked away from her. Was the sun brighter than it had been moments ago?

She leaned against the rail, her arm very close to his. "How long before the carriage will be here?"

Contentment bathed Blake in warmth. He wanted to linger next to Lily. "It will wait until you and the others are ready, but I have a question."

"As long as it has nothing to do with finishing schools." Her gaze teased him.

"Okay, I'll ask the other question." He took a deep breath. "I was thinking you and your sisters might enjoy an evening at the theater."

Another sideways glance. "Are you offering to escort us?"

"If I was, would you accept?" He held his breath, his heart pounding so hard he thought she might be able to hear it.

"Why certainly, sir. How could I resist such a sweet offer?" Her smile made his heart triple its speed.

"Why, Miss Anderson"—he fought to keep his voice light—"I do believe you have a bit of the debutante in you. Are you sure you haven't spent time in a finishing school yourself?"

Her giggle was music to his ears. She had been too serious of late.

As though she had read his mind, Lily sobered. "I need to ask you for something, too."

Now what? He braced himself for bad news. "Go ahead."

"I want you to consider contacting your family."

He should have known. "You don't know what you're asking."

She turned to face him. Her chocolate-brown eyes pleaded for him to listen. "Yes, I do. When you told me I should tell my family the truth, you were right. But before I could face them, I had to go to God and ask for His help in forgiving my father."

He felt her hand on his arm. He wanted to shake it off. He wanted to tell her to get in the carriage and leave him alone. To preserve their friendship, he folded his mouth into a straight line and said nothing.

"You were there when I needed you, Blake. I'll never be able to repay you for supporting me during a very difficult time. I want to offer you similar support." She squeezed his arm once before releasing it. "I'm sorry if I've upset you."

He shook his head. Maybe one day he would be able to talk about this subject. But that day was not now. He watched as she walked away from him. Then he turned back to the dock. He didn't know if that day would ever arrive.

❧

Lily looked in the mirror atop her dressing table and caught sight of Tamar's pursed lips. "Do I look that bad?"

Tamar shook her head. "I like your gray dress better. This is a special evening. You know you should dress up."

A knock on the door stopped Lily's protest. "Come in."

Mrs. Thornton opened the door, a broad smile wreathing her face.

It had been so good to see her friend again. Lily enjoyed the pampering she received at the Thorntons' home, but she valued even more the relationship she and Mrs. Thornton shared. Why couldn't Aunt Dahlia be a little more like her?

"Oh no, dear, you must wear the dress you bought on Canal Street. It will complement the little gift I brought for you to wear." She opened her hand to reveal a pair of exquisite pearl-gray hair combs.

Lily could feel her mouth drop open. "They're beautiful, but I cannot accept such an expensive gift."

Mrs. Thornton frowned. "I bought these last year on a whim. But I've never found anything to wear them with. You must accept them. It would make me very happy."

Tamar took the combs and set them on the dressing table. "They will be perfect with your dress, Miss Lily. You can at least wear them tonight."

"I suppose so." Lily didn't want to hurt Mrs. Thornton's feelings.

The casement clock on the mantel began to chime the hour. "I will leave you to change your dress." She whisked her skirt back through the doorway and disappeared.

Tamar picked up Camellia's hairbrush and used it to part Lily's hair.

"You and Mrs. Thornton are making too much of this outing. It's nothing more than the kindness of my business partner in wanting to entertain my sisters and me."

"And why not?" Tamar brushed her hair until it shone and then began twisting it up. "You have a handsome escort for a fancy night out. Who knows what magic could happen?"A shadowy emotion darkened Tamar's eyes. Was she envious?

A thrill of anticipation zipped through Lily at the thought of the surprise in store for her maid later this evening. She didn't know exactly what Jensen planned, but when he had asked for her permission to take Tamar out for the evening, she had given it gladly. Tamar deserved a better life, one that offered all the freedoms Lily and her sisters enjoyed.

In order to keep Jensen's plans secret, she adopted a casual attitude. "It's nothing special. I've half a mind to tell you to remove the combs and put away the gray dress."

Tamar's expression was so serene Lily wondered if she'd imagined the emotion she'd seen earlier. "You can tell yourself that falsehood if you want to, but I've seen Mr. Blake make you blush. And his gaze turns to you when he thinks no one else is looking. He's your beau, all right, or he would be if you'd give him a little encouragement."

A telltale blush rose toward Lily's cheeks. Why did she have to be so transparent? She grabbed her fan from the dressing table and swept it back and forth to cool her face.

Tamar sent a knowing look then helped Lily with the gray dress and nodded. "You look very nice."

Lily turned to the mirror and was surprised by her image. Her hair was pinned by the gray combs above her ears and cascaded in soft waves around her head, giving her a much softer look. Her dress, with its wide skirt and fancy stitched design, accentuated her small waist and looked most fashionable. Lily felt like a fraud. She was no beauty.

Confused by her thoughts, she decided to focus on Tamar. Now that her maid had an opportunity to escape the yoke of slavery, she wanted to make certain nothing stood in her way. She pointed her fan at the maid. "This situation cannot continue."

"What do you mean? Have I done something wrong?"

"Of course not. You've done nothing but care for Camellia, Jasmine, and me as if we were your own children."

A smile chased away the worried look on Tamar's face. "I couldn't love you any more than my own children."

"I know, Tamar. That's why I'm going to make certain you gain your freedom. The last time I suggested this, I thought you may have reacted so badly because Mr. Moreau was there."

Tamar stepped back, her head shaking. "That's not it at all, Miss Lily. I don't want him or anyone else to spend good money for me. Besides, if I was freed, I wouldn't be able to care for you or your sisters."

Deciding to dispense with the easier issue, she smiled. "Maybe not, but you'd be able to marry Jensen and have children of your own."

Tears shone in Tamar's dark-brown eyes. "I don't need to marry that man."

"So, it's fine for Blake to court me, but you don't deserve to be with the man you love?"

Silence filled the room as they looked at each other. Finally Tamar's gaze fell to the floor. "Sometimes I just want everything to go back to the way it used to be. Back to the way I felt before I ever met Jensen. But then, when I'm near him—" She twisted her hands in her apron. "He makes me want to have a different future."

"That's wonderful." Lily hugged Tamar, her heart practically bursting with happiness.

At first the older woman resisted, but then she returned Lily's embrace.

"Don't you see? You're in love with Jensen. I knew it! And the two of you are going to have a chance for happiness. You're going to have children of your own you can love as wonderfully as you've loved us for all these years."

Tamar shooed Lily out of the room. "Get on downstairs before Mr. Blake comes looking for you."

"I will, but only if you promise to give Jensen a chance." Lily waited for Tamar's nod before she skipped down the staircase. She found her sisters and their escorts in the front parlor. Jasmine was talking nonstop to Mr. and Mrs. Thornton about the evening ahead. Camellia sat on the sofa, her arms crossed and a pout on her face. One look at the disinterested expression on Jonah Thornton's face told Lily why. Camellia was not used to being ignored. Lily struggled to keep a straight face.

Blake leaned against the fireplace mantel, his tall black hat dangling from one hand. She had never seen him looking so elegant. The brass buttons of his striped waistcoat gleamed in the candlelight. His black boots had been polished to a mirror finish. Suddenly Lily was glad she'd worn her gray dress, especially when she saw the light of appreciation in Blake's eyes.

"The carriage is ready." Blake bowed and walked toward her.

Lily wanted to say something witty, but nothing came to mind. "You look very nice this evening."

His lips curled in a tender smile. "Thank you. So do you. You've done something different to your hair, haven't you?"

He had noticed. Lily touched a hand to one of the combs. "Mrs. Thornton loaned these to me for the evening."

Blake nodded. "Are you ready to depart?"

She smiled and placed her hand on his proffered arm. Not sure whether she was walking or floating, she passed through the doorway and into the foyer.

Tamar had been right. This was going to be a very special evening.

Chapter Forty-six

Freedom. The word had been an idea without substance to Tamar. At best it was a scary word, yet she found herself increasingly drawn to it.

She picked up Jasmine's pinafore and smoothed it with a gentle touch. Wouldn't it be wonderful to have a family of her own? But what would the Anderson sisters do without someone to watch over them?

Shaking her head, Tamar folded the pinafore and put it in Jasmine's trunk. She checked the room one last time to make sure everything had been put away before going down the narrow staircase used by the slaves.

The housekeeper met her at the back door. "You have a visitor."

Her heart leaped. "Is it Mr. Moreau?"

The older woman winked and nodded. "He's dressed up awful pretty, too. I'd say he's got courting on his mind."

Tamar ducked her head. If Jensen was dressed up, she didn't want to be wearing her apron. She grabbed at the strings holding it to her waist and wrestled with them.

"Let me help you." The housekeeper turned her around and untied the strings. "I'll put this in your room. You go on out to the kitchen and meet your young man."

Putting a hand on her hammering heart, Tamar walked through the garden and stepped into the bright, warm kitchen where most of the servants gathered in the evenings. Tonight was no exception. Two maids, the butler, and the cook were sitting around a large table. But the only person Tamar saw was standing next to the hearth.

He stepped forward, his brown eyes shining with love. “I’ve got plans for the evening.”

She cocked her head to one side. “You do?”

“Yes.”

Tamar raised her hand toward his hair. “I think your head may still be broken.”

Jensen captured her hand and placed it on his arm like she was a real lady. “I’m good as new. You didn’t have nothing else planned, did you?”

She couldn’t stop the giggle that slipped out. “What kind of plans could I have?”

“Good.” Pulling her out of the kitchen, away from the prying eyes and ears of the Thorntons’ staff, he escorted her to the outer entrance.

Her eyes stretched wide when she realized a hired cab awaited them. “Wait. I can’t leave. I don’t have permission.”

“Yes, you do. I talked with Miss Lily earlier. She said you could.”

She was free. For the evening at least.

Tamar let Jensen hand her into the cab. He climbed in and sat beside her, his closeness threatening her breath. “I can’t believe you did this. Lily didn’t say a word about it.”

“I asked her not to so’s I could surprise you.” He put his hat on his lap. “Are you surprised?”

Another giggle filled the air. “Of course. But are you sure?”

“I never been surer, Tamar.” His gaze caressed her. “I love you.”

“Don’t say those things.” She turned away and watched the passing scenery.

“I have to. Else my heart would explode. There’s lots I want to say to you, Tamar. But the most important is that I love you enough to buy your freedom.”

That brought her head back around. “You don’t have to do that. Lily promised to make sure I’m given my freedom.”

He rubbed his knuckle against her jaw. “I love you with all my heart. As soon as you’re free, I want to marry you.”

“Don’t say that. There are so many reasons we can’t get married.” Tamar tried to pull back, but he trapped her chin with long fingers.

“We belong together.”

“I’m too old and too dark.”

"I'll leave off my hat. The sun should help me look both older and darker." His grin was infectious.

Tamar found herself smiling at him. "I can't marry a man who's not a Christian."

"I have given my heart to Him." He waggled his brows at her. "I don't always do what I should. I just need a good woman to help keep me in line."

Infected by his jolly attitude, she summoned a fierce frown. "Well, if you want to be married to me, you'll have to change some. I'll not have anyone say I married a heathen."

He laughed out loud. Raising his other hand, he cupped her face. "I love you." He pressed a soft kiss on her lips.

Tamar felt like she was floating on a cloud. *So this is what the Bible meant about a man and a woman becoming one.* She could almost feel the joining of their souls.

The cab stopped, and Jensen let her go. "Are you ready?" He helped her out of the carriage and paid the driver.

They walked hand in hand down Gravier Street until they came to the St. Charles Theater. Her mouth dropped open at the size of the building. It could probably hold most of the citizens of New Orleans. Jensen led her past the line of carriages at the front entrance, walking toward the east side of the building. Part of her wished they could go inside, but Tamar knew that was impossible for a slave.

Refusing to let her thoughts spoil the evening, she looked toward the open doorway. The performance must have already started. She could hear someone singing. Dozens of people crowded around the door, jostling against each other to get a better position. They must have a view of the stage.

Jensen pointed to an empty bench a few feet away. "Why don't we sit over there?"

Tamar nodded. If they were very quiet, they would be able to hear almost every word. She couldn't think of any better way to spend the evening than sitting next to the man she loved.

Thankfulness filled her as she realized the truth. She loved Jensen Moreau. His arm encircled her waist and drew her close. If freedom offered other such delights, she would embrace it with a joyful heart.

Blake was a fool. All the gilded arches and velvet curtains of the theater were lost on him. He barely noticed the sparkling chandeliers or the crowds of tiara-crowned, bejeweled women. The only thing on his mind was that he was falling in love with a girl who was all wrong for him.

He glanced at her. Lily was leaning slightly forward, so caught up in the action on the stage that she had forgotten he was sitting next to her. Yes, he was an idiot.

Nothing about Lily should appeal to him. She was stubborn, idealistic, and a prude to boot. Never mind that she came with a ready-made family who would always be a big part of her life. Lily had a caring heart and a mind that worked at the speed of lightning, but those things shouldn't appeal to a man. He glanced at her again, his gaze caressing the fullness of her mouth and the jut of her determined chin. Funny how over the past months his idea of feminine beauty had changed.

A whisper from Jasmine at the front of the box drew his attention. She was seated next to Camellia and the Thorntons' son Jonah, while he and Lily were directly behind them. It was the perfect arrangement for chaperones.

When had he grown so old? And why was he spending his days surrounded by this motley crew of a family when he should be wining and dining lovely women from one end of the Mississippi River to the other?

Yet he found himself reluctant to sell his portion of the *Hattie Belle* to Lily. Although opportunities to open a gambling boat abounded, the thrill of gambling had faded to a distant fantasy. Blake had discovered he enjoyed the variety of alarms and challenges that chased Lily and her family.

Part of him even enjoyed listening to her father talk about his beliefs. Not that he would attend any more sermons in the dining room. But he did like asking Captain Henrick questions about faith in the modern world.

The curtain came down, and he joined the general applause even though he had no clue what had happened during the final act of *Richard Coeur-de-lion*. But when Lily turned to him, her brown eyes gleaming in the light of the sconces, he took pleasure from the knowledge that she had enjoyed the performance.

Her hand gripped his arm. "That was splendid. Thank you so much for taking us."

Blake covered her hand with his own. "I'm glad you liked it."

Jonah stood and stretched his arms over his head. "Their performance was a little unpolished. You should have seen the performance of *Don Giovanni* last month. The music was much better."

"I thought it was wonderful." Jasmine's eyes were even brighter than Lily's. She clasped the playbill. "I would like more than anything to become an actress like Miss Tabitha Barlow."

Camellia sniffed her disdain for the idea.

Blake felt the shudder that passed through Lily right before she pulled away from him. "That's ridiculous. I can't think of a more scandalous occupation for a young lady."

"It looks glamorous to me." Jasmine's chin lifted in the same manner Lily employed when she was determined to get her way.

"You'll feel differently when you grow up." Camellia tossed a smile toward Jonah, which the young man ignored.

Blake decided to step in before the discussion disintegrated into a quarrel. "I don't think we need to worry about such things tonight." He bent a cautionary gaze on Lily. "Let me help you with your cloak."

Jonah waved at someone on the opposite side of the theater. "Excuse me." He vaulted over the low wall that separated them from the pit before Blake could stop him.

With a sigh, Blake settled Lily's cloak around her shoulders. "I suppose he'll join us before too long." He helped the girls gather their wraps and gloves.

They exited the box, and he spotted Jonah with a group of youths about his age. Warning the others to wait for the carriage, he went to fetch the young man.

As he approached the group, they stopped talking, looking at him with suspicion. Did they think he was too old to join them? They couldn't be more than five years younger than he. Had the weight of experience aged him so much? For the second time that evening, he felt old. "Jonah, I need your help with the ladies."

Jonah rolled his eyes, garnering sympathetic looks from his friends, but he followed Blake back to the *porte cochére*. "I thought I would walk home to leave more room in the carriage."

"I appreciate your concern." Blake didn't try to hide his sarcasm. "But we have sufficient room."

They found the others without incident, and Blake guided them to the carriage, feeling like a sheepherder. On the way to the theater, the girls had sat on one bench while he and Jonah shared the opposite one. But somehow this time the girls managed to split up as they entered the carriage. Camellia sat on the forward-facing bench, Jasmine between her and Jonah. Lily sat by herself, leaving only one place for Blake, a development that made his heart beat a couple of extra times before returning to its normal rhythm. He settled in, his knee brushing hers through the material of her skirt.

Each time the carriage turned a corner, Lily's shoulder leaned against him. She smelled of almonds and honey, a light scent that teased his nostrils. He wouldn't care if the ride home lasted half the night.

Of course it didn't. But when Blake helped Lily alight from the carriage, their gazes met. She offered a secret smile that promised she had enjoyed the ride home as much as he.

He was an idiot, an idiot in love with Lily Anderson. It was time for him to make his intentions known.

❧

"It was so exciting, Papa." Jasmine's violet gaze was fastened on him, seated across from her at the Thorntons' dinner table later that evening. "Blondel gets free, and Lady Marguerite has a party, and then her soldiers rescue poor King Richard."

Lily exchanged a glance with Blake. They communicated without words—sharing their amusement at Jasmine's enthusiasm. Jonah Thornton may have found the evening beneath his standards, but the rest of them rated the music and acting delightful. It had also changed something between her and Blake. He had become a member of their family.

"Only because they tricked Florestan. He loved Laurette, and they used that against him." Camellia did not hesitate to set her younger sister straight.

Jasmine considered Camellia's words. "He got what he deserved for putting a king in jail."

Everyone laughed at her logic.

Jasmine looked a little put out, but she managed to smile. "It was magical. I'm going to sing in the opera when I grow up."

"I'm so glad you enjoyed it." Mrs. Thornton smiled at her youngest guest. "It is good to be so passionate. Perhaps one day you will become a great patron of the arts."

Lily appreciated the woman's kind words. They soothed Jasmine's sensibilities as well as her own concern that her youngest sister was too fervent in her response to the opera. All evening Jasmine had been humming the melody. Imagining her sister performing on stage was enough to cause nightmares. Although Lily's choice of occupation was not traditional, other ladies traveled on the river. If Jasmine decided to pursue a career on stage, she would be disappointed at how tawdry it was.

Mrs. Thornton placed her napkin beside her plate and rose, signaling that the ladies should retire. The gentlemen rose, too.

Lily glanced at Blake once more. How had she ever thought Jean Luc Champney interesting? He might have lived in Europe, but he seemed shallow compared with the man standing across from her.

Blake was a man of honor, and she prayed he would let go of his prejudice against God. Her father had told her about the conversations he'd had with Blake, conversations that let her know God was trying to reach him. It was enough for now. But would it be enough for a more permanent relationship?

So lost was she in her contemplation, Lily almost missed the slight motion Blake made with his head. She frowned at him. Again Blake tilted his head, his gaze intense. He must have some information to impart, probably about the *Hattie Belle*. Had they been robbed again? She nodded to him, praying his news was nothing serious.

Mrs. Thornton, Camellia, and Jasmine went to the front parlor.

Lily hung back until Blake joined her. "What's wrong?"

He shook his head and steered her toward the back of the house.

The air had cooled as night settled around them. Although the full moon had risen, its silver light did not impart warmth. Lily's arms were covered by long sleeves, but she wished she had a shawl. Maybe the problem wouldn't take long to solve.

They strolled along a dim path, saying nothing until they reached a stone bench. "Would you like to sit?" His voice sounded odd. Strained.

She sat and watched as he paced back and forth. "Whatever the problem is, Blake, you had best just tell me."

He stopped and looked at her, opened his mouth, shut it, and took another turn around their quiet corner of the garden.

"If you continue walking around in circles, one of us is going to become dizzy."

Moonlight touched his black hair as he sat beside her, taking her hands in his grasp. "I want to talk to you about the future."

Lily's heart missed a beat. "What?"

"We've made a lot of money on the *Hattie Belle*. I never thought shipping would be so lucrative, but you have pulled it off, Lily."

Did he want to end their partnership? She tugged on her hands, but he wouldn't release his hold. "I couldn't have done it alone."

He smiled. "I appreciate your kindness, but both of us know I had a completely different view of how to use the *Hattie Belle*."

Lily hoped she had mistaken Blake's intention. She hated the idea of living on the *Hattie Belle* without his reassuring presence. Who could she trust as much as she did this man? "It took both of us using the talents God gave us."

He leaned toward her, and Lily thought he was going to give her a brotherly hug. Anticipation warmed her. His hands released their grip, and his arms came around her shoulders. "Lily, you're a special woman." His head dropped lower. His eyelids drifted downward. And his lips covered hers.

She melted for a fraction of a second. But then reason returned. What was she doing? She pushed at his chest with enough force to stop his kiss. "S–stop, Blake." Was that breathy sound her voice? Lily cleared her throat. "I value your friendship deeply, but I cannot allow this."

Shock was evident in every line of his body. "I thought we understood each other."

Lily's mouth still tingled from his touch. She had never dreamed a kiss could feel so right—and so devastating. But she would have to consider the implications of her very confused emotions when she was alone. For now she needed to explain to this man why they were not right for each other. "Blake, you gave me the most excellent advice anyone could have offered at a time when I desperately needed it. You're the reason I've grown closer to God. You're the person who helped me see how far I'd strayed from Him. I'll always be grateful to you."

"I don't want your gratitude." He stood and faced the house. All she could see were his clenched hands behind his back, the same hands that had held her so gently moments ago.

"You're my best friend, Blake. You're the one who counseled me to tell my family the truth. I wish I had listened, as things would have been much easier."

He kicked at a stone, making her think of an angry child.

She hated being the cause of his anger. Hated hurting him. Praying for the right words, she drew another breath. "Letting this thing between us continue would be a lie."

He swung around. "A lie? What I feel for you is as real as that house. How can that be a lie?"

"I'm a Christian." She let her words sink in before continuing. "That means I can't link myself to someone who does not love God with his whole heart. I cannot put my eternal soul at risk for a transitory feeling. I beg you to understand."

"Understand?" He swallowed hard. Then his face smoothed out, becoming an emotionless mask. But the moonlight was bright enough to reveal the pain in his eyes.

Tears threatened to overwhelm Lily. With a wordless cry, she stood up and rushed past him to the house. Running up the stairs to her bedroom, she slammed the door and threw herself across the bed.

Hot tears streaked her cheeks and soaked the pillow. She didn't cry for herself but for the man she had deserted. The man who might never understand why she had rejected his love.

Chapter Forty-seven

Wondering why her father had summoned her, Lily pulled her cloak tighter as she plodded up to the pilothouse. The wind scraped at her cheeks and tugged at her skirt. The weather was a perfect reflection of her emotions.

She had seen Blake only once in the past week, the day of their departure. He'd moved out of the Thorntons' garçonièrre the day after he kissed her. She'd wanted to talk to him, explain why she had spurned his advances, but when she got to the boat, a single glance at his cold features destroyed that impulse.

Papa pulled a cord, and the long, low note of the steam whistle filled the cold air.

Lily stepped into the pilothouse and looked out over the water. Another stern-wheeler was churning south, riding low in the water. Bales of cotton were piled high on every available surface of the other boat. "How do passengers move about on that deck?"

He waved her forward, giving her a hug before answering. "I doubt they're carrying passengers. Their cargo alone will make the trip profitable."

The cotton must be getting wet from the water washing onto the deck. "If the boat doesn't sink before it makes port."

Her father withdrew his prized telescope from the inside pocket of his coat and held it up to his right eye. "She is riding low, but the pilot is taking his time. I doubt he'll sink her."

A feeling of peace stole over Lily as she and her father watched the boat until it passed them. She couldn't thank God enough for reuniting her with her father. "Did you need something from me, Papa?"

He studied her, his brown eyes filled with compassion. "I'm worried about you."

"Worried?" She lifted her chin and wished she had done a better job of hiding her sorrow. "Everything is going well. We found the perfect school for Camellia, we're making money faster than I dreamed possible, and you're with us. My family is reunited. What more could I want?"

Her ruse didn't work. "Water Lily, I know I haven't been around like I should have been for you and your sisters, but I'm not blind. Maybe God intended for me to be here now so I can help."

"I don't need your help, Pa–Papa." Trying to pass her stutter off as a reaction to the cold air, she shivered. "It's cold out here today, isn't it?"

He shook his head. "You can't fool me, honey. You and Blake spent a lot of time together in New Orleans. I tried to talk to him when he showed up here early one morning last week, but talking to that boy is like trying to swim upstream. When I saw how the two of you avoided each other yesterday and again this morning, I started to understand the problem." He cleared his throat. "He didn't try to take advantage of you, did he?"

Lily's cheeks felt as if they were glowing like twin flames. "No—"

"Good." The word cut off her explanation. "I would hate to have to toss that boy overboard."

Lily would have laughed, but his gaze told her he was not making a joke. "I care about him very much, Papa. But we have no future together other than as co-owners of the *Hattie Belle*."

"Is this because of his past?"

A sigh filled her chest. "Not exactly."

"Then what's the problem?"

"He's turned away from God."

A frown wrinkled her father's weathered brow. "Has he told you this? That he doesn't believe in God?"

She nodded, her heart breaking again as she remembered Blake's refusal to release the pain of his past and turn to God.

"That surprises me." Papa adjusted the ship's wheel to avoid a snag ahead. "He and I have spent some time together, you know. He's been as full of questions about God and Christ as anyone I've ever met. When someone is determined to avoid contact with God, he usually doesn't want to stay around Christians or give in to his curiosity."

His words buoyed her, offered her hope. But what if he was wrong? "He probably wants ammunition to use against Christians."

"I don't know, Water Lily. I only know that God doesn't want to bring either of you pain."

With great effort, she summoned a smile. "I know, Papa."

"Good." He focused on the horizon then returned his attention to her. "We need to ask God to reveal the truth to Blake, and not just for your sake. This is more important than whether the two of you love each other—it's about where he'll spend eternity."

Papa's words were stark, frightening. A shudder shook her. Lily looked at her father. "Can we pray right now?"

He held out his arms to her. "Of course we can. I can't think of a better time to do so."

❧

Blake watched Lily cross the gangplank and enter her grandmother's carriage. A piece of his heart traveled with her. He had to win her esteem. But was he ready to surrender control of his life? And if so, who was he surrendering to? The cold, uncaring God of his childhood or the warm, loving Savior that Captain Henrick and Lily worshipped?

He'd spent years chiseling out a life for himself, learning how to rely on his own strengths. Was he supposed to give all that up?

A hand clapped him on the back. Blake turned and met Captain Henrick's gaze. "You look like someone is tearing out your heart."

"I don't know what you're talking about." The accuracy of Captain Henrick's analogy stunned him. When had he grown so transparent? And what did his inability to hide his thoughts say about being able to return to the gambling tables? His future didn't look very hopeful. What was a washed-up gambler supposed to do? He couldn't stay here. Being around Lily without being able to claim her was harder than he'd thought it would be.

Captain Henrick shrugged. "If you say so." His glance went to the carriage that was pulling away.

Time to change the subject. "Why aren't you going to Les Fleurs with them?"

"I've spent a great deal of time on my knees since I turned to God, and I've learned a lot from that position."

"What are you talking about?"

"I'm talking about the way God uses weakness to His benefit."

He had Blake's full attention. "What kind of God wants weak followers?"

The smile on Captain Henrick's face widened. "The kind of God I serve." He closed his eyes as though thinking hard about his answer. " 'And he said unto me, My grace is sufficient for thee: for my strength is made perfect in weakness.' "

Frustration boiled in Blake's chest. "That makes absolutely no sense."

The captain opened his eyes. "Think about it like this, son. God is eternal. He doesn't think like we do. If you took the strongest person in the world and multiplied his strength a hundredfold, it would be as nothing to the God I serve. When Paul asked for the strength to overcome his weakness, God gave him the answer I just quoted to you."

"Then what's the point of striving for anything? Why not rely on God for everything we need?"

"Exactly right." Captain Henrick clapped his shoulder. "I knew you were close to understanding."

Blake had not expected the man to agree with him. He didn't understand why Lily's father was grinning, but then the truth hit him. He didn't have to control anything. All he had to do was turn to God. The God who was stronger than his doubts, his questions, his weaknesses, and even his strengths. Hope sprang up inside him, choking out the doubt and anger that had controlled his life for so many years. "You've given me a lot to think about."

"That's all I need to hear."

Blake wished Captain Henrick's eldest daughter felt the same way. But perhaps if he continued searching for the truth, perhaps God would show him the way to Lily's heart, too.

❧

Jean Luc's father pulled his pocket watch from his waistcoat. "You're late. . .again." He snapped the silver cover closed and replaced the timepiece.

One of the other clerks snickered.

Jean Luc wanted to turn on his heel and walk out. Why did he have to be so humiliated? Most fathers would appreciate his exemplary behavior. Jean Luc had taken such pains to please the man since the disastrous night when he'd lost his interest in the *Hattie Belle*. Yet all his father did was embarrass him in front of his employees. Tamping down his irritation, Jean Luc removed his gloves and hat. "I'm here now."

His father blew out a harsh breath. "None of my other employees arrive as late as you."

"Any time you want me to stop working, I will be most happy to oblige." Jean Luc sauntered to the small desk tucked into a corner of the office. He sat and pulled forward a sheet of paper, pretending to study it while his father continued to fume. A list of goods was handwritten in the margin of the bill of lading he held, but he had no idea whether someone had delivered the goods to Natchez or if they were being ordered from some other port. Nor did he care.

"I don't know why I put up with your impudence." His father stormed out, slamming the door.

Jean Luc sat back in his chair and crossed his ankles. A large window on the front of the office building showed passing carriages, carts, and horses. How he wished he were outside instead of stuck in this office. But as long as he needed funds, he would have to pretend to work for his father.

He hoped his pretense wouldn't be necessary much longer. His mother had told him they'd been invited to a party at Lily Anderson's home tomorrow evening. He needed to meet with Steenberg and arrange for another unfortunate incident. Perhaps something a little more damaging. He would offer to comfort Lily and see if he could convince her to give up her dangerous lifestyle. If he could present himself in the proper way, he should be able to convince her to turn over the management of her boat to him. It would only take a matter of weeks for him to cement his control. Then he could take his proper place in local society.

"Aren't you going to begin listing those goods in your ledger?" Another clerk, Randolph something-or-other, pointed to the pile of papers someone had stacked on his desk.

Jean Luc shook his head and leaned his chair back until only the back two legs touched the floor. "My eyes are crossed from trying to make sense of that top one. Why don't you be a good friend and take care of these for me?"

Randolph swallowed hard, his Adam's apple moving up and down.

"I have a stack of my own."

Letting his chair fall forward, Jean Luc picked up the neat stack and held them out to the fellow. "I'm sure you'll do a much better job than I."

A slight lift to Randolph's shoulder indicated acceptance.

Jean Luc dusted his hands and reached for his gloves. "I believe I'll go check on the ships that are supposed to be arriving today."

He left the office and whiled away the morning being fitted for a new pair of boots. After a leisurely lunch, he purchased a newspaper and took it to the park for perusal. After he finished his reading, Jean Luc strolled across the park, renewing acquaintance with several of the ladies he'd met over the past months. He managed to escape without too much trouble and decided he should visit his tailor to see if the new suit he had ordered would be ready for tomorrow evening's party.

When he finally made his way back to Champney Shipping, the office was closed. A pity. But what was he supposed to do? A gentleman had to keep his priorities straight.

As the sun was setting, Jean Luc made his way down to the docks, pleased to note that the *Hattie Belle*'s berth was at the far end of the waterfront. It shouldn't be difficult for his men to board her without being spotted.

He found Steenberg standing in an alley next to a waterfront warehouse, the brim of his hat pulled low over his face. "Do you have the money?"

Jean Luc ignored the ill-mannered question. "The party is set for tomorrow night. The whole family will be in attendance. Blake Matthews, too. Are you ready to get back on board?"

"All I need is the cash."

"I want you to make sure they cannot leave the next day." Jean Luc wished he could hire someone else. But at least the man in front of him knew how to keep his mouth shut. No one suspected that either of them was involved in the earlier robbery. "And make sure no one gets hurt."

"That guy sprung up out of nowhere." Steenberg put out his hand for the money. "But I managed to knock him out before he could see who I was."

"This time wear masks." Jean Luc counted out three bills.

"That's not enough money."

"Be glad I'm giving you anything, given your incompetence. You've failed me twice. Next time, I won't be as forgiving."

"But you need me." Steenberg stepped closer. "You don't want to get your hands dirty."

Jean Luc refused to be intimidated. "You'll get the rest when I am satisfied with the results."

Steenberg looked like he was going to argue but then shrugged and accepted the cash, tucking it into the pocket of his trousers. "Tell me exactly what you want done. I can wreck the boat so she won't move for a month or more."

Jean Luc considered the options. "Stay away from the paddle wheel. Those things take too long to repair. I'll leave it up to you. Just make sure the damage is not irreparable. I need Lily Anderson to turn to me for help. Then I'll be able to convince her to relinquish her interest in my boat."

"I'll make sure she comes crying to you." Steenberg's laugh was as irritating as his greed. "Did you write another love note for me to leave for her?"

"No." Jean Luc turned to go home. Then he stopped and looked at Steenberg. "Remember, if you do your job right, you won't need to be looking for any more handouts. I'll reinstate you as captain of the *Hattie Belle* as soon as the ownership reverts to me. But if you fail me one more time, you won't work on the river again."

Steenberg's face twisted, and for a moment Jean Luc feared for his life. His heart pounded as he wondered if he had been a fool to come here alone. What would stop this man from killing him and taking the rest of his money?

Jean Luc straightened his shoulders. If he allowed his fear to show, nothing would stop Steenberg. He wished he'd been smart enough to bring his pistol, but he hadn't thought of it as he was getting ready to go to his father's office.

Someone stepped out of the warehouse, breaking the hold the other man had on him. Jean Luc began walking away, his shoulders twitching as he wondered if he was about to be attacked.

He was halfway down Silver Street before he looked back over his shoulder. Steenberg was still looking at him, wearing a grin made up of equal parts greed and malice.

Wondering if he had made a terrible mistake, Jean Luc headed back up the hill. He would be glad when this was over.

Chapter Forty-eight

Blake loved holding Lily close. He wished he had the right to do so all the time.

She was wearing the same outfit she'd worn the night they kissed—well, the night he kissed her. But he had thought for a moment she had responded to the touch of his lips. Maybe that was why it hurt so much when she pushed him away.

"I hope you're enjoying yourself this evening." Lily's brown eyes searched his face. "I know you don't know many of the townspeople."

He wanted to laugh out loud at her naïveté. "You might be surprised how often I've sat opposite some of these men."

Her pink cheeks made him want to cut out his tongue.

He hadn't meant to make her feel bad. "I'm sorry."

She shook her head. "I should have realized."

They danced in silence for several minutes. Blake searched for something to talk about. What was wrong with him? He never had trouble making conversation. But Lily was a different matter. "Your sister seems to be having an exciting time."

Lily nodded and favored him with a crooked smile. "The young men are lined up to ask for her hand in a dance. I knew she would be popular. She is so beautiful."

"If you have a liking for porcelain dolls." Blake bent his head closer to hers, his mouth almost touching her ear. "I prefer a woman with determination, courage, and intelligence. A woman who can take on the world with a smile on her face."

She caught her breath, and her cheeks darkened, but this time he didn't regret being the cause for her discomfort. It was proof she did care for him. "You are quite the flatterer, Mr. Matthews."

"I am simply expressing my taste, Miss Anderson." He turned his head slightly, his lips ever so close to her cheek. She was adorably awkward and would have stumbled if he had not held her so close. Taking pity on her, he straightened, allowing a few inches between them. He didn't want to make her a target for the gossips.

When the music ended, he wanted to whisk her out to the veranda, but someone else was waiting to partner her. Jean Luc Champney. Smothering a snarl, he let her go and turned to find another partner. Maybe he could keep Lily's attention better if she realized other women found him attractive.

One dance led to another. Too bad Blake could not recall a single name of his dance partners. His brain had been numbed by all their banalities, flirtatious glances, and suggestive movements. None of them stood out in his memory, none except Lily.

Mrs. Blackstone, Lily's grandmother, had managed to introduce him to half the young ladies in attendance at what she was calling her "little dinner party." Where he came from, this evening would be described as a formal ball. From the full orchestra providing the music to the chaperones sitting in chairs along one wall of the ballroom, this evening had little in common with a simple dinner party.

A familiar voice hailing him made Blake's jaw tighten. He didn't want to have to exchange pleasantries with Jean Luc Champney, not after he'd had to watch the man fawn over Lily.

"I wanted to congratulate you on your success."

Blake bowed. "That's kind of you since it was born on your ill luck."

A polite smile camouflaged the scowl Blake's words had caused. "I hope all of that is behind us now. I have taken a position in my father's office to learn the shipping business from the inside. By the time I take to the water, I should know enough to make my own fortune."

"Good. Then perhaps we'll see you on the river soon."

"I hope so."

When Blake would have turned away, Mr. Champney put a hand on his arm. "I heard about the incident when you were docked here a few weeks back. I trust no lasting harm was done to the boat."

The hair on Blake's arm rose. How had this man heard of the burglary? Lily, Jensen, and he had decided to tell no one. Suspicion filled him. "Yes, but we have decided it was a random act of bored young aristocrats. The only thing they managed to do was destroy a couple of barrels of wheat. Since then, I have hired several guards to keep watch."

Jean Luc shook his head. "It's a shame you have to take such precautions. Perhaps one day the waterfront will be safe for everyone. Lily is so adventurous, but I worry about her remaining in that environment. I have tried to convince her that the river is no place for a lady."

Thinking of the note he had discovered in Lily's room, the one he had crumpled and later tossed overboard to keep Lily from seeing it, Blake gritted his teeth. "You need not worry about her or her sisters. Their safety is my primary concern." He glared at the other man, wondering what role he had played in the burglary.

"Forgive me, I didn't mean to insult you." Surprise raised Jean Luc's eyebrows, but the emotion seemed false to Blake.

He tried to temper his dislike of the man, but it was difficult. When he'd first met him, Jean Luc had been nothing more than a young man with more money than sense. Then Lily had put so much stock in Jean Luc's advice while she managed to ignore his at every turn.

He looked across the crowded room for her brown hair and gray dress, a fierce pain in his chest. Even though she had spurned him, his love burned as intensely as ever. "I'd better not catch you anywhere near the *Hattie Belle*. If I do, you'll find yourself treading water."

The polite mask disappeared as Jean Luc's face filled with bitterness and hatred. "If you were a gentleman, I would call you out for that threat."

"Lucky then that I am not."

"One of these days your luck will run out." Jean Luc's voice was little more than a growl. "I only hope I am there to see it." He turned and pushed his way through the crowd.

Blake watched him then decided it was time to make his excuses to Lily and return to the *Hattie Belle*. He had a sudden urge to make sure their boat was safe. He moved toward Mrs. Blackstone.

"Is there someone else I can introduce you to, Mr. Matthews?" Her widow's dress seemed dull in this room of pastel-skirted debutantes.

"Not at all." He bowed and reached for her hand. "I'm afraid I must take my leave. I need to check on the men I left aboard my boat."

"What is this about *our* boat?" Lily put extra emphasis on the word as she joined them.

Mrs. Blackstone put an arm around her granddaughter. "I won't have the two of you arguing in my home."

All of them laughed, and Blake winked at the two women. "I stand corrected."

"I've enjoyed meeting you, Mr. Matthews." Mrs. Blackstone's smile included both of them. "I hope you will not be a stranger. Anytime you and my granddaughter are in Natchez, I will expect to see you." She turned and left the two alone.

"I wish you would not go by yourself, Blake. I will be glad to join you."

Blake shook his head. "I don't think I need a protector."

"At least promise you will be careful."

He tweaked her nose. "Don't worry. Jensen is there, as well as the two men we hired. I'll be safer there than I have been amongst these matchmaking matrons."

Her frown lingered as he headed for the door, but Lily would probably forget about him when the other guests claimed her attention. He only hoped she avoided Jean Luc Champney. The thought of her dancing with him again made Blake's jaw harden. The self-absorbed Monsieur Champney was not a man to be trusted.

During the quiet ride to the dock, Blake began to think his overreaction could be attributed to a lack of sleep. Water lapped at the bank, its surface reflecting the light of the moon above. Natchez Under-the-Hill was rarely quiet, but sometimes in the hours before dawn, the community slumbered, exhausted by its wickedness. Even the stray dogs that normally wandered the streets had found safe places to rest.

Blake had to wake the liveryman to return his hired horse. After settling his account with the sleepy man, he walked the dark street to where the *Hattie Belle* was berthed, relieved to see her as quiet as the town.

"Jensen, where are you?" He crossed the gangplank and headed for the galley. He needed a cup of strong coffee if he was going to stay awake until the sun rose. The boat rocked under his feet, setting off a warning in Blake's mind. He brushed the feeling aside. Probably just a guard making his rounds.

Opening the door to the galley, Blake was blinded by bright lantern light. He raised his arm to shield his eyes and tried to look into the room. "How many lanterns do you—"

"What are you doing here?"

The voice sounded familiar, but Blake couldn't match it to any of the men he'd hired for the evening. He squinted, trying to see who was in the galley. He was so focused on who was in front of him that a blow to the back of his head caught him by surprise.

Fighting off the blackness that threatened to overtake him, Blake realized he'd been ambushed. The floor rushed up to smack him in the face, and the light became a dark chasm into which he fell. . .and fell. . . and fell.

Chapter Forty-nine

Jean Luc worried when he noticed Blake leaving. He glanced at a clock above the fireplace mantel. Steenberg should be through by now. At least he hoped so. He should have been done an hour ago. Blake would find nothing more than anonymous destruction.

Taking a deep, steadying breath, he moved toward Lily. Perhaps she would be more cordial now that her business partner was gone. He had noticed how her gaze followed every step the gambler took. He had never dreamed the two of them might have more than a business partnership.

Were they lovers? He rejected the idea. They had half a dozen chaperones on the boat. And he was experienced enough to know that Lily was still a wide-eyed innocent. He walked to where she stood talking to her grandmother. "May I have the pleasure of a dance with you, Miss Anderson?"

She glanced around before nodding. Was she looking for an excuse to turn him down? The polite smile on her face held little warmth as they moved to the center of the ballroom. They stood facing each other, waiting for the orchestra to begin.

"Your family must be pleased with the number of guests in attendance this evening."

Her smile warmed a fraction. "Yes, especially Camellia."

He looked to the pretty blond who was laughing and flirting with a group of young bucks. "You do not mind her popularity?"

"Of course not." Lily's brown gaze returned to him. "She's my sister. I love seeing her so happy."

Jean Luc realized he had offended her. . .again. A sigh filled his chest, but before he could begin an apology, a disturbance at the entrance to the ballroom claimed his attention.

A man had pushed his way past the servants. He stood swaying in the doorway, his clothing ragged.

"What's going on?" Lily began moving toward the man, her concern showing on her face.

Jean Luc followed her, as did most of the other people in the room. As he drew closer, he heard two words that struck fear into his heart. "Blaze. . .steamship." He gasped as realization flooded his mind. Steenberg had set the *Hattie Belle* on fire! He knew it! On the heels of his thought came remorse. What had he done?

Several of the women fainted, falling gracefully into the arms of the nearest men.

Jean Luc fought his way through them to a white-faced Lily. "Don't worry. I'll take care of this."

He didn't stay to see her reaction. What she or anyone else thought was secondary to his need to stop this disaster. He'd never meant for the boat to be destroyed or for anyone to die. All he'd ever wanted was to get his boat back and regain his father's approval.

As he tried to mount his horse, the enormity of Steenberg's actions pressed against Jean Luc's shoulders, threatening to pin him to the ground. He finally managed to struggle into the saddle, desperation strangling him as he pushed the horse to a gallop. The *Hattie Belle* could not be destroyed. If the stern-wheeler was lost, he would never be able to earn redemption.

❧

Blake tried to raise his hands to rub his aching head, but they were trapped at his side. What had happened? Why wouldn't his arms work? He struggled before realizing he was bound. Panic filled him before he managed to push it back. He needed to assess the situation.

Thinking back, he remembered the party at Lily's home, then boarding the *Hattie Belle*. . .and a bright light in the galley. He must have surprised another gang of thieves. They had attacked him and tied him up.

The floor swayed, telling him he was still on the boat. But where were the guards? And Jensen? Had they been overcome, too? Were they tied up in another part of the boat?

He pushed himself up, feeling much like an inchworm as he used the wall behind him for leverage. The stench of lamp oil burned his nose and throat, making him cough.

The noise must have brought one of his attackers closer. "I see you're awake."

He opened his eyes at the sound of the familiar voice. Standing over him was a recognizable figure, although he looked worn and bedraggled. "Steenberg."

The former captain laughed. "I told you I'd get even with you. I've been busy while you were taking your little nap." He set down his lantern.

Blake looked around to see if any of the other men were in the room with him. They weren't. Only he and Steenberg occupied the storage room. He poured all his energy into getting free of the ropes holding him. "I am guessing that. . .you take your orders from Jean Luc."

Steenberg's laugh died. "Jean Luc Champney doesn't control me. I just use his pocketbook to finance my future. He's got no idea what I'm planning to do to you and your boat."

Blake could feel one of the ropes loosening. He redoubled his efforts. If he could keep Steenberg talking until he could get free, he could overcome the man without much trouble. "Where are my men?"

"They're tied up and taking little naps of their own, but my plans have changed since we overpowered them." Steenberg pushed against a cargo barrel, toppling it with a loud crash. His smile returned. "One of my men gagged them and took them to the train station so they couldn't raise a ruckus. They'll be found in a few hours, but by then everything will be over."

"You'll never get away with this. And I'll make sure you never work on the river again."

"Those are some mighty fine words for a fellow who's not going to be alive much longer. Don't worry about me." The former captain stuck his thumbs in the waist of his pants and pulled in his stomach. "I've been bleeding Jean Luc for months now, doing jobs he's too soft to do himself. Even if someone suspects me, I can make a run for it. I've got enough money to leave this stinking town and never come back."

"Enjoy your freedom while you can." Blake gritted his teeth against the pain caused by his efforts to free himself. "I'll have the sheriff after you like I should have done in New Orleans."

The other man's grin didn't fade. He strutted around the tight space. "I knew that the minute I saw you. That's why I had to make new plans. You see, Jean Luc gave us orders not to destroy his precious boat. I went along because I didn't really care if we broke a few windows or blew the whole boat up, but everything changed when you walked in on us. Now I've stoked up the boiler and jammed her shut. She's already hissing like a bunch of alley cats."

His words struck fear in Blake's heart. Boiler explosions were the most deadly cause of accidents on the river. Worse than sandbars, snags, or even floods. When a boiler blew, the force was enough to throw fiery chunks of the boat hundreds of feet into the air. Then like lava from a volcano, the burning debris rained down on everything around. It was every river boatman's worst nightmare. For a moment he forgot his plan to escape. His cough returned.

"Yes, the smell is rather strong in here." Steenberg pushed over another barrel, and it crashed to the floor, spewing out its load of flour. "That's because we're going to set your boat on fire."

His threats brought Blake's mind back to earth. He couldn't afford to panic. "That sounds a bit redundant."

"I can't take the chance someone will arrive in time to stop the explosion." He pushed at Blake's leg with the toe of his boot. "You see, I don't like jails. And I'm not planning to spend any time in one."

The ropes around him refused to give. Could he talk Steenberg into loosening them? He coughed again. "Could I have some water?" Was that pitiful voice his?

Steenberg considered his request before shaking his head. "Don't you worry, though, it won't be long before your thirst is gone. I'd guess it's about time to put you out of your misery." He kicked over the lantern and walked out, leaving the door to the outside open.

His position in the room gave Blake a limited view of the sky, which was still as black and featureless as his winter cloak. He coughed again as the flames took hold and smoke began to rise around him. As the futility of the situation became apparent, his will to live bled away. He was going to die.

Anguish overtook him with the acknowledgment. Why now? So many things remained that he wished he had done, so many things he had yet to do. Was this all there was to life? Was he to end his life as the victim of a bloodthirsty crook? Did a man struggle and fight against the odds only to find himself facing death with no hope of redemption?

Sorrow and fear filled the empty spaces in his heart as Blake came face-to-face with his mortality. What was about to happen to him? Would he live on in some other form? A vision of hell rose up through the flames surrounding him. Why had he not repented when there was time? Why had he resisted the One who wanted to save him from eternal destruction? Why hadn't he realized the importance of faith until it was too late?

The flames licked higher, greedily consuming the space around him. Smoke wrapped its tendrils around him, choking out the air he needed to breathe, choking out all other considerations.

Blake slumped over as the heat intensified, regrets spinning away as death claimed him.

Chapter Fifty

Lily ran to her father. "We have to get to the river."

"I'll go. You stay here."

She refused to be left like some addled debutante. "I might be able to do something to help. You're going to need every able-bodied person you can muster, or every boat docked is liable to be lost, including ours."

He hesitated before nodding. "I'll get the buggy while you change out of that dress. But if you're not ready by the time I am, I'll leave you here."

Knowing his words were no idle threat, Lily pushed her way past their guests. Many of the men had already departed or were awaiting their carriages outside—not surprising since most of them depended on river traffic for their livelihoods.

Careless of the spectacle she might make, Lily took the steps at a dead run. When she reached her room, she jerked her skirt around so she could see the buttons and worked her way through them. Then she had to untie the ribbon holding her hoops to her waist. When she was finally free, she quickly donned one of her work skirts. The gray bodice would have to stay as Tamar was not here to help her and she could not reach the buttons.

She scurried back down the staircase, ignoring the raised eyebrows of the other women. Camellia was one of them, bless her heart. But her sister had always been much more concerned with her appearance than

Lily. Perhaps that came with being a beauty. If so, Lily was glad she was plain.

She ran to the stable, relieved to meet her father at the door. "I'm ready."

He held out a hand, and she pulled herself into the buggy. She was hardly seated before he whipped up the horse and they raced down the drive toward the river. It never took more than a few minutes to get to town, but tonight the ride seemed to last forever.

As they headed down the steep hill to the waterfront, her heart climbed into her throat. She could tell the *Hattie Belle* was on fire. Where was Blake? Was he one of the men tossing buckets of water into the flames?

Her father urged the horse faster, ignoring safety in his haste to reach the boat. He didn't pull up until they were almost on the men. Her gaze frantically searched their faces and figures, but she could find no sign of Blake. He must still be on the boat.

She leaped to the ground and raced to the gangplank, her father only a few steps behind her. At least the whole boat was not on fire yet, but it would burn to the waterline if God didn't provide a miraculous downpour.

Lily squinted, trying to see anyone through the billows of smoke. Then she caught a glimpse of someone in a dark coat. He was dragging something out of a room. Was it Blake? She knew almost instantly it was not. She could make out his dark hair, but his head was a different shape and his shoulders were not wide enough. He turned his head to cough, and she recognized him. "Jean Luc, what are you doing?"

"Get out of here." He coughed and turned again to pull at whatever he was dragging.

She and her father moved forward. Her eyes were streaming from the smoke, but she recognized Blake when they reached Jean Luc's side. He was bound in ropes and unconscious. Blood stained his face close to his hairline. He looked so pale she feared he might be dead.

Horror slammed through her at the thought of what Jean Luc had done to Blake. "Let go of him!" She tried to push Jean Luc away.

"Stop it, Lily. Do you think I'm the one who hurt him?" Jean Luc's dark gaze showed pain. "I'm trying to get him to safety."

"The two of you will have to work together." Her father stepped between them, his voice calm. "I've got to see about getting this boat out into the channel before it sets fire to everything docked here."

Lily's fear diminished a little because of his unruffled demeanor, but then the implications of his strategy hit her. Her father wouldn't survive if he stayed on the boat. "You can't do that, Papa."

"It's going to take all three of us to get Blake to safety." Jean Luc's voice was scratchy from exposure to the smoke.

Papa looked from Blake to the water. He nodded. "I'll come back as soon as we get him to the gangplank."

They tugged as a team, and Lily wondered if they were hurting Blake. But it didn't matter at this point. Ending up with broken bones was better than being burned alive. The smoke thickened as they moved toward the front of the boat. One step. . .pull. Another step. . .drag. She fell into a rhythm, ignoring the chaos around them. When they reached the end of the boat, the eager hands of several men lifted Blake's weight from between her and Papa and carried him to dry land.

That's when Lily felt the thrum of the paddle wheel. She looked around. "Where's Jean Luc?"

Her father's gaze followed hers, searching the deck around them. "He must be running the engine."

The wood crackled as flames licked greedily at the double doors leading to the staircase. The heat seemed to draw air from her lungs. She felt the tug of the boat as it began to inch away from the dock.

"Run!" Her father held out his hand, and she put hers in it. Together they dashed across the gangplank, barely making it before the whole thing fell into the river.

Slowly at first, then with increasing speed, the *Hattie Belle* began her final voyage. Lily's heart ached for Jean Luc. He was giving his life for the sake of others, showing he was a better man than she had ever dreamed. Tears streamed down her face as she caught sight of his figure in the pilothouse. "Jean Luc is a very brave man." Her voice broke, and her father cradled her in his arms.

After a few minutes, he leaned over and whispered in her ear. "There's a fellow standing here who seems mighty anxious to say something to you."

Lily raised her head, and her heart took wings. "Blake? Are you all right?"

He nodded, but the paleness of his face and the way he cradled one arm belied the gesture. "I'm sorry about the boat."

The meaning behind his words flashed across her mind. The boat was the only reason she and Blake were together. Without it, they had no reason to see each other. She would have no chance to convince him of God's love. He would have no reason to stay at her side. It wasn't like they were a married couple. He would be free to return to his former way of life and leave her to pick up the pieces.

An explosion rocked the water, and a blast of heat scorched Lily's face. "Jean Luc. . ." Horror and sadness filled her as her father put his arms back around her. They watched as flaming wood and metal splashed on the surface of the water and struck the surface of other boats.

She held her breath, fearing another boat might catch fire. Shadowy figures scurried around on their decks and doused the flames before they could take hold. Lily breathed a prayer of thankfulness to God for sparing them.

"I know where Jensen is."

"Is he. . . ?" Lily couldn't bring herself to complete the question.

"Not if Steenberg was telling the truth. He and the guards should be at the train depot."

Lily's head spun. "Steenberg?"

"He was getting even with me as he threatened when I dismissed him."

Knowing she would need time to absorb all the details about the night, she moved from the circle of her father's protection. "We need to get you back to Les Fleurs where someone can look at that arm."

He widened his stance as though he needed extra support. "First we need to find Jen—"

"You get some help for him. I'll take care of Jensen and the others." Papa walked away, calling out to one of the other men who huddled close to the empty berth where the *Hattie Belle* had been docked.

She turned her attention back to Blake and realized he was leaning to one side, much like a derelict boat. Lily stepped closer and grabbed the arm he was not favoring. At first he resisted leaning on her, but by the time they crossed the street to the buggy, she felt like she was supporting a mountain.

"I'm. . .s–sorry." Blake's voice was slurred.

Lily let out an impatient sound. "Don't be silly. You were nearly burned to a crisp. Just a few more steps and I'll help you get aboard. Then you can rest until we get home."

He didn't answer, which frightened her more than his apology. Blake was never at a loss for words. He must be more injured than he'd let on. Once they were both in the buggy, she slapped the reins and backed the buggy away from the somber crowd.

Blake sagged against her as they drove away, and Lily prayed with all her heart that he would recover. She couldn't imagine a life without his teasing smile and intriguing gaze. Or accept the idea that he might die before he became a Christian.

Blake was still in bed when someone knocked on the bedroom door. "Come in."

He expected one of the maids to enter with a cup of coffee and tell him breakfast was waiting for him downstairs. So when Lily entered, a breakfast tray carefully balanced between her hands, his mouth fell open. He grabbed at the bedcover, making sure his limbs were not exposed. He had never felt so vulnerable.

"I trust you are beginning to recover from your ordeal." She set the tray on a table at the foot of his bed and moved to where he lay.

Blake pushed himself up to a sitting position, keeping the cover tightly around him. He bit back a groan when his head bumped against the headboard. "You shouldn't have gone to so much trouble."

Lily walked to the window on one side of his bed and opened the curtains covering it. Weak light drifted into the room while she moved to the window on the other side of his bed and repeated her actions. "They caught Steenberg and his gang."

"What about Jean Luc?"

Her eyebrows crinkled in a frown. "He saved yours and Papa's lives."

Now it was Blake's turn to frown. Had Steenberg not told them about Jean Luc's role in the destruction of their boat?

"Such a heroic act. If he had not taken the boat out into the channel, the whole port would have gone up in flames when the boiler blew. A lot of people would have died if Jean Luc had not been so brave."

Every word she spoke was like a blow. How could he tell her the truth? And why should he? Blake didn't want to destroy her faith in the man. It was true that Jean Luc's actions had benefited the others. And since Jean Luc was dead, no one could bring him to justice for his attempts to harm the *Hattie Belle*. "I still haven't pieced together how you managed to get to the river."

She fluffed a pillow that had fallen on the floor. "Papa brought me in the same buggy that I used to get us back here."

Blake would have nodded, but he didn't want to aggravate the pounding in his head. "What I don't understand is how you went from dancing to rescuing me."

"One of the Champneys' slaves came in and said there was a boat on fire." She shrugged. "Nothing would have kept me in the ballroom."

He should have known that.

"Enough about me." She dropped the pillow on the bed and picked up the tray, settling it on his lap. "Are you recovered enough to feed yourself, or do you need some help?"

Blake's eyebrows rose. "Are you offering to be my nursemaid?"

Her blush was one of the things he loved most about Lily. That and her dogged determination. Like him, she had lost everything last night. Some women would have moaned and cried about the fire, but not Lily.

"How is your head?"

"It aches, but not too badly." He picked up his fork to prove that he was fine. The first taste of the fluffy scrambled eggs was delicious and seemed to light a ferocious hunger. Blake wolfed down the rest of his food and sat back with a sigh of contentment.

Lily reached for the tray. "I believe you are going to be fine."

Blake wrapped his hand around her wrist. "I don't know how you do it."

"What are you talking about?" She wouldn't meet his gaze, but she didn't try to pull away, either.

He didn't want to let her go, not until he understood her better. In all the months they had been together, he had never realized how strong she actually was. But now? "I don't have the energy to look on the bright side. All I can think about is that everything is gone. All my clothes, my cards, everything I owned was on the *Hattie Belle*."

She looked at him. Really looked at him. Her lips twitched, her smile appearing and disappearing like a shy child. "God can turn every tragedy into good."

Blake practically threw her hand away. His head pounded once more. "Is that all you have to say?"

She picked up the tray and moved away. "You asked the question."

Suddenly Blake knew what he had to do. "I'm leaving."

The tray dropped to the floor, making him wince and put a hand to his forehead. She looked at him, her face full of pain. "You can't leave. You're not well."

"It may take a day or two, but Camellia fixed me up pretty well last night. Besides, there's no reason for me to stay here any longer." He closed his eyes to keep from looking at her. He couldn't weaken. Couldn't let Lily's sweetness change his mind. Blake knew what he had to do.

The soft sound of his door closing made Blake open his eyes. She was gone. Now he realized that the pain in his chest was worse than the pain in his head. Blake sank into the soft, clean bed and groaned. He had to get away before he did something stupid. . .like kiss her again.

❧

Hopelessness claimed Lily. She knew she should not have expected anything else.

Two days after the destruction of the *Hattie Belle*, when it became obvious Jean Luc had died in the explosion, Monsieur and Madame Champney held a memorial service for their son. Her heart had gone out to the grieving couple. They seemed to have aged a decade. The only thing she could think of that might alleviate some of their pain was to tell them how brave Jean Luc had been, how he had sacrificed himself so no one else would die. They seemed to appreciate her words.

As sad as the service had been, Lily would have recovered from her sorrow. Then Blake announced that he was not going to stay in Natchez, and she fell into despondency, a yawning pit of blackness she couldn't seem to climb from.

She had said nothing as he recovered his strength, nothing when he bid them good-bye. What could she say? He would never change. He would not turn to God and become the man she could spend the rest of her life with.

The only reason he had stayed in the first place was because he was invested. . .in the *Hattie Belle*. Nothing else. If she had ever doubted that, Blake had proven it when he walked out of her life.

She sighed and looked out the parlor window. Clouds skittered across the sky. It was a gloomy day, one that matched her mood. Tears filled her eyes. Lily sniffed and tried to keep them at bay. She didn't want to waste any tears over Blake Matthews. Not when she was sure he'd already forgotten her. The door opened behind her, and she wiped at her eyes, wishing she'd brought a handkerchief.

" 'In every thing give thanks: for this is the will of God in Christ Jesus concerning you.' " Her father quoted the scripture quietly as he walked across the room.

His words brought back her answer to Blake when he bemoaned the loss of all his worldly goods. How self-righteous she had been when she told him that God turned tragedy into good. Lily had not realized that God would call on her to live her beliefs.

She twisted her lips into a smile and looked toward her father. "Thanks, Papa, for reminding me of His promise. I know it's true, but I'm finding it so hard to live that way when it feels like my heart has been torn out of my chest."

A frown appeared on his face. "I know it's not easy." He sat beside her on the sofa and patted her hand. "Especially when someone you care about is no longer at your side."

Determined not to cry, Lily folded her lips into a straight line and nodded. "I didn't realize how much I cared about Blake until he disappeared."

"God must have someone really special in mind for you, Water Lily. Someone who will love God with all his heart and love you as Christ loves the Church. It may be hard to believe right now, but you will be so happy with that man."

"I suppose so." Lily wished she could believe him. The hole Blake left in her life was an awfully big one to fill. He had challenged her to do her best, dared her to cling to her morals, and supported her when she least expected it.

Papa stood and walked to the window she'd been looking through. Silence gathered around them, deepening her feeling of dread. What was he thinking? Was he about to leave her, too? Lily wasn't sure she could handle two desertions in one week. "I need to check on Camellia and Jasmine."

He turned around as she was rising from the sofa. "Have you thought about your future?"

Here it was. Papa was not going to allow her to escape before he told her his plans. Lily shook her head. "Not much."

"I understand. You've suffered a huge blow. It takes time to get over loss and grief. But one of these days you're going to wake up and realize life is going on whether you like it or not. One of these days your faith is going to rise again to the surface."

She wondered if he planned to come back and visit his daughters once he returned to life on the river.

"I want you to know I am here for you, Lily." He walked back to her and put an arm around her waist. "If you want to buy another boat, I'll gladly captain it for you."

Touched by his offer, she returned his hug. "Thanks, Papa. I appreciate that. You're a great captain. It's a special talent God gifted you with. No matter which boat you guide, the passengers and crew will be in good hands."

He lifted her chin with a bent finger. "You've loved the river almost since you drew your first breath, but if this disaster has taken away your desire, I'll stay right here in Natchez with you and your sisters. I'm never going to desert you again."

"You would do that for us?" Her last doubts disappeared in a landslide of emotion. "I love you, Papa."

They hugged for several healing minutes. When they separated, Lily had to wipe her eyes again. Was she turning into one of those weak women she so despised? The ones who relied on tears to manipulate others?

Her grandmother opened the parlor door and started to enter. "Oh, I'm sorry. I didn't mean to interrupt."

Lily shook her head and smiled. "You're not interrupting us at all. Papa and I were talking about what we're going to do."

Grandmother looked from one of them to the other. "I hope you don't plan on leaving right away."

"Don't worry about that." Lily stepped forward and took her grandmother's hands into her own. "It's going to be a while before I'm ready to purchase another boat."

"Well, I can't say that I'm entirely unhappy to hear that. Although it saddens me to see you moping about, I still like having you around.

You've proven you are capable of taking care of yourself and your sisters. Your aunt and uncle may have suggestions for your future, but you will decide which path to follow."

Grandmother looked past her to where her father stood. "I hope you will stay with us, too, Henrick. My Rose loved you so much, and I hope you'll forgive us for keeping you separated from your children for all these years."

He cleared his throat. "Thank you. The past is behind us, and there's no reason to hold on to it. God has been so good to me, revealing Himself to me and giving me a reason to keep moving forward. He takes the worst circumstances and turns them into something beautiful. That's what I was telling Lily right before you came in."

"Amen." Grandmother released one of Lily's hands to reach out toward Henrick.

Lily's heart filled with love and thankfulness as she stood between her father and her grandmother. It was time to stop dwelling on her losses. She had a lot of things to be thankful for. The reconciliation of her relatives was proof that God could work out anything.

Peace settled on her shoulders with that realization, the peace that Christ had promised to all who believed in Him. She claimed that promise with all her heart, trusting that He would work out her future in a way more marvelous than she could imagine.

Chapter Fifty-two

Blake had never felt more alone in his life. He still remembered so clearly the day when Lily, along with her sisters, had appeared aboard the *Hattie Belle*, determined to get her clean and ready for travel. At that time he'd wondered if he would ever again enjoy peace and quiet. Now he wondered how he had ever enjoyed the solitude of his life before she. . .they entered it.

Even Jensen had deserted him, opting to stay near Tamar since she appeared more receptive to sharing her future with him. He hoped the two of them would marry and be happy.

He wanted to go back to Natchez. What was wrong with him? Lily had made her position clear before he left.

Blake left the room he had rented two weeks earlier when he'd decided to stop in Vicksburg. Walking toward the riverfront, he mused about the differences between Vicksburg and Natchez. Both were situated on high bluffs on the eastern side of the river, overlooking Louisiana lowlands on the west. But fewer plantation homes dotted the landscape of this town, and the dock was not as busy. Perhaps that was because Vicksburg had only been a settled area for a few decades.

At least he could play cards. Blake tipped his hat at a lady riding by in a carriage. For a moment his heart nearly stopped. Lily? She had the same light-brown hair brightened by golden strands that reflected the afternoon sun, but that was where the similarity ended.

Blake regained his composure and continued his trek to the waterfront. His footsteps dragged. He didn't feel like going to a gambling boat. The allure of gambling seemed to have faded now that he had enough money to live comfortably. Maybe he should consider buying a home and settling down. But that wouldn't solve his lack of companionship.

A flyer someone had tacked to an oak tree caught his attention. DISHEARTENED was the first word, followed by a question mark. He stopped to read further. The next line read, DISCOURAGED? and the third line was equally compelling: LONELY? The hair on the back of his neck rose. The sign might have been written for him.

Blake took a step forward and peered at the rest of the announcement. It was about a revival in Vicksburg beginning this very night and promised that all who came to listen to the Word as preached by Rev. Nathan Pierce would find the answers they'd been seeking. Blake almost passed it by, but what would he do with his evening? Perhaps this Pierce fellow had a message that would make him feel better.

He walked to the livery stable and rented a horse, getting instructions on how to reach the revival. As he rode past the outskirts of Vicksburg, he heard singing. It seemed to come from all around him, wonderful, uplifting chords. He couldn't make out the words, so he pushed his mount faster.

He reached the meeting place and felt like he'd been transported back in time. A brush arbor stood at the edge of a meadow, its roughhewn posts and leafy roof reminding him of his childhood. Early in his father's career as a preacher, the church had met in a similar arbor.

Blake almost turned back, but his arrival had been noticed by some of the congregation. He didn't want to seem like a coward, so he dismounted and tied his horse to a tree. He found a seat in the shady arbor as the preacher stepped up to the pulpit made out of a hickory post.

"Good evening." A tall, handsome man with a piercing gaze and blond hair stepped up to the podium as dusk settled on the meadow.

Some of the men in the congregation answered the preacher. "Good evening."

"I've come to Vicksburg to share a message of hope and redemption with all of you. A message that was first shared a long time before you and I came here. It's a message that all men need to hear. A promise that we can cling to even when it seems we've lost everything."

Blake leaned forward, his attention caught by the preacher's words.

"I'm sure a lot of you here tonight know who Daniel is."

Blake searched his memory. There was something about dreams and visions in that book of the Old Testament. A lions' den?

"Well, tonight I'm going to tell you a story about a set of young men who were his friends—Hananiah, Mishael, and Azariah. They were slaves of King Nebuchadnezzar, but they were also devout followers of the Most Holy God. So when King Nebuchadnezzar told them he wanted them to worship at the feet of a huge golden statue he'd made, they refused. This made King Nebuchadnezzar so angry he had them tied up and thrown into a fiery furnace."

The preacher paused and looked out over his congregation. It seemed to Blake the man was looking directly at him. "That's when things got really interesting. King Nebuchadnezzar looked at the furnace and saw that Hananiah, Mishael, and Azariah were no longer tied up. And they weren't alone in that furnace. Let me read this part to you directly from the Bible so you can hear it for yourself. 'Lo, I see four men loose, walking in the midst of the fire, and they have no hurt; and the form of the fourth is like the Son of God.'"

Blake's heart tripled its speed. This story was so familiar to him. He'd been bound and left for dead. He thought back to that night, to the despair that had claimed him before he lost consciousness. Like the three men in the Bible, he'd been rescued. He should have died that night, but God in His goodness spared him—sent others to pull him from the fire. He'd received a second chance, and here he was about to waste it.

As the preacher brought his sermon to a close, he asked all to bow their heads during his prayer. Then he invited anyone who had felt the hand of God on them to come forward and declare their faith.

Blake hesitated as others stood and made their way to the pulpit. Then he could not wait any longer. He stood and took a tentative step. It felt good. So he took another step. Joy was stalking him, making it difficult to restrain himself from running forward. When he reached the pulpit, Blake kneeled and bowed his head. He had learned from a young age what one said when giving one's heart to God, but tonight the words, the thoughts, had real meaning. He asked Jesus to come into his heart and felt the assurance flood his body. He was a new man.

The preacher put a hand on his head and prayed, giving thanks to God for saving another lost lamb. Blake had no idea how long he knelt there in front of the pulpit, but by the time he rose it was fully dark. He found his horse and rode back to the livery stable, wonder and excitement filling him.

He needed to tell someone, but who would care? *Lily.* The answer was in his heart as soon as the question formed. He needed to get back to Lily.

Blake thought of an advertisement he'd seen in the *Vicksburg Whig*, and everything came together as though God had planned it. Chills ran up his spine. God was omnipotent. Plans for surprising Lily filled his head as thankfulness flooded his heart. Blake knew exactly what he needed to do.

❧

Lily threw a kiss toward Jasmine as she mounted her dapple-gray mare and headed to town. The effort would be wasted. No boat her father had found so far was the right one. Too big, too small, or too decrepit, none fit the vision she had.

Now that she no longer had a partner, she didn't want a riverboat as large as the *Hattie Belle*. If she and her father could find something on a smaller scale, they could keep the crew to a minimum.

They would hire Tamar and Jensen, of course. They had gotten married right after Blake left. It was the one bright spot in Lily's life. She loved seeing Tamar blossom into a different person, walking taller with her shoulders back and head high. It was amazing what a combination of freedom and the love of a good man could do.

She wished Camellia would stay with them but had finally realized her sister would only be happy if she could attend the finishing school they had chosen in New Orleans. Perhaps they would at least curb some of her flirtatiousness. Lily was also concerned about losing her youngest sister. Jasmine seemed to be growing faster than the weeds in Grandmother's garden.

Lily reined in her thoughts as she descended the steep hill to the dock. Natchez Under-the-Hill was as busy as always, boats of all sizes vying for passengers and cargo before they once again braved the river currents. Why was it she always felt more alive when she was close to the river? Papa had nicknamed her well. She had to be on the water to thrive. Living with her relatives was not as difficult as it had once been, but this was where she belonged.

Papa's bright-red shirt and felt hat with its single feather made him easy to spot in the bustling area. He stood to one side of a new warehouse that partially blocked her view of the boats in the harbor. Lily walked her horse to where he stood and dismounted. "Where is this boat you've found?"

"It's not far." He gave her a kiss on the cheek, his eyes twinkling. "I think this one is going to be perfect."

Lily smiled at him. He was trying so hard. Even though she had climbed out of the despondency Blake's desertion had caused, it was difficult to regain her enthusiasm. "I hope you're right."

He tucked her hand into the crook of his arm, and they ambled toward the river. A bevy of steamboats bumped shoulders, their tall stacks puffing as muscular, sweating men filled them with cargo. Next to them were the smaller craft—the few flatboats, barges, and keelboats that struggled to survive alongside the larger boats. But where was the boat her father had brought her to see?

Then a boat caught her eye, a shiny white vessel with red lettering on the side. A pinprick of interest touched her. The boat was about half the size of the *Hattie Belle*, just what Lily had thought she might want to purchase. It only had three decks: the main deck, the boiler deck, and the hurricane deck. She would need to get closer, but from where she stood, the stern wheel looked as though it was in good condition. Maybe Papa had found the perfect boat this time.

Her eyes widened as she read the words stenciled on the side of the boat. She read the words out loud before looking at her father. "WATER LILY. What have you done?"

A wide grin crinkled the corners of his eyes. "I'm not the one." He spread his free arm out in an arc.

Lily's confused gaze followed the gesture. Her heart stopped as a familiar figure stepped out of the shadows and bowed in their direction. Blake. The man she thought she'd never see again.

She wanted to run across the gangplank, but her feet seemed to have forgotten how to move. She watched as he sauntered toward them, his stride as long and self-assured as ever. Her heart ached with love for him. The time they'd spent apart seemed to disappear as he reached her side.

"Hello, Lily." His voice sent a shiver through her.

Lily looked up at his face, her gaze tracing the lines of his cheeks, her fingers itching to feel the silkiness of his dark hair. With great difficulty she swallowed her emotions. "I love your new boat."

His eyebrows rose. "I was hoping it might be *our* boat."

She noted the emphasis on the pronoun, but a thousand questions arose. "I suppose I could buy into it, but who would own controlling interest? I'm not about to let you turn any investment of mine into a gambling casino."

He tilted his head, and his eyebrows climbed higher. He was not going to agree with her.

Lily braced herself for an argument.

Blake's eyes darkened in a way that made her heart leap. "Did you know that wives in Mississippi can own property?"

"What difference does that make?" Irritation colored her voice. "I'm not mar—" Her throat closed up as the implication of his question struck her.

Blake nodded. "It wouldn't have worked in New Orleans, Lily. I know that now. You were right to push me away. But I've found God. It's changed me so much. I'm not saying I'm perfect—"

"I'm sure of that." Lily recovered her equilibrium as joy exploded within her, a feeling so strong and so pure she knew it came from God. "But I've never wanted to love a perfect man."

"All I've been able to think about is sharing my life with you, living in His will." Blake moved closer and brushed a tendril of hair out of her face.

Lily turned to her father. "Papa?"

He shrugged. "Blake came to me yesterday and asked for permission to court you, but if you don't love him. . ."

"But I do. I do love him." She blushed as she spoke the words and looked up at Blake.

Slowly and with great care he took her hand from her father's arm and wrapped her in a hug. "I love you, too, my Water Lily."

Camellia

Aaron: I dedicate this book to my wonderful colleagues at Belhaven University. When Wesley College closed, I wondered if I would ever find another school where I could do more than just teach, where I could also minister to my students. God answered through you: Not only did you take me from working part-time to working full-time, you opened your hearts and took me in as one of your own. You will never understand how much this meant to me. I lost a family I had worked alongside for twenty years, but you replaced it with another that has become just as precious to me. Thank you for your love, support, encouragement, and full acceptance as a Blazer. I love you all.

Diane: For Lisa M. Davis, my sister from different parents. The hardest thing for me to do this year was tell you I was retiring from the Legislature. How could I give up the desk next to yours? How could I not talk to you every day? How could I leave you behind when we are best friends? When we count on each other to keep sane in the madness of the Capitol? Over the years, you've been there for me through hard times and good times. We've shared tears, laughter, and our deepest, darkest secrets. Even the phrase "town girl"—the one I use in my bio—came from you. And don't get me started on trips to the beach. Some things need to stay just between the two of us. The only reason I can bear to leave is the knowledge that nothing can break the bond between us. We may not talk as often, we certainly won't get to share the trivia of our daily lives. But I know when we do get together the time apart will disappear in an instant. Hang in there. I love you.

Acknowledgments

As always, we are so grateful to Becky Germany, Becky Fish, and the wonderful staff at Barbour Publishing. You truly make us feel like we belong.

Steve Laube, we couldn't do it without your invaluable assistance. . . and we wouldn't want to.

Bards of Faith, you are our anchor in the ocean of writing and publishing. Your friendships and prayers keep us grounded and fill our sails.

And most importantly, to our Lord and Savior Jesus Christ, all for You!

Chapter One

Boonville, Missouri
June 17, 1861

Jonah Thornton did not want to die.

His fingers cramped, and he loosened his grip on the trigger of his Sharps carbine. The butt of the rifle seemed grafted to his shoulder, an extra arm with deadly intent. He bent his head and sighted down the thirty-inch barrel, wondering if he could really pull the trigger. Wondering if he could take the life of another man. He raised his head and moved the rifle back to marching position, heel at waist level, barrel with bayonet over his shoulder.

A twig broke some distance away, and the tempo of Jonah's heart soared. Was it a scout looking for evidence of the force mustering in the area between the city of Boonville and the Mississippi River? Or a rabbit or deer foraging for an early morning meal?

His awareness stretched outward. Around him, the breaths of his fellow soldiers sounded loud, as did the whisper of gunpowder sliding into the throats of their muskets, followed by the snick of minie balls—a sound as deadly as a rattlesnake's tail. The moment was fast approaching when he would find out exactly what it meant to fight for his beliefs. Even to the point of risking his life in the protection of those beliefs.

Sweat sprouted on his forehead as he caught the rhythmic cadence of marching feet. The rest of the battalion was about to reach his position between two cornfields on the edge of Boonville. He had been aboard the first steamer to arrive before daybreak and had marched with the other troops toward the town where the Missouri State Guard and Governor Jackson waited.

The time to fight was upon them. His heart raced. Could he do it? Could he find the courage to leave his protected position? Could he jump to his feet and run forward when the order was given? Would the bullet from an unseen rifle tear through him? And if it didn't—if he somehow survived the assault—could he aim his own weapon at another human being and pull the trigger?

Jonah swallowed against the bitterness in his throat. *Lord, please let this end peaceably. Let them surrender without opening fire. Protect me and the other men. You know I don't want to kill. Fill them with fear and confusion so we might prevail without bloodshed. Amen.*

"Now!"

The single syllable catapulted Jonah to his feet. He ran without thought, almost propelled forward by the movement of the troops. They ran full tilt, up and over the ridge where the enemy soldiers were gathered. Cannons behind them boomed, but Jonah ignored the sound, centering his attention on one target, a man with short brown hair whose mouth had fallen open. Part of his brain noted the broad forehead, the lock of damp hair, and a pair of brown eyes wide with fear. Jonah reached for the rifle flung over his shoulder, bringing it around to his chest in one smooth movement. Tugging slightly on the trigger, he felt the movement as it began to move under the pressure.

A bullet whined past his ear, and one of the soldiers on the ridge crumpled. Still hesitating, he lifted his head slightly and realized the men on the ridge were running away from the charging soldiers. Jonah thought the battalion might prevail without further casualties until one of their officers began shouting. The fleeing soldiers halted and reached for their own weapons, apparently only now comprehending they could defend themselves.

Realizing the battle was not yet over, he sighted once more. His eyelids fluttered as he squeezed the trigger. The carbine slammed against his shoulder, and the intense fear that had been his constant companion for the past hour disappeared as the unfortunate man he had targeted jerked.

A surprised expression tautened the man's features. His rifle drooped as he looked down at his chest, at the dark stain spreading on his uniform. Then he looked up. His gaze slammed into Jonah. A scowl clouded his features. He raised his weapon a few inches before his features went slack and he crumbled to the ground.

Dead. The man was dead. He would never rise again, never laugh or speak or march again.

Horror filled Jonah as the realizations hammered him with the impact of the bullets flying between the two groups of men. He seemed frozen in the midst of the fierce fighting even though men continued to fire all around him. The sounds of battle faded, lost in the midst of the insistent ringing in his ears.

Nausea welled up, mixed with grief and remorse. He doubled over, and spasms shook him, turning his skin cold and clammy. When he thought the nausea had abated, he tried to push himself to his feet. But it was a futile effort as the horror overwhelmed him again, and his whole body convulsed once more.

It seemed to take forever before he regained control of his senses. Awareness of his surroundings crept back to him. The air was thick with smoke even though the deafening blasts of gunfire had been replaced by moans of pain.

Jonah pushed himself up and turned to survey the aftermath of the battle. Choking smoke hung low over the dirt road and clung to the few cornstalks remaining upright after the charge of the battalion. It blocked out the sun. Or had the sun set? Jonah wasn't sure of anything.

A hand clapped his shoulder, and Jonah's breath caught until he turned and recognized Cage, the dark-haired Arkansawyer who had befriended him when they met in Tennessee at the recruiting office.

"Are you all right?" His concerned gray gaze raked Jonah's face.

Hot tears pushed against his eyes, but Jonah clenched his jaw and nodded. He would not cry like a boy in short pants. He was a grown man, a soldier. He had to be all right.

Cage continued staring at him for a few moments before he nodded and cleared his throat. "You dropped this." He held out Jonah's rifle.

"Thanks." The single syllable scraped against his raw throat. When had he lost his weapon? A fine soldier he was turning out to be. Instead of reloading and killing more of their enemy, he'd run away. What if the battle had been won by their enemy? He'd likely be sprawled out on the ground, a bullet hole in his back. Jonah took his carbine from his friend's hand.

"You and I have talked about the necessity of war before." Cage nodded toward the road behind him. "We've prayed together about the Lord delivering us as He did the Israelites. 'In the world ye shall have tribulation—' "

" 'But be of good cheer; I have overcome the world.' " Jonah finished the quote for him.

Together they walked toward the riverbank to await the short voyage back to Jefferson City. Jonah knew he should be thankful for having such a strong Christian example as a friend. Over the past weeks they had spent time poring over the Word, reading from Cage's pocket Bible and discussing the significance of book, chapter, and verse.

But right now he wanted nothing more than to run from this world. To go back to New Orleans and the privileged life he'd enjoyed there. Why had he ever left home? And given the circumstances of his departure, would he ever be able to return?

"I don't know how we got separated on the way back." Cage's familiar drawl brought Jonah's head up.

Jonah could have told the other man he'd purposely searched out a corner on the crowded steamboat and turned his back on the soldiers. Shrugging, he looked toward the center of their encampment where, in spite of the warm evening air, the other soldiers sat laughing around a blazing campfire. Even if Cage was a close friend, Jonah didn't want to admit the shame keeping him apart from the others.

Cage looked at him for a moment before handing Jonah a tin plate and settling himself on the nearby trunk of a fallen hickory tree.

"You shouldn't look so glum. We won the battle this morning." Cage dug into his plate of beans with gusto. "According to what the others are saying, the Missouri State Guard has been routed. We beat them with a minimum of bloodshed, at least on our side. General Lyon has succeeded in subduing the Rebels before they could infect the whole state."

"I guess so." The words had little meaning tonight. Not when the memories were so sharp in his mind. Jonah knew he wouldn't be able to force a single bite of food past the lump in his throat. He picked up his hardtack and turned it over and over in his hand.

"Do you think you're going to find any answers there?" The other man's voice held a note of sarcasm.

Jonah shook his head and let the hard biscuit drop to his plate. "I'm not hungry."

"I see." Cage swallowed another mouthful.

Feeling his friend's gaze even in the deepening gloom, Jonah shrugged. "I can't get it out of my head. He was so young, so shocked. . ."

Cage's spoon clattered as it struck the edge of his tin plate. "That will pass, kid. And it'll be a little easier the next time."

"I'm not sure that's a good thing." Now that the words were out, Jonah wished he had not voiced them. Would his friend think he was a coward? And wouldn't that be a correct estimation? Tendrils of shame curdled his stomach as he thought of his reaction during the battle. The only reason he had not died was because the Lord had protected him for some unfathomable purpose. Jonah stared at the unappealing food on his lap and waited for Cage's condemning words.

"Jonah, you're reacting to the battle. Give yourself a little more credit." He nodded toward the group of men some distance away. "Do you think they condemn you? This was your first battle, and I assume the first time you killed something other than game."

"If I could've found the strength, I would have run away." Jonah's confession brought a tiny bit of relief. He looked up at Cage and saw understanding in the other man's eyes. He tightened his jaw to dam the flood of emotions threatening to overwhelm him.

"I know. Taking another man's life is a thing no Christian should have to face. But this world belongs to Satan. Remember what we read last week. Why do you think Paul spoke of the armor of God?" He closed his eyes for a moment, his eyebrows drawing together. " 'Wherefore take unto you the whole armour of God, that ye may be able to withstand in the evil day, and having done all, to stand.' "

The verse washed over Jonah like a wave, cleansing some of the fear and shame that had hung over him this evening.

"And Paul was in prison when he wrote those words."

Jonah closed his eyes and imagined being held in chains. The fear, the discomfort, the uncertainty that must have tried to settle on Paul. Had God whispered in the disciple's ear as he looked at the Roman centurion guarding the prison? Had He suggested the comparison that Paul would send to the Ephesians? They were words to sustain Christians by reminding them of God's protection even in this world of battles and rampant sin.

"Do you remember the different parts of the armor?" Cage's voice brought him back to the present.

Jonah thought for a minute. "Is truth one of them?"

Cage's grizzled head bobbed up and down. "That's right, and the breastplate of righteousness, boots made from the gospel of peace, a shield of faith, and the most important part of all. . ."

"If I remember rightly, it's my salvation." Jonah was feeling better than he'd felt since they had come back to camp on the bank of the fast-flowing Mississippi River.

"Yes." Cage's infectious smile was as bright as a beacon. He leaned over and rapped Jonah smartly on the head. "The helmet of salvation to be exact."

A chuckle filled his throat. It felt good to let it loose. For a moment his grief and shame lifted. Jonah almost felt human once again.

One of the other soldiers, a private with blond hair and a mustache, walked over to them. He bent and glanced at Jonah's full plate. "You going t'eat that?"

Jonah shook his head and started to hand his plate to the lanky man, but Cage grabbed his wrist before he could finish the motion. "You're going to need that food. You didn't eat much this morning. If you give away your supper, you may not last another battle."

The thought of future battles made Jonah's stomach clench. He looked at Cage, recognizing the experience in his gaze. He glanced up at the private. "Give me a few minutes to decide."

The man spat at the ground next to Jonah's left boot. "I never thought you Johnnys should be allowed to join." He stomped away and rejoined the men around the campfire. A couple of them glanced back toward Cage and Jonah, suspicion showing in their faces.

"I should have just given him the food."

"We can't buy their trust, Jonah. It's only natural for them to be suspicious of us. We are Southerners after all." Cage sighed and shrugged a shoulder. "Maybe one day they'll understand why we refused to fight with the Confederacy. Until then, we have to remember why we're Federal soldiers."

He knew Cage was right, but sometimes it was hard to bear. Had he done the right thing to volunteer his service to the Yankees? Yes. Jonah could not support slavery on any level, even though he dreaded the idea of facing a friend or relative on the battlefield. Would his convictions force him into killing someone he knew? Jonah prayed not.

Cage's grunt interrupted his circling thoughts. "Private Benton will survive. There's plenty of forage if he's hungry."

Jonah picked up his hardtack and gnawed at it. Letting the tough biscuit soak up the moisture from his beans only softened it a smidgen. His thoughts seemed as hard as the food in his mouth. It was fine to talk about the armor of God, but it still didn't answer all the questions and fears that had arisen because of the battle. "What does the Bible say about using weapons to kill someone else?"

"David was a great warrior, wasn't he?"

"Yes." Jonah was somewhat surprised by the question. Everyone knew about David's many battles.

"Wasn't he also called a 'man after God's own heart'?"

Of course. The oppressive doubt and shame lifted from Jonah's heart, if only for a moment. He might not be as strong as David, but he could still spend time reading the Bible his sister had given him for Christmas last year. Once again he regretted not bringing it with him on his trip to visit his brother, Eli. But he'd never thought he would go from Memphis to the front lines of the war between the North and the South.

Eli had tried to dissuade him from joining, but Jonah had been adamant. He had known his reasons for volunteering were valid. Too bad he'd never imagined what his choice would cost him—his self-confidence, his pride, and perhaps even his life.

Jonah lifted his thoughts heavenward and prayed his sacrifices would matter. And he entreated God to someday see him in the same way He had once seen David.

The food on his plate seemed more palatable after his prayer. Jonah filled his spoon and lifted it to his mouth, savoring the smoky flavor. Even his hardtack was tastier. His appetite reawakened. He shoveled in another mouthful and chewed. Energy flowed through him like a rising tide, and Jonah realized once more how blessed he was to have such a strong Christian as his friend.

❧

Jonah ran a finger underneath the scratchy blue-black collar of his uniform jacket before entering the general's office. Good thing he'd managed to get the white pants washed and pressed by a local washerwoman. He wanted to present the best possible image to his commanding officers.

The room, a gentleman's library in the house that had been commandeered, was crowded. Soldiers and officers stood in small knots, leaned against the walls, or sat in the leather chairs scattered about. Most of them did not notice his entrance, but his captain, Drew Poindexter, stepped forward and nodded briefly.

Jonah straightened his shoulders and snapped a salute.

Captain Poindexter returned his salute before turning to a large desk covered with papers and maps. "Sir, this is the man I told you about, Jonah Thornton."

Jonah swallowed hard and saluted once again as he met the piercing, coffee-colored gaze of Brigadier General Nathaniel Lyon. He had only seen the man from a distance before this morning. Why was he here now? What possible interest could this man have in him?

"At ease, son." General Lyon nodded toward a chair occupied by another soldier. "Major Eads, clear this room. I need a moment of privacy with Mr. Thornton."

Jonah let his arm drop but stood at attention as the major carried out the general's orders. His captain turned as if to leave, but the general stopped him with a raised hand. "I didn't mean you, Drew. This is your idea after all."

The room seemed much larger without the other occupants. The general leaned back in his chair and waved a hand at the pair of chairs in front of his desk. "How long have you been a soldier, Thornton?"

Jonah's mind raced. Had his deplorable behavior on the field of battle several days earlier been noted? He looked down at his feet. "Only a few months, sir."

"I want to commend you for choosing to serve your country in spite of the leanings of many of your fellow Southerners." The general's voice was not warm, but it was not as gruff as it had been when he addressed his subordinate.

Jonah risked a glance upward. The look on the man's narrow face was one of respect. Jonah responded with a dip of his head. "Thank you, sir."

General Lyon continued studying his face for a moment. Then he turned his attention to Captain Poindexter. "Why don't you tell Mr. Thornton your idea?"

Jonah swung his glance toward the captain on his right. Poindexter's jacket was unbuttoned, but his shirt was clean and crisp. His blond hair gleamed in the yellow light of a nearby lamp. "I. . .um. . .I don't want to embarrass you, Jonah, but I saw your reaction when you shot that fellow."

Hot blood burned Jonah's cheeks. The shame had begun to subside in the intervening days, but it resurged anew. What was he doing here? He should have listened to Eli, should have stayed in Memphis. . .remained neutral. . .avoided fighting for either side. But how could he ignore his convictions? He was not the type of man to hide out until the war ended. He could not abide the institution of slavery, could not support a society that depended on slavery to succeed. So he had joined the army and come to Missouri as ordered. Only to fail his first test. "I'm sorry, sir. It won't happen again."

A hand came down on his right shoulder. "Fighting is not the only way you can serve the Union."

"Yes, sir." What other way could there be? He had no naval skills, so they couldn't be thinking of putting him aboard a ship. Maybe they were intending to assign him to the rear, an assistant to the quartermaster. Jonah braced himself. After his experience on the battlefield, perhaps it would be a relief.

General Lyon leaned forward and steepled his hands. "One of the most valuable resources in any war is information."

A memory surfaced in Jonah's mind from the first time he and his brother had traveled to visit their grandparents in Natchez. One sunny afternoon, the two of them had gone exploring in a copse to the north of town. They had looked for dangerous Indians, scared squirrels out of hiding, and chased each other around the bases of monstrous oak trees. All the sorts of things youngsters found such fun. But the fun ended suddenly when Jonah broke through dense undergrowth at the edge of a drop-off. He remembered pinwheeling his arms and trying to keep from pitching forward into the ravine. An echo of the same stomach-clenching fear he felt that day enveloped him. "Exactly what are you saying, sir?"

The general frowned at him. "This war is going to be costly for both sides. One of the ways to shorten it is to have men infiltrate the rebel ranks and bring back information on their weapons, their plans, and their manpower."

"You want me to be a spy?"

Silence answered him. The general sat back once again, his gaze boring into Jonah's face. Captain Poindexter cleared his throat and shuffled his feet, the sound loud in the quiet room.

Tugging at his collar once again, Jonah's mind returned to the past. His brother had thrown an arm around him as he teetered on the edge of a lethal plunge, pulling him back from the precipice. But who would save him today? A spy? He'd never considered such an idea. Didn't want to consider it now.

"You'll be able to return to your family." Captain Poindexter's voice brought him back to the present.

"But I would have to lie to them."

"Yes." The general's voice was firm, uncompromising. "You will have to hide the truth."

"Your efforts could shorten the war. You would save lives, perhaps even the lives of your loved ones." Captain Poindexter's voice was less stern. He seemed to be asking Jonah rather than ordering his compliance with the plan.

The general stood up and walked around in front of his desk, waiting until Jonah and the captain also stood. "My first concern will never be with those who have rebelled against their government. It is with your loyalty. After all, you could well be a spy for the Confederacy."

Jonah felt like he'd been punched in the stomach. Hadn't he volunteered for service in the army? Hadn't he accepted the slurs and suspicions of the Northern soldiers while holding fast to his belief in the rightness of the Union's position? Many of his friends and family would consider him a traitor if they discovered that he'd become a Federal soldier. Smarting from the accusation, Jonah shook his head. "I have killed for the Union. Isn't that proof enough?"

The general shook his head. "The death of one nameless man would be a small price for a Confederate soldier to pay for the information he could gather while traveling with this army. If you want to prove your loyalty, you must be ready to do whatever service you are called upon to do."

Jonah's stomach twisted. This must be what his older brother had understood when Jonah announced his decision to fight for the United States. But Jonah thought he knew better, and in the end, Eli had yielded. He'd had such high hopes, such unrealistic visions of what his future would be. Jonah thought he had considered all the privations and sacrifices he might be called upon to give. He had wondered whether he might be able to shoot someone he knew. But this? The intimate, planned betrayal of his family? Could he be that loyal to his country? Jonah didn't know the answer. "I'd like some time to pray about this, sir."

General Lyon raised an eyebrow. He exchanged a glance with the captain before nodding. "Take all the time you need. . .as long as I have your answer by this time tomorrow. And I'm sure you know you cannot mention this to anyone outside of this room."

Jonah snapped a salute, holding his bent arm stiff until a nod from the general dismissed him. He turned sharply and marched out of the room, ignoring the whispered conversation behind him. His mind raced in circles as he considered the unappealing option he'd been given. What should he do?

Chapter Two

Les Fleurs Plantation
Natchez, Mississippi

"I have to go this term." Camellia Anderson couldn't keep the pleading tone out of her voice. Her eyes stung with unshed tears. "I'll be too old to go by the fall."

"I know how badly you want to attend the finishing school in New Orleans." Her older sister stood up and moved across the front parlor at Les Fleurs. Her skirts did not have the graceful sway Camellia had practiced for hours. Lily had never taken time to practice feminine arts.

Camellia turned away from her to watch the scene from the window. The unseasonably warm November afternoon had tempted the family to spend time on the front porch. Jasmine, their youngest sister, was entertaining the rest of the family by reading to them from her dog-eared copy of *Ivanhoe* by Sir Walter Scott. Her voice rose and fell, and her free hand was splayed across her chest in a melodramatic pose.

David Foster, the young boy she and her sisters had rescued from life on the street, stood beside Jasmine. His legs were planted widely, and as Camellia watched, he reached for an imaginary sword and brandished it in the air above his head.

She could hear Aunt Dahlia's distinctive laugh as the playacting continued. It was a shame their aunt had not come with them to the parlor. She would have lent her support to Camellia. But Lily had dragged her away from the others, bringing her inside the salon so they could "chat."

Camellia unfurled her fan and fluttered it in front of her face.

Straightening her spine and concentrating on forming a pleasant smile, she turned to face Lily once more. She wanted to stomp her foot in protest, but her aunt's insistence on decorum stayed the impulse. "You promised I could go, Lily." She was pleased with the blend of pleasantness and determination in her tone of voice.

"I know I did." Lily's gaze fell. "But I didn't know then that we would be in the middle of a war."

"The war has not come here, and it probably never will, not with our courageous soldiers fighting so fiercely. They won the battles at Fort Sumter and Manassas, after all. They've whipped those Yankee aggressors at nearly every turn. Who knows, the Northerners may realize by the end of the year that they cannot win. Then the war will be over, and we'll be able to resume our regular lives. I don't see any sense in putting off my future because of fighting going on so far away."

Silence fell on them as Camellia stopped speaking. In the quiet afternoon she could hear applause coming from the porch. Why couldn't Lily understand she had to get away from here? Away from her eccentric father and melodramatic younger sister. If she was ever going to find the kind of husband she dreamed of, it was going to be through the friendships she would make at a nice finishing school—one far from Natchez.

"These are dangerous days." Lily's words brought her back to the problem at hand. "With the Union navy blockading the gulf, who knows what may happen? I want to keep my family near. Except for Blake—you, Jasmine, and Papa are the most important people in my life."

Camellia sensed a weakness she could turn to her advantage. "If I'm so important to you, why are you trying to ruin my life?"

Lily's eyes widened, and her chin lifted. "Be reasonable. I'm not trying to hurt you. I just want you to be safe."

"I'll be very safe in New Orleans. The Thorntons and the Cartiers will watch out for me. Besides, if La Belle Demoiselle could not keep their students safe, I doubt they would still have any young ladies in attendance."

A sigh from her sister made Camellia's heart ache. She didn't like hurting Lily, but she had to persevere if she was to become a proper bride for a proper husband. Her time was running out. Soon her beauty would fade, and she would find herself without any prospects, much less the kind of husband she wanted to attract.

The type of man she dreamed of marrying would not accept less than perfect manners, perfect accomplishments, and perfect breeding from his fortunate spouse. And rightly so since he would offer the same benefits to her. He would be kind and handsome and rich, so rich that she would never have to set tables, polish silverware, or count linens. She could forget about all of the menial chores Lily made her and Jasmine do aboard the paddle wheeler.

"I wish you had been able to attend Mrs. Gossett's Finishing School last year."

Camellia sniffed. "It's not my fault she decided to close her school and return to Rhode Island."

"Of course not. But I could not blame her for returning to her home state after the death of her husband. During uncertain times most people want to be near their loved ones."

There it was again. The suggestion she would only be safe on her sister's riverboat. What could she say to convince Lily to let her go to New Orleans? No new argument came to mind, so she returned to her earlier logic. "A lot of people think the war will be over soon. And if that happens, you will have ruined my future for no reason at all."

Lily folded her arms over her chest. "I don't know what to do for the best. Blake and I have prayed for an answer."

Perhaps this was the opening she'd needed. "Didn't we find a wonderful school for me to attend that is close to the Thorntons' town house?"

"Yes."

Camellia caught her sister's gaze and held it. "Then why can you not accept that God has already answered your prayer? He wants me to attend the finishing school He led us to."

Lily shook her head. "I don't think it's that simple."

"I do." Camellia reached for one of her sister's hands, prying it loose and holding it against her heart. "This is my dream, Lily, my heart's desire. When you decided to avoid Mr. Adolphus Marvin's pursuit and purchase a steamboat, you chose the life you wanted to lead."

"But I did that so you and Jasmine and I—"

"You can try to convince the rest of our family that your decision was based on noble, high-sounding ideas, but I know how much you always loved the river. You become someone different when you're out there." Camellia released her sister's hand. "Even if Jasmine and I had not been around, you would have made the same decision."

Lily's eyes filled with tears. She nodded. "You may be right about that." She stepped closer and touched one of the corkscrew curls surrounding Camellia's face. "But I was determined to spare you the same misery as Aunt Dahlia and Uncle Phillip planned for me. I want both you and Jasmine to be happy and independent. I want you to have choices."

"Then why are you taking away my choice? Why are you insisting I conform to your rules?" Camellia placed her hand over her sister's. "Can't you see you're doing the same thing to me you claim Aunt Dahlia was doing to you?"

Lily sighed and pulled her hand away. She sat down in Grandmother's overstuffed chair, her head drooping.

For a moment Camellia felt like a beast. Who was she trying to fool? Lily had always put her sisters' needs ahead of her desires. She might have packed them up willy-nilly and brought them along with her, but she had also made sure they had everything they needed and many of the things they wanted. The very clothing she wore was paid for with money Lily had earned. Guilt knotted her stomach.

She opened her mouth to apologize for her manipulative words but was forestalled when Lily looked up. "All right."

The knots tightened even further, but Camellia swallowed hard and waited. She couldn't weaken now. Not when she was about to realize her dearest wish.

"Don't you have anything to say?"

Remembering to float downward like an autumn leaf, Camellia settled on the footstool next to Grandmother's chair. "Thank you so very much. Allowing me to stay in New Orleans is the best gift you've ever given me. I promise to make you proud of me, Lily." She rested her head against her sister's knees.

Lily laid a hand on her head and stroked her hair. "I am proud of you, Camellia. You are the most polished of all of us. Everyone says so. And you're so pretty. One of these days, some man is going to snap you up. He'll take you away from us and set you up in a beautiful house."

Camellia's eyelids drifted shut as she imagined the scene her sister described. She could see a big, fancy home—even grander than Les Fleurs. The formal dining room would seat a hundred guests, and she would preside over fancy dinners dressed in expensive jewelry and the most fashionable attire money could buy. The townspeople would be envious of her and her adoring husband. . .and they would have lovable children—a dozen at least. It wouldn't matter how her father dressed or what he did for a living, or why her sister had married a former gambler.

But none of her dreams would come true until she attended the finishing school. Camellia's eyes popped open, and she raised her head. "When can we leave for New Orleans?"

A laugh slipped from Lily's mouth. "Don't be in such a hurry, dear. You're going to need new dresses. I thought we could go shopping this week."

Camellia straightened and rose from the footstool. "I know how much you dislike shopping, Lily, so I've already asked Aunt Dahlia to take me."

"Oh." A world of hurt filled her sister's voice with the single syllable.

A blush burned Camellia's cheeks. How was she supposed to know her sister would volunteer to help her? Lily had never been interested in shopping. "I'm sorry. I can tell Aunt Dahlia you want to go along."

Shaking her head, Lily stood. "Blake was telling me this morning we need to make a quick trip to Greenville and pick up some furniture and deliver it to a plantation in Tangipahoa Parish."

Relief at Lily's words eased Camellia's discomfort. "So you can go with him instead of staying here to take care of me."

Lily's smile was a little shaky, but it solidified as she nodded. "You're right. But I want you to make plans to travel with us the following week for our scheduled trip to Memphis." She walked over to Camellia and put an arm around her waist. "I want you to spend a little time with us before you go off to school."

Normally Camellia would have refused to go along with her sister's plan, but she needed to focus on the greater goal. A few boring days spent aboard the steamboat was a small price to pay, even though she'd much rather stay here and get ready for her escape. As long as she and Aunt Dahlia finished the fittings next week, her clothing should be ready in time for the beginning of the term.

"You needn't be anxious. The school won't open for almost two months."

Camellia knew it was important to keep her tone cool and logical. "I don't see how you can blame me. Not after missing out last year."

"I wish we had gone ahead and enrolled you at La Belle." Lily's brown eyes seemed to be focused on the past. "But I didn't want to take a chance at putting you somewhere until I had the opportunity to thoroughly check Mrs. Dabbs's reputation in New Orleans. Besides, you were so anxious because of the classes you had already missed."

Hanging on to her temper with difficulty, Camellia pulled away from her sister's loose embrace. She didn't remember the events in the same way her sister did. Lily was the one who had been anxious. But she wasn't going to argue the point. It was ancient history, and she didn't want to roil the waters.

"Shall we go outside and tell the others?" Not waiting for an answer, Camellia floated across the parlor. At least she hoped she appeared to be floating. What was it Aunt Dahlia said? *"The road to a lady's success is trod with tiny footsteps."* Holding her head high, Camellia forced her feet to a deliberate pace. If she was going to succeed at La Belle Demoiselle, she would have to remember everything she had ever been taught about deportment and etiquette.

She preceded her sister into the hallway and out onto the porch. Blake and Uncle Phillip rose from their rockers as they arrived. Camellia met her aunt's concerned gaze with a tiny nod. Aunt Dahlia sat back, a satisfied smile on her lips.

Grandmother beckoned her to the empty chair beside her. "You have missed a fine rendition from Jasmine and David."

"Never fear, I've heard that scene several times." Camellia perched on the edge of the rocker, her spine as straight and rigid as a broomstick. "In fact, I have even been known to read the part of Ivanhoe when David is not available."

Poor David. He followed Jasmine around like a puppy. Camellia had no doubt he would lay down his life for the dark-haired girl he adored. And perhaps for that very reason, Jasmine treated him with offhanded disdain. She expected him to fall into every plan she conceived no matter his own desires or concerns. If he dared to cross her wishes, she would ban him from her presence. Eventually he would come back and ask her forgiveness, and the two of them would continue on as before. Camellia thought he would earn more respect from Jasmine if he refused to do her bidding from time to time. But that was apparently not to be.

"I have not been able to convince Camellia she would do better to wait awhile before attending the school in New Orleans." Lily's voice brought her musings to a halt.

She braced herself for her brother-in-law's frown. Blake Matthews didn't like anyone to contradict Lily. . .except himself, of course. In the first year of their marriage, Lily and her husband had spent a goodly amount of energy on arguments. But no matter what happened between the two of them, he was always eager to defend his wife against anyone who dared disagree with her.

Camellia was determined to learn from her older sister's example. Learn how *not* to act. When she married the man of her dreams, they wouldn't argue. She would be a dutiful wife. One who always put his needs ahead of her own. That was the way to conduct a marriage, not butting heads with one's spouse at every turn.

"Camellia has good reasons for being adamant." Aunt Dahlia punched her needle through the lacy handkerchief in her lap.

"I don't know, Dahlia." Uncle Phillip's long, manicured fingers worried at the cuff of his emerald-hued coat. "The Yankees seem determined to blockade the Gulf Coast and halt the flow of goods to and from Europe. They may well attack New Orleans to achieve their ends."

"I hadn't considered that possibility." Grandmother entered the discussion. Her voice carried a hint of a tremble, one that had become more noticeable in the months since Mississippi seceded from the Union.

Camellia's heart thudded, but she refused to let her consternation appear on her face. "If war does come to New Orleans, I'm sure our gallant soldiers will repulse them." Realizing her hands were clenched together in her lap, she forced them to relax into a more ladylike posture.

She'd had a lot of practice hiding her true feelings—ever since she had discovered that the man captaining her sister's steamboat was their father. Until that day she had thought he was dead, drowned in the same accident that took their mother. But he had survived. Faced with the prospect of raising three girls by himself, he had been forced to turn to his deceased wife's family for help. They had in turn wrung from him a promise to disappear from their lives, a promise Camellia wished had never been broken.

"I'm sure we could get to her before it came to a pitched battle." Her father tossed a smile in her direction. "Few men know the river as well as we do."

Guilt speared Camellia at his words. Perhaps she should not be so judgmental about Papa. He could have his uses. Her gaze drifted down the red shirt he always wore and stopped at the old-fashioned, wide-brimmed hat in his lap. If only he would not dress in such a ridiculous manner.

Jasmine pulled David onto the porch where the rest of them sat. Dropping his hand, she took a step forward, her violet eyes swirling with excitement. "I know. I could go with her."

Lily's gasp mingled with Blake's chuckle. "I don't see how that would keep Camellia safe."

Jasmine flung her ebony hair over her shoulder with a melodramatic sigh. "I was only trying to help."

Few things sounded worse to Camellia than the suggestion that her sister might accompany her to New Orleans. "Don't be silly. You're too young to attend a finishing school."

Aunt Dahlia and Uncle Phillip nodded while Grandmother and Papa exchanged a glance. Camellia sat up straighter in her rocker. Had she said something wrong? Should she not have expressed the truth in such plain language? "I'm sorry, Jasmine. I am sure you would be very welcome at La Belle Demoiselle."

"No, Camellia is right." Lily reached out to Jasmine and pulled her down onto her lap.

Camellia relaxed a tiny bit. Maybe a prayer would help. That's what the preacher had talked about last Sunday—about getting anything one asked for. Would God listen? Would He magically change the attitudes of her family? Asking for His help couldn't hurt matters. Not that she meant any disrespect.

She closed her eyes. *Lord, please forgive me for my wayward thoughts. I promise to be more circumspect if only You'll let me attend La Belle Demoiselle. It shouldn't be too much trouble for You. . . . Oh, and if You'll work this out for me, I promise to do something kind in return. I don't know exactly what, but maybe You have something in mind. Whatever it is, I'm sure we can work things out. . . .* Camellia hesitated. Should she add something else? She couldn't think of anything. *Amen.* As prayers went, it wasn't very eloquent, but maybe He would understand and give her her heart's desire.

Camellia opened her eyes and glanced around. Everyone looked the same except Jasmine, who had slumped back against Lily's shoulder and twisted her mouth into a pout.

Maybe God needed more time. She sure hoped He didn't wait too long.

❧

"What do you think of this color?" Camellia held up a length of gold silk for her aunt's approval.

Aunt Dahlia tilted her head as she considered the suggestion before nodding. "It should make a stunning ballroom ensemble with a white lace overskirt and dark gold ribbons."

Her smile widened as Camellia imagined entering a crowded ballroom on the arm of a dashing Confederate soldier. But then the dream crashed. "What if my escort is a soldier? Will the gold clash with his gray uniform?"

She held her breath as Aunt Dahlia frowned in concentration. "I don't believe so." Her aunt beckoned the owner of the dress shop to join them.

The tiny woman who ran the most fashionable shop in Natchez bustled over to them, a ticket book in her right hand and a pencil tucked into her elaborate coiffure. "You've chosen a marvelous cloth. Look at how it complements your niece's curls."

Aunt Dahlia nodded. "I know you won't have any of the suiting for men's attire, but do you have something the exact color of a soldier's uniform? My niece wants to be certain her dress will complement her escort's attire." The two women walked off, chattering about flounces, buttons, and ribbons.

Camellia was so glad her aunt was the one who had brought her to town. It wasn't that she didn't love Lily, but her sister would never understand or pay attention to all the implications of each decision they needed to make. She looked toward the counter, where the bolts of material they had already selected were piled high. By Christmas they would be transformed into day, tea, and walking dresses of white, periwinkle, jade, and jonquil. Tan broadcloth would become a riding habit for afternoon excursions. They had also ordered chemises, petticoats, and aprons from plain white cotton. She would have a short cape of black wool for fall and spring outings, as well as a long winter cloak made from a luscious length of figured navy velvet to replace the plain black wool one she currently used.

"Look at this, Camellia." Aunt Dahlia placed the bolt of gold silk on the counter and laid two swatches against it.

The pewter gray swatch was a nice contrast to the gold silk. The other swatch, a dull gold Camellia recognized as butternut, was more troublesome. She frowned but immediately forced her eyebrows back to a more pleasant position. She didn't want wrinkles. She pointed at the butternut-colored square. "I don't like that one."

"I know. Most uniforms are closer to this color." Aunt Dahlia picked up the gray swatch and held it in her hand while pointing to the square still resting on the bolt of gold material. "But what if your escort were to show up in that one?"

Camellia nodded and turned back to the table of displayed silks. She spotted another beautiful color, a bright cerulean-blue length of watered silk. "What about this one?" Her gaze met that of her aunt's, and both of them smiled at the same time.

"It's perfect. I only wish I were going to be there to see you when you enter the room on your handsome escort's arm." Aunt Dahlia walked to the table whose surface was covered with the latest dress patterns from Europe.

Following her to the table, Camellia sighed. "If only you could talk Uncle Phillip into moving to New Orleans."

"You're sweet, child. I know I shouldn't say it, but of all my nieces, you are the one who is dearest to my heart."

Camellia's lips turned up in a small smile. "I love you, too, Aunt Dahlia. I'll miss spending time with you, Uncle Phillip, and Grandmother, but we've talked about this. You know why I'm going."

Aunt Dahlia patted her hand. "You need some separation from your less. . .traditional relatives. I still find it hard to believe your sister has embraced Henrick so readily after the man all but abandoned the three of you."

Camellia glanced down at her shoes. She didn't want to point out that it was Grandfather's edict that had caused her father to disappear from their lives for so many years. She didn't want to defend the man at all.

"Don't worry." Aunt Dahlia had continued talking, unaware of her niece's inner turmoil. "I'll be busy looking for the perfect candidate to be your spouse while you're in New Orleans getting that extra bit of polish."

Thinking of the candidate her aunt and uncle had chosen for her older sister, Camellia shuddered. It was the reason Lily had purchased a steamboat and taken all three of them to live on the river. "I don't want you to try matching me to anyone like the old man you thought Lily should marry."

"Of course not." Aunt Dahlia's calculating gaze swept her from head to toe. "You are a very different girl than your sister—a beautiful gentlewoman. The man I choose for you will be of a completely different caliber. Lily, on the other hand, could have done much worse than to marry Adolphus."

Camellia remembered his atrocious sons and wondered.

Aunt Dahlia tittered and leaned closer. "As a matter of fact, she did do much worse." She glanced over her shoulder before continuing in a soft whisper. "You don't have to worry about him at all. It seems the Johnsons' oldest girl, Grace, has removed Adolphus from consideration. I have it on the best authority that they will announce their nuptials before the end of the year. I'm sure they'll host a party. Maybe we can attend it together before your departure."

"I don't think Lily will agree." Her fingers traced the outline of the topmost dress pattern lying on the counter. "She wants me to travel to Memphis with her before I start school."

"That's terrible." Aunt Dahlia shook her head and clucked her tongue. "Will she never stop interfering in your future?"

"I know, but it was the only way I could get her to agree to let me remain in New Orleans." Camellia's fingers drifted over the bolt of blue silk as she imagined the upcoming term. She would outshine every other girl at La Belle Demoiselle in a dress like this one. "At least it's only for a week, and then I'll be free to pursue my dreams."

The shop's owner returned to them then, and they began to discuss her new wardrobe. Camellia's head spun with plans and dreams as they picked and chose from the designs available. She felt like one of the princesses in Jasmine's dramas. And she would be. . .once she got to New Orleans.

Chapter Three

Lily was glad to be back on the river, even on a dreary day like this one. Winter had settled on them as they celebrated a subdued Christmas and ushered in the new year. The crisp morning air energized her as she watched the brown bank sliding past them.

A modest frame house perched on the western side of the river caught her eye. It amazed her how much the river had changed in the years since she'd first traveled its length as a young girl with her parents. Houses like the one they were passing dotted the landscape in ever-increasing numbers. She smiled and waved at a boy and girl who stood watching from the front porch. *Lord, please bless us with children of our own.*

A picture of the family's dinner table formed in her mind, the boy on one side of the table, his sister on the other. Their parents would be situated at either end. She could imagine them joining their hands as the father asked God to bless their meal. Then they would laugh and recount the day's adventures, perhaps even mentioning seeing *Water Lily* steam northward on the Mississippi River.

"You look awfully pensive on such a fine morning."

Lily jumped at the unexpected sound of her husband's voice. "Where did you come from?" She took a moment to study his masculine good looks. It never ceased to amaze her that such a wondrously handsome man had fallen in love with her, plain as she was. He could have turned the head of any female along the wide river, but he had chosen her to become his bride.

"I saw my beautiful wife standing out here all alone and came to see what might be on her mind." Blake pulled her into his arms and planted a warm kiss on her lips.

Lily melted against him as always, lost in the tender devotion he lavished on her. He was the best husband anyone could hope for—a man who sought God earnestly and worked hard to follow His leading. When they first met, he had not been as admirable in his outlook, but God had worked a miraculous change in Blake. He had taken a hardened gambler, a man who thought he didn't need anyone, and changed him into a thoughtful, kind, and generous disciple. Blake was always ready to tell anyone they met about Christ's death and resurrection and the difference His sacrifice made in the lives of all who accepted His free gift.

When he finally released her, Lily's cheeks burned in the cool air. "I love you."

"Of course you do." His eyes, bluer than the sky on a cloudless day, teased her. He wrapped her in his arms once more, this time resting his chin on her head. "I love you, too. . .more than I could ever have imagined."

A sigh of pure bliss filled Lily's lungs. She closed her eyes and thanked God for blessing her beyond anything she'd ever dreamed might be possible.

Their embrace lasted for several minutes before the long whistle of an approaching steamer separated them. Blake leaned against the rail, and she raised a hand to shade her eyes as the vessel drew nearer.

It had once been a merchant steamship much like the *Water Lily*, but unlike their boat, this one had become a warship. Steel plates covered the lower decks, featureless except for the cannons protruding from narrow openings along the side. Even the pilothouse and the great paddle wheel at the end of the boat were covered with shielding. The twin smokestacks belched black smoke, and cinders fell on the gray-suited soldiers who sat, walked, or lounged on the upper deck, their weapons close at hand.

Lily waved, even though her heart was heavy at this reminder of the terrible struggle that had been going on for nearly a full year. A few of them saluted or waved, but most of the group ignored her gesture.

She and Blake watched the boat until it disappeared around a bend in the river. "Where do you think they're going?"

Blake shrugged. "To defend one of the southern ports, I imagine."

"I'm so worried about letting Camellia attend school in New Orleans. I hate the idea of being unable to reach her."

The color of Blake's eyes seemed to change as a cloud briefly obscured the sun. "You've done everything you can to convince her, but your sister has her heart set on going to La Belle. If you don't let her have her way in this, she may strike out on her own." His lips curled in a quick smile. "She is an Anderson, after all."

Lily couldn't help the laughter that broke past her lips in response to her husband's not-so-subtle reminder of her own stubbornness. "But that was different. My aunt and uncle were trying to force me—"

"Trying to get you to do what they thought was in your best interest."

Her chin lifted. "I'm not trying to push Camellia into a loveless marriage."

"I know that, Lily. But you're the one who told me how adamant your sister is about going to that finishing school." He shrugged. "I don't see much wrong with letting her live in New Orleans. We have friends who will watch out for her safety, and if it becomes dangerous, we'll have the opportunity to rescue her and bring her safely back to Les Fleurs. Or keep her aboard with us if you want."

He was right. She knew he was right. But still she worried.

Blake dropped a reassuring kiss on her forehead. "Where is Camellia, anyway? I thought you wanted to spend all of your leisure time with her on this voyage since it will probably be the last one we manage before school begins."

"I sent her up to visit Papa." Lily glanced at the staircase behind his right shoulder. "She still seems so stilted and formal around him. I don't understand why. Camellia couldn't have felt the same way I did when I thought Papa had abandoned us. She seemed to get along well with him before she knew his real identity, and I would like to see them work out their differences before she goes away, before her heart hardens so much that—"

Blake's face, so warm and caring before her answer, hardened into a cold mask.

Remorse washed through her. "I'm sorry, Blake. . . . I didn't mean. . . . I wasn't trying to—"

He put a finger over her lips, silencing her apology. "It's okay, Lily. I suppose what I'm feeling is more guilt than anything else. Besides, we've had a similar discussion before when I was trying to get you to be more accepting of Henrick. I know I need to make peace with my own father."

Lily wanted to put her arms around Blake. She wanted to comfort him, tell him that she would always be there for him no matter what he decided to do about his relationship with his father. But she held her tongue and waited for him to finish. Her patience was rewarded after a long minute ticked by.

Blake sighed. "I just don't know if I'm ready to take that step yet. You cannot know what it was like—"

Unable to keep silent any longer, Lily interrupted him. "But I know what you're like, Blake. I've seen you grow closer to the Lord since we've been together. I love the time we spend together in devotion and prayer." She hesitated for a moment, trying to pick her words with care.

Blake smiled, but his eyes were filled with uncertainty. "But. . . ?"

Lily didn't want to cause Blake unnecessary pain, yet she owed him her honest opinion. "I can sense a hard place inside of you, a place you don't want to let Him touch. Maybe it's because I once harbored the same feelings toward my father that I recognize them in you." She put a hand on his arm, feeling the hard coil of his muscles under her fingers. "If you don't release the anger, it will consume you. I'm afraid it will make you someone different from the man I know and love. I don't want to see that happen to you. . .to us."

His head dropped toward his chest. "I know you're right, but it's not easy. I understand with my mind that I have to forgive my father, but I don't feel the truth of it in my heart. I've been praying about my father. So far, God has been silent on the subject. Maybe when things settle down some. . ."

Lily stood on her tiptoes and placed a whisper-light kiss on his cheek. "I love you, dearest, but you cannot continue to put this off. It's weighing on you too heavily."

"You're right, and I want to." His large, warm hand cupped her chin. "I have an idea."

She placed her hand over his and met his gaze, trying to encourage him. She loved him so much she felt her heart would burst, and she wanted him to see what was in her heart. "What is that?"

"Why don't you pray for God to show both of us the right time and the right way to deal with my father?"

Lily nodded. As long as both of them leaned on His strength, they would weather any storm. That knowledge also brought her a measure of peace regarding Camellia. The Lord would watch over all of them—whether they were in the same town or not.

❧

Camellia reached for another of the plates Tamar had scrubbed clean. "If I never had to spend another night on a steamboat, my life would be perfect."

"Don't you say such things." Tamar frowned at her as she continued her task. "This is your sister's chosen home."

"She can come and visit me once I get married." Camellia grimaced at the thought of her family creating a rumpus in her spotless, well-ordered plantation home. Papa's tall tales, Jasmine's dramatic posturing, and Lily's stubbornness would put an end to harmony. It would be a wonder if Camellia's husband didn't forbid their return after a single day in company with her family. "But only if she brings Aunt Dahlia and Uncle Phillip along as well."

The choked sound from the woman standing beside her made Camellia smile. Both of them knew the likelihood of Lily and Aunt Dahlia traveling together. The probability that at least one of them would expire during the journey—and not from natural causes—was extremely high.

Camellia reached for another plate to dry. "Why do you remain on the *Water Lily*?"

"Many reasons." Tamar's voice sounded serene, almost dreamy. "I suppose the main reason is that a wife's place is at the side of her husband."

The statement brought a nod from Camellia. She had finally gotten used to the romance between Blake's friend and the woman who had been a surrogate mother to her.

Tamar and Jensen first met on Lily and Blake's steamship the *Hattie Belle*. Jensen had been the cook on that ship, but Tamar was a slave, the slave who had taken care of Lily, Camellia, and Jasmine as though they were her own children. She had seemed content with her position. For as long as Camellia could remember, Tamar had been loving and kind, with a world of practical wisdom to impart to her charges.

Camellia had been surprised when her older sister went to their grandmother and asked for Tamar's freedom—and even more shocked when the newly freed woman announced she was going to marry Jensen. It gave her a whole new view of Tamar as a real person, not just the unassuming woman who made sure her clothing was mended and her hair arranged.

"But don't you want a regular home and children of your own?"

"Oh child, a home is wherever and whatever you make it. Besides, the good Lord blessed me with both of those things when He let me watch you and your sisters grow up." She sighed. "I wouldn't complain if He decided to give us a child of our own, but with things in such an uproar, I don't know if that's a good idea."

Now it was Camellia's turn to sigh. "The war affects us all, doesn't it?"

"Even though I'm free now, it may not always be that way. Who knows whether our children would be safe?" Tamar's voice was matter-of-fact.

Camellia's problems were small in comparison to Tamar's. The war had delayed her plans for the future, but whether she would be free to pursue her goals had never been in doubt.

Tamar swished her hands through the dishwater and pulled them out to reach for the towel Camellia was holding. "That's all of the dishes."

Jasmine ran into the small gallery. "We're about to dock!"

Camellia thrust her disturbing thoughts aside. Tamar was free. She had a husband and a good job. Untying her apron, she pulled it off and hung it on a peg to dry. "I'll meet you on deck, Jasmine. I just need to check my appearance."

"Looks are not the only thing that matters." Tamar's warning chased Camellia out of the room.

Ignoring the words, Camellia hurried to the room she shared with Jasmine. A glance in the mirror proved her concern was valid. Her hair was a mess, and her shirtwaist was wrinkled from leaning against the galley counter. It would take too long to heat a curling rod. Camellia ran her fingers through the blond ringlets and fastened them with combs so that they cascaded around her face.

A quick search in her trunks unearthed her short cloak. She could use it to hide the wrinkles in her blouse. Swinging it around her shoulders, she fastened the navy frog at the neck and checked her appearance once more.

Milky complexion, wide blue eyes, generous forehead, and long neck. She would turn heads as always. Men admired her while women hid their jealousy behind stiff smiles. It was her place in the world, a place she was determined to keep in spite of everything else.

She found both of her sisters and Jasmine's shadow, David, on deck, watching as their shipment was off-loaded by burly dockworkers. "How long will we be in Memphis?"

Lily glanced in her direction. "We'll stay with Eli and Renée Thornton tonight and leave in the morning."

Swallowing her groan, Camellia pinned a fake smile on her lips. She was not going to complain, even though she had no doubt Lily knew she didn't want to stay the night in Memphis. She wanted to get to New Orleans, get settled, and begin her school term.

"Don't worry." Jasmine stepped closer and grabbed her hand. "Papa says we'll get you there in time."

Camellia pulled her hand away. She didn't want to hear what Papa had to say about anything. What did her sisters see in him, anyway? All he did was tell stories about the way the river used to be. Or preach at them about turning the other cheek and forgiving other people hundreds of times when they were unpleasant. That was fine for him, but Camellia didn't see what good his talking did for her. Why should she be the one who forgave other people?

The one time she'd tried to talk to Lily about Papa's sermonizing, her older sister had gotten all serious and talked to her about letting go of the past like she had done. Camellia didn't have any problem with Papa's past. It was his present that bothered her. She'd much rather have Uncle Phillip for a father. He was a businessman. He knew how to dress, how to act at a dinner party, how to conduct himself in public. He would never be caught dressed like someone from the Revolutionary War. She busied herself comparing Uncle Phillip to Papa as they left the *Water Lily* and climbed into a rented carriage for the trip to Eli Thornton's home a few miles east of the harbor.

Jasmine chattered as usual, pointing out every building they passed as if they'd never before stayed in Memphis. How would others see them in the carriage? She was the pretty one, of course. Jasmine was the vivacious one. And Lily? Lily was just plain old Lily. Now that she had married Blake, her life had taken on a predictable pattern—one that Camellia would abhor, but one that seemed to bring her older sister happiness.

Chapter Four

Jonah's mouth was so dry he didn't think he would be able to deliver the code phrase. "May I inquire where you got that flower? Yellow is my favorite color."

"A shop on Beale Avenue purchases them especially for me. They are quite dear, but I don't mind the cost."

It was the correct response, the one that meant he was officially a spy. Jonah's shoulders tightened. His tongue felt too big for his mouth, and his breathing was choppy—as though he'd run all the way from his brother's store. He forced himself to take a slow, deep breath. "What happens next?"

He eyed the short man whom he named Mr. Brown for the color of his frock coat. He sported long brown sideburns, a bushy mustache, and a beard. If not for the bright yellow rosebud on his lapel, Jonah never would have given him a second glance. He supposed that was a good thing for a spy.

"You're going to New Orleans, a visit to your parents."

Jonah's blood chilled. He didn't like that this stranger knew so much about him and his family. "What will I do there?"

"Ferret out information about the rebel defenses—their weapons, plans, the number of soldiers present—and pass it along to your contact."

"How will I know him?"

The shorter man hesitated. Jonah thought he smiled, but it was hard to tell through the tangle of facial hair. "Your contact is not a man."

Jonah's eyebrows climbed high. "A female spy?" What type of lady would involve herself in such a dangerous pursuit?

"Why not? She's Colonel Poindexter's cousin, a widow who runs a school for the pampered daughters of rich Southern planters. That's why the captain was involved in choosing you. He has an interest in selecting an honest man, someone who won't betray his sister and can blend in with aristocratic society. You'll elicit all the information you can and give it to Mrs. Dabbs. She's responsible for getting the information to her brother. They'll be written in code, so even if a letter is intercepted, she won't fall under suspicion."

Wondering how he would avoid suspicion when delivering the information, Jonah nodded. When he had agreed to spy for the Union in June, he'd thought the general would send him out immediately. But that was before they received orders from President Lincoln to chase down the Missouri State Guard and stop them from consolidating a base in Missouri. They marched to Springfield, anxious to end the threat. But they had lost. Lost miserably. Catastrophically. So many men died. Even General Lyon was killed in a hail of bullets as he tried to rally his remaining men.

"You'll need to make haste to New Orleans. Even now the Federal navy is considering how to capture it. They need whatever information you can glean."

"I understand." He remembered the day Poindexter summoned him. Remembered the drawn look on the man's face. A colonel's eagle had replaced the captain's stripes on his shoulders, and his kindliness had all but disappeared under the weight of his new responsibilities. He gave Jonah the two phrases to memorize and sent him to Memphis to await further development.

Jonah had felt like the prodigal son on his arrival two days earlier. Of course, the prodigal son wasn't hiding dangerous facts from his family. Renée had prepared a feast, cementing his guilt because he knew the high prices she was paying for food, especially sugar from the plantations in the Caribbean. He'd barely been able to force down a morsel of the three-layered butter pecan cake topped with caramel icing. Or join in the happy conversation between Eli, Renée, and their three sons, Brandon, Cameron, and Remington. But no one seemed to notice anything odd.

"Is that all?" He wondered why he could not have received this instruction from Colonel Poindexter, but Jonah was too anxious to end this meeting to ask.

"Mrs. Dabbs's school is on Camp Street. Arrange to meet her alone and say, 'Mr. Lincoln could end all of this fighting if he would listen to reason.' "

Jonah nodded.

"Repeat the phrase, please."

He was not a child. Jonah opened his mouth to argue with the man but then hesitated. The knowing glint in "Mr. Brown's" eyes stopped him. He was much more experienced at spying. "Mr. Lincoln could end all of this fighting if he would listen to reason."

"Good. She will say, 'Yes, but I am afraid he is too stubborn to consider the desires of the South even though I write to him of my concerns.' " The other man looked at Jonah, a hint of his impatience evident in the shuffling of his feet.

"Yes, but I am afraid he is too stubborn to consider the desires of the South even though I write to him of my concerns."

The shorter man nodded once before glancing around at the quiet square. "Godspeed. May God be with us all."

When he turned and walked away, Jonah felt his stomach plunge. Was that how he would appear to some new recruit in a few months? Would he spend the rest of this war slinking around in the shadows and meeting other spies in deserted areas? Jonah began to pray as he left the square in the opposite direction "Mr. Brown" had taken. He prayed for the wisdom to outwit his friends and acquaintances. He prayed they would not be punished if he was caught. And he prayed that the war would end before he arrived in New Orleans.

Camellia was not surprised when Jonah Thornton took the seat next to hers even though he had several other choices. Most men would have chosen to sit next to the most beautiful woman in the room.

She intercepted a glance between Blake and Lily, seated at opposite ends of the table. Jasmine and David had their heads together across the table from her, and Papa sat between her and Lily. Either Jonah could choose to sit between David and Blake, or he could share her side of the table.

Satisfaction and self-confidence surged within her. She glanced at Jonah sideways, noting the well-brushed frock coat he wore over fawn-colored trousers. A white shirt, stiff collar, and silk tie completed his ensemble, showing that he was both a man of means and particular about his appearance.

"You are even lovelier than I remember, Miss Anderson." His eyes crinkled at the outside corners when he smiled. "I'm so glad you'll be in our fair city for several months."

Camellia could feel her heartbeat accelerating and wished she had brought her fan to dinner. It would have given her hands something to do and helped to hide the blush rising to her cheeks. "Thank you, Mr. Thornton. It is kind of you to say so."

Blake cleared his throat. "Let's bless this food."

Everyone bowed their heads, but Camellia peeked up at the man sitting next to her. Jonah Thornton might not have a plantation, but he was quite charming. She would enjoy bandying words with him during their trip to New Orleans. It was a pity they only had one more full day before reaching their destination. When Blake ended the blessing, she raised her head with the rest of the diners.

Lily uncovered a dish of sliced beef and passed it around the table. "How long has it been since we saw you, Mr. Thornton?"

Jonah's grass-green eyes narrowed as he considered her sister's question. "You were Miss Anderson still. And I was naught but a carefree partygoer." His smile invited all of them to join his regret over youthful indiscretions. "I wish you would call me Jonah." He glanced at Camellia for a moment before returning his gaze to the others at the table. "Mr. Thornton is my father, or perhaps Eli. I could never aspire to their heights of maturity."

Blake filled his plate with beef, creamed potatoes, and one of Tamar's fluffy biscuits. "Whether you aspire to become mature or not, you will find yourself growing old faster than you might believe possible."

"Pay no attention to my gloomy husband." Lily smiled in his direction. "He found a gray hair this morning and has felt the weight of his age ever since."

Everyone laughed at her comment, but Camellia was embarrassed for them. Why would Lily expose poor Blake to ridicule? And why did her sister think it was appropriate to speak of such intimate details in a family setting? Lily needed to attend finishing school even worse than

Camellia did. Not that she would. She was too busy sailing up and down the river, stopping at every port, and dwelling in the masculine world of shipping as though her gender did not matter.

Besides, if she did agree to attend, Lily would walk out after only a week of instruction. She had never seen a need to stand on ceremony. But speaking of Blake's dressing preparations went beyond what could be considered acceptable, even in the admittedly lax world of steamship travel.

"Will you be staying in New Orleans for an extended visit?" Camellia's father asked between bites of his dinner.

Jonah shrugged. "My plans are a bit unsettled at the moment. It depends on what entertainment may be had." He glanced toward her again, his gaze threatening to burn a hole in Camellia's face.

This time her blush was so heated that even Jasmine noticed it. "I think Jonah is sweet on you."

David's pale eyebrows disappeared into the thatch of white-blond hair on his forehead. Lily sputtered, Papa laughed heartily, and Blake frowned.

Camellia wanted to climb underneath the table. She tossed a scathing look at her younger sister. "You are embarrassing all of us, Jasmine. If you cannot hold your tongue, I hope Lily will send you to your room without your supper."

That stopped Papa's laugh and Lily's sputter.

Blake's frown disappeared as he reached for his water goblet. "I hope you will forgive Jasmine, Jonah. We are fairly free with our manners when we are *en famille*."

Camellia kept her gaze locked on her plate. She couldn't bear to look up at Jonah and see the condemnation in his eyes. The sooner she separated herself from her family the better.

"I don't mind." His deep voice sent shivers across her shoulders and down the length of her arms. "I consider it a compliment to be treated as one of the family."

Gathering her courage, Camellia risked a quick glance at him. Jonah's head was turned toward Blake, so she let her gaze linger on his profile. His chiseled jaw made him appear strong and capable. He sported a dimple in his chin that she could imagine tapping with her fan. His lips were full— Her thoughts came to an abrupt halt as he turned his head and their gazes clashed. His lazy, knowing smile taunted her. Jonah Thornton was too aware of his own attractiveness. It was a quality she did not appreciate.

Camellia sniffed and turned to engage Lily in conversation. "You don't have to come to La Belle Demoiselle with me. If you'll have my trunks delivered, I'm sure I can make my own way."

Jonah's arm was close enough to her own that Camellia felt it stiffen at her words. A tiny frown creased her brow before she remembered to smooth out the muscles. What could she have said to cause such a reaction in him?

"I'm not going to drop you off at the docks like a load of cargo, Camellia." Lily glanced toward Blake for confirmation before continuing. "I was planning on spending a few days with Jonah's family before returning to the river. Besides, did you think I had forgotten your birthday? We have always celebrated together, and this year will be no different."

Papa leaned across the table. "I believe the girl is ashamed of us." His wink included everyone at the table.

Now it was Camellia's turn to sputter. She thought she'd hidden her feelings better than that. Aunt Dahlia would be disappointed to learn she had been so transparent. "I am nothing of the sort." Even to her own ears, the words fell flat. She stopped and took a deep, calming breath. "I know how hard all of you work, and I was trying to make things easier. If any of you wish to accompany me to the school, I'm sure you are most welcome." With those words, she pushed her chair away from the table. "I'll go help Tamar with the dishes."

She was determined to show them she could rise above their taunts and accusations. If she was ashamed of certain members of her family, who could blame her? Debutantes, even ones as beautiful as she, had to be very assiduous in protecting their reputations or they would find themselves old maids while other, less objectionable females snatched up the best gentlemen.

Chapter Five

Camellia imagined that her patience was a ball of yarn like the one Mrs. Thornton held in her lap. Blue, of course, to match her eyes. Every now and then, like the roll of wool their hostess held, it threatened to break free, land on the floor, and unravel as it rolled toward the freedom of the front door. She had to concentrate on keeping her emotions in check or she would never be able to knit a future that matched her dream. A dream that was slipping away with each year that passed. She was eighteen today, a fact that had been celebrated during lunch with a festive cake and a song. Soon she would be too old to be considered a debutante. Soon she would be an old maid.

If only everyone would stop sitting about and help her get her belongings to La Belle Demoiselle. But here they remained, stationed in the front parlor of Mr. and Mrs. Thornton's town house, drinking tea and chatting without the least degree of urgency.

Mr. Thornton was reading his newspaper, Blake sat next to Lily on the sofa, and Jasmine was standing next to the window, looking out at the street. The only one missing was Jonah. She had not seen him since they arrived at his parents' home the day before. She couldn't really blame him, though, since his father had been less than enthusiastic about his return to New Orleans.

"You shouldn't worry about your sister. The war is not likely here." Mrs. Thornton's fingers worked nimbly as she spoke, her yarn turning into a lacy doily like the one covering the back of the chair in which Camellia sat. "Things are not as dire in New Orleans as you may have heard farther up the river."

Camellia glanced at Lily to see if she would accept Mrs. Thornton's reassurance. Her mauve day dress was Lily's nicest, but it was not as new or as fashionable as Camellia's pink one. Typical. Lily couldn't care less about fashions. All she wanted was something serviceable and modest.

"I know you're right, but leaving her here seems so risky." Lily tapped her spoon against the rim of her teacup before laying it on her saucer. "We know the Federal navy is eager to take this city. They have vowed to cut off trade between Europe and the South."

Mr. Thornton, sitting in a corner of the parlor, looked up. "Two forts lie between New Orleans and the Gulf of Mexico. They will defend us."

Blake shared a glance with Lily. "My wife cannot help herself. She's like a mother hen when it comes to her younger sisters."

"Sarah's here." Jasmine turned from the window, her excitement plain to see as she announced the arrival of the Thorntons' only daughter, Sarah Cartier.

Camellia shared her younger sister's enthusiasm. Now perhaps the others would be infused with some energy.

After a moment, the door to the parlor opened, and Sarah floated into the room. Camellia approved of her ensemble, a wool skirt and jacket of muted orange plaid befitting the winter season. "I was so excited to open Mama's note this morning. I hope you have not planned too many activities for your visit. I have dozens of ideas for things we can do."

Sarah dropped a quick kiss on her mother's cheek and waved a greeting at her father before turning to Lily. "Please tell me you will be here for a few days. I am having a little dinner party." She glanced toward Camellia, her dark eyes bright. "Nothing elaborate, but we plan to have musicians in case any of the younger people wish to dance."

Lily's gaze followed Sarah's. "I don't know. We are only here to see Camellia settled at her school."

Sarah clapped her hands. "La Belle Demoiselle, *n'est-ce pas*?"

Camellia nodded. She hoped to increase her understanding of French at the school. Of course she could translate simple phrases like the ones Sarah and Mrs. Thornton were always dropping into their conversations. By employing some herself, Camellia hoped to present a more continental persona.

"It is a very good school." Sarah kissed her fingers for emphasis and perched on the arm of Camellia's chair, giving her a quick hug. "But we must make sure you have sufficient clothes for the term, *non*?"

"You should see the number of trunks we off-loaded for her clothing." Blake's voice held a hint of mischief. "If she purchases anything else, she will have to store it in a separate room."

"Men." Sarah laughed. "They don't understand the things a female needs."

Camellia returned her smile. "I'm sure you're right."

"I want to go shopping, too." Jasmine crossed the room to stand near them.

Lily groaned. "Please don't tell me you've been infected with Camellia's fever to become a fashion plate. I've always hoped you would be a bit more down-to-earth."

Although Camellia could sympathize with Jasmine's desire to shop, she was also surprised by her younger sister's uncharacteristic statement. Perhaps she was reaching maturity. Jasmine could do worse than to follow her lead. In fact, as soon as she had secured her own future, Camellia would have to turn her attention to finding a worthy candidate to marry Jasmine. "You'll have to stop spending all your spare time with your nose in a book."

Jasmine tossed her dark hair over one shoulder in a gesture fit for a prima donna. "I enjoy reading."

Camellia thought of the tears Jasmine had shed when she finished the novel she'd been reading on their way to New Orleans. "Well, at least you might limit your reading to more uplifting material."

"*Uncle Tom's Cabin* was a very uplifting story."

Mr. and Mrs. Thornton gasped in unison, and Sarah slid off the arm of Camellia's chair to look at Lily and Blake. "You let her read such things?"

What was all the fuss about? It was only a novel, after all.

Mr. Thornton folded his newspaper and laid it on the table at his elbow. "False tales designed to demonize our way of life. It's written by a woman, after all, a liberal abolitionist with a political agenda."

Jasmine looked to Lily for support, but it was Blake who answered. "I've read the book myself. It has merit."

"I've never mistreated a slave in my life." Mr. Thornton's face reddened as he spat out the words. "I clothe and feed them, make sure all of their needs are met. And I daresay most men who own slaves are like me. It makes no more sense to whip a slave than to lame a horse."

"But you are an exception to the rule." Jonah's deep voice sent Camellia's heart bounding. When had he appeared? Leaning against the door frame, he looked more intense—and much more romantic—than he had seemed while they were aboard the *Water Lily*.

At least this time she had her fan. Camellia used it to cool her cheeks as she watched him straighten and saunter into the parlor. His green gaze ignored her to scan the room, stopping for a moment when he looked toward Blake but resting only when he met his father's angry stare.

"Do you think me a fool?" Mr. Thornton jumped to his feet. "I suppose you believe your travels have made you more knowledgeable than your father."

Jonah swept a low bow before him. "Who am I to argue with your opinion?"

The older man spluttered.

Camellia hid a smile behind her fan. Jonah's travels had made him more adept in social situations.

Mr. Thornton took a step toward his son, his demeanor threatening. "I don't know how I raised such an ardent abolitionist. It's about time you saw the world as it really is."

Jonah opened his mouth, and Camellia cringed at the anger she saw in his expression. Would the two men come to blows in front of them? She had heard about hot-blooded people who lived in New Orleans, but the Thorntons had never seemed quite so volatile. Not until now.

Sarah stepped between father and son, a warning look in her dark eyes. "This is not the time to air your personal differences. Think of your guests." She swept a hand around the room. "Do not make them more uncomfortable than you already have."

The tense moment stretched out until Camellia thought it would never end. Then Jonah nodded at his sister. "You're right. I apologize, Father. My passion for those who cannot protect themselves overcame my good sense."

As apologies went, it left a lot to be desired, but it seemed to appease Mr. Thornton. Without another word, he brushed past Jonah and left the parlor.

For a moment, Jonah's troubled gaze followed his father's exit. When Sarah threaded her arm through his, however, he smiled down at her. "One of these days, he will have to realize he cannot control me."

"No matter how old you get, Jonah, he will always be your father." She glanced around the room.

Mrs. Thornton resumed her needlework. "Weren't you planning a shopping excursion?" Her practical question gave everyone a new focus.

Sarah separated herself from her brother and shooed Camellia and her sisters out of the parlor.

For the first time she could ever remember, Camellia didn't want to go shopping. It wasn't because she already had the necessary items for beginning the school term, nor did her eagerness to get to La Belle Demoiselle play into her reluctance. She wanted to spend more time with Jonah, regain the admiring attention he had showered on her during the trip from Memphis. He was so intense, so exciting to be around. Even when his eyes seemed filled with green lightning, she found herself drawn to the man.

Of course nothing could ever develop between them beyond a light flirtation. She had her sights set on a much bigger prize than Jonah Thornton. He had neither job nor military rank, proving his lack of ambition. She adopted a pleasant smile even while scolding herself for her reluctance.

As she and her sisters donned their cloaks and gloves, Camellia made a mental list of the reasons she could not be attracted to him. Jonah had no plantation and no prospects other than running his parents' shipping business. She wanted someone of deep conviction who believed in a cause and was ready to risk everything for it. Not someone who stood on the sidelines and pointed a finger of blame at the men who were fighting for their beliefs.

Satisfied with her logic, Camellia pushed Jonah from her mind. She couldn't wait for La Belle Demoiselle to open its doors.

Chapter Six

Camellia's excitement collapsed like an unstarched petticoat when Lily suggested Papa might want to accompany them to La Belle Demoiselle. She would rather be scalded with a pot of boiling water than have to face the ridicule of her peers and the teachers at the school when they realized what a character the man was. She cast a desperate glance around the breakfast table, but no one seemed aware of her consternation. "Perhaps I should go alone."

Lily's jaw dropped open. "What?"

If she had been trying to be the center of attention, Camellia had succeeded beyond her wildest dreams. Everyone was staring at her as if she had grown an extra head. "I. . .I don't want to be any trouble."

Blake raised an eyebrow before returning his attention to the food on his plate. "I doubt your sister will send you off by yourself."

"Of course not." Mrs. Thornton smiled.

"I saw them loading your trunks into the wagon as I came through the courtyard." Jonah added the information with a hint of mischief in his voice. "Perhaps you could ride on it instead."

"Jonah!" Mrs. Thornton shook her head at her son. "You are being ridiculous. Of course Camellia will ride with the rest of us in the carriage."

When Camellia saw the moisture in Jasmine's expressive eyes, she felt even worse. Why did everything have to be so difficult? Her family seemed determined to punish her for wanting to break away, wanting to have a life of her own. She pushed back from the table. "Thank you for the delicious breakfast."

"And for your wonderful hospitality." Lily put her napkin on the table next to her plate. "You cannot imagine how much easier I feel because you are here to watch over my sister."

"Never fear." Mrs. Thornton leaned across the corner of the table and patted Lily's hand.

Camellia ignored the sardonic look in Jonah's eyes and wondered if she could slip away before anyone realized she was gone. Probably not. Unless she wanted to ride in the wagon as Jonah had suggested. Camellia's ears burned at the thought of arriving on such a pedestrian conveyance. Perhaps there were worse things than having to introduce her papa.

She went upstairs to the bedroom she had been sharing with Jasmine to gather her cloak and check to make sure she was presentable. Staring into the mirror, Camellia tried to imagine what life would be like at the school. Now that the day had finally arrived, she found herself oddly reluctant to forge ahead.

"I'm going to miss you." Jasmine had entered the room without making a sound and came to stand behind Camellia's left shoulder.

"It's not like I'll be gone for a long time. The school term will end in a few months, and I'll return to Natchez." She turned and held out her arms, enfolding Jasmine and dropping a kiss on her forehead. "But I don't want you to get any older until then."

"I won't." Jasmine could usually be counted on to giggle at her silliness, but this morning she seemed more somber. Her lower lip protruded slightly, and her violet eyes were shadowed. "Please don't forget about us."

"As if I could." Camellia leaned back and stared into her sister's eyes. "I know you don't understand why this is so important to me, but I promise to come home again."

"Lily says you'll probably be married before the end of the year." Jasmine's dark eyes filled with tears again.

What a wonderful idea. Camellia was glad her sister was prepared for that eventuality. But this was not the time to admit as much to her younger sister. "Don't worry so. It will be your turn before too much longer."

Jasmine shrugged her shoulders. "I don't ever want to get married."

Feeling the full weight of her eighteen years, Camellia drew on her own experience. "You're a warm and caring young lady who is not quite grown up yet, but wait and see. One day you'll wake up and realize that a home and children are exactly what you want most."

Jasmine didn't look convinced, but she did not argue the point, instead looking around for her cloak and bonnet.

Once she was sure they were both ready to leave, Camellia took a deep breath. She would go through with this. Nothing, not even a marauding Yankee army, was going to stand in her way.

❧

Mrs. Thornton arranged her skirts with care in the crowded carriage. "I'm glad you could arrange your schedule to accompany us, Jonah."

Ignoring the beautiful Camellia, whose skirts were taking up the majority of the bench he shared with her, Jonah leaned his head back and closed his eyes. "I am happy to be of service." The thick irony in his voice was carefully contrived. None of the four females in the carriage could suspect his real motive for joining them.

"How far away is the school?" Lily was sandwiched between his mother and Jasmine. She sounded as uncomfortable as she probably was.

"Not too far," his mother answered. "The Garden District is not as close to the river as our town house, but it is a lovely area."

"Why is it called La Belle?"

Jonah lifted his head, wondering why Lily encouraged Jasmine's never-ending curiosity. One of these days it would likely put her into a perilous situation, much like those faced by an inquisitive feline. It was a pity Jasmine could not boast nine lives. She would probably need several.

"The name is La Belle Demoiselle." His mother answered the question. "It means the beautiful young girl. The man who built it, Mr. Peter Hand, was a successful architect with a very young bride. I have heard that he named his home for her. When Mrs. Dabbs, the present owner of the house, decided to open a school for young girls, she decided to use the original name."

"How romantic." Camellia leaned forward and stared out of the window as though counting the minutes until their arrival.

Wouldn't she be shocked to discover the other side of her romantic headmistress? Jonah ran through the code phrase to make sure he would not stumble when the time came to alert the woman to his identity. He hoped she was more experienced at this spying game than he. If not, the North was in serious trouble.

❧

The last one out of the carriage, Camellia put her hand in Jonah's and caught her breath. *Tranquil. . .tranquil as the surface of a pond.* The mantra helped her present a calm face even though her heart felt as though it was about to jump out of her chest. The quick squeeze he gave her gloved fingers did not help matters. What was it about this man that affected her so? Why did her cheeks burn in spite of the cold wind swirling through the quiet neighborhood?

As soon as her slippers touched the raised sidewalk, she pulled her hand from his and looked around, determined to minimize the contact. In an effort to regain control, she focused on the ornate iron fence surrounding the school property. "Is that a snowflake design?"

"Oui." Mrs. Thornton touched the gate with a gloved hand. "The story is that Mr. Hand's young wife was from New York, and she missed the beautiful winters of her youth. So he ordered the fence to ease her homesickness."

Jasmine had been quiet all the way to the school, but she brightened at Mrs. Thornton's explanation. "How romantic."

A grunt from Jonah showed his lack of appreciation for Mr. Hand's gesture. Typical.

Camellia couldn't resist adding her own interpretation. "When a marriage is based on mutual love, such wonderful gestures become commonplace."

Lily nodded her agreement, but Jonah rolled his eyes before opening the gate for the ladies.

Lacy iron formed arches between the black columns that framed the first-story porch and the second-story balcony. They reminded Camellia of picture frames. She could see herself standing on the balcony. Her soldier-fiancé would have an arm around her, and they would be facing each other as they exchanged sweet words of love and devotion.

A jerk on her arm ended the pleasant daydream. "Are you going to stand out here in the cold all morning?" Jonah's frown was like a slap.

"Of course not." She lifted her skirts and climbed the steps to the front porch, her head high. How dare he criticize her? This was her time. She was not going to let him destroy her anticipation.

A black woman wearing a dark dress and a fancy white apron met them at the front door. Mrs. Thornton introduced herself and explained the reason for their arrival, handing her calling card to the servant.

While they waited for Mrs. Dabbs to send for them, Camellia looked around the stylishly appointed foyer. A silver tray filled with other calling cards rested on a small table to her right. Above it was a rococo mirror. Several chairs lined the wall next to the table, a place for visitors to sit while they waited to see if the lady of the house was receiving guests.

A door opened farther down the hall, and a tall, spare woman appeared. She was probably about the same age as Aunt Dahlia, but that was the only similarity Camellia could find between them. Mrs. Dabbs moved more slowly than her aunt would, her hands folded at her waist. Her hair, parted in the center, was very dark except for a stunning stripe of snow-white tresses beginning at the V of her widow's peak. Each step she took was small and deliberate, conveying her authority and self-confidence.

"Bienvenue, monsieur and mesdames, á mon ecôle." Her accent was as impressive as her entrance. Camellia wondered if she had spent time in France.

"Merci, Madame Dabbs. *Me permettre d'introduire. . . ."*

The words washed over Camellia. One day she would be able to carry on a conversation like the one between Mrs. Thornton and Mrs. Dabbs. It was a pity she had not studied French when she was younger, but her relatives had never seen a need for her to learn the language.

Mrs. Thornton switched to English and introduced Jonah, Lily, and Jasmine. Then she turned to her and nodded. "And this beautiful lady is of course your new pupil, Miss Camellia Anderson."

"Mademoiselle Anderson, it is a pleasure to meet you." She spoke without any trace of accent, slipping from one language to another with an ease Camellia envied.

Camellia could feel the weight of Mrs. Dabbs's assessing gaze as she curtsied.

When she straightened, the lady was smiling at her. "We are going to have such a wonderful spring, my dear. Your things arrived earlier, and they have been taken to your bedroom upstairs. Say farewell to your family, and I will take you to meet your roommate."

So soon? Her nose tingled as she turned to face the others. Parting from her sisters was going to be harder than she had realized. It wasn't like remaining behind at Les Fleurs while Lily and Jasmine took an overnight trip to Memphis or Baton Rouge. She wouldn't see her sisters for months.

The tight smile on Lily's face was an indication of her older sister's emotions. She was probably already regretting her decision. And Jasmine looked as though she might burst into tears at any moment.

"Thank you so much for letting me do this." She hugged Lily and Jasmine at the same time. "I love both of you very much."

"We love you, too." Jasmine's voice was a bare whisper.

Lily's arms tightened around her. "Are you sure you want to do this?"

Camellia nodded, her head rubbing against theirs.

"Then you'd better get upstairs before I drag you back to the carriage." Lily released her and raised her chin. "But remember that I can come get you at any time. All you have to do is get a message to the Thorntons."

"Now, now." Mrs. Dabbs stepped between them, cutting off Camellia's escape route. "Your sister will be very happy here. All of my students enjoy themselves."

Allowing herself to be pulled toward the staircase, Camellia heard a whisper from the second floor. She glanced upward and caught a glimpse of a heart-shaped face surrounded by a cloud of dark hair before it disappeared around a wall. One of the other students. She looked about Jasmine's age. Camellia glanced back over her shoulder at her younger sister, wishing for a brief instant that she would remain behind.

Then reality intruded. Jasmine would never be happy here. She barely tolerated the lessons she received aboard the *Water Lily*. La Belle Demoiselle was not the place for either of her sisters. But it was the perfect place for Camellia. She felt lighter as she moved away from the first floor, as though each step upward was freeing her, freeing her to become an irresistible combination of style and grace that would complement her physical beauty.

She looked up and met Jonah's gaze. She wished she could think of something to say that would wipe away the half smile on his face. She had no reason to blush. It wasn't like he could read her thoughts.

Jonah shook his head and turned his attention to Mrs. Dabbs. "If something happens, you will send a note around to my parents' home."

She tilted her head and stared at him. "Of course, but I believe we're safe enough here."

Camellia wondered why Mrs. Dabbs's reassurance made Jonah straighten his posture. He threw his shoulders back, looking almost like a soldier for a moment. "Mr. Lincoln could end all of this fighting if he would listen to reason."

"Yes, but I am afraid he is too stubborn to consider the desires of the South even though I write to him of my concerns."

Camellia's eyes widened. "You send letters to Abraham Lincoln?"

"Why not?" Mrs. Dabbs's smile softened her question. "If I don't ask him to stop this war, how can I expect him to grant my dearest wish?"

"How indeed?" Lily looked impressed by the lady's calm logic. "Perhaps all of us should follow your example."

Mrs. Dabbs nodded in agreement. "I encourage all of my students to do so."

"Do you really think your letters reach Mr. Lincoln's desk?" Jasmine's eyes were wide at the thought.

"I am sure of it. I grew up in Maryland, you know. It is not so far from the White House. And I got to see one of the debates between Mr. Lincoln and Mr. Douglas a few years ago. He struck me then as a man who is very approachable." Then she seemed to add as an afterthought, "As does our own president, Mr. Davis."

Lily pulled on her gloves. "Well, I hope one of them pays attention to any pleas you send. I am afraid there will be no winner in this war."

Chapter Seven

Two large beds filled the room, and a banked fire pulled dampness from the air and made the space feel warm and inviting. Camellia's trunks were nowhere to be seen, and she wondered where they might be. A large wooden desk took center stage in the room, with several books stacked on top of it and a pair of ladder-back chairs tucked on either side. A rocker filled another corner, but there was still plenty of room to move around.

Camellia looked for the girl she had caught a glimpse of as they came upstairs. Was she going to be her roommate? Pushing the question aside for the moment, she removed her gloves and hat, tossing them on the nearest bed as she moved into the room.

Mrs. Dabbs cleared her throat. "You must not get in the habit of scattering your belongings about. At least a dozen young ladies will be attending classes this spring term. You'll want to avoid the possibility of mixing up your things with someone else's."

A blush heated Camellia's cheeks. "I'm sorry."

With a wave of her hand and a quick smile, the older lady excused her actions.

Camellia snatched up her hat and gloves and looked around for a better place to put them.

"I had closets installed in all of the bedrooms last year." Mrs. Dabbs took Camellia's hat and walked to a bank of doors on the far side of the room. When she pulled on them, they parted, folding back like the spines of a fan.

Camellia's jaw dropped when she realized several of her new outfits hung from a bar inside the wooden box. "How ingenious." Her skirts looked ready to be worn. They were not crushed from lying on top of one another.

Mrs. Dabbs laid her hat and gloves on a shelf at the top of the closet before turning and dusting her hands together. "There. That's much better. One of the first lessons most of my girls learn is how to take care of their clothes. During these uncertain times, you must learn to fend for yourselves."

Camellia didn't understand the other woman's logic. She would never have to do without slaves or servants. But she was not going to start the term with an argument. She nodded and won an approving smile from Mrs. Dabbs.

"Jane Watkins, your roommate, arrived late last night. Like you, she comes from Mississippi. I'm sure you'll get along famously." Mrs. Dabbs moved to the door. "I'll ask her to come up and help you settle in before dinner. We won't start classes until tomorrow, as two of the local girls won't be here until this afternoon."

Removing her cloak, Camellia started to toss it across the foot of her bed. But then she stopped and looked toward the door. She would be a model student, learning everything Mrs. Dabbs offered whether she agreed with the lady or not.

Walking across the room, she pushed on one of the closet doors. It didn't budge. She stepped back and considered the problem. Did it act like a fan? She looked toward the floor but saw nothing except wooden planks. Raising her gaze slowly upward, she spied a pair of depressions—one on each door. She placed her fingers in one and tugged, her lips curving upward in a triumphant smile as the door glided open.

She didn't think closets would catch on. Her skirts looked odd—deflated—suspended from hooks that ran along the walls of the closet. The flounces bunched together, and the arms of her shirtwaists hung empty. Her clothing looked like it belonged on a scarecrow. With a sigh, she bunched up her cloak and tried to fit it on an empty hook. It slithered to the floor as soon as she let go of it.

"Here, let me help you."

Camellia jumped at the unexpected sound of a voice. Her ringlets bounced around her face as she turned to the front of the bedroom. Taking in the pretty girl who must be Jane, she wondered if they were going to be rivals.

Sunlight poured into the room from a large window and seemed to set Jane's thick auburn hair aflame. She stepped up to the closet and took Camellia's cloak, shook it out, and hung it on the offending hook by its collar. "There. It only takes a little practice to get the hang of this."

She giggled, her brown eyes dancing. "Get it? You'll soon get the *hang* of it."

A nervous laugh gurgled up Camellia's throat.

"Oh good. I was hoping my roommate would have a sense of humor." Jane put a hand on Camellia's arm and pulled her toward one of the beds. "You're quite beautiful, you know. I should be jealous, but that would make living with you so uncomfortable."

Camellia took in her roommate's curvaceous figure. From her long neck to her tiny waist, Jane was the very embodiment of femininity. She had thought the other girl's eyes were brown, but now that she was close to her, she realized they were more hazel. "You're pretty, too."

Jane waved away the compliment with a quick motion. "I've always wanted curls like yours, but no matter how much effort I expend, my hair has more in common with a mop than a corkscrew."

Unable to resist the urge to laugh, Camellia felt the tension and fear fading. Jane was not going to be a rival. Whatever sadness had lingered at parting from her sisters disappeared. "Your hair gleams, though, while mine is as dull as wash water."

Her new friend's mouth tightened, and the green flecks in her eyes dimmed. "I have an idea."

"What?" Assuming an equally serious expression, Camellia straightened her spine.

"I assume you're here for the same reason I am—to find the perfect husband."

Camellia wasn't sure if she was ready for this much frankness. She waited for Jane to continue.

"Think about it, Camellia. Not every man wants a vivacious, redheaded beauty on his arm."

Both of them were perched on the edge of the bed, their skirts billowing around them. Camellia thought they would present a nice picture—one dark, the other fair. Her eyes widened. She looked at Jane, who nodded. "I believe you may be the smartest girl I've ever met."

Jane squealed and fell on her neck. "Between us, we'll attract every available man in the city of New Orleans."

"Why stop there?" Camellia emerged from the embrace with a sigh. "I have my heart set on marrying a hero, someone who is willing to fight for his beliefs."

Jumping up from the bed, Jane squealed again and reached for her hand. "I cannot believe it."

"What?"

"My brother. You have to meet my brother. He's rich, handsome, and a soldier." She ran to the desk and pulled out a chair. "I'm going to write to him right away. I can't wait until we're sisters."

Camellia watched as she bent over a piece of stationery, excitement building in her. She'd known coming to La Belle Demoiselle was the right move, but she'd never dreamed she would find the perfect husband on the day of her arrival. "What's your brother's name?"

"Thaddeus. . .Thaddeus Watkins. But everyone calls him Thad."

Mrs. Thad Watkins. She extended her hand and imagined a large ring on her fourth finger. Fate had ordained her future. Maybe she'd been foolish to spend so much energy regretting the necessity of putting off her education for a year. Everything was working out perfectly.

Jonah was sick of parties. He was tired of sifting through bits and pieces of information and trying to decide what was important enough to pass along to Mrs. Dabbs. At least he'd been able to report the encouraging news that the work on the two ironclads being built in the New Orleans harbor was at a standstill. Getting the supplies through Admiral Farragut's blockade had proven more difficult than expected. Furthermore, many of the men who were formerly employed as shipbuilders had volunteered in the Confederate army.

Last night he had learned that a portion of the New Orleans forces were being sent northward, further weakening the city's defenses. He needed to get that information to Mrs. Dabbs right away. If the Union showed up today, he believed they could take over the city without firing a single shot.

"Did I overhear you ordering that your horse be saddled?" His mother's question interrupted his thoughts. "I am planning to visit

Mary Lee Thompson's mother and thought you might like to join me. You seemed to be taken with her at your sister's party last week."

"No, thank you. I'm going to La Belle to check on Camellia Anderson."

"Again?" Her gaze searched his face. "You have been to see her several times in the past month. I thought the first time that it was just your sense of obligation to Lily, but I am beginning to wonder if you have other reasons to frequent the school."

Another of the problems with being a spy was the lying, especially to people he cared about. "She's pretty, but I have no interest other than that of an older brother. Besides, she has her sights set on a much bigger prize."

A frown crossed his mother's face. "I don't know why she wouldn't be flattered by your attention. Why don't you take her some flowers? Young ladies always like romantic gestures."

"Thank you for the advice, Mother."

"I know, I know. You don't need your mother telling you how to act."

At least he knew enough about the female gender to not respond to that comment.

"Why don't you invite Camellia over for a weekend visit?" His mother seemed to have taken his silence as an invitation to meddle. "I'm sure she would like to get away from the school for a few days."

"She seems pretty happy at La Belle." As soon as he made the statement, Jonah could have bitten off his tongue. Even to his own ears, he sounded too much like a jealous suitor. "I'll invite her if you wish."

"Excellent. Sarah would probably like to see her, too. And we'll all go to church together. Perhaps I can even convince your father to join us."

"I doubt that. Father cannot abide the pastor's cooperationist leanings. The last time he went with us, I thought he was going to have an apoplexy."

"He is a man of strong principles."

"It's a shame he's chosen the wrong ones."

She considered him for a moment before answering. "Youth is a glorious time. You know all the answers and could solve all of the world's problems if only you were in charge." She pursed her lips. "But things are not that simple. Your father is an ardent supporter of states' rights. He believes the federal government has grown too powerful, and he doesn't want to be ruled by the politicians in Washington."

"He would rather be ruled by the rich planters instead?"

Silence fell between them, filled with tension. Jonah wondered if other families suffered the same divisions, argued the same issues.

"Your father is a good man." His mother's voice was tender.

The tension leached out of Jonah's shoulders. He smiled at her and pushed back from the table. "I should be back in an hour or so."

Her eyes, a darker shade of green than his, were luminous with unshed tears. "I love you."

He moved to her side of the table and dropped a kiss on the cheek she raised to him. "I love you, too, Mother."

"Now go. And don't let Camellia get away from you. If you wait too long, she may fall for some other fellow's smooth talk."

It was time to make his escape before his well-meaning parent sent out invitations for a wedding. "I promise you my heart is not pining for the beauteous Miss Anderson. I'm not ready to marry anyone."

"If you change your mind, you will let me know, won't you?"

"Of course. You'll be the first." He left the house then, snagging his greatcoat on his way to the stable. A misty rain chilled the air as he threaded his way through the congested streets.

A feeling of anticipation surprised him. He wanted to get this errand behind him, didn't he? Of course he did. It must have been all the silly talk from his mother about other suitors that had him thinking of Camellia Anderson.

That was it. Jonah pulled back on his horse's reins and moved out of the flow of traffic. He had no feelings about her at all. Visiting Camellia was nothing but a ruse to protect him from exposure. He didn't even enjoy being around her. In fact, he hoped she would turn down his mother's invitation. The idea of being around her for an extended period of time filled him with nothing more than dismay, perhaps even repugnance.

Once this war was over, he would turn his attention to marriage, and when he did, it would be to someone much more serious about life. A girl who had strong faith and exhibited the qualities enumerated in the book of Proverbs. Camellia probably had no idea how to be a proper wife, and he had no desire to teach her.

Satisfied with his logic, Jonah clucked his tongue and encouraged his mount forward once more, eventually arriving in the quieter portion of the city where Mrs. Dabbs's school was located. The trick was to keep his mind on the job the military had given him. Maybe after he left the school, he would visit the Custom House to discover what the enterprising blockade runners had managed to slip past the Union navy. Feeling much more in control of himself, Jonah dismounted and tied his horse to an ornate post outside of the school. All he had to do was politely ask Camellia to visit. Then he could get on with the real reason for his visit.

Chapter Eight

"I don't understand why we have to practice needlepoint." Camellia punched her needle through the piece of cotton, almost stabbing her knee through her skirt and the multiple layers of petticoats she wore. "I already know how to sew."

Mrs. Dabbs was helping Camellia with a knot in her thread. "This is not about sewing. It's about beautifying your home with handmade art."

"Every well-bred lady should be able to ply a needle with skill." Pauline, a short girl with olive skin and a long nose, added her opinion.

Fourteen-year-old Molly nodded. Camellia thought of the girl as Pauline's shadow. She had an unfortunate lisp, so she didn't speak often. Next to her sat bespectacled Catherine, who was probably doing a better job than Camellia even though she was practically as blind as a bat.

Even Jane seemed to be enjoying their lesson. She held her handwork up to the light, and Camellia could see how even each stitch was in the five-pointed star and the circle surrounding it.

She sighed and pulled her needle back through even as she realized the points of her star had an odd tilt and her circle was decidedly lopsided. She would much rather be practicing her penmanship or even adding up columns of numbers. At least those skills had some bearing on her future. If she needed artwork for her home, she would commission an artist to paint a portrait of her to be hung above the mantel in the front parlor.

A knock at the door brought Camellia back to the present. Mademoiselle Brigitte Laurent, Mrs. Dabbs's assistant, entered the room and looked straight at her. *"Excusez-moi,* Mademoiselle Anderson, *vous avez un visiteur."* The girl looked over her shoulder and blushed.

"Merci." Camellia thanked her in French without effort. Her accent was getting much better. She caught Jane's inquisitive glance and shrugged. She had no idea who might be asking for her. Standing up, she moved to place her handwork in her seat, but it was stuck on something.

A giggle from one of the other girls made her look down.

"Oh no!" The groan came when she realized she had sewn her star to her dress. Now everyone could see how poor her needlework was. She tried to jerk the pitiful cloth free, but she had no luck. She had never been so embarrassed in her life. A blush burned her throat and cheeks.

"I see you're sporting a new style."

Camellia looked toward the door and wished she had not gotten out of bed this morning. Her embarrassment increased tenfold—a hundredfold—as she saw the sardonic grin on Jonah Thornton's face. She wanted to jump out the window, sink beneath the carpets, or at least run away from the derisive laughter. Even Mrs. Dabbs had a hand over her mouth, her eyes dancing.

"Let me help you." Jane pulled out a pair of scissors and snipped the threads holding the needlework to her dress.

Bless Jane, her only friend in the world. Even though her cheeks were still flaming, Camellia lifted her chin. "I have always been an innovative thinker."

Jonah bowed, although his grin was still wide. "I look forward to seeing all the debutantes following your lead."

The smothered giggles stopped as Mrs. Dabbs stood. "How pleasant to see you again, Mr. Thornton." She nodded at Camellia. "Why don't you and Jane show Mr. Thornton the visitors' parlor? Mademoiselle Laurent will order the tea service."

Grabbing her friend by the hand, Camellia hurried to comply with the instructions. Anything to put distance between her and their stitchery lessons. She pulled Jane past Jonah before he could say anything derogatory, leading the way to a small parlor just off the central staircase.

A cheerful fire crackled in the fireplace, its flames dispelling the February chill. A small sofa provided seating for an intimate conversation, while a single straight-backed chair some distance away was for a chaperone. Camellia sank onto the sofa, her cheeks beginning to cool. She motioned for Jane to sit next to her, but her friend shook her head and moved to the chaperone's chair.

Did Jane think Jonah was a suitor? Far from it. Although she had considered him a possibility at one time, it had not taken her long to discover he was like a bothersome gnat she would like to swat. She was still staring daggers at Jane as he entered the room, having taken his sweet time to traverse the hallway.

Her heart stopped for a brief moment as their gazes met. He *was* handsome; she had to allow him that. She remembered the first time she'd seen him, his deep auburn locks stylishly disheveled, his emerald eyes swirling with mystery and challenge. But that had been years ago—almost two whole years—and she had become much more sophisticated since then.

In an effort to prove how little she cared, Camellia spread her skirts out to cover the length of the sofa. Of course he didn't understand that she wanted him to stand.

He simply raised one supercilious eyebrow and towered over her. "I'm happy to see how much you've learned about decorum since you came to La Belle."

Camellia's shocked gaze met his and read the determination stamped there. Suddenly she realized that Jonah was no longer the carefree younger son. He was a man fully grown. She huffed her irritation but gathered in her skirt. "Please sit down, Mr. Thornton."

"Thank you for the offer, Miss Anderson, but I believe I'll stand." He moved to the fireplace and leaned one shoulder against the mantel.

Infuriating man. One of these days she would get the better of him. Maybe she would even make him fall in love with her. Once she knew his heart was in her hands, she would make him beg for mercy. Then she would marry someone else, and Jonah would live out the rest of his days a broken shell of his former self.

With her plan in mind, Camellia fluttered her eyelashes at Jonah. "It's so pleasant to see you on this dreary day."

His grin widened.

Hanging on to her temper with all her might, Camellia forced herself to smile back at him. "How are your parents?"

He pushed away from the mantel, and she hoped it was because his backside was burning. After making a circle around the room, his gaze flitting from window to door, he sat next to her on the sofa. "My mother sends her regards. She and my father would like for you to come and stay with them for the first weekend next month."

Since the moment Jonah had arrived at La Belle Demoiselle today, Camellia had felt like the very ground under her feet was shifting. His statement, however, changed all that. Her world steadied. He must have told his mother he would like to court her, and sweet Mrs. Thornton had extended the invitation so he would have ample opportunity. This was a game she knew very well how to play. She would turn him down and allow herself to be persuaded by his heartfelt pleas.

She leaned against the back of the sofa and turned her head toward Jane, giving her a broad wink as a cue. "Don't we already have plans for that particular weekend?"

Jane shook her head. "I don't—"

Camellia interrupted her friend. "Oh yes, the trip to Lake Pontchartrain is scheduled for that weekend, is it not?"

Jane folded her lips together and shot her a fearful look.

Camellia turned back to Jonah only to find him not even paying any attention to her. He was looking over his shoulder at the door to the parlor. Was he interested in someone else?

A sharp pain clenched her heart, stealing her breath for a moment. Was she mistaken about Jonah's interest? "I believe my roommate is correct after all, Mr. Thornton."

"What's that?" He turned back to her, his eyes unfocused.

Had he been drinking? He was certainly acting oddly. Camellia straightened her spine. "I said I will—" She broke off as a thought occurred to her. "That is, Jane and I will be able to come for a visit on that weekend."

He nodded. "Good."

Mademoiselle Laurent entered with the tea tray, and Jane pulled her chair closer to the low, ornate table in front of the sofa. Camellia narrowed her eyes and watched to see if any secret glances passed between Mrs. Dabbs's assistant and Jonah. Neither of them seemed to notice the other, but was their nonchalance suspicious?

Camellia waited until the assistant left before pouring the tea and offering Jonah the tray of sweets. "Have you written to Mr. Lincoln?"

An odd expression crossed his face. Fear? It was gone so quickly she wondered if she had imagined it. "I have been too busy for that."

"I suppose your father must appreciate your help at his office."

"I'm not working." Jonah shook his head and glanced over his shoulder again.

Who was he expecting? Camellia looked at Jane and shrugged. "Then what is it that occupies your time?"

He looked back at her. "Escorting my sister and my mother to their numerous social engagements."

"I see." She wanted to ask him how he could waste his time in frivolity. Didn't he know they were at war? Had he no patriotic feelings? She rose from the sofa, forcing him to follow suit. "It's been nice seeing you, but Jane and I must get back to our class."

"Yes." Jonah gave her his full attention. "You certainly need all the instruction you can get."

Camellia snapped her mouth shut on the words that threatened to escape. Never before had she so clearly understood the command to not cast pearls before swine. She would make certain she followed it in her future dealings with Jonah Thornton.

Jonah lingered in the parlor after Camellia stormed out. He should be ashamed of himself for baiting her, but he found the temptation irresistible. A chuckle slipped out as he considered the girl. Of course, she brought a great deal of it on herself by insisting on adhering to all the rules of society.

"It's good to hear you laugh." Mrs. Dabbs entered the room and closed the door behind her.

He shook his head. "Not while I'm on such serious business."

"Do you have new information for me?"

"Yes. Last night I learned that General Lovell's request for additional troops to defend the city has been refused for now."

Mrs. Dabbs clasped her hands in front of her chest. "That's good news for us."

"Yes, but we cannot get overconfident. The Confederacy will not give up the city unless the Union can act quickly. The troops will eventually arrive, and then it will take a pitched battle to capture New Orleans."

The older woman grew more serious. "Many lives will be lost if that happens."

"Yes."

"Can you find out exactly when the troops will be sent?"

Jonah sighed. "I don't know. I'll try."

Her sigh echoed his. "I know it's difficult, but remember that we have a worthy goal."

"You are right." He bowed and turned to depart.

Mrs. Dabbs stopped him with a hand on his arm. "I pray for your safety every night. I know God is watching over us."

"Thank you, Mrs. Dabbs. You are truly a remarkable woman." As he left, Jonah compared Camellia's personality to that of her headmistress. She would do well to emulate Mrs. Dabbs in all areas—skill, comportment, and faith. If only she could let go of her self-importance.

Chapter Nine

"I cannot believe the soldiers need any more bandages." Pauline folded her arms over her chest and sat back. "We've rolled thousands already. Enough to stretch from here to Virginia. What can they possibly need more bandages for?"

All the blood drained from Jane's face.

"Ith for doctorth to wrap around the hurth." Molly was finally beginning to talk more often in spite of her lisp, and she no longer absorbed every word spouted by the overbearing Pauline.

Camellia reached out a hand to her friend. "Don't think about it."

Jane nodded and looked at Mrs. Dabbs. "May I be excused?"

Mrs. Dabbs gave her permission, and silence fell on the room while Jane rose and slipped out of the room, closing the door with a sharp click.

Poor little Catherine's eyes grew monstrously large behind her spectacles, and a fat tear rolled down her cheek. She was a very high-strung child.

Pauline was more resilient. She rolled her eyes. "What's the matter with her?"

"How can you be so insensitive?" Camellia's hands balled into fists. She loved Jane like a sister. "Jane has never done anything to you. Don't you know her brother is a soldier? One of these bandages could be used on wounds he sustains in a battle."

"I'm sorry." Pauline's dark face blanched. "I didn't think—"

"That's right. You didn't think. You never think about anything if it doesn't affect you." Camellia could feel the blood pounding in her head.

"Enough." Mrs. Dabbs pointed to the pile of cloth strips. "If you cannot be civil to each other, then you will finish your tasks in silence."

Camellia enjoyed the practical job of rolling bandages much more than stitching stars or circles. Where would this roll go? What hands would unroll it and gently wrap it around a wounded soldier? Would this bandage save his life? She hoped so. She hoped the nameless soldier would sense the love and caring wrapped into the spiral of cotton.

Half an hour passed, and her roommate had not returned. Camellia was about to go in search of her when the door opened and Jane rejoined them. Her eyes and nose bore indications of a tearful interlude.

Reaching for a fresh strip, Camellia sent a threatening look at Pauline. She had better not say anything else untoward. Camellia wasn't afraid of her or her family.

A rustling sound brought her head up. One of the servants had opened the door, but Camellia hardly saw her for the vision standing directly behind her. He was beautiful. Tall, with shoulders so wide they looked like they would fill a doorway. His face was all angles, from his square chin to his high cheekbones. His dark eyes surveyed the room and zeroed in on one face. Camellia barely had time to register the way his smile was reflected in those delicious eyes before a feminine squeal startled her.

Jane launched herself toward the stranger and threw herself into his arms. Had she forgotten to tell her best friend about this man she obviously loved? Wistful envy filled Camellia. What a fortunate girl she was to be adored by such a fine specimen of a man. And a soldier at that. He didn't even need the gray uniform—he would have been equally handsome in civilian attire.

"Jane!" Mrs. Dabbs's shocked tones separated the two at the door.

Jane's tears were back. They trickled down her face, reddening her eyelids and nose all over again. But the wide smile on her friend's face told Camellia this time her tears were of the joyful variety.

The tall man reached into his pocket and produced a handkerchief that he offered to her.

Jane wiped her face clean and took a deep breath. "I'm sorry, Mrs. Dabbs. Please allow me to introduce a very special man." She sent him an adoring glance and reached for his hand, drawing him farther into the room. "This is my brother, Captain Thaddeus Watkins."

Camellia's heart tripled its speed. Jane's brother? The man her best friend wanted her to meet? Her whole world turned upside down. Her earlier envy turned into anticipation. He *was* the man of her dreams. Handsome, rich, and a soldier. Captain Thaddeus Watkins was almost too good to be true. She would need to be on her best behavior.

As Captain Watkins exchanged pleasantries with Mrs. Dabbs, Camellia realized that even his deep voice was perfect. When Jane dragged him across the room to stand in front of her, Camellia wondered if she was going to swoon. If she did, would he be impressed with her delicate femininity or repulsed by her weakness?

"My sister has written to me of her bosom friend." His eyes were like a cup of warm cocoa. "I have to admit she didn't exaggerate your beauty."

"I am happy to meet you, Captain. Your sister speaks so highly of you." Camellia thought she could look into his face for hours on end. For the rest of her life.

"I didn't mean to interrupt you ladies—"

"Don't give it a thought, Captain." Mrs. Dabbs beamed at him. "We were about to take our afternoon tea. I hope you'll join us."

Three parallel lines appeared in his noble brow when Jane's brother frowned. Camellia longed to smooth them away with her fingers.

"I don't want to intrude. I wanted to let Jane know that I've been stationed at Chalmette. With your permission, I will come back and visit tomorrow."

His manners were impeccable, too. Camellia knew as well as she knew her name that she was in love with Thaddeus Watkins. She hoped he didn't disagree, because she was certain they would one day become husband and wife. From the admiration in his eyes as he gazed at her over the top of his sister's head, Camellia suspected he wouldn't put up much resistance.

❧

"I have butterflies in my stomach." Camellia put her hand on the waist of her blue-gray walking dress.

"I'm just glad you want to go with me." Jane tweaked the flounce on her skirt, part of the gold ensemble that complemented her burnished auburn hair. "I promise we won't spend the whole evening talking of family members you've never heard of."

"Don't worry about that. I will be content to be next to my best friend."

They left the room together, descending the staircase with their arms around each other's waist. Camellia was aware of the picture they presented. Jane was glowing, prettier than Camellia had ever seen her. It was a good thing they were not competing for Thad's affections. Not that he could resist Camellia when she put her mind to attracting him. No one could.

He stood in the foyer, even handsomer than she remembered. His gray uniform was pressed, and he had his slouch hat tucked under his right arm. He lifted his head and watched as they floated down, his eyes glowing with appreciation.

Camellia's heart soared. She and Jane reached him at the same time, but she stepped away to allow him to hug and kiss his sister.

When he turned toward her, she sank into a deep curtsy to exhibit her gracefulness. Straightening, she extended her gloved hand for his salute.

He bent and placed a kiss on her knuckles. "I'm the luckiest man in New Orleans."

A tiny splinter of disappointment buried itself in her mind. Where was the tingle she had expected from his touch? Was it because of her glove? A more daring man might have turned her hand over and placed a kiss on the inside of her wrist. Camellia shook her head to banish the thought and allowed her lips to curve into an admiring smile. "We are the lucky ones to be escorted by a true hero."

"I'm thankful to have two of the people I love the most right here with me." Jane's pleasure was reflected in her radiant smile.

The captain helped them with their cloaks. Did his hands linger a second or two as he settled the dark velvet across her shoulders? Camellia hoped she was not imagining the tiny detail. Whether she tingled at his touch or not, she still knew Thaddeus was the man she was destined to marry.

The sun was setting as they arrived in the Vieux Carre, embarrassing the sky into a deep blush. Camellia wished she could emulate it as Captain Watkins handed her out of the carriage. She needed to get rid of her gloves. Perhaps she could leave them behind in the hotel during their meal. Frozen fingers would be a small price to pay to feel his skin on hers.

Soldiers wearing uniforms of all styles and states of repair filled the lobby. They stood in small knots, laughing and talking. But as Camellia and Jane gave their coats over to be held for them, the conversations hushed. She looked around to see that they were the center of attention. Unsettled, she looked at the captain.

His smile comforted her. "I cannot blame them for looking when I can hardly tear my own eyes from your face."

Camellia wanted to blush. That's what she was supposed to do when a man complimented her, but her heart continued its steady pace. She grabbed the fan dangling from her wrist and opened it to hide her lack of emotional upheaval.

One of the men separated himself from the others and moved toward them. His hair was so white Camellia at first thought he was an older gentlemen, but as he drew closer, she realized her mistake. He was about the same age as Jane's brother, but his freckled face was nowhere near as handsome. "Thad, you rascal, you didn't tell anyone you would be entertaining two ladies."

The captain made a face but turned to the man who had hailed him. "Jane, Miss Anderson, allow me to introduce Lieutenant Harold Baxter, a bold scoundrel who does not mind presuming on the barest of acquaintance."

Camellia didn't realize he only had one arm until he bowed and his coat sleeve dangled free. She glanced away and caught the expression of sympathy on Jane's face. It shamed her into donning a smile and turning back to the lieutenant.

"Harry, this is my sister, Jane, and her friend, Miss Camellia Anderson."

The lieutenant grinned at them. "If I weren't bold, I'd never get to meet the prettiest girls."

Other men began drifting in their direction, their gazes curious. Lieutenant Baxter held out his good arm to Jane, and he winked at Thad. "I think we'd better get these two ladies into the dining room before we are overrun by the less enterprising officers present."

Jane's brother opened his mouth to say something but was forestalled when she put her hand on the other soldier's good arm. With a good-natured shrug, Thad offered his arm to Camellia. "Don't think this means you can join us for dinner."

Lieutenant Baxter's infectious laughter drifted back over his shoulder.

Captain Watkins chuckled and leaned his head toward Camellia's. "I hope you don't mind. The poor fellow has had a rough time."

"Did he lose his arm in battle?"

"Yes, he fought with the Army of North Virginia at Manassas." The captain's face tightened. "All teasing aside, he is a good man. He and I have become fast friends since we met."

Lieutenant Baxter was helping Jane into one of the three seats as they reached the square table covered by a snowy tablecloth. A waiter dragged a fourth chair toward them, a sour look on his face.

Camellia moved toward the chair opposite Jane's, but the captain redirected her footsteps with a slight pressure on her arm and pulled out the chair on his sister's right. Then he took the seat opposite Jane, leaving the chair on his sister's left open for the lieutenant.

"Afraid to let me sit next to Miss Anderson, are you?" Lieutenant Baxter winked at her. "I can understand your fear. I'm so much more handsome than you."

His joke set the tone for the evening. Camellia could not remember ever giggling so much. Their meal was delicious, too: rack of lamb with sprigs of mint that reminded her of the meals Jensen prepared on her sister's first riverboat.

Lieutenant Baxter leaned back and sipped from his water goblet as the waiter removed his empty plate. "I still can't believe any finishing schools are still operating in the city or that your families will allow you to attend."

Camellia looked away. This conversation made her think of the time and effort she'd had to expend to convince Lily that she would be safe.

"Why not, Lieutenant Baxter?" Jane asked. "My parents believe it's important for us to continue ordinary life as much as possible."

He raised his sandy-white eyebrows. "I thought we were on a first-name basis since we've broken bread together."

"Harry." Jane looked down at the table as she spoke.

"Much better." He grew serious. "The city is filled with people who want to help the North destroy our way of life."

"Really?" Jane looked at her brother for confirmation.

Thad cleared his throat. "Let's not frighten the ladies. We don't want them to worry."

"I'm not worried." Camellia summoned a confident smile for Jane's benefit. "Not when we have such fine men defending us."

"You may rest assured that both of you will be safe no matter what happens." Thad's smile was aimed at both of them. "I promise."

Camellia finally felt a shiver rush through her at his words. How exciting to feel protected. She reached under the table for Jane's hand and gave it a reassuring squeeze. Everything was going to be just fine.

The lieutenant tried to include himself in the carriage ride to La Belle Demoiselle, but Thad sent him back inside with a wave of his hand. Camellia wouldn't have admitted it to Jane, but she was relieved. Although Harry was an entertaining dinner companion, she had no desire to listen to any more of his tall tales.

Remembering to leave her gloves in her reticule, Camellia sat next to Jane, leaving the opposite bench for Thad. She pleated the folds of her cloak and wondered if he would try to take her hand.

Darkness and silence intermingled as the carriage left the lights of town behind. She searched her memory for some interesting topic to introduce, not wanting to bore Thad with conversation about the weather or their studies.

"Spring will be here before we know it." So he couldn't think of anything either.

Then an idea came to her, sparked by his mention of spring. "Mrs. Dabbs told us this morning that we are going to host a gala as soon as the weather warms a little."

She couldn't see Thad in the dark, but she heard the rustle of his coat as he nodded. "What does Mrs. Dabbs consider a gala to be?"

"It's going to be a fancy ball," Jane answered. "We'll get to dress up in our fanciest ball gowns."

Camellia tilted her head and raised her voice a few notes in imitation of their headmistress. " 'It will give you girls the opportunity to practice the skills I've been teaching you this term.' "

Jane giggled at her imitation, and Camellia decided Jasmine's penchant for playacting must have rubbed off on her. Her friend's laughter rewarded her silliness.

Her eyes must be getting accustomed to the gloom, because she could make out Thad's features as he leaned toward them. "I'm certain you already have an escort, Camellia."

"No, she doesn't."

Camellia hoped he couldn't see her blush. Why had her friend been so quick to answer? If Thad thought someone else was interested in escorting her, it would sharpen his desire to win her affections. Or so Aunt Dahlia had always said. She stifled a sigh and tried for a nonchalant tone. "I'm not sure if any of us will have escorts since it's to be held at the school."

His hand covered hers, stilling her nervous movements. Jane might have seen the gesture, but she was looking toward the window.

Camellia's fingers fluttered under his large, warm touch. Exhilaration sent the butterflies moving about her stomach again. Now what? Should she pull her hand away or allow it to remain under his?

"My military duties will keep me occupied tomorrow, but may I call on you Saturday?" His low voice swept her away on a heady tide of success, making her almost forget her roommate was in the carriage with them.

"We can't." Jane's voice intruded in their moment like a dash of icy water.

Camellia jerked her hand away and buried it under the folds of her cloak. Her mind was still spinning. She wanted to say something, but her mouth didn't want to cooperate.

"We're going to the Thorntons' town house for the weekend, remember?"

The Thorntons' home. Of course. Jonah Thornton and his family. But how would she explain to Thad the relationship between her and the Thorntons? Camellia chewed on her lower lip as she considered how to turn the situation to her advantage. Aunt Dahlia's words came back to her as the carriage slowed and pulled up under the porte cochere.

Thad slid across the seat and reached for the door.

Taking a deep breath for courage, Camellia leaned forward and put her cold hand on his. "Wait. Perhaps you can come for dinner at the Thorntons' home Saturday evening."

He shot her an odd look. "But I don't know the Thorntons. I would not dare show up on their doorstep uninvited."

"But I know they would love to meet you. Mr. Thornton is an avid supporter of the Cause. As soon as he discovers that Jane has a brother who is a *captain*. . ." She put extra emphasis on the word and paused as though overcome. "Well, suffice it to say he would be most put out with me if I didn't invite you."

"When you put it like that. . ." His smile warmed her heart.

This was going to be perfect. He would have eyes for no one but her. By the time of the gala next month, he would be ready to propose.

She needed to get inside and start preparing. Aunt Dahlia would be so proud.

Chapter Ten

Jonah's mother studied him during the drive to La Belle. "I'm not sure why you thought it necessary to come along this morning."

"Are you saying I'm not welcome?"

"Of course not. But you cannot be that anxious to see dear Camellia again, not when she is about to spend the entire weekend with us."

He yawned to cover his inner turmoil and looked out the window. Bright sunlight heralded the impending arrival of spring. Before much more time passed, it would be summer, and the Confederate forces would arrive to bolster New Orleans' weak defenses. If the Union did not strike soon, it would be too late. The work on the ironclads in the port might be slow, but it was progressing. Now, right now, was the time to take the city. The local newspapers had carried news of the Union victories at Fort Henry and Fort Donelson in February. They even speculated that the real target was New Orleans and warned that an invading force could be expected to travel from Tennessee to attack the city. So why did the Federal forces hesitate?

Jonah fostered a smile and turned to face his mother. "Perhaps I have an ulterior motive for joining you."

Her gaze sharpened. "Oh? Is there something or someone you want to tell me about?"

For a moment, he wanted to confess his true agenda, wanted to tell his parent exactly why he had volunteered to come with her to pick up the girls. Mother was not as ardent in her support of the South as Father, and having someone he trusted to confide in would lessen the heavy burden of guilt and uncertainty.

The words burned his throat, but he choked them back. Telling her might bring him some relief, but at what cost? Involving his mother would force her to be complicit. He did not have that right. "What if I said I wanted to spend more time with the only lady who truly holds my heart in her hand?"

She sat back and laughed. "When did you become such a charmer?"

"You wound me. Are you trying to say I have not always been a pleasant fellow?"

"Of course not. But since you came back to New Orleans, you have been different. I've never known you to attend so many parties. Your father and I have begun to hope you are ready to pick a bride and settle down. And we would be delighted if your choice was a certain beautiful young student. You know how much we love all three of the Anderson girls."

His mouth tightened. "We've spoken of this before. Camellia Anderson is beautiful, but I want more in the woman I choose for a wife. Now if we were speaking of her older sister, Lily, it would be a different matter. She is a woman I admire greatly for her strong faith, her morals, and her independent spirit."

"Yes, but I can see some of those same qualities in Camellia. She only needs a strong Christian man to give her direction."

The carriage stopped then, ending their conversation, though her words echoed in his mind. As Jonah helped his mother alight, he wondered if it might be true. Was he being too hard on Camellia? Was she just young and in need of a guiding hand?

He followed his mother into La Belle Demoiselle, his eyes widening at a pile of luggage that filled the foyer. He wondered whether one of the girls had been expelled or perhaps called back home by her family. Easing his way past the stack, he nodded to the assistant, whose name he couldn't remember. Miss Lacy? Latrobe? It was on the tip of his tongue.

"Welcome, Monsieur Thornton." She smiled at him before continuing. "Madame. The young ladies are in the visitors' parlor, awaiting your arrival."

Jonah could feel his mother's speculative gaze on him, but he ignored her as he nodded. "Thank you, miss. I know the way." He strode down the hall and held the door open for his mother to precede him. Both Camellia and her friend were seated on the sofa, their heads together as they studied some magazine. He had to admit they made a pleasing picture.

Camellia stood and hurried to his mother as she entered the room, hugging her with an affection that seemed sincere. "Thank you so much for inviting us to stay with you."

"You are most welcome. I don't know why I waited so long." His mother touched Camellia's cheek. "But we will make up for my oversight by filling this weekend with a great many activities."

"We are prepared." Camellia looked back at Jane and gestured for her to join them. "Please allow me to introduce Miss Jane Watkins, my dearest friend and roommate. She is from Vicksburg."

Jonah slipped out of the room as the ladies got acquainted. He had a note to give Mrs. Dabbs—a list of the armaments planned for the *C. S. Mississippi*, the ironclad that was most likely to threaten U.S. naval ships once it was completed.

The headmistress must have gotten word of his arrival, because she was waiting for him in the hallway. "I have planned a picnic for next week. Will you have the girls back before then?"

"We'll have them back here by dark on Sunday." He pulled the note from his pocket, careful to keep it hidden in case they were being observed, and slipped it into Mrs. Dabbs's hand as he bowed over it.

"That's good, then." She wrapped her fingers around the piece of paper. "I know they'll have a nice visit with your family."

He nodded and turned away, his heart pounding as he returned to the visitors' parlor. He prayed the information would get into the right hands. Slipping back into the room a bare two minutes after his departure, Jonah was relieved to see the ladies had not missed him. He donned a bored expression and waited for a chance to interrupt.

"Are you sure you won't mind an additional guest for dinner?" Camellia's question put him on alert. What was she planning?

His mother tossed a look in his direction before responding. "Of course not, dear. Captain Watkins sounds like a fine gentleman. I'm sure my husband will be delighted to meet him."

Jonah frowned. Camellia might be a close friend of the family, but inviting a guest into his parents' home before asking their permission was ridiculous. His mother might not mind her effrontery, but he did. "I thought this was a finishing school."

Camellia turned toward him, her face wearing a look of indignation. "What is your point, sir?"

"My point is that any *child* would know better than to invite a guest to a gathering at which she is not the hostess."

Her eyes darkened, reminding him of a stormy sky. "I don't see why it's any concern of yours. He is Jane's brother and has only recently arrived in New Orleans. Your mother does not mind if Captain Watkins comes, so I don't see why you should take exception to the idea."

"My mother is far too gracious to tell you to your face that you have gone beyond the limits of acceptable behavior."

"Jonah." Mother's voice was gentle, but it stopped him from continuing his reproach. The look she gave him was full of understanding and something else. Did she pity him? Why? Did she think he had another reason for protesting Camellia's behavior?

Jonah snapped his mouth shut. Maybe she thought he was upset because this fellow was a soldier and he was not. He wanted to tell her, tell all of them, that he *was* a soldier. But his lips were sealed by the oath he'd taken.

If she did not mind Camellia's invitation to a stranger, he could not very well continue to chastise the girl. Jonah glanced around the room. "Do you have any bags for me to load into the carriage?"

Jane and Camellia exchanged a glance. What now?

Camellia lifted her chin, her gaze still exhibiting a desire to challenge him. "Our things are in the hallway."

Jonah spluttered. "The hallway? Do you mean to tell me that mountain of luggage is what you consider necessary for a two-day visit?"

"I want to be at my best no matter what you may think." She turned up her nose at him.

"It's not all hers." Jane came to her friend's rescue. "One of them belongs to me."

"And the other dozen belong to Camellia." Jonah sighed and reached for the door handle. He'd better see to getting the bags loaded or they would be at the school until midnight.

Jonah knew the first minute he saw Thad Watkins that the two of them were not going to be friends. He disliked everything about him, from his gray uniform to the way he looked at Camellia—like a wolf considering the lamb that was about to be its next meal. He practically drooled on her hand when he kissed it. And she must be an idiot to simper and preen so. Couldn't she see that he wanted to devour her?

When they'd been seated at dinner, Jonah had not been surprised to discover that the captain had been given the seat to his father's right, the space reserved for the guest of honor. His sister, Sarah, was sitting between Thad and her husband. Camellia was sitting opposite Thad and did not appear to realize anyone else had joined them for dinner. Especially not him, the man sitting next to her. She had barely spoken a word to him all evening. Perhaps she was still smarting over his amazement at the number of bags she had brought for her weekend stay.

Jonah thought she would be better served to follow her friend's example. Ironic that Jane was the hero's sister, as she had none of his brash egotism. Seated on his left side, Miss Watkins was a refined lady. She didn't flirt or try to monopolize his attention like Camellia and her "war hero." She divided her attention equally between Jonah and his mother as was proper. She had obviously paid much closer attention to their lessons on etiquette.

"What happened then?" Camellia batted her eyelashes quickly enough to raise a breeze.

Jonah's father leaned forward as though waiting for Thad's answer. He had a gleam in his eyes that seemed to disappear when he looked at his son. "What did that Yankee do when he saw you had him surrounded?"

Thad chuckled. "He dropped his weapon, fell to his knees, and begged us to let him join the Confederacy. It seems old Abe Lincoln hadn't paid him a dime in the eighteen months that he'd been a soldier."

Papa laughed out loud, leaning back and slapping his knee. "That's why the South is going to win this war. We'll never bow to Washington's tyranny. Even the Yankees know it. That's why he wanted to join up with the winning side."

Jonah could not keep silent any longer. "The newspapers don't seem to share your optimism. I read again this morning that many experts think General Grant will come knocking on our doorsteps at any moment."

Sarah, always eager to avoid family strife, frowned a warning at him.

But Jonah didn't care. They all needed to face the truth. The South was not on the winning side. It was only a matter of time. Lincoln was not going to let this country be split apart. He would keep fighting for however long it took to preserve the Union.

Instead of arguing with Jonah as expected, his father turned back to Thad. "It's true that New Orleans is very vulnerable to attack. Every time I turn around, more of our local boys are being pulled away to defend some backwoods town in Georgia or South Carolina. Abraham Lincoln has been very vocal about his plans to control the Mississippi River. Our trade with Europe is the lifeblood of the South. If we lose the river, I'm afraid we'll lose the war."

Thad's eyes narrowed. "Yes, sir, you are right. I'm not at liberty to say much, but I can assure you steps are being taken. New Orleans has not been forgotten."

"I hope you're right, young man." Jonah's father sighed. "But however this war turns out, I want you to know how proud I am of your service. I wish I could join you out on the battlefield myself, but I'm too old."

"You look like you're in your prime to me, sir."

Jonah wanted to groan aloud. Would his father fall for such blatant flattery? From the pleased look on his face, apparently he would. Right now he was probably wishing Thad was his son. But Jonah could not let that disturb him. He had prayed for wisdom before he made his decision about which side to join. He had to keep faith that God would continue to lead him.

A wisp of an idea slipped through Jonah's roiling thoughts. Thad knew things, things that could be useful to Jonah's superiors. Of all Jonah's acquaintances, none remained here who were officers in the Confederate army. He needed to use this one connection to full advantage, no matter what it cost him personally.

Jonah's mother picked up a spoon and tapped it against the rim of her plate. "That's enough talk of war and fighting. We will learn of the girls' activities at their school. Jane, why don't you tell us what you are studying."

She looked as frightened as the soldier Thad had told them about, surrounded by the enemy. "I. . .um. . .we've worked on our musical skills."

"That sounds wonderful. Do you play the piano?"

Jane shook her head, her auburn hair gleaming in the light of the candelabra that hung above the dining table.

"Don't be so modest." Camellia leaned forward, looking past Jonah. "Jane is an accomplished harpist, and she sings like an angel."

Jonah could hear the affection in her voice as she praised her friend. He found that commendable. Of course, she knew she didn't have to compete with Jane for the captain's attention. In his experience, young ladies could be quite ruthless in disparaging each other as they pursued the attentions of prospective suitors. Camellia might not be as generous with her praise if the captain and Jane were not brother and sister.

Sarah smiled at the blushing Jane. "You'll have to sing for us later this evening, Miss Watkins. I would be most happy to accompany you on my parents' piano."

Jane reached for her water and took a healthy gulp.

"Their graduation will be a formal ball." Captain Watkins's statement drew everyone's attention away from Jane.

A rising tide of irritation made Jonah want to growl. Did he have to look at Camellia with such longing?

"Miss Anderson has agreed to let me be her escort." His smug voice taunted Jonah.

Would this meal never end? Barred from reintroducing a military topic by his mother's earlier comment, all Jonah could do was think about the captain dancing with Camellia, holding her close. He shook his head to clear it of the vision. He would have to find a reason to attend their ball. . .so he could learn more from Thad, of course.

Jonah listened to the conversation flowing around him. Sarah offered to take the girls shopping for a special outfit. He expected Miss Fashion Plate to jump at the chance, but she didn't. Jane explained why when she told them about the dress Camellia had brought with her from Natchez. The ladies discussed fabrics and colors, cooing over matching ribbons and lace and all manner of folderol. How long could they continue to talk about clothes? Even his surgeon brother-in-law looked like he was about to fall asleep.

Finally his mother took pity on the men by announcing it was time for the ladies to retire. After they left the dining room, Thad and Father returned to their discussion of the war. Jonah listened carefully but discovered nothing new.

Jonah excused himself and went to his flat. Of course sleep eluded him. Until Jonah thought to get out his Bible. Opening it to the Old

Testament, he read about the trials of Joseph. At least Jonah had not been sold into slavery by his siblings. Yet Joseph had never given up his faith. And God had rewarded him and, through him, his people.

Slipping back into his bed, Jonah prayed for patience and faith like Joseph's. His anxiety lessened, and his eyes drifted shut. God would help him see the way.

Chapter Eleven

Camellia checked her appearance in the mirror. A row of tiny buttons on the front of her dress were covered in matching crimson material. She loved the tiny lines of gold that lent a striped appearance to the fabric. The sleeves, daringly simple and straight, were adorned with a single ruched band before ending halfway between her elbow and wrist. But the neckline was too plain. Draping a white scarf across the bodice, she turned to ask Jane's opinion of her embellishment, surprised by the worried frown on her friend's face. "Don't be anxious. The Thorntons' church has so many nice people. They've always welcomed me and my sisters."

Jane hid a yawn behind her hand. "I hope I don't fall asleep during the sermon."

"I promise to pinch you before you begin snoring."

"I don't snore." Jane pointed a finger at her. "You are a different matter, however. Your snoring would put a locomotive to shame."

Camellia shook her head. "That wasn't me. It was you."

They continued to banter as they headed downstairs to meet the others. Sarah and Dr. Cartier had returned home, of course, and would meet them at the church. But Camellia was surprised to see only Mrs. Thornton and Jonah awaiting them in the foyer. Mrs. Thornton was already wearing a dark cloak that hid the color and cut of her dress. Jonah wore a bottle-green coat that stretched across his broad shoulders.

An embroidered waistcoat and striped trousers completed his outfit, marking him as a gentleman of fashion.

Dragging her gaze away from his compelling features, she looked around the foyer. "Where is Mr. Thornton?"

Mrs. Thornton shook her head. "He's stopped attending services for now."

Jonah held Jane's cape for her, taking his sweet time with her friend. Determined to show she didn't need anyone's help, Camellia managed to get the heavy material of her own cloak across her shoulders without twisting her arms completely off.

"The pastor dared to express his support for abolition from the pulpit." Jonah's voice was as sour as ever. Did he always have to be so sarcastic?

Jane fastened the button at the top of her cloak and sent a grateful look in his direction. "Our pastor in the Garden District has not addressed that subject at all."

"Pastor Nolan is a good shepherd for our little flock." Mrs. Thornton pulled on her gloves. "He is a man of conscience, and his spiritual message is always applicable to our lives, even if we disagree with his political views. Coming together with other Christians is a directive from the New Testament that I will not ignore. Especially during these troubled times. I don't know how people survive when they do not have the support of a church to sustain them."

Camellia nodded. "We attend a church just around the corner from La Belle Demoiselle, even when the weather is inclement. You should see all of us following behind Mrs. Dabbs and Mademoiselle Laurent."

"Like a colorful line of ducklings?" Jonah's half smile had returned. "I'm certain you turn all the heads in your neighborhood."

She was not going to let him rile her this morning. Let him poke fun all he wanted. This was Sunday, and she was determined to be more circumspect. Didn't the Bible say something about heaping coals on someone's head? "I hadn't thought of it in exactly that way, but you're right, Jonah."

The surprise on his face at her agreement was delicious. A victory over the supercilious man at last. Squelching her glee, as it might not be considered very Christian, Camellia sailed through the door he opened and into the bright spring sunlight.

Their path to the church roughly paralleled the crescent path of the river, taking them past several shuttered homes. New Orleans had changed since Louisiana had seceded from the Union. Men had volunteered to fight, and their wives and children had fled to the safety of extended families. Those with Northern roots escaped the South rather than swear fealty to the Confederacy, leaving behind the lives they had established during the lucrative heyday of international shipping and trade. The weed-choked lawns made Camellia wonder if anything would ever be the same again. Would the residents return once the war ended? Or would those who survived remain in the new lives they had crafted? Who would one day live in these abandoned homes?

When they arrived, the pastor and his wife were standing at the front door of the whitewashed building. After brief introductions, they moved inside.

Even the church seemed subdued. The majority of those in attendance were ladies and children. Camellia wondered if that was because the men had volunteered to fight or if they, like Mr. Thornton, refused to attend.

Mrs. Thornton led the way to a vacant pew near the front, crimping her skirts to navigate the narrow space.

Camellia had meant to sit between Mrs. Thornton and Jane but somehow ended up behind her friend, meaning she would be trapped between Jane and Jonah. She wondered if she could manage to ignore him the whole time. It shouldn't be too hard. Straightening her spine, she folded her gloved hands in her lap. Presenting an attitude of humility was always appropriate in church.

" 'Thou wilt shew me the path of life: in thy presence is fulness of joy; at thy right hand there are pleasures for evermore.' " The words thundered out of the pastor's mouth, making Camellia forget all about the man sitting next to her. The reverend's gaze lifted from the Bible he held in his right hand, and he studied the congregation. "I don't know about the rest of you who are in attendance today, but I am spending hours on my knees praying for America's future."

A shifting among the pews signaled discomfort from at least some of the people. Or was that the Holy Spirit? Camellia held herself very still. If God was here with them, she didn't want Him thinking she wasn't listening.

"If we don't pay attention to God's Word, this country is doomed."

"Amen!" A male voice from somewhere behind them startled Jane.

A nervous giggle formed in Camellia's chest. She tamped it down and managed to resist the temptation of glancing at her friend, unsure if she could maintain proper decorum otherwise.

"Last night as I studied my Bible for the right message to bring to you, I was drawn to the middle of my Bible." The pastor reclaimed her attention. "I read this verse, and it got me to thinking about paths and the nature of the steps we take. Then I turned to Proverbs, the book of good advice we should all read at least once a month."

Camellia twisted her gloved fingers together, concentrating on the smooth feel of the silky material in the palm of her hand. The leather corner of a Bible appeared within her field of vision. Jonah's Bible. Curiosity turned her gaze toward the words his finger was underlining as the pastor read the verse.

" 'There is a way which seemeth right unto a man, but the end thereof are the ways of death.' "

She shuddered. Some parts of the Bible didn't appeal to her at all. Why did God have to go to all the trouble of making the way to Him so difficult? Why couldn't He make things simple? If she was running the world, things would be different. Her cheeks heated at the errant thoughts. Should she apologize to God? Was He listening that closely to her thoughts? Would He smite her where she sat?

A breathless moment of fear made her freeze again. Nothing happened, and she relaxed.

Jonah closed his Bible, his fingers stroking the worn leather cover. The book was old, worn, well used.

It sparked a new thought in her mind. Was the Bible outdated? Was it too old? They lived in a modern world, a world that would confuse the people in the Bible. She sat straighter. Maybe that was it. Maybe the Bible wasn't relevant anymore. Maybe God had instituted a new system.

The pastor had been droning on for a while now, talking about how they were all going to end in destruction. He'd probably start talking about weeping and teeth gnashing in a minute. She should have stayed at the town house with Mr. Thornton. She could understand why he refused to come.

Her head drooped lower as she studied a line of tiny stitches. It was a good thing she didn't have to make her own dresses. She caught the giggle before it escaped, but a hiccup managed to break free.

Jane elbowed her. "What are you doing?"

Jonah turned his head and looked at them, his frown stopping her answer.

Camellia pouted at him and pulled on the cuff of her glove. He didn't have to be so sanctimonious. She'd like to run his world for a little while. Send him racing down a path that no one else was on. Or was that what God had already done to him?

Her eyes narrowed, but before she could continue the thought, the pastor asked for everyone to bow their heads. After he prayed for a little while, his words running together in her mind, the pastor ended the prayer. Then it was over.

They gathered their things and began to file out of the church. Jonah offered his arm to his mother.

Jane touched Camellia's arm as they moved to follow. "Tell me what you were doing during the service."

Camellia shrugged. "Nothing much. Just trying to stay awake."

Jane shot a look at her. "I didn't have much trouble."

Ignoring her friend's censure, Camellia raised her voice so the Thorntons could hear her question. "Do you think we're on the right path?"

She could see Jonah's shoulder tighten.

It was all the encouragement she needed to continue. "I'm not sure this is the right way. It may be the path that leads to destruction."

Mrs. Thornton looked over her shoulder at them. "I'm so glad you took the sermon to heart, Camellia. I was afraid you might find the message troubling."

"No, of course not." Camellia silenced the voice inside her head. "I may not agree with his whole message, but I know he believes what he says."

Jonah stopped walking for a minute then seemed to recover himself. He continued on until they reached his family's home. But she could almost feel the storm brewing in him.

"I need to speak to you for a moment, Camellia." He practically dragged her from the foyer, his fingers making certain she didn't escape.

Camellia refused to be intimidated. Jonah held no power over her. She took a stance in the center of the room, shoulders back, head high. Aunt Dahlia would be proud of her. "What is wrong?"

"You may not. . . . No, let me start again. You obviously do not value the message you heard today."

"I don't see why the path to God has to be narrow and strewn with briars." She pulled off her gloves and held them in one hand. "And if it is, who is to say the South is not following the right path? After all, we are the smaller group. Does that make us the ones with the right answer?"

He sighed. "Is that really what you believe? That God smiles on the South and the Southern way of life?"

"If you're so sure we're wrong, why do you stay?"

His mouth closed in a straight line.

Camellia could sense she was about to win. She let her mouth relax into a smile. "Are you going to answer me?"

"You wouldn't understand if I did. Your ears have been closed. Your eyes can't see." He turned on his heel and walked out of the room.

The victory she had sensed felt hollow, empty. She slapped her gloves against her empty palm and blew out a breath of disgust. How like a man. He would never admit she might be right.

Chapter Twelve

On the Mississippi River near St. Louis

John Champion tossed another piece of wood into the boiler and slammed the door shut. "Do you want me to add more?"

The engineer pushed back his black cap and scratched his head. "No, that'll do her fer now."

Nodding, John pushed his sleeves back down and fastened them.

"Don't see why ya bother with that." The shorter man shook his head. "Ya gonna have to roll 'em up again or replace that shirt soon."

It was a habit born of his earlier years, but one John seemed unable to break. Even though it had been two years since he had last seen his home, it was hard to forgo some routines. "I'll roll them up when I have to."

The engineer's puzzled look made John laugh as he left the engine room and wound his way through hogsheads of sugar from southern Louisiana. Captain Pecanty should make a good profit this voyage. Sugar was worth its weight in gold since supply had been cut off by the Union blockade in the Gulf of Mexico. That meant John would also earn more.

Not that he had much need for money these days. Working on the *Catfish* ensured him a serviceable bunk and plenty of food. He usually stayed on the boat with the Pecantys instead of visiting the gambling dens that lined many of the towns along the river. Keeping to himself had grown easier and easier the longer he remained on the steamship.

A warm breeze pushed his hair down into his eyes. He reached up and brushed it back with an impatient gesture.

"If you didn't wear it so long, it wouldn't bother you." The feminine voice brought his head around. Almost as wide as she was tall, Naomi Pecanty had twinkling green eyes, a smile as wide as the river they rode upon, and a caring heart as steady and strong as the paddle wheel steering them northward.

She never came up on his right side, the side that bore the reminder of past sins. It was an indication of her thoughtfulness. Mrs. Naomi never asked him about the disfiguring scars that marred one side of his face. She and her husband were not the kind to ask many questions about a man's past, a fact that suited John to a T. But that hadn't stopped the kindly woman from presenting him a scarf last Christmas to serve the dual purpose of keeping his head and neck warm while covering a goodly portion of the rough, purplish-red skin left by the explosion.

"I like it long." He leaned against the wooden rail and looked out at the green hills. Of course the lock fell down into his eyes again, but this time John ignored it. He could almost feel her disapproving look. The silence lengthened until he finally gave up, sighed, and pushed back the hair once more. "Did you come up front to advise me on fashion?"

"No." The gentle tone of her voice made him feel guilty for his gruff tone. "I need to ask a favor of you."

"A favor?" He glanced sideways and met her gaze.

Something swirled in those eyes, something that made his shoulders tense. John wanted to walk away, but he couldn't. The woman next to him had practically adopted him the moment she joined the crew as the cook.

Yankees had raided her home, taking the livestock, looting the garden, and burning down the house she and Captain Pecanty had built. They decided she would be safer on the boat, so Mrs. Naomi took over the kitchen duties. John had gained at least ten pounds since she'd come on board.

"I need some supplies from Devore's in Cape Girardeau."

Their next stop would be at the small town in southern Missouri—a regular destination on their voyages. He fumbled for an excuse. "I don't know. I doubt I would come back with the right supplies."

"I made out a list for you." She pulled a folded slip of paper from her sleeve.

Tommy Bender, a short man with dirty blond hair and light blue eyes, came down the stairs and moved past them with a toothy grin. "Is dinner about ready?"

"Not yet." Mrs. Naomi returned his smile. "Biscuits will be ready at sunset."

"Don't let John eat all of 'em before the rest of us get to the dinner table."

John frowned. He should be used to the ribbing from the rest of the crew, but he wished they would simply leave him alone.

"I won't." Mrs. Naomi pushed the list toward him.

John took it and stuffed it into a pocket. It seemed the time to object had passed. He supposed he could do as his employer's wife wished. As he walked away from the rail, his shoulders twitched. Why did it feel like he had a target painted on his back?

New Orleans

Camellia tucked a bit of hair under her nightcap and leaned back against her pillow. "What do you think of Jonah Thornton?"

Jane blew out their candle and shrugged. "He seems like a nice man."

Tilting her head, Camellia tried to decide if Jane was hiding her feelings. Her tone of voice was calm and matter-of-fact. But she must have been impressed with Jonah. He was quite handsome, after all. And he had been nothing but kind and courteous to Jane. He had never called her an impolite child, laughed at her faux pas, or castigated her for the number of trunks she needed for her clothing. If Jonah had been half as nice to Camellia as he had been to her roommate. . .

Camellia shook her head before the thought could complete itself. She needed to concentrate on Jane's needs. "He's well connected, you know. His family is quite popular. Sarah, his sister, hosts the grandest parties."

The bed sagged as Jane settled next to her.

A faint glow from the fireplace on the far wall was the only illumination in the room. Camellia pulled the cover up to her chin and waited for an answer.

"Yes, I'm sure you're right." Jane stopped speaking.

"But?" The word echoed in the room, but no answer came.

After several moments, Jane cleared her throat. "Nothing really.

It's just that Mr. Thornton seems so. . .so serious."

"Is that all?" Camellia let out the breath she hadn't realized she had been holding. "What he needs is a pretty young lady to help lighten that serious nature."

Her mind went back to the night when Lily and Blake had taken them to the theater. How young she had been back then. And how debonair Jonah Thornton had seemed. He'd been dashing and mysterious—grave one moment and carefree the next. He had been exactly the type of beau she wanted to snag. Camellia could feel her cheeks growing warm as she considered how he must have perceived her back then—the gauche younger sister of an unconventional family. She had made little secret of her admiration, but Jonah Thornton hadn't been interested in her. He'd never been interested in her. And he never would be. Not that she wanted him to be. . .although it would have been satisfying for him to pursue her, if only so she could ignore his advances.

She could feel Jane's gaze in the shadowy room. Camellia sniffed. "I think you should encourage him. The two of you would make a wonderful couple."

"I'd much rather spend time with someone who makes me laugh."

"Jonah is quite clever. You've only seen him at his worst." The thick down mattress made it difficult to turn over, but after a moment Camellia managed to face her friend. "It's the war, don't you see? It's made everyone too serious. As soon as our brave Confederate soldiers whip those meddlesome Yankees, everything will go back to the way it was before."

"Sometimes I don't think anything will ever be like it was before the war. Sometimes I'm afraid the South will lose and—"

"Don't say that," Camellia said, interrupting her friend's words. "Don't even think it. What would your brother think to hear you say such things?"

"I know, but that's why I don't want to spend my time with someone so. . .so intense."

The break in Jane's words made Camellia wonder if the other girl was about to start crying. She could feel her own throat tightening. If she didn't redirect their conversation right away, they would both end up bawling like a couple of hungry babies. "That's why I think Jonah would be perfect for you. I could understand your hesitation if he was a soldier like your brother. Sending them both away to fight would be difficult for anyone. But Jonah Thornton is not a soldier. He's not even interested in the war." She stopped and reached for Jane's hand under the cover. "Do you think he doesn't want to fight because he's a—a coward? I hadn't thought of that."

Jane's cold fingers gripped her warmer hand. "I don't know Jonah like you do, but from the limited amount of time I've been around him, he doesn't strike me as the sort of man who would be afraid to fight."

Camellia breathed a sigh of relief to have the idea dispelled. She nodded even though she wasn't sure if Jane could see the motion.

"I think you may be misled by appearances." Jane's voice no longer sounded as choked with emotion. "Sometimes it can take more courage to go against popular opinion than to don a uniform."

Camellia pushed up onto one elbow. "Can you see now why I think you and Jonah would make a perfect couple? You have seen something about him that I never have."

"I don't know." Jane giggled. "From the sparks that always seem to fly between the two of you, I wonder if you're not more interested in Mr. Thornton than you are my brother."

"Don't be silly." Camellia collapsed against her pillow, her low-pitched giggle harmonizing with Jane's. "Captain Watkins is wonderful. He's exactly the kind of man I hope to marry someday."

"That's good. I would much rather have you for a sister than a friend."

"I hope to be both."

A knock on the door quieted both girls. They had no desire to be chastised by either Mrs. Dabbs or her assistant.

As Camellia drifted toward sleep, she considered Jane's words. Was Jonah as brave as Captain Thaddeus Watkins? The idea seemed ludicrous. How could a man who had never fought a day in his life compare well against someone who braved danger and death in the quest for freedom for his home? The answer was simple. He couldn't.

Chapter Thirteen

Jonah dismounted and tethered his horse before entering La Belle Demoiselle. He wondered how Camellia would respond to his visit. Just when he thought he had figured her out, she surprised him. She was as tantalizing as the first hint of spring after a long, cold winter. As refreshing as a cool breeze in the hottest part of the summer. But she wasn't the girl for him. If he ever decided to settle down and raise a family, he would not choose a young woman like Camellia. He wanted a wife who shared his faith, his ideals, and his values. Not someone as vain and shallow as she.

His heartbeat picked up with each step he took toward the house, probably because of his errand. What would Camellia think when she found out he was paying yet another visit to her school? Would she think he was pursuing her? If so, she was going to be disappointed. He had a totally different goal in mind—one that would dispel all of her pretensions.

Jonah gave his hat to the assistant who answered the door, happy to remember her name today. "Hello, Miss Laurent. I'm here to see Miss Watkins."

"Yes, sir. I'll check with Mrs. Dabbs." The girl led him to the visitors' parlor before scurrying toward the back of the school.

A pendulum clock on the mantel marked the minutes while he waited. Jonah was about to go in search of Mrs. Dabbs and her charges when the lady appeared at the door, Jane behind her. The older lady carried a basket of handwork, apparently something to occupy her while she chaperoned her charge. He gave both of them his winningest smile, a smile that barely faltered when Camellia's blond ringlets and familiar features came into view behind her friend. Why was she with Jane? His plan would not be as easy to carry out if she was going to remain in the room. He'd counted on letting her friend tell her his errand later.

"Good morning, Mr. Thornton." Mrs. Dabbs swept into the room, a question in her gaze.

She must be wondering if he had more information to pass along to her. A slight shake of his head gave her the answer.

The reason for this visit was different. He needed to secure a valid reason for attending the end-of-the-term dance. And he needed to get as close to Captain Watkins as possible. "It's a beautiful day," he said.

He bowed at all three of them as they took seats in the parlor. The younger girls sat on the sofa next to each other while he and Mrs. Dabbs sat in chairs across from them.

Camellia unfurled her fan and fluttered it with practiced ease. "Are your parents well?"

Jonah nodded at her but turned to Jane as he made his answer. "As well as can be expected since their lovely guests departed." He sent the auburn-haired beauty a smoldering look, one he remembered from his earlier days. One that had always gotten a positive response from females, whether in ballrooms or parlors.

His effort was wasted as Jane's brown gaze swept past him and settled on something behind him. "How kind of you, sir. We very much enjoyed our weekend, didn't we, Camellia?"

He wanted to look back over his shoulder to see if someone else had entered and was about to cuff him. Managing to control the impulse, his gaze clashed with the sparkling blue gaze of the minx sitting beside Jane.

Camellia's eyes danced as though she read his thoughts. "Yes, indeed. Your mother and father are *two* of my favorite people."

He swallowed a grin at the barbed comment. He got the message. He was not one of her favorite people. Jonah raised an eyebrow. "I'm sure they would want me to return the compliment." Which was not to say he would. Miss Anderson was not the only one who could use double meanings to make a point.

A slave entered with a tea tray and set it down on the table between the sofa and his chair.

"Would you care to serve?"

Jane's eyes opened wide in response to Mrs. Dabbs's question. "I think it's Camellia's turn."

"Very well." Mrs. Dabbs nodded to Camellia and reached for her embroidery, effectively divorcing herself from the conversation.

Closing her fan with a snap, Camellia rolled her eyes and reached for the teapot. "Would you care for sugar, Mr. Thornton?"

"What need have I for sugar when I'm surrounded by such sweet temperaments?"

Camellia tossed him a dirty look, one that made his smile widen.

Jane looked from one of them to the other, her brow wrinkled. She was a beauty but apparently did not understand the joy of verbal sparring with a worthy opponent.

Jonah reached out to accept the cup Camellia offered. "How are your needlework skills progressing?"

The liquid threatened to overcome the lip of the porcelain cup as she jerked. "How dare you," she hissed between clenched teeth, practically dropping the cup and saucer into his hand.

"You would be amazed at Camellia's talents." Jane came to her defense. "She understands mathematics and medicine better than anyone else here."

Jonah nodded. "A family trait she shares with her sister Lily."

"I know you didn't come today to speak of my family, Mr. Thornton." Camellia held out a tray of sweets.

Balancing his tea on one knee, Jonah picked out a cream-topped cookie. "How right you are. My reason for visiting is to ascertain whether or not Miss Watkins would allow me to be her escort for your school gala."

Jane lifted her cup and drank instead of looking at him. What was the matter with the girl? Did she find him repulsive? Did she have an escort already?

"She would love to go with you." Camellia stepped into the uncomfortable moment. "Wouldn't you, Jane?"

Mrs. Dabbs's needle stopped, and she put her embroidery down. "How kind of you, Mr. Thornton. I have to admit I have been concerned about whether or not our ball would be a success this year. So many of our Southern gentlemen are not available to act as partners."

"They are more concerned with protecting their families and homes from marauders."

Trust Camellia to take every opportunity to point out his apparent unwillingness to fight. Jonah tamped down his irritation. What was it about her disdain that made him want to defend himself?

"Camellia, you need to mind your manners." Mrs. Dabbs frowned. "Your sentiments are not shared by all."

"They are shared by those who are loyal to the South." The thump of Camellia's cup against the serving tray emphasized her words.

"God gave each of us different talents." Jane seemed to be a natural peacemaker, ready to diffuse tension. "I think those who remain at home may sometimes have the harder road."

Her championship didn't soothe him much. Jonah still wanted to blast Camellia for her ignorance. Couldn't she understand how wrongheaded she was? Or was she incapable of seeing beyond her own comfort to the needs of those enslaved to support her way of life?

Mrs. Dabbs stood. "How right you are, Jane. I'm sure you are looking forward to your entrance on Mr. Thornton's strong arm."

Jonah tried to keep his gaze centered on the girl as she nodded, but something drew his attention to Camellia. Was she pouting because her loyal friend had the effrontery to disagree with her disparaging words? Or was she the tiniest bit disappointed because he was not paying her the homage she seemed to feel was her right?

"Thank you for the honor, Mr. Thornton."

"The pleasure is all mine." He stood and bowed to her. "I'll leave you ladies to return to your studies."

Camellia's gaze burned as he took Jane's hand and dropped a kiss on it. But her glower only made him lengthen his salute.

A knock brought everyone's attention to the door. It opened and revealed the crisp gray uniform of a Confederate soldier.

Jonah recognized the beefy face of Captain Watkins before the man got all the way into the room. His teeth grated together.

Camellia rose and met the soldier in the middle of the parlor. She extended her hand, and the captain bowed over it.

Jonah didn't like being on this side of the glower. But he had not drooled over Miss Watkins's hand. And he had a responsibility to Camellia. He might not be her relative, but as a friend of the family, he had a duty to make sure her reputation was safe. He cleared his throat.

Captain Watkins took the hint, dropping her hand and bowing to the rest of the parlor's occupants. "Hello."

To give himself the chance to regain his composure, Jonah made a show of pulling out his pocket watch. "It's been a delightful visit, but I am going to have to say good-bye. My father is expecting me at the office prior to lunch."

"We enjoyed your visit." Mrs. Dabbs rose and walked with him to the parlor door. "Please feel free to drop by at any time."

"Thank you." He bowed and left, his resolve hardening as he heard the laughter and chatter between the captain and the girls.

All the way to his father's office, Jonah lectured himself. He had a job to do here in New Orleans. A job that had nothing to do with flirtatious females. The sooner he got the needed information and returned to the battlefield, the better his life would be.

Camellia brushed her hands together as if she had completed a satisfying chore. Although he had left on his own, seeing the back of the irritating Mr. Thornton was reason to feel satisfied.

She turned back to the charming captain. His chocolate-colored eyes brimmed with flattering consideration. Very different from the sarcastic green gaze and supercilious attitude of their recent guest. She felt sorry for Jane. Her friend was bound to be miserable with him as an escort to their ball. But she would make sure Jane enjoyed herself as much as possible. How could she do any less for her best friend when she was going to have the night of her life?

Captain Watkins was nothing like Jonah Thornton. Although both men were handsome and polished in their manners, the similarities ended there. Most girls would be delighted to attract the captain's attention, even without him wearing an officer's uniform. With it, he became the type of beau every young lady wished for.

Excitement coursed through her as she shared a glance with Jane. Wouldn't it be wonderful if the two of them became sisters? Of course that would only be a formality. They really were sisters. She felt as close to Jane as she ever had to Lily or even Jasmine. She and Jane were so much alike. They wanted the same things from life, and they weren't afraid to work for their goals.

"If you would care to join me?" His brown eyes caught her attention.

Captured by the admiration in his gaze, Camellia felt like she was lost in time. Thaddeus Watkins. A sigh filled her. Captain Wonderful would be a more fitting name for the man. He was so handsome. She could stare into his eyes forever. And he never poked or prodded her like the man who had just departed. No, this man could be counted on to be a gentleman rather than an irritation. Her gaze traced the outline of his insignia, and her mind recounted the other main difference between the two. It didn't matter how many excuses the others were willing to give for Jonah's actions; he was a coward. Captain Watkins believed in giving more than lip service to the things he believed in.

"Camellia seems to have lost her tongue, but I can assure you it's because she's excited at the prospect you have offered." Mrs. Dabbs's voice brought her back to earth. "Even though they have lessons, I generally set aside some time for leisure activities for the students. She has my permission as long as she and Jane wish to go."

She could see Jane's encouraging nod from the corner of her eye, and even though she had no idea exactly what she was agreeing to, Camellia took a deep breath. "Yes, Captain. We would be delighted."

"That's good, then. I'll pick you and Jane up prior to two o'clock. The troops will be performing maneuvers in Jackson Square. If you've never seen it before, I think you'll be quite impressed."

The smile that turned up her lips was genuine. She would be impressed with any destination he chose, as long as he was there to protect her. Before she could get caught up in the daydreaming his handsome physique seemed to encourage, Camellia nodded. She needed to focus or he might decide she was an empty-headed ninny, one of those giggling young women who had no ability to carry on a conversation. "I'm sure you are right. How kind of you to take time out of your busy day to escort us."

"It will be my pleasure." His smile was wide, showing his straight, white teeth.

Camellia felt like she would float across the parlor floor once teatime was over. No need to worry about the length of her stride or the sway of her skirt. Happiness would keep her feet several inches above the wooden planks.

Jane served tea to her brother with all the aplomb Mrs. Dabbs expected. He sat and conversed with them for another ten minutes before rising.

Camellia wanted to ask him to remain a little longer but knew she could not say anything of the sort. She watched him kiss Jane's cheek and bow to Mrs. Dabbs. Then he crossed to her.

She fumbled with her fan, her heart threatening to burst out of her chest. "I'm sorry to see you leave us."

"Only for a little while." He flashed that beautiful smile at her and took her hand in his. With a smooth movement, he planted a warm kiss on her skin.

Camellia's breath caught. Now that no one was looking on with disapproval, she could get lost in the moment. Her heart stopped beating altogether. This must be love. The tingling of her skin was proof. She was in love with Captain Watkins. And if the look in his dark eyes was a mirror of his desire, he felt the same way about her.

He straightened and turned to march out of the room, his stride strong and even. Everything about him was perfect.

This man had been designed specifically for her, according to her deepest desires. And she was going to do everything in her power to make certain he knew it, too. She would make him the best wife possible. How long would it be before she could claim the title of Mrs. Thaddeus Watkins?

Chapter Fourteen

The air in New Orleans had a distinct flavor all its own—a mixture of seafood from the fish market and tropical fruit from nearby plantations, with an underlying hint of the smoky odor of burning pitch used to ward off dreaded yellow fever outbreaks. Camellia raised her scented handkerchief to her nose to block out the unpleasant odors.

Captain Watkins pulled back on the reins of the restive horses leading their open barouche. "I should have procured a closed carriage."

Camellia shook her head and lowered the handkerchief, careful to take shallow breaths. A lady would never be so gauche as to agree that her escort was less than exemplary. "I'm enjoying the sunshine."

"Back home it's rarely this warm so early in the year." Jane, seated between Camellia and the captain, added her opinion. "We would have missed this wondrous weather inside a closed vehicle."

Traffic had slowed as they neared Jackson Square. Apparently most of the townspeople would be present to show their support for the Confederate forces. Ladies in large bonnets and larger skirts were escorted by men in long frock coats and followed by one or more slaves. Tradesmen and street vendors hawked everything from sweet pralines to meat pies to ready-made boots. With all the activity continuing unchecked, it was hard to believe the Union blockade had affected the flow of goods at all.

As they inched forward, Camellia realized their carriage was garnering some attention. The occupants of other carriages fluttered handkerchiefs in greeting even though they were strangers. Perhaps because of the gray uniform Captain Watkins wore.

As they neared Jackson Square, beggars crowded around them, asking for a few cents for food. Thinking of David Foster and how narrowly he had avoided becoming one of them, Camellia reached into her reticule and pulled out two folded bills.

Jane put a hand on her arm. "What are you doing?"

"We have so much. I cannot see their young, gaunt faces but that my heart is not touched."

Captain Watkins leaned forward and met her gaze. "That is laudable, Miss Anderson, but you have to be careful or one beggar will grab your purse whilst you are giving money to another."

A tiny little bubble of irritation disrupted her pleasure in the outing. Did Captain Watkins think she was an empty-headed idiot? She handed over the money to the grubby hand reaching toward the carriage seat without comment. The bubble popped after a moment. Thad was probably only being careful. She ought to be pleased with his warning instead of finding fault. Camellia summoned a smile that she turned on both of the Watkins siblings. "Thank you. I'll be more careful in the future."

The captain expertly guided their carriage to the St. Charles Hotel and handed the reins to a hostler before jumping to the ground. He came around to Camellia's side of the carriage and reached a hand up to help her.

She stepped down, coming within an inch of touching his chest.

"Steady now." His face, close enough to touch the brim of her bonnet, made Camellia's heart thump. His sideburns were neatly trimmed, not bushy like some she had seen. A shadow of stubble outlined his upper lip and the square shape of his chin.

Hot blood rushed up to her cheeks as his warm, appreciative gaze met hers. Her feet touched the ground, and he gave her hand a quick squeeze before releasing it. Needing the distraction of her fan, Camellia untied the ribbon holding her fan around her wrist and opened it. The air pushing against her face cooled it as the captain turned his attention to Jane.

She glanced around at the crowd, soaking in the festive air. A familiar voice called out her name, and Camellia turned. "Look, it's

Mrs. Thornton and her daughter, Mrs. Cartier." She smiled and waved, forgetting that she still had her fan open. An errant breeze snagged the fabric and jerked it from her hand. Without thinking, she stepped forward to catch it before it landed on the dusty street.

"Camellia, watch out!"

Jane's scream brought her head up in time to see a pair of horses galloping toward her. The men on their backs were glaring at each other instead of watching the road ahead of them. Camellia stumbled, her hands lifted above her head in an instinctive gesture, her skirts not allowing her the freedom of running to safety.

Hands circled her waist and jerked her sideways. Dizziness assailed her as she was swung in an arc. Strong arms twirled her about as though she were a child.

An unladylike *oomph* escaped her lips as she was crushed against a hard, masculine chest. Camellia's first thought was that the captain had saved her from certain death. The second was how safe she felt with his arms encircling her.

"Are you hurt?" The voice that tickled her ear was not right. It wasn't the captain's deep drawl.

Camellia bent her head back and met the bright green gaze of the wrong man. "Jonah." She struggled in his embrace. What on earth was he doing here? And how had he come to save her when it should have been Captain Watkins?

Before he could say anything more, everyone was crowding around them. Someone pulled Camellia from Jonah's arms, and he moved back a few feet. But she could still feel the weight of his gaze. And his cologne clung to her, reminding her of their closeness.

"Thank You, Lord, for protecting Camellia." Mrs. Thornton looked as though she had aged a year in the past few minutes.

Mrs. Cartier nodded her agreement. "He sent you over here, Jonah, so you could save her."

"And I thought I came to search out seats for the exhibition." His voice was full of its usual sarcasm, but Camellia had seen the concern in his eyes. Did he use sarcasm as a shield?

Before she could consider that question, Jane wrapped her in a hug. "I don't know what I would've done if you'd been hurt."

"It was my own fault." Camellia returned her hug, her mind occupied with the sight she must be. Her hat hung crookedly over her forehead, one flower dangling in front of her nose. Her flounce was dirty and possibly torn. Her fan was gone, probably smashed into tiny pieces by the very hooves that nearly got her. . .would have gotten her if not for Jonah.

Captain Watkins shook his head, a fierce frown darkening his brow. "No, I'm the one to blame. I should have been paying more attention."

Camellia heard the disgusted sound Jonah made. She might agree with Jonah, but Captain Watkins knew enough about etiquette to assume responsibility. If she disagreed with him, would she be usurping his position as the person in charge? He was obviously distraught.

"It doesn't matter who is at fault." Jane stepped between them, her voice calm. "What matters is that disaster was averted. And for that, I wish to thank you, Mr. Thornton."

"Yes." Captain Watkins turned to Jonah. "Thank you for doing what I should have done."

Jonah bowed. "I was happy to be of service, and now if you will excuse us, I need to return to my errand."

"Wait a moment, please." Jane's gaze raked Camellia's face, reminding her of her bedraggled appearance. "I don't believe I feel like observing the soldiers any longer. Perhaps you and your family can use the seats my brother arranged."

Everyone tried to argue, but Jane was adamant.

To tell the truth, Camellia felt relief. Her head ached, and she wished for nothing more than a quiet place to rest it. When Captain Watkins added his voice to Jane's, she acquiesced.

Seeing that their seats would not be used, Jonah and the two ladies agreed to take them. Mrs. Thornton promised to check on her the following day, and Mrs. Cartier invited her to visit her husband's clinic if she was not improved.

The drive back was quiet. Jane patted her hand several times but said nothing. Captain Watkins kept leaning forward to glance at her. After the fourth time, Camellia wanted to ask him if she had grown an extra head. She bit her lip instead and stared forward. He was probably upset because he'd not been the one to save her.

Camellia understood. She was disappointed, too. If he had been the one to rescue her, she might not have minded the destruction of her hat, her fan. . .and her self-esteem.

❧

"May I help you, Mr. . . ?" The young woman came around the end of the counter, tilting her head and eyeing him with ill-concealed curiosity.

"John—" He barely stopped himself from sweeping a bow, a gesture the clerk at Devore's General Store would find odd. At least he'd managed to give her his name without stuttering. An accomplishment given the circumstances. Since landing a job on the *Catfish*, he had not spoken to many females, certainly not marriageable ones. He had stayed away from society as much as possible to hide his disfigurement. . . and to avoid temptation. "My name is John Champion." By now he should be less self-conscious, but the lie tasted sour on his tongue.

On long, dark nights when the scars on his face wouldn't let him sleep, doubts haunted John. He had been given a second chance. He wanted to do the right thing. To be worthy of the opportunity. He was determined not to make the same mistakes this time.

Mrs. Naomi was not helping, though. His boss's wife must consider herself a matchmaker. He did not doubt she had sent him to town for one purpose. . .to meet the girl standing in front of him.

"It's a pleasure to meet you, Mr. Champion." Her mouth shifted, slowly blooming into a smile that transformed her face.

Amazing how pretty she was. . . . But. . .her face seemed somehow familiar. Had they met before? Impossible. John searched his memory but came up empty.

Shifting his weight onto his right foot, he turned his body so she couldn't see the scar. It was a tactic he'd learned to spare others when they took on passengers. He wished he could grow side-whiskers on his right cheek to keep from frightening women and children, but the thick scar tissue made that an impossibility.

A curtain over an alcove in the back of the store moved, and a man wearing a white apron appeared. His brown eyes combed the store, settling on the two of them. His mustache twitched over his smile. "Anna, are you helping our customer?"

"Yes sir, Mr. Devore," Anna answered the man before turning her azure gaze back to John, her smile widening even further. "What can we do for you?"

He shouldn't return her smile. She might take his gesture as encouragement. But then again, he would probably never see her after today. They would be heading south soon, and by the time they stopped at Cape Girardeau again, she'd probably be married. So he smiled. And it felt good. As good as the first glint of sunshine on frost-covered ground.

The twinkle in her eyes made his heart turn over.

John wished he'd taken extra care with his appearance. He was clean. He bathed more often than most of the rest of the crew—a holdover from his earlier life. And he'd combed his hair. But his clothing was worn and faded, and his shoes were free of polish. He found himself hoping she would overlook his shortcomings as he fumbled for the list Mrs. Naomi had given him. "Here." He held out the folded sheet to her, noticing the creamy texture of her hand in comparison to his sun-darkened skin.

She nodded.

As she took the paper from him, his fingers grazed her palm. A tingle spread from the contact, racing up his arm and burrowing into his chest.

Her eyes widened for a brief moment, and their color went from sky-blue to the darker hues of a wave out in the open ocean. Had she felt it, too?

A bell above the door tinkled as another customer entered the store.

Anna turned to smile at the thin, sour-faced lady who had come in. The same sweet welcome she'd offered him was now expended on the new customer, and John's heartbeat returned to its normal, steady rhythm as he realized the clerk's nature had misled him. She didn't feel any more attraction to him than anyone else. She was just doing her job, greeting the customers and taking care of their needs.

The manager stepped from behind the counter and offered to help the female customer.

As John waited for Anna to fill his order, he let his gaze wander around the store. Two other customers arrived, their syrupy drawls reminding him of the Deep South. . .home. He ducked behind a display of shaving cream, not wanting to hear their gasps if they caught sight of his face.

"Mr. Champion?"

John spun around at the sound.

She stood only a foot away, her gaze caught on his face, his right cheek.

John wanted to sink through the floor. How had he missed her approach? Feeling exposed, he tried to turn away, to hide his ugliness from her.

"You poor dear." Her voice stopped him.

John looked down at her and found no revulsion, no horror. Only sympathy filled her face.

He was unmanned by the kindness of it. Most females turned away if they caught sight of his cheek—one had even fainted dead away. Children gave him a wide berth, their frightened faces turned into their mothers' skirts. Men were easier. They ignored the scars as though they did not exist.

Anna's hand reached up and softly grazed the mottled skin. "Does it hurt?"

His mouth was so dry John wasn't sure he could say anything. He shook his head, unable to admit pain that might make him seem weak to her. He looked into her eyes, lost himself in the tenderness he saw. His walls, the protection that he had slowly built over the past months, tumbled down like Jericho.

As though she realized the impropriety of touching him, Anna jerked her hand away. "I'm sorry."

"Don't be." He poured all his gratitude into the two words. How could he explain to her that he no longer felt so beastly? He might still wear the mark of Cain, but her acceptance and sympathy made his lot more bearable. He took her hand in his and lifted it to his lips, pressing a kiss on her soft skin. "Thank you."

Her breath caught, and her cheeks glowed.

John had never seen a more beautiful sight in the world. No other female could hold a candle to this tenderhearted young woman. And he knew in an instant he was in love. In love for the first time in his life. With a girl he knew only as Anna.

Chapter Fifteen

The temporary walls between the parlor and the first-floor classrooms had been removed this afternoon, and large potted plants were brought inside to decorate the large area where the ball would take place. Camellia and Jane were supposed to be napping in preparation for the festivities, but they had been unable to relax. Instead they crept downstairs to gaze at the ballroom and imagine what the evening would bring.

Jane sat in one of the chairs that lined the walls. "Are you disappointed that your family couldn't attend?"

"Not at all." Camellia took the chair next to her. She was happy with the separation between her colorful steamboat family and the social world of La Belle Demoiselle. "But I know you wish your mother was able to come."

A sigh answered her. "I'm just so worried about the situation at Willow Grove."

"Do you really think the slaves at your plantation might revolt?"

"It's happened at other places."

"That's true." Camellia reached out and took Jane's hand in hers. "But that was because of cruel owners and miserable conditions. I'm sure your parents are good to their slaves. Like at my grandmother's home. They have no reason to be unhappy."

Jane squeezed her fingers, her features relaxing as she nodded.

"Besides, we'll be going there as soon as Thad can get permission to escort us. I'm so glad you'll be with me. We're going to have so much fun."

Camellia was excited, too. It wouldn't be like Natchez where everyone knew her and her family. And of course she was looking forward to spending time with Thad. . .and Jane.

"What are you girls doing down here?" Mrs. Dabbs's voice made the two of them start.

"We were curious." Camellia stood to take the blame. It had been her idea to come downstairs, after all.

Jane stood beside her. "We'll go back to our room."

Mrs. Dabbs shook her head. "Since the two of you don't feel like sleeping, I could use some help. I have a thousand details to see to before tonight."

"What can we do?"

"Go put on your aprons and come back down." Mrs. Dabbs waved a hand toward the dining room on the other side of the hall. "The silverware needs to be polished, and then you can inspect the crystal for cracks or smudges."

Jane didn't look very happy with the instructions, but Camellia was glad for something practical to do. It would help pass the time until they dressed for the evening. The tasks were something she would be expected to oversee when she gave her own parties. She hurried her roommate upstairs, grabbed a starched apron, and returned to the first floor.

As she entered the dining room, however, Camellia began to understand Jane's reluctance. She had never seen such a pile of silver. It would take them an hour or more to finish polishing and probably as much time to inspect the crystal lined up on the sideboard. "We'd better get started." She took a seat and reached for a polishing cloth and the nearest spoon.

"Have you ever been kissed by a man?"

Jane's question startled her. "Sure I have."

"I mean someone besides your family."

Camellia's cheeks warmed. "No, of course not. Have you?"

Jane shook her head. "I wonder what it feels like."

"My sister seems to like it." Camellia could feel a deeper flush coming up now. "At least I'm sure Blake is the type of man to like kissing a lot, and she seems happy with him."

"Maybe my brother will kiss you tonight."

The skin on Camellia's arms tingled and rose like gooseflesh. Would he try? If he did, should she let him? "I'm not sure I'd like that."

Jane's mouth drooped in a pout. "I thought you wanted to be my sister. I don't think your romance will go very far if you're not willing to be kissed."

"Aunt Dahlia says a lady shouldn't let a suitor become too familiar or he'll take advantage of her innocence."

Jane's right eyebrow rose. "I don't care what your aunt says—I want to know I'm in love before I get married. It'll be too late if I discover I don't like his kisses after."

Camellia's heart, which had been fluttering, suddenly felt heavy in her chest. Jane wanted Jonah to kiss her? She wanted him to hold her close and press his lips on hers? She dropped the knife she'd been polishing, and it clattered to the floor. She leaned over to retrieve it. By the time she sat back up, she had recovered her equilibrium. "I doubt Mrs. Dabbs will let us go off alone with anyone. Can you imagine the scandal?"

Jane giggled. "I guess not, but it sure is exciting to think about."

Camellia didn't feel excited at all. In fact, she wasn't even looking forward to the ball now. She glanced toward Jane, who was concentrating on rubbing a dull spot from the handle of a serving spoon. And she wasn't sure she wanted to join her roommate at her family's plantation. Maybe she would beg off and stay here with the Thornton family until Lily could collect her. That way she wouldn't have to watch Jane flirt with anyone.

❧

The stays were so tight Camellia could hardly catch her breath.

Brigitte stepped back to reach for the hooped skirt that would form the basis for Camellia's evening gown. "*Bien. Vous sera magnifique.* . . . Beautiful."

"Merci, mademoiselle." Camellia tried to take a deep breath, but the boning around her ribs and waist would not allow it. "Can you loosen this a bit?"

Brigitte shook her head, her lips folded into a straight line as she tightened the waist of the hoop skirt.

"It will be better after a moment." Jane was already dressed, her maroon velvet gown a sharp contrast to her milky skin. One of the maids was combing her hair into elaborate swirls.

Camellia ignored the stab of jealousy. She refused to envy Jane. In fact, she would help her all she could. "I've never seen you look lovelier." Another petticoat cut off her view for a moment before it settled around her waist. Brigitte cinched it with expert fingers.

"You will surely outshine me in that dress."

"I don't know." Camellia panted while another petticoat followed the first. Then it was time for her ball gown. The silk sighed as it drifted down. It was as cool as springwater, and she knew it was a flattering color for her, but still. . . "If I look half as lovely as you, I'll be satisfied."

"Don't be silly." Jane turned her head back and forth to admire her new hairstyle. "You're at least twice as pretty as I am."

"Between us, we'll attract all of the male attention."

Brigitte clucked her tongue, looking for all the world like Mrs. Dabbs in spite of her darker hair and unlined face. But she didn't say anything.

Camellia was glad. She wasn't in the mood for a scold. Tonight was going to be difficult enough. She took Jane's place at the dressing table, concentrating on her breathing as the maid twisted her hair into a knot. Of course it sprang loose the minute the maid reached for hairpins. "My hair will never lay smooth."

Jane's smiling face appeared in the mirror in front of her. "You don't need smooth hair to be the belle of the ball. Just wait and see. You'll never get to sit down."

The maid finally managed to subdue the largest portion of her hair, but stray tendrils formed corkscrews around her face and at her neck. With that she would have to be satisfied. Jane passed her white gloves and a lacy gold fan to complete her outfit.

"Is it time to go downstairs?" Jane glanced toward Brigitte for the answer. Receiving a nod, she linked arms with Camellia. "Let's go see what my brother thinks of the woman he's going to marry."

Chapter Sixteen

Camellia and Jane were still giggling as they descended the stairs, so Camellia failed to realize some of the guests had already arrived.

"Well, if it isn't the two loveliest debutantes in New Orleans." Captain Watkins's deep voice stopped Camellia in midgiggle.

She stood still, forcing Jane to do the same or risk tumbling down six or seven steps. "Oh dear."

Jane looked from her brother to her friend, a wide smile on her face. She leaned toward Camellia. "I think it's a bit early for you to be calling him that."

Camellia's cheeks flamed. She glanced toward the small group of people in the foyer. Had anyone heard Jane's teasing remark? Captain Watkins, standing head and shoulders above the other soldiers who had come with him, did not show any evidence of having heard the words. His dark eyes were full of appreciation.

Finally, Camellia realized everyone must think she had turned into a statue. What would Aunt Dahlia say if she could see her niece frozen with fear? She would tell her to get down to her guests and present a friendly, welcoming face. The internal lecture helped her to release her strong grip on Jane's arm. Camellia took a deep breath and stepped out, her slippered feet moving as trained. She must float as though lifted a few inches above the ground. "I hope you will forgive our tardiness." She glanced past the captain toward Mrs. Dabbs, who had taken up a position at the front door.

Captain Watkins bent over her hand. "You are worth waiting for."

His voice was pitched low and, combined with the emotion in his dark eyes, caused excitement to spread upward from her stomach, bringing a rush of warm blood with it. "Th–Thank you, Captain."

Jane cleared her throat. "It's nice to see you, too, Thad."

He winked at his sister. "You look lovely as always, Sister. You're doing something different with your hair."

Camellia nodded. "Doesn't she look even more beautiful than usual?"

"Excuse me." A plaintive voice from behind Captain Watkins drew her attention to the rest of the soldiers. "I believe we should be introduced to these two ladies."

Captain Watkins's grimace made Camellia smile. She watched his features as he turned to face the man. "If you insist. This is my sister, Miss Watkins. I warn you that I will not tolerate any of you breaking her heart or treating her with the least disrespect. The same holds true for her friend and mine, Miss Anderson. Not that I plan to let you have much chance to monopolize her."

The men groaned at his words, each one bowing as Captain Watkins rattled off their names. Camellia recognized Lieutenant Baxter, the man who had dined with them last month, but the rest were a mishmash of names and faces. She might have managed one or two others, but Captain Watkins appropriated her hand as he practically spirited her away from the foyer.

With all of the candles glowing, the large room had been transformed into a magical setting akin to one from a fairy-tale world. The musicians had not started playing yet, so Camellia and the captain moved toward a section of empty chairs.

Camellia sat and arranged her skirts around her. Her waist felt pinched, but she ignored it. The admiration in her escort's gaze was worth her pain. "I'm so glad you came tonight."

Captain Watkins reached for her hand, encompassing it in both of his. "I wouldn't have missed it for the world."

Aware of the looks from some of the other students, she pulled her hand free. "Mrs. Dabbs must be delighted that you brought so many of your friends."

"Now that was a true sacrifice." He smiled at her, his teeth even and white, his eyes gleaming. "I hope I won't have to compete with them too much for your attention."

Heat warmed her cheeks once more, and Camellia glanced away. Her gaze traveled around the room as she considered how to answer him. Should she be coy? He was making his interest in her obvious. Perhaps she should let him know how much she admired him. But would that make him lose interest? For a moment she wished Aunt Dahlia had been able to come to New Orleans. She would know exactly how to advise her. But she hadn't, so Camellia had no choice but to follow her instincts. She opened her fan and let it rest against her chin in an attitude of deep thought. "I wouldn't want any of our brave soldiers to feel slighted."

The captain straightened his spine.

Camellia raised her fan to hide her smile. His reaction, the fierce frown on his face and the way he glanced about the room, told her she'd responded in the best way possible.

The musicians began playing, and the others in attendance poured into the room from the foyer. Camellia looked around and saw that Jonah had arrived. But he was not standing near Jane. Instead he was chatting with some of Captain Watkins's buddies. That was odd. What could he possibly have in common with them? She filed away the question for future consideration as the captain stood.

"Please dance with me." He held out a hand.

Camellia put away her fan, fumbling to draw out the moment. The captain knew she would accept his invitation, but why be in a hurry? By the time she put her hand in his, several couples had already taken positions on the dance floor.

She noticed that Jonah did not break away from the group he was conversing with. Jane, however, did not seem to mind. She was too busy smiling at a handsome soldier in a butternut-hued uniform who was leading her toward the other dancers.

Camellia curtsied as the captain bowed, then joined her right hand to his left and stepped forward. As the piece continued, she discovered that he was an accomplished partner. Their conversation was limited by the steps of the dance, but he never seemed to take his gaze from her face.

When the musicians struck the final chord, she expected him to take her back to the chairs, but he did not move away from the dance floor. "If you do not promise me more dances, I will simply keep you away from the rest of those dogs."

"Of course I will dance with you again." Camellia released the material of her gown, allowing it to settle around her. "You are my escort. To refuse you would be rude."

His face relaxed into his signature smile. "And I know you would never be rude."

"Never," she agreed.

He took her arm as the musicians began their next song. "Excellent."

And so the evening continued. Camellia did dance with other men, but she spent most of her time in Captain Watkins's arms. They did not stray from the strictures of propriety, however.

She could not say the same about Jonah. He had not approached her at all, but he had danced with every other girl in the room. Even some of the older ladies—the mothers, aunts, and sisters of the students. He had partnered with Mrs. Dabbs once, making that lady color and giggle like one of her pupils. Yes, Jonah had been quite the ladies' man this evening.

As Captain Watkins swirled her around the room in one of the few waltzes of the evening, she noticed Jonah had taken Jane onto the floor. He held her very close. Too close. Why wasn't Mrs. Dabbs separating them? She had done so with other men who had gotten a little too daring. Couldn't she see how inappropriately they were acting? Jonah's mouth was practically grazing Jane's ear. Camellia stumbled as she craned her head to watch them.

Captain Watkins caught her, keeping her upright when she would have fallen. "Are you tired?"

Camellia looked into his dark brown eyes, thankful he'd stopped her from making a spectacle of herself. He was kind, too. Considerate of her. "No, it's nothing. I just wondered if Mrs. Dabbs was going to stop Jonah and Ja—"

Her words were cut off as her partner swept her into a sudden turn, a turn that allowed him to see how close Jonah and his sister were dancing.

"That Cajun conniver. I should have known he would take advantage of Jane's innocence." The captain's words were laced with anger.

His anger was nothing compared to the fire that leapt to her cheeks. "Whether Jonah Thornton is a Cajun or not has nothing to say to the matter. Besides, I know your sister well enough to realize she is capable of using him to draw someone else's attention. Lieutenant Baxter, for instance."

"I can't believe you're defending him." The captain's cheeks were as red as her own, and his blazing eyes bored a hole in her. "And you call yourself Jane's friend? I cannot believe you would blame her for his poor behavior."

Camellia was so irritated with his patronizing tone that she forgot they were in the middle of a waltz. She pulled away from the captain and turned on her heel. When she saw the shocked expression of the other people in the ballroom, it was too late. For a brief instant, she considered fainting. But no. She could not bring herself to fall to the dirty floor and soil her beautiful gown. Instead she picked up her skirt and ran from the room, her eyes burning from the tears that threatened to escape.

❧

"Can you get a note out tomorrow concerning General Johnston's troops?" Jonah whispered the words to Mrs. Dabbs as they moved toward the dance floor.

"I suppose so. Are you certain the information is correct? I can hardly believe they would move a major force so far south after all these months."

Jonah nodded, his gaze centered on a rotund gentleman who was partnering with his daughter. The girl looked terrified, and he winced in sympathy as her stumbling footsteps landed on her father's feet. "I loitered near your buffet table and struck up a conversation with a soldier named Baxter. While he was talking, I overheard the captain and some of his cronies discussing it. You must send a warning. I only hope it's not too late."

The music ended then, and he moved forward to intercept Miss Watkins. It was time for him to reassume his role as the smitten escort. She was an amenable young lady, but she seemed as shallow and self-serving as Camellia. What was it about young women that made them focus on such frivolities as fashion and etiquette even while their country was tearing itself apart? Couldn't they see that their privileged world was based on a vile, destructive institution?

As they danced, he found himself unable to keep his gaze on Miss Watkins. He was too distracted by Camellia's flamboyant dress and the way her hair floated about her heart-shaped face as the captain swirled her about the dance floor. She was easily the most beautiful girl in the room. A fact borne out by the number of men eager to dance with her.

She had not sat out a single dance. But it seemed to him she glowed with happiness as the captain partnered with her. Why was she so animated when the captain held her? And why did Jonah care who brought a smile to her face?

"Don't you agree, Mr. Thornton?"

Jonah dragged his attention back to Miss Watkins and wondered what she had been saying. "If you say so, Miss Watkins."

A slight frown marred her brow, so he executed several quick turns. At the same time, he tightened his hold on her waist and brought his head closer to hers, moves that should redirect her thoughts. "Will you be leaving New Orleans right away, or can I expect to see you here the next time I come to call?"

Satisfaction settled on her face, replacing the frown. Good. Better for her to count him a conquest than to wonder what really held his attention. "My brother is hoping to escort me and Camellia to Vicksburg by the end of the month. He has asked his superiors for a short leave." She giggled. "If you come before then, I will be here."

Further confirmation of the arrival of fresh troops. The smile on Jonah's face felt frozen. The Confederate leaders would not allow Captain Watkins to take leave unless they believed he would not be needed. Which would be true if General Johnston came to bolster the flagging number of defenders. Now was the time for the Federal troops to take the city. New Orleans would have no choice but surrender if Union soldiers arrived before Johnston's troops. They could cut off the South's supply lines and end the war before the year was half over. He prayed his superiors would take advantage of the information being funneled to them. Perhaps his subterfuge could end at that time, the slaves could be freed, and life could return to less battle-some days.

A commotion on the far side of the ballroom brought his head up. He was surprised to see Camellia jerk her arm away from her escort's and dash out of the room. It wasn't like her to cause a scene. She always strove hard to appear perfect. It was one of the reasons he could never resist teasing her—to witness her struggle between the desire to put him in his place and the need to maintain her flawless facade. What had happened? Had Captain Watkins offended her? Or was there another reason for her public faux pas? What could have made her break the primary rule of her very existence? The questions crowded his mind as the musicians finished playing the waltz.

Miss Watkins leaned on his arm as Jonah escorted her from the dance floor. Her brother was standing next to a large potted plant, talking to a few of his Confederate friends, so he steered Miss Watkins in that direction.

"You seem preoccupied this evening. Have I said something to upset you?" Miss Watkins pouted at him, her lips drooping.

Jonah realized she must be unaware of the disturbance between her brother and Camellia, or she would not still be trying to flirt with him. Had her back been turned to them the whole time? She would find out soon enough why the others were whispering, but for now he hoped she would remain unaware. He needed a little time to figure out what had gone wrong. "Of course not. I'm sorry. You must think me quite rude. I enjoyed our dance."

"I'm certain a polished gentleman like you must find our party boring and prosaic." Her voice was light, but he detected a slight edge to the words.

Jonah opened his mouth to answer her but was distracted by the conversation taking place a few feet away.

"Her actions show how temperamental a pretty girl can be. She'll soon learn she cannot control a man." Captain Watkins slapped one of his friends on the shoulder, and all of the group laughed.

Any answer he would have given to the girl on his arm was forgotten because of the captain's callous statement. Was he speaking of Camellia? What had he said to her? A part of Jonah wanted to confront the man right then, but he decided his first duty was to check on Camellia. Once he knew she was okay and found out exactly what the captain had said or done, he could decide the proper action to take.

"Please excuse me." He bowed to Miss Watkins, straightened, and cleared his throat to get the attention of the laughing men. "I'm certain most of these fine gentlemen are eager to partner with you."

Captain Watkins crossed his arms over his chest as the eager soldiers crowded around his sister.

Jonah's eyes narrowed as they searched the man's face. At least he could not have done her any physical harm in the middle of the ballroom. But if he'd been cruel to Camellia, Jonah would make sure he answered for it.

Turning away, he hurried to the door and into the hallway, looking left and right for any sign of Camellia. Seeing nothing, he decided to check the first-floor rooms that were not in use for the party. He crossed the hall and tried the first door. The room was dimly lit, but the yellow light of an oil lamp atop the fireplace mantel showed him floor-to-ceiling shelves lined with books. The library. "Camellia? Are you in here?"

A sniffle answered him.

Jonah's mouth tightened. She *was* crying. He entered the room and closed the door behind him. It might not be proper to shut himself in with her, but Jonah knew Camellia wouldn't want anyone to see her crying. He looked about until he spotted the bright material of her gown.

She stood beside a tall window, one hand strangling the heavy velvet drapes.

Jonah closed the distance between them and put a comforting hand on her shoulder. "It's okay, Camellia."

"Go away." She spat out the words and shrugged his hand off with an impatient motion. "Leave me alone."

He sighed. "I'll leave you alone as soon as you tell me what's going on."

She twisted to face him. "It has nothing to do with you."

"Anything that hurts you involves me." Jonah wanted to pull her into his arms and hold her close. He could see the vulnerability in her large blue eyes, could trace the pain down the wet paths on her tearstained cheeks. "Did he insult your honor?"

A brittle laugh escaped her. "Of course not. Captain Watkins did nothing wrong. All he did was defend his sister's honor."

Confusion made Jonah frown. He tilted his head as he tried to understand what she had said. Why would Captain Watkins feel the need to defend his sister? Camellia would never attack the girl. They were close friends.

Before he could puzzle out the answer, she pointed a finger at his chest. "Why did you come tonight?" Her voice was pitched low, some emotion making her tremble.

The question put him on the defensive. Did she suspect the truth? He thought he had fooled everyone. Jonah's heart was heavy in his chest. But then he realized she couldn't have any idea he was a spy. Camellia was a staunch supporter of the Confederacy. If she suspected the truth, she'd tell the soldiers to arrest him. Jonah cast about in his mind for a suitable answer, but only three words came to him. Three words that told a truth even if they didn't disclose everything. "To see you."

Her mouth formed a perfect O of shock. Her blue eyes widened.

Silence filled the room as she absorbed his words. Then she shook her head. "You have some other reason. Your mother must have put the idea in your head. You only care to belittle me and my dreams. You and I both know this isn't the kind of party you generally attend."

"You don't know me at all, do you?" Jonah stepped back. "You judge me for my boyhood days. Can you not see that I am different now? I like to think I have gained a little maturity in the past few years."

Camellia shrugged, her pale shoulders catching the light of the lamp on the mantel.

"I was a child, but now I'm a man. I've put away childish things." He hesitated a moment, gathering his thoughts. "Christ is the One who guides me, not the ambitions of this world."

Her pale brows drew together.

Jonah straightened his shoulders and waited to hear the question he could almost see quivering on her full lips. He sent a quick prayer heavenward that he could properly answer whatever troubled her. That he could help turn her thoughts toward God and the real reason for existence.

She cocked her head, her curls falling across the curve of her cheek. "Is that why you're not a soldier?"

Surprise spread through him as she watched him through narrowed eyes. He almost laughed out loud. Camellia was obviously not ready to change.

The impulse to tell her the whole truth tempted him to speak. The confession would be so easy. Sharing his secret with someone he knew would be a luxury. Temptation filled him, but with an effort Jonah turned his back on the desire.

What if Camellia didn't turn him in? Then she would be a traitor to the Confederacy. Did he really want to put her life in danger for his own sake? Shame replaced his earlier surprise. "No." The single syllable was harsh even to him. Jonah swallowed and tried again. "No, that's not it at—"

"Are you afraid?"

Jonah wondered how they had gotten so far from talking about the importance of faith. "You can think what you like, Camellia. The truth is that my reasons are private."

Her gaze pierced him, leaving Jonah feeling exposed. He supposed he should credit her with looking beneath the surface for a deeper answer. But why did she have to pick tonight? Why was she searching for truth now when she'd accepted him so easily in the past? Was it some kind of test for him? A temptation placed in front of him to see if he would yield?

"I see." She turned away from him and took a step toward the door.

"Wait, Camellia." Jonah put a hand on her shoulder once more, halting her forward movement. "I'm sorry. I didn't mean to offend you."

"Don't worry about that. I'm not offended." She allowed him to turn her to face him, but she kept her gaze centered on the carpet.

He pulled her closer, intoxicated by the feel of her soft skin under his fingers and the flowery fragrance of her perfume. "I think it's time for you to realize that I can be a good friend."

"I have plenty of friends already." She glared up at him. "And I don't need the friendship of a coward anyway."

Her words bounced off of him like the first drops of a spring shower. Jonah knew he should release her, but he didn't seem to have any control over his body. He stepped closer to her, close enough to see the slight tremble in her lower lip.

Their gazes met, and her anger faded, replaced by something warmer. Something that drew his head down. His hand moved from her shoulder to cup her chin, his thumb grazing the edge of her mouth. Her eyelids drooped in response to his touch, and Jonah leaned in and let his lips cover hers.

Gently he explored her mouth with his own, teasing her, feeling her response as the kiss deepened. His heart felt as though it was about to burst from his chest. Somehow his arms had wrapped around her tiny waist, pulling her to him.

When her lips parted slightly under his, a warning bell clanged in Jonah's head. He could not allow their embrace to continue. She was too young, too innocent. Besides, hadn't he followed her in here to find out if she needed his protection?

Jonah made his hands push her away. She needed more protection from him than from the captain who had made her flee in the first place. "I'm sorry."

Her gaze fled from his, and she caught her breath with a sound between a gasp and a sob. Raising a hand to her mouth, Camellia scrubbed at her lips as though she wanted to wipe away the feel of their kiss.

He was a heel. A worm. He had taken advantage of her. Hating himself, Jonah brushed past her and exited the library. If he'd come across any other man doing what he'd just done, Jonah would have demanded satisfaction. Or at least a proposal of marriage to protect her reputation. He certainly wouldn't have allowed the fellow to slink away without repercussions.

Hesitating a moment as he considered his options, Jonah strode to the front door and jerked it open. He couldn't do anything now except put some distance between them.

Chapter Seventeen

The war didn't completely stop commerce on the river. Captain Pecanty had permission from both the Union and the Confederacy to travel on the river as long as he did not transport slaves, weapons, soldiers, or suspicious cargo. Lately, each time they made a landing, they had to allow an inspection by some authority and often lost a percentage of their cargo that was deemed to be "suspicious." It might be nails, copper wiring, sugar—anything was subject to seizure. Once they had even been commandeered as a transport ship for several wounded soldiers.

Today they had lost a hogshead of flour to the frowning Union commander. According to Mrs. Naomi, it was a small price to pay for an overnight stop in Cape Girardeau, one of her favorite landings.

Since the beginning of spring, it had become one of John's favorites, too. Miss Anna Matthews would be there, and perhaps she would be able to spend a little time with him before they had to leave. He could hardly wait to see her.

"Let's get this leather loaded." Captain Pecanty brought his attention back to the boat and the task at hand.

Two other steamboats floated next to them, a tin-clad armored boat, cannons bristling from every side, and a small, squat tugboat that had seen better days. Last year this dock would have been covered with boats, but the war had changed all that.

"They've put up another fort." Mrs. Naomi appeared from the galley in her "visiting" dress, a black bombazine with rosettes along its hem, as they finished loading the cargo. "That makes four."

The rest of the crew scattered, most of them heading to one or another of the saloons for entertainment while a few returned to the boat to stand guard.

John watched as the captain helped Mrs. Naomi climb onto the front of the wagon and then took his place beside her.

"You are coming with us, aren't you?" Mrs. Naomi sent a speaking glance his way. "I know that a certain young lady will be anxious to see you."

John ducked his head while Captain Pecanty laughed. "Leave the boy alone, Naomi. He doesn't need you to be a matchmaker, and I don't need to lose such an able-bodied crewman." He climbed up next to his wife and grabbed the reins. "But you can ride with us if you like, John."

Deciding he'd rather wash up before visiting Devore's General Store, John shook his head and waved them off. He grinned at the disgruntled look on Mrs. Naomi's face. She might have been instrumental in introducing him to Anna, but she didn't need to know how effective her strategy had been.

Devore's had several shoppers when he entered, the tinkling bell announcing his arrival. John looked about for Anna, and his heart quickened when he spotted the shining tresses of her amber-colored hair. She was helping a couple of Union soldiers find candles, so he leaned against a nearby shelf and waited. Anna was kind and patient with the men, deflecting any personal questions with ease.

As soon as she sent the men to the counter to pay for their goods, she turned toward him, her smile appearing like the first rays of the rising sun. "Hello."

"Hi. I hope you're doing well this afternoon." John took her hand and raised it to his lips, placing a soft kiss on her wrist.

Her soft intake of breath was followed by a blush, and Anna looked away from him. "I'm so glad to see you again."

John thought her embarrassment was charming. But that was not surprising. He found everything about her charming. "It's good to see you, too."

Silence enveloped them for a moment while John watched her staring at her left foot as it drew a small circle on the wood floor of the general store.

Anna looked up at him from the corner of her eye. "Do you have a list for me today?"

"Not today." He stepped toward her and took one of her hands in his. "I was hoping you could take a walk with me."

She giggled and glanced at her foot once more. "I'll have to ask Mr. Devore."

The bell over the door jingled as the soldiers left, their purchases under their arms. Her employer frowned in their direction and moved from behind his cash register. "Is that man bothering you, Anna?"

Her eyes widened, and she shook her head. "No, sir. I. . .he—" She stopped and gulped. "I mean, M–Mr. Champion has asked if he might take me for a walk."

John held out his hand to the older man. "If you can spare your assistant, Mr. Devore, I promise to bring her back as soon as you say."

Mr. Devore gripped his hand and shook it. "I don't know if her father would approve. He's the preacher in these parts, you know."

"No, sir." In fact, he knew very little about Anna's home life. But that was something he'd like to remedy. "If you think it would be better, I can apply to him for permission."

Mr. Devore studied him for a couple of minutes before shaking his head. "I think it will be all right, if she wants to go with you."

Anna nodded, the emphatic movement dislodging a lock of her hair from behind one of her ears.

John's smile felt more natural than it had for years. "Thank you, Mr. Devore. I'll take good care of her."

He opened the door for her to pass through and offered his elbow, leading her southward, toward a river bluff hosting one of the four forts built by the Union. "How have you been?"

"It's been a rather difficult summer."

Protectiveness flooded him. John wanted to protect this young woman. It was a foreign idea, but one he could not deny. He wanted to take care of Anna and make sure nothing ever disturbed her again. "Is it Mr. Devore? Is he difficult to work for?"

"Of course not. Don Devore treats me like a daughter, as does his wife, Norma Jean." Her laughter calmed his concern.

"What, then? What dragon can I slay to win your heart?"

She glanced at him and then toward someone walking toward them. A blue-uniformed soldier approached them, his rifle perched on his shoulder. As he passed them, John couldn't help but notice the bold way he stared at Anna.

As soon as they were far enough away for privacy, John halted and turned to face her. "Have the soldiers been bothering you?"

"What?" She shook her head. "No. It's nothing like that. It's just that my aunt has been ill. She has been like a mother to me since my own mother died."

John's ire began to fade. Sympathy took its place. He took her hands in his and rubbed them. "I'm so sorry. Is there anything I can do?"

She gave him a calculating look. "As a matter of fact. . .there is something."

"What? Do you need money? An extra hand back home? I'll do anything in my power."

Her smile appeared inch by inch, and her hands clung to his. "Come to church with me tomorrow morning."

She couldn't have surprised him more if she'd asked him to bring her the sun or moon. John didn't want to disappoint her, but he couldn't go to church, couldn't go anywhere with that many staring eyes. But he found it impossible to express his concern, so he fell back on an easier excuse. "I don't have a suit to wear."

Her face fell. Anna pulled her hands from his and stepped back. "I see."

John's heart clenched. But what else could he do?

❧

John tugged on his borrowed coat one last time before stepping into the small whitewashed church. Two rows of pews marched toward the wooden pulpit, each crowded with the townspeople. Captain Pecanty and Mrs. Naomi had left the *Catfish* ahead of him, but he couldn't see their familiar faces in this sea of strangers.

What was he doing here? John would rather have faced the danger from a cauldron of boiling oil than walk down the aisle to the only empty seat he could spy. Why had he come?

As expected, he heard the gasps of the females on his right as they caught sight of the ruined side of his face, saw the way they put protective arms around their children. This was a terrible mistake. John turned on his heel, unable to continue in the face of their collective horror.

Before he could finish the move, however, the soft touch of a hand stopped him. "Please don't go." Anna's eyes echoed the plea in her words before she turned and speared one of the repulsed ladies with a glare. "You're welcome here."

John let her pull him toward the front. She sat on the first pew and looked up at him, expectation brightening her soft-green gaze. He sat and tried to ignore the whispers behind them. This was as bad as he had imagined.

Her perfume swirled around him as she leaned close. "I'm glad you came."

Suddenly the reaction of the others in the room didn't seem as important.

The Reverend Enoch Matthews entered the sanctuary, and every conversation died away as he strode down the aisle. Anna's father was a tall man with salt-and-pepper hair, whose eyes were the exact same shade as hers. He stepped up to the pulpit and laid his Bible upon it before surveying the people in the pews. "Good morning."

The people answered his greeting in a single voice, the deeper tones of the men blending with the higher notes of the women and children. "Good morning."

John started, unused to such a responsive audience.

"Let us give thanks to God for the overflowing blessings He showers on us." Pastor Matthews bowed his head and began to pray, his words flowing over John like a cleansing cascade.

He listened as Anna's father spoke to God as though they were personally acquainted. He started by praising God for His sovereignty, His loving-kindness, and His free gift of grace. The older man continued with praises for a list of things. . .everything from sleeping well to the brave soldiers who protected them from bushwhackers, the rebel guerrillas who preyed on citizens in the border states. He asked for guidance and wisdom as the church faced the challenges and opportunities of the day. He asked God to forgive them in accordance to the forgiveness they offered to others. By the time he reached the end of his prayer, the pastor's voice reverberated around the room. John was sure they had traveled all the way to heaven.

Pastor Matthews looked up once more, his face serious. "I have spoken to many of you about the future. I've listened to your fears and prayed with you for loved ones who are fighting to keep our country whole. I've shed tears with you when you found some of those same names on the lists of missing, wounded, or dead. But today, I'm here to remind you that God knew about all of this before you were even born."

He paused, his gaze moving slowly around the room. "I can see the doubt on your faces. How could God allow such pain? How could He let such terrible things happen to us if He truly loves us?"

John was riveted by the questions. He wanted to stand up and shout his agreement. What kind of God allowed such terrible things to happen to His people? He touched the skin on his right cheek. His punishment was different. He had earned it with his past deeds. But what of those who led upright, principled, honorable lives? Why were their lives full of pain?

The pastor opened his Bible and began reading from Psalm 139: " 'Whither shall I go from thy spirit? or whither shall I flee from thy presence? If I ascend up into heaven, thou art there: if I make my bed in hell, behold, thou art there. If I take the wings of the morning, and dwell in the uttermost parts of the sea; even there shall thy hand lead me, and thy right hand shall hold me. If I say, Surely the darkness shall cover me; even the night shall be light about me. Yea, the darkness hideth not from thee; but the night shineth as the day: the darkness and the light are both alike to thee. For thou hast possessed my reins: thou hast covered me in my mother's womb. I will praise thee; for I am fearfully and wonderfully made: marvelous are thy works; and that my soul knoweth right well.'

"Do you understand what this means?" the pastor asked. "The Lord God, the greatest being in existence, knew each of you before your own mothers did. And He loves you. He loves you so very much. More even than the love you feel for your children." He glanced toward the first pew, his gaze gliding past John and landing on Anna's face. "And I know how deep that love is. I know also that God's love puts my puny feelings to shame.

"This whole psalm is one I turn to often. I would read the whole chapter to you this morning, but I want to challenge each of you to go home today and read it for yourselves. Read each word. Ponder the power of our God who knows every breath each of us takes. Not just my breath. . .or Anna's. No, he also knows the breath of this stranger who has joined us this morning. He knows why this man is here and each step that led him to this place."

John's mouth dropped open. He wished more than ever that he had stayed on the *Catfish*. He wished he had found a seat in the back of the sanctuary, a place of anonymity. But somehow he knew God wanted him at this place, at this moment. The words might be issuing from the pastor's mouth, but they were coming directly from God.

Heat enveloped him. His collar was strangling him. John pulled at it with a desperate finger and wondered if he could escape. Anna must have sensed his anguish, because she touched his hand with hers. The touch did not immediately eliminate his vulnerability, but the desperation eased a bit—enough for him to remain seated on the pew.

"After you finish studying this psalm, I want you to turn to the words of the prophet Jeremiah. I want you to read my favorite verse, chapter 29, verse 11. 'For I know the thoughts that I think toward you, saith the Lord, thoughts of peace, and not of evil, to give you an expected end.' God wants you to come to Him. He made you. He is your father. Gladden His heart by turning to Him this morning. Repent and join the ranks of His fruitful children. Jesus is standing at the door and knocking. Won't you invite Him in?"

John could feel the words seeping into his soul. He was a beloved child of the Father. Even with his dark and painful past, he could still turn to God. He dropped his head and prayed to the Father to forgive his sins. He told God he wanted to be a different man. He wanted to start over and live the rest of his life according to His direction. He wanted Christ in his heart.

Tears threatened to overwhelm John, but he fought them back. Someone brushed past his left arm. John looked up and saw that two other men had come to the front of the church and were on their knees in front of the podium. Pastor Matthews was standing in front of them, his hands spread in front of him, palms up. They were praying together, a wonderful prayer of new beginnings. More than he had wanted anything in his life, John wanted to join them.

He put his hands against the pew and pushed himself up. At first he couldn't believe it was actually him moving. It seemed Something. . .Someone stronger than he was helping to lift him from the mire of his past. John stepped forward and fell to his knees, his heart full of hope—a clean, refreshing, full hope—for the first time in his life.

"Lord God," the pastor's voice washed over him, "these men come to You with repentance and hope in their hearts. They want to turn their lives over to You. They are seeking You and calling on Your promise to dwell within them forevermore. They were sinners, but now they want to be washed clean in Your holy, cleansing blood. Thank You, Lord, for speaking to their hearts and bringing them to You. We are grateful for these new brothers of the faith. Be with them as they begin these new paths to Your glory. Amen."

When John opened his eyes, the pastor was looking over their heads at the others in the church. "What a glorious morning this is. We get to welcome three more sheep into the fold."

John pushed himself up, dusted off the knees of his slacks, and turned to see Anna at his elbow.

Her face glowed with joy. "I'm so happy for you, John."

Pastor Matthews joined them. "Is this the young man you've told me about?"

"Yes, Father. This is John Champion."

"I'm pleased to meet you, John Champion." The pastor shook his hand.

John wanted to tell them the truth right then. The compulsion was very strong to come clean on this day of new beginnings. But fear grabbed him again. If he told them his real name, he would be stepping back into his past. He would be mired in his previous life. He might even once again become the monster he had been. So he nodded. "It's my pleasure, sir."

Reverend Matthews then left them to speak to others of his congregation.

Anna took one of his hands and squeezed it, her face full of joy. "Isn't it wonderful to be a Christian?"

Touched by the sincerity of her voice, John smiled. "Yes, it is. I can hardly believe how. . .how content I feel."

"I know. Walking with the Lord is a privilege." She waved one hand in an arc. "You're reborn, and from here on you can live a life of praise and thanksgiving, sure of your eternal home."

Before he could answer her, the Pecantys joined them. Mrs. Naomi hugged him, and the captain shook his hand. For a little while, John forgot the scars on his face. He forgot about his past and focused on his future. A future that was looking brighter than ever.

Chapter Eighteen

Even though almost two weeks had passed since the formal ball, Camellia's lips still tingled if she allowed herself to remember Jonah's kiss. His touch had been tender, the complete opposite of his cold voice.

"I'm sorry." The icy tone and the remorse in his eyes had thumped her back to reality.

She was sorry, too. Sorry she hadn't slapped him for taking advantage of their relationship in such a way.

Camellia had wanted to confide in her best friend, but how could she when he was supposed to have been Jane's escort? How could she admit she had been swept away by his touch? That kissing was much more delightful than they'd ever imagined?

The answer was simple. She couldn't. No one could know what had happened in this very room.

This afternoon was the first time she'd returned to the library. Mrs. Dabbs was working with some of the others on their penmanship but had sent Camellia to finish her sampler. Jane had received permission to join her.

Camellia's gaze strayed to the corner where she and Jonah had stood. With a bit of imagination, she could once again feel his warm hand on her shoulder. What had come over her? She'd been angry with Jonah Thornton right until the point at which he wrapped her in his arms. Until her mind stopped thinking and her feelings took over. Why?

What magic did Jonah have to so easily make her forget everything? Why had she felt so safe in his embrace?

"Do you think Thad will come to call this afternoon?" Jane's voice brought her out of her spinning thoughts.

Camellia shoved her needle through the square of fabric she held, careful not to stitch it to her gown as she had earlier this year. At least the time at La Belle Demoiselle had improved her sewing skills, even if she still didn't care for samplers. "I don't know."

"What about Mr. Thornton?"

A hot flush burst upward and burned her cheeks. Did Jane suspect something? "What about him?" Camellia winced at the defensive note in her voice. "I mean. . .I'm sure he has many more important things to do than frequent the school."

Jane glanced her way. "Are you feeling feverish? When Pauline's parents came to collect her last week, I overheard them tell Mrs. Dabbs that yellow jack is expected to be worse than ever this year."

Camellia rolled her eyes. "We'll be gone to Vicksburg before there's any danger."

"I suppose you're right." The two of them worked in silence for a little while, the mantel clock ticking away the minutes as the afternoon passed. "Thad has been busy lately with some secret plan, but he said he hopes to have some free time before the end of the month."

A knock at the front door made them look up.

"Who do you think that is?" Jane's brown eyes twinkled with excitement.

"Probably one of those soldiers who seemed so smitten with you at the ball."

Both of them giggled and put away their needlework. It didn't take long before footsteps echoed in the hallway. Whoever had answered the door was coming for them.

Camellia's heartbeat increased. What if it was Jonah? What would she say to him? How could she face him?

The door burst open, and Brigitte rushed inside, her cap hanging on to her curls by a single pin and a wild look in her eyes. "*C'est une catastrophe.* Come quick."

"A disaster?" Camellia translated the phrase as she and Jane rushed out of the library. Had someone been hurt? Had a doctor been called to attend one of the students? "Who's hurt?"

"Non, non." Brigitte shook her head, and her cap flew free, landing on the floor. With a cluck of her tongue, the flustered woman scooped it up before beckoning them to follow. "Soldiers are here. *Vite.* Hurry."

As they rushed behind her, their hands clasped, Camellia heard thumps and bumps coming from upstairs. It sounded as though the second floor had been invaded. What was going on?

Brigitte passed the door to the visitors' parlor and the private parlor, heading toward the dining room behind the stairwell. As she opened the oak door, the sound of feminine sobbing was punctuated by the deeper sound of male voices. "I have brought the last two."

Jane stopped in her tracks, her grasp holding Camellia back. "I'm scared."

"Camellia? Jane?" Camellia recognized Mrs. Dabbs's voice, although it sounded strained to her ears.

"Don't be scared." Wishing she could follow her own advice, Camellia swallowed against the lump in her throat and pulled on Jane's hand. "It's going to be all right." She took the last steps to the open doorway and glanced inside, shock making her let go of Jane. What she saw did not calm her.

The remaining students were congregated in the far corner of the room. Three soldiers surrounded Mrs. Dabbs, their rifles pointed toward the ceiling. But the serious cast to their features was more than a little intimidating. Brigitte's eyes were large in her face as she positioned herself between the soldiers and the students as though intent on protecting them.

But what protection did any of them need? These were not invading Yankees. These soldiers wore the gray uniforms of the Confederacy.

Mrs. Dabbs stood as Camellia and Jane entered the room.

One of the soldiers, his face hidden by a thick brown beard, swung the point of his rifle down. The bayonet flashed in the light coming from the windows.

Red splotches stained Mrs. Dabbs's cheeks. "Put that weapon away before you hurt someone."

He looked toward the taller one, who shrugged. After a moment, he shifted the weapon so it rested on his shoulder. "Is this all of them?"

Mrs. Dabbs sent him a disdainful glance. "I have seven students remaining. Count for yourself."

"What's going on?" Camellia took a step toward Mrs. Dabbs.

The tall soldier, who had blue eyes and a freckled face, frowned at her.

Camellia ignored him, moving forward and taking the older woman's hands in her own. They were as cold as icicles. "Are you all right?"

"Yes, dear." Mrs. Dabbs sighed. "But I'm afraid these gentlemen are going to insist on my accompanying them. As the oldest student, you'll need to help Mademoiselle Laurent notify everyone that the school is closing immediately. Thank goodness many of them have already departed. You should have no trouble getting the rest of them to their relatives."

"But why?"

A noise at the door took Mrs. Dabbs's attention away from her face. An exclamation from behind her brought Camellia's head around. Jane had run to the door and flung herself on the man standing there.

Relief spread through Camellia, and she squeezed Mrs. Dabbs's hands. "Captain Watkins, thank goodness. Now everything will be fine."

He hugged his sister briefly, keeping one arm around her as he entered the room. He ignored everyone else as he nodded to the soldiers in the room. "I'll take over in here. Riley, Hamilton, stand guard at the front door. Don't let anyone in or out until I've cleared them. Adkins, go help the search out back."

The three men hurried to do his bidding.

Camellia let go of Mrs. Dabbs's hands and summoned a bright smile for his benefit. He was forgiven for his boorish behavior the last time she'd seen him. "I'm so glad you're here."

"And I wish you and Jane were not." His handsome mouth did not relax into a smile. He didn't look angry. But he glanced toward Mrs. Dabbs, and his face hardened. "I wish I could spare all of you girls, but your families will no doubt read of it in the newspaper. Traitors cannot be tolerated. Not when so much is at stake."

Camellia put a hand to her mouth. It couldn't be true. But then she saw the defiant gleam in Mrs. Dabbs's eyes. The lady looked as though she was proud of her actions. Camellia took a step away from her.

Jane sidled to her and put an arm around Camellia's waist as she directed a question toward their teacher. "What have you done?"

Mrs. Dabbs rolled her eyes. "Why don't you ask the brave captain?" She directed a frown at him. "I assume you have thoroughly searched the rooms upstairs?"

Captain Watkins nodded. Then he looked at Camellia and his sister.

"We intercepted a letter she tried to send to Captain Poindexter, a man who happens to be her cousin."

That didn't sound too bad. Camellia supposed she had relatives who were Yankees. Would she be arrested if she wrote to one of them? She sent a questioning gaze toward the captain.

"It contained information we planted during her party."

Now he had everyone's attention. Even the younger girls stopped sniffling to listen to his story.

"We've had reports of a traitor—maybe one person, maybe more—who is passing information to the Yankees about our troop movements. Of course the letters are in code. They appear to be innocent, but in reality they are detailed descriptions of our plans, weapons, and troop strength. We got a lead on Poindexter and decided to set a trap, something that would flush out the guilty party. We planted false information about the impending arrival in New Orleans of General Joseph Johnston and his troops. Then we waited for someone to take the bait."

He drew a folded sheet of stationery from his coat pocket and opened it with a snap. "This is all the proof we need to arrest Mrs. Dabbs. It's taken more than a week, but we finally broke her code. This letter warns her cousin of Johnston's arrival and begs him to come and conquer the city while our defenses are weak."

Camellia's stomach clenched so hard she felt nauseated. "What will happen to her?"

"We'll take her to prison." The captain's eyes blazed with scorn. "I hope they hang her."

Jane gasped, and several of the students began crying again.

Camellia tightened her jaw against the nausea, reminding herself that she had to be strong for the other girls. She could feel their gazes on her, awaiting her response. "We'll pray for her."

Captain Watkins's expression softened a smidgen. "Your sympathy is admirable if misplaced. I'll check on you and Jane as soon as I can." He took Mrs. Dabbs's arm and urged her to the door.

As he led their schoolteacher away, Camellia turned toward the distraught students, wondering what had driven Mrs. Dabbs to take such drastic steps. Why had she turned on the system that supported her students? Her school?

And what did this turn of events say about Camellia's ability to judge others? She had respected Mrs. Dabbs more than most, as much as Aunt

Dahlia. She could no longer trust anyone, even if her own powers of discernment said differently.

❧

"I hope Thad doesn't arrive before we get back from delivering Molly to her parents." Camellia glanced toward the little girl who huddled in one corner of the carriage.

"I'm sure he'll wait." Jane coughed and waved a scented handkerchief in front of her face. "The smoke seems worse than this morning."

Camellia nodded her agreement. "I wish they would stop ringing the alarm bells. Surely no one in New Orleans is unaware of the danger." She thought about the report Brigitte had brought them while they were getting ready to leave.

Mrs. Dabbs's assistant had gone to Jackson Square to discover why the alarm was being sounded. Apparently everyone expected the Yankees to arrive at any moment. The shipyards across the river at Algiers were in flames. Bales of cotton had been dragged out of warehouses and put to the torch. Even boats on the river had been set afire and loosed from their moorings to drift down the river.

"I hope my parents are all right." Tears puddled in Molly's eyes.

"I know you're frightened." Camellia hid her fear behind a brief smile. "Don't worry. I doubt the Yankees are really coming. Don't you remember all of the handsome soldiers who came to dance with us?"

Molly looked a little happier as she nodded.

"Those silly Yankees wouldn't dare to attack them, now, would they?"

Molly shook her head and sat up straight as the carriage made a turn. "Are we there?"

Camellia leaned forward, careful to keep her spine straight as she'd been taught. No matter what the future held, she was determined to present a polished and serene image. A curve in the drive showed her a double row of moss-draped oaks, a fitting entrance to a grand plantation home. " I believe we are."

She and Jane helped gather Molly's belongings, but before they could alight, a short lady with dark curls and worried brown eyes was at the door to the carriage. When Camellia saw the woman's rounded stomach, she realized why Molly's mother had not been able to come collect her daughter. She was going to have a baby, a little brother or sister for Molly.

"Merci. My husband is in the army, but we have much room if you would like to stay here with us."

For a moment Camellia was tempted to take up Molly's mother on her offer. Farther from town, the air seemed clearer, the danger not so immediate. They could hide out here and hope the war would pass them by.

But then a picture of Thad's earnest face appeared in her mind. His dark eyes boring a hole into her, his arms coming around her, his lips—Camellia slammed the door on the memory—not of Thad but of Jonah. Why was he the one she thought of?

No matter, they had to go back to the school or *Thad* would be worried. She shook her head. "We have family in town."

The older woman nodded her understanding. Putting an arm around her daughter's waist, she led Molly between a pair of white columns and onto a shady porch. They both turned and waved as the coachman backed the carriage and began the drive to town.

When a bend in the drive hid the graceful, two-story home from sight, Camellia turned to Jane. "What do you think will happen to them?"

"We should pray for their safety." Jane sighed.

As the carriage trundled through the countryside, each retreated into her own thoughts. Camellia wondered why everything had changed. Why was her life so out of control? No matter what she did, nothing ever worked out as planned.

First she was kissed by the wrong man. Then Thad, the man she hoped to marry, appeared to arrest Mrs. Dabbs. He had single-handedly closed down the school, although she supposed she couldn't blame Thad for his actions. But couldn't they have just intercepted the letters and waited to arrest Mrs. Dabbs once the term was completely over? And now the Yankees were practically knocking at their front door. How much worse could things get?

The thoughts continued to roll in her mind until the carriage came to a halt. "What now?"

Jane's eyes widened. "Do you think it's. . .Yankees?"

A shudder passed through Camellia. "I hope not."

The coachman climbed down and opened the door between them. His dark face was drawn in a frown. "There's some kind of speechifying going on up on the Levee Road. I can't get through right now. Did you ladies want to get out and walk about while we wait?"

Without waiting for Jane's agreement, Camellia moved toward the door. She needed to get out of the stuffy carriage. As soon as her feet touched the ground, she looked about. A crowd had gathered around a man of average height whose mustache blended with his side-whiskers. Curiosity drove her forward.

"Wait for me." Jane's voice came from behind her.

The heat pounded on her shoulders, and the smoke was worse once more. Camellia choked back the urge to cough. When Jane drew even with her, they linked their arms and picked their way around the ruts in the road to stand on the outskirts of the crowd.

The man tugged on his uniform and cleared his throat. "That's why I feel it would be best to withdraw from the city."

A collective groan greeted his statement. One of the ladies fainted. Her escort caught her and lowered her to the ground before returning his attention to the man speaking.

"We will be within easy reach should you need our military support, but I don't want the Yankee navy bombing the city. If no one remains within New Orleans but workingmen, women, and children, I believe they will not take action against you."

Camellia was horrified at his suggestion. Without a military presence, the city would undoubtedly fall into Yankee control. Since her sister was directly involved in the world of commerce, she understood what it would mean to the South to lose the city. The free flow of arms and goods would be halted. It would be a devastating blow, one that might mean the end of the war, the end of everything that mattered to her.

Chapter Nineteen

"You cannot remain here all alone." Jonah held on to his patience with an effort. The woman standing in front of him had to understand the dangers she and her friend might face. "Now that Admiral Farragut has landed, New Orleans must surrender to the inevitable."

Camellia opened her mouth and closed it with a snap. "If you believe that, you're an idiot. Our soldiers will defend us."

"Is that what you think? Do you expect Captain Watkins to ride in on a white horse and save the day?"

Her eyes darkened, distracting him.

All he wanted to do was take her in his arms once more and feel her soft curves yielding to him. Jonah shook his head to clear it. This was definitely not the time to be thinking about romance. He needed to convince Camellia and Jane to leave the school and take up residence with his family where he could keep an eye on them. Just to make sure they were safe, of course.

"I'm sorry. I shouldn't have said that." He pivoted and walked to the far side of the visitors' parlor, his footsteps echoing in the empty house. Maybe some distance would help him keep his focus.

She sniffed. Had he made her cry? Jonah glanced over his shoulder, relieved to see that her lips were folded in a straight line. She might be angry, but at least she wasn't falling apart.

A thought occurred to him. Was she angry with him because of this afternoon? Or was she upset about the way he'd acted the last time they were together? "Camellia, I'm sorry for what happened that night, and I know what you must think of—"

A disdainful roll of her eyes stopped his words and made his jaw tighten.

Jonah took a deep breath and began again. "I promise I won't come near you if you'll only consent to moving to the town house. Father will fuss about the Federals, and Mother will fuss over you and Miss Watkins—"

"Jane. Her name is Jane."

He was glad to get past the apology, so Jonah ignored the needling tone in her voice. "You and *Jane* cannot remain here without Mrs. Dabbs."

"We couldn't very well abandon the younger girls to suit your sense of propriety." Camellia raised her chin in a defiant gesture. "Jane and I have spent the past two days getting messages out to the families of the other girls and delivering the ones who could not be picked up."

Jonah sighed. "It's not my sense of propriety, Camellia. I'm impressed that you took it upon yourself to reunite the remaining students with their families or send them home, but that responsibility is completed. I saw no sign of any servants, so I assume they've run away. It's time for you to leave, too. Thieves are taking advantage of the confusion and panic to break into homes and steal whatever they can find. And they don't care if they hurt someone in the process."

"Wait a minute." Camellia's chin lowered a notch, and her gaze studied him. "How did you know Mrs. Dabbs wasn't here? We haven't told anyone, and it hasn't been in the newspapers."

She was too quick for her own good. Jonah could hardly tell her he'd received a report from another sympathizer who was stationed at the prison. Nor could he kiss her again to distract her. He looked away, his mind grasping for a plausible answer. "That captain sent me a note about it and asked me to make sure the two of you were safe."

The suspicion on her face didn't abate. "Why would he do that? When did the two of you become such fast friends?"

He forced a laugh. "I wouldn't call our relationship friendly, but you're the one who introduced him to my family. He was worried about you and couldn't check on you himself. It's no wonder he contacted my father."

"I thought you said he sent a note to you."

"I—I meant that I read Father's note." Jonah summoned up all the innocence he could muster and met her gaze openly. It was time to put her on the defensive. "Why are you so concerned about how he addressed the message? What really matters is that you and Miss. . .Jane pack a bag or two. I could not bring the wagon through the streets, so don't pack too much." He held his breath as he watched the emotions play across her features.

She finally shrugged and moved to the door. "I don't suppose we have much choice. But I'm going to take Thad to task when I see him next for sending a note to you—or your parents—when he couldn't be bothered with letting us know what was going on. Jane and I have been worried sick about him since he failed to show up yesterday afternoon as expected."

"I'm sure he wanted to." Jonah kept his tone light. "Go on and get your things. We need to leave as soon as possible."

The moment the door closed behind Camellia, Jonah collapsed onto the striped damask sofa. That had been a close one. He would have to send a missive to the captain reassuring the man about the girls' whereabouts. And he would have to hope his subterfuge was not discovered.

As long as Camellia was around, Jonah would also have to watch every word he uttered. If she realized his true mission, she would run straight to Captain Watkins with the information. Then his usefulness as a spy would be over. He wouldn't be able to rescue Mrs. Dabbs, and he'd probably have to run for his life to escape imprisonment or hanging.

"Mayor Monroe sent a note back that if Farragut didn't like the flags flying over our government buildings, he would have to remove them himself." Mr. Thornton's laughter rocked the carriage.

Camellia hoped the noise their host was making wouldn't bring unwanted attention to them. Fog and smoke swirled outside the window, barely visible in the predawn hours. She stretched her senses to their utmost, trying to hear above the *clip-clop* of their horse's hooves on the pavement. Did a shadow detach itself from the alley they passed, or was it only her imagination?

"Are you sure the boat will leave this morning?" Jane's question brought her attention back to the interior of the carriage.

Accustomed to the dark, she saw Jonah's nod. "Don't worry. Everything's arranged."

Why did his voice sound so kind when he addressed Jane? When Jonah spoke to her, which had been an infrequent occurrence over the past three days, it had been in distant monosyllables. When she had asked if he'd seen the Yankee boat, he'd answered yes. When she questioned him about further messages from Captain Watkins, he'd simply said no. No explanation, no comment. As though they were strangers. It was very perplexing.

As she returned her gaze to the dark landscape, Camellia's thoughts turned to home. Wouldn't Lily be amused that she was so anxious to board a steamboat? A pang speared her. She couldn't wait to see precious Jasmine. Had her baby sister memorized any more dramas? Or had she grown out of that fascination? She had no doubt that Lily and Blake were still happy in their odd, argumentative way. And what about Aunt Dahlia and Uncle Phillip? Had they found her a better suitor than Thaddeus Watkins, Esquire? She couldn't wait to show all of them how much she'd matured. Even Grandmother would be impressed by her improved skills.

If only she'd been able to convince Mrs. Thornton to come with them. But the lady had refused, stating that she would not abandon her husband and children. Camellia shuddered to think of any of them caught between the opposing forces. The men in the family would try to protect Mrs. Thornton and her daughter, but would it be enough?

She would have to pray that the Yankee admiral would give up and slink away. Wasn't it enough that his ships were blockading Confederate waters? Did he have to threaten the cities, too?

Camellia glanced toward Jonah and wondered what he would say if she voiced her opinion. Would he stick to monosyllables then? She was tempted by the idea of engaging him in a discussion, even if it was an argument.

She knew she should be thankful he was keeping his distance from her. They could not afford a repeat of that moment in the library at La Belle Demoiselle. Her cheeks heated, and a chill that had nothing to do with the damp morning air raced through her. A part of her wanted to repeat the experience, if only to prove that the emotions of that night had been a result of the excitement of the dance rather than a response to his kiss.

A shout interrupted her thoughts and brought Camellia's attention back to her surroundings. The carriage came to a halt as they reached the port. How different it looked without all the steamships lined up along the docks. Before the war, she would not have been able to see the oak trees on the west bank, but as the sun began to rise above the horizon, she could easily make out the widespread limbs and gnarled trunks lining the opposite shore.

The pungent odor of burned cotton seemed to hang over them as Jonah opened the door and jumped out, turning to offer a hand to assist them.

Camellia waited for Jane to alight then took Jonah's hand. She realized her mistake as soon as her bare hand touched his. No admonition to be as tranquil as a lake's surface could stop her reaction. Grabbing hold of a lightning bolt could not have caused a greater sensation. A flash in Jonah's dark eyes told her he had felt the same thrill. Time stretched out as she leaned against his strength, as she relied on him to keep her from tumbling to the damp pavement. Then her foot touched the ground, and the moment ended. Her heart was fluttering in her chest like a frightened bird. What had happened? What power was it that Jonah had over her? Why could the mere touch of his hand cause such a furor?

Jerking away from him, Camellia caught her breath and looked around them. The fog dampened all sounds, giving the area an eerie, deserted feel. Gooseflesh arose on her arms. She wanted to reach for Jonah's solid form again but moved closer to Jane instead. "Where is the boat?"

Behind her, the horse whinnied and the coach creaked as Mr. Thornton disembarked. "It ought to be right over there."

"I don't see anything." Concern filled Jonah's deep voice. "I thought he was going to wait here for us."

Jane put an arm around Camellia's waist. "Perhaps he had to move to a berth farther down the river?"

Mr. Thornton walked to the water's edge and raised a hand to his brow, searching in both directions for any sign of the boat. "Nothing. I don't see anything but water."

Camellia's heart sank. Would they not be able to escape after all?

A bright light shone from the opposite bank, piercing the fog that seemed to grow denser with every passing moment.

She pointed toward it. "Is that the boat?"

"That doesn't make sense." Jonah took up a position on the other side of Jane. She could almost feel the tension rolling off him. "Why would it be on the west bank?"

Camellia squinted, trying to discover the source of the light. It seemed to expand, becoming several points of brightness. Was that the effect of the fog? Or something more ominous?

"I think it's a fire." Jane whispered the words as though afraid to say them out loud.

The lights jumped higher and spread out wider at the same time, casting a yellow reflection on the dark water of the river. For a moment she thought someone might have set fire to one of the old oaks, but then Camellia recognized the outline being made—a steamship.

A blast rent the air, and the sky filled with burning debris.

"Watch out!" Jonah turned and caught both of them in his arms, bending his torso to form a barrier between them and the dangerous missiles.

She could hear the thunks and splashes as the pieces rained down all around them, but Camellia was more aware of the scent of Jonah's cologne, the strength of his arms, and his protective stance than the danger they were in.

As soon as the noises abated, he dropped his arms from them. "Father? Father, are you all right?"

"I'm fine." Mr. Thornton was no longer standing where he had been.

Camellia looked around, relieved when she saw Jonah's father and the coachman emerging from the space under the carriage. "There they are."

"Look." Jane's voice brought their attention back to the river.

The decks of the steamer were completely enwrapped in a blanket of flames. The paddle wheel still churned, however, its great blades pushing through the muddy water and sending the boat downriver.

Camellia looked for the name on its side, her heart sliding downward as she made out the last three letters: H–O–E. "It's the *Ivanhoe*." Her voice cracked on the last word.

"Don't worry." Jonah stepped toward her. "We'll get you out of New Orleans."

"How?"

"We'll find another boat."

Camellia wanted to believe him, but his eyes told her a different story. "There aren't any more boats."

He put a hand under her arm and guided her back toward the carriage. "I'll do whatever is necessary, Camellia. If I have to carry you out of here on my back, I'll see that you reach your family safely. You can count on me."

And somehow she knew she could.

Chapter Twenty

Jonah wondered how the mayor could continue refusing to bow to Admiral Farragut now that everyone knew both forts guarding the river below the city had surrendered. It was only a matter of time before troops arrived and put the city under marshal law. He ought to be proud that his work had helped make a bloodless victory possible.

Even his father had accepted the inevitable and freed their slaves. A couple of the older ones stayed, but most of them were happy to seek out brighter futures than they had once dreamed possible. Jonah had given them all the cash he could collect, a gesture he hoped would help them during these difficult times.

A knock on the front door went unanswered for a moment until he rose with a grin. Along with his parents, he was going to have to remember to wait on himself. He crossed the marble floor of the foyer and pulled the door open, a frown drawing his eyebrows together when he recognized their visitor. "Captain Watkins."

"Are my sister and Miss Anderson staying with you?"

Jonah bowed and stepped back begrudgingly. "They're safe." He wanted to voice the unspoken words *thanks to my efforts* but decided that would be an unchristian remark.

"Captain Watkins!" Camellia didn't run to the door, but she moved faster than her usual sedate pace.

Jane followed, her smile mirroring the wide one Camellia wore. The two girls pulled Thad into the parlor.

Jonah decided to ask if anyone in the kitchen could prepare a tea tray. As he waited for Selma to finish steeping the tea, he wondered what conversation was going on in the parlor.

"We got a few more pralines, Master Jonah, but no cookies to go on the tray."

Maybe that would keep the captain from returning. But Jonah knew better. They could forgo tea altogether for that matter. He was here to regale Camellia and Jane with his derring-do. He would gloss over the conditions under which the Confederates held poor Mrs. Dabbs with the excuse that he didn't want to upset the girls.

Jonah gulped as a new thought hit him. If Camellia thought to upbraid him for his supposed message to the Thornton household, she would find out Jonah had made up that story. Grabbing the tray from Selma, he hurried back to the parlor, the rattle of the china announcing his arrival.

". . .and how much longer the city can hold out." Captain Watkins sat on the sofa between Camellia and Jane.

Jonah's father and mother sat across the tea table from them in the pair of overstuffed chairs. Jonah was relieved to see his parents in the parlor, as it meant the conversation would be centered on the war.

"As long as it takes." Father banged his hand on the arm of his chair. "We're not a bunch of sniveling cowards like the men at those forts. I still find it hard to believe they surrendered without a fight."

A fact for which Jonah was profoundly thankful. He attributed the event to God's intervention. As He had done to the enemies of the Israelites, God had filled the Confederate soldiers with a spirit of fear. According to the reports Jonah had heard, they had spiked or dismounted the cannons, insisting on surrender no matter what their superiors promised. The route to the city was open, and he expected to see troop ships sailing into the port city any day.

"Unfortunately, our batteries at Chalmette are intended to revoke an attack by land. There's nothing we can do to protect the city at this point."

Jonah put the tray on the tea table and straightened. "So what will you do?"

What the captain might have answered was lost as the sound of marching feet outside grabbed their attention.

Jonah was the first to the door. He wrenched it open and strode to the sidewalk, followed by his parents and their guests.

Soldiers marched through the street, their faces stern, the brass buttons on their blue uniforms gleaming under the noonday sun. The familiar red and white stripes of the U.S. flag waved bravely above their heads.

"This is a disgrace." His father's voice was gritty with disgust. "A day of shame for the South."

"It's the end of the war." Relief flooded Jonah. Southerners would have to realize they could not win now. They could return to their homes, free their slaves, and vow fealty to their country.

Captain Watkins rested a hand on his sidearm. "Not quite."

What was the idiot going to do? Fight the Union all by himself? Jonah failed to see how Camellia could admire the captain.

"Come, girls. Let's get out of the street." Mother's voice was quiet, emotionless. "The rest of you should come inside, too. No need to risk being shot."

Jonah ignored her suggestion, watching until the soldiers disappeared from sight. He supposed they were headed to city hall to replace the Louisiana state flag.

It was over. Without access to the Gulf of Mexico, the blockades would succeed in stopping the movement of troops and goods. He had no doubt May 1, 1862, would go down in the history books as the day the War Between the States was won.

Camellia turned over and punched her pillow. Settling back with a sigh, she studied the ceiling and wondered why sleep was so elusive. Was it because of the soldiers they'd seen marching through the streets? What would happen tomorrow? And when would they ever get out of the city? No Confederate steamships would come; that was for certain. Not unless they intended to fight the Union navy.

According to both Jonah and Thad, all was lost for this city and probably for the war. While a part of her mourned the defeat, another part of her was glad it was ending. Maybe now her life could get back on an even keel. Thad would be able to woo her without the distraction of his military duties. Yes, the more she thought of it, the better things were looking.

She rose from her bed and looked out the window, noting the rain that had begun falling. A figure on the street caught her attention. Her hand went to her throat. The stories of looters had begun to abate, but the danger was still there. Another figure joined the first, slipping from shadow to shadow as they traveled down the street and onto the Thorntons' front lawn.

A scream rose to her throat but then halted when she saw the smaller figure raise a hand to knock on the door. Burglars wouldn't knock, would they? She ran to her bed and pulled on her dressing gown. She used the tinderbox on the mantel to light a candle then slipped out of her room, one hand guarding the flame while the other grasped the balustrade.

Light flowed up the spiral staircase, indicating the late-night visitors had roused someone in the household. Voices from below were hushed, but she heard her name clearly. The voice was familiar. Her feet moved faster, and Camellia was suddenly glad she'd been unable to sleep.

"Lily?" She reached the foyer and threw herself at her sister, excitement stripping away her decorum and the training she'd received at La Belle Demoiselle. But for the moment she didn't care. Camellia wrapped her arms around Lily and squeezed her like a fresh lemon. "What are you doing here?"

Lily returned her hug. "We came to get you, of course." Her voice choked. "Did you think we wouldn't?"

"I'm so glad you're here." She leaned back a little, her smile encompassing her brother-in-law as well.

"Why don't you come into the parlor and tell us all about it." Camellia had not realized Mrs. Thornton was in the foyer until she spoke.

Lily shook her head. "We don't have much time. You'll need to pack one set of clothing, Camellia. Your other things can come to Natchez by wagon."

"I understand."

"What? No argument?" Blake's blue gaze held a twinkle. "I'm beginning to think that school was a good idea after all."

"What's going on down here?" Jane looked down on them from the first-floor landing.

Camellia beckoned to her friend. "Come down and meet my family." She performed the introductions, leaving out the fact that Jane's brother was the man she was going to marry.

Lily and Blake exchanged a glance, some wordless communication passing between them. "We'll gladly take you with us, Miss Watkins, if you wish."

"I hate to leave, but I do think it would be best. Thank you."

"Then both of you had better get upstairs." Blake gestured toward the stairwell with his chin. "And remember you cannot bring more than one valise each."

Camellia rushed to do his bidding, wadding up underclothing, a nightgown, and a shirtwaist and stuffing them into the bag she had stored under her bed a week earlier. She dragged on her smallest hoops and tied them loosely around her waist. Her black skirt looked a little lopsided, but perhaps no one would notice.

By the time she returned to the parlor, it seemed everyone in the household was awake. Even Jonah had come over from his *garçonnier*, his auburn hair gleaming in the candlelight. He was standing in a corner of the room, talking to her brother-in-law. Was he going to come with them? The thought made her heart race.

Mr. Thornton was asking Lily about commerce north of the city, a subject that seemed unimportant to Camellia. As steeped as she had been in the standoff between the mayor and the Yankee admiral, she had forgotten the rest of the world might continue business as usual. When he saw her, however, he stopped. "I'd better call for the carriage."

Jonah raised a hand to stop his father. "I'll drive them."

"It's not too far for us to walk." Blake took Camellia's valise from her. "As soon as your friend is ready, we'll leave."

Jane entered the room as though on cue, a bit of lace trailing from her valise. "I'm here."

"I insist on taking you. It'll be much safer." Jonah straightened and moved to the door. "I'll meet everyone outside in a few minutes." Since no one argued, he disappeared through the door.

At least he would be with them a few more minutes. Now that it was time to go, sadness swept through Camellia. She hugged both of the Thorntons and thanked them for their hospitality.

Lily hugged them, too. "Are you sure you won't come with us?"

"Not now." Mr. Thornton shook his head. "Maybe in a week or two when we can be certain our daughter and our home are safe."

Blake handed the ladies into the carriage before joining Jonah up front. Since they had no lantern, Camellia knew it would take both of them to avoid obstacles.

She peppered Lily with questions on the way to the river, learning that Jensen and Tamar had stayed on board to protect the *Water Lily*. Seeing their former nanny and her husband would be more pleasant than dealing with her father once more. Odd how when she'd been wishing to sail away from New Orleans, Camellia had not once considered the most colorful member of her family. A familiar vise settled around her chest. It was a reminder of the reason she'd fled to New Orleans in the first place. How had she ever forgotten that?

Yet when she looked out the carriage window to see the white decks and tall stern-wheeler of her sister's steamship, Camellia wanted to applaud. Safety was finally within reach.

The carriage halted, and Jonah pulled open the door. Mindful of her experience the last time he'd helped her out of a vehicle, Camellia pulled back. Jonah handed Jane out. Then Blake appeared and caught Lily around the waist, pulling her out amid giggles and whispered demands that he be more serious.

Camellia rolled her eyes, but inside a part of her rejoiced to be near them once more. She moved to the door quickly and stepped down without any assistance. It might not have been her most graceful exit, but at least Jonah's touch didn't electrify her.

Her father, Jensen, and Tamar stood at the rail of the boat, waving toward the dock.

Camellia returned the gesture, moving closer to Jane. "It won't be long now before we'll be back in Confederate-controlled territory."

A grunt made Camellia look behind her. A nearby lamp played against the planes of Jonah's face, highlighting his disgust. Why? Because of her words? Even if he wouldn't fight, he still supported the Confederacy. . .didn't he? He had chosen to return here. What other reason could he have for remaining?

The answer to her question smashed into her with the force of a runaway train. He didn't like the Confederacy, was opposed to all of its goals. He didn't want independence, and he was here to make sure the Cause failed. The reason he'd come to La Belle Demoiselle so often had nothing to do with her or Jane. He had come to pass along information to Mrs. Dabbs. All the little incidents, all the glances, words, and gestures played through her mind, ending with the kiss. Was that nothing more than another of his lies?

Jane crossed the gangplank with dainty footsteps while Camellia, thoroughly shaken by the monumental realization, stared at Jonah, not wanting to believe he could have betrayed his country, his friends, his family.

"What's the matter with you?" His whisper came out sharp, like the buzz of a wasp.

Camellia shook her head. "You're a spy." She watched him carefully, hoping he would deny the accusation.

His shoulders drooped. "You don't understand anything."

No denial. No attempt to hide the truth now that it was too late for her to do anything about it. "I ought to send a note to Thad."

"Camellia, my work here is done. The city is in the hands of the United States."

"If not for people like you and Mrs. Dabbs, New Orleans might still be safe."

"Or thousands could be dead, including my family." He sighed. "Why do you think Farragut has not bombarded us with his cannons?"

He stepped closer to her, wrapping his hands around her upper arms and squeezing them with gentle strength. "Because of people like me who assured him there's no need. You haven't seen the horrors of war. . .the destruction and death. What I've done has spared New Orleans. Can't you see that?"

Madness. Even now, even when she knew how he had lied to her, Camellia wanted to lean into him. She wanted to rest her head against his broad chest and let his argument convince her. But she couldn't. "I see nothing but your betrayal of the people who care for you." She stepped back, wondering if he would try to stop her.

But he released his hold on her arms. "I wish you weren't going. Not now. Not like this."

The words were soft, tempting. Like the look on his face. But what could she believe from a man who lied to everyone around him?

Camellia grabbed her skirts and ran across the gangplank, eager to put physical distance between them. Tamar was there, and Camellia fell into the older woman's arms, thankful for the familiar welcome from the woman who had raised her and her sisters. But the ache in her chest did not ease. Overwhelmed by a loss she didn't completely understand, Camellia sobbed into Tamar's collar.

"There, there." Tamar patted her back. "You're safe now, dearest."

The words were empty to Camellia. In the last few days, everything had changed. Two people very close to her—her teacher and her. . .what was Jonah to her exactly?—had proven to be the opposite of what she had thought. She didn't think she would ever feel safe again.

Chapter Twenty-one

"You're here!" A feminine squeal split the morning air, and weight landed on Camellia's bed.

Disoriented for a moment by the familiar walls of the bedroom she had grown up in, Camellia squinted at the dark-haired girl perched on her bed. Almond-shaped eyes the color of violets stared back at her. "Jasmine."

It was the only encouragement her younger sister needed to launch herself at Camellia and envelop her in a tight embrace.

The nightmare of the dark journey home began to fade. She was home. Home where everything was still normal. The scourge of war and soldiers and traitorous spies had not touched Natchez, and she hoped it never would.

Emerging from Jasmine's hug, Camellia leaned back and stretched her arms over her head. "What time is it?"

"Noon."

The single word caught her in midyawn. "It can't be that late."

"Grandmother said we should let everyone sleep this morning." Jasmine hopped off the bed and went to the pair of long windows on the far side of the bed. She pulled back the claret-hued curtains, and golden sunlight flooded the bedroom. "But everyone else is up, even your friend Miss Watkins. So Aunt Dahlia said I could come wake you."

Camellia pushed back the quilt and swung her legs over the edge of the bed. "Find something for me to wear, please. I had to leave nearly everything in New Orleans."

"There should be an old outfit around here somewhere." Jasmine moved to the bureau, opening and closing drawers in her search.

Surveying the familiar room, Camellia was comforted by the floral wallpaper, marble mantel, cane-backed chair, and dressing table. It was good to be home. She sat in front of the mirror and unbraided her hair.

"You don't look much different." Jasmine held up a white shirtwaist and a gray wool skirt with a patched hem. "What did you learn at that fancy school?"

"Too much to tell you about right now." Camellia dragged a brush through her hair to remove snarls. "Where are the servants?"

"Uncle Phillip said they were a danger, what with all the rumors of an uprising, so he shipped them to some island in the Caribbean."

The brush halted. Obviously not all things had remained the same during her absence. "Who does the chores?"

"Cook is still here, and we hire out some of the work, like the laundry." Jasmine took the brush from her hand and started pulling back the curly locks. "I help Grandmother with her buttons, and all of us have chores in the house. When Lily and Blake are here, things are much easier."

"What about the fields? Surely we are not reduced to picking cotton or cutting sugar cane."

"No, silly." Jasmine giggled. "Uncle Phillip hires workers, some black, some white. Everyone who has not gone to fight in the war needs work. Everything has gotten very dear because of the blockade."

"Why didn't anyone tell me what was going on?" Camellia thought of the letters she had received. Not a hint of any troubles had been apparent. Feeling chastised and a little miffed, she dressed in silence.

Jasmine continued chattering, however, apparently unaware of her sister's emotions.

As they trod downstairs, Camellia trailed her hand along the rail of the stairwell, noticing it lacked its usual glossy sheen. Would she be reduced to dusting the woodwork and polishing the silver?

A vision formed in her imagination. She wore an apron and carried a dustpan in one hand and a broom in the other as she welcomed guests to Les Fleurs. What kind of suitor could she hope to attract in such a situation? Maybe Aunt Dahlia could give her some advice.

Feeling a tiny bit better, Camellia took a deep breath, threw back her shoulders, and followed her sister into the front parlor. Whatever the future held, she would face it with the aplomb and gentility she had learned at La Belle Demoiselle.

❧

Camellia set the pitcher of lemonade on the tray and picked it up with both hands.

"You sure you can handle that by yourself?" Tamar watched her with a doubtful expression on her face.

"Don't worry. I made the lemonade, didn't I?" Proud of her accomplishment, Camellia walked out of the kitchen and around the side of the house to take the refreshment to Aunt Dahlia and Jane on the front porch. She kept one eye on the grass and the other on the slices of lemon threatening to slosh over the top of the pitcher. Arriving without mishap, she set the laden tray onto the table between the rockers.

Aunt Dahlia was crocheting a doily while Jane was working on the sampler she'd managed to bring with her from New Orleans two days earlier.

"There you are." Aunt Dahlia pulled on the spindle of white thread and continued looping it. "I was about to come in search of you."

Camellia shook her head, and several ringlets came loose. She swept them away from her face with an impatient hand. "I hope I didn't keep you waiting too long."

"Not at all." Jane put her sampler in her lap and smiled. "Your timing is impeccable as always."

The sound of an approaching horse stopped Camellia's answer as she turned to see who was coming up the drive. Gray fronds of Spanish moss obscured the rider as he rode between the oak trees that lined both sides of the path, but she could tell he was a soldier from the gray uniform he wore. She raised a hand to shade her eyes.

Jane gasped. "It's Thad." Her needlework hit the floor as she jumped from the rocker and raced down the steps just as Thad reached the house.

He dismounted and held out his arms, folding them around his sister and dropping a kiss on her head.

"Well." Disapproval filled the single syllable from Aunt Dahlia.

"Captain Watkins is Jane's brother," Camellia explained as she smiled on the two of them.

"Oh. I should have noticed the resemblance right away."

Camellia nodded and descended the steps with less exuberance than her friend had showed. But she didn't try to hide her pleasure.

The captain kept one arm around his sister but bowed to her. "I'm happy to see you and my sister are safe."

"I could say the same about you. When we left New Orleans, we didn't know if you would be taken prisoner by the Yankees."

"Were you worried about me, Miss Anderson?"

Jane rolled her eyes. "Of course she was. We all were. I hated leaving you, but when Camellia's family asked me to accompany them, I thought it best to go."

He squeezed his sister once more before letting go of her. "Thank you for making sure she is safe."

Camellia's cheeks warmed under his approving gaze. "L–Let me introduce you to my aunt."

Captain Watkins tucked his cap under one arm and followed the two of them to the front porch.

Camellia performed the introductions and served lemonade as Jane peppered him with questions.

Aunt Dahlia's fingers once again twisted her thread as her rocker moved back and forth. "I still cannot believe the Yankees have taken New Orleans."

"It should not have happened." The captain shook his head, a mixture of sadness and anger pulling at his features. "But now we must concentrate on taking it back into the Confederacy and regaining our base of operations there."

Hope blossomed in Camellia. "I knew all was not lost."

"No, indeed." He sipped from his glass. "Our first step will be to retake Forts Jackson and St. Phillips to the south. Once we cut off the support of the ships that have their guns trained on the city, they will realize their mistake and withdraw."

"Is that the mission that brings you to us, Captain?" Aunt Dahlia stopped her handwork for a moment while she waited for his answer.

Thad looked down at his glass of lemonade. "I really can't talk about my mission. I hope you understand."

"Of course we do." Jane reached for his hand.

Aunt Dahlia frowned. "Do you think we cannot hold our tongues?"

It was time to turn the conversation in a different direction. Camellia leaned forward. "Thank you so much for sending Jonah Thornton to collect us after Mrs. Dabbs was arrested."

One of Thad's eyebrows rose. "What?"

Camellia should have known. Jonah had lied even about that. He had not one truthful bone in his whole traitorous body. Her mouth tightened. "I thought Jonah said you had sent him a note. I must have misunderstood."

His gaze remained on her a few moments.

During that time, the temptation to blurt out the truth was strong. But she could not do it. What would happen to Mr. and Mrs. Thornton once New Orleans was retaken by the Confederates? Would they pay the price for their son's stupidity? She couldn't afford the luxury of confessing what she knew to Thad. He would be honor bound to pass the information along to his superiors. No, this was one secret she had to keep.

"You will not believe how harrowing our trip to Natchez was." Jane's statement ended the uncomfortable moment. She began to describe the way she and Camellia had boarded the *Water Lily* and the trip through the darkness.

The captain listened intently, making exclamations at the right points and sitting back when she finished. "I can only conclude that God was on your side."

"My papa is a very religious man," Camellia offered. "Perhaps his prayers were heard."

"He is a very sweet man, too." Jane smiled in her direction. "But Camellia's whole family is wonderful. They've taken me in without complaint."

"I'm glad for that, Sister, but I can get you a berth on the boat that will take me north. I know you're enjoying your visit to this beautiful home, but our parents must be worried about your welfare."

Camellia sent a desperate look toward her friend. Without Jane around, what would she do with her time?

Before she could express her concern, the other women in her family came outside, and Captain Watkins stood. She cringed at Lily's brown skin, but at least Grandmother and Jasmine looked presentable. Performing the introductions, Camellia watched the captain's reactions, pleased when he seemed so accepting, even of Lily's life on a steamboat.

If this was a test, he had passed it with flying colors. Aunt Dahlia smiled at her, her meaning clear. Captain Watkins was an excellent candidate for a husband.

Looking back at Thad, she wondered. Only a few short weeks ago she would have agreed. He was handsome, polite, wealthy—all the things a girl should want in a husband. Of course he was the perfect mate. A Confederate soldier for goodness' sake. He was exactly the man she'd always dreamed of marrying. Wasn't he?

Chapter Twenty-two

This riverboat was more spacious than the *Water Lily*. Camellia's fingers straightened the sterling knife on the right side of her plate. It caught the light of the chandelier above their table, almost seeming to throw off sparks as it moved. The linen cloth covering the table was spotless, the crystal sparkled, and the china was decorated with a delicate floral design. Aboard the *Kosciusko* she could almost forget the war that had wrought such change in her life.

A white-gloved hand filled her goblet with water and then withdrew. Another hand, this one female, removed her napkin from the table, shook it, and placed it on Camellia's lap. She could grow used to such deference. It was much better than having to clean dirty dishes as she'd once done aboard her sister's boat.

"I'm honored your family entrusted me with your care." Thad's voice brought her out of the past.

Camellia smiled at him. "I'm honored to be escorted by a true hero of the Confederacy."

"I don't know about all that." He looked troubled, as though uncertain of himself. Or was he concerned for the future?

The desire to ease his concerns filled her. Was this what it would feel like to be married? Being a helpmeet to such an honorable man would be a wonderful way to spend her life.

His hand rested on the table next to the assortment of forks on the left side of his plate.

Camellia reached to pick up her goblet and let her hand brush against his. The contact brought a sense of daring. . .but no romantic thrill. Thad's eyebrows climbed up toward his hairline, and a blush heated her cheeks. She had been too forward.

"I haven't written to our parents." Jane's voice came from Thad's far side. "They're going to be surprised when we show up on their doorstep."

Thad turned away from her to answer his sister's comment.

Camellia took a deep breath and brought her goblet to her lips. As she sipped the cool water, she wondered if her misstep would cause him to reconsider his pursuit. The platters of food on the laden table lost their appeal. What if Thad considered her too forward?

A young man on her left cleared his throat and asked her to pass the saltcellar. Camellia complied. He looked about her age, his cheeks still showing the roundness of youth. His auburn hair gleamed richly in the glow from the chandelier. He looked like a younger, more innocent version of Jonah Thornton, bringing a smile to her face. He blushed and shook a copious amount of salt on his serving of roast duck. The incident reminded her of the usual effect her attention had on members of the opposite sex. If she set her mind to it, she could certainly win her way back into Thad's affections.

"Where are you going?" The young man's voice cracked in the middle of his query.

"I'm visiting friends in Vicksburg."

He looked taken aback by her answer. "This is a perilous time to be making social visits."

Camellia dabbed her mouth with her napkin as she considered him, watching as his cheeks turned a deeper shade of red. "Our escort will see that we arrive safely at our destination."

"Of course." The young man took a bite of his dinner. An expression of shock widened his eyes.

Camellia watched as his Adam's apple worked up and down and the corners of his mouth turned down. She hid her smile and took pity on him. Looking behind her at the line of white-coated servers, she signaled to one and asked for a fresh plate.

He threw her a thankful glance and started his dinner afresh, paying much closer attention to the amount of salt he applied to his food.

When dinner was over, Jane and Camellia joined the other ladies in their lounge.

"How much longer will our trip be?" Jane settled in one of the upholstered chairs.

Camellia shrugged as she sat next to her. "It depends on how many stops the captain makes, but we should arrive before dark."

"I hope so." A short, older lady sniffed. "All of our lives are in danger from those marauding Yankees, especially after dark."

"My brother, an officer, is aboard." Jane crossed her legs at the ankles. "He'll make sure no one gets aboard without proper papers."

"I'm scared, Ma." A young girl with brown hair the color of Mississippi mud buried her face in her mother's lap. "I don't want them Yankees to get me."

A black woman in a dark dress and starched apron entered the room with a laden tea tray balanced in her hands.

Camellia waited for her to put the tray on the low table in the middle of the room and then depart before answering. "You don't have to worry about Yankees. Did you see all the men in their handsome uniforms at dinner? They'll protect us."

"That's right." Her mother stroked her daughter's hair. "And you remember what your pa said about them old Yankees. It'll take a dozen of them to fight just one of our soldiers. If they see how many we have on board with us, they'll run away and hide."

Camellia thought of Jonah. He was the only Yankee she knew. But was a Yankee sympathizer the same thing as a Yankee soldier? She thought of his strength of character and his physical prowess. If Jonah was typical of the caliber of man fighting for the North, they were in for a desperate fight.

Even if he wasn't, the rebel forces had run when the Yankees showed up with one little boat at the dock in New Orleans. The soldiers at Fort Jackson and Fort St. Philip had also surrendered without a fight. They had not even tried to stop the Yankee navy from steaming up the river to take the city.

Maybe what this mother was saying to her child was wrong. Camellia was beginning to wonder if it took a dozen Confederates to overcome one Yankee. And if that was the way of it, they would all be Yankees before long.

❧

"Natchez has fallen." Thad crumpled the newspaper between his hands and threw it into the fireplace. "I cannot believe they didn't fight. Why have the cannons on the bluff if they are not going to use them?"

Camellia's stomach knotted. She felt as though they were running across a bridge that was disintegrating immediately behind them. If Natchez had fallen, would Vicksburg be next? She looked at Jane and her mother and saw the same fear mirrored on their faces.

"I must go on to Memphis immediately." Thad's announcement made all three of the women gasp. "The Confederacy needs every able-bodied man now."

"But what will happen to us?" His mother rose and moved across the room to stare out the window of her home.

Camellia knew she was not really looking at the rolling hills outside or the well-tended grounds surrounding her plantation. The faint movement of the older woman's shoulders indicated that she was choking back tears.

Jane got up and went to her, putting an arm around her mother's tiny waist. "It's going to be all right, Mama. I'm here now. You won't be alone."

"No." Mrs. Watkins broke away from her daughter and turned from the window. She faced her son with a determined look. "You must take Jane and Camellia with you."

Thad frowned. "Impossible. I won't be able to protect them once I have rejoined my regiment."

"The danger from the encroaching navy is greater. If they continue to advance this quickly, it won't be long before they are knocking on my door."

Camellia considered their options. There must be some place they could go. Would Lily and Blake come to Vicksburg to rescue them as they had in New Orleans? It might be better to wait here and see. Thinking of her sister put her in mind of stops they had made in the past. "I have it."

All three of the Watkinses turned to her.

"Mr. and Mrs. Thornton have a son in Memphis. Eli and his wife, Renée, will take us in. Surely we'll be safe with them." She turned to Mrs. Watkins. "You can go with us, too."

Mrs. Watkins's lips turned up, but sadness filled her eyes. "I cannot leave my home."

"Mama, you can't stay here alo—" A catch in Jane's voice stopped her for a moment. She gulped and raised her chin before continuing. "It won't be safe for you if the Yankees really do come."

"Don't worry about me. Your father will have returned from Barbados before long. I am determined that he will have a home to return to." Mrs. Watkins took a deep breath and nodded. "I'll keep everything running here."

"Then I won't leave you behind." Jane was a younger version of her mother's determination.

Camellia could feel pride and admiration filling her. The women of the Confederacy were as strong in their way as their husbands and sons.

"Don't be silly." Mrs. Watkins summoned a frown for her daughter. "I can manage here until your father returns, and I will sleep much better knowing you and Camellia are safe."

"I think Mama is right." Thad nodded. "You and Camellia can come with me to Memphis. I'll make sure you are safe with Camellia's friends. Once the South has retaken Natchez, Baton Rouge, and New Orleans, you can return. I'm certain it will only be a matter of days or weeks before things return to normal. As soon as our troops arrive from Virginia, we'll push those Yankees out of our waterways and restore order."

Camellia smiled in his direction. As long as men like Thad were in charge, she could rest easy. The South would overcome even these dark days. "I'll write a message to my family in Natchez. I don't know if packets will be allowed back into the city, but in case they are, I would like them to know where they can find me."

Mrs. Watkins smiled in her direction. "They will appreciate any news. I know how much I awaited letters from Jane and Thad when we were apart."

Jane sighed. "I can't believe we need to pack our belongings so soon."

"Limit yourselves to one trunk each." Thad raised his eyebrows toward his sister.

Camellia's mind flew back in time. Her cheeks burned at the memory of Jonah's incredulous voice as he surveyed the mountain of luggage she'd packed for the weekend with his parents. What innocent days those seemed in retrospect, when all she had to worry about was fashion and etiquette.

Well, she knew better now. A lady might desire all the comforts of home when traveling, but as long as she had a few basic necessities, she could get by. Camellia wondered what new lessons she would learn as the war dragged on. And what her life would look like once the fighting finally ended. Would she find herself married to Thad or someone like him? Or would she remain single, becoming a burden to her family as her beauty faded?

Everything seemed to be careening out of control. As she prepared to flee once more, Camellia found herself wishing for stability and some measure of normalcy. She wished to return to the past. She even wished for the days she'd spent with her sisters aboard Lily's boat.

Given her disdain for life on the river, she could imagine the shock her sisters would exhibit if they had any inkling of her thoughts. But that did not protect her from the yearning inside her, a yearning for something she would probably never again enjoy.

Chapter Twenty-three

Jonah's heart thudded in his chest as he made out the shape of four, no, five Union ironclads. Their armored plates and bristling gun ports became more distinct as the sky lightened. He prayed the Confederate officers would realize the overwhelming odds against them and surrender. If they did not, the South would lose many brave men in the ensuing battle. And he might be one of them since his officers had once again sent him into enemy territory as a spy. That was how he found himself on this Confederate ship, locked in a fierce battle near Memphis.

The eastern horizon glowed pink as the sun began to rise, but before it could make its appearance, the boom of a cannon drew his attention. A deadly whistle accompanied it as the missile passed over their heads and crashed into the bank behind their cotton-clad ram.

Jonah prayed for God's protection. It was the only thing that would keep them alive on their outgunned, out-armored boat.

"Man your stations." The command from above sent him and the other sailors running.

Another explosion rent the air. Another missile whistled past them. But when it splashed into the water, Jonah could tell it was closer than the first shot. The Yankees were closing in. They would sink this ship in a matter of minutes.

"Cannoners post!" At least he wasn't part of the seven-man team who would have to man the cannons on either end of the ship. "Solid shot load!"

The deck shuddered under Jonah's feet as twin explosions announced their intention to fight. The sky above was filled with smoke so dense and gray he could no longer tell the time of day.

Jonah wondered if he should jump overboard and take his chances in the strong currents of the river. Or should he remain aboard and try to convince the commander to surrender? The side of the Union ironclad expanded, growing larger and larger until he could see nothing but its dark hull in front and above them. Too late. He was too late to do any good at all.

"Brace for impact," the Confederate officer warned the crew.

Jonah slung his rifle over one shoulder and wrapped his arms around the tall mast at the stern. He closed his eyes and prayed, the words lost in the sounds of battle raging around him. Then it happened. As their prow rammed into the side of the ironclad, a cannon found them. It slammed through the tall stacks of cotton and pierced the deck with devastating results.

Water gushed upward in a dirty fountain as it mixed with coal, splintered wood, and blood. Jonah tried to hold on to the mast, but he was thrown away from it like a droplet of water shaken from a dog's back. He scrambled for another purchase as he slid headfirst toward the edge of the steamship. In the last possible instant, his questing fingers latched onto something. What they found was not important. What mattered was that he had not plunged into the muddy water between the two ships. That way was certain death.

Another barrage of cannon fire warned him the danger was not past. Screams of fear and pain were punctuated by the endless booms of the cannons. He managed to drag himself to his knees and look around. The deck was on fire, and he saw several men lowering buckets to the river. The attempt to stop the deadly flames was doomed. The ship was sinking faster than he would have thought possible. He had failed, completely and utterly. He would not be able to save a single life.

Explosions rocked the water around them, but at least the ironclad had drawn back some. It gave the sailors a better chance to escape in the river without being caught up in the churning water of the paddle wheels or rammed by the heavy hulls. As he crossed to the starboard side of the boat, a groan stopped him.

Jonah glanced around, his eyes streaming from the thick smoke enveloping the ship. At first he saw nothing, but then the groan came again, and he saw a slight movement to his right. A young man, a boy really, lay on the deck, his legs pinned beneath the heavy mast that must have broken during the battle. Jonah fell to his knees to assess the situation.

"I think my leg's broke." The boy coughed. "I don't wanta die."

"You're not going to die." Jonah made the promise even though he had no idea how to keep it. He glanced around them, looking for something to use as a lever. Several men staggered past them, but no one stopped. Each was fighting to save his life, climbing to the far side of the boat as it listed at an ever-steeper angle.

Remembering the rifle on his back, Jonah pulled it forward and wedged it under the mast. Pushing with all of his strength, he managed to move it an inch. "Can you move?"

The boy stopped moaning and pushed up onto his elbows. He managed to move a few inches. The battle faded around them as hope shone on his face. After a few minutes of sweating and grunting, he pulled free.

Jonah released his hold on the mast with relief. Placing an arm around the boy, he helped him stand. "Is it broken?"

The boy shook his head.

"Praise God."

They limped together to the edge. The black water of the river was full—bobbing heads, debris, oil. Jonah took a deep breath, pushed the boy, and jumped. Water closed around his head, and the whine of bullets whizzed past him. Fear pushed him forward. Something slammed against his legs, catching him and trying to drag him under. Then another obstacle hit his shoulders, his chest, his head. Jonah couldn't tell any longer which direction he should be swimming. His lungs ached to breathe. It was done. Fear was replaced by sadness that he had failed to do so many things.

"*Today shalt thou be with me in paradise.*" The promise brought peace and acceptance to Jonah as he lost consciousness.

❧

Camellia thought Thad was as handsome in regular clothes as when he donned his uniform. But on this voyage, he was in disguise. If the packet they were traveling on was stopped by Union forces, he would appear to be nothing more than an escort for his sister and her. Of course anyone searching his bags would know better, but that was a remote possibility since this portion of the river was still controlled by the Confederacy.

She watched the way he sipped coffee from a china cup. His exceptional manners were apparent even in this prosaic setting. Their breakfast came without frills—black coffee, dry biscuits, and a piece of jerked pork that Camellia had no intention of touching. She crumbled the edge of her cold biscuit with a thumb and finger. "When should we arrive in Memphis?"

"Later than I had hoped." He set down his cup and smiled in her direction. "The captain delayed our departure because of a rumor that the Union navy is headed this way."

Jane pushed her plate to one side, apparently as unimpressed as Camellia with the plain fare. "I hope we have not made a mistake to leave Mama alone in Vicksburg."

"I worry about her, too." Thad's brows lowered. "But she was quite insistent."

Silence enveloped them. Camellia wondered about her own family. The reports from Natchez were encouraging. . .as encouraging as possible considering they were in the hands of the enemy. Since the town had surrendered without a fight, most homes were safe. No casualties, no injuries. While a part of her wished the city council had not given up so easily, she was relieved at the lack of bloodshed.

Shouts from outside drew her attention to the window. Crewmen ran back and forth, pointing at something in the river.

She pushed her chair back and stood, aware that both Thad and Jane had done the same. "What's happened?"

"I have no idea." Thad strode to the door and opened it.

Camellia and Jane stood immediately behind him, both trying to hear what was being said.

Someone was in the river.

"We have to help the poor soul." She tried to push past Thad.

"Wait, Camellia." Thad put a hand on her arm. "This could be a ruse to draw passengers out where they can be picked off by sharpshooters in the woods."

Her heart faltered, but then she frowned. "If that's the case, it seems they would have picked off a few of the crewmen already." Pulling her arm free of his grip, Camellia stepped to the edge of the boat. What she saw made her stomach heave. A gray uniform was draped across a large tree trunk floating in the water. The poor soldier's head hung down, hiding his face, but she would recognize those distinctive auburn curls anywhere. She ran to one of the crewmen who had a boat hook in his hand. "Please help him. I know that man."

"What?" Thad had followed her outside.

"Yes." She pointed at the form as it drew even with the boat. "That's Jonah Thornton."

The captain shouted an order to halt the boat while the crewman snagged Jonah's sleeve.

Camellia winced as they dragged his limp body aboard. Was he dead? Her heart stopped beating at the thought. He couldn't be dead. Half-forgotten prayers surfaced as the men laid him on his back. Jonah's face was as white as fish scales, and his eyelids remained closed. Was he breathing?

Ignoring her hoops, Camellia dropped to the deck next to him and took Jonah's cold hand in her own. "Bring me some blankets." She put her head against his chest and listened, not daring to draw a breath for fear of missing some evidence of life.

Dimly, slowly, his heartbeat sounded. He was alive.

"Thank You, God," she whispered as someone spread a blanket over him.

"What's wrong with him?" Jane stood next to her. "Is he dead?"

Camellia shook her head. She didn't see any evidence of a gunshot wound. "His heart's beating."

Thad pulled her up and took her place on the deck, sliding his arms under Jonah's shoulders. "Someone take his legs. Let's get this man to a bed."

Camellia and Jane followed him, their hands linked.

"What on earth is Jonah doing here?" Jane's question echoed her own. "And why is he in uniform? I thought he wasn't the fighting type."

If he had decided to join the army, he certainly wouldn't have joined the Confederacy. Not when his convictions had led him to spy on his friends and neighbors. He was a traitor. His uniform was more likely a disguise to allow him to infiltrate new areas and send vital information to the Union. She should be glad he was wounded. In fact, she ought to be hoping for his demise. But though Camellia considered herself a patriot, she could not go that far.

Thad carried Jonah into a room reserved for passengers. "You girls stay out here."

Camellia opened her mouth to argue, but seeing the look on Thad's face, she remained silent.

"Trust me. I'll take care of your friend and let you know how he's doing." He kicked the door closed.

Jane pulled on Camellia's hand. "Let's go back upstairs. Maybe we can learn more about what's going on while Thad sees to Jonah."

They climbed the stairs to the main deck. Only a handful of passengers had joined them on this trip. They stood in a cluster at the bow of the boat, whispering and pointing at something in the water. Did someone else need to be rescued?

Camellia stepped to the rail, relieved when she saw that a small fishing boat had pulled up alongside the packet. "What's going on?"

"There's been a huge battle at Memphis." A man with a large mustache pulled off his spectacles and wiped them with a handkerchief before continuing. "The Confederate navy was scuttled in little more than an hour."

Jane gasped, and Camellia felt like crying. Their hope for a safe harbor had been snatched from them once again. What would they do now?

Chapter Twenty-Four

No doctor traveled with them, so nursing their half-drowned passenger fell to Jane and Camellia. As the men discussed the next move to be taken, the two friends cleaned the scrapes and scratches on Jonah's face and limbs. After an hour or so, Camellia sent Jane to find out what was going on while she stayed behind to watch over Jonah.

He was so still she could hardly believe he was still alive. Yet she could see the faint rise and fall of his chest under the bedcovers. If he would simply open his eyes and smile at her. Her anger and frustration faded away as she sat next to his bed and watched him breathe. She wanted him to wake up, if only so she could turn him over to Thad.

That would serve Jonah right. While she might be able to admire him for standing up for his principles and joining the wrong side of the war, she could not understand how he could reconcile those same principles to the lies he'd told his family and friends while he spied on them. She could only conclude he had no principles at all. So why did she want him to awaken so desperately?

The door opened, and Jane entered. "They've decided to remain here for the rest of the day and await further news."

Camellia wondered what they hoped to hear. Did they think the original report of complete defeat was wrong? The fishermen had seemed to her to have very detailed information about the battle just north of Memphis, including the number and names of the Union ironclads.

"How's our patient?"

"Much the same." Camellia dipped her cloth in a bowl beside the bed and wrung it out before placing it on Jonah's forehead again. "He still won't awaken."

"Don't worry." Jane hugged her before slipping into the chair on the opposite side of Jonah's bed. "He's strong. I'm sure he'll pull through."

"I hope you're right."

Silence invaded the room. As the day wore on, Camellia prayed. She tried to bargain with God, but she could not think of anything to offer Him equal to Jonah's life.

Jane cleared her throat. "You should get something to eat."

"I'm fine." The growl of her stomach belied her words, but Camellia ignored the sound. "Why don't you take a break?"

The door opened, and Thad's shoulders filled the space. "Is he any better?"

"He's no worse," Jane answered for both of them.

"Perhaps in his mind he's still in the belly of the whale."

Camellia looked up at Thad's words. "Like Jonah in the Bible?"

Thad nodded. "Jonah of Nineveh spent three days and three nights there. Maybe your friend is frightened of waking up and finding himself swallowed alive. Maybe he'll wake up in a few days all rested and ready to return to the fighting."

Her heart took wing, and Camellia sent a grateful smile toward Thad. "I hope you're right."

He held out a hand to her. "I'm sure that's all it is. We found no sign of a serious injury. Jonah Thornton is just showing us how stubborn he is."

Camellia allowed him to pull her up.

"I think it's time you took a break."

"I'm fine."

"I know that very well, Miss Camellia Anderson." He smiled down at her. "Few women would expend so much energy over an unresponsive soldier. You're a shining example of patience and hope. But even though you are very fine indeed, I believe you should come with me now for a walk around the deck. Jane will let us know if Jonah's situation changes."

Allowing herself to be pulled out of the room was a little like departing from her family when she left to attend finishing school. But she knew Thad was right. She had been stooped over Jonah's bed for hours. With one last glance at his pale face, she turned and left on Thad's arm. As she walked, the knots and kinks in her back, arms, and chest began to loosen. "Have you any more news?"

"Yes, and it's not good."

Camellia felt her worries descend once more. "What will we do? Where can we go that is safe?"

"The captain has an idea about that." He patted the hand resting on his arm. "Are you familiar with Jacksonport in Arkansas?"

She shook her head. "Where is it?"

"It's on the White River. We'll overnight here and return south tomorrow to the place where the White River empties into the Mississippi. As soon as we leave the main course of the river, I think we'll be safer. Although we'll have to take our time and make sure the Yankees haven't gotten ahead of us once more, it should be an uneventful voyage. And the advantage is that the passengers can disembark there. I can join the forces in Jacksonport and return to my duties knowing you and Jane are safe."

Camellia nodded. Perhaps Jacksonport boasted a doctor who would know how to treat Jonah's injuries.

As though he could read her mind, Thad sent a keen glance in her direction. "I know you and Jane are not experienced nurses, but I appreciate your efforts with Mr. Thornton. Who knows? One day I may be the unconscious soldier in need of care." He raised her hand to his lips and pressed a warm kiss on it. "I would like to think it might come from someone as lovely and caring as you."

Blushing, Camellia looked away. If only Thad realized what kind of man Jonah really was, he'd probably throw him back into the river. But she couldn't tell him what she knew about Jonah. The information she was hiding from Thad was like a wall between them. A wall she wasn't sure she wanted to breach.

❧

The little packet crept around the curves in the river, sliding down its length like a snake, taking to the bayous whenever other boats were spotted.

Camellia kept watch over Jonah, but he remained unchanged. This morning Jane had brought her sewing basket with her and was even now busily plying her needle. Wishing for something to divert her own attention, Camellia decided to go look for writing paper and a pen. She could send word to her family of her whereabouts so they wouldn't worry.

"I'll be back in a few moments." She spoke in a normal voice. Perhaps they were being too quiet in the room since they wanted Jonah to awaken.

Jane nodded.

Camellia walked down the passageway of the small boat and decided to take a turn on the lower deck to breathe some fresh air. The river here was so wide it looked like a long lake. Oak, walnut, sweet gum, and magnolia trees shaded the banks, their wide trunks making a convenient cover for their boat. Of course, they also provided excellent hiding places for ambushes. Even though the day was warm, her thoughts made the skin on her arms prickle.

"We're about to reach the mouth of the White River." Thad's deep voice made her jump. "I'm sorry, I didn't mean to startle you."

A giggle threatened to escape, but Camellia managed to choke it down. "It wasn't your fault. It's just so quiet. I was thinking about soldiers hiding in the woods with their rifles trained on us." She leaned against the rail and tried to see past the wall of hardwoods.

Thad moved closer, his arm brushing hers.

A tingle that had nothing to do with warfare spread from her fingers upward, and Camellia caught her breath. Was she actually beginning to feel something truly romantic for Thad?

If he noticed, he said nothing.

They stood that way for several minutes, neither speaking, as the river widened even further. The riverboat turned westward and poured steam into its engines to break free of the Mississippi's powerful current. After several moments, the water narrowed, the trees closing in on either side of them.

A crewman appeared with a sounding weight and began taking readings, calling out the depths in a distinct voice so the captain could avoid shallows and sandbars. From having watched her own father on Lily's steamship, Camellia knew this captain would also be keeping an eye out for snags formed by fallen trees and floating debris.

The thrash of the paddle wheel faded into the background as the sounds of the swamp surrounded them. The plop of alligators and snakes falling into the water as they fled for safer bayous. The caw of birds warning their brethren of approaching danger. The scream of a large cat, either a panther or a bobcat. The swamp was a place of darkness, danger, and mystery.

Camellia moved a tiny bit closer to Thad for security, her heart thundering. She didn't like swamps.

Thad slid an arm around her and pulled her close. His presence was warm and reassuring. His closeness calmed her heart and allowed her to breathe more easily.

She let her head fall onto his shoulder, so tired from her vigil at Jonah's bedside that she didn't give a thought to the impropriety of her action. Or what signal she was sending to Thad.

His hand under her chin should have been a warning. When Camellia looked up to see what he needed, she realized what was happening. Thad's gaze scalded her, setting off a warning in her head. But it was too late for her to fight now. Besides, wasn't this what she wanted? Thad was an honorable man. Kissing her would be tantamount to a betrothal. She would become Mrs. Thad Watkins, perhaps before they even returned to the waters of the Mississippi.

So why did her body stiffen in protest? Why did she pull free of his embrace? Why did she lower her head and turn away? Camellia couldn't understand the instinct, but she also couldn't resist it. "I–I'm sorry."

"Camellia, forgive me." He reached for her. "I didn't mean any disrespect."

"I know you didn't." She twisted her hands together and wished she had never left Jonah's side. "Let's just forget about this. We can go on as before, can't we?"

Confusion filled his handsome face. He opened his mouth, but before he could put his thoughts into words, a shout interrupted them.

"Torpedo!"

The single word made him turn his attention to the water. What had almost happened was forgotten as they both searched for a glimpse of the threat.

"There it is."

Camellia squinted. All she could see was an empty barrel floating on the surface of the water some distance away. It didn't look particularly dangerous to her.

"Get back inside." Thad shouted the command at her as he rushed up to the hurricane deck. "All stop. All stop!"

Curiosity kept her at the rail. The paddle wheel fell silent, but they continued drifting toward the barrel, their forward motion stronger than the river's current.

Thad ran back downstairs with a bundle of dyed cloth in his arms. He didn't slow down to tell her again to leave the deck, instead running to the flagpole. With efficient movements, he lowered the white flag they had been flying and tied on the corners of the material from his bundle below it. She watched as his strong arms worked the ropes and a new flag spread out over his head.

It took her a moment to realize what Thad had done. A bright red background was crossed by a blue X with white stars on it, the flag of the Confederacy. Thad was flying their true colors, hoping the torpedo was being manned by a Confederate soldier.

She held her breath as they drew even with the barrel. It scraped the hull of the packet, the sound distinctive in the thick air, but it didn't explode. Then they were past it.

Camellia closed her eyes for a moment. She was thankful Thad was so smart. If not for his quick action, they might now be sinking into a watery grave.

Two near disasters in such a short time weakened her knees. She needed time to calm her emotions. To think about what had almost happened.

She ought to linger on the deck and see if Thad returned to take up the conversation about their future. But she took the cowardly route, returning to her room.

How could she explain her muddled feelings to him when she didn't understand them herself? Thad was everything she'd dreamed of, but was he the right man for her?

Chapter Twenty-five

Jonah floated in inky blackness, the screams of dying men all around him. It was too much to bear. The pain was physical and emotional as well. He didn't want to live any longer. He wanted to join those who had gone before him. Jonah wanted to sing in a celestial choir and walk on streets of gold. He wanted to enter the mansion Jesus had prepared for him.

The first emotion to hit him as he opened his eyes was disappointment. Heaven should not be dark. He turned his head and was surprised to see Camellia sitting beside him. What was she doing here? She was far too young, so full of life and beauty. "Are you dead, too?" His voice was cracked and dry, a mere shadow of what it had once been.

But the sound seemed to please Camellia. Her mouth widened in a smile, a genuine smile of gratitude and happiness. Her warmth eased some of his physical pain. "Of course not, and neither are you." She reached for his hand, her fingers encircling his wrist, causing his pulse to skyrocket.

"I don't understand."

"I'm not surprised." Camellia let go of his hand and shook a finger at him. "You had us terrified that you wouldn't wake up at all. You didn't seem to be seriously hurt, but you wouldn't wake up even for meals."

"How long have I been asleep?" He tried to prop himself up on his elbows, but his arms refused to support the weight of his upper body.

She reached for a pitcher and glass from a small table next to his bed. The splash of the liquid made him realize how dry his throat felt. She held the glass to his lips, her free hand supporting his head and shoulders so he could swallow the water without choking.

Jonah still sputtered a little, unaccustomed to having someone else control the glass.

"It's good to see you drinking on your own." Camellia moved the water away from his mouth and gave him a moment to breathe. "For three days and three nights we've had to coax broth into you, feeding you one spoonful at a time."

"What?" The urge to rise from the bed swept him again. "I have to get up."

Camellia put a hand on his shoulder, holding him down with little trouble. He was as weak as a newborn babe.

"Not so fast. Didn't you hear what I said? Your body needs to recover its strength. Don't worry. You don't have any battles to fight today."

"Where am I?" Jonah fought against her grasp.

Her frown deepened. "Aboard a packet bound for Jacksonport, Arkansas. We fished you out of the water after the battle in Memphis. A battle we lost because of the efforts of men like you."

The sting of her words was like a physical slap. He fell back against the pillows, his breath coming in gasps. "You don't understand anything."

"I think you've forgotten how much I do understand, Mr. Thornton." She set the glass on the table with a punctuating *thump*. "I may not understand everything that's transpired since we parted in New Orleans some months ago, but I know exactly why we found you masquerading in a Confederate uniform when we pulled you from the water."

Dread of prison or a hanging filled him. "Have you already told them who I am?"

Her face hardened. "Of course. I could hardly do less. Did you think I would try to hide your identity?"

"I see." His mouth grew dry all over again, as though it were filled with cotton bolls. "I suppose I should be thankful I'm not already in leg irons."

"Yes, indeed." She turned from him, her chin held high, her golden curls bouncing with the strength of her convictions. "I'll make certain that the situation is remedied before you regain your strength. We can't afford to allow a traitor to escape."

He had no answer for her, so Jonah remained silent.

Camellia busied herself with folding a towel and placing it on the table that held the water pitcher. Then she filled a spoon with some kind of concoction from a small brown bottle and tipped it against his mouth.

Jonah drank reflexively, making a face as the bitter draught slid across his tongue. He coughed, wishing for another swallow of water but determined to conceal his weakness.

"Why did you do it?" She put down the spoon and reached for his glass of water, holding it to his lips.

Another cough rattled him, but Jonah managed to drink. His chest relaxed as the cool moisture spread through his body. When she took away the glass, he had regained the strength he needed to answer her. "Become a spy, you mean?"

Camellia nodded, her harsh expression at odds with the gentle touch of her hand on his brow.

"It's not like I awoke one morning and decided I should lie to my family and friends in the service of my country."

She blew out a sharp breath. "You live in the South."

"Yes, the southern part of the United States of America. Not some cobbled-together rebellion that has but one purpose—the continuation of slavery."

"You twist everything about until it makes no sense. Why can't you be like everyone else and simply accept that we are trying to preserve our freedom, our way of life?"

Jonah wanted to answer her, but the room was growing fuzzy, distant. He couldn't keep his eyes open any longer. Yet even as he sank into oblivion, Camellia's face hovered over him, but it looked as though a long tunnel had formed between them. She was saying something to him, and her hand reached through the tunnel to touch his cheek. Turning his face into her hand, he relaxed and let the void take him to a more peaceful place.

❧

"Jonah seems better." Camellia looked toward Thad. "We've managed to get more food down him, but I wish we were in Jacksonport. Jane and I aren't doctors."

Thad pushed his empty plate away and tossed his napkin on it. "We're taking things much slower than normal. We have to spend most of our time in bayous and shallow waterways to avoid falling into enemy hands. The boilers need fresh wood every day, and the snags are worse because the snag-boats have been pressed into service for one side of the war or the other."

"Have you seen any more torpedoes?" Jane's eyes were shadowed by lack of sleep and worry.

Camellia knew the same could be said for her. Both she and Jane had worn themselves out taking care of Jonah. They divided their time between sitting at his bedside, preparing and feeding him nourishing broths, and administering medicinal concoctions the cook made for them.

Those who had remained on the packet worked hard each day, even old Mr. Carlton, the silver-haired man who walked with a cane. Several of the passengers and one of the original crewmen had decided to take their chances on land after the near disaster with the first torpedo. Only five men had remained on board the packet—the captain, the engineer, the cook, Thad, and Mr. Carlton.

"Not since the one on Wednesday," Thad answered his sister.

Camellia pushed a curl back with her right hand. Her coiffure had suffered from the lack of proper facilities and the help of a lady's maid. She had learned to thread a ribbon around her head to keep her hair out of her face. Aunt Dahlia would be appalled, but then, Aunt Dahlia had never had to survive aboard a boat without any of the basic necessities. Deciding to dwell on more positive matters, she summoned a smile. "What fine stories we'll have to share with your parents and my family about this excursion."

Mr. Carlton nodded and pushed his chair from the small table at which they sat. "If that handsome fella there didn't have an eye on you, little missy, I'd try to woo you myself."

A blush heated Camellia's cheeks. She found it impossible to look toward Thad. Since the day he'd almost kissed her, she had kept some distance between them. That wasn't hard to do, of course, since she had to see to Jonah. She began to gather the dishes from the table, having fallen back into the habit she'd learned when living aboard Lily and Blake's steamship. "Come along, Jane. We need to check on the rabbit stew for Jonah."

A male chuckle followed them out of the dining room, but Camellia didn't look back to see if it came from Mr. Carlton or Thad. In the past she might have remained with the men and flirted with both of them. But now she had more important matters to see to.

❧

The next time Jonah awoke, Jane Watkins was sitting beside his bed. He coughed, and she held a glass of water to his lips as Camellia had done. He told himself he was not disappointed that Jane's hand was the one supporting his shoulders. Had he only dreamed Camellia had caressed his cheek as he fell asleep?

"Good afternoon, Mr. Thornton. I hope you're truly on the mend now."

After he'd drunk enough to moisten the inside of his mouth, Jonah indicated he was done with a shake of his head. She removed the glass and let his head fall back against the pillow.

He sent a smile in her direction. "Thank you."

"You're very welcome."

Jonah studied the young woman, a beauty in her own way. Did she feel any kindness toward him? Would she help him escape? Would the time she had spent around him and his family influence her decision? She was certainly being considerate of him now. But that might change as he got stronger. If she was filled with the same misplaced zeal for rebellion that had infected Camellia, she would never countenance his escape.

The door to his room opened, and Jonah squinted toward the newcomer. His heart climbed up toward his throat when he recognized Jane's brother in full dress uniform. Whether or not he could convince Jane or Camellia to help him became immaterial. As long as Captain Watkins was aboard, Jonah's chances of escaping dwindled to nothing but a vain hope.

"How is the patient today?"

"He's awake." Jane smiled at Thad. "Why don't you ask him yourself?"

Thad nodded and entered the room. "How do you feel?"

"Tolerably well, I suppose. Camellia said y'all fished me from the river."

"Yes." Thad sat on the end of his bed. "You were a pretty sad sight. I was all for leaving you behind, but the girls would not hear of it."

"Thad!" Jane's scandalized response made Thad smile and raise an eyebrow.

Realizing the man was trying to introduce a note of levity, Jonah managed to force his parched lips into a weak grin. "I don't blame you. I probably would have done the same thing if you had been the one in the water."

Thad laughed out loud and slapped the bed. "At least you're strong enough to give as good as you get. The girls have been nursing you nonstop this past week. If you recover your health, you have them to thank for it."

Jonah hid his surprise that so many more days had passed. "I'm thankful to both of them."

Thad turned his attention to his sister. "Why don't you go and get Camellia? I have a couple of things to say to your patient."

Both of them watched her leave the room. Jonah tried to brace himself for the worst. Though his chest felt heavy with congestion, at least he was a little stronger than the last time he'd awakened. But was he strong enough to face what was coming? If he'd been unconscious for another three days, their boat would have had plenty of time to arrive in Jacksonport. Would Thad arrest him now and have him dragged away to a prison? He tried to choke down his cough, but it would not be denied. When the paroxysm ended, he lay back against his pillow and waited to hear the bad news.

"That's a bad cough, Thornton. I hope it won't delay your return to action." Thad stood and moved to the chair his sister had vacated. "I have to admit I had my doubts about you when we met in New Orleans. But in light of the fact that you've decided to volunteer, I am willing to put our differences aside. The Confederacy can use every able-bodied man whose heart is in the right place."

Shock held him still. Camellia had not spilled his secret after all. If he could keep his wits about him, he might yet escape hanging or prison. Jonah's grin turned rueful. While he didn't want to mislead Thad, it was necessary. "You're right about that. I'm glad you're willing to overlook my past, and I want you to know I'm determined to do my part to finish this war."

"Good. I'm glad that's settled." Thad put a hand on the doorknob. "The girls seem to think your body is mending well. You've had plenty of time to catch up on your sleep, so I'll hope to see you on deck in a day or two. I could use the careful eye of another soldier."

Jonah's head fell back on the pillow once more as Thad left him alone. He closed his eyes and began a prayer of thanksgiving. It was only through God's grace that he'd not been found out. His grace and the unfathomable intentions of a Southern belle who had little reason to protect him.

Chapter Twenty-six

John watched each bend in the river as they once again approached Cape Girardeau. It had been too long since he last saw Anna, but he'd thought of her every moment of those weeks. The sound of rain on the surface of the river became the tinkling noise of her laughter. He imagined building a home for the two of them. A home filled with faith, love, and laughter. It was a dream that he hoped would one day become a reality.

The walls of the southernmost fort came into view, the formidable black eyes of its cannons unblinking.

"Are you going to ask that girl to marry you?" Mrs. Naomi's voice startled him.

He couldn't keep the grin from his face. "Who told you such a thing?"

"I'm a woman." Her eyes twinkled. "No one had to tell me."

John sobered. "Do you think she'll have me?"

"You and I've been working together for more than a year now. I know people well enough to tell the difference between a scoundrel and an honest, Christian man. If that young lady doesn't snap you up, she's not half as smart as she looks." Mrs. Naomi laughed and patted his hand. "Don't you worry. She'll fall in your arms as soon as you open them for her."

The captain signaled that it was time for the crew to begin making preparations for their landing, so John moved away from Mrs. Naomi. He picked up a coil of rope and twisted it into a loop, throwing it over his shoulder and measuring the distance to the pier. The large paddle wheel slowed and changed the direction of its rotation. Churning the water in reverse, it slowed the *Catfish* and brought her closer to land. John tossed his rope expertly, catching the upright piling on the first try. He heard two other crewmen toss separate ropes, and soon they had the boat securely tied.

He waited with barely leashed patience as their ship was inspected by the harbormaster and a couple of Union soldiers. As soon as they were cleared, he went onshore and strode up the hill to the central part of town. The sun was sinking toward the western horizon, but he calculated it was only about three in the afternoon. Anna should still be at work.

The moment John pushed open the door, he knew something was wrong. Devore's looked like an unkempt child. Items were crowded every which way on the normally orderly shelves, and a film of dust dulled the shiny counter behind which she and Mr. Devore usually stood. The latter was helping a female customer, but John could not see Anna anywhere. Another lady stood in her place behind the counter. His heart thudded to a stop. Where was Anna? Had there been an accident? Was she sick?

Lord, please let her be safe and healthy. The plea filled John's head. He walked to the counter, his mind dwelling on the macabre possibilities. They lived in a dangerous time. Anything could have happened to her—a snakebite, the attack of a wild animal, yellow jack fever. His mind spun.

"Are you all right?" The lady in Anna's place looked at John with concern. From Anna's descriptions, he knew the attractive woman must be Norma Devore, Don's wife.

More concern washed over him as he realized she must be assisting her husband due to Anna's not being able to work. "I'm fine. I was hoping to see Anna. I'm John Champion."

"Anna's at home," Mrs. Devore said. "Her father had an accident, and she's been nursing him."

At least she was not hurt—or worse, dead. John thanked the woman and hurried out of the store without asking any more details. He had to get to Anna. Make sure she had what she needed. His gaze remained fixed on the road in front of his feet, the prayer in his mind becoming wordless as he cast his cares before his Lord.

A knock on the door of the Matthewses' place brought a middle-aged woman to the door, Anna's aunt Tessie.

"Is Anna home?"

Before she could answer, John heard a sound in the hall behind her. Aunt Tessie stepped back, and there she was in front of him. His Anna. His gaze took in her appearance in an instant, cataloging the dark circles under her eyes, the droop of her shoulders, and the desperation in her gaze.

"John?" Her expression eased a little. "I can't believe you're really here."

Aunt Tessie finally took care of the social amenities as he and Anna could only stare at each other. "Come in, young man." He then noticed the same mixture of weariness and fear in her face, too. "Why don't you take him to the parlor, and I'll see if I can fix a tray for the two of you."

John followed Anna down the hall, noticing the general air of disorder here, too. "How is your father?"

Anna shook her head and opened the door to the parlor. She sat down in a rocker that dwarfed her and leaned back. "He's failing." A catch in her voice made John want to gather her in his arms and comfort her. "I don't know what to do. Aunt Tessie is doing everything she can, but she's still recovering from her illness."

"What happened?"

"Pa was cutting down a tree out back because it had begun to lean and he was worried it might fall and take down part of the house." Anna parroted the words as though she'd told the story many times before. "I don't know exactly how, but the tree fell the wrong way, and Pa was caught underneath it. Aunt Tessie was resting in her bedroom and couldn't hear him calling for help. By the time I got home several hours later, he was b–barely hanging on."

John closed his eyes for a moment, seeking words of comfort for her. Something that would let her know how much he regretted everything that had happened to her and her family. "I'm here now, and I'll do anything I can to help you."

She looked up at him, her eyes watery with unshed tears. "Thank you, John. Just seeing you is a blessing to me."

"What can I do?"

"Pray. Pray that God won't take my pa until he and my brother have made their peace with each other."

John frowned. "You have a brother? You've never mentioned a brother before."

"I haven't seen him in nearly a decade. The last letter I had from him is more than five years old."

"Where is he?"

She shrugged. "The last time Blake wrote to us, he was living in a town in Mississippi. . .Natchez or Vicksburg, I can't remember exactly."

"Blake Matthews is your brother?" John's knees weakened, and he collapsed on the nearby sofa. In all of his dreams of what this day would bring, he'd never imagined such a calamity. He'd never thought a nightmare of gargantuan proportions would swallow his future whole. He'd never thought that the woman he'd fallen in love with would bring his doom on him.

Camellia watched as Jonah's health returned slowly over the next days. His deep cough still worried her, but he shrugged it off with a quip. He even spent a few hours each day sitting in one of the two chairs in his room, his legs modestly covered with a blanket whenever she or Jane was with him.

Today, however, he had spent the morning sitting up, so now he rested in his bed as he finished the light lunch she had brought.

When Jane left them alone while he ate, Camellia decided to tackle the subject they had both avoided since he'd first awakened. "I don't understand how you can betray everyone you care for."

His sigh was long and led to another cough. As soon as it passed, he picked up his tray and handed it to her. "You do understand that a soldier must follow orders, right?"

"Yes."

"Thad is following his orders, isn't he? He might choose to get you and his sister to safety before completing his mission, but he cannot. His duty must come before family obligations or others will suffer."

"Yes, but—" A sudden jerk of the boat threw Camellia forward. The tray hit the far wall, and she sprawled across his lap with an unladylike grunt.

"I know you find me attractive, Miss Anderson, but you really must control yourself." Jonah's laughter brought his cough back.

Camellia bounced off of him as though she had springs under her. "I'm sorry."

As soon as he stopped coughing, he raised his head and stared at her.

"I can't say that I am."

Her face flamed. Trust the man to make a joke at her expense. Shouts and the sound of feet running down the passageway provided her with a needed distraction. She moved to the door and peeked out. "I wonder what's happened."

"It's time for me to get out of this bed and find out."

A rustle behind her brought Camellia's head back around. Jonah had thrown his sheet back and was putting his feet to the floor. She gasped at the sight of his bare legs sticking out from the tail of his nightshirt. "Jonah!"

"You may want to leave if you don't want to be offended." His voice was grim and determined. "I refuse to lie here and wait to find out what disaster has overtaken us now."

Camellia picked up her skirts and fled. As she ran to the room she shared with Jane, she realized the paddle wheel was not churning. Had they hit another snag? A sandbar? She threw open the door and found her friend trying to lace up the back of her dress. "Let me help."

"Do you know what's going on?" Jane looked over her shoulder, a concerned look on her face. "Have we finally made it to Jacksonport?"

"I don't know." Camellia finished with the lacing. "Let's go see."

The main deck was empty. Camellia glanced at Jane, who reached for her hand. Had the men deserted them? That made no sense. Thad would not leave them voluntarily. Her heart thumped.

"We must get free. We may lose another day." Thad's voice came from the far side of the boat.

Jane and Camellia followed the sound to discover the men, even Jonah, standing in ankle-deep water just off the bow. That's when she realized that the packet was sitting at an angle. They had run up onto a sandbar. She looked at the gangplank that had been swung to the bank to allow the men to see the extent of the damage done.

"I didn't realize we were on a schedule." Jonah's voice was still weak, but he had managed to negotiate the gangplank, a definite improvement.

Jane squeezed her hand and pulled her forward. "What's wrong?"

The captain scratched his head, dislodging the slouch hat he wore. "I was trying to avoid a snag and ran us into more trouble."

Another of the men sighed. "We'd better get busy."

"Can we help?" Camellia hoped the answer would be no.

Jonah laughed and exchanged a glance with Thad. "Not unless you can handle a shovel."

"Look at that." Jane's voice sounded sad to Camellia.

She looked toward the bank and saw what had drawn her friend's attention. A stunning plantation had once commanded a view of this bend in the river. All that remained of it, however, was a burned-out shell. The spreading limbs of live oak trees formed a path from the bank of the river to the front steps. Five tall columns were spread out as silent sentinels across what had once been an inviting veranda edged with a profusion of azaleas, bougainvillea, and roses.

Visions of slave uprisings and Yankee marauders made Camellia's head spin. "I wonder what happened there."

Mr. Carlton stomped out to join them, his gaze surveying the ruined estate. "Most likely lightning." He pointed with his cane at a tree Camellia had not noticed earlier, its trunk blackened, its bare limbs reaching toward the sky. "See the hole in that wall? Once the fire breached the house, it was too late to do anything. It would have burned in less than an hour."

Camellia turned to Jane. "Are you feeling adventurous?"

"Not me." Jane shook her head and shrank back.

"Come on. We can spend the afternoon exploring while the men do their work." Camellia drew her forward. "It'll be fun."

Jane squealed as the gangplank bounced under their feet, the river water rushing a few inches beneath their feet. "I don't think this is a good idea."

Thad shook his head and waded back to the bank, meeting them before they got halfway across the narrow wooden planks. Walking three abreast was impossible, so he took his sister's arm and guided her to the bank. Then he turned back to where Camellia stood with one hand clutching the packet's rail. Instead of offering her his hand, he bent and scooped her into his arms.

Caught off guard by his unexpected action, she had no choice but to rest her head against his chest.

Mr. Carlton chuckled and she heard the *tap-tap* of his cane as he moved away. The captain was giving instructions to his crewmen, ignoring the women and Thad.

Jonah was a different matter, however. He stood at the end of the gangplank, his face a mask of fury.

Thad put her feet on the ground, his hand settling around her waist. "Is there a problem?"

Jonah's hands clenched and unclenched. "As a friend of Camellia's family, I can be considered a chaperone. I don't know how you've been comporting yourself while I've been indisposed, but I'll thank you to act like a gentleman now."

Stepping away from her, Thad straightened his shoulders. "My actions are in keeping with the man who will one day be Camellia's husband."

Camellia's mouth dropped open, but before she could say anything, she saw Jonah sway.

His complexion had grayed to almost the same hue as his uniform. His gaze went to her face. "You're engaged to be married?"

"I am not." She shot a look of warning toward Thad. "And this is not the time or place to discuss such matters."

To his credit, Thad moved to Jonah and steadied him. "I'm sorry if I spoke out of turn, Camellia, but it cannot be a secret that I care about you greatly. And now that we've spent all this time practically alone on the river, everyone will expect us to—"

"Enough." She stomped her foot on the ground, coughing at the dust it raised. "You might make the same argument about myself and Jonah, or even Jonah and your sister. We've been adequately chaperoned the whole time, so I will hear no more on the matter."

Both Jonah and Thad looked at her, their faces slack. Then Thad glared at Jonah. "You ought to get inside before you fall over and I have to carry you, too."

Jonah snorted but never took his gaze off her face. Even as she walked toward the ruined house, she could feel a prickle on the back of her neck. Why did the man have such fire in his eyes? And why did she feel so bruised? She ought to be glad two men were vying for her attention, but all she felt was persecution. She hadn't done anything to deserve their attention or their scorn. She would not feel guilty.

Mist had settled on the water overnight. Now it rose in wraithlike tendrils, first hiding then revealing the surface of the river.

Jonah settled into a chair provided by the engineer and watched as the plantation home receded in the distance. It had taken the men all night to move enough sand for their boat to float free. How much longer would it take them to reach Jacksonport? And what would happen to him when they did?

"How do you feel this morning?" Camellia's voice pulled him away from his thoughts.

Jonah looked at her, standing so demurely in front of him. He had thought her beautiful when she wore glittering finery, but she was even more so out here on the river without her fancy coiffures and fancier dresses. Her eyes were bluer than the sky, her lips as soft as the petals of a rose. Even though she looked as delicate as porcelain, he knew better. Many women would have spent their time weeping and bemoaning the danger and privations of this trip. Camellia had not complained even once. He could not afford to give in to the tenderness flooding him. "Not as tired as your fiancé."

"Don't call him that. Thad spoke out of turn."

Her denial made his heart pound. "Are you saying you don't love him?"

She looked past his shoulder, a frown on her lovely face. "I. . . Oh, I don't know how I feel. I always thought I would marry someone like Thad, but now I don't know."

"He's a good man—honorable and caring. You could do worse for a husband." What impulse made him defend the Confederate soldier? She could see for herself what kind of man Thad was. Jonah didn't need to push her in that direction. But somehow her happiness was important to him, more important than his own.

Her head shot up at that. "Are you saying you want me to be engaged to him?"

"Only if it will make you happy." Jonah sighed. "I've known you for years, Camellia. I've seen you during good times and hard times. I've seen you act the part of a supremely egotistical debutante. Your physical beauty is undeniable, but at times I've thought I glimpsed something else in you. . .something admirable, something warm and caring and honest."

A tear slipped free and trickled down the curve of Camellia's cheek.

Jonah's breath caught. "I'm sorry. I didn't mean to make you cry. I only want you to be sure you love Thad before you agree to marry him."

She rubbed a finger across her cheek. "Sometimes I don't know what I'm doing. I think about that sermon. Do you remember? The one at your church where the pastor talked about the narrow path that leads to salvation. I thought he was being silly. Everyone I knew felt the same way. We all believed in the South, the Cause. But I'm not so sure anymore. War is a harsh, scary thing. How many men will give their lives for an ideal that has nothing to do with God? How many lives will be ruined when husbands, brothers, or sons never come home again?"

Jonah took a deep breath. He didn't want to say the wrong thing now. Their conversation had taken a much more serious turn, a turn that could lead her either to a closer relationship with Christ or to a life of discontent that ended in eternal destruction.

He closed his eyes and prayed for the right message to give her. She was the missing lamb, the one the Shepherd left His flock to find. For the first time, Jonah understood why the Shepherd would risk everything to bring one lost lamb back into the fold. "Hundreds, even thousands will be affected before the war is over. It's the nature of war."

Her gaze came back to him. "That's the real reason, isn't it?"

"I believe the South is wrong. I believe the soul of every person is precious to God, no matter the color of a person's skin. I believe slavery is an abomination that must end if our country is to survive." Jonah paused. Should he tell her everything? Let her see how far he would go. . .had gone? "Even before the war began, my brother, Eli, and I helped slaves escape to safe havens. He didn't want me to volunteer to fight because he understood what you are just now seeing, the death and destruction. But I couldn't stand on the sidelines. Following God's urging is more important than my comforts, my life, or even my family."

Emotions chased each other across her face—fear, knowledge, understanding, and finally determination. "What can I do to help?"

Her question made him want to shout with joy. And in that moment, he knew why Thad's announcement had caused him so much pain. He was deeply, completely, irrevocably in love with Camellia Anderson. If she married someone else, it would be a disaster of monumental proportions. He wanted to extract a promise from her to wait for him. He wanted her to vow not to marry Thad. But he could not. He would not. So he shrugged. "Keep your eyes and ears open. God will give you the answer in His time."

Chapter Twenty-seven

The landing at Jacksonport should have been crowded with townspeople and soldiers in the morning, but Camellia could see no sign of activity.

White tents littered a clearing nearby; lazy tendrils of smoke rose from cooling campfires. Gray-coated soldiers with bayonets attached to their rifles patrolled the edges of the camp, their faces hard as they watched the packet approach the empty landing.

As soon as the gangplank was lowered, Thad marched across it and headed toward a tent over which a Confederate flag waved.

Jane came to stand next to Camellia and placed an arm around her waist. "You've seemed different these past few days. Is that scene with my brother troubling you?"

Camellia would have liked to blame her problems on such an easy target, but she could not be untruthful to her best friend. "No."

The other girl was silent, as though waiting for an explanation. But Camellia had none to give her. She couldn't reveal her changed feelings about the war and slavery without exposing Jonah, and she couldn't very well ask her friend to betray her brother by hiding Jonah's secret.

"I suppose we're all tired."

Camellia sighed. "It has been a long trip."

"At least Jonah seems back to normal. Even his cough is easing."

Thanking God in her heart, Camellia smiled. "That's true. Perhaps we have bright futures as nurses."

Jane shivered. "I don't think I have the stomach for it."

"You don't find it rewarding to see Jonah's recovery?"

"Of course I do, but it's not like he had any gaping wounds or sores. His problems were more internal."

Thad's reappearance stopped their conversation. He was escorted by an older man, a civilian.

"Here they come. I wonder what your brother has learned."

They soon found out. Jacksonport had been in the hands of the Union until only a few days earlier. Camellia wondered what might have happened if they had arrived then. Would they have been taken prisoner, or would Jonah have come forward and worked to ensure their freedom?

The Confederate commander who had retaken the town had a number of wounded on his hands, and he needed to arrange transport back to Vicksburg where they could receive proper care. Even though their packet was small, he thought it would meet his requirements.

Thad described the proposition as a choice, but Camellia viewed it as a command. They would transport the wounded soldiers to Vicksburg whether they wanted to or not.

She and Jane spent the afternoon scrubbing out the unused guest quarters. Soldiers drove nails into the walls and hung hammocks inside the cleaned quarters. By the time the sun was setting, the boat was almost ready.

The commander's assistant, a pale man with a long beard and pale eyes, joined them for dinner. It was a fancier dinner than they had enjoyed for the weeks they'd been on the White River. Colonel Thomas Scoggins regaled them with stories of battles and skirmishes they had managed to avoid in their time on the river.

As a result, Camellia found herself unable to eat any of the fried squirrel or rice. From the colonel's descriptions, they would surely encounter Union gunboats if they tried to return to the Mississippi. Would she and Jane spend the rest of the war in this small town in Arkansas?

"I'm surprised Mr. Thornton is not present for dinner this evening." Mr. Carlton's innocent comment set Camellia's heart thumping. "I would have thought he would be anxious to make a report of the activities at Memphis."

Colonel Scoggins raised an eyebrow. "Who is this?"

Thad explained how they had fished Jonah from the river after the battle above Memphis and watched him sleep for three days and nights. Colonel Scoggins expressed a desire to interview Jonah, and the conversation at the table became more general.

But Camellia knew it didn't bode well for Jonah. She had to warn him and see that he avoided talking with the sharp-eyed soldier. She had no intention of seeing him hanged for his actions—not now that she understood the truth.

❧

Two days later the packet had taken on a whole new identity. Fresh paint blazoned the word Hospital on the housing that protected the paddle wheel, declaring to all that she should be allowed to pass without being fired upon. Camellia hoped both armies would respect the packet's purpose.

She had never been more tired in her life. Her legs hurt, her arms felt too heavy to lift, and her neck was as stiff as a board. And still the wounded and sick were brought onto the boat in a never-ending flood. Women from the town came aboard, too, with offerings of fresh bandages, soap, and herbal remedies.

The doctor had Jane and Camellia organize their supplies and start a list of their patients' names. Along with Mr. Carlton and some of the other crewmen, they talked to the men, holding their hands, cleaning their faces, and making them as comfortable as possible. The stench was nearly unbearable, but somehow Camellia managed to get around the crowded room.

Jonah caught her in the passageway at noon on the second day. "I want you to come to the dining hall with me."

"I don't have time to eat." She tried to push past him but was halted when he spread his legs and crossed his arms over his chest. "Get out of my way."

He uncrossed his arms and touched her cheek with a gentle finger. "You cannot keep spending all your time with the wounded."

"That's what Thad told me when I was tending you."

Jonah's head snapped back as though she had slapped him.

Remorse flooded Camellia. "I'm sorry."

"Don't be. I don't mean to irritate you, Camellia. But I'm worried about your health. You're exhausted." He took her by the shoulders and turned her to face one of the passageway windows. "Look at yourself. If you keep up this pace, you'll expire before those men in there."

Tears burned her eyes. Couldn't he see she was doing this because of him? Because he had helped her see the truth? "What do you want from me?"

"Come with me." He dropped his hands from her shoulders and pulled her toward the exit. "I have something I need to tell you, and spending an afternoon in the sunshine will make you feel better."

The fresh air did smell good. And the warmth of the sun on her skin was a welcome relief. Strangers, the soldiers who came and went from the Confederate headquarters in a never-ending flow, watched them disembark. But no one challenged Jonah. Had he convinced them that he was one of them? Was he even now gathering information that would be used to defeat them? "Where are you taking me?"

Jonah didn't answer her, just kept a guiding hand under her elbow. They walked down the dusty street, passing a mercantile and half-a-dozen houses. And still he walked. Over a slight rise, through a valley of tall grasses.

Camellia was beginning to think her legs would fall off. "I have to stop."

"It's not much farther now." Jonah's promise encouraged her to continue.

Finally he turned into the woods, following a path only he could see. Trees surrounded them, hiding them from civilization. She could hear something new ahead of them, a sound like thunder. Where was he taking her?

And then she saw it. The thunder was water rushing across huge boulders. "A waterfall?"

Their gazes met. He looked like a mischievous kid. "One of the local men told me about this place. I thought I would offer to stand guard while you refresh yourself." He held out his hand, his palm open to show her a sliver of soap.

Suddenly the layers of grit and grime on her skin were intolerable. She took the soap from him, imagining the feeling of the cleansing water surrounding her. "Really?"

He nodded and turned his back to the waterfall. "Be careful. I'd hate to have to offend your modesty."

Camellia felt her blush, though she knew he couldn't see it under the dirt. She moved to a pool at the base of the waterfall and stripped off her clothing one layer at a time. Dressed only in her chemise, she stuck a toe in the water. It was cool, as refreshing as she'd hoped. She glanced back over her shoulder to make certain Jonah was not watching. His back was barely discernible among the tree limbs. Satisfied, she walked forward. The water climbed to her waist then to her neck. Camellia held her breath and plunged her head into the water. She lathered the soap and used it to melt the dirt and grime. She rinsed the suds away and started over again, scrubbing her scalp, her skin, every part of her body she could reach.

"Are you still in the water?" Jonah's voice reminded her of his presence.

"Yes. It's wonderful, Jonah." She rinsed the soap off a second time and stepped out of the pool. Getting dressed was not easy, but with a bit of squirming and straining she managed the laces and buttons.

Squeezing the water out of her curls, Camellia walked back up the path to the place where she had parted from Jonah. "Where are you?"

He appeared from behind a large oak. "Right here." His crooked smile made her breath catch.

"Thank you."

"Did you enjoy yourself?" He offered his arm.

Camellia nodded. "It was worth the walk. I feel I could take on the whole world again."

They wandered down the path again, at peace with each other. The sun was beginning to approach the western horizon.

Jonah sighed and stopped walking just short of the town's edge. "I have to leave."

Although she'd been expecting this moment from the start, Camellia's heart fell. "When?"

"Now. A couple of days ago Colonel Scoggins sent a messenger to my battalion to report my survival. As soon as he realizes my commanding officer doesn't have any record of me, he'll realize I'm a spy." Jonah heaved a sigh. "I wish I could stay, but it's impossible."

"I could go with you." The words slipped out before Camellia could stop them.

He shook his head. "Thad will take care of you."

Camellia promised herself she would not cry. She would not let him see how his refusal hurt her or how much she would miss him. She choked back her emotions. "Godspeed, then."

"Camellia, I want you t—" He bit off the word and shook his head. "Thad is a good man. You could do worse than marry him."

She shook her head. "Please don't say such things." They had been through so much together. The memory of his kiss came back to her with startling clarity. She wanted to do nothing more than repeat the experience. Before she could talk herself out of it, Camellia lifted herself on tiptoe and pressed her lips against Jonah's.

After a brief hesitation, his arms embraced her, holding her close. His lips moved on hers, and a shock like lightning shot through her. Time stood still as the bond between them strengthened. For a moment she seemed to melt into him, become a part of him in some way that she didn't understand. Then it was over.

Jonah put his hands on her shoulders and slowly pushed her away. "I have to go." His voice was rough, but she could see the remorse in his gaze. Then he turned on his heel and walked away, disappearing into the woods without a backward glance.

Pain tore through her, and Camellia sank to her knees and wept. She wept for past mistakes and present dreams; she wept for lost causes and separate pathways. But mostly she wept for the brave man who would not shirk his duty no matter the cost.

Chapter Twenty-eight

The note was delivered by a young boy who put Lily in mind of David, the child they had rescued from the streets of Natchez Under-the-Hill. Dirty and barefoot, he was another of the "throwaway" children who should be staying at the foundling home. She must remember to mention him to the orphanage's matron.

"I have a note here for y'all. The scary man said you'd pay me for it." He held up the folded sheet.

Lily frowned. "The scary man?"

The child nodded, his brown eyes solemn.

Wondering who had given the child a note, Lily shrugged. She reached for the reticule at her waist and drew out a gold coin. "Is this enough for your long walk?"

The child's eyes widened at the generous offering. "Yes, ma'am."

She held out the coin, smiling as he snatched it from her hand.

He handed her the note and skipped off the veranda. Lily imagined the tales he would share tonight in whatever hovel sheltered him. Perhaps the money would buy him a good meal and a real bed or stretch to a new pair of shoes. She hoped so.

Returning to the front parlor, she sat next to Blake. "I had hoped this would be a note from Camellia, but it's addressed to you."

Blake took the note from her hand. "One of my admirers, no doubt."

She punched his arm.

"Lily, control yourself, please." Aunt Dahlia sniffed.

Blake adopted an angelic expression and nodded. "Thank you. I have told Lily again and again that she should adopt your manners."

The older woman preened, and Lily felt like punching his arm again. If she had followed Aunt Dahlia's advice, they never would have met. She never would have purchased half interest in a steamboat, and he probably would have been shot by some unhappy gambler by now. Deciding to take the higher road, she forced her lips into a congenial smile. "Are you going to open your note?"

His unrepentant grin teased her.

Lily folded her hands in her lap and gazed at the fireplace. She refused to be drawn into further tomfoolery.

Blake sighed and pulled a small knife from the pocket of his trousers.

Aunt Dahlia gasped and fanned herself, apparently overcome to find a lethal weapon in their parlor.

Lily regaled her aunt and grandmother with a description of the boy and his "scary man" while her husband perused the note. She didn't realize anything was wrong until the sheet of paper drifted to the floor. She turned to look at her husband, surprised to see the anguish in his navy-blue eyes. "What is it?"

Blake shook his head and leaned back against the sofa, his hand covering his eyes. Was he crying?

Lily scooped up the note and read it:

Dear Mr. Matthews,

I am sorry to inform you that your father has suffered a serious accident and is not expected to recover. By the time you receive this note, it may already be too late, but your sister has expressed a desire for your help, as she has no other male relative to support her during these trying and dangerous times. As a friend of the family, I have taken it upon myself to contact you and request that you repair immediately to your family's home in Cape Girardeau.

The note was signed with a flourishing *J*.

Grandmother put down her teacup. "What has happened?"

"It's Blake's father. He's been in some sort of accident."

"Your father?" Aunt Dahlia looked at the man beside her. "I thought you were an orphan."

Blake lowered his hand, and Lily noticed that the skin under his eyes seemed moist. The urge to protect her husband took hold of her. "Blake had a difficult childhood and had to break free from his family."

Aunt Dahlia's jaw fell. After a moment, she snapped it shut. "I suppose I shouldn't be surprised."

What she left unsaid was a phrase Lily had heard often enough. . . *from a gambler*. She frowned at her relative. "Not everyone is as comfortable or blessed as we have been. Blake deserves your admiration for succeeding in spite of the setbacks he's faced."

Blake patted her hand. "It's all right, Lily. You don't have to defend me. I have never corrected your relatives' mistaken assumptions about my past."

"But—"

A look from him stopped her words. "I believe the time has come for me to take your advice." He stood and reached for the note.

Lily bent her wrist away from his hand. "Don't think I'm going to let you take this trip alone."

Grandmother cleared her throat and sent a look in Aunt Dahlia's direction. "I believe we need to inspect the linens upstairs." It was her tactful way of offering them privacy.

Aunt Dahlia's mouth curved downward, but she nodded and rose from her rocker.

Lily waited until both of them exited the parlor before returning her attention to her husband. "We can pick up Camellia on the way. I think it's time she rejoined her family. I really miss her."

"It's too dangerous for you to come. Every day we receive more reports of battles and skirmishes along the river." He reached for the note once more.

Shaking her head, Lily stood and held her hand behind her back. "You are no more impervious to bullets than I."

"Lily, be reasonable. I must go." He cupped her chin with one hand.

She refused to be swayed by his tenderness. "I suppose you mean to take *my* boat and *my* father."

"I can catch a ride on a different boat. Captains will be eager to travel north for goods they can sell to us at inflated prices." He slid his hand down the length of her arm, raising gooseflesh.

Lily shivered and failed to hold on to the note.

Blake snatched it from her hand and stepped back, a teasing smile on his lips.

"I can't stop you if that's what you want to do." Lily returned his smile with deceptive humility. "But whether you're aboard or not, the *Water Lily* will be making a trip to Cape Girardeau."

Camellia wept for the first soldier whose shroud-covered body slid into the dark waters of the river. She cried over the next one, too. But then her heart seemed to scab over, hardened by experience. Fever swept the packet ship, and more of them died. Helplessly, she swabbed their foreheads and listened as they spoke of home.

"I'm afraid Michael won't last another day." One of the soldiers traveling with them whispered the information as she took his place beside Michael's hammock.

Camellia nodded and removed the warm cloth from the patient's forehead, dropping it into a pan with other dirty cloths. Later she would boil the contents of this pan in a large pot with lye soap. "I think they might do better if we could carry them to the deck." Replacing the soiled cloth with a fresh one, she thought of the way she'd felt that bittersweet day when Jonah had taken her to the waterfall.

How impossibly far away that moment of hope seemed to her now. Jonah was gone, and all that was left was sickness, pain, and death. Helplessness and hopelessness were her constant companions. Sometimes she felt she would lose her mind.

Moving to the next hammock, Camellia peeled the dirty cloth from the soldier's head, wrung out a fresh one, and laid it gently across his face. As she turned away, however, this man put a hot, dry hand around her wrist. "Are you an angel?"

Camellia shook her head.

"I've never seen anyone as pretty as you."

"Of course you haven't." Michael coughed, and she turned back to look at him again, noticing the gray cast to his face. "That's 'cause she *is* an angel, only she can't tell anyone."

Her heart broke again as she put a hand on his shoulder. No one could say these men weren't brave. Even now, as their broken bodies failed, they could find something to make each other smile. "Of course I'm not an angel. I'm just a girl from Natchez."

"Didn't I tell you?" Michael nodded before sinking back against the hammock. "She can't tell anyone what she really is."

Shaking her head, Camellia looked up and saw Thad entering the sickroom. He looked troubled, and her heart pounded in response. How much more would they have to bear before this nightmare ended? She picked up her bowl of rags and moved toward him.

"We need to talk." His voice was as grim as his face. His back was as straight as a ramrod as he escorted her out of the sickroom.

"What has happened?"

They walked through the passageway to the deck. Camellia glanced about for evidence of a new threat, but she could see nothing more than the trees and banks they were sliding past.

"We've received news about Jonah Thornton. It appears he's been masquerading. . ."

Camellia's mind spun as Thad talked. Had Jonah been apprehended by the Confederates? A vision of his lifeless body dangling from a hangman's noose sprang to life in her mind. She couldn't seem to catch her breath. Couldn't make sense of the words flowing from Thad. What would she do without Jonah? Without seeing that half smile of his, the fire in his green eyes? What about his parents? His sister? The brother in Memphis?

"If I see his conniving face again, I'll put a bullet in him myself."

The truth burst upon her like the blast of a torpedo. He was not dead. Was not even languishing in a Confederate prison. Her heartbeat quickened. Jonah was alive. And free. Something of her joy must have shown on Camellia's face, because Thad stopped talking and frowned at her. "You don't seem surprised at my news." His brown gaze pierced her.

Camellia realized she had best step warily if she didn't want to be branded a spy herself. "Jonah told me there was a problem with his enlistment."

A harsh laugh from the man beside her stopped her careful words. "The problem with his enlistment is that it's a sham. Wait a minute. . . ."

She looked up at him.

Thad was gazing into the distance, his mind busy with implications. "He's the missing piece!"

"What do you mean?" Camellia forced the words through her tight throat.

"He's the one who was passing classified information to Mrs. Dabbs. And he's the one who most likely orchestrated her escape before we left New Orleans." Thad no longer looked suspicious of her. His gaze settled on her hair, and he reached up to tuck a stray strand into her bun. "It all makes sense now."

Before Camellia could say anything, he bowed to her. "I have to report this to my commanding officer. He needs to know exactly how nefarious Jonah Thornton really is."

She watched Thad march away and wondered where it would all end. Would Thad someday kill Jonah?

Guilt assailed her, and she felt her heart being torn in two parts. Thad was a good man. He had all the qualifications to make her happy. But her heart wanted to be near Jonah. If only he wanted the same thing, too.

Chapter Twenty-nine

Thunder rumbled in the distance as the packet-turned-hospital reached the Mississippi River. Camellia wondered if it came from the dark clouds in the sky or yet another confrontation between the United States and the Confederacy. She leaned against the rail and turned her face to the wind.

"It won't be long before we reach Vicksburg." Jane came up behind her and removed her apron.

"I wonder if the Union navy has taken it as well."

"Thad says no. Vicksburg may be the only city the Confederacy can hold, but it will never fall into the hands of the Yankees."

Camellia wondered if Thad could be wrong. But she had seen the high bluffs. She had heard the men talking about Vicksburg's refusal to surrender even after New Orleans, Natchez, and Baton Rouge had fallen. And she could see for herself the ardent desperation of Confederate soldiers to win the war against all odds.

Ahead of them the river seemed to come to an end, so deep was its curve. The hairpin curve just above Vicksburg.

Jane's dark hair whipped around her head in the brisk wind. "Isn't it ironic that we tried to stay away from the fighting but only managed to get ourselves mired in it?"

"I read something about that in my Bible this morning."

"I'm not surprised. You've spent more time with your nose stuck in your Bible during this trip than you did the whole time we were at La Belle." Her fingers tried to tuck the errant strands back into her coiffure. "Exactly what do you hope to find?"

"Answers." Camellia sniffed. "Isn't the Bible supposed to have all the answers?"

"I suppose so. . .if you're a preacher."

"The book of Proverbs has good advice for everyone."

Jane wrinkled her nose. "I suppose you're right, but you have to weed through all the ones that don't apply to get to the good ones."

Camellia could remember thinking the same way, so she knew nothing she said would change Jane's mind. All she could do was pray for her friend to have an awakening that would open Jane's heart and mind to the importance of each verse in the Bible.

Thad walked up to them, and Jane moved over to make a space between her and Camellia. He stepped into it. "What are my two favorite ladies discussing?"

The question made Camellia's brows rise. This was the Thad she remembered from New Orleans—the kind, debonair escort with a ready quip and winning smile. She liked him much better than the angry, bitter man who spoke of vengeance and reprisals.

"We were talking about the Bible," Jane answered.

He looked up at the sky and pursed his lips. " 'Blessed are the peacemakers: for they shall be called the children of God.' "

Camellia wondered why that verse had sprung to his mind. Did he wish to be a peacemaker? This was indeed a change, one that could only be wrought by God. She looked at him with new eyes. "Can you imagine listening to Jesus on that hillside?"

Thad looked at her, his gaze seeming to penetrate to her very soul. "His words are no less valid today or they wouldn't be included in the Bible."

Jane's voice broke the deepening spell between them. "I'm beginning to think we're at church."

Camellia turned back to the vista. "Look, there's the city."

A boat bristling with cannons approached them, and Thad sighed. "I'd best leave you two to pack your belongings while I go reassure those gentlemen that we are no threat."

Jane left to do as her brother suggested, but Camellia didn't care if she never saw any of the clothing she'd brought on this trip. Most of it was too filthy to even be given away. As soon as she got back to civilization, she would order a whole new wardrobe.

Men in worn gray uniforms walked past her with serious looks on their faces. Camellia watched as they checked every nook and cranny of the boat. Thad talked with one of the other officers. Eventually the soldiers left, and the boat continued to the port. As they drew nearer, her gaze swept the boats tied together at the dock. Tugs and schooners towered over canoes and pirogues. The distinctive smokestacks of other steamships filled the air with black steam and cinders. At least this area seemed untouched by the war.

Her breath caught when she noticed the lettering on one of the steamships. It couldn't be. And yet there it was. The *Water Lily*. Her family was in Vicksburg. Camellia's heart leapt in her chest. She wanted to shout at the captain to hurry.

Jane came back to the deck. "I'm ready."

"Look." Camellia pointed to her sister's boat. "My family is here."

"I'm happy for you." Jane gave her a brief hug. "I hope this doesn't mean you're planning to leave me after we land."

The unalloyed joy she'd felt was pierced by sadness. She put an arm around her friend. "Maybe we can all go back to Natchez together."

A shake of her friend's head negated that idea. And Camellia understood why. It was the war. Jane would want to remain on Confederate soil so she could stay in touch with her brother, the soldier, and her father, the blockade runner.

"Maybe your family has fled to Vicksburg, and all of us can stay here."

Given her sister and brother-in-law's views, Camellia doubted that possibility, but she kept her own counsel. And prayed for God to work out the things she could not see. A feeling of peace settled on her shoulders as the verse she'd read that morning came back to her. *"A man's heart deviseth his way: but the Lord directeth his steps."*

"Camellia! Look, there she is!"

She waved her arm in a wide arc. "Lily! Blake!" Her feet flew across the gangplank. As soon as they hit the dock, she was caught up in a three-way hug.

"Are you hurt? Where have you been?" Lily's question melded with Blake's.

Laughing, Camellia added one of her own. "How long have you been here?"

Before they could answer, another person joined them. "I know this wretched creature is not my dainty Camellia."

Freezing at the sound of her father's voice, Camellia turned. And smiled. "I'm afraid it's me."

He opened his arms, and she walked into them. For the first time since she'd learned this man's real identity, she felt a connection with him.

Lily and Blake crowded around them. Questions and answers flew through the air like the gulls that followed behind fishing boats. By the time all of the stories had been sorted out, the packet was empty. Camellia looked around for Jane and Thad.

"Your friends have gone to their home ahead of us." Blake answered the question in her gaze. "We rented rooms in a hotel downtown, but we'll ask them to join us for dinner if you'd like."

"Of course she would like." Lily smiled at her. "She's in love with that handsome soldier, remember? That's the reason we let her go to Vicksburg."

Camellia opened her mouth to disagree but decided this was not the time to try to explain her divided loyalties. "But I have nothing to wear."

"Never fear." Her father's eyes twinkled. "Your sister brought one or two of the things that arrived from New Orleans after you left."

Lily nodded. "One or two trunks, he means. You should have heard Jensen complaining about their weight."

"Jensen is with you?"

"And Tamar, too. They are watching Jasmine." Blake put two fingers in his mouth and whistled. A carriage rolled away from the curb toward them, and all four of them climbed in.

A short ride later brought them into the central part of Vicksburg. Camellia was conscious of the stares her tattered garments and gnarled hair garnered in the lobby, but her family closed ranks around her and whisked her to a room. It looked huge to her, with a four-poster bed, two bureaus, a dressing table, and a sofa.

She turned to look at Lily who had followed her into the room. "Who's staying with me?"

"No one." Lily hugged her once more. "This whole place is for you."

Camellia perched on the edge of the sofa. "I feel like a princess."

"And you're going to look like one, too. But first, why don't you relax and take a nap. You've lost so much weight."

"I know. I've become a hag."

"No, no." Lily sat next to her and put a hand on her shoulder. "You're beautiful. All you need is a little rest, some fresh food, and your clothes. You'll feel better in no time."

It felt good to wash her face and hands, to strip off her clothes and choose something from the bureau Lily had filled with the clothing from her trunks. It felt even better to climb into the soft bed and pull the cover up to her chin.

The only things that remained troublesome were the grass-green eyes that chased her into oblivion.

"I wish you weren't leaving in the morning." Thad's soulful brown gaze pricked her conscience. "We need you. . .*I* need you. . .here."

Camellia stepped back as required by the dance and curtsied. Her smile was not as firm as it should have been. She took two steps forward and curtsied again. "I have to go with my sister. She's upset that I left Vicksburg with you last time."

"I know. But that was my fault. I should have realized the danger."

"Don't be silly." Her smile relaxed into a more natural curve as she sought to allay his guilt. "No one could have known what would happen in Memphis. Lily should be glad you were there to protect us on our trip to Jacksonport."

The music ended. Thad offered her an elbow and escorted her from the dance floor. Camellia was immediately besieged by other handsome soldiers. She was the most popular girl at the party. She should be giddy with excitement, but a strange emptiness filled her with each new partner. Some stepped on her toes while others regaled her with stories of their exploits on the field of battle. She had never been so ready to leave a party.

Jane and Thad talked nonstop on the way back to the hotel, neither noticing that Camellia hardly spoke. When the carriage came to a halt, she gathered her wrap and reached for the door handle.

"I'll be right back, Jane." Thad's hand covered hers on the handle.

Camellia jerked her hand away as though his touch burned it.

Jane settled in the far corner of the carriage. "Don't hurry on my account. I may even take a nap." She lowered one eyelid at Camellia before turning her head away.

Thad stepped down, unaware of the byplay between Jane and Camellia. He reached a hand toward her, and Camellia allowed him to help her from the carriage.

"Thank you for a lovely evening." She turned to go inside.

His hand encircled her elbow. "Wait a moment."

She sighed. "I know what you're going to say, Thad. I'm sorry I can't stay in Vicksburg, but it's out of the question. My family needs—" Her mouth dropped open when she turned to look up at him, ending the speech she'd prepared.

Thad had dropped to one knee. His head was lower than her shoulder.

"Please get up, Thad."

"No." He reached for her hand, raising it to his lips and placing a warm kiss on it. "I have something to ask you, Camellia."

She wanted to pull her hand away, but his grip was too strong. "Thad, please. You're embarrassing me."

"Camellia, you are the most beautiful woman I've ever met. But that's not the best thing about you. Looks fade, but not the things in here." He thumped his chest with his free hand. "You care about others. I've watched you under the most extreme of circumstances. You didn't break. You never complained or whined."

"Neither did Jane."

His smile lifted only a corner of his mouth. "I'm not in love with my sister, Camellia. Now will you hush and let me finish?"

She gave him a slow nod.

Another carriage pulled up at the front of the hotel, and a couple got out. They stared at Camellia and Thad. The woman giggled.

"Camellia, I love you." His words came faster. "Please say you'll marry me and make me the happiest man alive."

"I. . .uh. . .I don't know what to say, Thad."

He stood and brushed dirt from the knees of his trousers. He didn't pull her into his arms but stood with his arms hanging loose at his side. "The obvious answer is yes."

She shook her head. "I can't. . ."

"Don't answer right now." He put a finger on her lips. "Not unless you're going to give me an emphatic yes."

Camellia couldn't bear to see the hurt in his eyes, so she looked past his shoulder and remained silent.

"I thought so." He turned to walk toward the hotel entrance and held the door open for her. "Just promise me you'll think about your answer while you're gone."

Tears sprang to her eyes. What woman would be silly enough to turn him down? Yet she couldn't accept his offer. Not until she sorted out her muddled feelings. "We've been living in each other's pockets for more than a month now. I think spending some time apart is a good idea."

Silently, he bowed and watched her with his sad brown eyes.

Camellia entered the hotel and went to her room. As the maid helped her undress, her mind kept going over Thad's proposal. She knew she'd done the right thing by not accepting him. So why did she feel like she'd kicked an innocent puppy?

Chapter Thirty

"You need to get out of that sunshine before you turn yo' skin as dark as mine." Tamar stood at the entrance to the parlor.

Camellia blinked away her drowsiness. "I'll go get a hat."

"T'ain't no hat to protect you from the glare off the water. You need to get inside here and help with the mending."

Making a face, Camellia pushed herself out of the chair she had been resting in. "I can't sew at all."

"Humph. A fine job they did at that fancy school, then. Now you go help your sister. I'm going to check on Jasmine and make sure she's doing the schoolwork Lily assigned." Tamar disappeared into the shady interior.

Camellia wondered if Tamar ever worried about losing her freedom. She had lived most of her life as the property of Camellia's grandparents, and she had never seemed unhappy with her situation. She had lavished affection on all three of her charges. But that had been before Lily bought a steamship and before Tamar fell in love with Jensen. Camellia had been thrilled when the woman who raised her gained her freedom and married Jensen, Blake's friend and employee.

Their situation gave the issue of slavery a human face. If Tamar had remained a slave, she would have had to petition Grandmother for the right to marry. How many other Tamars and Jensens were denied the chance for happiness because of slavery? The question made her heart ache and brought Jonah's arguments back to her. Yet without slavery, so many plantations would fail. Was there not some middle ground that would work for everyone?

Putting away the question for later, Camellia moved into the parlor, pulled out a chair, and sat next to her sister.

"Oh good. I can use an extra hand." Lily nodded her head at the pile of starched linen and clean socks that hid the surface of the table in front of her. "I don't know how I can get so far behind."

Camellia made a face. "I'd rather be scrubbing the deck outside."

"I know you've never enjoyed handwork, but surely you learned enough at La Belle to be able to sew a straight line." Lily handed her a needle and some thread. "Why don't you show me what they taught you?"

"I doubt you'll be impressed." Catching her tongue between her teeth, Camellia concentrated on threading the needle. Nostalgia brought a sad smile to her face as she recalled the day she'd sown her sampler to her skirt. Life had seemed so much simpler then. . .before she'd seen the ugly face of war. Camellia glanced toward her sister. "Do you ever wish you could go back into the past?"

Lily shook her head. "I'm happy to be where I am. If you spend time always looking back over your shoulder at what was, you'll miss out on a lot."

"I just wish things were not so complicated."

"It's true that adults have more responsibilities than children." Lily inspected the napkin she was working on. "But many of our problems are as simple as theirs."

Camellia huffed her disbelief.

"No, it's true. We tend to think everything is complicated. Think about how the Pharisees tried to trip up Jesus. They asked him to list the commandments in order of importance."

"How complicated could that be? There are only ten commandments, after all."

Lily raised her eyebrows. "Whole volumes of laws have been written to support those ten rules, but that's not even the point. Jesus pointed out a simple answer. He said that we must first love God with all our hearts, souls, minds, and strength. Secondly, we are to love our neighbors as ourselves. He told the Pharisees to forget about everything else and concentrate on those two things alone."

"It can't be that easy."

"I didn't say it was easy, Camellia. I said it was simple. Even the most ardent Christians may struggle at times with loving God with everything in them. And it's extremely difficult to love someone who is trying to harm you."

"But if everyone did the same thing. . ." Camellia let her voice trail off, trying to imagine a world without strife.

"Someday we will. When Christ comes again, everyone will bow to Him."

Another thought occurred to her. "If everyone will bow to Him then, why do we worry about following His Word now? I mean, if everyone will be saved when He comes back, what difference does it make how we live?"

"I didn't say everyone would be saved. Christ promised that some will claim to be His children, but He will not know them. Those pitiful souls will be separated from God for all eternity." She shivered and reached for another cloth to mend. "I know you believe in God and that He sent His Son, Jesus Christ, to die for your sins, Camellia. Listen to God, always keeping your heart in repentance toward Him. Love Him and love the people around you. God will take care of the rest."

It sounded too easy to Camellia. And how was she supposed to apply her sister's advice to the problem she was facing? What answer was she going to give Thad the next time she saw him?

"Camellia, I've prayed a lot about your future." Lily hesitated before continuing. "I worried that you might not have the right priorities in mind. But I've seen the difference in you since the beginning of the year, and I have confidence you are seeking the path God intends you to follow. It will not be the same path as mine or Jasmine's, but that's as it should be."

Her sister's words washed over Camellia like a cleansing flood. If Lily believed in her, she must be doing something right. The little voice trying to insist that she still didn't know what to do was firmly squashed. She didn't need to make the decision today, after all. Once they arrived at Blake's family home, they would probably stay at least a month. Perhaps she would figure out what to do before the voyage home.

❧

"Heave to." The order was punctuated by a blast from a cannon.

Blake bounded up the steps from the engine room, his gaze landing on Lily before swinging to the gunboat stationed near their bow. "Are you all right?"

Papa stared down at them from the hurricane deck. "You may want to shut off the boiler and weigh anchor before those fellows get nervous."

Jensen appeared from the galley and moved toward the anchor, releasing the pin with a minimum of effort.

Blake disappeared down the steps into the engine room once again, and Lily heard the hiss of steam being vented. The paddle wheel stopped, and they were still in the water, ready to be boarded.

The tin-clad steamer, not much larger than the *Water Lily*, was fully outfitted for battle. Three large cannons poked muzzles through the tin that offered protection to the sailors manning them. She could still see smoke rising from the one that had fired a warning shot past them.

Both wooden decks and the pilothouse were encased in sheets of tin that would stop a hail of bullets. As she watched, sailors in dark blue poured from the interior of the ship, bayonetted rifles in their arms. Above them the familiar flag of the United States waved its colors.

Blake came up next to her and slipped a comforting arm around her waist. "You should probably go inside with Tamar and your sister while your father and I talk to the officers."

"I'm not afraid of them."

"That's not the issue here, Lily." Blake kept his tone light, but his fingers squeezed a warning. "I don't want the captain or his men to be distracted. Let me show them our papers, and we'll be on our way in no time. Both of us want to reach Cape Girardeau before the sun sets."

She cupped his chin with her hand. "Just make sure you don't get shot or impressed. I wouldn't relish being left on the bank while the Union navy sails away with my boat."

Camellia, Jasmine, and Tamar met her at the door to the parlor.

"What will happen now?" Camellia's face was as white as a bleached napkin.

Tamar didn't look as concerned as she had the night they crept into New Orleans to rescue Camellia and Jane. She stood next to the doorway, her legs spread and her arms crossed over her chest.

Lily encouraged them to sit down, enclosing Jasmine in her arms. The men would talk to the sailors, show them the papers that cleared the *Water Lily* for travel along the Mississippi and Ohio Rivers. Before leaving Natchez, she and Blake had signed sworn statements of fealty to the United States to receive their clearance. At the time she had thought it an unnecessary precaution to take. They had never been stopped by either side before. But now she was glad Blake had insisted.

The minutes passed slowly, but Lily took comfort in the fact that no one was shouting or shooting. She closed her eyes and prayed for the safety of their crew and the men on the gunboat. Peace blanketed her as she took her petition to God, and Lily opened her eyes.

Camellia had moved to the window and was watching the action through a slit in the curtains.

"What's going on?"

"Not much. One of the Yankees—"

"Federals," Lily corrected her sister.

Camellia sighed and started over. "One of the *Federals* is talking to Blake. . . . Now he's going back to his boat. . . . Blake's waving at our father. . . . I don't see Jensen."

The sound of the anchor chain as it was being wound back up told them what Jensen was doing.

"I'll be back." Lily released Jasmine, rose, and put her hand on the door, surprised when it moved under her hand. Had a deserter sneaked on board while the two boats were lying side by side? She took a step back, breathing a sigh of relief when Blake's dark hair and blue eyes appeared.

"Are all of you going to lollygag in here the rest of the afternoon?" His smile teased her. "If this is the effect your debutante sister is going to have on you, we'll have to leave her in Cape Girardeau."

Lily rolled her eyes. "And to think I was praying for your safety."

"And a good thing, too." He caught her in a hug and dropped a quick kiss on her forehead. "That was the USS *Rattler*. Her captain is spoiling for a battle and seemed a bit put out that we weren't blockade runners or spies."

She looked at him more closely to see if he was still teasing. What she saw made her heart stutter. Whatever had transpired outside had been a close-run thing. Visions of Blake, Jensen, and Papa being carried off in chains while strangers in blue uniforms commandeered the *Water Lily* took form in her head. Lily closed her eyes and thanked God for His protection before following her husband to the engine room.

The sun had not quite sunk below the horizon as they passed under the guns of a fort south of Cape Girardeau and began looking for an overnight berth. The dock was crowded with warships—steamers, screw steamers, and schooners. All flew the Stars and Stripes, and most bore evidence of contact with Confederates.

They tied up at the end of a pier, and Blake met with the harbormaster before returning to report to the others. "He says we can stay here tonight, but tomorrow we'll need to come back and move to make way for ships that are currently out on patrol."

Lily nodded. "Does he know where your family is?"

"He's heard of a sick preacher who lives a couple of miles downstream."

"Do you think that's him?"

Blake shrugged. "It's as good a place to start as any. After we get the boat settled tomorrow morning, I'll walk down there and see whether or not it's my father's home."

Touching his arm, Lily gave him an encouraging smile. "I'm glad we're finally here. As soon as we find your father, we'll get him on the road to recovery."

"I hope you're right." Blake put an arm around her waist. "But no matter what we find, I know God will help us face it."

She rested her head on his shoulder. "I love you."

"I love you, too."

The kiss he dropped on her cheek was sweeter than honey. How blessed she was to have such a godly man as her husband.

Chapter Thirty-one

Blake pointed toward the river. "If we're about to reach my father's house, we could move the *Water Lily* over there and tie her up."

Lily nodded. "It would be nice to have Papa, Jensen, and Tamar close at hand."

Feeling a trickle of sweat down her back, Camellia wished they would reach the house. She had told Lily she could stay on the *Water Lily* as Jasmine was, but her older sister had insisted she wanted Camellia with her.

It seemed they had been walking an hour. At first Camellia had enjoyed the view of the colorful hills. The reds, golds, greens, and browns of the leaves made them look as though God had rained paint down on them. But all these months on board one riverboat or another had meant little walking. Her legs ached, she was huffing like a racehorse, and one of her hat pins was drilling a hole into her head.

"Is that it?"

Lily's question brought her head up. A small house squatted at the end of a twisty lane. Camellia frowned. It looked like a face to her. The door was a nose flanked by two window "eyes." The steps up to the porch looked like a mouth, and the roof continued the image with its brown shingles rising steeply above the porch in imitation of a head of hair. It was smaller than Lily and Blake's boat.

Blake bounded up the steps and knocked on the front door, but Lily and Camellia waited on the lane behind him.

After a moment, the door opened a crack. Camellia thought it might be a woman who answered, but she wasn't certain.

Blake said something, and the door flew open.

A girl about Camellia's age flung herself into Blake's arms and hugged him tightly. "It's a miracle."

Blake put his arms around her and bent his head. "How have you been, Anna?"

After a moment, he turned and waved to Lily and Camellia. "I have some special ladies I'd like you to meet."

Camellia planted a smile on her lips as he performed the introductions. After hugging Lily and welcoming her to the family, Blake's sister turned to her. "You're ever so beautiful, Camellia. I hope we're going to be good friends as well as sisters-in-law."

She noticed Anna's threadbare cuffs and the old-fashioned cut to the dress that was partially hidden by her apron. She looked tired, too, and her figure was certainly not as rounded as Camellia's. But she did have a pleasant face and natural gracefulness. With a little time and effort, she could be made into a very presentable young lady. "I'm sure we will."

Anna waved them into the house. "Aunt Tessie, come to the parlor. I have the most wonderful surprise for you."

The older woman who came to greet them had silver-touched brown hair and light blue eyes. Her smile was warm and welcoming as she surveyed them. Then her expression froze as she recognized who stood in the doorway to the parlor. "Ezekiel." Joy rose in her face like the first rays of the morning sun. "You've come home to us."

Ezekiel? Camellia saw the frown on Blake's face even though it was quickly absorbed into a smile of recognition. "Aunt Tessie, you've not aged a day since I was fourteen."

She waved a hand at him. "Go on with you, Ezekiel. You still haven't lost that slick tongue of yours."

"Aunt Tessie." Anna's voice brimmed with concern. "You know Blake prefers to be called by his middle name."

"I know, I know. But old habits die hard. You'll always be Ezekiel to me, dear, but I'll try to remember." Blake's aunt hugged him before turning to Lily and Camellia. "And who are these lovely ladies?"

"This is my wife, Lily, and Camellia, her—"

Aunt Tessie's shriek interrupted him. "You've gone and gotten married!"

Camellia watched, bemused, as Blake's aunt pulled Lily out of her curtsy and wrapped her in an enthusiastic embrace. Then it was her turn to be bear-hugged. At least she could set aside the concern that her family might embarrass Blake. If this lady was any indication, his family had at least as many eccentric characters as hers.

"God bless the two of you for bringing Ezek—" She halted and shook her head. "Blake back to us."

The parlor was small. A sofa, whose worn covering was imperfectly disguised by several doilies, looked like a castoff. The rest of the furniture looked old, too, including several wooden chairs that boasted neither cushion nor upholstery. At least the tables in the room gleamed with furniture polish, somewhat softening the air of spartan frontier existence.

Camellia and Lily sat next to each other on the sofa, leaving sufficient room for Blake to join them. Anna and Aunt Tessie took two of the straight-backed chairs.

"You're an answer to prayer." Anna twisted her hands in her apron.

"Pa?" Blake's voice trembled with the single syllable.

Anna looked out the window for a minute as though gathering her thoughts. "He's growing weaker every day. After the accident, his leg wouldn't heal, and the doctor had to. . .had to remove it. Since then, it seems he's lost the will to live." She put a hand up and swiped at a tear.

"I've tried every remedy I know to help him recover, but your father's an obstinate man." The aunt continued the explanation while Anna recovered her composure. "I'm at my wits' end, as is your sister. But perhaps all that is about to change now. Maybe seeing you will give him a reason to get out of his bed and resume his life."

Blake's face looked as though it had turned to stone. Wasn't that why they were here? Lily had told her that Blake and his father had had an argument years ago. This trip was supposed to give him a chance to make amends. So why did he look so frozen? "I won't feed his ego just to keep him alive."

The words fell into the silent room, and Camellia wished she could be somewhere else. Was there something she could say to diffuse the tension? The weather? The trip to Cape Girardeau? Nothing seemed appropriate, so she kept her gaze trained on her lap and waited.

"No one's asking you to lie to Pa." Anna stood and paced across the room, her stride too wide to be considered proper for a young lady. Mrs. Dabbs would have corrected her, but no one said a word in this parlor. "But I hope you can find it in your heart to forgive him for whatever wrong he's done to you."

Blake stood and walked to his sister. Camellia looked up and caught the determined look on her brother-in-law's face. "I'll do my best." His words, like his face, were filled with determination. "That's all I can promise."

Anna reached up and touched his cheek. "That's all anyone can ask of you."

"How long will you and your family be staying with us?" The aunt turned her attention to Lily.

Lily glanced at her husband for an answer, but he was still talking to his sister. "I'm not really certain. We weren't sure what the situation would be. The note Blake received was rather cryptic."

"You received a note?"

"Yes." Lily took a deep breath. "The note said Reverend Matthews was very sick and that y'all needed Blake's support."

A frown appeared on the aunt's face. "I wonder who sent the note? It had to be someone who knows us and who knew Blake and where he was."

Lily shrugged. "I'm just glad whoever it was took the time to let us know. Blake would have been distraught if he'd learned about this when it was too late to help."

"We'll be happy to have you as long as you'll stay." Anna left her brother and walked to the door. "I'm going to let Pa know you're here before I leave for my job at Devore's. I'll be back before dark."

"Oh no." Her aunt also stood. "Your lunch is not ready yet. I forgot all about it in the excitement."

The two of them exited the room.

Lily stood and moved toward Blake. "Are you okay, dear?"

"I suppose so." His tone was bleak. "So much has changed since I left."

Camellia stood and cleared her throat. "I think I'll go see if I can help someone do something."

Neither of them said anything, so she exited and looked around the foyer. What was she supposed to do with herself now?

❧

Blake felt his shoulders tense as he passed through the doorway into his father's bedroom. The curtains were drawn, seeming to shut out light, hope. . .and life. In the dimly lit interior, he could make out the posters at each corner of his father's bed, but he could not make out the man's form behind the thick bed curtains hanging between them. "Pa?"

"Who's there?" The voice was querulous and shaky.

Blake's memory of his father's voice was much stronger, deeper, frightening. He glanced at Aunt Tessie, who was sitting a few feet away from the bed, a book in her lap. "It's your son come to visit you."

"Ezekiel?"

Blake grimaced at the name. He'd hated it as a child. Even after his parents had told him about the prophet he'd been named for. Ma had taken pity on him and began calling him by his middle name—her maiden name—Blake. But Pa had never called him anything else. "Yes, it's me, sir."

Silence filled the room. Blake wondered if the man had fainted from shock. Or was he struck dumb with horror?

Long, pale fingers pulled back one of the bed curtains a few inches. Blake could feel the chill of his father's gaze. It reminded him of the past—of being pierced by his parent's wrathful looks and fiery accusations. The hand fell back. "Why did you come?"

"Enoch," Aunt Tessie said as she rose from her chair and placed her book on it, "that's no way to treat your only son."

" 'The son shall not bear the iniquity of the father, neither shall the father bear the iniquity of the son: the righteousness of the righteous shall be upon him, and the wickedness of the wicked shall be upon him.' "

Blake's ears burned as he realized his father was quoting from the book of Ezekiel. He knew because he'd turned to that same verse many times as a young man. It had been comforting to him then to believe that his father's sins wouldn't be passed on to him. He had enough sins of his own to be concerned about. "If you're trying to say that I should not blame my mistakes on you, then you don't need to worry. I'm man enough to take responsibility for my mistakes. But I am not sure God will judge either of us righteous."

A whispery sound came from behind the curtains as his father apparently shifted his position in the bed. This time when the fingers appeared, they jerked back the cloth between Blake and his father.

Schooling his features to show none of his surprise, Blake looked at the man who had always stirred such fear in him. Propped into a sitting position with pillows behind him, his pa seemed much less frightening now. Wispy tendrils of graying hair fell over his forehead. His cheeks were gaunt from privation, and his faded blue eyes seemed filled with sorrow and regret. His mouth worked, but no words issued from it.

The years of bitterness seemed to melt away as Blake looked at his father's bent shoulders and lined face. Should he bow? Offer his hand? Try to hug the feeble man? Uncertainty kept him rooted to the floor a few feet away from the edge of his father's bed.

"I've prayed for this day." His father reached out his arms. "Please say you'll forgive me."

In all the times Blake had imagined facing his father, he'd never once thought the man would ask him for forgiveness. He'd expected a thundering scold, a litany of his shortcomings, or perhaps a demand that he leave immediately. He shook his head. "It wasn't all your fault, Pa. I shouldn't have run away."

"I've missed you, Son."

Blake moved toward the bed and hugged his father, his own eyes filled with tears. "I'm sorry it took me so long to come home."

"The important thing is that you're here now." Aunt Tessie's practical voice reminded Blake she was still in the room. "God has a way of working things out once we give Him our obedience." Her words resounded with faith and truth.

Blake closed his eyes and thanked God for giving him and his father this moment, this chance to heal the wounds of the past. "I know you've had a hard time over the past few months, Pa."

"They took my leg, Ezekiel. I'll never walk again." His father's voice was choked with unshed tears. "I'll never stand at the podium and look out over my church."

"I know, Pa." Blake straightened and took his father's hands in his own. "But we'll make some crutches for you. With prayer and hard work, we'll have you moving around this house like you always did. By spring you'll be back in your church telling them about doing all things through Christ."

Pa looked down at the sheet covering him and said nothing.

"That's right. God's got a lot of things for you to do. If He didn't, you'd be gone from here." Aunt Tessie pulled back a curtain to let the afternoon light into the room. "It's about time you remembered you're here for His purposes, and I'm pretty sure He didn't intend for you to lie about in here any longer."

Watching his father's head and shoulders rise at his aunt's words, Blake felt hope flooding him with the thought that it wasn't too late. His father's indomitable spirit might return. And he intended to stay here long enough to see that it did. No matter what difficulties they had ahead of them, they would face them together.

Facing difficulties together reminded him that his father had a few other surprises in store for him. "Pa, I've changed a lot since the last time we saw each other, and I owe a lot of that to a young lady I want you to meet. Her name is Lily. . .Lily Matthews."

"You're married." It was more a statement than a question.

Blake nodded.

"Well, go get her." His father leaned back against the pillows and closed his eyes.

Concerned that he had overtaxed his father's strength, Blake patted his hand. "It can wait, Pa. You rest a bit. She'll still be here when you wake up. We're not going to leave anytime soon."

"Good."

Blake leaned closer to hear his father's whisper.

"I want to thank her for bringing my son back to me."

Chapter Thirty-two

Camellia looked up from the letter she'd been trying to compose as Lily and Aunt Tessie, as she'd insisted Camellia call her, entered the warm parlor. "How is Mr. Matthews feeling this morning?"

Lily looked more than a little unsettled, her face paler than normal.

"He's feverish." The older woman's face wore a worried frown. "I'm going to the kitchen to prepare some tea that should reduce his fever and make him more comfortable."

Camellia put down her letter, her mind going back to the voyage from Jacksonport to Vicksburg and her helplessness as the sick and wounded soldiers grew weaker. She wanted to learn how to treat illness, how to mend young men instead of grieving over their deaths.

The letter to Jane could wait another day. "May I come with you? I'd like to learn more about making medicinal concoctions."

"Of course you can." Aunt Tessie gave her an approving nod before glancing toward Lily. "Would you like to come with us?"

Lily shook her head. "I'm not very good in the kitchen. Unless you think you'll need my help, I'd like to walk over to the boat and check on Papa, Jasmine, Jensen, and Tamar. I want to make sure they haven't had any problems since Blake and I saw them last week."

"Of course, dear." She beckoned Camellia toward the hall, where they headed to the back entrance and outside.

The air was cold, quickening their footsteps as they crossed the distance between the house and the separate, one-room kitchen. Warmth replaced the chill as they entered the functional room, and Camellia breathed in the mixture of pleasant smells. Coals smoldered in the fireplace that took up one wall, their heat warming her cold cheeks.

She glanced up at the copper pots and black, cast-iron cookware suspended from the ceiling beams overhead. A pair of shelves on the wall to her left was crowded with jugs, tall bottles, ladles, clay crocks, and tin plates. Sitting in a corner beneath the shelves, a wooden butter churn waited for fresh cream. To her right, she noted a tall safe holding bowls, baskets, and an impressive supply of canned vegetables. The fourth wall was used for drying. Herbs with their stems pointing toward the ceiling were fastened in neat bundles, hanging between and over two long tables next to the safe. The plank surface of one of the tables held labeled jars filled with leaves, seeds, creams, ointments, and wood shavings.

Aunt Tessie handed her an apron before she walked to the table with the labeled jars. She picked one up and shook it before removing the lid. "I'll need you to draw some water and put it on the fire to boil."

Camellia tied her apron strings and picked up a black kettle from the hearth. She worked the pump as Aunt Tessie got out some cheesecloth and filled it with curls of bark. "How did you learn about taking care of people?" Camellia asked.

"Experience mostly." The older woman waved a hand toward the safe. "My mother taught me which herbs, flowers, and roots to grow or gather. Sweet myrtle for congestion, aloe for burns, willow bark for fever, and many others. Most of the plants out there in the woods can be used as remedies, but you also need to know which ones to avoid."

"Will you teach me?" Camellia suspended the kettle on the cooking arm and waited for Aunt Tessie to drop in her packet of willow bark before swinging it over the coals.

"I'd be delighted to. Anna has never had time or the inclination to learn."

While they waited for the kettle to boil, Aunt Tessie began the lesson. It didn't take long for Camellia to realize she would need to take notes, so she ran back to the parlor to retrieve her stationery and writing implements. By the time she recorded the information from Aunt Tessie, the tea was ready.

Aunt Tessie arranged the teapot, cup, and saucer on a serving tray. "If you will get some of the ginger cookies from that jar, we'll be ready to take this to my brother."

Camellia followed the older lady up the stairs, opening the bedroom door for her. "Do you want me to wait out here?"

"No. Come on in and help me check our patient's dressing." Aunt Tessie put down the tray and turned to Mr. Matthews's bed.

Embarrassment attacked her as Miss Tessie examined Mr. Matthews's leg, but that disappeared as she concentrated on the wound and learned how to check for infection. Black sutures held the skin together where the leg had been removed below the man's knee. She could not imagine what pain he must have gone through.

Their patient was querulous and restive until they pulled the bedcovers back over him. "I don't want any of that nasty swill of yours, Tessie."

"Come now, Mr. Matthews." Camellia smiled at him. "I am anxious to see how effective our remedy will be."

He frowned but didn't resist as she plumped up his pillows and helped him sit in a more upright position. "We've got some ginger cookies for you, too. What if we dip one of them in the tea to sweeten it some?"

"I suppose."

She flattered his efforts and coaxed him to continue trying until he downed a full cup of the willow bark tea.

"You have a natural talent," Aunt Tessie complimented her as they left the bedroom. "And you're so pretty that men seem to naturally want to please you."

Camellia almost stumbled on the next step. She grabbed hold of the balustrade to keep from tumbling to the floor. Was her physical beauty an attribute God had given her for some reason other than snagging a rich husband? Like a stone plopping into a quiet pond, the thought rippled through her past assumptions, changing them forever. Had Aunt Dahlia been wrong in advising her to pursue wealth and ease as her primary goal in life? Jonah's face flashed in front of her, and she heard again his condemnation of her shallow dreams and plans. He'd been right all along.

Aunt Tessie stopped and looked over her shoulder. "Are you dizzy?"

"No. I j–just realized something." How could she explain what had happened? Her life had changed. She felt like a veil had been ripped away and now she could see the banality of her existence. Nothing would ever be the same again.

Raising an eyebrow at the enigmatic answer, the older woman continued her descent.

After a moment, Camellia loosened her grip and followed her to the first floor. She didn't have time right now to ponder her epiphany. She had a lot of things to learn if she was going to fulfill her purpose.

❧

"His name is John. . .John Champion." Anna's pale green eyes seemed to have caught a spark from the nearby fireplace. Her smile was at once tentative and hopeful. "He is a very handsome man, even with his scar. . . ." She blushed. "At least he is to me."

Imagining someone who looked like Tamar's husband, Jensen, Camellia tried not to cringe. She was determined to avoid making assumptions based on appearance as she once would have done. "What kind of work does he do?"

She followed Anna's glance around the room, but everyone else was engrossed in their own conversations. Aunt Tessie and Blake were talking about his father, making plans for a special wheeled chair to help him move about. Blake's father considered his next play on a chessboard while Lily and Jasmine sat opposite him, joining forces in an attempt to defeat him.

"He works on the *Catfish*."

An image of a saddle being placed over the back fin of a splashing fish took form in her mind before Camellia realized Anna must be referring to a steamboat. "He works on the river."

"Yes, and he should be coming to town within the next week or so." Anna gazed into the distance and sighed. "His captain generally comes through here before the Missouri River freezes and puts a stop to northbound travel."

"Maybe you can invite him to dinner so all of us can meet him," Aunt Tessie piped in.

The opportunity of getting to know this man intrigued Camellia, too. She would like to see if he cared for Anna or if the romance was one-sided. He didn't sound like much of a Lothario, but Anna was such an innocent when it came to matters of the heart. How could she be otherwise, living on the edge of the frontier?

A vague sense of discontent had begun to awaken in Camellia as the end of the year approached. Neither Blake nor Lily seemed anxious to return south. Papa, along with Jasmine, had left Jensen and Tamar to guard the *Water Lily* and moved into the Matthewses' home, which was beginning to feel quite crowded. He led the worship service at the church in town and spent the rest of his time helping out with the chores that had been left undone after Mr. Matthews's accident.

Jasmine and Lily cleaned house, Anna worked at the store, and Aunt Tessie spent most of her time in the kitchen, preparing meals for the large household. She had told Camellia she felt free to do so as her pupil was taking such good care of her brother. Reverend Matthews's recuperation had occupied Camellia's time. . .until now. Since he was doing better, she found herself with too much time on her hands. She had written to Jane and to Thad, and she helped out with the chores, but she wanted to do more. She wanted to do something meaningful.

"He won't come." Anna's sad voice dragged her back to their discussion. "But he does attend church if his boat is still here on a Sunday."

Making a face, Camellia considered the young woman sitting next to her. "That's good, but it would show more serious intentions if he were to come calling at your home."

"I've invited him before, but he always refuses."

Camellia put a finger on her chin as an idea popped into her head. "We'll have to see what we can do to fix that problem."

"What do you mean?" Anna's concern was apparent in the frown on her face.

"I'm not very adept with hairstyles, but we can go to the *Water Lily* and ask Tamar to do one of her special arrangements." She looked at Anna's shapeless gray wool dress, her excitement growing as she considered the possibilities. "We'll need to see if any of my clothes will fit you."

"I—I don't know if that's a good idea."

"Trust me." Camellia imagined the finished product. She would take Anna's pleasant looks and turn her into a real belle. If he was not toying with her affections, this man for whom Anna pined would have to declare his intentions or risk losing her to some other suitor. "It's a wonderful idea."

She stood and glanced toward Lily. "Anna and I will be upstairs."

"That's nice." Lily waved at them before returning to her game.

Camellia grabbed Anna's hand and dragged her up the staircase and into the bedroom she shared with Jasmine. "I think you should wear my blue-and-beige walking dress. The cut is very modern, and the colors will complement your skin."

"I don't think I would dare wear one of your dresses to Devore's. What if I spilled something on it?" Anna's eyes rounded as Camellia held up the silk gown. "I could never replace such a beautiful dress."

"You don't have to replace it, silly. All you have to do is wear it to work." She held the dress up to Anna's neck. "This will make your beau realize what a lucky man he is."

Anna blushed. "I. . .I don't—"

"Do you want him to notice you?"

Anna nodded.

"Do you want him to hold your hand and give you compliments?"

Another nod.

"Then you're going to have to trust me. I have a great deal more experience in these things than you. If you'll do what I suggest, you'll soon have Mr. Champion bowing to your every whim."

"But I'll never be as pretty as you."

"To a man who loves you, you will be prettier than any other woman born." Camellia smiled in her direction. "We just have to make sure he realizes that he does love you. Then you'll see. Your Mr. Champion won't have eyes for anyone else."

Over the next several days, Camellia coached Anna in the ways to walk, talk, and flirt with a fan. She called on all of the lessons she'd received at La Belle Demoiselle. She walked with Anna to the store each morning and watched her interact with the customers, dispensing advice and tips after each visitor departed. By the time Blake and Lily came to collect her around noon, the store would be filled with eager customers.

It took until the middle of December, but Anna was now much more polished and self-confident. She could exchange banter with the customers while taking care of their shopping needs. Mr. Devore was happy with the increase in sales and encouraged Anna to listen to her sister-in-law's advice.

Soldiers came by more often and spent more time, and more money, each visit. Anna blamed this phenomenon on Camellia's presence more than any changes in her. But Camellia gave all the credit to her sister-in-law as winter settled in around them.

Anna had blossomed, even though the weather was not warm at all. As long as she followed Camellia's advice, she would surely be a bride by the time spring returned to Missouri.

Chapter Thirty-three

John strode into the store, hope riding high in his heart. He'd begun to think they would never reach Cape Girardeau before the Mississippi became impassable. Every bend in the river seemed to harbor yet another Union ironclad that wished to check their cargo and crew. They had spent more time docked each day than actually moving along the river. But they were finally here.

At least the delay meant he didn't have to worry about running into Blake. That would be a disaster of untold proportions. He felt certain the man would have come and gone in the months since he'd received word about his father's accident. He only hoped Blake was able to lift some of the burden from Anna's shoulders.

Worry nibbled at the edge of his mind as John wondered if Anna was still in Cape Girardeau. What if her father had died? What if she and her aunt had gone to Natchez with Blake? It was a possibility that had occurred to him some weeks ago. He didn't know what he would do if Anna was forever removed from his life. But a return to Natchez was out of the question. Everyone would be far better off if he never went ashore in that town again.

The little bell tinkled as he pushed open the door. John's heart clenched in his chest when he saw a pretty blond standing behind the counter. He could not see her face as her back was turned to him, but she was not his Anna.

A rustle of skirts from the end of the main aisle was accompanied by a quick intake of breath. "John, is it really you?"

His heart began beating once more as he turned and saw her. "Anna." He reached for her hand as he searched her face.

"I was beginning to worry something had happened to the *Catfish*." Her slow smile spread across her face, and her beautiful eyes filled with joy and welcome.

John felt like he'd come home. "It was a slow trip. The war, you know."

"You weren't caught in any battles, were you?"

He shook his head. "But every inch of the boat has been searched over and over again by suspicious officers. Not even a Confederate grasshopper could have traveled with us to Missouri."

Her giggle was like music. Was it his imagination, or had Anna undergone a change since his last visit? He couldn't quite put his finger on it, but something was different.

"I have someone I want you to meet." She put a hand on his arm and pulled him to the counter. "A new member of my family."

The blond who had been standing next to Mr. Devore looked up as they approached, a smile of welcome on her face.

Dismay and fear mingled in John's chest. He tried to separate himself from Anna, but she would not release him. He couldn't break free without drawing even more attention to himself.

"Don't be shy, John. You're going to love her."

He should have seen this coming. He should have made inquiries before walking into the store. But he'd been so focused on seeing Anna. And he'd been certain enough time had passed. Trapped by his impetuousness, John still realized all was not lost. The girl at the counter might not even recognize him. For the first time, he found himself glad for the scars that obscured his features. He managed a shaky smile as Anna introduced him, but not much more.

He needed to escape, get out of the store, get out of town. His pleasure at seeing Anna was overcome by the necessity of keeping his identity hidden. "I'm sorry, but I have to leave now."

Lily's younger sister frowned at his abrupt announcement.

Disappointment stole Anna's smile. "Is something wrong?"

John shook his head. "I'll come back later." He pulled his arm free and began to back away.

As he reached the front door, the bell tinkled, and a couple entered the store. Out of habit, he turned the burned side of his face away to keep from frightening the female.

She was chattering at her escort but stopped in midsentence with a gasp as she caught sight of him. "Jean Luc?"

With those two words, his whole world crashed around him.

❧

"Stay out here, Camellia." Lily ignored the huff of irritation from her sister and strode to the stockroom door.

Anna was already in the room, turning up a lamp to bring light into the windowless room. Blake was right behind her, and Jean Luc lagged farther behind.

Lily was impressed by the cleanliness of the spacious area and the order in which Mr. Devore kept his extra stock. Floor-to-ceiling shelves held everything from baking soda to jewelry, all neatly labeled. It must make reordering simple.

Blake snapped the door shut as soon as Jean Luc entered. His brows were pulled down by a ferocious frown, and he stood with his feet spread and his arms crossed over his chest.

Anna moved away from the lamp and faced her brother. "I don't understand what's going on. How do you know John?"

"First of all, his name is not John." Blake spat out the words. "He's Jean Luc Champney, a wastrel, a thief, and a scoundrel. He has tried to cheat me out of everything I ever cared for."

Lily was as surprised as Anna by Blake's denunciation. "He saved your life and mine that night after the *Hattie Belle* was set on fire."

"It's more likely he was trying to cover up his own culpability and failed to get off the boat in time."

Anna looked from one of them to the other before turning to Jean Luc. "Please, would someone start at the beginning?"

"I will." Jean Luc stepped forward, his shoulders drooping. "I deserve all of your brother's scorn and enmity. I've done things. . .terrible things. I thought at one time that I could start over, leave behind all the mess I caused, and begin my life with a clean slate."

Lily's heart fell as she heard the man's confession. She prayed for guidance to navigate the murky currents of their shared past. Peace settled over her like a warm fur coat. Glancing toward Blake, she could see the condemnation on his face. She stepped closer to him, letting her shoulder rub his arm.

"It all started the night I lost my boat in a card game."

"Half a boat," Blake said, correcting Jean Luc's statement.

Jean Luc nodded. "My father was very angry, even threatening to keep me away from his business. Then Lily bought the other half of the boat, a controlling half, and I decided I could regain the *Hattie Belle* through her."

Lily put a hand to her chest. Jean Luc had never been romantically interested in her. The realization stung, but looking back over the events of the past, she realized she was more than happy with the way God had worked things out. And very thankful she hadn't lost her heart to him.

"When all my efforts failed, I hired a couple of men to tear up a couple of the staterooms." Jean Luc turned to her, confusion apparent in the twist of his eyebrows. "Even that didn't stop you. So I hired them again and told them to do more damage, enough to keep your boat docked for a few days until I could figure out another way to succeed."

The disappointment of learning Jean Luc had not been enamored of her faded as she listened to his tale in growing horror. "You set the *Hattie Belle* on fire?"

"That was never my intention."

"You see now why Jean Luc isn't an acceptable suitor for my sister." Blake's voice was smug. "He's dangerous. He needs to be locked up for trying to destroy our livelihood and for attempted murder."

"I cannot argue with you." Jean Luc held up his hands, crossed at the wrist, and bowed his head. "I'll go with you to the constable. I'll confess to my misdeeds."

"Wait a moment." Lily stepped between the two men. "That story is all fine and dandy, but it has a few holes in it."

"I don't know what you're talking about." Blake kept his voice low.

"I'm talking about the fact that I never heard this from you." She pointed a finger at her husband. "I'm talking about your letting me believe Captain Steenberg and his henchmen were the culprits. You never mentioned that Jean Luc had any part in the mess they left."

"Why should I?" Blake shrugged. "He was dead. Why upset his grieving parents further? You and the rest of the town were saying he was a hero for sacrificing his life to save our lives and the other boats in the harbor. I didn't see any reason to reveal the truth."

Lily tried to set aside her feelings of betrayal to consider Blake's explanation from a logical standpoint. Would she have done the same thing? She didn't know. "I still wish you had told me. Now I have to wonder what other things you have failed to tell me about because you see no need to 'reveal the truth.' "

Blake's arms fell to his side. He looked startled by her words. "I'm sorry. I thought I was protecting you."

"I would have thought you would know I'm not some delicate flower that needs to be protected from the bumps and bruises of life."

An arresting look entered his blue eyes. "You may be able to stand on your own, but you must allow me to protect you. It's my right and my pleasure as your husband."

"Rest assured we'll talk about this later when we're alone, but what we need to focus on right now is Jean Luc and Anna."

"You needn't worry about that." Anna stepped directly in front of Jean Luc. "Did you set my brother's boat on fire?"

He straightened his shoulders, his facial features showing resignation. "Not directly, but it was still my fault."

"Did you try to murder Blake?"

"No." The word shot out of him like the blast from a cannon. He glanced at Lily. "I was trying to free him, remember? I knew someone had to get the boat out into the river, so as soon as I knew you and Blake were safe, I went to the pilothouse."

Lily nodded. "I remember."

"It's true he was not the one who tied me up."

"I almost died that night." Jean Luc touched the scarred side of his face. "When I woke up in a strange town, I thought God had given me a second chance. I returned to Natchez several months later, but everyone thought I was dead. It was wrong of me to try to escape the consequences of my terrible decisions. I know that now. I see that it was cowardice on my part, a desire to escape punishment. But at that time, I convinced myself it would be kinder for my parents. They had gone through so much already. I was content to make a living on the river. I knew I didn't deserve anything more because of what I'd done. But then I met you, Anna, and everything changed. I fell in love with you. . .with your honesty and purity."

A new thought occurred to Lily. "You're the one who sent us the note about Blake's father."

Blake's head jerked as if from a slap.

Jean Luc nodded. "Anna was struggling to survive. She needed your help."

"Didn't you think I would recognize you when I saw you here?"

"I thought you might have left again when I didn't see your boat in the harbor." Jean Luc shrugged his shoulders. "Besides, I couldn't stay away from her any longer."

Blake put his hands on his sister's shoulders and moved her to the side before pointing an accusing finger at Jean Luc. "You'd better learn how to stay away from her, because I'm telling you now that you won't be seeing her again."

Anna gasped. "Blake, please. I'm a grown woman. I can make my own decisions."

"No, he's right." Jean Luc lifted his chin. "You're much too good for me."

"Yes, she is."

Lily could feel the heat of her husband's anger from where she stood a foot away. Jean Luc looked so dejected. While she could not agree with his decision to run from his problems, she could understand how high a price he'd paid for his actions. At this moment, he reminded her of her father. He'd run away when he should have stayed and persevered.

Blake reached for his sister's elbow, but Lily stopped him with a shake of her head. "While I appreciate your concern for your sister, you should give Anna the chance to decide her own future now that she knows the truth about Jean Luc."

He turned his frown on her, but Lily would not back down. She knew she was right about this. Reaching for his hand, she pulled him toward the door. "Let's leave them here to thrash out their problems."

"That's a good idea." Blake's frown did not abate at all. "And I can use the time to hunt down the sheriff and lodge a complaint against him."

Lily seemed to be the only one who heard his threat. She shook her head, dragged the door open, and pushed him through it. "You have five minutes. I doubt I can hold my husband off for any longer than that."

❧

"I'll never understand women." Blake took aim at the piece of wood on the chopping block and split it with his ax.

"I don't think we're meant to." Henrick Anderson picked up the two halves and placed them on the growing pile of firewood. "It's our job to love them and protect them. But as for understanding them. . ."

"Lily is barely speaking to me. She seems to think I had some nefarious reason to keep her in the dark about Jean Luc's treachery."

"Did you?"

Blake grunted. "Of course not. The *Hattie Belle* was gone. By the time I woke up, everyone was saying what a noble thing he'd done to sacrifice his own life for the sake of the other boat owners. Like everyone else, I thought the man was dead. I thought he was beyond taking responsibility for his actions, and I didn't see why his parents should suffer for his misdeeds."

"That sounds logical to me."

"Then why is Lily so miffed?" Blake put another piece of wood on the block. "Why can't she see the truth?"

"She probably can." Henrick chuckled. "But if I know my eldest daughter, she is wondering if there are other things you've been less than truthful about. For your own good reasons, of course."

"That's ridiculous." Blake concentrated on his chore for several minutes—splitting the wood released some of his irritation.

Sweat trickled into his eyes, and he stopped to wipe his brow. "I don't understand Anna, either. She ought to be glad she found out who 'John Champion' really was before she committed herself to him."

"The girl's heart is bruised if not broken." Henrick spoke gently. "Since Jean Luc has disappeared—"

"A fact she seems to blame on me."

"Yes, well. . .I'm sure you didn't arrange for his boat to leave Cape Girardeau, but you probably weren't unhappy to learn of the man's departure."

Of course he wasn't unhappy. Blake didn't want to have to go to the authorities and swear out a complaint against the man. And he wouldn't. . .as long as Jean Luc stayed away from Anna. He put down the ax, crossed his arms over his chest, and waited for Henrick to continue.

"So now that Jean Luc is gone, you're a convenient target for her disappointment."

"That makes no sense at all."

Henrick shrugged. "As I said, it's our job to love the women in our lives, not understand them."

The man sounded just like Camellia—shallow, foolish Camellia—the girl who had told him earlier this morning that he should bide his time. She'd actually suggested he might give the other two women a little time to recover from their disappointments instead of trying to defend his actions. When had she become so mature? When had she grown more levelheaded than Lily?

First she had become Aunt Tessie's assistant, nursing his father and learning how to make remedies. Then she had taken Anna under her wing and showed her how to be more self-confident. Now she was dispensing advice to him. It made absolutely no sense.

"This world would be a sorry place without the ladies." Henrick chuckled again. "Logical or not, we're much better off with them than without them."

"That's easy for you to say." Blake glanced toward the house. "You're not married to a single one of them, nor do you have a sister to watch over."

"No, only three daughters. And I thank God every day for putting them back in my life."

The older man's words struck a chord in his heart. Shame hit Blake. He should be focusing on his blessings—having a wife and a sister who loved him in spite of his shortcomings. They might be put out with him now, but one day they would forgive him. At least he hoped they would.

Chapter Thirty-four

Mrs. Naomi plopped down beside Jean Luc as he whittled a piece of driftwood. "What are you making?"

Hunching a shoulder, he looked at the pattern of grains. "A bird, I guess."

"A seagull!" She clapped her hands together. "You have a fine talent at whittling."

Jean Luc shrugged. What did it matter? His life had come to another dead end. He never should have fallen in love with Anna Matthews. He should have kept to himself, kept his heart free of entanglements. Hadn't he learned yet that he had nothing to offer others? Blake had been right when he'd condemned Jean Luc. He couldn't blame the man for his anger or for the way Anna had run from him that day.

"You've been moping around here for more than a week." Mrs. Naomi's soft voice pulled him from his roiling thoughts.

Jean Luc looked at the river, its muddy surface sliding past them. "I don't know what to do."

"We'll be back in Cape Girardeau by Christmas Eve. Why don't you plan on going to the church service? Your sweet Anna should be there."

"I can't."

Mrs. Naomi squinted at him. "I don't understand what happened between you and that young lady, but I know how much you care for her. And it seemed to me she was taken with you, too."

"That was before her brother told her about my past. He knew me when I was a different man. I tried to hurt him and his wife. And I almost succeeded in getting all three of us killed."

"I see." Mrs. Naomi put a hand on his arm. "I have to admit that sounds pretty awful."

Jean Luc grunted as the knife in his hand slipped and pinked his thumb. A dot of red appeared in the fleshy center of the appendage. He concentrated on it to keep his emotions at bay. When he was sure he could speak without betraying himself, he looked at her kindly face. The captain's wife had been a good friend to him, almost a second mother. But how could she understand? "It was—and is—inexcusable."

"You have given your life to Jesus, haven't you?"

He shrugged. "I guess so."

"No." She shook her head. "There's no guessing when it comes to this. Either you are a child of God or you are not. Jesus died on the cross because He is committed to saving you from eternal damnation. If you've asked Him into your heart, He's washed away your past sins. Even God does not see them anymore."

"But the earthly consequences are still there."

"Yes, and you have to face up to those. But always remember that Jesus loves you. He knows not only what you did but also every thought inside that thick head of yours. And He still has His arms wide open to you."

A faint hope entered Jean Luc's chest. In the turmoil of having to admit his past, he'd neglected Christ's love and acceptance.

Mrs. Naomi winked at him. "As soon as we dock, I want you to go to that girl and lay your heart in front of her. If she rejects you, it will hurt, but you can survive her rejection with God's love to sustain you."

Jean Luc flattened his palm and studied the spread wings of the bird he'd whittled. He could feel his own heart soaring with the freedom Mrs. Naomi's words were bringing to him. "You're a very wise woman."

"I couldn't sit still and let the devil convince you with his lies. He'd like nothing better than to separate you from God, but don't you let him get away with it. No matter what happens in Cape Girardeau, you can always lean on Him."

He offered the seagull to her, but Mrs. Naomi shook her head. "You're going to need a gift to give your girl for Christmas."

Jean Luc smiled. For the first time since seeing Blake and Lily, he began to believe everything might turn out all right.

❦

"When are we going back to Mississippi?" Camellia looked down at her feet as they walked the path to the church on Christmas Eve.

Lily thought for a moment her younger sister had returned to the immature girl she'd once been, the girl who thought of nothing beyond the next social occasion and the newest fashion plates. Then the likely reason for Camellia's question occurred to her. "Are you missing that handsome Captain Watkins?"

"No, that's not it." Camellia lifted her skirts to avoid a puddle. "I would like to see Jane of course."

"Of course." Blake joined the conversation as they walked three abreast.

Lily frowned at him before returning her attention to Camellia. "I've been so impressed with you, Camellia. You've always had a tender heart when it comes to taking care of others, but now you've turned that talent into a calling. You've learned so much about healing and effective treatments. You should be proud of yourself."

"That's just it." Camellia sighed. "Blake's father is getting better now. He really doesn't need me anymore. I want to be useful. I want to make a difference. If you're right and God has given me a calling, I need to find a way to use it. I thought I was helping Anna, but now look at her. She's practically walking on air since Jean Luc showed up this afternoon."

"I know." Lily glanced toward the couple walking a few yards ahead of them, their heads inclined toward each other. "Isn't it romantic?"

"I don't see why everyone else is so pleased to see Jean Luc and my sister together," Blake complained. "Have all of you forgotten what he did?"

Lily planted her feet in the path and tugged on his arm to make him face her. "Your sister is happier right now than she's been since the day she discovered who Jean Luc really was."

"I always thought you had a soft place in your heart for that man, but you're letting your emotions rule your head."

"That's like the pot calling the kettle black." Lily heard Camellia mutter something and move away. She waited a moment until she was sure no one would overhear her words. "If you're wondering whether or not I ever loved Jean Luc Champney, you can rest easy. Yes, I did have a bit of a soft spot for him. His parents tried to force him into their idea of a proper future the same way my aunt Dahlia and uncle Phillip tried to do to me. But that's all it ever was." She pointed a finger at him. "You're the only man I've ever loved."

"I didn't mean—"

"While we're on the subject of Jean Luc, I want to point out a few things for you to consider. First is that he has lost a lot more than you or I have. Sure, we lost the *Hattie Belle*, but I thought you were happy on the *Water Lily*. I know I have been. And God has blessed us abundantly. We have family and friends and a life that has not been spent hiding from our past."

She could see that her words were beginning to get through to her husband. He was finally starting to understand why she'd been so put out with him lately. She had waited for him to discover these truths for himself, but maybe she should have been more direct back when they first found out whom Anna had fallen in love with.

"So you think he should be forgiven? Allowed to escape the consequences of his actions?"

"What I think is that we are not supposed to judge him. Anna has told us he's a Christian. He is our brother as surely as Anna, Camellia, and Jasmine are our sisters. By taking on the role of judge, you are inviting bitterness to creep back into your soul." She took hold of one of his hands and held it to her cheek. "You have only recently rooted out the bitterness you had against your father. Can't you see that you are inviting more pain into your life—our lives—by holding on to this anger against Jean Luc?"

He raised his other hand and cupped her face. "You're a very smart woman, Lily Matthews."

"That's right." Happiness brought a wide smile to her lips. "And don't you ever forget it."

Blake laughed with her, dropped a light kiss on her lips, and grasped her hand in his larger one. "I have the feeling that if I dare to forget, you'll remind me."

❧

Henrick read the story of Christ's birth from the Gospel of Luke to the church that evening. As he spoke of the wonder of that night, the promises of the host of angels, and the birth of the world's hope, Blake closed his eyes and prayed.

He laid at Christ's feet the anger he'd been carrying toward Jean Luc and the worry that his sister had fallen in love with the wrong man. He asked for forgiveness and felt Christ's answer deep inside. Peace and reverence filled him.

By the time the service was over, he knew what he had to do. As they left the church, he asked Henrick to take all of the girls home while he talked with Jean Luc. He could see Lily's worried frown and Jean Luc's fear, but he smiled at both of them, shooing his wife away as he waited for the church to empty.

"I'm sorry about what I did to you and Lily." Jean Luc shuffled his feet and looked at the door with longing.

Blake sat down in one of the empty pews. "I'm sorry, too. I'm sorry you felt cheated and that you had to pay such a high price for your immaturity."

As the words rolled off his tongue, he praised God inwardly. It was only through His power that Blake could utter such phrases and mean them.

"Thank you for understanding."

"You are the one who sent me that note about my father, aren't you?"

Jean Luc nodded. "I didn't know she was your sister. Not until the day she told me that she wished her brother was here in Cape Girardeau. When she told me your name, I couldn't believe it."

Blake tried to imagine what the man must have felt. He wondered if he would have done the same thing if he'd been in Jean Luc's shoes. "It must have been a hard thing for you, knowing you would have to face your past."

With a sigh, Jean Luc sat in the pew opposite Blake. "I knew I had to do it. I still hoped to evade you, you know. I stayed away from Devore's for several months, even when the *Catfish* docked here. I wasn't sure Anna would still be here."

"Why did you come back?"

"I love your sister."

The four words were spoken with an intensity Blake could not ignore. He remembered too well the feeling that he had to get back to Lily no matter the cost. He held his hand out to Jean Luc, who took it after a brief hesitation. "You're invited to come back to our home tomorrow and have dinner with us."

Jean Luc's hope shone as bright as the sunrise. Even the scars on the right side of his face couldn't detract from his joy. "Thank you, Blake. I promise to make your sister happy."

"I still have hope she'll turn you down." Blake clapped him on the shoulder and rose, smiling at the other man to show that his words were not to be taken seriously. He had the feeling his sister was going to accept Jean Luc's offer, and he was beginning to find peace with the idea of welcoming him into the family.

❧

The food on the Matthews family's table was as sumptuous as any of the meals Jean Luc had eaten with his parents, but the atmosphere was very different.

Anna presented him with a platter filled with succulent slices of meat. "Did you try any of the roast duck? It's one of Aunt Tessie's specialties."

Jean Luc patted his stomach. "I couldn't eat another bite if I had to."

She nodded and returned the platter to an empty space on the far side of her plate. "I'm glad you came."

"I'm happier to be here than you can imagine." He touched his napkin to his mouth. "It's the best Christmas I've ever enjoyed."

"Excuse me." Blake stood and tapped his water goblet with a spoon to get their attention. "Now that we've all enjoyed a wonderful meal, my wife and I have an announcement to share with you."

Camellia, sitting on his left, squeaked and put both hands over her mouth. Did she already know what Blake was about to say?

Jean Luc turned his attention to the foot of the table as Lily stood next to her husband, her gaze locked on his face. Blake took her hand and brought it to his lips, kissing her knuckles in an open display of affection that surprised Jean Luc. He loved Anna. He knew that for certain. He could not imagine a future without her in it. But he wasn't sure he would ever feel comfortable letting others see his feelings so clearly.

Lily blushed and tugged her hand away, apparently sharing some of Jean Luc's discomfort. But the affection in her eyes never dimmed.

Blake turned his attention back to the other diners. "Lily just told me this morning that we're going to have a baby."

The room filled with noise. The women squealed and pushed back their chairs, even Anna. They surrounded Lily and practically carried her out of the room, their eager questions and exclamations trailing behind them.

"Congratulations." Lily's father raised his glass to Blake. "Having a child is one of the most rewarding, challenging experiences you'll ever have."

Blake's father nodded. "I'm happy for you, Son. I know you'll be a good father."

"Coming from you, Pa, that means a lot to me." Blake cleared his throat, and Jean Luc thought he saw the sparkle of a tear in the man's eye.

Jensen cleared his throat and stood, offering a hand to Blake. "Congratulations."

"I'm happy for you." Jean Luc added his voice to the other men's. "You're a lucky man."

"Not lucky." Blake exchanged a glance with him. "I'm blessed beyond imagining." The joy radiating from Blake was nearly as warm as the fire in the parlor as they joined the ladies.

Anna looked up as Jean Luc approached her, her expression shifting between uncertainty, excitement, and affection.

"Could you show me the way to your father's library? I wanted to look for a particular volume he mentioned during dinner." Jean Luc knew his excuse was weak, but it was the only way he could think of to separate her from her family for a few minutes.

Anna nodded and rose from her chair. As she put her hand on his arm, he could feel the weight of Blake's gaze. He smiled in what he hoped was a conciliatory way. "We'll be right back."

The lamp in the hallway flickered as they passed it. Anna stopped long enough to pick up one of the tallow candles lying next to the lamp and light it before leading him to a door at the end of the hall. "The library's in here."

Instead of entering the room, Jean Luc reached in his pocket and drew out the carved seagull, holding it in his open palm to present it to her. "I'm sorry, but I couldn't find a box to hold this."

Her mouth formed an O of surprise. "For me?"

"Yes." His throat closed up. Jean Luc swallowed hard and wondered what to say next.

Anna took the tiny bird and held it up. "It's beautiful."

"Not as beautiful as you." Remembering what he'd planned to do, Jean Luc dropped to one knee in front of Anna. His heart threatened to explode out of his chest as he took her free hand in his, but he was determined to say the words he'd been practicing since Blake invited him for dinner the day before. "Anna, I have admired you since we first met. You're dedicated, resourceful, hardworking, and a woman of abiding faith. When I look at you, I see the gentle side of Jesus, and I find hope for a happiness I know I don't deserve. I love you, and I hope you'll consider spending the rest of your life at my side."

Silence answered him. Jean Luc's pulse sped up further. Was she going to reject him? He looked up at her and saw tears in her eyes.

"Anna, why are you crying? Don't you understand? I want you to marry me."

"Yes, I understand, John—Jean Luc, and I would like to. . ." Her voice faded into silence, and she shook her head.

He could hear the resignation in her voice and knew she was about to turn down his offer. His heart clenched. "Do you love me?"

Anna nodded.

His pain diminished somewhat. If she loved him, surely they could work out any other problems.

"I'll marry you—"

He stood and tried to take her in his arms, but Anna held him off with an outstretched arm. "Please let me finish."

Jean Luc nodded and stepped back to give her some breathing room.

"I fell in love with you before I really knew who you were, and now that I do, I find myself concerned about the past you hid from me. I cannot marry you until you have dealt with that past." Her gaze begged him to understand her words. "It's not right for your parents to be grieving your death. As soon as the river opens up again, you need to return to them and let them know the truth. Then I'll marry you."

Now it was his turn to be silent. Could he do it? Could he return to Natchez and face them? Could he bear their condemnation? Calm filled him, the whisper of Christ reassuring him. He would not be alone no matter what happened. "I'll do it."

"Good." Her smile of approval warmed him. "There's one other thing."

Jean Luc raised an eyebrow. "I'm beginning to feel like Jason and the Argonauts."

Anna giggled. "I don't need a golden fleece. I want to go to Natchez with you. I want to meet your parents and be there to support you."

This time when he moved to embrace her, Anna did not demur. He wrapped his arms around her and held her close to his heart. When he covered her lips with his own, emotion welled up in him. Love, tenderness, protectiveness, and a myriad of other feelings he couldn't even name. All he knew was that he, like Blake, was blessed beyond all imagining.

Chapter Thirty-five

Camellia was tired of chaperoning "the lovebirds," as Blake called Anna and Jean Luc. She'd been given that responsibility in Cape Girardeau when Jean Luc left his ship and took up residence at a boardinghouse in town. Now that they were back aboard the *Water Lily*, she could relax. There were way too many people aboard for the lovebirds to need an assigned chaperone.

Bidding Aunt Tessie and Reverend Matthews good-bye the day before had pulled at her heartstrings, but as soon as the paddle wheel began churning the muddy water, Camellia began looking forward to returning to Mississippi.

With an hour to fill and warm sunshine outside, she wandered up to the pilothouse to see what her father and Jasmine were doing. As she stepped onto the hurricane deck, she heard her little sister's voice.

"Why did Jesus want to make people suffer?"

Papa was standing behind the wheel, but he took his gaze from the river and frowned at Jasmine. "Who told you Jesus wants anyone to suffer?"

"Blake's papa said it yesterday in church."

He frowned for a moment before understanding dawned on his face. "Oh no, Jasmine, you misunderstood what he was talking about. Jesus was not happy with His disciples because they weren't letting some youngsters through to talk to Him. He told them to let the children come closer. That's what it means when the Bible says, 'Suffer the children to come unto me.' And He reminded His disciples that all of us have to believe in Him with the same open faith that children have."

Camellia didn't know why she hung back a bit. She only knew she didn't want to interrupt their conversation. She stood at the top of the stairwell, feeling the importance of this moment in her heart.

"So He liked children?"

"Yep. In fact, He loved them. And He loves you, too."

Jasmine tossed her hair over one shoulder with a flick of her wrist. "I love Him, too, Papa. I want to be close to Him like those children in the Bible."

Her sister's words took Camellia back to the day she had confessed her faith in Jesus. She had been even younger than Jasmine was now, but she had known exactly what she was doing.

"Tell me what you know about Jesus."

Why was Papa questioning Jasmine? Why didn't he tell her she was saved?

"He is God's Son who was born a long, long time ago in a stable. When He grew up, He did miracles like healing people who were sick or lame or blind. The important people were upset with Him, and they killed Him and buried Him in a cave."

"That's very good, Jasmine. I can tell that you've been listening closely in church. So why do we talk about Him? After all, He's been dead for a long time."

"No, He hasn't." Jasmine looked toward her father. "When His mama went to the cave where He was buried, He wasn't there anymore."

"Where was He?"

Camellia could see Jasmine's shoulders bend forward as she considered how to answer Papa's question.

"He rose from the grave and told His friends not to worry. He said He was going to heaven to make houses for them."

"That's exactly right, honey. I'm so excited for you." Papa hugged Jasmine. "Once you ask Jesus into your heart, the rest of your life will be different. Are you ready to take that step?"

Camellia's little sister nodded. "Yes, Papa, I want Jesus to fill me up with His love."

Unable to contain her joy, Camellia clapped her hands. Both Papa and Jasmine turned to where she stood. She ran forward and embraced both of them. "I'm so happy for you, Jasmine."

"Let's pray together." Papa glanced back at the river to check their progress. Then he put an arm around each of them and closed his eyes. "Father God, we come into Your presence with hearts of thankfulness, praise, and joy. We give thanks for these my daughters who are Your children. Thank You for revealing Yourself to them, and thank You for letting me witness their abiding faith firsthand. Please accept Jasmine into Your fold and watch over her as You do for all your children. Keep us ever mindful of You and Your wondrous plans for our lives. . . . Amen."

"Amen." Camellia and Jasmine chorused the word at the same time.

Looking out on the winding river ahead of their boat, Camellia thanked God again for this day, her sister's faith, and the wonderful Christian examples in their family. On a beautiful morning like this one, everything seemed perfect. Even the war seemed a continent away.

❧

"Grant is obsessed with winning Vicksburg."

Jonah stared at his brother across the counter at the shipping office. Eli had aged a decade since the war began. His hairline had faded back, making him look more like Father, and the furrows on his forehead had deepened since the last time they'd been together. "Yes, but for good reason. If we can only gain control of Vicksburg, we'll choke off the supply lines and communications of the Confederacy."

"I know." Eli put a hand over his mouth and coughed long and hard. When the paroxysm was over, he drew a handkerchief from his pocket and wiped his forehead.

Jonah wondered if the physical changes in his brother were more from illness than advancing age. "You sound terrible."

"I'm better than I was a week ago." He reached for the goblet sitting on the desk in front of him and took a long swallow of water. "Renée and I have both recovered, but the children are still struggling with fever and chills. We are just thankful it's not yellow fever."

A shudder passed through Jonah at the dread his brother's words caused. With the privations of war and the arrival of summer, an outbreak of yellow fever was likely.

Eli put down his water. "You're not going to get me off the subject of General Grant. Is it true he's trying to dig a tunnel around the city of Vicksburg?"

"Yes, it's true." Jonah sighed. Concentrating on the campaign strategy of his leaders was better than worrying about the future.

"Does he think he's trying to change the course of a meandering stream? That's the Mississippi, the Father of Waters. He must have no concept of its strength. The spring rains have already begun. The floods will wipe out his efforts and probably kill a lot of good men."

"I know. The water is already threatening the dikes at New Orleans."

"You've been to New Orleans?" Eli's expression turned eager. "Is Sarah still holding court? How are Mama and Papa?"

"Well enough, although Father almost shot me when he realized I was wearing a Union uniform."

Eli chuckled. His cough returned with a vengeance.

Jonah wished he could do something to ease his sibling's symptoms. The thought took him back to the days when Camellia tended him so gently. Nostalgia and yearning swept through him, but he'd become adept at pushing those feelings to the back of his mind. "I think you should go upstairs and rest." He pushed himself up from the leather chair on the opposite side of his brother's desk.

"Visiting with you is as good as any tonic my wife has given me." Eli stood, too, stepping around his desk to give Jonah a hug.

"What does your doctor say?"

Eli threw him a rueful glance. "Doctor? We've not seen one of those for the past month."

"There's help at the fort."

"But they're needed to tend the soldiers."

"That's a ridiculous notion. I can find someone to at least prescribe a remedy for your cough."

"Don't worry about us. God will provide."

Jonah put a hand on Eli's shoulder. "Perhaps He is providing. . . through a brother with the right connections."

"Just pray for us."

"Always." The love he felt for his sibling swelled up. Before Jonah could form the words to express his affections, someone knocked on the library door.

Eli's frown returned as one of his servants poked her head into the library. "I'm sorry to disturb you, sir, but you have visitors."

"I thought I left instructions that we are not receiving."

The young woman bobbed her head. "They are from out of town."

No matter who the visitors were, they would not want to remain in a sick household. Jonah looked at his brother. "Why don't you let me go and explain the situation?"

"I wouldn't mind your support." Eli swallowed hard to suppress yet another cough, and the two of them walked to the parlor.

When they entered the room, the first person Jonah saw was Blake Matthews. His heartbeat increased a notch. Then he realized that two ladies were with the man—and one of them was the only woman who'd ever turned his world upside down. His mouth turned as dry as a desert. "Camellia."

While Eli greeted Blake and Lily, Jonah could hardly keep his eyes from devouring Camellia. She was wearing a yellow dress almost the same color as her hair. In combination, they formed a halo around her that made him think of angels.

His brother indicated the sofa and chairs. While he explained the situation in his home, Jonah took a seat next to her. A thousand contradictory impulses attacked him.

"What are you doing here?" Her voice was barely more than a whisper.

"This is my brother's home." He saw her cheeks redden and wished he could recall the words. He hadn't meant his answer to sound so insolent.

"Of course. I just thought you would be in Confederate territory somewhere gathering information. But I see you are wearing your true colors now."

The venom in her words opened a gulf as wide as the river between them. A gulf he knew he couldn't bridge. She was as dedicated to preserving the Old South as he was to changing it.

"I thought you would be in Vicksburg with people who think like you do." The sarcasm in his voice was a mask for the pain in his heart. Why did this one woman cause so much emotional turmoil in him? She didn't even have to try to be aggravating. Her presence in his brother's parlor was enough.

"As a matter of fact, I've spent the last several months in Cape Girardeau."

His jaw dropped. "With Yankees? Have you had a change of heart?"

"Not that it's any of your business, but Blake's family lives there. His father was in a bad way, so we went up to see if we could help."

Jonah snapped his mouth shut. She was right. She didn't owe him an explanation. He had absolutely no claim on her. But that didn't stop the curiosity consuming him.

"Camellia." Her older sister's voice interrupted their private conversation. "Did you hear that? Eli, my sister has learned so much about taking care of the sick and infirm that she now carries her own medicine bag. It's chock-full of everything your poor family could need."

Eli's gaze met his own. A thankful prayer filled Jonah's heart at the answer God had sent before they'd even made their requests. Perhaps he would even get a chance to explore the changes in Camellia while she was here.

Chapter Thirty-six

Camellia hummed a song as she climbed the stairs, a tray with bowls of warm broth in her hands. Although she missed her sisters, taking care of the Thornton boys and Renée had filled her time.

Blake had returned to the *Water Lily* with Lily and Jasmine as soon as they realized the danger, but he had come to check on her and the Thornton family daily.

She bumped open the boys' bedroom with a hip. "How are y'all doing this afternoon?"

Brandon and Cameron were out of bed, studying their lessons in one corner of the room. Remington, the youngest, had been the first one to catch the croup, and he was the slowest to recover from its ravages.

Setting the tray between the two older boys, she walked to Remington's narrow bed. He was propped against several pillows, his dark hair falling over his forehead. "I'm ready to get up."

Although she sympathized with him, Camellia shook her head. "One more day to make sure the fever doesn't return."

He groaned and rolled his eyes. "It's not fair. Cameron and Brandon don't have to stay in bed."

"At least you don't have to read this awful poetry." Brandon made a face at the book in his hands.

"Or find the answers to equations," Cameron chimed in. He put down his pencil and reached for one of the bowls of broth. "This smells great."

Remington looked toward the table. "Can I at least get up and eat at the table?"

"Your fever is gone." Camellia reached for his wrist and checked his pulse. It was no longer rapid and thready. "I think it will be all right."

Pleasure entered his face, but the youngster did not throw off his covers. "You'll need to leave, then. I only have on my nightshirt."

Camellia nodded. "Be careful, though, and get right back into bed as soon as you're done." Exiting the room, she checked on Renée before heading back to the first floor. Everyone was on the mend. She should be able to rejoin her family in the next day or two.

She saw Jonah before she was halfway down the staircase, and her cheeks flamed in reaction to his intense gaze. Why did he always affect her this way? Straightening her shoulders and taking a deep breath, Camellia continued her descent after a brief pause. She wanted to check her appearance before facing him, but retreat was not an option. "Hello, Jonah."

He nodded his head in greeting. "I was looking for Eli."

Of course he was not here to see her. Why should he be? Jonah had left her behind after she'd thrown herself at him the last time they were together alone. Her pride rescued her from making a fool of herself again. "He's at the shipping office."

"I'm glad to hear that. How are your other patients?" Jonah's gaze slammed into her.

Trying to keep her heart intact, Camellia told herself his eyes were the color of wet moss in a swamp. "Mostly recovered. They don't really need me anymore."

"I'm sure you'll be glad to be back with your family."

"Yes, Blake and Lily have promised to stop in Vicksburg so I can check on Thad and Jane."

His lips lost their supercilious curve. "You must be kidding. I cannot imagine the Rebels will let you make a landing."

"Don't worry." She wondered if he regretted telling her to fix her interest with Thad. Or did he even remember giving her advice? The incident that seemed so clear in her memory apparently had no place in his. "Blake has spent some time in Vicksburg, and he has friends who will vouch for us."

"I hope you don't intend to stay there. General Grant has made that town his main target. When Vicksburg falls, the town's residents may well pay a high price for their resistance."

She could not believe the man's effrontery. Who did he think he was to attempt to advise her? "It's really none of your business what my plans are."

Green fire seemed to shoot from his eyes. "You really haven't changed at all, have you, Camellia? I should have known it was only a vain hope on my part that you might have set aside your childish tendencies, but you are a socialite at heart, and you will never change."

His words struck her heart with deadly force, their power shattering the protective wall she'd erected between them. Tears burned at the corners of her eyes. "At least when the South wins this war, I'll have Thad to care for me. I'll be surrounded by my loved ones while you either flee northward or land in prison for your betrayal of our way of life."

The color washed out of his face, and Camellia realized she'd gone too far. She opened her mouth to take the words back, but it was too late. Jonah turned on his heel and strode out of the house, slamming the door behind him.

Camellia sank onto the bottom step and rocked back and forth as anguish burned her heart. She ought to be glad they had been so honest with each other. Now she knew without a doubt they could never be happy together. But as she considered her future, she wondered if she could be happy without him.

"Good morning, sunshine." Renée's familiar greeting brought Camellia's head up.

She planted a smile on her face for her friend's benefit. "I'm happy to see you up and about."

"Not as glad as I am to be out of my bedchamber." The short, dark-haired woman was pale, but Camellia could see the determination in her eyes. "I don't know how to thank you for all you've done since you got here."

Even though sadness lingered deep inside her heart, Camellia felt a sense of contentment in the knowledge her skills had helped the Thornton family recover their health. "It's my pleasure."

"Have you seen Brandon and Cameron?"

"They've gone to open the shop with Blake and Eli." Camellia rose from her place at the table and went to the sideboard to help Renée get some breakfast.

Renée pointed to the toast. "I think that's all I want to eat."

Her nursing sense took over. "You need something more substantial than that." Camellia spooned scrambled eggs onto the other woman's plate and added a slice of cured ham.

"That's enough." Renée laughed. "I don't want to be as large as a cow."

Remington dashed into the room then, his normal high spirits in evidence since he'd thrown off the effects of his illness. "I've finished my lessons. May I walk to Pa's shop?"

Renée kissed him on the forehead. "I'm glad you feel so much better, but I think you'd better stay inside today."

"Aww, Mama." He broke away from her, picked up a plate, and filled it with slices of crisp bacon.

Camellia put Renée's plate on the table and returned to her seat. "Blake said Jasmine and Lily are planning to visit again this morning."

"Really?" Remington was already chewing on bacon as he sat next to her. "I like Jasmine. She's funny."

Camellia and Renée exchanged a glance. Camellia doubted her sister would appreciate his description of the impromptu theatrics she'd performed for him during her visit the day before.

She sipped her coffee as she listened to Remington's rapid-fire comments and his mother's calm responses. Renée obviously knew how to respond to boyish enthusiasm.

"How much longer will you stay with us?" Renée's question interrupted her musings.

"Lily is anxious to get to Natchez."

"I can understand that. She'll want her family around her when the baby comes."

Camellia nodded. As long as she had the chance to visit with the Watkinses in Vicksburg. She had no doubt she could wrangle an invitation from Jane to stay with them. And Lily seemed amenable to allowing her to remain behind since she'd conceived the idea that Camellia was in love with Thad. And she was. . .or at least she would be as soon as she was near him again.

A flash of lightning, followed by the crash of thunder, made all three of them jump.

Remington's voice rose an octave. "Is that cannon fire?"

Camellia glanced toward the window and shook her head. "It's just another spring storm."

Renée shook her head as rain peppered the window. "I feel sorry for the soldiers outside in this deluge."

Where was Jonah? The question trembled on Camellia's tongue, but she could not voice it. She had not seen the man since Tuesday. Not that she cared, but she did want to apologize for her angry remarks. He had a right to his opinion the same as she did.

Had he been sent somewhere to spy once more? Or was he on board one of the naval ships? She shuddered to think of his pointing a cannon at the bluffs of Vicksburg.

"It's been a stormy spring." Renée pushed back from the table. "Eli says the river is high now and likely to flood."

"Lily will probably be more anxious than ever to depart." Camellia put down her coffee cup. "I suppose I'd better get my things packed."

Renée sighed. "I wish we had more time to visit now that I'm feeling better. I can never repay you for taking care of me and my household."

"You would do the same for us." Camellia folded her napkin and put it on the table. "In fact, Eli's parents—his entire family—have done the same for us already."

"They are a wonderful, giving, faith-filled family." Renée stood and shook out her skirt. "I am worried about Jonah, however."

Camellia's heart thumped. Had he been hurt again? Was that why he had not returned to his brother's home? Was he wounded? Her hands itched for her bag of medicines. If he was hurt, she wanted to treat him now that she actually knew what to do to speed up his healing. "Where is he?" Raindrops peppered the windows, and Camellia noticed how dark it had grown in the dining room.

Renée moved to light some of the candles in the room. "He's gone south where the fighting is the worst."

Which probably meant he'd once again donned his Confederate uniform and gone in search of information to pass along to the Union. She wondered if he would be caught this time.

"Eli and I pray for him every night, and for all of the soldiers fighting in this terrible war." Renée hesitated a moment before continuing. "I hope you don't mind that Lily told me about your Confederate beau. I know you have a good heart, dear, and you cannot be responsible for the person it chooses."

Camellia's cheeks felt as bright as the candles Renée had lit. She wanted to blurt out the truth. Of course she cared for Thad and worried about him. He was her best friend's brother. And he was handsome. . .and rich. . .and a good man, besides. The type of man she'd always yearned to marry. The type of man she would marry. Her head could and would rule over the desires of her heart.

Chapter Thirty-seven

"We have family in Natchez." Lily felt like a parrot. How many times had she explained to the hard-faced Union soldier?

"Yes, ma'am, I appreciate that fact. But I need you to understand what's going on here."

Lily glanced past his right shoulder to the ships forming a floating city next to the bank. Soldiers, covered wagons, and horses made a raucous caravan of supplies from boat deck to the city of tents set some distance from the water's edge. "It looks like a great deal of enterprise to me. Do you plan to have a permanent settlement here?"

"That's not for me to say."

"Of course not." Lily tapped a foot as she waited for Blake and his Union escort to return from their inspection of the *Water Lily*. A movement in her stomach made her put a hand on her midsection.

The officer's gaze followed her movement, and an expression of surprise and awe came over his face. "Why don't you sit down, ma'am?"

"I believe I shall." Lily tried to reassure her sisters and Anna with a look of confidence as she returned to the seat she'd vacated when the Union soldiers first boarded their boat.

Camellia's gaze burned Lily's shoulders as she sat.

Anna reached out a hand to her. "God will protect us."

"Of course." Lily squeezed her hand before releasing it. "We'll be on our way in a few minutes."

"I hope so." Camellia picked at the lace on her sleeve.

Lily frowned at her sister as the soldier stepped out into the passageway. "Be careful what you say. I don't want us delayed any more than necessary."

Shouts from outside drew their attention to the single window. A string of logs had been laid to form a path for people on foot. One of them had apparently sunk under the weight of the foot traffic, leaving three hapless men standing thigh deep in thick, black mud. Their plight was causing great merriment from others as they tried to escape to drier ground.

After watching their lack of progress for a minute or two, Lily turned her attention back to the others. "Those poor men. I don't understand why everyone is laughing instead of offering to help them."

Blake strode into the parlor. "We'll be under way in a minute. Next stop, Vicksburg."

Jasmine clapped her hands, while Anna and Camellia looked relieved.

Lily stood and moved toward him. "Perhaps we should try to bypass the port there to avoid further delays."

"We cannot." Camellia tossed a desperate glance in her direction. "I must check on Jane and her family."

"I know we planned to do that, but I'm not sure the Confederates will even allow us to land there."

"But we have to try. I haven't received a letter from Jane since Christmas, and I'm very worried about her. Please, you must let me go see about her."

Lily glanced at her husband's tight face. She could tell he was leery of making the attempt. "Why don't we wait and see what the situation is in Vicksburg? Then we can decide our best course."

Camellia's eyes filled with tears, but she nodded, her heart obviously broken at the news that she might not get to see her beau.

Lily's own heart ached for her. She left her husband's side and sat down next to her sister. "We'll do everything we can to check on them."

"Thank you." Camellia pulled a handkerchief from the sleeve of her gown and used it to dash away the tears trying to escape her eyes.

Jasmine moved toward them, too, her dark eyes troubled.

Lily put her arms around both of her sisters. The hug they shared warmed her. "I love y'all so much. I'd do anything to make you happy."

As the *Water Lily* chugged away from the Yankee encampment, she thought about the families that had been torn apart by the war and sent a prayer of thanks to God for keeping the three of them together.

❧

Camellia ran the last few steps to the picket fence that surrounded Jane's family home. As she reached for the gate latch, the front door flew open, and a glad cry came from the young woman standing there.

"Jane!" Camellia picked up her skirts and dashed forward.

Jane met her in the middle of the front lawn, and the two friends embraced. "I can't believe it's really you."

"I know. It's been so long." Camellia leaned back and frowned. "Why didn't you answer any of my letters?"

A frown marred Jane's pretty face. "I didn't receive any correspondence from you at all. I thought you had forgotten all about me once you and your family went north."

"I wrote to you every week, telling you all about Blake's family and Cape Girardeau."

"None of them got through." Jane shrugged. "So I had no direction to put on a letter to you. But come inside, and you can tell me all about it."

"I only have half an hour to visit. Then I must return to the docks or Lily and Blake will come looking for me."

"Half an hour? That's not nearly enough time. You cannot leave me again so soon. Why don't you plan on staying for a while? I know my mother and Thad would love to see you."

Camellia gave her a hug. "I was hoping you would invite me. Maybe together we can convince my family I should stay."

"It will be perfect. Thad comes by to check on us every day, so your family can have no qualms about your safety." Jane pulled her up the steps and into her home. "I'll collect Mother and my cloak, and we'll go to the boat together to convince them."

Carried forward on the wave of her friend's enthusiasm, Camellia watched as her plan came to fruition. Jane's mother, an older version of her daughter, accompanied them to the *Water Lily* to convince Blake and Lily to let her remain. She didn't feel any pangs of regret as she stood next to her trunks and waved good-bye to her family.

On the ride back to the Watkinses' home, Camellia asked them what had been happening since she last saw them.

"We lost the steeple of the Baptist church to a Yankee shell." Jane pointed out the window. "And some of our slaves have dug a cave area for the family. We've retreated to it twice this winter."

Mrs. Watkins shuddered. "It's a terrible inconvenience."

"But better than braving death when the shelling begins."

Camellia couldn't imagine the fear these women had faced. "You are both very brave."

"Thad tells us to pretend we are staying in a medieval castle." Jane rolled her eyes. "I cannot quite manage that, but it is an adventure to make the place habitable."

Would she have to go to the cave? A frisson of fear slid through Camellia. Perhaps she should not have been so hasty to insist on remaining. At the end, Lily and Blake had left the decision up to her. Camellia had not hesitated at all, but now she wondered if she'd been foolish. Deciding it was too late to question her choice, she sat back against the cushions and prayed for God's protection.

Feeling better because of the peace that entered her heart, Camellia listened to Jane and her mother discussing the high prices and scarcity of even the most basic foods. Flour and sugar were almost impossible to find and certainly beyond the means of any but the richest of Vicksburg's inhabitants.

"Miss Claiborne told me last week that her father has taken apart their smokehouse," Jane reported.

Camellia asked, "Why ever would he do such a thing?"

Mrs. Watkins sniffed. "They boil the wood for water for broth."

"Are things so desperate?"

The carriage slowed to a halt as Jane nodded. "We may have to consider doing the same thing."

Camellia shook her head. She waited for Mrs. Watkins to disembark before turning to her friend. "I hope we can visit the hospital later."

"Of course." Jane climbed down and straightened her skirts. "I go over there nearly every afternoon. It's my Christian duty to offer succor to our brave soldiers."

The prospect of becoming involved with the hospital made Camellia feel much better. No matter what privations she might face, it would be worth it if she helped their soldiers heal. Aunt Tessie had taught her so much. She welcomed the chance to put her skills to work.

❧

The hospital slouching at one end of Pearl Street had serviced the sick and infirm for about ten years. Sunlight peeked between a pair of dark clouds and highlighted the ill-tended lawn, giving the area a foreboding air. Some of the windows had been covered with boards, probably to replace windowpanes shattered by enemy shells.

As the carriage dropped them off, Camellia wrapped her hand around the handle of her bag of medicines and ointments and lifted her chin. No matter how grim the setting or how difficult her self-appointed tasks, she was determined to make use of the talent God had given her.

A nun greeted Jane at the door, her face enclosed in a white wimple. "Thank you so much for coming again today, Miss Watkins. I know how much your visits mean to our young men."

"It's the least we can do, Sister Alice. We may not be able to fight in the battles, but we can support those who do."

Camellia waited behind them as the sister mentioned some of the men whom Jane must have visited in the past.

"Please excuse me." Jane turned to her and pulled her forward. "This is my dearest friend, Camellia Anderson."

"Welcome, Miss Anderson. It's kind of you to volunteer."

"I am eager to be of service, Sister."

Before the nun could answer, a groan from the room behind her focused all of them on the reason for being at the hospital. Sister Alice nodded and turned to the open door. Jane pulled her skirt close to her legs and followed the nun into the first room.

The smell reminded Camellia of the horrendous days on their trip from Jacksonport. But the number of patients then had been much lower than the number of men whose cots filled every available inch of floor space. Little room remained between the cots to allow them to maneuver. Now Camellia understood why Jane had insisted they leave off their hoops. Their voluminous skirts would have seriously impeded their progress.

The first bed they came to held a young man with dark, feverish eyes.

"Hello, Ray." The nun bent over him, raising her voice to counteract the moans coming from the other cots. "Look who I brought to see you today."

The poor fellow seemed oblivious to them. He moved his head

back and forth on his pillow and made unintelligible noises, something between a grunt and a moan. He was obviously in a great deal of pain. His cheeks were splotchy, and his eyes bore a bright, fevered glaze.

"He seems much worse today, poor thing." The nun straightened and looked toward them. "I prayed with him last night, but today he is not even coherent."

Camellia put a hand on his forehead. His fever was dangerously high. If they didn't do something to remedy the situation, he would likely die before the day was out. Reaching for the bag at her feet, she opened it and looked for her bag of mint leaves. "Do you have a bowl of water and some clean rags?"

Sister Alice's face froze for a moment as she considered Camellia's question, but then she nodded and disappeared from the sickroom, returning a moment later with the required items.

Camellia sprinkled some of the crushed leaves into the water and stirred, watching as the water turned green. She soaked the rag in the treatment, pulled it out, wrung the excess water from it, and placed it on the soldier's forehead.

The result was immediate. He stopped tossing his head, and the glaze in his eyes dimmed a little.

She was relieved to see the calming effect of her treatment.

"You're an answer to prayer." The nun's voice was filled with joy and wonder. "We've been running low on supplies, and no one has the time or temerity to venture into the woods to collect fresh herbs."

Her hope gave Camellia a feeling of satisfaction. This was the Lord's doing. He had put her in this place at this time to do His will. It was an exciting, humbling idea. "I don't have enough for everyone, but we can begin by treating the most serious cases."

"This is wonderful." The nun steepled her hands and bowed her head. "Thank You, Lord, for providing in our time of terrible need." She was silent for a moment as she communed with God. Then she raised her head, determination in every line of her face. "Let's get to the kitchen and see what we can do."

Camellia closed her bag and nodded. She glanced toward Jane, who was already moving to another bed where she took the hand of the soldier and began talking to him in a cheerful manner. Each of them had something she could offer the men here. She hoped it would be enough to make a difference.

The hours sped by as she measured out dosages and gave them to the patients according to their needs. She ran out of willow bark first then camphor. By the time they left the hospital, her bag of medicines was much lighter, and every muscle in Camellia's back ached. But satisfaction overrode her pain. "We make a good team."

"I don't know that my part is important." Jane glanced at her. "But I cannot believe how much you learned in Missouri. You are saving lives."

"Don't be so modest. I may have some medicine to help relieve them, but you give them hope by talking to them and reminding them of their homes and families. Without the will to get stronger, no amount of medicine can heal them."

Camellia could see that her words had struck a chord with Jane. Her head lifted, and tears made her eyes gleam in the dusky light of late afternoon.

Jane reached for her hand and gave it a quick squeeze. "I'm so glad you've returned to Vicksburg. And I know someone else who will be equally delighted to see you."

Knowing her friend was referring to Thad, Camellia smiled. "I can't wait to see him, too."

"General Pemberton keeps him fairly busy, but I hope he'll be at home for dinner tonight."

Camellia looked down at the soiled material of her gown. "I hope I brought enough clothes with me."

Laughing, Jane linked arms with her. "If not, we'll have to share like we did at La Belle."

The words brought back happy memories. Her life had taken so many unexpected turns since then. Suddenly the time she'd spent in New Orleans seemed unimportant. But without it, she never would have formed this link with Jane. In these uncertain days, such friendships seemed especially important, so she was determined to treasure this one.

Chapter Thirty-eight

Dinner had almost ended when Thad Watkins appeared in the entrance to the dining room. "Am I too late to dine with you?"

His mother shook her head, the dark curls on either side of her jaw quivering. "Of course not."

"Look who has come to join us." Jane pointed toward her.

"Camellia?" He turned his handsome face in her direction. "Is it really you?"

She pushed back her chair and stood. "It's so nice to see you, Captain Watkins."

Thad took two long strides to reach her and wrapped her in his arms.

Jane giggled, but when Camellia emerged from his embrace, she caught the look of disapproval from his mother. Her face heated, and she stepped back to put a proper distance between them. Her heart was pounding so fast in her chest, she felt like she'd run across the city. Putting a hand on her chest, she glanced back up at him.

"You're as beautiful as ever." His eyes made her think of warm chocolate.

She couldn't help the thrill that shot through her in response to his compliment and admiring gaze. "We're embarrassing your mother."

He cleared his throat and looked past her to his parent. "Please excuse my enthusiasm, Mother. I forgot myself for a moment in the excitement of seeing her here."

"Even though we are caught in the midst of war, we must not forget propriety. If we do, then it will not matter whether or not we win."

He left Camellia to move to his mother's chair and drop a kiss on her raised cheek. "You're right as always. Please forgive me. I promise to be more circumspect."

Camellia slid back into her chair and put her napkin back in her lap while one of the servants laid a fresh setting for Thad. Her heartbeat returned to normal as she watched him interact with his family.

The shadow of a beard darkened his chin, giving him a slightly dangerous look. But his smile was as bright as ever. "How have you been since leaving Vicksburg last fall?"

Jane passed him a basket of yeast rolls. "Camellia has learned how to be a doctor."

"Is that right?" His smile dimmed a bit.

"Not really." She shot a look of warning to Jane. Thad might not approve of women doing such masculine work. "You remember my brother-in-law, Blake Matthews?"

He nodded.

"We went to visit his family in Cape Girardeau, Missouri, because his father had been in an accident. Blake's aunt was caring for him, and she showed me some of the basic treatments she used."

"Don't be so modest, Camellia." Jane turned to her brother. "Even Sister Alice was impressed with her today. She has asked us to come back to the hospital again in the morning."

"I don't know if that's such a good idea." Thad's face wore a frown as his gaze moved between the two of them. "Now that it's growing warmer, yellow fever may settle on the hospital. I wouldn't want to see either of you getting sick."

"I agree." Mrs. Watkins pushed back her chair. "I think we should plan an outing instead."

"That's an excellent idea, Mother. I can ask for a few hours off tomorrow and take you ladies on a picnic."

Jane clapped her hands, but Camellia felt little enthusiasm for the idea. "But we promised Sister Al—"

"Don't worry about that." Thad put down his fork. "I'll send a note explaining that you've been detained. She ought not be so dependent on you anyway. I'm certain the doctors at the hospital have more than enough experience to take care of our soldiers."

Unable to protest further in the face of their enthusiasm, Camellia desisted. She didn't like the idea of disappointing the nun, but she was not free to follow her own inclinations. Perhaps she could at least use the outing to gather fresh herbs and roots to replace what she had used today. As her host and hostesses began to make plans, she made a mental list of what she would need. She was determined to use her time wisely and continue the work God had set for her to do.

❧

A distant thunderstorm woke Camellia from her troubled dreams. She stretched her hands over her head and wondered if it would rain all day. She was so tired of spring showers that turned the streets into muddy bayous and raised the level of the waterways surrounding the city. The storm would also put an end to the picnic and to her plan to gather medicaments.

Another clap of thunder sounded, this time much closer. She looked toward her window. The thick curtains stopped her from seeing much, but flashes of lightning shone around their edge.

As they faded, someone began banging on her bedroom door.

Camellia sat up and pulled the sheet up to her chin. "Who's there?"

"Camellia, wake up." She recognized Thad's deep voice. What was he doing outside her bedchamber? "Get dressed quickly and come downstairs."

She heard his footsteps as he walked away. What was going on? She pushed back the covers and put her bare feet on the floor.

Another knock on the door heralded one of the maids, who entered with a lit candle. "I'ma help you dress, ma'am." The girl sounded terrified. "We's all going to the caves."

More claps of thunder sounded, and Camellia realized what she was hearing was not the sound of nature. The city was under attack. The house shook as a mortar struck somewhere nearby. Would the next one land on top of the Watkinses' home?

The maid used her candle to light a three-pronged candlestick on the mantel. The additional light chased away some of the shadows in the room, making it easier for the two women to work.

The maid picked up the navy blue skirt she'd worn at dinner the evening before and shook it out. Camellia started to untie the collar of her dressing gown but realized it could serve as a chemise. The skirt went on over it, and she thrust her arms into the matching blouse, buttoning the cuffs with trembling fingers as the maid addressed the back closures Camellia could not reach. In record time, she was presentable, even though her hair was in a single braid and her nightcap was still attached to her head. The screams of the mortar fire made her head pound as she grabbed her bag of medicines and ran down the stairs.

Thad was pacing in the foyer.

"What's happening?" She had to raise her voice to be heard over the noise.

Thad looked grim. "It looks like the whole Yankee fleet has decided to converge here. But don't worry. We're too high above the river for them to be able to send soldiers into the city. The poor fellows would be mowed down by our boys before they got halfway up the bluff."

His reassurance brought her some relief. "Then what are they doing?"

"Probably just trying to rob us of a good night's sleep."

Jane tromped down the stairs, her hair still in a braid like Camellia's. "Then they are succeeding."

Mrs. Watkins was right behind her. She carried a candle in one hand and an ornate box that probably held her jewelry in the other. "Are we ready to go?"

Thad nodded and opened the front door.

Billowing smoke made all of them cough. Camellia couldn't see much through it except for the red and yellow flames from a nearby house that had caught fire. She climbed into the carriage after Mrs. Watkins and Jane, moving far enough over for Thad to sit next to her on the rear-facing bench.

"I can't come with you." He stood for a moment in the opening to the carriage, his face drawn.

Mrs. Watkins put down her jewelry box and reached for her son's hand. "You can't send us to the caves alone."

"It will be all right, Mother. You know Thad has a duty to fulfill." Jane pulled her mother back. "We'll be safe in the cave."

Thad threw a relieved glance at his sister before turning to Camellia. "I'm afraid we'll have to postpone our picnic."

Another mortar screamed overhead as if making fun of his statement. She waited until it sailed past before answering him. "Don't worry about that or about us. Jane and I will take care of your mother. You need to focus on keeping yourself and your men safe."

He took her hand and raised it to his lips. "Thank you for being so brave."

Although she didn't feel particularly brave at the moment, Camellia summoned a smile. "We'll be praying for you."

As soon as he let go of her hand, Thad stepped back and slammed the door shut. They heard his command to the driver, and the carriage moved forward.

She closed her eyes and began to pray that God would protect them and allow them to survive the night.

The ride through town was slow but steady. The shelling seemed a little less constant as they escaped the center of Vicksburg.

Swaying with the movement of the carriage, Camellia finished her prayer and opened her eyes.

Mrs. Watkins slumped in a corner, her handkerchief hiding her face.

Jane peered out of the carriage window, looking for all the world like she was no more frightened than if they were making a morning call. "We're almost there." The carriage stopped, and she pushed open the door without waiting for the coachman to dismount. "Come along, Mother. The sooner we're inside, the better you'll feel."

The cave was not as bad as Camellia had imagined. She had to bend over to navigate the entrance, but once inside, she found the roof sufficiently high so that she could straighten. Some of the household slaves must have already come over and lit the candles that glowed from alcoves in the wall. The dirt floor was covered with a rug, and several wooden chairs had been brought from the house.

"The bedrooms are separate from this room." Jane pointed to a corridor to her right. "We only dug two of them—one for females and one for any men."

"What about your slaves?"

Mrs. Watkins looked at her as though she'd grown an extra head. "What about them?"

Camellia glanced around for a secondary corridor. "Where do they sleep?"

"Outside. They're much hardier than you think."

She cringed at the cold note in the older lady's voice. Did she think the slaves didn't need protection, too? They were the ones who had dug the cave system for the family. It was inconceivable to her that Mrs. Watkins hadn't thought to provide a safe place for them to shelter. Yet she wondered if Aunt Dahlia and Uncle Phillip wouldn't agree with Mrs. Watkins's assessment. Camellia glanced at Jane and saw the same incomprehension in her friend's gaze. Was she the only one who thought the slaves deserved space in the cave?

Another anchor to her long-held affection for the Southern way of life fell away. Camellia could not imagine thinking so little of other human beings.

Mrs. Watkins yawned. "I think I'll lie down a little while. Do you have anything for a headache in that bag of yours?"

Camellia considered the question before nodding. "I have some chamomile for a soothing tea. Is there somewhere I can brew it?"

"We have a fire pit right next to the entrance." Jane took her mother's arm and headed for the back. "I'll come out to assist you as soon as I help Mother get comfortable."

Camellia picked up her bag and retraced her steps, taking a deep breath as she emerged into the cool predawn air. Several of the slaves were sitting around the fire Jane had mentioned, but they scrambled to their feet as she approached. "I'm sorry to disturb you, but I need to prepare some tea for your mistress." Spotting a pot to one side of the fire, she moved toward it. "Is there any water already drawn?"

The little maid who had helped her dress stepped forward. "Yes, Miss Anderson. I can fill that from one of the buckets."

"If you'll show me where they are, I'll be glad to do it for myself." Even as she spoke, Camellia realized how much she had changed in the months since she'd left New Orleans. The haughty student at La Belle Demoiselle was gone. Hopefully, she would never return.

Chapter Thirty-nine

Jean Luc wanted to turn and run from his parents' house. His throat was tight with fear. Why had he come? Why hadn't he said no to Anna?

Because she was right. The answer in his head didn't quiet his fear, but it did give him the strength to raise his hand and knock. They had talked about this moment several times during the voyage from Cape Girardeau, and he'd thought he was ready. But now he wasn't so sure.

"I'm right here with you, and so is God."

Anna's whispered reminder buoyed him. He reached for her hand, squeezing it to show his appreciation.

The door opened a few inches, and the familiar face of their butler appeared. "We have a side entrance for tradesmen."

"I'm not a tradesman." Jean Luc turned his head so the man could see the unscarred side of his face.

The butler gasped. "Master Champney? Is it really you?"

Jean Luc nodded. The butler pulled the door open the rest of the way and bowed. "Your ma and pa are in the library, sir. And they're gonna be so happy."

The welcoming look in the older man's eyes warmed him further. "Thank you, Carson. I hope you're right."

"Oh yes, sir. You're gonna be the prodigal son for sure."

Offering his arm to Anna, Jean Luc stepped over the threshold. "I'll announce myself."

Carson bowed once more and reached out a hand for Jean Luc's hat.

The house seemed unchanged, as though frozen in time. Ornate furniture from Europe clogged the hall, and his long-dead ancestors stared down at him as he escorted his fiancée toward the room the butler had indicated. He stopped for a moment and faced Anna. "Let's say a prayer."

"Of course." Her smile was as slow as ever, dawning with the stately radiance of the sunrise.

He took her hands in his own and bowed his head. He didn't know exactly what he wanted to say to God, but after a moment the words seemed to flow out of him. "Lord, thank You for this woman who is lending her strength to me. Please help my parents forgive me for deceiving them, and help them understand why I did what I did. I know how wrong it was, and I'm sorry for hurting them. Please help me to be the son they deserve, one who honors them in the way You always intended. Thank You, Lord, for hearing me. . . . Amen."

"Amen," Anna echoed. She stood on tiptoe and planted a feather-soft kiss on his cheek. "I'm so proud of you."

Jean Luc took a deep breath and pushed the library door open. His father was seated at his mahogany desk, a pile of papers in front of him. He looked up as the door opened. "What is it?"

His mother, seated in her favorite chair next to a southern-facing window, gasped and dropped the needlework in her hand.

"Papa? Mama? It's me, Jean Luc."

His father rocked back in his chair as though blown back by a high wind. "Jean Luc?"

Mama sprang from her chair and took a step forward before crumpling to the floor.

All three of them rushed to her side. Jean Luc picked up her head and shoulders and placed them on his lap. Anna bent over him and waved a handkerchief in front of his mother's face.

Papa fell to his knees on the other side of Mama. He picked up one of her hands and chafed it, but his dark eyes devoured Jean Luc's face. "Is it really you, my son?"

He nodded, overwhelmed by so many emotions he could not speak.

His mother's eyelids fluttered open, and a beautiful smile swept across her face. "You have come back to us."

Both of the men helped her regain her feet and led her back to her chair.

"Your mother never truly believed you were dead."

"I am so sorry. I didn't want to bring more shame to you," Jean Luc blurted out, forgetting the speech he'd practiced. "I almost died in the explosion of the *Hattie Belle*. When I came to, I was so ashamed of what I'd done. Of the pain I had caused my friends and family. . . . I didn't know what else to do except disappear."

His mother put a hand on his arm. "You should have known that we would rather have you with us no matter what happened. We love you, Jean Luc. Nothing you do or fail to do can ever change that."

"She's right." His father held out his arms to him. "I am the one who should be asking for forgiveness. I realize now how hard I was on you."

Jean Luc stepped into the embrace, hugging the dear man with all his might. "No, Papa. You were right to expect me to be a man. I'm the one who let both of you down."

"No, it was my fault."

"Why don't you all agree that none of us are perfect except Jesus?" Anna's calm voice broke through their conversation. "That is why He died for us, after all. We have many things to forgive of one another."

His parents looked toward Anna as though they'd only just realized she was in the room. Breaking free of his father's hold, Jean Luc swept a hand in her direction. "Please allow me to introduce Miss Anna Matthews, the reason I finally found the courage to return to you and the woman who has agreed to become my wife."

A brief pause filled the room. His parents looked at each other and smiled.

Mama pushed herself up from her chair and put an arm around each of them. "Welcome to our family, Miss Anna Matthews. We've been waiting for you for a very long time."

And Jean Luc knew everything was going to be all right.

❧

"Port Gibson has fallen, and still Pemberton won't send us out to face the Yanks." Thad paced across his mother's parlor, pounding one of his fists into a cupped palm. "He's going to cost us the whole war."

"Perhaps he thinks you need to stay here and protect the citizens of Vicksburg." Mrs. Watkins poured warm tea into a cup and offered it to her daughter.

Jane took the proffered cup. “I heard he’s nothing more than a transported Yankee himself.”

Camellia knew she should probably keep her opinions to herself, but she didn’t think the man’s reputation should be shredded by gossip. “I thought he was a hero in the Mexican War.”

“That’s true.” Thad stopped his pacing. “But it’s also true that two of his brothers are fighting for the Union.”

Not wanting to start an argument, she desisted. Sometimes she caught Thad looking at her with a question in his gaze as if he still wondered exactly when she’d discovered that Jonah was a Union sympathizer. He wouldn’t be happy if he knew the truth. But she had no intention of telling him. Nor did she have any intention of telling him about the time she’d spent with Jonah and his brother’s family in Memphis right before coming here.

“Don’t you agree, Camellia?”

She came out of the fog of her thoughts when she heard her name. All three were looking at her. “I’m sorry. I missed what you said.”

“We were discussing whether or not we should leave Vicksburg.” Jane put down her tea. “I think we should remain here and do whatever we can at the hospital.”

Camellia nodded. She and Jane had spent a great deal of time working with the soldiers. “Besides, you’ve always said we are safe here. With its high bluffs and command of the river, Vicksburg will stand strong until the war is over.”

Thad looked troubled as he considered them. “I don’t know if that will hold true now that Grant and his army have gained a foothold in Mississippi. Especially since our general seems content to remain hiding in his garrison.”

“I don’t want to be so far from you, either.” Mrs. Watkins nibbled at a cookie, one of the last they were likely to have given the rising cost of sugar. “We have our cave to run to in case of need.”

“If you’re certain, I must admit that I like knowing you are close by.” Thad sat down on the sofa near Camellia’s chair. “But I want you to promise that you’ll consider limiting your time with the soldiers at the hospital.”

Camellia’s heart fell to her toes. She didn’t like to cause further worry when Thad had so much on his mind. “The doctors have begun to rely on Jane and me to take care of the cases that are not so desperate.

Every day more soldiers are being brought in." She put a hand on his arm. "If you could see them in such pain and fear."

He covered her hand with his own. "Your tender heart is leading you astray, Camellia. I know you want to help, and I know you think that you are filling a need, but I want you to consider your health and your reputation, as well as Jane's." His gaze was sincere.

Camellia wanted to yield to him, but she couldn't form the words to tell him so. "I cannot stop going."

"Why? Why is this so important that you will risk my displeasure and my sister's well-being?"

Camellia pulled her hand from underneath his. "If you would come by and see what we do, perhaps you could understand."

"I don't have time for sightseeing. I am doing all I can to keep the Confederacy together." His voice hardened. "I don't want to forbid you, Camellia. I'd much rather you stopped voluntarily."

"Thad! You cannot mean what you're saying. Camellia and I are not in any danger, nor are we risking our reputations."

Jane's interjection stopped Camellia from answering him directly. But he had chosen the wrong way to win her compliance. No matter what happened, she was determined to continue her work at the hospital. He had no power to force her compliance, and if he tried to stop her, she would simply remove her belongings to one of the hotels in town and continue her work. Her shoulders straightened.

Thad held up both hands. "I'm sorry. I shouldn't have said that. I suppose it's just an effect of the strain I'm under."

Camellia kept her hands relaxed in her lap. She would not let him see how angry he had made her. Over the past weeks, she had thought she might actually be falling in love with Thad Watkins. But she had been mistaken. She could never marry a man who did not think her work as important as his own. Nor could she be married to someone with such a strict notion of what was acceptable behavior for a lady.

It wasn't as if she wanted to go dancing down the street in her nightclothes. She was trying to provide succor and support for wounded Southern soldiers. One day he might be wounded himself. While she did not wish such an eventuality on him, she thought if it happened, he might finally understand why she would not stop her work.

Jonah chewed on a piece of hardtack and wondered when the army would move again. They had forced the Confederates to retreat all along their route inland across central Mississippi. Some said they would be going south next, to Port Hudson, where they would join up with General Banks and overrun the stronghold before moving to Vicksburg with a force greater than that of the Confederates.

After spending more than a week bivouacked in the small village of Port Gibson, Jonah found himself agreeing with the ones who thought Grant would continue forward to Jackson, the capital city of Mississippi, and cut off the railroad supply lines running between there and Vicksburg. If he managed that, the city on the river would be cut off from all hope of success.

Cage, the man who had first befriended him when they fought side by side in Missouri, limped over to where he sat and lowered himself to the ground. "We'll be on the march again before the end of day."

"Where to?"

"Edwards Station." Cage nodded to the north.

Satisfaction filled him. Grant was not going to wait for Banks. He was going with his bold plan to put a stranglehold on Vicksburg and force its capitulation. "I told you so."

Cage bumped him with his elbow. "No one likes a smart aleck."

"I can't help it if I'm smarter than you." Jonah laughed at his friend.

"And I can't help it if someone knocks the stuffing out of you."

Jonah sobered. "You've been a good friend, Cage. Your friendship is one of the few things I will treasure from this war."

"You can try to flatter me all you want, but I've seen who you truly are. You're nothing but a know-all and a pain, besides." Cage's grin took the bite out of his complaint. "But I guess I've invested this much time in saving your sorry hide, so I may as well continue watching your back for a little while longer."

Shouts ended their conversation as the men around them began gathering their meager belongings and wrapping them into their bedrolls. It was time to march.

Tossing his hardtack into a knapsack, Jonah stood and looked out across the unplanted fields surrounding the army. He wondered what the people in Port Gibson would do for food next winter. How long could they continue fighting against a superior force? When would they realize that they could not, would not win? He hoped it would be soon.

"Have you gotten any letters from your lady love?" Cage fell in beside him.

Jonah rolled his eyes. "Just because I kissed a girl doesn't mean I'm in love with her."

"Oh, ho!" Cage's eyes grew wide. "You kissed her? And she's an innocent?"

"Of course she is. She's a family friend. Her sister and my sister might be kin they are so close."

"Then you must be serious about her."

"I am not. She's all wrong for me." Jonah ran a finger under the collar of his uniform, wishing the wool didn't sting. Or was that his conscience? Why had he kissed Camellia? And not just once, but two times. As Cage had pointed out, she was an innocent.

He could close his eyes and still feel the wonder of that first kiss—the way her lips had parted in surprise and the way she had felt in his arms. And when he'd left her in Jacksonport, he'd done it again. And again she had responded to his caress as though there was some connection between them.

Perhaps he should have kissed her again in Memphis. Maybe that would have halted the harsh words between them. But if he had, he might have lost all control over his senses. He might have asked her to marry him. And he didn't want to find himself chained to some spoiled beauty for the rest of his life.

Cage was watching him, his gaze understanding. "Sometimes the heart knows what the head will not admit."

"Her faith is nothing more than a sham. She has no ideas in her head except clothes and money and finding a husband. Camellia Anderson is definitely not the type of woman I should marry."

"What you should do is not always the best thing."

Jonah looked at him. "Would you stop spouting such nonsense? You are not even married yourself. What do you know about it?"

Cage looked out over the fields, his gaze vacant. Then he shook himself and looked toward Jonah. "I once fell in love with a girl, but I let her get away from me. I thought she was not good enough for me, not serious enough, too focused on worldly matters."

It sounded to Jonah that the man must have met Camellia or

someone very like her. "What happened?"

He shrugged. "She married another man and is a wonderful wife to him. I saw that what I had mistaken for materialism was nothing more than immaturity."

Later that night when they bedded down, Jonah thought about Cage's story. Was he making a mistake to resist Camellia? Or was he being careful not to become unequally yoked?

Jonah wasn't sure, so he began to pray for an answer from the One who knew exactly what was in Camellia's heart. He prayed for discernment and wisdom, and he prayed for the patience to wait for God's answer.

Chapter Forty

The sound of marching feet brought Jane and Camellia out onto the front porch. Line after line of gray-coated soldiers passed the house, bayonets resting on their shoulders.

Jane pulled a handkerchief from the sleeve of her blouse and waved it at them. Grins and salutes answered her gesture. "Aren't they handsome?"

Camellia felt sick to her stomach. Yes, these men were clean and well outfitted. They seemed spirited and eager to get to the battlefield. But she couldn't help thinking about their destination. Fighting, killing, or perhaps meeting death itself. How many of the men now writhing in pain at the hospital across town had marched off in the same manner? "I wish I could tell them to turn back."

Jane stopped waving at them and turned to look at Camellia. "What?"

"Don't you see? Your own brother is amongst these soldiers. Aren't you worried about him? How many of these handsome men will return to Vicksburg? How many of them will soon be nothing more than corpses lying on a blood-soaked field?"

"That's not something you should be thinking about right now. Think about the victory they will win for us."

Camellia shook her head. "Whether the army wins a victory or not, many of these men—perhaps even Thad—will come back to us with grievous wounds. . .if they return at all."

"I knew it!" Jane grinned at her. "You're in love with Thad."

She couldn't believe her friend had drawn that conclusion from her words. "I am not in love with your brother. I'm only worried about him like I am about all of these men."

"I don't care what you say. I know the truth." Jane stuffed her handkerchief back into her sleeve. "You're only angry with him because he doesn't want us to continue going to the hospital. But don't worry. You'll soon change his mind."

"I don't want to change his mind because I'm not in love with him." Camellia's temper rose in reaction to Jane's teasing and her concern about all of the soldiers. She clenched her jaw and pointed a finger at Jane. "And if you make comments like that to him, you'll be leading him to believe something that is completely, absolutely, totally false."

Jane lost her smile. "Are you trying to throw me off by denying your feelings?"

"No. I am telling you the truth." Her irritation faded as she saw the hurt look in her friend's eyes. "Look at me, Jane. You know me better than most. Do I look like I am lying to you?"

They locked gazes, and Camellia tried to communicate all of the frustration and sadness she felt. A part of her would like to fall in love with Thad, but that was the old Camellia, the girl who wanted nothing more than a pampered lifestyle as the privileged wife of a planter. Now she knew she wanted more from life. She wanted to make a difference. And being married to someone like Thad would prevent her from even trying to reach her goals.

Jane sniffed. "I suppose not."

"Good. Then please respect my feelings." Camellia put an arm around Jane's waist. "I care for Thad like a brother, not as the man I want to marry."

"Are you in love with someone else?"

The question caught her completely by surprise. All of a sudden she could see Jonah Thornton's green eyes, auburn hair, and crooked grin. She could almost hear his distinct New Orleans drawl and feel his hand touching her cheek right before he kissed her. She tried to banish the memory and concentrate on answering Jane, but it was no use. Her cheeks flamed.

Jane's gaze sharpened. She stepped back and frowned. "You are! Who is it? You cannot hide it from me. Is it one of the doctors at the hospital? Is that why you are so anxious to keep going there?" Her mouth dropped open. "Or is it one of our patients? It's that tall, dark-haired, extremely handsome captain. What is his name. . . ? Oh, Luke Talbot."

Relieved that her friend had not discerned the truth, Camellia shook her head. "Of course not. He's married. Didn't you see the pretty girl who came to the hospital to visit him? I hope he doesn't have to lose his leg."

One of the passing soldiers called out to them, and Jane let the subject drop. As she waved to him, Camellia's mind whirled. She suspected the interrogation was only postponed, and she would have to do a better job of guarding her heart if she was going to keep her feelings a secret. At least until she sorted them out for herself. She didn't love Jonah Thornton, did she?

She couldn't. It had to be a mistake. Maybe it was because he'd kissed her. That had to be the explanation. She felt connected to him because he'd taken advantage of her. . .twice. No longer seeing the waves of young men marching past them, Camellia rubbed the back of her hand across her mouth. She would eradicate whatever connection might have been forged between them. It couldn't be love. Could not. The last time she'd seen Jonah, they had argued like a couple of children. She had barely thought of him since then.

As the parade of soldiers dwindled, she began to feel a little better. Jane turned back to the front door, and Camellia followed her inside. If her silly heart insisted on maintaining a connection to the wrong man, she would take one of the herbs in her bag for purging impurities. She had no other choice. Because no matter what her feelings might be toward Jonah Thornton, she was certain he felt nothing but disdain for her.

&

"Why don't they surrender?" Lily tossed the newspaper on the table and pushed her chair back. She was so worried about Camellia. Why had she let her sister and Mrs. Watkins convince her that the area would be safe? If she ever got Camellia under her wing again, she would not let her out of her sight until the war was over. . .if ever.

Blake shook his head. "The Confederates know that losing Vicksburg will split their forces in two. They will be a house divided."

"But they cannot win against Grant's forces. They may have the upper ground, but he can starve them. And I don't doubt that he will if he is forced to."

Aunt Dahlia, sitting on the opposite side of the table, moaned. "You should have brought the girl back here to me. I always knew your traipsing all over the country with your sisters would come to no good end. And now poor Camellia is paying the price for your stubbornness."

The words should not have come as a surprise to her. Aunt Dahlia would never approve of her unconventionality. Uncle Phillip was nodding his agreement with his wife's condemnation. She supposed they had forgotten how her decision to operate a successful steamship had helped support their lifestyle here at Les Fleurs.

"You cannot blame Camellia's situation on Lily." Grandmother sent a disapproving glance at her daughter and son-in-law. "The girl was determined to stay with the friend she made at that fancy finishing school that you encouraged her to attend."

"She's in love with Thad Watkins." Lily tried to push herself up from the dining chair, but her protruding abdomen made the maneuver impossible.

Blake and Papa both saw her difficulty and moved to assist her.

"Thank you." She managed a shaky smile for their efforts. Taking a deep breath, she turned her attention back to her aunt. "While Captain Watkins is not the man I would have chosen for my sister, I know he and his family will do everything in their power to keep Camellia safe."

Aunt Dahlia's face was pinched with worry. Lily knew she should be more sympathetic. Camellia had always been her favorite of the sisters. Lily was too plain, and Jasmine's black hair and violet eyes were too exotic for acceptance into the highest levels of local Natchez society. Camellia's blond curls, creamy complexion, and cornflower-blue eyes made her the perfect candidate. If the war had not come along, she had no doubt Camellia would have been the most popular girl in the city.

"I think you should go after her." Aunt Dahlia's suggestion was like an arrow through her heart. "Put that boat of yours to good use for once."

Blake put an arm around his wife's shoulders while speaking to Aunt Dahlia. "I think you have lost your mind."

Both Aunt Dahlia and Uncle Phillip looked shocked, but Lily could feel a bubble of laughter trying to escape her throat. Trust Blake to support her even though he'd argued against leaving Camellia in

Vicksburg. She leaned against his shoulder and sent him a thankful look.

"The Confederate batteries will shoot at anything that is moving up or down the river right now. When we passed through that area in March, things were already perilous. The only thing we could accomplish by taking the *Water Lily* to Vicksburg is to get her rammed or shot to pieces."

Grandmother cleared her throat to gain their attention. "Maybe her brave Confederate officer would escort her to Natchez if you sent a request."

Now Aunt Dahlia looked scandalized. "I hope you're not suggesting that she travel alone with a man. Her reputation could never survive such scandalous behavior."

"I'm not as worried about her reputation as I am her life." Lily rubbed her belly with a gentle hand as the baby inside shifted. "I would feel much better if she were here with us, but I don't see how we can accomplish that right now."

Papa returned to his place at the table. "We'll have to leave it in God's hands."

Lily nodded. "You're right as always, Papa. God will protect her as He does all of His children."

She had spent a great deal of time talking to God about her concerns as the situation worsened over the past two months. He had not answered her prayer with words, but His peace brought her some comfort.

Still, it was hard not to worry as they followed the progress of the battles taking place to their north. According to the reports of the local newspaper, General Grant had burned a swath through the countryside, isolating Vicksburg from all hope of support. After two unsuccessful assaults, he had decided to lay siege to the city. Lily could not begin to imagine the conditions her sister was experiencing.

"I think you need to lie down for an hour." Blake's voice tickled her ear.

Wondering how she would ever relax enough to sleep, Lily allowed him to lead her from the dining room. "Do you think we could get word to Captain Watkins?"

"I doubt it." His gaze was kind. "But I have thought of someone who might be able to help."

Lily stopped walking. "Who?"

"The Thorntons' youngest son, Jonah."

"Jonah? I doubt he would be any use to us at all."

The look in Blake's eyes told her he knew something she didn't.

Lily stomped her right foot. "Tell me."

He shrugged. "Eli told me he joined the Union army. He's currently with Grant's army and may be in a position to reach Camellia."

Excitement and hope coursed through her blood. Lily threw her arms around her husband, hugging him as close as she could with the baby between them.

A pang caught her by surprise, and Lily tensed.

"What is it?"

Blake's voice seemed to come from a distance as yet another pain struck, stealing her breath with its strength. Lily doubled over and grabbed her abdomen, trying to keep her composure as the truth became apparent to her. "You'd better send for the doctor. I think the baby's coming."

Chapter Forty-one

"Jonah Thornton! I have a message for Jonah Thornton."

The voice called him from a dream, a dream of secret waterfalls and stolen kisses. With a groan, he rolled over and peeked out from the opening of his tent. "I'm Jonah Thornton."

The messenger's head turned as Jonah pushed himself up. He was young but carried his satchel with obvious pride. Reaching inside it, he produced a white envelope with Jonah's name printed in bold black letters.

"Thank you."

The boy's salute was crisp. Then he looked inside his bag and read the next name. "Tom Waterford! I have a message. . ."

Jonah put his finger under the seal to break it.

"A love letter?" Cage's drawl held a teasing note. "It's about time for the ladies to catch up with you."

His gaze dropped to the bottom of the letter and read the signature. His lips curled. "Yes, and her name is Blake Matthews."

Both of them laughed at the suspicious looks from some of the nearby soldiers.

Jonah raised his voice to explain. "*His* wife and my sister are close friends." He glanced at the stationery in his right hand:

Dear Jonah,

Lily and I are sending this note to you in the hope that you can help her sister Camellia. You may remember she is the sister whom we came to remove from New Orleans as the city was being occupied by Union forces.

Jonah rolled his eyes. If only Blake knew how closely acquainted he was with the middle Anderson sister, he would probably demand satisfaction instead of sending him a polite letter.

A few months ago, during a trip from Memphis to Natchez, we allowed her to visit friends in Vicksburg. After we reached Natchez, the situation on the river deteriorated further, and we have been unable to secure passage for her or permission to return to Vicksburg.

She is trapped within the confines of the city, and we are unable to reach her. If you could ascertain her whereabouts and conditions and report them to us, we would be very grateful.

Also, if you speak to her directly, you might wish to convey the happy news that she is an aunt to the most handsome little boy named Noah.

We appreciate your help in this matter and remain prayerfully hopeful that we may all survive this war.

With sincerest thanks,
Blake Matthews

Jonah's heart was beating so hard it felt as if it might jump from his chest.

"What's the matter?" Cage touched his arm. "Your face is as white as a field of cotton."

Unable to express the fear that had taken hold of him, Jonah shook his head. He had wondered from time to time where Camellia was. She had even told him she was planning to visit her friend and that pompous captain. But he'd never really thought her family would have allowed her to stay. Perhaps stop by for an afternoon visit, but then she should have gotten right back onto her sister's boat and sailed away to safety. "I have to talk to Grant."

Cage pulled his hand back as though he'd been burned. "General Grant?"

Jonah nodded. He had to sneak into the city and see Camellia to safety. In the past month, the situation inside the city had gotten bad. While the soldiers sniped at each other from their positions in the ravines and on the hillsides, no food had passed into the city for several weeks. The rumor was that the civilians and soldiers had been reduced to eating mule in place of beef and pork and that all the cats and dogs in the city had disappeared.

The townspeople had moved into caves to escape the shells falling into the city. He had to get to her, no matter the cost.

Camellia couldn't remember ever being so tired in her life. Her hand went to the small of her back, and she massaged the area.

"How long has it been since you rested?" Sister Alice touched her shoulder.

Looking out the window, she was surprised to see the sun dipping low on the horizon. "I'm not sure."

The nun frowned her displeasure. "You look ready to drop."

"Where's Jane?"

The nun pointed past the rows of cots. "The last time I saw her, she was sitting by some of the new arrivals."

A sigh filled Camellia's chest. Would the steady stream of sick and wounded soldiers never end?

"I'll go find her." Camellia checked the forehead of a soldier who had lost his left arm to a minie ball. It was cooler than yesterday. She pulled a notebook out of her bag and made a notation.

Sister Alice's habit bounced as she tapped her foot. "You need to leave right now, or you'll have to walk back in the dark."

"Yes, ma'am." Camellia smiled at the older lady. Sister Alice could be a tough drill sergeant, but her motives were always good. "I just have to tell Dr. Dickson I'm leaving."

"I'll tell him. You go on."

She knew when she was outmaneuvered. Walking to the outer room, Camellia collected Jane. "Let's go home."

Jane made a face. "You mean to the cave."

"It's safer than staying in town." As if to emphasize her statement, the whistle of a missile made both of them freeze.

The sound had become so common in the past weeks they could tell when it passed their location. The floor shook ahead of the *boom* as it hit another part of the city. Camellia hoped Willow Grove was unharmed.

"Let's go." Jane's dark tresses were limp, and her eyes no longer held a sparkle. It had been ground out of her by the death and sickness they encountered on a daily basis, compounded by the heat of summer, the uncomfortable sleeping cots in the cave, and the lack of proper nutrition.

Obed, the large, quiet slave who had been assigned to accompany them back and forth from the hospital, met them as they stepped outside. Camellia wondered what he did all day while they were inside. She was glad to have his escort, as the soldiers who seemed to inhabit every street of the city might have been a problem otherwise.

Jane kicked a pebble ahead of them. "I wonder how long it will take before the Yankees give up and go home."

"Is that what you really think will happen?"

"Either that or General Johnston's reinforcements will arrive. Thad says if they come, we will squash them between the two legs of our army." She slapped her hands together to illustrate the maneuver. "Vicksburg will never fall."

Another shell whistled overhead. Camellia looked up and saw its arc. No danger. She continued walking. "I don't know. They seem very determined."

They finished their walk in silence. Camellia wanted to reach out to her friend, but she didn't know how. It seemed they had grown in different directions. Jane still wanted the South to win. She didn't see anything wrong with their old lifestyle and couldn't wait to resume it.

Although Camellia deplored the war, she welcomed the change she believed it would bring. She wanted freedom for all slaves. She didn't want to return to the past, not since her eyes had been opened. Balls and fancy gowns had lost their attraction, as had every other aspect of a life of privilege. She wanted to spend her life in more serious pursuits.

Mrs. Watkins greeted them at the entrance to the cave. "I have a wonderful surprise for you girls."

Camellia and Jane exchanged a glance. All either of them wanted to do was eat a little and fall into bed. They'd both had a long day. And tomorrow wouldn't be any shorter or easier.

"What's the surprise?"

Mrs. Watkins giggled like a young girl. "Your brother has brought us a roast."

Tiredness receded as Camellia's mouth watered. For the past week, they'd subsisted on turnips and canned beans. "Where did he find a roast?"

"Who cares?" Mrs. Watkins led the way into the main room. "I thought you girls were never going to get here, and Thad insisted we had to wait for you."

The room that served as a dining room and a parlor had undergone a dramatic change since they'd left this morning. The large dining table from the house took up most of the space. It had been covered with a white cloth that reached to the floor. A pair of silver candelabra sat on either side of a tall vase of fresh flowers that dominated the center of the table. Four place settings, two on each of the long sides of the table, invited them to take seats and dine, really dine, for the first time since they'd retreated to the cave.

Thad stepped out of the shadows, a look of expectation on his handsome face.

Camellia wished for a moment she could be in love with him. But then sanity returned. Thad would make an excellent husband for someone. . .but not her.

"Welcome." He bowed and indicated the table. "If you ladies will take your seats, I'll check on our dinner."

Jane sat on the far side of the table. Before Camellia could slip into the seat next to her, Mrs. Watkins blocked her path. "Why don't you sit on this side? I know Thad would rather sit next to a pretty girl than his mother."

"I thought he was unhappy with me because of our time at the hospital."

Mrs. Watkins sat down next to her daughter and put her napkin in her lap. "He's past all that. His friends are impressed with the work you and Jane are doing. He told me so while we were waiting for y'all."

Camellia folded her lips into a straight line. Was she supposed to be mollified because Thad's friends had judged her actions acceptable? She managed to swallow her irritation as Thad returned, followed by three slaves.

He was so proud of his efforts. And she had to admit the food was outstanding. Thad was charming, telling them amusing stories about men answering roll call wearing only one boot or with a shirt on wrong side out.

Camellia laughed in the appropriate places, but her eyelids were threatening to close in spite of her best efforts. She held her napkin in front of her mouth to hide a yawn. "I'm afraid I must excuse myself." Camellia pushed back her chair.

Thad jumped to his feet and helped her, ever the gentleman. "I have something I need to discuss with you if you have a moment."

Tiredness washed through her. All Camellia wanted to do was climb into her cot, but a glance at Thad's tense features made her ignore her desire. "Is something wrong?"

"No, but I need to seek your advice on a private matter." His smile appeared as he offered his elbow. "Let's step outside."

When they reached the entrance to the cave, a cool breeze lifted the hair from the back of her neck. A group of slaves huddled near the cooking fire, their voices too low for them to hear.

Thad walked her away from them, to the edge of the light from their cave. She sat on a convenient boulder and watched as he paced back and forth in front of her. Another yawn threatened to crack her jaw. If Thad didn't hurry, she would fall asleep before he got started.

When he knelt before her, however, Camellia's sleepiness fled. Thad took possession of her left hand. "I don't know how much longer our troops can hold out. It's only a matter of time until we have to surrender to the Yankees. I'll be taken prisoner, but I'm very worried about what may happen to you."

"Please, Thad." Camellia tried to pull her hand from his grasp, but Thad would not release it.

"Let me finish before you say anything."

She sighed. "Go on, then."

"Mother and Jane have the protection of our family name. It will stop the Yankees from harming them. But you do not have a male protector nearby, and I think we should remedy that. You are a beautiful woman, accomplished and strong. It would give me great pleasure if you would agree to become my wife."

Camellia squeezed his hand. "While I am flattered by your offer, I must refuse. I am fond of you, Thad, and I admire your steadfastness, but I do not love you in that way."

"I will teach you to love me."

Her empathy disappeared, as did the desire to let him down easily. "That's not possible. My heart belongs to another man."

He let go of her then, his face slack with surprise. "Who is he? Is he one of the doctors at the hospital?"

Camellia thought of kindly old Dr. Dickson, who must be at least midway through his forties. "No. And I warn you to stop guessing before you further insult me. I appreciate your offer, but it cannot be."

Thad stood and brushed dirt off his trousers. "Why not?"

"You are going to make some lucky girl very happy." She put a hand on his arm. "And I really wish I was that girl, but we want different things for our lives. Since I've been working at the hospital, I've realized how much I can contribute beyond my looks."

"I rather like your looks."

She grinned at him, relieved when he grinned back. "Thank you for the compliment, Captain. You are quite attractive yourself."

He tilted his head to one side. "In that case. . ."

Camellia pushed herself up from the boulder. "Don't you see? We have a great friendship, but there's no spark between us. When I marry, I want it to be because I cannot stand the idea of living without him."

"You've given me a lot to think about, Camellia." He walked her back to the cave opening. "I'm sorry things didn't work out between us."

"Me, too."

As he strode back toward his station, she thought his step was not that of a man who was crushed by disappointment. That was a relief. She didn't want to hurt Thad, and she hoped he would find a wonderful girl he couldn't live without.

Searching out her own cot, Camellia completed her toilette with a minimum of fuss and climbed into bed, her eyelids closing the moment her head rested on the pillow.

Chapter Forty-two

A loud explosion woke Camellia, the concussion throwing her to the floor. For a moment she couldn't get her bearings. The darkness of the cave was absolute. She felt around her until her hand closed over the foot of her cot. "Jane?"

She heard the snick of a tinderbox, and a candle's flame dispelled the darkness. "Are you okay?"

Camellia nodded. She threw a wrapper over her gown and slid her feet into slippers. "That was close." The idea of being buried alive inside the cave made her heart pound.

Someone came rushing in, and her breath caught. Had the Yankees finally overrun them? But the face that appeared in their doorway belonged to one of the maids. "Please come quick, Miss Camellia. Someone's been hurt."

Grabbing her bag, Camellia followed without question. Was it Mrs. Watkins? Or one of the families who lived in a nearby cave? She prayed as she ran, leaning on God for the courage and strength to meet whatever awaited her.

The sky outside was much lighter than she'd expected after the gloom of the cave. The first rays of the sun peeked above the horizon. That was the direction they headed, toward the field of wildflowers and the old oak tree that had become a shelter for many of the slaves.

The oak tree looked odd to her, and then Camellia realized what was wrong. It was canted, leaning at an angle. Her breath caught, and she came to an abrupt halt.

"Come with me, Miss Camellia." The maid tugged on her arm. "Obed's bleeding real bad. Can you help him?"

"I'll try." Camellia ran to a small knot of women, pushing her way through them until she could see Obed's familiar face.

The wound was nasty. Flayed skin exposed muscle and bone. She used the belt of her wrapper to stop the bleeding and began cleaning the wound. Obed's face was turning gray, and she worried he was dying. "Hang on, Obed. I'm working as fast as I can."

His eyes opened, and he managed a shaky smile. "I'm not gonna go anywhere unless you say I can, Miss Camellia."

She threaded a needle and stitched up the worst of the wounds. At least the bones had not broken. The worst effect would be the loss of blood. If she could get Obed stitched up well enough, he should be okay.

She was finishing her work as a shadow fell across Obed's body. "What are you doing out here?"

Camellia looked up and saw the appalled faces of Jane and her mother. "Obed was hit by a bomb."

"His people will take care of him." Mrs. Watkins's voice was cold. Wasn't she worried about the man at all? Obed had worked for her family for years.

"His *people* have no medical supplies or experience."

Jane rolled her eyes. "Come back to the cave."

"I will when I'm through."

Several moments passed in silence. Camellia mopped up the blood and leaned back on her heels to see what else she needed to do.

"Come along, Mother. We can't make her come with us."

"I don't know what she expects us to do." Mrs. Watkins's voice floated back to her. "We can hardly keep body and soul together. It's all the fault of the Yankees. If they would just go away, we could resume our lives as before."

"Then I pray the Yankees never go away." Camellia's gaze met Obed's. The kindness and patience apparent on his face made her want to weep.

"Me, too, Miss Camellia. Me, too."

❧

The boat, Jonah's exit out of the city, was secure from the view of Confederate pickets. He'd gotten the location of Willow Grove from a bewildered prisoner they'd captured a few days earlier. All he needed to do now was get into the city, collect Camellia, and escape without being caught.

"I can set off a small mine at the end of one of our tunnels." Cage held up a torch to show him an artillery shell with a long lead.

Jonah remembered an earlier attempt to gain entrance through one of the tunnels they'd dug underneath the feet of the Confederates. "What will stop someone from shooting me as I emerge?"

"We've learned from our mistakes. This tunnel goes further than that last one. It burrows underneath their defensive positions and continues another quarter of a mile. You should come out somewhere close to the center of the city."

"No matter where it comes out, someone will hear the explosion and come to investigate." Jonah wanted to get Camellia out, not get them both killed.

Cage shook his head. "We'll time it to go off at the same time as a barrage of cannon fire. No one will notice. I guarantee it. Do you think I want you to get shot?"

"Of course not." Jonah clapped his friend on the shoulder. "When can we do it?"

"Give me five minutes."

Jonah went to his tent and pulled out the Confederate uniform he'd worn during the battle near Memphis. It was more than a little tattered, but that shouldn't raise any suspicions. He doubted any of the soldiers defending Vicksburg looked any better. He dressed quickly and met Cage at the mouth of the tunnel. "Are you ready?"

Cage nodded. "As soon as they start firing, I'll blow the entrance. I'll be praying for you."

"No matter what happens, I appreciate your help."

From a distance they heard the order to fire. The night sky lit up as one cannon after another belched out their deadly missiles.

"Godspeed." Cage pressed the detonator.

Dropping into a hunch, Jonah crabbed his way through the tunnel. He prayed for God's protection, prayed that he might reach Camellia, prayed that they might escape safely. The dim circle of the tunnel mouth came into view, and Jonah's heart climbed into his throat. This was the most dangerous time. He stopped to listen for a moment, trying to ascertain if anyone had noticed the explosion and was waiting for him to emerge.

Another round of shells exploded overhead, and he pushed forward, bursting from the ground with all the speed he could muster. Half expecting to meet the blast of a rifle, he rolled in a ball and tried to protect his head. . .and tumbled down a small rise to lie in the middle of someone's backyard.

No one was awaiting him. Jonah breathed a prayer of thanks and pushed himself to his feet. Now if he was seen, he would be just one of the occupying soldiers. He pulled his cap from the pocket of his trousers and put it on, pulling the bill down to hide his features. The chances of running into someone who knew him were not high, but he didn't want to take any unnecessary risks.

Willow Grove had been described as tall and yellow, with columns and a white picket fence. He looked around but found no house to match that description. Time to explore the neighborhood.

No dogs barked at him as he traveled the streets of the town. No cats slinked in the shadows. The only people he saw were dressed in uniforms like his own. He saluted when appropriate and moved past them with the confidence of a man who had a specific destination. It was a tactic that served him well.

Nearly an hour passed before he came upon a house matching the description he'd been given. It was dark, of course. The front door was locked, but a window next to it opened easily, and Jonah stepped into the parlor.

Moving as silently as he could manage, Jonah checked the rooms downstairs. By the time he climbed the stairs, he was certain the house was empty. If they had moved to a cave, he had no idea how to find Camellia. Desperation filled him as he checked bedroom after bedroom. What was he going to do?

"Stop right there, thief." The sound came from the landing behind him. It was a voice he remembered. "Raise your hands and turn around slowly."

Jonah did as ordered. "Hi, Thad. Is this the way you treat your friends?"

"You!" Thad raised the rifle an inch. "I ought to shoot you right here."

"But you don't want to get blood all over the floor, right?"

Thad's mouth twitched a little, and the deadly bore lowered until it was aimed at Jonah's chest instead of his head.

Jonah didn't know if that was much of an improvement.

"What are you doing here?"

"I came to collect Camellia, and your sister, too, if you trust me to get her out of here."

The rifle lowered a few inches more. "You're not going anywhere except prison."

"I can't." Jonah let his hands down. "I hear you have a flea problem there, and I'm terribly allergic."

"You'll be laughing from the other side of your mouth soon. I'm not going to let you slip away again. You've betrayed your people, and you have to pay the price."

It was time to make a decision. If it came to hand-to-hand combat, he felt like he could get the weapon away from Thad, but he might kill him in the process. Then he would never find Camellia, and if he did, she might never forgive him for killing the lout. *Lord, what should I do?*

"Get your hands back up." Thad gestured with his rifle.

Jonah obeyed him, although he only lifted his hands to the height of his shoulders. He rocked forward onto the balls of his feet in preparation to grab the rifle away from Thad. "Do you plan to parade me through town?"

"Th—" Whatever Thad was about to say was lost forever in the screaming whistle of a shell and a burst of light.

The explosion that followed catapulted Jonah through the air. Then the floor rose up to meet him, and everything went black.

Chapter Forty-three

"Thad hasn't been to see us in several days." Mrs. Watkins looked toward her daughter, ignoring Camellia as she'd done for several days. Ever since Obed had been hurt.

Jane pulled at the collar of her gown. "I know. He may be avoiding us." She gave Camellia a piercing look full of accusation.

The night sky lit up with a barrage of shells. Only a few weeks ago, the three women would have run inside the cave for shelter, but now they waited and watched before moving. The direction was wrong to threaten them, so they kept their seats at the mouth of their cave.

Mrs. Watkins waved her fan in front of her face. "The Yankees don't want us to get any sleep tonight."

Camellia wondered if the woman blamed her for the Yankees' persistence. Probably. She felt very unwelcome in their cave.

She and Jane were still going to the hospital every day. They'd come to an agreement to avoid discussing the slaves' right to equal consideration since it was obvious they would never agree on that subject.

They had patched up their friendship, and Camellia was beginning to feel much better. So much so that she had made the mistake of telling her about Thad's proposal. She didn't think her friend would ever forgive her for "breaking Thad's heart." No matter how much Camellia tried to explain that Thad didn't really love her, Jane was determined to defend her brother.

So here she was, stuck living with two women who obviously wished her gone. Camellia wondered how much longer the siege could go on. The soldiers were so weak from starvation that she wondered how they kept alert. Surely General Pemberton would see the futility of continuing to hold out. Vicksburg might be unassailable, but starvation would kill as surely as bullets and mortars.

One of the women who lived nearby came running toward them, her skirts raising a cloud of dust. "Lawson came by a few minutes ago and gave us some bad news."

Camellia's heart fell. What now?

"It's Willow Grove. It was hit by those infernal Yankees." The woman put a hand to her chest and gasped for air before continuing. "It didn't catch fire, thank the good Lord, but your roof is gone."

Jane jumped from her seat and looked toward her mother. "We need to go see about our things."

Mrs. Watkins's face shone white in the light of the torch. "I can't. . . . I don't. . .feel right."

She slumped forward and toppled from the chair.

Jane ran to her, turning her mother over and chafing her hand.

Camellia knelt beside her, wishing she had her medicines. She checked the older lady's wrist. The pulse was weak but steady. "I'm sure she's overheated. You stay here. I'll get a cool cloth, and we'll have her feeling better right away."

It took a quarter hour, but they managed to get a weepy Mrs. Watkins into her bed.

Camellia and Jane stepped outside the cave to discuss their next move. "You stay here and watch your mother. I'll go check on the house and report back to you."

Jane tossed her a grateful look. "Would you?"

"I'll be back before you know it." Camellia set off for town at a brisk pace, a torch in her hand.

The picket fence looked as fresh as it had when she first arrived in Vicksburg. How long ago that seemed. She tucked away her thoughts for consideration later. Right now she had to focus on her task—checking on the house and reporting back to the others.

A window stood ajar. A result of the explosion? She stepped through it into the parlor, holding the torch in front of her while she looked for a candle. Why had she not brought a candelabrum with her?

A satisfied sound escaped her lips as she found a box of candles near the hearth. Lighting one from the failing light of the torch, she took stock. This room looked untouched. Camellia exited and looked up, surprised in spite of herself to see stars twinkling above her head.

The roof had an enormous hole. They would have to get someone here immediately to patch that before a summer thunderstorm drenched the interior of the house.

Foreboding stole over her. Camellia tried to dismiss the feeling as a result of the destruction, but something raised the hair on her arms. Something was wrong in the house. Clenching her jaw, she considered the stairs. They looked secure. She put her foot on the first step, her heart pounding in her chest.

Was that a rustle from the second-floor landing? Probably a mouse or some other small rodent. At least she hoped it was. Lecturing herself silently, she continued moving upward. She would take a quick look around and leave. She and Jane could come back in the morning for a more thorough investigation.

Having made that promise, Camellia rushed up the last few steps. The wallpaper was blackened and smelled awful. It would probably have to be stripped.

Camellia's foot struck something soft, and she almost fell. Her candle showed her a gray uniform. Had someone been in the house when the shell struck it?

A groan made her catch her breath. "Thad? Is that you?" She leaned over the man, careful to keep wax from dripping on him. His features looked odd in the candlelight. Not odd. Wrong. His hair was auburn, his chin shorter. He looked like. . .like Jonah Thornton.

"Jonah?" She touched his face with a trembling finger. "Jonah? What have you done?" Tears blurred her vision. What was he doing in Willow Grove? In Vicksburg?

She snuffed out the candle and put it down on the floor next to his prone body. "Jonah, wake up. Please, you can't die. I love you." She felt the truth of her words reverberate through her. The pain nearly tore her in two.

Camellia put his head in her lap and rocked back and forth. "God, I don't know why Jonah is here, but I beg You to please let him live. Give me the chance to tell him the truth. I promise, God, that I won't let the opportunity escape this time. Only please give Jonah back—"

A hand fell on her shoulder, ending her prayer with a gasp.

Camellia looked back over her shoulder and saw Thad standing behind her. She bent her body further, trying to protect Jonah from him. "Go away. I'll take care of this man."

"I know who he is, Camellia." Thad's hand squeezed her shoulder before letting go. "He was here before the blast. He came to rescue you."

More tears threatened. Jonah was hurt because of her? After what she'd said to him? The clinical part of her mind protected her from the deepening pain. "Would you get some candles? I need to see how badly he's hurt."

Thad nodded and clomped down the stairs.

As soon as Thad reached the first floor, the man in her lap stirred. "Jonah? Do you hurt anywhere?"

He grinned up at her. "I've felt better, but being this close to you almost makes the pain worth it."

Anger replaced her fear. Camellia pushed him out of her lap. "You're not hurt at all. Have you been conscious the whole time?"

"Ow!" He rubbed the back of his head.

"How much did you hear?" She stood and brushed the dirt off her dress.

Jonah scrambled to his feet. He put a hand under her chin. "Enough to know that you're leaving Vicksburg with me tonight."

A part of Camellia wanted to push his hand away, but she was caught by the look in his eyes. "I am?"

"Yes, you are." Thad had come back upstairs more quietly than he'd departed. "Both of us heard you, Camellia. I know now why you turned down my offer."

She finally found the strength to push Jonah's hand away. "I'm sorry, Thad."

"Don't be." He sighed. "I think I realized the truth when I first saw Jonah here. I was so angry. I wanted him to pay for taking you away from me. But then when I came to and heard your voice. . . I'll always carry the shame of what I tried to do to him."

Camellia started to move to him, but Jonah put a hand on her arm. When she looked at him, he shook his head.

"Don't be so hard on yourself." Jonah's voice was gravelly. "I might have done the same thing in your place."

A slight smile appeared on Thad's face. "Thank you for that. Do you need help getting out of here?"

Jonah seemed completely recovered as he looked up to judge the amount of light in the sky. "I think we can still make it if we hurry."

The two men needed to stop talking about her as if she wasn't even here. "What about my medicine? My clothes?"

Thad and Jonah shared a look. A look that mixed empathy and disdain. Thad turned away, but not before she saw the grin on his face.

"You'll have to leave all that here." Jonah put an arm around her waist. "I'll buy you all the clothes your heart desires, and New Orleans has several apothecary shops, so don't worry about your medicines. We have to leave right now."

"I have one more thing to do." She pulled away from him and walked to where Thad stood.

He turned to face her. "You really do need to leave, you know."

"Thank you." She put a hand on his cheek. "I'll never forget this."

Thad pressed a quick kiss into her palm. "And I'll never forget you." He looked to Jonah. "Take care of her."

Jonah nodded and held out his hand. "Are you ready?"

Camellia put her hand in his. "Yes."

They walked hand in hand through the town and passed two sentries, neither of whom questioned their apparent early morning tryst. One of the men even had the temerity to wink at them. Camellia wondered if her cheeks were rosier than the predawn sky.

Jonah leaned over and put his lips on her ear. "Getting out of town is a lot easier than getting in."

When she was sure they were far enough from the sentries to speak openly, she turned to him. "How did you manage to get in at all?"

"I crawled through a tunnel." He described his efforts briefly before taking her in his arms.

"I'm so sorry for the things I said to you in Memphis. I understand now why you cannot support the South and what it stands for." She stared at the gray collar of his Confederate uniform, thankful it was only a costume. "I've seen the futility of the fighting—the death and pain men are causing each other. When I thought you were a casualty—" The horror of those moments threatened to overwhelm her again. "You shouldn't have put yourself at risk for my sake."

"I would have crawled a dozen miles farther and faced even death itself to rescue you." He put a finger under her chin and lifted it until their gazes met. "I love you, Camellia Anderson. I love the strong, committed woman of faith and integrity you've become."

"I love you, too, Jonah Thornton. I think I always have."

When his lips closed over hers, Camellia wondered how and why she'd ever resisted Jonah. He was the perfect hero for her—a gentle man with a heart of gold, a will of iron, and a love for the Lord that would always guide him. She thanked God for keeping him safe and for opening her eyes to the truth so that they could be together—together serving Him in all of their endeavors, no matter what the future held.

Epilogue

Natchez, Mississippi
July 1865

"Why is the boat rocking so much?" Camellia asked the question over her shoulder, her blue gaze meeting Lily's in the reflection of the mirror. "We haven't broken away from the dock, have we?"

Lily stood in the doorway and watched as Tamar arranged Camellia's blond curls around her face. She had always been the beauty of the family, but her face glowed with excitement on this, the day of her wedding. "Don't worry. I'm sure it's only the guests arriving and moving around in the main parlor." Perhaps a change of subject would calm the bride's nerves. "Wasn't it nice of Jean Luc's parents to offer their luxury steamship for your wedding? It's a shame Jean Luc and Anna could not come, but they've been busy in Missouri since the baby was born."

Camellia's expression bunched. Apparently she would not fall for Lily's ploy. "What about Mr. and Mrs. Thornton? And Jonah? Is he ready?"

Lily sympathized with the concern she detected in her sister's voice. She could remember her own wedding day. The fear of the unknown. . .the concern over the future. . .wondering if she was making a huge mistake. Of course all of that had disappeared when she saw the look of adoration in Blake's face as he stood tall and straight in front of the altar. And the same would be true for Camellia.

"Of course he's ready." Tamar answered the question for Lily. "Jonah loves you. He loves you the way Blake loves Lily."

"And the way Jensen loves you, Tamar." Lily smiled and moved toward the fancy dress suspended from a wooden rod in one corner of the stateroom. The skirt consisted of three deep flounces, each edged with wide lace. A bodice of matching white silk was decorated with floral fasteners and had short, puffed sleeves. Across the bed pillows lay the lace veil that would drift behind Camellia as she floated down the aisle in front of her friends and family. "You'll be a beautiful bride, dearest."

Camellia's expression mellowed, and a dreamy look replaced the concern in her eyes. "I've wanted to be married since I was a little girl."

"I have to admit I once worried you might select a husband for the wrong reasons, but you resisted the temptation to choose status over substance." Lily turned to the dressing table and reached to give her sister a hug. "Jonah Thornton is a fine Christian man. I know the two of you will keep God at the center of your lives, and He will bless your union."

"Amen." Tamar tweaked an errant curl into place.

Tears sparkled at the corners of Camellia's eyes.

"Don't you go crying and mess up that beautiful face." Tamar shook a finger at Camellia's reflection. "Tears aren't what you want to remember about your wedding day."

Camellia sniffed. "You're right."

"What's going on in here?" Jasmine bounded into the room with the enthusiasm and energy of youth. "Are you crying, Camellia?"

Camellia shook her head and dabbed at her eyes with the lace handkerchief Tamar handed to her.

Lily smiled at both of them, but her words were directed toward her youngest sister. "You'll understand better when it's your turn to get married."

"I'm not going to get married." Jasmine turned up her nose. "I'm going to be an actress with my own show and loads of admirers."

Tamar gasped, but Lily was not surprised. Her youngest sister had a talent for dramatic pronouncements. "That's good. You're too young to be thinking of marriage anyway."

Jasmine flipped her hair over one shoulder, her exotic violet-hued eyes scornful. "I don't care how old I am, I'll never get married. I want to be free to follow my dreams."

Lily exchanged a knowing glance with Camellia. Jasmine's words mirrored the sentiments each of them had once expressed. Camellia had used the same reasoning when she wished to go to the finishing school in New Orleans, and Lily had used it when explaining to her relatives why she had bought her first riverboat. But both she and Camellia had been much older than Jasmine was now. "Let's not worry about that. Today is Camellia's special day. The whole town is coming to share in her joy."

Chastened by the reminder, Jasmine nodded and lowered her nose. "You're right."

Lily's stomach churned, and she spread a hand over it below the blue ribbon around her waist. A thrill shot through her. She was expecting again, she was sure of it. But as she'd told Jasmine, today was not the day to focus on anything except Camellia and Jonah's happiness. Her announcement could wait. Even Blake didn't know yet.

A knock on the door was followed by Blake's voice. "Are you ladies ready? Everyone is here, and there's a nervous young fellow pacing the deck above you."

"We'll be up in a few minutes." Lily carefully took the wedding dress from its hanger, and she and Tamar lifted it over Camellia's curls. "Tell Jonah not to worry."

They heard his footsteps move away and breathed a collective sigh before turning to the next task—fastening the tiny pearl buttons on the back of the dress as well as the florets on the bodice.

Jasmine brought over a pair of white kid gloves and handed them to Camellia as Tamar and Lily secured the long veil in Camellia's hair.

When they finished, Lily stepped back to admire the picture her sister made. "You are so beautiful, inside and out."

Camellia took a deep breath, smiled, and nodded. "Thank you for letting me find my own way to happiness, Lily."

Lily nodded, and she sent a prayer of thanksgiving to God for their blessings. She opened her arms and gathered both of her sisters close for a hug.

"Now, don't you mess up Camellia's dress." Tamar's admonition ended the hug. "Lily, you and Jasmine go on to the parlor. I'll follow to make sure Camellia's train is straight when she makes her grand entrance."

Lily hesitated a moment, but then she felt Jasmine's arm around her waist. It was time to let Camellia go start her own family. She pulled Jasmine closer as they made their way to the crowded main room.

More than one hundred chairs were arranged in neat rows, and nearly every seat was occupied. It seemed the whole town had decided to attend Camellia and Jonah's wedding.

She and Jasmine took two chairs on the front row next to David and Blake, who was holding Noah. Grandmother was seated past them, with Aunt Dahlia and Uncle Phillip filling out the row.

Papa stood next to the podium, his smile as wide as the Mississippi. Jonah, standing next to him, still looked a little pale.

No wonder, given the fact that he'd only returned to Natchez from the war a month earlier. When Lily and the rest of the family tried to convince him to wait until he fully regained his health before marrying Camellia, he had replied that he had waited far too long already. He would marry his bride as soon as his parents arrived from New Orleans.

Lily leaned forward and looked to her left, sending a smile toward Mr. and Mrs. Thornton. Who would have thought that the friendship they had offered so many years ago would end in the union of their families? God, of course. It amazed Lily that she could be so blind to His purpose until she looked back in time. But seeing His guiding hand was a comfort she relied upon. No matter what circumstances or challenges they faced, He was always there.

Her thoughts were cut off as the buzz of conversation died down. She looked back to the entrance of the room and saw Camellia standing in the doorway, her skirts flowing around her like fluffy white clouds. Lily and the others stood and watched as she advanced, seeming to float forward like a cloud. When she reached the front of the room, Jonah stepped toward her, his adoration for Camellia plain to see.

He took her hands in his own, staring into her eyes as though she was the only person in the room. He repeated his vows as instructed, never looking away from her. When Papa pronounced them man and wife, Jonah swept back Camellia's veil with one hand and captured her face with the other. His whole attitude was one of love and devotion. What a wonderful man Camellia had fallen in love with.

"I love you." Blake whispered the words in her ear as he put an arm around Lily's shoulders.

Looking up at her husband, Lily thanked God again for her

blessings—for giving her a dream and helping her to follow it. "I love you, too."

Lily's heart seemed likely to burst from happiness as she returned her attention to Camellia and Jonah. They ended their first kiss as a married couple. Jonah tucked his bride's hand under his arm, grinning at the audience as Papa introduced them.

Mr. and Mrs. Jonah Thornton began their new life. . .together.

Jasmine

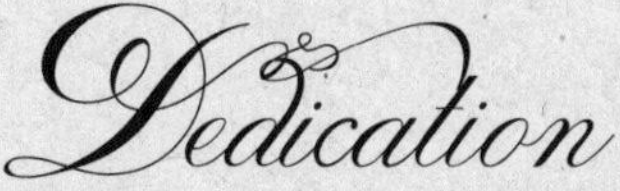

Diane—It is funny how things turn out sometimes. I wrote this dedication to be used in Camellia before deciding to save it for the final novel in the series. It breaks my heart that you died before you ever saw it. Rest in peace, darling, until we are reunited in heaven. For Edward Gene Ashley, April 15, 1952–November 28, 2012:

For Gene—the man who holds my heart. If I had looked the world over, I could not have found a spouse better than you. You enrich my life beyond anything I could have imagined when I was single. It took a long time for God to bring us together, but I cannot regret those years because I know He was molding each of us to become what the other needed. Thanks for forgiving my shortcomings, overlooking my faults, and encouraging me to pursue this dream of writing novels. Each day I get to spend with you is a treasure. We may not always see eye-to-eye, but that does not matter because we love and respect each other. You have taught me so much about patience, peace, and how wonderful love can be between a man and a woman. No one gets me like you do. No one else sees my warts with quite so much clarity. Yet you still love me. You are my hero. If I started today and filled up every hour telling you all the reasons I love being your wife, I would never get to the end of the list. I hope we get to spend many more years loving each other. I love you. . .more.

Aaron—I honor my friend who fully supported his wife's writing in a partnership. Thank you, Gene.

Acknowledgments

We would like to thank Becky Germany, Becky Fish, and the team at Barbour for believing in us and our journeys along the Mississippi River. We also thank our agent and friend, Steve Laube, for helping to make our writing dreams come true. For our support group, the Bards of Faith, God put you in our lives for many reasons beyond writing. Thank you for being His instruments. And for our readers, we thank you so, so, so much. We do it for Him, but we have you in mind always.

Chapter One

Sandwich, Illinois
April 15, 1870

Ducking behind a horse trough, David Foster pulled out his weapon and aimed it toward the opposite side of the street. A bullet dug a hole in the dirt a bare inch from his foot. David narrowed his eyes against the dust it kicked up and pulled his body in tight. "Put down your weapon and raise your hands."

He could see Cole Hardy's face peeking past the curled brim of a hat—a lady's hat with posies tucked into the headband. The poor woman wearing the incongruous headpiece was an innocent passerby Cole had grabbed when David first tried to arrest him. The outlaw brandished his pistol and laughed. "You're not going to take me alive, Pinkerton."

Even though it wasn't his name, David had grown used to the title in the past weeks. The others employed by the famous private detective agency said it was a part of the job.

David looked around the end of the trough to judge the distance between him and Hardy. "Let the woman go, Cole. She has nothing to do with this."

"My name's the Whiskey Kid." The man's voice held a plaintive note.

A grin slid across David's face in spite of the dangerous situation. Criminals could be so childish. As if their development had ended at age five even though their bodies continued to mature. Perhaps by appealing to the outlaw's ego, he could diffuse the situation. "How did you get that name, Whiskey?"

The woman he held whimpered, a sound combined of fear and pain.

"Shut up," Cole hissed at his hostage.

From his limited view of the pair, David could see her face pale even further as the outlaw tightened his hold. While he waited for an answer to his question, David considered how to protect her. If he shot at Cole, he might hit her instead. His best option was to get the man talking. "If I'm going to call you something other than the name your ma gave you, I want to know why."

"It's because I kin drink more than anyone else around and still keep my wits about me."

"Is that right?" David wondered if the man was drunk right now. If he was, his aim would be shaky. Of course his temper would be on a short fuse. "And I guess your skill has gotten you a lot of admiration over the years."

David risked leaning out a few inches farther and studied what he could see of his opponent. The kid looked only fifteen years old, but he was probably about twenty-one, the same age as David. The leader of a local gang of outlaws terrorizing the area, Cole Hardy had shot down the former sheriff and two of his deputies to establish control. He might be young, but he was still a murderer.

The day the town of Sandwich buried their law enforcement officers, a telegram from the local bank president arrived at the Pinkerton National Detective Agency—a plea for help that David had been selected to answer.

"Come on out here, Pinkerton, and I'll show you my real skills."

Another bullet struck the ground and made David duck for cover. At least the bullet had missed him again. Sweat trickled down his face, mixing with the dust. He would need a bath when this was over. Wiping his face with his free hand, David pushed his hat back. It was time to see if he couldn't push Cole a little harder—see if he could get the lady free. "Where I come from, real men don't hide behind women's skirts. Why don't you let her go, and you and I can discuss the matter man-to-man."

The only response to his taunt was silence. He leaned forward again, hoping Cole wasn't smart or sober enough to be waiting for his face to show once more.

Something had happened to draw Cole's attention away from the trough where David hid. He was looking over his shoulder, maintaining the barest grasp on the back of the woman's neck.

David waved a hand to make sure she could see him and gestured with a jerk of his head to run. Fear entered her eyes, gleaming through a sheen of tears. He smiled for encouragement and received a whisper of a nod from her. He held his breath as she pulled away with a sudden jerk and went running down the street.

Cole Hardy whipped his head back around, cursed, and pointed his weapon at David. In the split second before the outlaw fired, David squeezed his trigger. The other man spun in the opposite direction as the bullet tore through his thigh. His shot went wild. David was up and running toward him as the outlaw hit the dusty road.

"You shot me." Pain twisted Cole's face, and he curled up into a ball, his spent weapon forgotten. "It hurts."

David picked up the gun and shoved it into his belt. He holstered his own weapon, looking to see what had taken Cole's attention away from his captive in the moments before she had escaped. Illinois Bank was painted on the plate glass window, but no one stood there.

With a mental shrug, David bent to inspect Cole's wound. "You're lucky I didn't shoot you in the heart. You'll live to face a judge for the murders you committed."

A door creaked open, bringing David's attention back to the bank. Two men, their hands raised high, stepped across the threshold, followed by a grim-faced man who held an ancient-looking shotgun in his hands. "Git on out there so the Pinkerton man can escort all you to jail."

David stood and settled his bowler on his head more firmly. "I'll take those men off your hands, but the doctor will have to sew this one up before he gets carted off to jail." He pointed his pistol at the two uninjured outlaws and marched them toward the end of the main street to the sheriff's office.

People stepped outside and watched them move past the various businesses of Sandwich. Their faces showed varying degrees of relief, shame, and hope. A young boy dashed past, shouting for his pa to come look. Ladies stood in little groups of two or three, their bonnets shading their faces but not obscuring their admiring glances.

He reached the jailhouse without mishap and herded the two men inside. An empty desk and two barred rooms greeted them. Where was the sheriff? Or whoever represented the law since the sheriff was murdered.

"Both of you can get in that cell." He closed the door behind them and walked to the desk, opening the drawer and fishing out a ring of keys.

By the time he had them secure, the grim man who had held his shotgun on the two gang members entered the sheriff's office. He looked different now—more jovial and relaxed. David assumed he was the banker who had sent a wire to the agency.

"Now our law-abiding citizens won't have to hide themselves anymore." The man held out his left hand. "I'm Mr. Morton Winthrop at your service. I don't suppose you'd consider staying here in Sandwich for a spell? We need a new sheriff."

David waited for Mr. Winthrop to pause before introducing himself. "Where is your sheriff?"

"Dead." One of the prisoners answered him with a cackle, exposing a number of broken or missing teeth. "Cole done kilt him last week."

The other gang member, shorter and meaner looking, nodded. "And yer next."

Mr. Winthrop shook his head. "You can see why we're having a bit of a problem choosing a new sheriff. . .but a man like you can handle himself. And Sandwich has a fine collection of pretty young misses, any of whom would make you a good wife."

An image sprang to David's mind. A girl with coal black hair, violet eyes, and a complexion as fair as a bowl of milk. "I'm not interested in finding a wife or in staying in Sandwich."

"Woo-hoo, I'd like me one of them gals." Tall-and-toothless stood with his face pressed between the bars of the cell.

"Mind your own business." Mr. Winthrop sneered at the man. "I wasn't talking to the likes of you or your partner."

The front door swung open, and two men brought Cole Hardy in on a stretcher.

One of them looked to Winthrop. "Where should we put him?"

As Winthrop sputtered, David slipped past the men with the stretcher, feeling Cole Hardy's angry stare all the way out the door. Turning right, he walked down the street to the hotel, the only two-story building in Sandwich.

The sun would set soon. He couldn't get back to Chicago tonight, so he decided he could get that bath, eat some supper, and retire early. Tomorrow he would get an early start. The people of Sandwich could handle the Whiskey Kid and his followers. David had done what he was hired to do.

Breathing a sigh of relief to enter the relative coolness of the hotel, David tossed a couple of coins on the front counter and asked for bathwater to be delivered to his room.

"I'd be happy to bring it myself." The girl at the counter was the daughter of the proprietor—single and dangerous. She was rather pretty, if a man liked his women with wheat-colored hair and glittering blue eyes. He was more fond of dark-haired women.

Besides, like he'd told Mr. Winthrop, David had no intention of finding himself a wife here. "That's all right. If you don't have a servant to carry the water, I can go to the barbershop." He ran a hand over his chin. "I need a shave anyway."

She pushed out her red lips in a pout. "Pa can bring the water."

"That's okay." The hair on the back of his neck rose in response to the predatory look in her eyes. He would also ask the barber if he could get a decent meal at any other place in town. David had plans for his future, plans that had nothing to do with being caught by a man-hungry female in Sandwich.

❧

Chicago

Pinkerton code:
Accept no bribes
Never compromise with criminals
Partner with local law enforcement agencies
Refuse divorce cases or cases that initiate scandals of clients
Turn down reward money
Never raise fees without the client's pre-knowledge
Apprise clients on an ongoing basis

David could recite by memory the words stitched on the framed handwork hanging on his supervisor's wall. They had been drilled into his head when he joined the agency. They were the first thing he was taught, along with the methods for catching criminals.

Homer Bastrup glared at him over the top of his wire-rimmed glasses for a moment before nodding. His bulldog face relaxed into a smile. Removing the glasses, he carefully folded the legs and placed them in a leather case.

"Good job." The large man's voice boomed through the suite of offices located on the second floor of the Pinkerton National Detective Agency. Several of the detectives whose desks were stationed outside his door raised their heads. "This is the kind of report I wish all my men would turn in."

The heads dropped again, and David thought he could hear the scratch of pens on paper in the sudden silence. "Thank you, sir." The approval on his supervisor's face brought home the importance of his recent success. It made his hard work worth the effort.

"Mr. Winthrop was very complimentary. He sent a letter saying you did an excellent job in protecting the citizens while addressing the problem." Mr. Bastrup tapped a sheet of stationery with a beefy finger.

"He even asked if you might be willing to return to Sandwich as their sheriff."

"That's very kind of Mr. Winthrop. He made my job easier by holding a weapon on the gang members after I shot their leader."

"Are you interested in returning to Sandwich?"

"I don't think that's a good idea. I like living here in Chicago." David hoped to make a career for himself with the Pinkerton agency. Chasing down criminals and making sure they were put in prison was a noble occupation, and one he seemed to have some aptitude for.

He was proud to be a Pinkerton detective. The agency had the largest collection of information anywhere about crimes and criminals in the United States. Thanks to their efforts, America was a safer place for law-abiding citizens. "We never sleep"—the motto of the Pinkerton agency—was proven true over and over as murderers, thieves, and anarchists were arrested in ever-growing numbers.

The older man reached for a fountain pen, scratching his name at the bottom of the final page of David's report with a flourish. "Those men who held up your stagecoach last fall got quite a surprise. Your story is much like Allan's. He got involved in detective work when he helped the Kane County sheriff capture a gang of counterfeiters."

David was familiar with the story of how Mr. Pinkerton had become a deputy sheriff before forming the agency with his brother Robert. The three-story building that housed their agency was a testament to their hard work and success. "As they say, 'It's an ill wind that blows no good.'"

The trip back from San Francisco had been difficult even before the incident Mr. Bastrup mentioned. David had traveled out there to reconcile with his father. That was a mistake that had cost him both time and money. On the long trip back, a pair of masked riders held up the mail coach. All the passengers were ordered out of the coach and told to empty their purses and pockets. Waiting for the right opportunity, he managed to pull his weapon, wound one of the robbers, and capture the other.

"How would you feel about a trip to New Orleans?"

The question caught David off guard. Most of the cases he'd worked were much closer to home. "Sir?"

Mr. Bastrup's wise brown eyes seemed to see right through him. "You're familiar with that part of the world, aren't you?"

Memories flooded David. The flavor of fresh fish; the smell of burning coal; warm, lazy days watching the splash of a paddlewheel. . . "I grew up in the South."

"You still talk like your mouth is full of cotton."

David had heard that complaint often since making Chicago his home. "The people back there say I sound like a Yankee."

A hint of a smile lighted Mr. Bastrup's face as he opened one of his desk drawers and pulled out a thick folder. "You may remember hearing about a rash of bank robberies in Chicago last year. Just about the time our agency was hired, before we could find out if the robberies were connected to each other, they stopped."

David watched the older man's face as frustration and anger replaced his moment of humor. Mr. Bastrup was dedicated to his job. For him it was a personal insult for someone to get away with a crime. As tenacious as a snapping turtle, he rarely failed.

"Now the same thing is happening in New Orleans. One of the bank officers wants to hire our agency. They need help getting their money back, and it seems the police force down there isn't having much luck. When I talked to Mr. Pinkerton about this assignment, I told him I think there may be a connection between the robbery there and what happened here. He agreed and told me about another incident in Vidalia, Louisiana, across the Mississippi River from Natchez. Isn't that where you're from?"

David didn't want to nod. He had no desire to discuss Natchez or even think about the people there. But Mr. Bastrup knew the answer. He tilted his head.

"I thought so." Bastrup slammed a fist on his desk for emphasis, making David's shoulder even more tense. "The robbers take their time and hit the banks when they are most vulnerable. We have to stop them. Let people know their money is safe. I want an agent down there who can put them in jail where they belong."

An odd mix of feelings assailed David as he listened to his supervisor. He was equally anxious to catch the bank robbers, but he wasn't certain if he wanted to return to the South. He had come to Chicago for many reasons, not the least of which was to start a new life. He no longer had any family ties. He was free to go anywhere, even to Europe if he wanted. Was going back to the area where he'd grown up a good idea? His heart said yes; his mind, no. "Do you need an answer now?"

A frown drew Mr. Bastrup's eyebrows together. "Most of the detectives out there would jump at the chance I'm offering you. I thought you were a man of ambition. Do you really want to become a manager here, or are you satisfied working small cases in remote areas?"

When his supervisor laid out the options, David realized he didn't have much choice. "I'll do it."

"Good." Mr. Bastrup handed him the folder. "Here's all the information we gathered in Chicago. Maybe you'll see something we missed. And you should probably check out that bank that was robbed in Vidalia. They might have some new lead. If nothing else, it'll give you an opportunity to visit your family in Natchez before you continue on to New Orleans."

David started to correct him about his family situation, but he simply said, "Thank you for trusting me." He stood and tucked the folder under his arm. "I'll do my best."

Bastrup grunted. "I expect good things from you. If you want more responsibility, you'll have to earn it. Mr. Pinkerton demands it from himself and from his agents."

As he walked from the room, David wondered at the irony. He had thought he could break free of his past. Unresolved questions returned to his mind. Would the people in Natchez treat him differently now that he was a full-fledged detective? His life had taken so many turns that it made him dizzy to consider all the twists and turns. Where would this venture take him?

Chapter Two

Natchez, Mississippi

My dance card is full." Jasmine Anderson snapped together the spines of her fan so David wouldn't see that several of them had no partner written on them. Why had Camellia decided to order fans instead of using the traditional dance cards that could be more easily hidden? Dangling from her wrist, its weight seemed to chide her for being untruthful. She wished she could use the silly thing to cool her cheeks. Why was the room so warm when the month of May had barely begun?

Jasmine set her jaw and glared up at him. She would not yield to temptation. David had no right to expect her to swoon with excitement because he had shown up at the last minute. At one time she might have considered a proposal from him—a temporary bout of madness, no doubt. She had been foolish enough to listen to his plans and dream of a future together. But no more. She was done pining for him.

A slight smile emerged from the corner of his lips but did not continue up to his eyes, eyes as green as maidenhair ferns. Eyes that held a hint of sadness. Why should he be sad? He was the one who had gone adventuring and left her to molder here in the backwaters.

Something had changed in him since he decided to move to Chicago and become a detective. And she didn't like it at all. In spite of her determination to remain at arm's length from him, she wished David could remain the staunch friend and ally he'd been. She was the same, after all. What had happened to the boy who had known her better than anyone else? Was he still inside there somewhere? Or had he ceased to be her David the moment he left town?

No matter the answers to all those questions, he should not have appeared so suddenly tonight. He should have had the decency to call on her yesterday or at least earlier this afternoon—before the ball started—like her other dance partners. Did he think he should get special consideration because of a handful of empty promises?

If that's what he thought, she would disabuse him of the notion right now. "I'm sorry, David. If I'd known you would be here. . ." She let the words trail off.

"Of course. I understand." His voice was steady and his smile widened, but his green eyes stayed sober. He bowed briefly. "I apologize for my presumption."

She was saved from further conversation with him by the appearance of William Smalley, her next dance partner. She welcomed his arrival with a determined smile. She refused to compare him to David. A proper gentleman, Mr. Smalley had called on her several days ago and secured her hand for this dance. Never mind that he was not as tall or broad shouldered as David. He was a very nice man, and she was looking forward to their dance.

"I believe our quadrille is beginning." Although William held out his right hand in invitation, his uncertain brown gaze darted from her face to David's.

"Of course." Jasmine put her hand on his arm and allowed herself to be swept onto the dance floor as the music began.

"You are looking exceptionally lovely this evening, Miss Anderson." William's smile was much more flattering and genuine than David's had been. It soothed her ruffled nerves.

Jasmine curtsied to him before turning to the gentleman on her right and curtsying again as the dance required. "Thank you, Mr. Smalley."

The orchestra's music could not quite drown out the conversations in the crowded ballroom, but at least out here they had room to breathe. Waiting for their turn to cross the square, she pulled at the cuff of her elbow-length glove. What was wrong with her? She should not be so nervous. It wasn't like this was her first ball. Since the end of the war she had attended dozens of similar affairs with her sister Camellia. At the age of twenty some would consider her an old maid, but Jasmine was determined to take her time before selecting a husband. Or she might decide to remain single. No law demanded that she marry, after all.

Tapping her foot in rhythm to the music, Jasmine swept out onto the floor with all the enthusiasm she could muster. As she and her partner neared the far end of their square, she held out her left hand for him to grasp. His right hand rested lightly on her waist as they executed the turn. In perfect coordination, they crossed the center once more to return to their original position. Then it was time to promenade.

Mr. Smalley was an excellent partner. Jasmine was beginning to enjoy herself in earnest, her gaze sweeping the room for sight of either of her older sisters. Both Lily and Camellia were dancing in another square, their husbands at their sides.

The turn of a man's blond head drew her attention. David! He was leaning toward another female and smiling. His eyes crinkled in the way she remembered. The way they should have crinkled when he was smiling at her.

Betrayal swept through her like a spring flood. Jasmine missed her next step and stumbled. If not for Mr. Smalley's tightened grip on her waist, she might have actually fallen to the floor like a graceless child.

"Are you all right, Miss Anderson?" His whispered question brushed past her ear.

She answered him with a nod. "Thanks to your quick thinking, sir."

"It's kind of you to say so." His face beamed, and his chest expanded with pride and satisfaction.

"I apologize. I must have been distracted. I promise I'm not usually so clumsy."

His eyes widened, and he swallowed hard. "You're never clumsy, Miss Anderson. Quite the opposite, in fact."

They reached the point in their square where they had begun, and Jasmine breathed a sigh of relief. Concentrating on the other dancers, she refused to let her mind wander to what she'd seen David Foster doing. It was none of her business anyway. Let him flirt with whatever girl he wished. He'd made it quite clear when he moved to Chicago what their friendship meant to him—nothing. He may have hinted at returning for her, but he'd never done so. And her heart had mended.

The quadrille came to its conclusion without further mishaps, and Mr. Smalley escorted her from the dance floor. Jasmine was quickly inundated with other young men who wished to dance with her. Laughing with all the skill she could muster, Jasmine allowed one or two to pen their names to the empty spines on her fan. No green-eyed traitor was going to ruin her night.

By the time the orchestra took its first break, her feet ached and her lips felt cracked from all the smiling she'd done. She spied a pair of empty chairs next to a large vase of cut flowers and hurried toward them. Sitting down with a sigh of relief, she stretched her toes as far as her shoes would allow. It would be nice if she could reach down and rub her arches, but Camellia—ever the stickler for proper behavior—would have a fit of apoplexy if she saw her sister doing anything so gauche.

"You seem to be the belle of the ball tonight." Lily's voice interrupted her moment of solitude.

Tucking her feet away, Jasmine glanced up at her oldest sister. Lily's light brown hair was pulled back into its usual bun, but it gleamed in the light of nearby candles. "Isn't that what you and Camellia want? Both of you seem insistent on introducing me to suitors so I'll wed and no longer be a burden to you."

"Don't be a goose." Lily sat down in the chair next to her, the dove gray silk of her dress sighing like the flutter of birds' wings. "You'll never be a burden to me. All I want is for you to be as happy as I am."

"And marriage is supposed to make that happen?"

Before Lily could answer, a shadow fell over their corner. Jasmine frowned as her other sister approached them. Camellia was resplendent as always. A true Southern belle, she wore a gown of light blue watered silk that matched the color of her eyes. Her golden hair was dressed in the latest style—pulled straight back to the crown of her head and allowed to cascade around her face in a profusion of ringlets. "Here the two of you are. I wondered if you were hiding."

Jasmine sighed. If she tried to arrange her hair that way, it would have looked like a rat's nest. But Camellia's natural curls could always be depended upon to look just right. "I believe you can count your ball a success."

Camellia's blue gaze swept the ballroom. "Who would want to miss such a festive evening? Did I see David here awhile ago?"

"I saw him at the docks this afternoon and invited him to come." Lily unfurled the fan each of the ladies had been given at the beginning of the ball—it was noticeably empty of partners' names—and waved it back and forth. "He didn't seem certain if he could make it. Did you speak to him, Jasmine?"

"Only for a moment." Jasmine's hands clenched in her lap. "I've been so busy dancing."

Camellia frowned at her. "I hope you weren't rude. David considers us his family, you know."

"I don't know why." Jasmine rolled her eyes. "He and I may have been playmates as children, but he's hardly been here since last summer."

"I'm sure it's been difficult for him. I wish his father had not died before David tracked him down." Lily's brown eyes moistened. "We all know what it's like to be separated from our parents."

Guilt assailed Jasmine. She grew up thinking her father had died in the same accident that took their mother's life. When he had reappeared eleven years ago, all their lives had changed. Lily had let go of her bitterness, Camellia had focused on her future, and Jasmine had welcomed Papa into her life with an open heart. She had accepted his viewpoint on everything from river traffic to faith. Of course, she was an adult now. She still respected her father, but she was beginning to see that the world could not be viewed as simply as he had once taught her.

She nodded to a far corner of the ballroom where a knot of dowagers and middle-aged courtiers had gathered. "It looks like Aunt Dahlia is still holding court. No wonder she was so eager for you to have this ball."

"I wonder where Uncle Phillip has gotten off to." Camellia pleated the material of her skirt, her blue gaze fastened on something farther away than their mother's sister. "I for one am glad to see her so animated. Since Grandmother died, she has become more frail somehow. Some days I worry that she will wilt like an unwatered flower."

"I doubt Aunt Dahlia is going to fade away." Lily's voice was practical as always. "She's as strong willed as ever. She may well outlive all of us."

Camellia tilted her head and considered her older sister. "The two of you have always rubbed each other the wrong way. Can you not forgive her for trying to marry you to the wrong man?"

"You can't think I would nurse a grudge like that." Lily's fan swept back and forth with enough speed to raise a breeze. "I forgave her many years ago. But she still expects me to go along with whatever strategy or plan comes to her fevered mind. Last week she told me that Magnolia needed to begin comportment lessons. My daughter is too young to be made to worry about such things. She's only four."

Deciding her two sisters might need someone to play the peacemaker, Jasmine cleared her throat. "And the two of you call me melodramatic?"

Both of her sisters stopped glaring at each other and turned to her. Lily was the first to respond. A smile broke through her frown. She nodded at Jasmine. "You make an excellent point."

Camellia looked as though she'd like to continue discussing the matter, but Jasmine raised an eyebrow and glanced toward the other guests. After a moment her shoulders relaxed. "I should find Jonah. He's supposed to dance with me after this break."

Jasmine and Lily watched her move across the dance floor in search of her husband, her gown barely swaying in spite of all the hoops under it.

"I cannot believe how warm this room is." Lily redoubled the speed of her fan and frowned at Jasmine. "Where is your fan? Has some lovelorn boy stolen it away from you?"

Jasmine's cheeks heated. She had stashed it in a corner of the library earlier, unwilling to hold onto the evidence of her lie to David. "I. . . It's around here somewhere."

Her oldest sister raised her right eyebrow in a mannerism she had picked up from her husband. It conveyed her skepticism quite plainly.

Unwilling to admit the truth, Jasmine pushed herself up from her chair. "I believe the orchestra is ready to begin again." Without another word she escaped Lily's probing gaze, smiling widely at the young man she hoped was coming to collect her for the next dance.

The rest of the evening passed in a blur of mazurkas, waltzes, and polkas. By the time the ballroom emptied out, Jasmine was certain she had danced away at least an inch of her height. Everything hurt—feet, legs, arms—even her head. She could hardly wait to pull the hairpins out, exchange her ball gown for a nightgown, and seek her bed.

Uncle Phillip and Aunt Dahlia led the way as they all headed upstairs for the night. Jasmine yawned and put a hand to her aching head. "Don't expect to see me before noon."

Camellia glanced back over her shoulder at her younger sister. "I'm sure all of us feel the same way."

"*I'm* sure the children will have us up earlier than that." Lily put her hand on Blake's arm.

He laughed, the deep sound echoing in the quiet stairwell. "And I'm sure you'll want me to keep them busy while you get dressed."

"Would you? That would be grand."

Jasmine heard her brother-in-law mumble something but didn't quite catch what he said as she reached her bedroom door. It didn't really matter anyway. Lily and Blake were always carrying on like children.

With impatient fingers, she jerked her hair free from the pins restraining it as a sleepy maid helped her undress. "Thanks for staying up so late, Lynette. Go on to bed now."

The room darkened as the maid left, and Jasmine sighed her relief. She had gotten through the evening even though David Foster's presence had made it a trial. Normally she wouldn't have taken part in every dance, but because she'd told him that she had no dances open, she'd had little choice. A wry smile crossed her face. She supposed she had no one to blame for her aches but her own incautious tongue.

As she drifted to sleep, a Bible verse her father had once taught her floated through her mind. *"In the multitude of words there wanteth not sin: but he that refraineth his lips is wise."* Her last thought was that she was not as wise as she thought. . .according to the Bible anyway.

Chapter Three

I think we should pay a visit to Anna and Jean Luc." Blake Matthews pushed his chair away from the dining table.

"That's a good idea." Lily finished the last bite of her toast and washed it down with a sip of strong, dark coffee. "I noticed they weren't at the ball last night."

She wasn't surprised at the absence of Blake's sister and brother-in-law. They had only come back to Natchez last month, and she had hoped they might attend, even though some sticklers might have raised their eyebrows. Glancing toward her husband, she could tell he was thinking the same thing. So often their minds traveled the same pathways. Lily supposed it was a result of working together so closely. . .and of being married for ten years.

"It would have been a good opportunity to reintroduce them to the people here." Blake tapped a foot on the floor. "But I suppose they were worried about keeping up appearances."

Lily placed her napkin on the table next to her plate. "I tried to tell Anna that no one would think anything amiss if they were seen at a family party. I know they are still in mourning for Jean Luc's father, but that doesn't mean they have to avoid every social gathering."

Aunt Dahlia frowned at Lily's words. "I don't know what this world is coming to. You young people don't have any respect at all for traditions that have been followed for centuries."

"It's a brave new world, Aunt Dahlia." Camellia handed a soft, warm biscuit to Amaryllis, her two-year-old daughter. "We've left the old ways behind."

Lily was surprised at her sister's agreement. In the past Camellia had always been determined to cling to rules and regulations, but her marriage to Jonah had brought about some much-needed changes in her sister's personality. It was a pity the same could not be said for Aunt Dahlia. But she and Uncle Phillip still adhered to the practices that had been in effect prior to the war.

She sent a stern glance to her oldest child, Noah. "You need to practice your sums while we're gone, young man."

Jasmine rushed into the dining room at that point, her expression harried. "Good morning."

She reached across Magnolia and grabbed a piece of dry toast.

"Why don't you sit and break your fast like a real lady?" Disapproval filled Camellia's voice and her face.

"No time." Jasmine stood behind her niece's chair and munched on the toast. "I'm already late."

A harrumph from Aunt Dahlia showed her agreement with Camellia.

Deciding to allow her younger sister the benefit of the doubt, Lily frowned at the other two women before turning a smile to Jasmine. "Where are you off to?"

"The orphanage." Jasmine dusted crumbs from her hands, her bread gone. "We have practice beginning at nine."

Blake pulled out his pocket watch. "It's 8:50. I'm afraid you're going to be late whether you sit and eat or not."

"I know." Jasmine blew them a kiss. "Don't expect me for lunch, Camellia. I'll eat at the orphanage." With that parting shot she left, disappearing before anyone had time to stop her.

"Phillip, don't you agree that girl is allowed far too much freedom?"

Uncle Phillip didn't emerge from his newspaper but gave a grunt that his wife took as agreement.

"I suppose that means Jasmine won't go visiting with us this morning." Lily picked up Benjamin, her baby, and excused herself from the dining room. She was eager to make her escape before Aunt Dahlia started in on one of her diatribes. She knew it would lead to her favorite list of deficiencies since the end of the war.

Like others of her age and social status, her aunt imbued the pre-war days with a golden glow that had little to do with reality. If Aunt Dahlia had her way, slavery would be reinstated and Jefferson Davis would still be the president of the Confederacy. No matter what anyone said, she was not likely to change her opinion. Although Lily felt sorry for her, she didn't want to be trapped into either arguing with the older woman or tacitly agreeing with her beliefs.

As she reached the nursery door, Lily heard footsteps coming up the staircase and turned to see who was coming.

Blake appeared at the top of the stairs, their daughter, Magnolia, in his arms and Noah walking as close to his father as possible.

The sight of her family warmed Lily's heart. God had blessed them so.

Her husband's teasing blue gaze met hers. "I can't believe you abandoned me and two of your children to a homily on the waywardness of today's young people."

"Benjamin was growing fussy." Lily stepped into the nursery, depositing her youngest son on his bed while she gathered clean clothes and a fresh diaper. "Besides, you seem to have escaped unscathed."

Blake followed her into the room, handing their daughter over to the nanny, who would watch all of the children. He settled Noah at his desk with a lesson on mathematics while Lily readied Benjamin for his nap in a wicker bassinet. Magnolia and her cousin Amaryllis played with their dolls in one corner of the room under the nanny's indulgent gaze.

Listening to them was almost like traveling back in time to her own childhood, when Lily and her sisters had played together in this very same room. After a few moments, her husband put his arm around her waist and pulled her from the nursery. "How long before we can leave?"

"I just have to put on a cap and get my parasol."

Blake dropped a quick kiss on her cheek. "I'll go get the buggy ready and meet you downstairs."

By the time Lily had gathered her things and stepped out into the warm morning, Blake was sitting in the buggy with the reins in his hands. She climbed up beside him and settled herself as he guided the horse down the lane to the main road.

"I wonder if Jean Luc and Anna will stay in Natchez or if they plan on taking his mother back to Cape Girardeau." Lily glanced at her husband's face. What a boon it would be to have both of their families living in the same town. Of course, given the number of trips they took to deliver people and goods up and down the Mississippi, they were sure to see all of their relatives from time to time. But she rather liked the idea of getting to know Blake's sister better, which was more likely to happen if she and Jean Luc remained in Natchez.

"I hope so." Blake spared her a quick glance before returning his gaze to the road ahead. "I doubt it would do his mother much good to be uprooted from the home she's lived in all these years."

"And Jean Luc could take over his father's shipping business." Lily caught her breath as an idea burst on her with the suddenness of a summer thunderstorm. "Maybe we could even help to make sure he's successful."

"Perhaps."

Lily looked at her husband again, noticing the tightness around his jaw. He could not be worried that Jean Luc was still the malicious person who had once tried to wreck their first boat, the boat that had brought the two of them together. That had been more than ten years ago. In the intervening years, Jean Luc had proved his trustworthiness again and again. Besides, he was the father of Blake's only nephew. "I know you've forgiven him, Blake, but have you put the past behind you?"

"Of course I have." Blake moved the reins to his left hand and put his right hand over hers. "In fact, Jean Luc and I have talked several times over the past few years about the future of river traffic."

His tone of voice was ominous, striking a chord of fear in Lily's heart. "What do you mean?"

Blake's hand squeezed her cold fingers. "You must have noticed how the number of boats has decreased for the past year or so."

"People are just recovering from the war." Lily refused to accept his interpretation of the reduced traffic. Sometimes they might go an afternoon without seeing another boat, but it was unusual. They didn't see as many of the smaller vessels, but that was because the larger boats could navigate better and transport merchandise more economically. "River traffic is going to come back. It has to. It's only been a few years. Think of all the boats we see every time we go to New Orleans."

He pulled back on the horse's reins and turned to give her his full attention. "I know how much you love the river, darling. And I'm sure we can continue to move cargo in *Water Lily*. But you have to realize things are changing. The railroads are a good alternative for a lot of businessmen. More and more bridges will crisscross the river as people out West demand better service. The flaw in our waterways is the difficulty in reaching all destinations. Railroads will always go places that riverboats cannot."

The irony of the situation was not lost on Lily as she listened to Blake explain his logic. Hadn't she just been feeling sorry for Aunt Dahlia because she would not accept the inevitability of change? Was God trying to tell Lily that she should deal with the log in her eye before trying to remove the mote in her aunt's eye? She took a deep, steadying breath. "I'm sure we can make a life for ourselves anywhere, Blake."

"That's my practical Lily." He loosened the reins once more, and the horse picked up speed. "People will always want to seek a better life in new places, and they will need more supplies shipped to them no matter the method of transportation."

Lily bit her lip as she tried to imagine making a home on one of the smoking, belching beasts that threatened her lifestyle. She didn't much like the rumble they made crossing the tall bridges the *Water Lily* glided under. Could she trade gentle breezes and swift-flowing water for hot cinders and soot? Could trains even accommodate a family like their riverboat could?

Yet the idea of visiting new destinations was somewhat intriguing.

Perhaps looking into a different mode of transportation was a good idea. With a lift of her chin, she decided that she would first trust God and then her husband and follow. . .no matter the destination.

❧

David took a battered envelope from his breast pocket and studied its limp edges. He knew the contents of the note inside. Had memorized the words months earlier when he'd first received the letter originally addressed to his deceased mother.

"What do you have there?" Marguerite Trahan, the assistant at Mercy House Orphanage stepped into the parlor, her dark gaze full of curiosity.

He tucked the letter back into his pocket and turned to the girl who had become his friend when both of them lived here as children. "Nothing of importance."

Marguerite was a sweet young woman, with the dark hair and eyes of her Cajun heritage. Even though she had spent many years on the Mississippi side of the river, her voice still held a hint of an accent. "Is that so, *cher*? Then why the long face?"

David met her stare with one of his own. The air in the parlor thickened as the silence between them lengthened.

She cleared her throat but did not drop her gaze. "You look like a man with a heavy burden."

Part of him yearned to confide in her. More than anyone else in his life, Marguerite understood what it meant to have no family. Perhaps if he talked to her, he could move past the pervading feeling of aloneness that had stalked him for the past months. Not that he felt this bad all the time. Last night's encounter with Jasmine and her sisters had brought back his feelings of inadequacy. A wall stood between him and her family, a wall that he seemed unable to scale. She tilted her head to one side, making him think of a bird. "Does this have to do with that father of yours? Did you find him?"

Her questions pierced him, bringing the grief of loss crashing down on him. He tightened his chin against the tears that threatened. If his father had taught him anything before leaving, it had been that men had to be strong. . .always. David pulled the note from his pocket once more, turning it over in his hands. "I was too late."

Children ran past the doorway, talking and laughing, their voices filling the air as they clattered outside to play in the yard.

Inside the parlor, silence dominated the room. He dragged his gaze from the door to look at Marguerite. He was surprised by the comprehension in her face.

She stepped toward him and placed a gentle hand on his arm. "I'm sorry."

David wondered why it had to be Marguerite who showed him such sympathy. Why not Jasmine? She had known about his father's death, but where was her concern over his loss? His heart twisted. Jasmine was too caught up in her plays and dramas. Playacting was her answer to all of life's questions. Would she never grow up?

"Thanks." David summoned a smile for Marguerite's sake. He wasn't supposed to hurt this badly. Not for a father who hadn't cared anything about him. "It's probably just as well. He was pretty sick when he sent this note. I doubt he would have wanted me to see him that way."

"It might have been easier for you if you could have made your peace with him."

Shamed by his roiling emotions, David wondered what he had expected from his father. He shook off Marguerite's hand and walked to the window, his gaze looking past the children outside as his mind piled up all the reasons he could never have made his peace with the man.

Pa had abandoned him and Ma years ago. Sure, he'd promised he would come back for them as soon as he made a fortune digging for gold. But like so many who had followed the lure of easy riches, he'd failed. And he had failed those who relied on him—the only people in the world who loved him. "All my Pa was ever good for was empty promises."

Marguerite sat down in a narrow chair on the far side of the room. "At least you had a father."

The wistfulness of her words was not lost on him, but David knew there were worse things than not having a father.

"If you could call him that. I had to pay off his debts once I finally tracked down the house he lived in." David heard the hatred in his own voice. It stopped him for a brief instant, but then he realized that he should hate the man. Jeremy Foster had not been a father. Or a husband, for that matter. He'd been a selfish, foolish man who knew nothing about love. "He deserved to die all alone for the pain he caused me and my mother."

Marguerite sighed. "I know he hurt you, David. But you need to forgive him."

He rounded on her then. "Forgive him? Why should I forgive him? His desertion changed my life."

"Yes." She unfolded from the chair, her movements graceful. "But if you don't forgive him, you'll never be free."

"I know that the Bible agrees with you, Marguerite. But God couldn't mean I should just forgive Pa. My mother had to—" He choked, unable to continue for a moment. "She had to make a living in Natchez Under-the-Hill. If not for the Anderson girls—for their acceptance of me—I don't know what would have happened to me." The words were bitter in his throat. Talking about his past was hard, but he wanted Marguerite to understand. He wasn't a bad person. His pa was the villain.

She smiled at him, a world of knowledge and peace in her gaze. "If you don't find a way to forgiveness, it will kill you. Your Pa is already dead. He can't feel your wrath. Who will it hurt if you forgive him?"

The heat trying to consume him ebbed a little. David yearned for the same peace she had found. Was forgiveness the only way to get it?

"I know you're a Christian, David."

"Of course I am." He had never let his parents' poor decisions get in the way of his beliefs. He knew God loved him. He knew Christ had been born a man and died on the cross to save all sinners.

"God gave so much so you and I could spend eternity with Him. He's your real father. He's the one you can turn to." She smiled at him, a radiant smile that offered promise and hope. "I'll be praying that you let Him show you the way to forgiveness."

He wanted to grasp the promise in her words. But something held him back. Some inner spirit that whispered he shouldn't have to forgive a man who had wronged him to such an extent.

"Why don't you talk to Lily and Blake?" Marguerite's voice seemed to come from far away even though he knew they were still standing in the parlor. "They've been like family to you."

David shook his head. "It's not the same. I know you understand the hope that one day you and your parents can be together again. No matter what they've done, as long as they're out there, you can't abandon them. Lily and her family are special to me, but on some level, I'll always be the discarded kid they felt sorry for. I've never been one of them."

"I think you're wrong, David. They love you. Talk to them. Tell them how you feel. Maybe they'll help you understand what I'm having a hard time communicating to you."

Understanding was not the problem. David understood that his father had been a worthless bum and that he and his mother had paid the price for the man's shiftlessness. While his father had chased the illusion of easy wealth, David had depended on the charity of others for food and shelter. "Lily and Blake took me in. I owe them a debt of gratitude I'll never be able to repay."

She frowned at him. "Then what about Jasmine?"

"What about Jasmine?"

Her laughter was musical. "Come on, David. You're not fooling me. You've always been sweet on that girl."

He lifted a shoulder. "You are a hopeless romantic. Please don't read anything into my association with Jasmine except for a childish infatuation. Jasmine had all the things I did not—wealth, security, and a family who cared for her. She cannot understand my feelings."

A noise at the door took his attention away from Marguerite. His heart climbed into his throat as he saw Jasmine standing there. What had she heard? Did she know they'd been discussing her? Had she heard his confession of infatuation? But that would be no surprise to her. Jasmine had to know how much he adored—*had* adored her. Even as he told himself that the attraction between them was a thing of the past, he knew better. He would always love her, even if she had tired of waiting for him.

"Excuse me, I was looking for Miss Deborah." Her face was frozen, not giving any inkling of her thoughts.

Marguerite stepped between him and the door. "I believe she's in the back parlor, working with some of the older girls on their needlework."

Jasmine nodded, but her gaze was still fastened on him. Were her cheeks paler than when he'd seen her last night, or was it his imagination?

David ran a finger around the collar of his shirt. Why had he given in to the temptation of confiding in someone? "I've got to go. I have business in town."

"Feel free to stop by anytime, David." Marguerite sent a knowing glance his way.

He shook his head. He was not about to confide in Jasmine Anderson. "Tell Miss Deborah I'll come back this afternoon when she's not so busy."

David jammed his bowler on his head and stalked past both women. When would he learn to keep his own counsel? A fine detective he was turning out to be, spilling his guts the first time someone was kind to him. It was a good thing Mr. Bastrup was in Chicago.

David wondered when he would ever learn the harsh lesson that he was all alone. Like always. And he always would be. Except for God, of course. He sent a rueful glance toward the sky. "But God, it sure would be nice to have someone down here to care about me."

Chapter Four

Lily accepted a cup of tea from Anna and balanced it on her knees. "I'm sorry you couldn't come last night."

"We appreciated your invitation, didn't we, Mama Champney?" Anna glanced toward Jean Luc's mother.

Dressed in unrelieved black, the widow was pale and listless. The elder Mrs. Champney's attention was not on her guests but on her lap and the lace handkerchief she was twisting into a tight spiral.

Lily's heart ached for the evidence of the other woman's grief. She would have to remember to say a special prayer for her.

"What?" Mrs. Champney looked up and glanced around the parlor as though she had no idea where she was.

"I said we appreciated the invitation to the ball at Les Fleurs."

"Yes." The older lady's wistful gaze fastened on Lily's face. "Dashiell and I used to have such nice parties."

Unshed tears made Lily clear her throat before answering. "Yes, the whole town talks about the fancy balls and masquerades you've hosted. Not to mention your famous galas on one or another of your boats."

The barest hint of a smile on Mrs. Champney's lips quivered before disappearing. "You're sweet to say so."

The conversation died again as the ladies sipped their tea. Lily glanced around the large parlor that was still swathed in black cloth to mourn Mr. Champney's death. The mirrors and pictures were hidden, as was the outside. She found herself wishing she could pull back the drapes and open the window to let in some sunlight and fresh air. She would rather have gone to walk the garden with her husband and Jean Luc than remain in this dark, stuffy room.

The door opened, and she looked up, hoping her thought had brought her husband back to the parlor. Instead she saw the familiar face of Aunt Tessie, Anna and Blake's aunt. She rose as the lady entered the room, putting down her teacup and moving across the room to offer a hug.

Aunt Tessie never seemed to age. The few wrinkles on her face had more to do with smiles than sagging skin, and her light blue eyes were as sharp as ever. The silver streaks in her hair were a bit more numerous than the last time Lily had seen Aunt Tessie, but they were still outnumbered by light brown strands. Perhaps it was her posture—so straight and tall—that gave her the appearance of a younger lady. Whatever the reason, Lily hoped she would age as gracefully as Aunt Tessie.

"You must tell me all about my great-niece and nephews." Aunt Tessie sat in a chair next to Lily and accepted a cup of tea from Anna. "I imagine Noah has grown several inches since I saw him last."

"Closer to a foot." Lily picked up her tea once more. "Magnolia is not far behind him, and even Benjamin is growing like a weed."

Anna's face lifted with her smile. "I know what you mean. Achille seems to get taller even while he's asleep."

The conversation picked up then as they compared notes and shared stories of their children's accomplishments. Even Mrs. Champney emerged from her miasma long enough to recount a story of the fine mess of fresh fish Jean Luc and his son had caught for dinner a few days earlier.

Lily countered with a story of the large turtle Noah and Magnolia had discovered in an estuary and sneaked aboard the *Water Lily* during a recent trip. Of course the reptile had gotten out of their quarters during a meal and caused enough havoc with the crew that their cook, Jensen, had suggested he could make gumbo with the turtle her children had adopted.

Jean Luc and Blake reentered the room as she was describing Jensen's relief to find that the turtle had "escaped"—with the help of her distressed children—before he had a chance to make good on his threat.

Blake leaned against the fireplace, his gaze darting between his sister and aunt as though he was considering how to broach a difficult topic. He turned down the offer of tea and cookies, patting his flat stomach with a rueful gaze that made even Mrs. Champney smile. "I am most impressed with your son's understanding of the shipping business, ma'am. You must be proud of him."

"Yes." She reached for Jean Luc, who had taken a seat next to her on the sofa, bringing his hand to her cheek. "He's the best parts of his father and has far exceeded our hopes for him."

Jean Luc shrugged, but Lily saw a gleam in his eye that might have been a tear. He brushed a hand across his face before sending a smile toward his mother.

"He and I have been discussing a joint venture that we both believe will strengthen Champney Shipping and ensure that it remains in business for years to come—but perhaps with a new name." Blake pushed away from the mantel and came to stand next to the chair Lily sat in. He put a hand on her shoulder. "A decade ago my wife had the foresight to purchase a boat and chisel out a life for herself and her family on the Mississippi."

Lily looked up at him, her heart nearly exploding with joy. "It was a joint venture."

"Exactly. Partnerships are often successful because one person's strengths can fill gaps made by the other's weaknesses." The look in his blue eyes bathed her in so much approval Lily hardly minded the way he had manipulated her.

"Blake and I have been talking about a partnership I believe would be equally beneficial for both of our families." Jean Luc sat forward, his handsome face eager. His excitement seemed to invade the dark room, holding grief at bay if only for a short time. "The United States is growing by leaps and bounds. Now that the scars of war are healing, people are anxious to make up for lost time. They're building homes and businesses in what used to be uninhabited frontier. Whole new towns are springing up, and with them comes the need for everything from nails to barber chairs."

Lily could feel her stomach turn over as she looked at her husband. Words they had spoken on the way over here flooded into her mind. But perhaps she was jumping to conclusions. She would withhold judgment until she understood exactly what the two men were proposing. "You want us to invest in Champney Shipping?"

Blake shook his head. "We thought it would be better to create a new company—one that will focus on rail transportation instead of the river."

"Rail?" Anna looked confused, her gaze seeking comfort from her husband's face.

Lily put a hand to her chest to calm the pounding of her heart. "Isn't this rather sudden?"

"How long did it take you to decide to purchase the *Hattie Belle*?" Blake's eyes danced as he reminded her of the early days when they had first discovered they each owned part of a large riverboat.

This was different! she wanted to protest, but the words stuck in her throat. She swallowed hard and considered how to answer her husband. "Not. . .long." She didn't want to make the admission, but honesty compelled her to be truthful. "But I knew—"

Jean Luc raised a hand and stopped her sputtering. "The way my father told it, you didn't even know you had a partner until after you bought him out."

"I think it's a splendid idea." Aunt Tessie joined the conversation, making Lily feel like she was the only one resisting the notion. "I've been worried about all of you for years. The river is a harsh place with so many dangers—snags, floods, and storms to name a few. Lily, you and Blake have children who rely on you to care for them. Maybe it's time for you to settle down somewhere and make a permanent home for them. I'm not talking about Les Fleurs. While I'm certain Camellia welcomes your company, you should have an estate of your own."

Lily sat back and nearly overset her teacup. Catching it with one hand, she considered what Aunt Tessie had said. The idea of selling their boat—their home—pained her. She had been raised at Les Fleurs, but she had claimed her adulthood on the riverboat. Besides that, what would her father do? She couldn't imagine him giving up his life on the river. Would she have to choose between her father and her husband?

"Why don't we all give the matter some thought?" Anna's voice was calm and matter-of-fact. She set her teacup on the tray.

Blake nodded. "You're right, Sister. I think it's an option to consider, but we don't have to decide anything today. We have enough business to keep us afloat for some time. In fact, we'll be leaving for New Orleans by the end of the week."

The conversation around her grew more general, but Lily's mind was focused on the idea of buying or building a home. She had no idea where she would even want to live if they sold the *Water Lily*. Natchez might be a place Camellia loved, but for Lily it had been a relief to leave the self-important planters behind. New Orleans? While there was much to commend that city, she didn't relish the idea. Blake's father had settled near Cape Girardeau, Missouri, but Blake had never been interested in living there.

The sound of Anna clapping her hands drew Lily back to the conversation. "You should go with my brother and Lily."

Aunt Tessie's gaze bumped into her own. Lily scrambled for a proper response. She thought they had been talking about the upcoming trip south, hadn't they? "Have you ever been to New Orleans?"

"No." Aunt Tessie lifted her shoulders in a shrug. "I've always wanted to travel, but I never have found the time."

"Do you have room to take on a passenger?" Jean Luc asked.

Lily thought it was a great idea. "Of course we have room for such a pleasant companion, don't we, Blake."

"I don't know." Aunt Tessie glanced toward her niece. "Anna probably needs me to stay here and help with the baby."

"Don't be silly." Anna looked at her husband for confirmation before continuing. "Mama Champney, Jean Luc, and I can handle matters here. You go have a wonderful time."

"We'd love for you to come with us." Blake winked at his aunt. "But don't be surprised if you find yourself washing dishes or setting tables."

"Ignore your nephew." Lily's glare should have burned him to a crisp. She didn't want his aunt to get the wrong idea. "We'd love to have you with us. I won't let him put you to work."

"I wouldn't mind that a bit." Aunt Tessie's eyes were bright with excitement. "I might even get to spend some extra time with my great-nephews and great-niece."

Lily need not have worried that Aunt Tessie would misunderstand her nephew's teasing words. She could feel her irritation draining away.

Jean Luc stood and brushed a hand across his wife's shoulder. "It's settled then. As long as you'll be okay, Aunt Tessie will go with Blake and Lily at the end of the week." He shot a speaking glance toward Blake. "You and I can get together again once you return."

As she and Blake gathered their things and took their leave of the Champneys, Lily couldn't stop her mind from considering once more the idea of giving up life on the river. Could she do it? Should she? What would she really be giving up? While she enjoyed the challenges of life on the river, did she owe it to her children to give them a more normal childhood? The questions swirled inside her mind like an eddying current on the river.

She knew she'd have to spend some time talking to God about what to do. He had led her this far. He would certainly be there to guide her in the future.

❧

"I'm worried about your future, Jasmine." Lily watched as her youngest sister picked up a doll she used to play with—one of Magnolia's favorites now—and placed it on a shelf.

The children were playing outside under Camellia's watchful eye, except for Benjamin, who was napping nearby while Lily and Jasmine straightened the nursery.

"By the time I was your age—"

"I know. You were already a successful businesswoman with a boat and crew to manage." Jasmine picked up the toy soldiers that belonged to Noah. "And Camellia was choosing amongst her numerous suitors for the best possible match."

Silence filled the spacious room as Lily considered what to say next. She didn't know how to talk to Jasmine anymore. A part of her longed for bygone days when her sister was a happy-go-lucky girl with a penchant for adventure. "What do you want from me?"

"I want to go to Chicago, or New York, or even San Francisco—anywhere that I can act on a real stage in front of a real audience." A wistful sigh and downcast eyes accompanied Jasmine's answer.

Lily had thought it difficult when Camellia wanted to attend a finishing school in New Orleans during the thorny days preceding the war. That was nothing compared to the idea of sending Jasmine to some far-off city. Nightmare scenarios filled her imagination. "I thought you were happy with the Shakespearean play you and the other young people are putting on for the community. It was your idea. And I am so proud of you for wanting to help the orphanage by donating the proceeds to them. Miss Deborah told me she hopes to purchase a new stove and pay for several other repairs."

Jasmine meandered to the window. "It's fine, but I want to be as famous as 'The Divine Sarah.' And that's not likely to happen here in Natchez, performing in a homemade production to benefit the orphanage."

"I'd say she is more infamous than famous." Lily walked up behind her sister and looked out over the plantation grounds. "What would Aunt Dahlia have to say about a niece who performs on the stage and has the reputation of a Sarah Bernhardt? The poor thing is liable to have a fit of apoplexy."

A choked giggle from Jasmine brought her some hope. If she could get her sister laughing, maybe they could work together to find a compromise to satisfy Jasmine's need for recognition while keeping her safe from harm.

Lily snapped her fingers as a new idea occurred to her. "What if we plan a trip to Chicago this winter?"

"Do you mean it?" Jasmine swung around, her violet eyes practically glowing with excitement.

"Yes." Lily's excitement built as her vague idea began to take form. "We could ask Camellia and Tamar to go with us, too. We could spend at least a week, maybe even two there."

The excitement disappeared from Jasmine's expressive eyes. "Unless you plan on leaving me behind, that wouldn't be enough time to accomplish anything."

"I'm afraid anything longer is out of the question." Lily frowned at the windowpane. "Maybe we could have David escort us. He would be the perfect one to make sure you were safe if we did have to leave."

"Don't be silly. David Foster doesn't want to be saddled with someone like me."

Lily was surprised at the venom in Jasmine's voice. "What do you mean? That boy has worshipped the ground you walk on since both of you were children. He's pulled you out of more scrapes than I can count."

"Maybe so." Jasmine pulled at the material of her cuff. "But I have it on the best authority that he has no interest in me anymore."

"Who told you that? Some jealous debutante? You should know better than to listen to gossip."

A deep sadness came over Jasmine, and she sighed. "I wasn't listening to gossip, Sissy. He said it himself."

It had been a decade since Jasmine used her pet name for Lily. Aunt Dahlia had forbidden it in public, and Lily thought her sister had outgrown it. Protectiveness was her first response, followed swiftly by betrayal and anger. "I can hardly believe his ingratitude. David has always been welcome in this house and in our lives. For him to say such a mean thing to you is inexcusable. The next time I see him, I'm going to give him a piece of my mind."

Jasmine's eyes widened. "Please don't."

"He deserves much worse. Wait until Blake hears about this."

"You can't say anything to David. He didn't mean to hurt my feelings. He didn't know I was in the room when he said it." Jasmine's chin quivered. "Besides all that, he has a right to his opinion. Everyone has that right. If he has outgrown his feelings for me, I'd rather know it."

Lily pulled her sister into a hug. Jasmine's arms went around her, and the poor thing began crying like her heart was breaking. She rubbed her sister's back in a comforting motion while she wondered how she could have been so wrong.

It had to be a misunderstanding. She had watched David grow up. That man loved Jasmine more than he loved his own life. Sure he'd been away from Natchez for a time, but no one changed that much. And at the ball the other night, he had made a beeline for Jasmine. "Don't worry, sweetheart."

The tears ceased a little later. Jasmine pulled away, sniffed, and began fishing for something.

"What's the matter?"

Jasmine shook her head. "I need a handkerchief."

"Here, use mine." Lily pulled a rumpled square of cloth from her skirt pocket and watched as Jasmine mopped her face with it.

"Thanks." Jasmine tucked the handkerchief into her sleeve. "I'm sorry I fell apart. It was just a shock to hear David describe me as nothing more than a childish infatuation. He said it with such contempt. Like he wished he'd never met me."

Lily brushed a strand of hair back from Jasmine's temple. "The more you tell me, the more I'm inclined to believe something else is going on here. David may be going through something we know nothing about."

"I'll bet Marguerite Trahan knows about it, whatever it is. That's who he was confiding in."

Patting her sister on the shoulder, Lily shook her head. "If you don't want me to talk to him about what he said, I hope you will. He probably has a reasonable explanation. Maybe he's trying to make you jealous. You were a bit cool to him the other night during the ball." The more she thought about it, the more convinced Lily became that David was either put out by Jasmine's refusal to dance or trying to draw her attention.

"I don't think I can."

Lily raised an eyebrow. "If you don't, I will."

That brought Jasmine's chin up. Good. She hoped her sister would confront David. And Lily would be there to comfort her if David really was falling in love with someone else.

As she moved to go outside and collect her other two children so she could get them ready for lunch, Lily wondered why life had to be so complicated. Why couldn't things run as smoothly as they did when the family was on the river? Their biggest problems then were a cranky boiler or passenger. No prickly questions of love or heartbreak.

She could hardly wait to get to New Orleans. Maybe her friends in that city could offer sage advice or some way to redirect Jasmine's energy. She didn't want her sister to continue pining about, dreaming of a future that would only lead to heartbreak and disappointment.

Chapter Five

Jasmine peeked out at the audience. Miss Deborah, the lady who had run Mercy House since before Jasmine was born, sat on the front row. Her hair was pulled back in a tight bun, and her kindly face wore a wide smile.

Jasmine didn't even mind seeing Miss Deborah's assistant, Marguerite, occupying the seat next to her. Beyond her were Jean Luc Champney with his wife and mother. David's blond hair was visible on the second row. He sat with Papa, Lily, Camellia, and the rest of her family. Beyond them she could hear the rustle of the audience, but she couldn't make out the faces.

"Are you ready, Cordelia?"

Recognizing her character's name, Jasmine swung around and curtsied to Cedrick Wilson, who was playing King Lear, the title character in Shakespeare's play. A flowing white beard had been glued to his face and obscured everything below his brown eyes. He tugged on the beard with one hand as he waited for her response.

Jasmine glanced down at her own outfit and some of her pre-performance excitement ebbed. Miss Deborah and Tamar had done an excellent job sewing the various costumes for their project. Camellia had not liked the idea of using material taken from the rag bins at Les Fleurs, and Jasmine had wanted to agree with her. She would have loved a fancy costume, complete with flowing robes and a conical hat. But then ever-practical Lily had suggested that the money they would spend on new cloth would do much better going to replace the orphanage roof.

"Buck up, Jasmine." Cedrick's voice teased her. "You don't die until the end of the play."

She raised an eyebrow at him. "I have a lot on my mind."

Cedrick was the handsome younger son of one of the wealthiest plantation owners in Natchez. Jasmine had been flattered when he set aside his philandering tendencies to spend time helping with their production. For a while her family had thought he might be trying to fix his interest with her, but Cedrick had never been anything but a friend. She valued his friendship but knew, as he apparently did, that they had no warmer feelings toward each other.

"I think the whole town is out there." He inclined his head toward the audience.

Jasmine followed his gaze. "What else is there to do in Natchez?"

He raised an eyebrow but didn't answer. He didn't have to. She had spent enough time at the docks to hear about the "entertainments" available at the various inns and gambling saloons.

The voice of the stage manager interrupted their whispered conversation. "Take your places everyone."

As the play began, Cedrick took her hand and squeezed it. Jasmine mouthed the opening words along with the actors playing the parts of the dukes of Kent and Gloucester, George Reed and Tom Hayes. "I've never seen anyone more focused than you, Jasmine. I—"

Other actors joined them, including Ellen Tate and Wendy Jeffers, who were playing King Lear's older daughters, Goneril and Regan.

"Is it time for our entrance?" Ellen asked.

Cedrick nodded and dropped Jasmine's hand. As she followed him and the others onto the stage, Jasmine wished for a moment that he were interested in her. At least Cedrick understood what made her heart pound with anticipation. He didn't try to convince her to let go of her dreams. He would probably even support her desire to leave Natchez. But she didn't have time for romance. She had a career to pursue.

"Love, and be silent." Jasmine's first words were a bit shaky. She needed to forget everything else. She could not fail now, or Lily would never take her seriously. When it came time to speak again, she put everything into the words. They soared over the audience, bringing the reaction she had hoped for and setting up the Bard's tragedy.

The curtain rose and fell, each scene tightening the knot until none of the characters could succeed. From her place off-stage in "prison," Jasmine realized her eyes had adjusted to the dim light in the audience. She could see a few of the women dabbing at their eyes with handkerchiefs, and her heart lifted. This might be a ragtag group of actors and their stage might be nothing more than a raised dais with homemade curtains, but still they were managing to elicit emotion from the audience.

By the time the curtain fell for the final time, Jasmine knew they were a success. Cedrick winked as he took her hand and led her to the center of the stage. They waited as the other actors crowded around them—from the smallest of the children who'd spoken no lines to those who had memorized dozens of speeches over the past weeks—all proud of the work they had done to ensure the orphanage would continue operating.

The curtain rose, and applause began in earnest. Cedrick pulled her with him as he stepped forward. She curtsied while he bowed, wishing he would not be so attentive now. Everyone would think they had an understanding.

Jasmine forced her mouth into a wide smile and concentrated on the future. One day she would perform in front of a real audience. She would stand in front of a heavy curtain made of rich crimson velvet and bow to a full theater of well-educated patrons who had paid hefty prices for the chance to watch her perform.

Instead of enjoying this moment, Jasmine found herself wondering if Lily would ever allow her to follow her own dreams. She wanted more, much more, than what Natchez had to offer. She wanted fame. She wanted to see her name on a theater marquis, to be feted and adored by people from all over America. From all over the world, actually.

Aunt Dahlia might not approve, but that wouldn't stop Jasmine. She would not be ashamed of her own dreams even if her family didn't support them. Providing entertainment to others was a time-honored tradition. It gave people chances to forget for a while their boring, humdrum lives.

Since she'd been a youngster, Jasmine had found satisfaction in performing for others. Family and friends all told her she was talented. If only Lily would let her go to Chicago or New York—anywhere that would give her a chance to see her dreams come true. Why couldn't anyone else understand that? Was she always to be alone?

❧

David stood back a little as Jasmine's family congratulated her. He wished he understood why she had such a strong hold on his heart in spite of everything. She was beautiful, of course. But he had met beautiful women in both California and Illinois. No one intrigued him like the dark-haired minx who was accepting the compliments of her family with an attitude adopted from British royalty.

Jasmine Anderson was far from perfect. She was headstrong. A grin formed on his lips. He couldn't really blame her for that. None of the Anderson sisters could be described as wallflowers, despite their floral names. Lily was a riverboat owner. Camellia had spent part of the War Between the States nursing soldiers on a riverboat and had been at Vicksburg while it was under siege. He supposed Jasmine was simply following in her older sisters' footsteps.

But did she have to trample on his heart at the same time?

"What did you think of the performance?" Marguerite's voice startled him.

"Impressive." He bowed to her. "Did the orphanage benefit?"

"Oh, yes." Her dark gaze turned toward Jasmine. "Your Jasmine is quite the center of attention this evening."

He could feel heat rising to his face. "I thought I told you there's nothing between us. She's not my Jasmine. . .apparently she never has been."

Marguerite tilted her head. "I know what you said, but I can read the signs for myself. If you're not careful, that girl will tear out your heart and leave you a bitter man."

"I don't think that's any of your concern." He regretted the cold words as soon as they left his mouth.

Marguerite's eyes widened. Then she nodded. "I'm sorry if I overstepped the boundaries of our friendship."

He put out a hand to stop her, but it was too late. Marguerite moved toward Miss Deborah and began gathering the children. He ought to catch up to her. Apologize. But he couldn't bring himself to do it. Marguerite was getting too close to the truth for his comfort.

It was time for him to leave Natchez anyway. He should have headed to New Orleans a day or two ago, but he'd wanted to see the play.

With a disgusted shake of his head, David moved away from the crowd surrounding Jasmine. She would never miss his presence. She had more attention than any of the rest of the cast. Even "King Lear" had not received so many compliments.

Blake Matthews broke free of the crowd and moved toward David. "Lily sent me to invite you to dinner with us at the Bluff."

"Thanks, but I don't—"

"You really expect me to tell Lily you won't come?" Blake put an arm around his shoulder. "Do you know how much discord your refusal will cause?"

David chuckled. "We can't have that." He would rather have returned to his room to brood over his wayward heart, but he didn't want to upset Lily. She'd been so good to him over the years. "I'll get my horse and meet you there."

"Excellent." Blake pulled his arm away and pointed at David. "If you don't show up, I will have to come looking for you."

Both men laughed. David's spirit lifted a bit. If he could keep his distance from the star of the evening, it might be good for him to get out.

He retrieved his rented horse from a nearby stable and rode down Washington Street past stately homes. A dog raced along the length of one iron fence, barking until David and his horse passed the border of the home's lot.

He arrived at the Bluff, a two-story building hunched on the edge of the bluff it was named for, overlooking the rushing waters of the Mississippi. Tethering his horse, he tugged on his neckcloth. Why had he agreed to come? He might have defected if not for the arrival of his hosts.

The restaurant looked as though it was being besieged, as at least a dozen people descended on it from the three carriages. Mrs. Champney was followed by her son, Jean Luc, and her daughter-in-law, Anna. Anna's aunt alit and stood looking up at her escort, Jasmine's father Henrick Anderson. Jasmine's aunt Dahlia and uncle Phillip were the first to disembark from the next carriage, followed by Camellia and her husband, Jonah. The final carriage contained Lily and Blake and Jasmine, who seemed to be still riding high on her success.

David stepped forward to offer her his arm, but she swept past him, her little nose in the air.

Camellia rescued him from embarrassment when she put her hand on his arm. "We can always count on you to be the gentleman, David. I have missed you since you left us for California and Illinois."

Recovering his wits, David smiled and answered the questions she peppered him with. By the time they were all seated, he found himself on Camellia's left hand. Aunt Dahlia sat on his left. He could see Jasmine's dark hair some distance away and drew a breath of relief. At least he would not have to worry about being snubbed again.

"Lily says you are a policeman." Dahlia claimed his attention with her statement.

David shook his head. "I'm more of a detective."

"What's the difference?"

"Policemen are paid by the city. My employer is paid by the people who need his help."

Her husband, Phillip, leaned forward. "So you are a mercenary?"

David supposed it was a fair question. Picking up his fork and spearing an olive, he considered how to answer the man. "Except that I am not a soldier, sir, I guess you can say that is a proper title for what we do."

"David's organization is quite famous." Camellia joined the conversation. "He's a Pinkerton."

Both Dahlia and Phillip frowned at him as though they'd never heard of the agency at all. Camellia patted his hand. "I do miss you, though. No one can keep Jasmine in check like you can."

"I don't know about that. Jasmine is high-spirited, but she's always known how to get what she wants." David glanced toward the girl in question.

She threw back her head and laughed at that moment, showing the full length of her white neck.

The waiter standing nearby couldn't take his eyes off her. David wanted to take the fellow out back and explain basic manners. A pain in his hand made him look down. His fork was no longer as straight as it had been.

He looked up and caught Camellia's understanding gaze. "Your sentiments are nothing to be ashamed of, David. Jasmine is too naive to realize her effect on those around her. I'm afraid she is headed for trouble, but she will not listen to us. Perhaps you might have better luck."

Wondering what he could say to Jasmine that might make a difference, David concentrated on the food on his plate. She would never listen to him, and he wasn't sure he wanted to put himself in the position of being ignored or worse. "I'm leaving for New Orleans in the next day or two. I doubt there will be time for me to do much."

Lily, sitting on the opposite side of the table, looked up. "You're going to New Orleans? Then you must go with us. It will be like old times. We'll have such fun reminiscing."

"I thought you were going to Memphis."

Lily shook her head.

Feeling like a butterfly caught in a windstorm, David shrugged. "How can I say no?"

He looked toward the far end of the table once more, and his gaze clashed with Jasmine's. In them he read a challenge. A challenge he was loath to accept.

Chapter Six

"At least we're not carrying many passengers this trip." Jasmine smiled at her nephew Noah. "You won't have as many chores as we used to have when your mama and papa had their first boat."

"Papa says that's bad news." Noah's bright blue gaze, so much like his father's, watched her scrub a greasy spot from one of the dining tables.

"Your papa and your grandpapa are in agreement on that."

The boy frowned. "Do they know about the chores?"

Jasmine laughed. She could understand why her sisters enjoyed having their children around them. "Maybe not."

She moved to another table and bent over it, scrubbing with a strong arm. The smells from the galley made her mouth water. Picking up a fresh tablecloth from the stack she and Noah had brought into the dining room, Jasmine shook it out and spread it over the table with a deft move that came from years of practice.

"Why do you wipe the table if you're going to put a cloth on it, too?" Noah pushed one of the chairs toward the table.

"So everything will be clean."

He frowned as though trying to grasp the concept of cleaning what would not be seen. Jasmine laughed and ruffled his dark hair with her fingers. "You'll understand when you're older."

The familiar words brought a frown to her face. It was exactly what Lily used to say all the time when she was younger. When had she become the responsible one? The grown-up?

"There you are!" Aunt Tessie breezed into the room and pointed at Noah. "I've been looking all over for you, young man. It's time for your mathematics lesson."

Noah cast a desperate look at Jasmine.

In spite of the empathy she felt, all Jasmine could do was shrug. "It won't be so bad."

Noah's shoulders fell. He looked so pitiful.

Aunt Tessie put a hand on his shoulder and smiled at him. "Come along."

Jasmine watched them leave before returning to her work. Noah was growing up so fast. Funny how childhood seemed so endless to the child and so quick to adults.

"This doesn't look like the right activity for a famous actress."

The deep voice sent gooseflesh running up her arms. Jasmine took a deep breath before turning to face David Foster. "You're quite the comedian."

The look on his face made her regret her waspish tone of voice.

"I'm sorry, David. I didn't mean that the way it came out."

A strained smile appeared on his face. "I'm not sure why you're so angry with me."

What could she answer? The truth was too painful. She had missed him much more than he had missed her. "Who said I was angry?"

His gaze challenged her words.

Jasmine lifted her chin, dredging up a measure of self-preservation. She would not be manipulated.

"Your sisters are worried about you."

He only thought she'd been angry with him before. His meddling words made her blood boil. She could feel the fire in her eyes. How dare

David presume to speak to her as though they were still as close as they'd been growing up? "What my sisters may or may not think isn't any of your business."

"You're right, of course." He sounded resigned. As though he knew he was in the wrong. The stubborn thrust of his jaw, however, told her how determined he was to continue meddling. "I care about you, Jasmine. I don't want to see you hurt."

She knew she should calm herself, but concentrating on what was wrong between them gave her the excuse to maintain a certain distance from him. It protected her heart. "You don't have to worry about me. I know exactly what I want and how to get it."

David picked up a stack of dinner plates and distributed them on the tables like a dealer would a deck of cards.

So he was not going to say anything? Fine. Two could play at that game. She picked up the salad and dinner forks, placing them to the left of the plates he distributed. As they worked, her ire faded, replaced by their comfortable rhythm. It seemed so natural, so normal. He put one knife and two spoons to the right of each place setting while she folded the linen napkins into neat triangles and set them in the center of each plate.

As Jasmine gathered the leftover implements, David moved to stand near her. "When we were young, I thought you were the most beautiful, most intelligent, most loving person in the world."

"Yes, I heard you telling Marguerite that you've outgrown your childish infatuation." She tried to keep the hurt from her voice.

He put a finger under her chin and lifted her face so that their gazes met. His eyes had not changed. They were as green as a pine thicket. They promised peace and rest and happiness.

Jasmine thought she might melt into a puddle at his feet. She even imagined for a brief instant what it would feel like for their lips to meet. Her eyelids grew heavy. She wanted to lean into him, draw on his strength.

In that instant something changed between them. David was no longer the safe and predictable childhood friend that she loved. He was. . .something much more dangerous.

Her heart galloped like a runaway horse. The feeling was heady, exciting, almost the same feeling she got right before a performance. She could feel herself weakening. . .leaning toward him.

When David stepped back, her heart stopped its furious pace. It seemed to stop beating at all. Jasmine felt it stand still, crack, and shatter into a million pieces, taking with it dreams she'd never before recognized.

"Jasmine, I. . ."

She turned away from him. No matter what his words, she didn't want to hear them. She had to defend herself. "Don't worry, David. You don't have to apologize. It's not as though we're romantically involved. How could we be? You're the brother my sisters and I always wanted, so I suppose I shouldn't be surprised they wanted you to talk to me."

His mouth tightened, and the same eyes that had been so tender a few seconds before spat green sparks toward her. "How can you be so flippant? Do I matter so little to you? Does anything matter to you at all?"

The words nicked her, but Jasmine raised her chin. Let him think what he wanted. Why should she care? When she was famous and had dozens of men begging for her attention, David Foster would see who was right. Then he would be sorry for treating her like a wayward child. She marched out of the dining room without a backward glance, self-righteousness helping her to keep her head high.

❧

"Trust God to straighten out your path." Tamar snapped a handful of beans and dropped the pieces into the large pan on her lap. "If you look to Him for guidance, He'll help you succeed."

Jasmine knew the words were true. And they sounded like excellent advice. . .for someone who wanted a conventional life. "You sound like Papa and Lily. But what if God listens to them instead of me? I know they don't want me to be an actress."

Tamar's dark face was dear to her. She had been more a mother than a servant to her and her two sisters. When Lily had secured Tamar's freedom almost a dozen years earlier, it had been a moment of celebration for all of them. Her marriage to Jensen, a close friend of Blake's, had been as sweet as caramel icing. Now she and Jensen made their home with Lily and Blake on the river, their happiness apparent in their actions and words. "Where did you ever get the idea that God shows favor to one of his children over the other?"

Jasmine shrugged. "Isn't it obvious? Some people are rich. Others have nothing. He shows favor to them, doesn't He? And I know both Papa and Lily are better Christians than I am. So it makes sense that He would listen to—"

Tamar's laugh interrupted her words. "Child, child. You do have the oddest way of looking at life. People are not more or less Christian. We either accept Jesus and His free gift or we do not." She put her pan on the table and reached for Jasmine's hands. "Do you have Jesus in your heart?"

Jasmine remembered the day Papa had led her to Christ. She remembered the incredible lightness she'd experienced when she turned her life over to Him. But since then He'd become less and less a part of her daily routine. "Of course I do." She silenced her conscience with an effort and met Tamar's gaze.

"Then you should know that He places as much importance on your hopes and dreams as He does on those of your sister or your father."

She wanted to believe what Tamar said. But it made no sense. Everyone had a favorite. Camellia was Aunt Dahlia's favorite niece. Grandfather, a man who had spent little time with her, had lavished Lily with his love and attention. Jasmine knew she had been Grandmother's favorite. Grandmother always said she was most like their mother, Rose, even though the portrait of her in the upper hallway at Les Fleurs showed more resemblance to Camellia. Mama's hair had been blond, not dark like Jasmine's. Nor were her eyes as dark. Grandmother had obviously been mistaken in her assessment.

It was time to turn the conversation in a different direction. "Do you think I'm a good actress?"

Tamar sat back and released Jasmine's hands. "God's given you many gifts, like He does all of His children. He'll show you how to use them. . .if you'll let Him." She picked up her pan and began snapping beans once more. "Lily told me you want to go to Chicago."

Irritation blew through Jasmine like a hot wind. Was there no one Lily had not discussed her with? First David and now Tamar. Was she to expect a homily from Blake next? "So the two of you talked about what should be done with me?"

"Your sister wants the best for you."

Click, click, splatter. More beans joined the growing pile in the pan.

Jasmine felt hemmed in on all sides. "Is it so wrong to want to use my God-given talents?"

"Of course not." *Click, click, splatter.* "But maybe you should try to find a way that will ease Lily's worries. She only wants what's best for you."

Frustration pushed Jasmine out of the chair. She walked to the doorway and looked out at the river sliding past them. She wished she could float away on that current, escape her overprotective family. If only they would let her go.

"Could you try for a job in New Orleans?"

The thought had occurred to Jasmine from time to time. New Orleans was a cosmopolitan city with many opportunities. But if she did start to gain notoriety, Lily would drag her back to Natchez, certain some nonexistent disaster was about to befall her. "I don't think that will work."

"I'll pray about it." Tamar sent her a sympathetic smile. "God is certain to see a way that we haven't considered."

Escaping from the galley, Jasmine wondered how Lily had managed to get most everyone on this boat to tell her the same thing. Was it some ploy to convince her to give up her dreams? She glanced up at the sky. Clouds obscured the sun, but its heat made the air sticky and warm, like a damp sponge surrounded her. Wishing for a fan, Jasmine considered going to her room, but the effort seemed too great. She'd have to return there soon enough to change for dinner.

Would God really listen to her? Over the years she'd come to see Him as a white-bearded king sitting on His throne in heaven—kindly but distant. Wouldn't He be busy with others? People with more pressing needs than hers?

When she had first become a Christian, she'd talked to Him on a daily basis, asking Him to watch over her loved ones and petitioning Him for her heart's desires. But somewhere along the way she had fallen out of the habit of praying every day. And little by little God and Christ and the Bible had become less important to her.

Closing her eyes, Jasmine leaned against the rail. She felt a little silly praying out here in the open. Maybe she should go to her room. Besides, God would probably laugh at her anyway. What could she promise Him in exchange for making her dreams come true?

Her eyes popped open of their own accord, and she took a step back, wiping her hands on her skirt. She would pray this evening, when the time was right.

Chapter Seven

David washed his face and stared into the mirror hanging on the wall. He was so foolish. No amount of water would wash away the words he'd flung at Jasmine earlier. Why had he even thought he could talk to her? Why hadn't he kept his mouth shut? He had enough to worry about with his assignment. He needed to focus on that instead of Jasmine.

For a moment he'd dared dream they might have a future together. That she might return his feelings after all. But she would never see him as anything but the homeless kid she'd rescued. A companion maybe. A brother certainly. But not a man she could love. No matter what he did, no matter what he accomplished, he would never be someone she adored.

When he saw her at dinner, he would be polite. Distant. He wouldn't give her the chance to wound him again.

He picked up a white towel and turned it over in his hands, his gaze tracing the blue curlicues that spelled out *Water Lily*. The towels were finer than what Lily and Blake had supplied back when he traveled with them.

Who had done the handwork? Lily was too busy with running the boat and raising her children, and Camellia never could sew an even line. Had Jasmine's fingers been the ones to stitch the letters into the linen? He could almost see her seated in a rocker next to the fireplace, her midnight-dark hair held back loosely with a ribbon as she leaned over an embroidery hoop.

A smile slipped into place as the scene became more detailed in his imagination. He would be reading a book on the far side of the fireplace. Maybe they would have a child playing on a knotted rug between them—

No! He had to stop this foolishness. Jasmine was following her own path, and it was not one he wished to tread with her. He would purge her from his mind and heart.

With careful movements, he folded the linen cloth and put it next to his washbasin before moving to his bed and reaching for his valise. Digging past his nightclothes and stockings, he felt for the hard edge of his Bible. He sat on the edge of his bed, his fingers finding the ribbon bookmark as he closed his eyes. "Lord, please give me peace about her. Help me follow You wherever You lead." He sat still in the room and let his mind relax as he thought about God. The sounds of the boat and the river faded away as peace filled him. After a period of time, he opened his eyes and began to read.

One verse leaped up at him. *"For I know the thoughts that I think toward you, saith the Lord, thoughts of peace, and not of evil, to give you an expected end."* The ache in his heart faded further. God knew what he needed and would provide it. "Thank You, Lord."

He closed the Bible and left it sitting on the bed as he continued dressing. No matter what happened, he could face life with calm certainty. God had spoken through His Word, a promise that David knew he could claim.

Shrugging into his coat, David checked his appearance one last time, winking at the reflection in the mirror. God had brought him this far. All he had to do now was forego trying to win Jasmine's affections. Like Jehoshaphat had done when the Edomites, the Ammonites, and the Moabites gathered against him, he would allow God to fight his battles for him. This ensured ultimate victory.

The sound of the dinner bell made his stomach rumble. David left his room and strode down the narrow passageway.

Jensen's scarred face was the first one he saw as he entered the dining room. "I wasn't sure you would still be cooking for Lily and Blake."

"Look at you all gone and grown up." The older man might give the appearance of a pirate to a stranger, but David knew his true nature. David held out his right hand, but Jensen ignored the gesture, pulling him into a bear hug instead. "Tell me what you've been doing with yourself."

Feeling like he'd not matured a day as he emerged from the older man's grasp, David shrugged. The boat shifted under his feet, and he automatically adjusted his stance to compensate. "I've been up in Chicago."

Jensen's bushy eyebrows lowered, emphasizing the scar over his left eye. In past years David would have been intimidated by the look indicating skepticism. "Come to the galley when you finish your dinner. I want to hear what's been keeping you so far from the people who care about you."

Not sure if he would have time since he calculated that the *Water Lily* would reach port in a couple of hours, David replied, "I'll do my best." He took a seat at one of the tables as the other diners began to file in.

A bald man with a wide mustache sat to his right, while a younger fellow dressed in the sober suit of a professional businessman sat on his left. The other two chairs at the table were taken by two redheaded females who appeared to be mother and daughter.

The bald man nodded to them and introduced himself as Albert Culbertson. Weldon Brown was the name of the younger man. He also told them he was a photographer and offered his services to them at a reduced rate.

The ladies were Mrs. Bertha Dickinson and her daughter, Adina. As he introduced himself, David noticed that Adina seemed quite taken by the dapper photographer. Her mother also noticed and immediately engaged Mr. Brown in a rigorous interrogation as to his pedigree and prospects.

All conversations stopped when Jasmine and her family arrived. Blake welcomed the guests and asked everyone to bow their heads for the blessing.

He had barely uttered, "Amen," before Mr. Culbertson picked up his napkin and tucked it into his shirt collar. "I hope you ladies have a male relative meeting you at the docks."

Mrs. Dickinson shook her head. "My husband would have come with us, but an unexpected matter detained him. He'll be joining us in a few days, however."

Mr. Culbertson looked grave at this news. "You know how dangerous it is to be unescorted, don't you? Even before the war, women had to be suspicious of strangers, but now that we've been overrun by carpetbaggers and scalawags, it's much worse."

Mr. Brown cleared his throat. "You shouldn't frighten the ladies. I'm certain they'll be safe enough in a New Orleans hotel."

"Which shows how little you know. I've been traveling these waters for years now, and I can tell you this part of the country is a nest for the worst thieves in the country."

Even though the older lady looked frightened, Adina seemed nothing more than curious. "What do you mean?" she asked.

"A long curve just south of Natchez has long been known as Dead Man's Curve because of all the unwary travelers whose bodies have been found there." Enjoying the attention, Mr. Culbertson smoothed his mustache with two fingers. "The innkeepers at Natchez Under-the-Hill offer cheap rates and then murder their guests, tossing them into the river from trapdoors."

The daughter turned to her mother. "I told you we should have stayed at home until Papa could come. No amount of European imports are worth dying over."

"All of that is ancient history." David would rather have kept silent, but he could not bear to see both females so concerned for their safety. "Most towns have cleaned out the criminal element. You'll be as safe in those places as in your home."

"I don't know where you get your opinion, sir." The mustached storyteller tossed him a disdainful glance. "While those inns may not be murdering helpless souls, bank robbers—probably Confederate deserters for the most part—are very active now. I heard of a robbery across the river from Natchez in Vidalia just a few weeks ago."

David had visited the bank in question as Mr. Bastrup had suggested, so he probably knew more about the robbery than the man beside him. But that didn't mean he could erase the fear in the ladies' faces. Or could he?

"That was far from here. And I've met the sheriff there. He'll probably make an arrest before long."

Mr. Culbertson snickered. "He's more likely to be in league with them. Why else would a gang of robbers be able to get away so easily?"

"Nevertheless, they will be caught." David found the man's foot with his own and stepped on it with some force. "I'm certain these ladies will rest more easily knowing that."

After a grunt and an angry glance that David met with a warning stare, the man took a deep breath and nodded his agreement. "Of course you're right. I apologize. I didn't mean to frighten you."

The ladies exchanged a worried glance. The mother put her fork down on the table and pushed her chair back. "I am feeling a bit out of sorts, Adina. I believe we should retire to our stateroom and rest."

Adina cast a sorrowful glance toward the photographer before nodding her agreement.

David was the first one to stand and bow to them, regret filling his heart because he'd been unable to reassure the ladies. As he watched them make their way around the other tables, his gaze clashed with Jasmine's. He shrugged his shoulders at her frown. Was she so eager to condemn him when she knew nothing about what had just happened?

Before hopelessness could overtake him once more, David took a steadying breath. Hadn't he promised God a little while earlier that he would wait on Him? What had happened to his resolve? He smiled at Jasmine. Let her think what she wanted, he wouldn't let her boorish behavior upset him.

❧

Walking out onto the deck, David leaned against the rail. A leafy curtain of tall trees gave the illusion that the *Water Lily* traveled through an uninhabited wilderness while showy white magnolia blooms filled the air with their sweet fragrance. During the months he'd spent in Chicago, David had forgotten how green and beautiful the landscape was along the river.

He didn't realize he wasn't alone until a hand clapped him on the shoulder. He turned and looked into Blake's bright blue eyes.

"You look more relaxed than at the restaurant the other night."

"Can you blame me? You didn't have to sit next to Jasmine's aunt Dahlia." David grinned to soften his words.

"I'm sure she had plenty of gossip to share since you haven't seen her for a while." Blake whistled. "It's a wonder your ears still work."

"I know." David pulled on one of his lobes and made a face. "It was touch and go for a while."

"The rest of the family sends their thanks for the pleasant meal." Blake's laughter blended with his.

A splash close to the boat made them look at the muddy brown surface of the river. A ring of concentric circles showed where a fish had broken the surface in its quest for a meal.

As silence enveloped them, Marguerite's advice returned to David. Should he talk to Blake about his feelings? The idea yanked the smile from his lips. What could he say? That he didn't feel like a part of the family? That he'd been naive enough to hope his irresponsible parents might one day get back together and welcome him into a loving home? The very idea of being so candid made his skin crawl.

"Are you doing okay?" Blake's question was hesitant, as though he too wrestled with uncomfortable emotions. "I hated to hear about your father. I know how much you hoped to see him once more."

"I'm fine. It's not like Pa and I were close."

Another silence developed, broken by Blake's sigh a few moments later. "Have I ever told you about my own father?"

David shook his head. Even though he'd spent so much time around Blake and the others aboard the *Water Lily*, he'd always thought they led wonderful, nearly perfect lives.

"We were estranged for years. I thought he was wrong in the way he raised me, and I ran away from him as soon as I could. I blamed him for all of my troubles, holding him responsible because I misunderstood him. I was full of bitterness right up until the day I forgave him. Looking back at it now, I wish I hadn't wasted so much time. Forgiving him lifted a huge weight off of me."

How could Blake compare their experiences? "Your situation was different from mine."

"That's true." David could feel Blake's gaze probing his face. "I'm the one who abandoned my father, not the other way around. And I had the chance to talk to my father about the past. I know it's hard, but that doesn't change the fact you still need to forgive your father."

David turned suspicious eyes toward the older man. Had Marguerite blabbed to him about David's reservations? No. Marguerite wouldn't betray his confidence. "Why should I forgive him? If he hadn't run away, my life and my mother's would have been much different."

"Yes, your life would've been different. Whether it would have been better or worse is something we'll never know."

Surprise rocked David. He'd never thought that his life might have been harder if Pa had stayed in Natchez. He'd always been too angry about being deserted.

"But you have a duty to forgive him anyway because you're a Christian." Blake spoke softly, but his words might have been daggers aimed at David's heart.

A sense of betrayal made him defensive. He pushed away the idea that he might be better off because of his father's absence. "It still feels wrong. I shouldn't have to forgive him when he's the one who did wrong. I was only a child. I had no choice."

"I know how hard it seems right now. I struggled with the same sense of unfairness even though I was the one who ran away." Blake's voice roughened. He stopped talking and cleared his throat. "I blamed God. I thought He should have given me a better home, a father who would care for his family's physical needs over their spiritual welfare. I couldn't see that the man who raised me wasn't the problem. I was too busy running away. Even after Lily and I met—after I fell in love with her—I didn't understand how my refusal to face the past affected my future."

David swallowed hard as he listened to Blake's confession. He'd never seen the struggles Blake was describing. He'd always thought Blake and Lily knew how to deal with every challenge. Sure, they'd argued from time to time. Who didn't? "What changed?"

"God called me to Him. He filled my life with Christians and used them to speak to me, to be examples for me." Blake's chuckle held no mirth. "But I was hardheaded. Running away seemed easier than listening to Him. It took losing everything I held dear before I finally surrendered my life to Him."

Taking a deep breath, David turned toward Blake. "And once you did, everything worked out. But that won't happen for me. It's too late. I used to dream my pa would come back to Natchez, get me and Ma, and we'd live together like a real family."

"I'm sorry your dream didn't come true."

David didn't know what he'd expected from Blake. Derision? Disbelief? Certainly not sympathetic understanding. Blake's response gave him the courage to continue. "I think that's why I never quite accepted you and Lily as my family. Don't get me wrong. I know how good you've been to me, how much I owe you."

"You don't owe us anything, David. We may not be your blood relatives, but that doesn't affect our love for you. You're like a younger brother to me. Forget this debt nonsense. You're one of the family."

How could David explain his sense of separateness? "When Ma passed away, I still thought maybe Pa would show up. I thought we could do the kinds of things your family does—work together, rely on each other, love each other without reservation. I even thought we could go fishing and hunting together. Create a family of our own. When I got to California, though, I had to face the truth. Once I buried Pa, I decided to make a break with the past. I walked away from all that you and Lily have done for me."

"Nothing you can say will change my mind." Blake draped an arm over his shoulders. "I know you're not perfect. None of us is. Lily and I are proud of the man you've become. We've watched you and Jasmine grow up together. Lily has even wondered from time to time if the two of you. . ."

David heaved a sigh of resignation. "I don't think that will happen—"

"You don't have to explain anything to me." Blake's voice cut off his protest. "I'm not trying to interfere in your life. I just want you to know how much I care about you and pray for your success. We all miss getting to see you now that you've become a successful Pinkerton detective, but we're thrilled to see you happy with what you're doing with your life."

David wondered why Blake's compliments made him feel so uneasy. He felt like a fraud. The reason he'd made the decision to become a detective was not as straightforward as Blake made it sound. In some ways he thought he might even be doing what Blake had done. He might be using his job to avoid dealing with the past. He circled back to the real question in his mind. "What if I don't know how to forgive my father or how to let go of the past?"

"It will come to you, David." Blake squeezed his shoulders before releasing him. "There's a story in Mark about Jesus telling a father that He could heal his son if the father believed. The father cried out 'Lord, I believe; help thou mine unbelief.' That scripture is important to me because it says that all we have to do is take the first step. Christ will help us cross the bridge. He is the Way."

But what was the first step? How could he forgive a father who was dead? He was alone, an orphan. He was a victim separated from the rest of the world by circumstances beyond his control. And that was the real reason for him to start a new life in Chicago, away from anyone who knew his past.

Blake didn't really understand. No one could. He was as isolated as he'd always been. The only thing David could cling to was the hope of making a difference through his work as a Pinkerton.

❧

Fog, gray and mysterious, wreathed the trees on the west bank of the river as Papa and Blake brought the *Water Lily* up against the dock.

The sun was about to make its exit, but people crowded the waterfront. Tall-masted schooners, their sails furled, rubbed against the docks as cargo was loaded into their holds. Beside them, tall smokestacks belched smoky tendrils into the air. Smaller rafts and even a few pirogues bobbed between the larger vessels like tiny fish in a large pond. Looking out at the hustle-bustle, Lily found it easy to discount Blake's opinion that river traffic was on the wane.

Blake's deep voice surprised her. "I know what you're thinking."

Lily felt his arm go around her waist, imparting warmth and strength. She leaned into him, thanking God once again for the life they shared. She glanced sideways at him. "I was wondering if Aunt Tessie can watch Benjamin as well as Noah and Magnolia."

"Is that right? Are you worried about Aunt Tessie or our children?" His eyes, as blue as the sky, teased her. "I would have guessed something different. You aren't looking at all of this activity and discounting the idea that we should get out of the steamship business, are you?"

A blush warmed her cheeks. "How can you know that?"

"You, my dearest wife, are as transparent as a new windowpane, in spite of the fact that muddy water practically runs through your veins." He dropped a light kiss on her lips. "Besides, if I didn't know what your thoughts were after a decade of living and working with you, I'd have to be deaf and blind."

She tried to pretend outrage, but a bubble of laughter in her chest demanded escape. He joined in, and the merriment they shared washed away the fear that had stalked her since he had first mentioned a change in future vocation.

"It does look like shipping is still a thriving business." Lily heard the note of wistfulness in her voice. Was she clinging to something in spite of the evidence? Or was Blake wrong?

"Don't you remember how it was before the war?" His voice was gentle, coaxing her agreement.

Lifting her chin, she nodded. "Business has come back since the war ended, though. Perhaps not quite as much as it was before. But after the heavy toll taken on both people and ships during the war, what do you expect? The ships will return, and we'll be in high cotton again."

He didn't answer her in words, but his silence shouted disagreement. She might have pulled away, but his arm drew her even closer.

They stood like that for several precious moments. Lily knew they both had a lot to do over the next hour or two, but she found herself wishing she could stay right where she was, hoping life would continue as it had for the past decade. They had endured difficulties and hardships like everyone else in the country, but they had survived. Did her husband expect her to simply give up now?

In an effort to breach the silence, she decided to focus on another problem that had been bothering her since they left Natchez. "Jasmine and David still seem to be at odds with each other."

Blake raised an eyebrow but accepted the change of subject. "I don't understand either of them. They were so close before he went off to try to reconcile with his father."

"I know. It's a shame." Lily sighed. "He's lost so much."

Blake nodded. "I talked to him earlier. He's struggling with some tough issues, but he'll figure things out eventually. He's a good man."

She loved that Blake had cared enough to ask David. "At one time I hoped perhaps he and Jasmine would fall in love. They always seemed to get along well together when they were children and up until he went out West. Do you think it's because of his job? His work is dangerous. Maybe he doesn't want to expose Jasmine. Or maybe she's the one who doesn't want to be tied to a lawman."

"I don't know what the problem is, but the two of them will have to work it out on their own." Blake's mouth quirked upward in the crooked smile so dear to her. "I can remember a time or two way back in the past when you and I didn't see eye to eye. Neither of us would have welcomed outside advice on how to run our lives."

"That's true." Lily leaned her head against Blake's shoulder. "But were we ever quite so stiff with each other as they have been on this trip?"

Before he could answer the question, passengers began appearing on deck, coming from their staterooms or one of the two lounges.

With a reluctant sigh, Lily pulled away from her husband. "I left the children with Tamar and Jensen, so I'd better go collect them."

"I thought you were going to ask Aunt Tessie to keep an eye on them for you."

She rolled her eyes. "I told you I'm worried about overloading her."

"I wouldn't concern myself with that. From the amount of time my aunt and your father are spending together, I think you can count on his helping out if she runs into any complications."

Lily halted in midstride and turned to him, her eyes wide. "What are you talking about?"

"I hope you don't mind, but I think Henrick may be smitten with her."

"Of course I don't mind." Lily hugged herself. "I just can't believe you noticed something like that before I did."

He grinned. "One of these days you're going to have to admit that I can see beyond the end of my nose." Without waiting for her reply, he bounded up the stairs to the hurricane deck.

Lily shook her head and set out once again for the galley.

Jasmine met her at the door, Benjamin squirming in her arms. She could see Tamar and Magnolia stirring a pot at the stove. Noah sat on a bench close to them, aimlessly swinging his legs.

Noah jumped up as soon as he saw her. "Mama, will you tell Aunt Jasmine it's time for Bible study."

Smiling at her firstborn, Lily shook her head and took Benjamin from Jasmine. "I'm proud of you for remembering, but we're docked now. I'm afraid we'll have to wait until we get to the Thorntons'."

Jasmine said nothing as Lily gathered her children and began herding them to the stateroom that served as their nursery. When Lily glanced back to see what had caused her sister's uncustomary silence, she realized Jasmine's wide eyes were fixed on something extraordinary. "What is it?"

"A floating theater!" The excitement in Jasmine's voice didn't bode well.

"I don't see any reason for your excitement." Lily looked past the motionless paddlewheel and spotted the gaudy barge decorated with streamers and flags. Lanterns cast a yellow light on the large signs proclaiming the exhibits and dramas available at all hours of the day and night. "Lately, there's always one or another of those boats stopping in Natchez. Most of them are full of drunks and ladies of ill repute."

Jasmine crossed her arms over her chest and tapped her foot on the deck. "I shouldn't be surprised at your attitude. You'll never change—" With a sob she bit off whatever she was going to say and whirled around.

"Wait." Why did her sister have to be so melodramatic about everything? Lily hadn't meant to evoke such a response. She wanted to run after Jasmine, but her children were also clamoring for her attention.

Benjamin patted her cheek with a chubby hand. "Mama?"

Her heart melted as she looked at him. "Yes, sweetheart, I'm listening to you."

Maybe once they were all settled at the Thorntons', she could devote some time to Jasmine's needs. Beginning to wonder if bringing her to New Orleans had been a mistake after all, Lily sighed. Only the good Lord knew what she could do to make Jasmine happy.

Chapter Eight

Jasmine ignored David's hand as she stepped out of the rented carriage. What did she care if no one understood her? She was beginning to think Lily and the rest were conspiring against her. Even Aunt Tessie seemed distant. And Papa had barely said a word to her the whole time they were on the boat. She sailed through the wrought-iron gate and entered the shady courtyard that separated the Thorntons' townhouse from the street.

The door opened, and Mrs. Thornton—*Tante* Charlotte to her and David—stepped onto the veranda, her arms wide and welcoming. "Come let me see you, cher. Let me see how beautiful you have grown since your last visit."

Jasmine began to feel a little better as she allowed Jonah's mother to hug her and draw her inside. "Tante Charlotte, you're the real beauty. You'll have to teach me how to stop aging."

Tante Charlotte laughed and turned to greet the rest of the group. Soon they were all ensconced in the back parlor, a room that seemed as familiar to Jasmine as those of Les Fleurs.

"Lloyd will be home in a few minutes, and we can all go to the dining room to eat." Tante Charlotte had to raise her voice to be heard over the noise of so many conversations occurring simultaneously in the crowed space.

Jasmine had taken a place beside Tante Charlotte on a shorter settee, while Papa and Jensen were perched on the edges of two straight-backed chairs. Aunt Tessie, Tamar, and Lily were seated on the sofa—the latter with Benjamin on her lap. Blake stood behind Lily, one hand on her shoulder, and David stood next to a small round table, claiming that he preferred to stand after spending so much time sitting while aboard the *Water Lily*. Noah and Magnolia sat on stools dragged in from the garden.

"My goodness, I could hear you from outside, Maman." Tante Charlotte's daughter, Sarah, breezed into the parlor, adding more chaos as everyone tried to greet her at once.

"Don't think you can keep all of these guests to yourself." Sarah swept her arm out wide, barely missing a collision with David. "I will take sweet Jasmine and her David to my house."

Jasmine opened her mouth to protest that David did not belong to her or any female, but Sarah rushed on in her usual impetuous manner. "I can also offer rooms to Henrick and Miss Matthews. In fact, I can take the whole family to stay with me."

"I was planning to stay at a hotel." David inserted his statement when Sarah stopped for a quick breath.

"Nonsense." She wagged a finger at him. "You are family. You will not stay in some hotel."

An odd look crossed his face. If Jasmine didn't know better, she would have thought he felt honored to be counted a member of the family. But that was ridiculous. David had practically grown up with them. No matter that they were not blood related, he was one of them.

Whatever he felt was now hidden from view. "You are most generous, but I insist. I have work to do while I'm in New Orleans. I don't want to disturb you with my comings and goings at all hours."

Sarah's smile peeked out. "You will be in our garçonnière, of course. It has a separate entrance, so you may stay out all night or come in as the sun rises. You won't disturb anyone."

"I agree with Sarah. Of course the same is true if you would rather stay here, David. No one will ever know your schedule." Tante Charlotte turned her attention to Sarah, her brow furrowed. "However, I will not allow you to take all of my guests away. I have plenty of room for everyone else."

Sarah looked as though she wanted to argue the point, but she was forestalled when Jensen cleared his throat. "Thank you for your hospitality, but Tamar and I will stay on the *Water Lily* as usual. Someone must meet with the new passengers and keep the boat safe from pickpockets and looters."

Blake exchanged a glance with Jensen. "If you want to stay here, I can hire someone to watch the boat."

Jensen shook his head. "That's our home as much as yours. I don't trust anyone else to protect it like I would."

Sarah clapped her hands to regain everyone's attention. "Who else will come to stay at my home?"

"I promised to help with the children, so I'll need to be wherever they are." Aunt Tessie smiled at Sarah. "It was the main reason I came."

Sarah turned to Papa. "How about you, Henrick? Would you like to share the garçonnière with David?"

He glanced toward the sofa before answering, making Jasmine wonder whose attention he sought. "I think I will remain here, if your parents have room for me."

"It's settled then." Tante Charlotte snapped her fingers for emphasis. "You may have Jasmine and David, but you must bring them to me when I ask."

Sarah agreed and reached a hand out to Jasmine. "Come with me to point out which bags should go with us."

Jasmine could hardly contain her excitement. With Sarah as her hostess, she would be much freer to embrace life. Even though she enjoyed the Thorntons and their home, she could hardly wait to leave.

By the time they had the luggage sorted, Tante Charlotte's husband, *Oncle* Lloyd, had arrived. Even though it had not been that long since Jasmine had seen him, his dark hair did seem to have gained a few more white strands. His hug was as affectionate as ever, and his dark eyes still gleamed with intelligence.

When the greetings were over, Jasmine discovered that Noah and Magnolia had been taken to the nursery on the third floor of the Thorntons' spacious townhouse by one of the maids. Now everyone else was waiting on the two children to return before going in to dinner.

Jasmine remembered the dining room as being spacious, but she wondered if they would all fit at the table.

Oncle Lloyd took his place at the head of the table after helping Tante Charlotte to her seat at the opposite end. The two married couples—Lily and Blake and Tamar and Jensen—took up the left side of the table while the other five—Sarah, Papa, Aunt Tessie, David, and she—squeezed together on the right side of the table.

"I can sit with the children upstairs." Jasmine didn't want to rub elbows with David. Her suggestion caused a stir.

Aunt Tessie, on the other side of David, pushed her chair back. "You stay. I should be the one to go upstairs—"

"No one will be banished to the nursery." Tante Charlotte frowned at them. "We are all family here."

"Bow your heads." Oncle Lloyd's command was stern. No one at the table dared argue. "Lord, we give thanks for the bountiful blessings You shower on us. Thank You for this gathering of family and friends. Please banish the spirit of discontent among us and help us to be ever mindful of Your love for all. Amen."

Feeling properly chastised for bringing the spirit of discontent to the Thorntons' home, Jasmine kept her attention centered on her plate of fresh vegetables and braised beef. Several conversations went on around her.

David handed her a basket filled with crusty rolls, holding onto it a second or two as she reached for it. Was he trying to bait her? She refused to meet his gaze as the silent tug of war ended.

"It's been awhile since you visited with us, David." Tante Charlotte spoke as she took the basket from Jasmine. "Tell me what has been keeping you busy."

Jasmine could see David's hands as he spread butter onto his roll. "I am working in Chicago now, so I don't get to spend as much time in Natchez."

"David has taken a job with the Pinkerton National Detective Agency." Blake's voice was full of encouragement and pride.

"A growing area of the country." Oncle Lloyd joined the conversation from the far end of the table. "Plenty of opportunities open to hardworking young men. I've thought of opening a shipping office up there, but I've never taken the time to go that far north."

"I would be happy to show you around, sir."

Jasmine wondered what kind of home David lived in. Did he rent rooms at a boardinghouse or had he purchased a home of his own? Did he live close to the agency's office or on the outskirts of Chicago? Shame hit her as she realized how little she actually knew about his life anymore. When had they grown so far apart?

"Eli is thinking of closing down the office in Memphis. He believes railroads are the key to the future."

"Is that right? I am surprised to hear that he is ready to abandon the family business." The tension in Lily's voice brought Jasmine's head up.

What was going on here? She saw Blake and her sister exchange a glance.

He covered Lily's hand with his own. "Perhaps after we visit with the attorney here, we should go to Memphis and talk to Eli."

Papa leaned forward. "I find it hard to believe people will exchange their luxurious accommodations on riverboats for smoky, dangerous rides across the country."

"If not for the gold discovered in California, I doubt many would try it." Aunt Tessie spoke with authority. "It's dangerous, too. Thieves and bandits rob trains, taking the passengers' possessions from them by force."

"Mr. Pinkerton has been hired by several of the operators to provide safety." David's voice, so close to her, startled Jasmine.

She glanced sideways at him, suddenly able to see him confronting dangerous men on a trek out West. And able to see him lying face down on a dusty prairie, dead at the hands of a ruthless bandit. Jasmine shuddered.

David must have felt the movement. He looked down at her, concern on his face.

For a moment their differences and arguments faded away. She could see the longing in his eyes. It called to her. Jasmine wanted to comfort him, tell him that everything would be all right. She opened her mouth to find the right words.

But then his expression changed, hardened into a cold mask. He became once more the stranger she didn't understand at all. A man who appeared without warning. A man who had nothing in common with her childhood friend.

Jasmine turned a shoulder on him and gave her attention to Tante Charlotte for the rest of the meal. She would not mourn the friendship they had shared. She and David wanted very different things from life. Very different things.

David woke with the dawn. Rising from his bed, he walked to the window of the Cartiers' apartment and pushed back the curtain.

The city was not fully awake, but wagons carrying milk, cream, and eggs trundled through the streets on their routes, and stumbling revelers picked their way past vegetable vendors. Soon the streets would fill with all manner of carriages and characters—businessmen on important errands, sailors returning to their ships to earn enough for their next shore leaves, and pickpockets looking for easy marks in the rushing, oblivious crowds.

Letting the curtain drop, he thought he had a lot in common with the separate building that was attached to the Cartiers' home. He had no real connection to Jasmine's family, no real connection to any family. He could come and go through life, and no one would take much notice.

A small voice inside whispered that he did matter to Someone. He mattered to God, his Maker. The thought comforted him, gave him the push he needed to get dressed and get on with his mission.

As David left the apartment, he planned a route to take him to the telegraph office and the bank. The smell of freshly baked bread made his stomach growl, so he decided that breakfast was the first stop he would make.

Entering a small café on St. Charles Street, he ordered a baguette and a cup of dark, chicory coffee. The warm, crusty bread calmed his hunger pangs, and the coffee chased away the cobwebs of sleepiness. The warmth of the day was beginning to make itself felt as he left the café and caught a horse-drawn omnibus to Canal Street.

The Daily Telegraph was a large building. Sandwiched between a saddlery and a millinery store, it stood four stories tall. David thanked the driver and disembarked on Canal Street in front of the building. He tugged on his coat to make sure it was not wrinkled and entered with a deep breath.

A slender man with dark hair and hazel eyes stood inside the doorway. "May we be of service?"

David removed his hat and tucked it under his arm. "I need to send a telegraph to Chicago."

"Yes, sir." The employee pointed him to a window on the far side of the large, columned foyer.

Taking his place in line, David considered the most concise way to send his information. He needed to let Mr. Bastrup know he was in New Orleans and would report further progress as he could. By the time he made it to the window, he had the basics worked out. "Good morning."

"What's the message?" The man on the other side had stooped shoulders, a balding head, and deep-set eyes. He looked bored as he listened to David. "Direction?"

"Mr. Homer Bastrup, Pinkerton National Detective Agency, Chicago, Illinois."

Disinterest dropped away, and the telegraph officer straightened his shoulders. "You're a Pinkerton?"

David raised his chin an inch before letting it fall back to a normal position.

"I've never met a Pinkerton before." Avid interest sharpened the man's gaze. He glanced back over his shoulder before leaning closer to David. "Are you on a job?" His question came out in a whisper.

"Didn't you know?" David winked at the man and flashed his badge. "We never sleep."

The telegraph officer guffawed.

After his message was sent, David turned to leave. Several people watched him as he made his way through the lobby. Some even stepped aside to open a path to the front door. David's shoulders itched, and he wondered whether any of the men here were connected to the bank robberies. He hoped not, or his mission would be over before he even got started.

He walked down Canal Street toward the river until he reached Royal Street. Turning right, he left the busyness behind. At the next corner, he found his destination—Citizen's Bank of Louisiana.

The interior of the bank was posh, quiet, designed to invest prospective customers with the assurance that their money would be safe inside. A shiny marble floor gleamed in filtered sunlight. Two counters were strategically placed in the center of the room for customers who wished to fill out paperwork.

David noticed all the details as he strode to the teller window. "I need to speak with your manager, please."

The young man gulped, his Adam's apple moving up and down in his throat. His nose and ears seemed too large for his narrow face. "D—do you have an appointment?"

"No." David pulled his badge out once again and showed it to the boy. "But I think he's expecting me."

Another gulp. "Yes, sir." He closed his cash drawer and disappeared from view.

While he was waiting, David studied what he could see of the area behind the teller windows. The vault looked sturdy enough. The steel door stood open at the moment, but he could see it was at least a foot thick. A large handle and a round dial would lock it closed. Steel bars provided an extra measure of security, essentially enclosing the safe in a jail cell.

"Good morning, sir." A tall man with salt-and-pepper hair and a neatly trimmed mustache approached the counter, the teller a step behind him. "May I help you?"

"I've come from Chicago to investigate your robbery."

Surprise widened the man's eyes. "You're too late. Didn't you know they caught the man?"

David took a step back. "What?"

"That's right. He's moldering in jail right now. I went down there a couple of days ago to identify him." The manager tapped his temple with one finger. "I don't forget a face once I've seen it."

Had he come all this way for nothing? Disappointment was David's first reaction. He shoved it away. Better to focus on the success of the local law enforcement officers. He should be glad for them. But it was a letdown all the same.

"He was arrested for disturbing the peace. When they brought him in, he had one of our bags on him. He denied being involved, but I recognized the scoundrel the moment I saw him."

"He acted alone?"

The manager's chest deflated a little. "No."

David felt a stirring of interest. Perhaps he could still do something here.

The other man thrust his chin out. "He was the ringleader, though. Now that he's in custody, the others will run for the hills."

Wanting to point out to the fellow that Louisiana—especially southern Louisiana—was short on hills, David held his lips together with effort. Citizen's Bank was the customer. He had no right to express his disdain for their manager's shortsightedness. Besides, it would only be his irritation speaking. This was serious business. He needed to keep his emotions at bay and do his job. People he didn't even know were counting on him to follow through.

"Thank you, Mr. . ."

"Hebert. Émile Hebert."

David dipped his head. "Mr. Hebert, I'm very happy the robber was caught. If you don't mind, I'd like to meet with him before I make my report."

Hebert shrugged. "I suppose it will be okay. As long as there's no charge."

"Don't worry. We won't charge you for anything unless you agree."

"In that case, go ahead. It may be a waste of your time, but I suppose you realize that."

A hint of an idea occurred to David. He smiled at the bank manager. "You could be right. I just want to make sure I tie up any loose ends before I make the trip back to Chicago."

He exited the bank with quick steps. His day was going to be longer than he had expected.

Chapter Nine

Camellia Thornton pushed back a lock of hair and leaned over the table where the younger children were copying the alphabet onto their slates. She enjoyed working with the sharecroppers' children, offering them tools that would ensure them brighter futures. One day soon she would begin bringing Amaryllis to the schoolhouse and including her in the lessons she prepared for these children.

Mary, one of her youngest students, caught her tongue between her teeth, her gaze focused on her slate. She glanced up as Camellia walked toward her side of the table. "Am I doing it right, Mrs. Camellia?"

Glancing at the line of letters, Camellia rewarded the child with a bright smile. "You have most of the letters right, but you've mixed up *B* and *D*. It's something I had trouble with when I was your age." She rubbed the bottom of each letter with the heel of her hand and watched as the child wrote them in once more, praising her when she succeeded.

As she went to another side of the table to help twin siblings Abraham and Zipporah, another of the younger children—a boy named Bobby—tugged on Mary's braid. Camellia started to chastise Bobby but stopped when Mary stuck her tongue out at the child and returned her attention to her slate. It might be better to ignore the byplay since Mary didn't seem overly concerned.

Camellia had arranged the children around the table according to their ages, which ranged from five to twelve. The older children often helped her with the younger ones, learning not only the current lesson but also how to pass their knowledge along to others.

She noted a couple of empty chairs and wondered if their parents had insisted the children work today instead of coming to school. Although most of the sharecroppers were grateful to send their children to school, one or two of them balked from time to time, deciding they needed the extra hands with planting or harvesting more than they needed educated children.

"Mrs. Camellia, what is that smell?" Abraham Shasta was a ten-year-old with cheeks the color of mahogany and a heart of gold. He and Zipporah always sat side-by-side in the schoolroom and were inseparable, even when working or playing outside.

Camellia glanced toward the window, surprised to see that the air was hazy. "I don't know."

Zipporah lifted her nose and sniffed. "It smells like a cookstove to me."

This morning when Camellia had walked to the schoolhouse, no clouds had been evident. Had a thunderstorm overtaken the plantation while they studied? She walked away from the children to investigate further.

With each step she took, the air became more pungent. Her heartbeat tripled its speed, threatening to jump out of her chest as she wrenched the door open. Smoke—dense and gray—crept between the gnarled trunks of the oaks surrounding their cabin. It writhed through the upper limbs, ruffling the leaves and obscuring the sky. Her mind screamed the dreaded word as she shut the door with a snap, *Fire!*

What should she do? Where was the fire? Should they run or remain in the cabin?She chewed on her lower lip as she considered the wooden walls of their schoolhouse cabin. If the fire came too close, this place would burn up in a few seconds. She couldn't take any chances with these children's lives at stake.

Maintaining a calm façade to keep from frightening the students, she made up her mind. They would go to the big house and raise the alarm.

An idea came to her, and Camellia clapped her hands for attention. "We're going to have a parade this morning just like the ones on the Fourth of July. Quickly now, I need you to gather your things and form a line."

Concerned faces turned toward her—some black, some white—a fair representation of the families who drew their livelihood from the plantation grounds since she and Jonah had implemented their sharecropping system. "James, you and Charity help Mary and Bobby. I'll hold Dorcas's hand." She pointed Abraham toward his sister. "You and Zipporah will be at the head of the line. Hold hands and march with your knees high like the soldiers do. No running."

The children followed her directions, their voices hushed and their eyes betraying some fear. Praying that the fire was far enough away to ensure their safety rather than running rampant between them and the plantation home, she nodded toward Abraham. "Go. March to the big house."

Dorcas's hand was so small in hers. Would the five-year-old, the youngest of her students, be able to keep up? She was not much older than Amaryllis. Her little legs would not be able to keep up, especially if they had to run for cover. Picking the child up, she settled Dorcas on her hip, glanced around the schoolhouse one last time, and stepped through the doorway.

The heat from the fire was noticeable, but a quick glance around did not reveal the hungry lick of flames. Gray smoke and blackened cinders filled the air, obscuring everything. With her hearing stretched to its limit, she thought she caught the snap and crackle of the fire behind them, on the far side of the cabin. "Follow the path to the big house."

She could barely see Abraham and Zipporah some five yards ahead. James had picked up Mary, but Charity and Bobby were walking hand-in-hand directly in front of her. Dorcas cried against her shoulder as they picked their way down the path. The walk to her home only took a couple of minutes each afternoon, but today the distance seemed to stretch out endlessly ahead of them, as though they were caught in a nightmare. Finally they topped the rise between the big house and the cabin. The smoke had not yet reached this far, and Camellia breathed a sigh of relief as they half-ran, half-marched forward.

When they reached the front lawn, she saw Aunt Dahlia rocking in one of the chairs scattered across the front porch, Amaryllis in her lap. Camellia rushed up the steps toward them. "What's happened?"

"Thank goodness you're safe," Aunt Dahlia's voice squeaked. She cleared her throat before continuing. "Someone came to the house a few minutes ago and said the back field is burning. Jonah and your uncle Phillip have gone to see what can be done."

At least it wasn't harvest time. Perhaps some of the crops would survive. Camellia set Dorcas on her feet. "I have to go help them."

"Don't be ridiculous." Aunt Dahlia stopped rocking. "You mustn't forget you're a lady. Besides, you're needed here. Who do you expect to keep watch over all of these children you insist on coddling?"

"Charity and Zipporah can watch them." Camellia ignored her aunt's complaint and waved the older boys toward her. She loved her aunt, but they seemed to disagree on many things these days, including the necessity of educating the sharecroppers' children. She was beginning to fully understand why Aunt Dahlia and Lily had never gotten along. "I'll go see what I can do to help control the damage."

With an expression as sour as buttermilk, Aunt Dahlia shook her head and began rocking once more. "You grow more like your sister with each passing day."

"Thank you for that compliment." Without waiting for a reply, Camellia turned and headed back the way she had come. When she topped the rise between the house and the woods, her heart launched itself upward into her throat. The schoolhouse cabin was ablaze. If she and the children hadn't left right away, they might be caught in that conflagration now.

She started running toward the springhouse to help with the bucket brigade that she prayed was already channeling water to douse the hungry flames. If they didn't get it stopped soon, her family might lose everything.

❧

Jasmine wandered through the exquisite rooms in the Cartiers' impressive mansion on Prytania Street in the Garden District. She had not seen David since they arrived yesterday evening. He had not joined her and the Cartiers for breakfast, and he had been absent during lunch.

Dr. Cartier, one of the most renowned surgeons in the city, had gone to the hospital to see some patients after lunch. Sarah had told her he would probably not return before nightfall, when they would all go to dinner at a popular restaurant. She had also promised to take Jasmine shopping in an hour or two, as soon as she finished meeting with the housekeeper about menus for the next few days.

All of which meant that Jasmine was bored. She should have stayed in Natchez. In fact, now she couldn't remember why she'd let Lily talk her into coming. The exciting city outside the Cartiers' front door might as well be a thousand miles away for all the good it did her. Could she go for a walk on her own? Do a little shopping? No. Lily had insisted she not be allowed out of the Cartiers' home without an escort.

Jasmine kicked her skirt out in front of her, her feeling of misuse growing with every moment. When would she ever get to do what she wanted to do? She was stuck in a world between—too young to venture forth alone or to be included in whatever business it was that had Lily so distracted and far too old to take part in the childish world of her nephews and niece. She needed a companion. Someone who had similar interests. A partner in adventure. Someone like David Foster.

Where was he when she needed him? Jasmine bit her bottom lip. Dare she send a note to him? Housed in the garçonnière, he had a separate entrance that allowed him privacy. It was an odd arrangement outside of Louisiana but one that many families of either Creole or Cajun heritage adopted, from the wealthy members of society to the middle-class businessmen.

Infused with a sense of purpose, she headed to the back parlor where she thought she'd seen a writing desk. Sarah wouldn't mind if she used a piece of stationery. But as she drew nearer, another problem occurred to

Jasmine. What would she say? Could she plead with him to rescue her from inactivity? Would he understand? Come to her rescue? Or would he ignore the note altogether?

Jasmine turned around and walked toward the foyer. She couldn't do it. She would simply have to hold onto her patience a little while longer. Perhaps Sarah would be done before long.

The open door of Dr. Cartier's library drew her attention. She slipped inside, her interest piqued by the walls of floor-to-ceiling bookshelves. They were crammed with every manner of reading material. She moved to the nearest one and began perusing titles. The arrangement seemed to reflect Sarah's haphazard personality more than her staid husband's. Medical books rubbed shoulders with Beadle's dime novels. Classical literature was shelved with books on animal husbandry and at least one tome on popular architectural styles. Shaking her head at the chaotic arrangement, Jasmine selected a dime novel. Aunt Dahlia would have a fit if she knew. But Aunt Dahlia was in Natchez.

She was so engrossed in the description of western frontier life that she didn't hear Sarah calling for her at first. Closing the salmon-colored cover, she slipped the book back onto the shelf and hurried into the hallway.

"There you are." Sarah skipped down the stairs as though she and Magnolia were the same age. Her dress for the afternoon was a bright concoction of white satin under a layer of yellow tulle. Blue organza flowers scattered across the skirt matched the ribbons laced through her cosmopolitan hairstyle. "I have been looking for you all over. Are you ready for our outing? I thought you would enjoy a drive to Place Gravier. It's a park named for Jean Gravier, who donated the land."

Jasmine immediately forgot her woes as excitement filled her. She didn't care where they went as long as she was no longer trapped inside. "Yes, I would adore an outing."

Although Sarah was wearing a dashing hat with a tall crown, she was several inches shorter than Jasmine. But that didn't stop her from patting Jasmine's cheek with a gloved hand. "Poor dear. I've been ignoring you, *non*?"

The older woman clucked her tongue and shook her head, putting her hat in danger of toppling from its lofty heights. "I promise to make it up to you."

Like a leaf caught in a swift current, Jasmine followed Sarah across the foyer. She might have little control over her destination, but it was bound to be an exciting ride.

A cabriolet stood outside the front door, its hood folded back so the two ladies would have a wide view during their drive. Jasmine cast a doubtful glance at her hostess's hat, wondering if it would survive the buffeting of a brisk drive. But as it turned out, she need not have worried. Sarah Cartier might be a whirlwind when it came to her duties as a hostess, but she drove her carriage with all the deliberate speed of a tortoise. Their vehicle crept down the street, earning rude comments from one or two of the drivers stuck behind them. By the time they turned into the park, Jasmine's ears burned with embarrassment.

"I don't know why everyone is in such a hurry." Sarah flourished the whip in her hand but did not direct it toward their horse. "I believe all this rushing about is why people grow ill during warm months. Poor Kenneth is so overworked from April until October that I worry about his health."

Jasmine nodded, her head swiveling back and forth to take in the sights. Ladies and gentlemen strolled about the shady paths of the park or rested on benches. A young girl in a rough cotton shift exhorted gentlemen to purchase flowers from her basket for the women they escorted. A young fellow was being tugged down the path by a large dog on a leash, his arm extended to a degree that made Jasmine wince in sympathy.

A desultory breeze ruffled the leaves on the oak trees and teased Jasmine's collar. "Do you drive here every day?"

"Oh no." Sarah's mouth formed a perfect O when she spoke.

Jasmine wanted to imitate the gesture but managed to restrain herself. She filed away the expression for future use. She had read an article the other day about how the most successful actors studied people to learn how to portray emotions on the stage. She had determined immediately to adopt the habit as she could see the benefits to be derived from it.

"I usually have a coachman drive me to the park, but I wanted to show your pretty face to all of my friends."

An oncoming carriage drew even with them and stopped as the lady inside poked her driver with her parasol. "It's nice to see you this afternoon, Sarah."

"Jasmine, I want you to meet one of my dearest friends, Madame Cécile LeBlanc." Sarah turned to the lady in the other carriage. "Cécile, this is the youngest sister of my brother's wife, Camellia, Miss Jasmine Anderson."

The other lady, dressed in a pink figured silk dress with short sleeves that exposed most of her upper arms, squinted toward Jasmine. "*Enchanté*, *mademoiselle*."

Jasmine was glad for Camellia's insistence that she learn a few French phrases for just such social occasions. "*Merci, madame. Comment allez-vous?*"

The other lady nodded her approval. "*Je vais bien*. I am well." She looked at Sarah. "She is indeed beautiful and smart, too. Our poor debutantes will tear their flounces in despair."

Sarah beamed with pride as though she was personally responsible for Jasmine's looks and behavior. "I have told you of their older sister who owns her own steamboat, Mrs. Lily Matthews."

Madame's dark gaze studied Jasmine with interest. "*Oui*."

"Usually Jasmine stays with my parents when her family is in town, but I insisted she stay with me this time. I hope she will remain with us for a few weeks at least so we can attend some parties. You know how much these young girls enjoy dancing and flirting with handsome young men."

A protest trembled on the tip of her tongue. Camellia was the sister who enjoyed parties. She enjoyed every aspect of the social whirl—from selecting the invitations and hiring the orchestra to sipping lemonade and chatting with the other women about their new gowns. Jasmine could dance, but she got enough of parties at home. And the idea of spending a whole evening at a ball where she would know no one made her shudder. "I'm not certain what Lily's plans are."

"I know." Madame LeBlanc's cocoa-colored eyes sparkled with

excitement. "You should bring her to the theater this evening."

This sounded much more promising. Jasmine straightened her spine. "I'd love to see a play."

"But Kenneth and I didn't purchase tickets for this season." Sarah shook her head. "We find it such a crush, and the performances are sometimes too risqué for my tastes. I'm sorry, Jasmine. If I'd thought of it earlier, Kenneth might have been able to procure tickets for us, but I doubt there's time now."

Disappointment filled Jasmine at Sarah's admission. Her smile drooped in spite of her best efforts. A trip to the theater would have been a perfect way to spend the evening.

"I have the solution." Madame LeBlanc waved her hand like the magic wand of a fairy godmother. "Monsieur LeBlanc and I always purchase extra tickets, and we are not attending this evening. I will send them around to you, and then you will not have to disappoint your guest."

"I don't know what to say." Sarah's voice was hesitant. "I will gladly purchase the tickets."

"Don't be silly."

Jasmine's excitement returned full force. Madame LeBlanc's offer was almost too good to be true. Her hopeful gaze met Sarah's.

With a Gallic shrug, her hostess acquiesced. "Thank you, Cécile. You are very thoughtful."

Feeling like she could float on a cloud all the way back to the Cartiers' home, Jasmine turned to Madame LeBlanc. It took her a moment to remember the way to say thank you in French. "Merci *beaucoup*."

"*C'est ne rien,* cher. *Comment adorable.* She is adorable, Sarah." Madame LeBlanc prodded the coachman's back once more to indicate she was ready to leave. As they pulled away, she leaned out of her carriage window. "In fact, I have an idea to arrange a special surprise for your young visitor. She will be *aux anges.*"

Jasmine wondered what surprise Sarah's friend was planning. Whatever it was, it could not compare with a night at the theater. Nothing could compare with a treat like that.

Chapter Ten

Les Fleurs

The fire yielded slowly to their efforts. Someone along the line reported that the men had lit a backfire. Camellia knew of the idea to "fight fire with fire" even though it made little sense to her. Would the strategy work, or would it cause even more destruction? She lifted buckets of water until her arms felt wooden and her back ached worse than when she was expecting her child.

The sun had passed its zenith when Jonah appeared, his face so grimy she almost didn't recognize him.

Camellia forgot her aches in the rush to check on him. "Are you okay? Is it over? Was anyone hurt?"

He put an arm around her shoulders and hugged her close. "I'm fine."

Camellia broke free and filled a dipper with water from the spring.

Jonah drank greedily before continuing. "We had some scary moments. We lost several cabins, and some of the crops were scorched, but we managed to dig a trench that enclosed the worst of the blaze. The bucket brigade and a backfire did the rest."

As long as he was safe, she didn't much care about the rest of the estate. Crops could be replanted; houses could be rebuilt.

"We need to send for the doctor."

Camellia took a mental inventory of her medical supplies to keep fear at bay. "Where are you hurt?"

His smile reassured her. "I only have a few scrapes, but Amos was burned when a limb fell on him, and I'm sure we'll have some other injuries to sort out before the day is over."

Nahum Shasta walked to where they stood. A brawny man with short-cropped hair, he was Abraham and Zipporah's father and the new foreman. "Jonah, I've got something here you need to see."

"I'll go back to the house and gather some things," Camellia said. "Get anyone who's hurt to come there."

He dropped a quick kiss on her cheek before they separated.

Camellia passed along the information to the women before heading back to the main house. She gathered wheat flour to cover the cleaned burns, needle and thread for any cuts, soap and fresh water, and clean cotton strips for finishing.

Jonah and Nahum brought in the first patient on a litter, and Camellia directed them upstairs to the guest wing.

"Shouldn't you wait for the doctor?" Aunt Dahlia stood at the parlor door. "I don't think it's a good idea to take men like that into the bosom of your family."

Camellia knew what her aunt meant. The man on the stretcher was black. She tried to remember that her aunt had been raised during a different time, but her temper flared. "He risked his life to help put out a fire threatening our home—the very room to which he is being carried. What would you have me do? Leave him on the front lawn?"

"I didn't intend—" The glare Camellia tossed at her stopped Aunt Dahlia midsentence. She fell back a step, her eyes wide.

Trying not to feel guilty for her harsh tone, Camellia sighed. "Please send the doctor up as soon as he arrives."

Aunt Dahlia nodded.

Camellia climbed the steps and found that the men had transferred the patient to the bed.

Nahum dipped his head as she moved toward the center of the room. "Your sheets may not come clean, Mrs. Thornton."

"Don't worry about that." She spared a smile for Nahum before turning to the man on the bed. "We'll have him comfortable in no time."

Jonah and Nahum moved back as she investigated her patient.

His wary eyes watched her with doubt. His chest and arms had been burned. Although not deep, the large area of burned skin concerned her.

Camellia hoped the doctor would arrive soon. She could dress the wounds, but she had no laudanum to ease his pain. "What's your name?"

"Simeon." His skin was the color of café au lait, his eyes hazel.

"Well, Simeon, I want you to relax a little." She reached for the bowl of clean water. "Have you ever been treated by a lady before?"

The frown on his wide brow eased a little. "No, ma'am. 'Cept for my ma when I was a little boy."

"My wife has a lot of experience." Jonah stepped closer. "You're in good hands."

"Yes, sir." His gaze swiveled from Jonah back to her. "I'm sorry 'bout your bed, ma'am."

Camellia made a shushing noise as she continued her work. When she was satisfied that all dirt and debris had been removed, she sprinkled the wounds with flour. Then Jonah and Nahum helped Simeon sit up so she could wrap the cotton bandages around his chest.

The doctor arrived as she was tying the final knot, his black bag held in one hand. Jonah and Nahum left them alone. She held her breath as the doctor inspected her work, prying at the edges of the bandages and grunting as he checked Simeon's pulse and temperature. Finally he glanced up at her over the edge of his oval spectacles. "If you ever wish to work at my practice, Mrs. Thornton, you are more than welcome."

"Thank you, Doctor." She watched as he measured out a dose of laudanum. "It's been awhile since I had to deal with anything more serious than cuts and bruises."

"I know you worked with patients during the war, and you've certainly not lost your touch." He capped his bottle and left it on the dresser. "If he wakes during the night, you can give him one more spoonful." The doctor closed his bag and moved to the door, inclining his head to indicate that Camellia should precede him. "What happened to him?"

Camellia told the doctor about the fire.

He shook his head. "Do you have other patients I should see?"

"I don't know for certain. My aunt may have suffered a fit of apoplexy by now."

He turned his chuckle into a cough. "Never fear, I will check on Miss Dahlia on my way out. I may have a little something to calm overwrought nerves. Why don't you wash up? You look ready to fall over."

"I concur with your diagnosis." Jonah's voice came from the shadowy hall. Bathed and in a fresh suit, her husband looked much refreshed. "And I intend to see that my wife follows your instructions to the letter."

Shaking her head, Camellia watched as the doctor made his way to the first floor. "I should see to the others before—"

Jonah put a finger over her mouth. "You heard the doctor. You will not be allowed downstairs until you make use of the warm bath waiting in our bedroom."

Recognizing the firm tone in her husband's voice, Camellia nodded. Besides, the idea of washing the grime from her skin sounded blissful. "Are you sure no one else needs to be seen?"

Instead of answering, Jonah swept her into his arms.

"What are you doing?"

"Making sure you follow orders." He stopped long enough to open the door before depositing her on the edge of their bed. "Do you need help undressing?"

Camellia could feel her cheeks heat. "I believe I can manage on my own."

"If you're sure..." The look in his eyes was positively wicked.

Fleeing to the dressing screen, Camellia began removing her clothing with racehorse speed. She heard the bedroom door close and giggled. As she climbed into the bathtub, she thanked God for bringing Jonah into her life. He was the only man in the world who could make her laugh on a day like this one.

David was led to the cell by Constable Louis Longineaux. He was young and looked like he needed to gain some weight so he could fill out his uniform—a double-breasted frock coat of a rather garish orange hue and matching trousers. The left lapel of his coat boasted a metal badge in the shape of a star with a crescent surrounding it, the standard emblem of the Metropolitan Police Force.

Ignoring the rude remarks of the prisoners they passed in the dreary hallway, David matched his pace to the young constable's. His nose stung from the noxious odors of waste and filth. As a detective he'd seen the inside of many prisons, but none quite so grimy. The walls were streaked with water and green slime, and decay and hopelessness permeated the air. "Has the prisoner had any visitors?"

"No." The constable stumbled over a loose brick in the floor, setting his ring of keys to jingling before he regained his balance. "I reckon he's a loner. Or maybe none of his friends know what happened to him."

Before he could ask more questions, they reached their destination in a dank corner of the jail. Longineaux rattled his keys and selected one to insert into the lock. "Wake up, Charlie. You got a visitor."

Charles "Charlie" Petrie lay on one of the two cots in the cell, his hands under his head. When he heard the door open, he sat up and swung his legs to the floor.

Several days' growth of a dark beard hid the shape of his chin. His hair was a mess, standing at odd angles around his head and giving him the look of a madman. His eyes reminded David of a cat—almond-shaped and so light a shade of brown they might be called yellow. They glowed in the dim light of the cell, tracking the constable's movements even though the prisoner's head didn't move.

"Whatcha' mean? I got no friends in New Orleans."

David noticed the way he pronounced the city's name. The prisoner said it as two separate words—New Orleenz. A native like Constable Longineaux would have said N'awlins.

"No one said I was a friend." David stepped into the cell and gestured to the constable to lock him in. "You can come back in about half an hour. I should be done by then."

"You sure you'll still be alive?" Petrie's feline gaze skewered him.

David resisted the urge to touch his gun. His holster was empty—a rule enforced with all visitors, even Pinkerton detectives—but he felt secure in his ability to protect himself, even in such close quarters. "I'm not worried."

Longineaux left them alone, and David glanced around the room. It was sparsely furnished—a pair of cots, a chamber pot, and a narrow window so grimy it let in little sunlight. Deciding not to lean against the wall, David sat on the unoccupied cot.

Charlie Petrie didn't say anything, but his gaze bored a hole into David's chest.

Accustomed to anger and belligerence, David took his attitude in stride. He wasn't here to make a new friend, after all. He took a moment to size the other man up before beginning his interrogation. "So you're the man who planned and executed a successful robbery at Citizen's Bank?" He put a hint of disbelief in his voice.

Petrie sneered, his face seeming even more catlike as he wrinkled his nose. "If you say so."

"I'm asking." David took a notebook from his coat pocket. "I have to complete a report. It would help me immensely if you would tell me about the robbery."

Crossing his arms over his chest, Petrie leaned against the wall behind him. "What do you want to know?"

"I don't know." Chewing on the nib of a pencil, David looked up at nothing in particular. He wanted Petrie to think he was a bit of a simpleton. "Why don't you start with the number of men involved in the robbery."

"Just me."

David scratched his head. "Is that right? What about the others who came in with you and held guns on the staff? Are you telling me they were strangers you met on the street as you walked into the bank?"

"Yep. I had me an idea to slip in right quick and empty out the safe.

Those fellows offered to help for a cut of the money." Petrie relaxed as he talked.

"I see." David wrote a couple of words down in his book.

"You could say I've got one of them friendly faces. Folks walk up to me all the time and ask if they can help out."

David let the prisoner continue his story, inserting approving noises here and there to keep him talking.

"Say, what are you writing down in that book about me?"

"Hmmm." David looked up. "Oh, it's nothing much. Kinda boring. My boss likes for me to wrap things up in a nice package so he'll know where to put the file after you're dead."

Petrie's jaw dropped. "What are you talking about?"

"Armed robbery is a serious charge. I was hoping maybe we could talk about a reduced sentence if you knew something to lead me to the others who were at the bank." David shrugged. "But since you didn't know them, and you're not a member of a gang, you really don't know anything I can use."

A crafty look entered the man's yellow eyes. "I might be willing to talk a little more if it would save me from the hangman's noose."

Petrie was an example of the adage "There is no honor among thieves." Few criminals possessed a high moral code. Most of them would be willing to sell their mothers for a jug of whiskey.

"You can talk your head off all the way to the gallows, and it won't make a bit of difference." David closed his notebook and returned it to his pocket. "It's a shame really."

Petrie pushed himself forward, leaning toward David. "You've got to listen to me."

"Why should I?" David stood. "I have enough information for your file. Thank you for your time."

"Wait." Petrie's jaw worked, evidence of the strong emotions passing through him. "What if I was lying? What if I really did know those men? What if I could lead you to them? What if you made a big arrest and got yourself a nice promotion? You'd like that, wouldn't you?"

"Of course I would." David met Petrie's gaze. "But if you were lying then, how can I believe anything you tell me now?"

Petrie rocked back on the cot.

David could practically hear the wheels of the man's brain grinding as he considered his options.

"I don't know much. I ain't been a part of the gang for long. Only since they showed up in New Orleans a few weeks ago."

David's pulse spiked. He'd lost hope that Charlie Petrie might be part of the gang that had been robbing banks up and down the Mississippi River valley. Anyone dumb enough to be caught in a bar with evidence on him didn't seem like much of a mastermind. He had decided that at best Petrie was a junior member of the gang. At worst he would have no connection at all to the robbers David was tracking. He needed to keep his interest well hidden. "So you really don't know anything at all, do you?"

"That's not true." Petrie thrust his chin up, defiance evident in every muscle of his body. Even his beard seemed to bristle with it. "I don't know exactly where they hide out, but I can get a message to them. . . draw them out. Then you can spring your trap."

"I don't know. . . ."

The arrival of Constable Longineaux could not have been better timed. David could see the anxiety in Charlie Petrie's yellow eyes. He would let the man sit for a day or two while he talked with the police chief. Together, they could work out a plan. Something that would stop Charlie Petrie and his gang from ever again preying on innocent people.

Chapter Eleven

Jumping to her feet as the final curtain fell, Jasmine brought her hands together with enthusiasm. She didn't care that none of the others in their box stood. Lily was probably frowning, but it didn't matter. Nothing could undermine her delight in the performance. As the applause of the audience began to die down, she returned to her front-row seat. "I wish it wasn't over."

Sarah leaned toward her. "Kenneth and I are enjoying watching you enjoy the play. You're a breath of fresh air. I had almost forgotten how much fun the theater can be."

Jasmine felt a bit like a brown sparrow sitting next to a peacock. When she first walked downstairs this evening, she had been more than satisfied with her navy blue frock. Six flounces edged in bias-cut lace decorated the skirt. The bodice was unadorned except for a single row of buttons, a narrow collar, and a rosette of the same silk faille as her dress. Her jewelry was a single strand of matching pearls, and her hair had been pulled back in a simple style that allowed soft ringlets to touch her shoulders.

But Sarah's dress put hers to shame. It might have been shipped directly from Paris. Forest green in color, the silk gown nipped in her waist and exposed her dimpled shoulders. The flounce was caught up high on the skirt and cascaded toward the floor in elegant folds. A diamond collar sparkled around her neck, complementing the glittering earbobs that dripped from her ears. She looked like a plate from a fashion magazine.

Sarah touched Jasmine's elbow with the tip of her fan. "Would you like to go backstage to meet Miss Barlow?"

Jasmine's jaw dropped. She couldn't imagine anything any more thrilling.

Lily leaned forward from her seat on the second row. "You'd better close your mouth before an insect flies into it." Her whisper fell into one of those sudden silences that sometimes happens even in large crowds.

The people in the next box glanced in Jasmine's direction as a result of her sister's warning. She heard a chuckle from Blake behind her and saw the smile on Kenneth's face. A tide of hot blood stung her cheeks. Wanting to bring her hands up to hide her embarrassment, Jasmine trained her gaze on the floor. She wished Lily and Blake had stayed at the Thorntons' house tonight. The outing would be much more pleasurable without her sister's constant poking and prodding.

Sarah came to her rescue. "Don't be so hard on the girl." Her dress rustled as she stood and looped her arm through Jasmine's. "Madame LeBlanc arranged it for you, but if you don't wish to go, I will understand."

"Oh, no." Jasmine bit her lip. "I mean, yes, please. I would like that above all things." The very idea of meeting one of the talented people she'd just seen on the stage made her heart race. She lifted her free hand to check her hair and realized it was shaking. Hoping no one else had seen it, she allowed her arm to drop back to her side. This was the most exciting moment of her life. But she didn't have to advertise that fact to her naysayer sister.

"Good." Sarah turned to Kenneth. "Why don't you take Lily and Blake outside to the carriage? We won't be long."

"Actually, Lily and I have decided to go back to the Thorntons' alone instead of making you drive back to the French Quarter to drop us off."

Kenneth looked toward his wife, a frown on his normally calm face. "Aren't we going to Bonhomie for dinner?"

Jasmine could see her dream of visiting the backstage area slipping between her fingers. Life was so unfair. Why did Lily have to spoil things?

"I hope you won't change your plans because of us." Lily hid a yawn behind her fan. "I am so tired this evening. I suppose I'm getting too old for all of this excitement."

"Jasmine may have a conniption if she doesn't get to visit with that actress." Blake smiled to remove the sting from his words.

Dr. Cartier's frown deepened until everyone laughed. He was so serious—an odd spouse for someone as animated as Sarah.

Holding her breath, Jasmine looked at Sarah, who leaned toward her husband and whispered something in his ear.

Kenneth nodded. "We insist you take the carriage home. I will arrange for a cab while the ladies are visiting."

"That makes no sense." Blake settled his wife's cloak around her shoulders. "I can get a cab for Lily and me."

Kenneth and Sarah exchanged a glance. She lifted her shoulders, and he nodded before turning to Blake. "I'd be most happy to take you home while the ladies are visiting the actors backstage."

Blake's refusal was polite but resolute. By the time Sarah's husband agreed, Jasmine wanted to scream her frustration. "Can we go now?"

Laughing at Jasmine's obvious fervor, Sarah nodded and led the way out of the box. They were immediately caught up in throngs of laughing, chattering people who were making their way toward the building exits. By the time they made it to the relative quiet of the dressing rooms located in the back of the theater, Jasmine felt bruised by the effort. But she would have turned around and done it again if necessary.

Sarah explained to one of the workers that they were supposed to meet Miss Barlow in her dressing room. The man looked them over with a raised eyebrow before directing them down a hallway.

Several young men crowded around one of the doorways, jostling with good-natured rivalry in their attempts to gain entry into one of the dressing rooms. As they drew closer, Jasmine realized it must be Miss

Barlow's room. She had never imagined such a throng all seeking the same goal. Would they be able to see the actress, after all?

"May I be of service to you young ladies?" A tall figure separated from one of the shadowy corners of the hallway.

When he came fully into view, Jasmine thought she might faint. She recognized him—the actor who portrayed the hero, Vance Hargrove. He was even more handsome up close than he'd been on the stage.

Sarah seemed unfazed by his good looks or fame as she nodded and once again explained their objective.

Mr. Hargrove bowed. "She is inundated for the moment, but perhaps you ladies would care to join me for dinner. We can return here in an hour or so once her admirers have cleared out. I'm certain Miss Barlow would be delighted to spend time visiting with such charming ladies."

Sarah shook her head. "I'm afra—"

The opportunity of a lifetime was within her grasp. Unable to let it slip past, Jasmine interrupted Sarah's response. "Perhaps you could join us for dinner instead, Mr. Hargrove. I would love to ask some questions about the theater." Fear struck as she wondered what had possessed her to be so forward. What would Mr. Hargrove think of her?

A smile appeared on the man's handsome face, lending him a worldly look. "Are you perhaps an aspiring actress, Miss. . . ?" He held onto the last syllable, inviting her to offer her name.

"Jasmine. Jasmine Anderson." She curtsied as gracefully as possible in the narrow confines of the hallway.

Mr. Hargrove took her hand in his and brought it to his lips. As he placed a lingering kiss on her knuckles, his soulful gaze seemed to consume her. "What a lovely name for a lovely girl."

He turned to Sarah. "And this gorgeous young creature must be your sister."

A sharp pang ate at Jasmine's heart as Mr. Hargrove took Sarah's hand and kissed it with the same lingering attention.

But Sarah didn't seem to mind. She fluttered her eyelashes at the man as he straightened. "You are quite the flatterer, are you not, Monsieur Hargrove?"

He put a hand to his chest and staggered back a step. "You wound me, mademoiselle. If I cannot remark on beauty where I see it, what use is this tongue?"

Sarah laughed. "How would you earn wages without it?"

"This is very true." He winked at her before turning his attention back to Jasmine. "If you can convince your sister to include me in your family party, I would be most delighted to join you."

Jasmine's pang intensified. She wished for a moment she'd paid more attention to Camellia's advice about learning the art of flirtation. But she had never needed it before this evening. Could she even flutter her eyelashes? "I'm sure Mrs. Cartier wouldn't mind."

From the odd expression on the actor's face, Jasmine's attempt to flutter was not going well. She closed her eyes for a brief moment as she realized how gauche she must appear to him. When she opened them, he had recovered his aplomb. He bowed to her and offered his arm. . .to Sarah. Didn't he hear her say that Sarah was a married lady? Jasmine trudged behind them and wondered how she might regain Mr. Hargrove's attention.

"My heart is broken to learn that some other man has stolen your affections. Dare I hope that your family forced you into a marriage with a doddering old fool who is at the point of demise?" His voice was pitched low, but Jasmine had no trouble overhearing him.

Sarah giggled and rapped his hand with her fan. "You are a rascal. Dr. Cartier won my heart a decade ago."

"He is in poor health, though?"

"My husband is in the prime of his life."

Mr. Hargrove shook his head. "Then I am doomed to worship you from afar."

Jasmine rolled her eyes. By the time they found Kenneth and performed the introductions, she was wishing she'd not been so impetuous.

The drive to the restaurant changed her opinion slightly as Mr. Hargrove recounted several humorous stories of past performances. He accompanied his tales with admiring glances in her direction. By the time the coachman pulled up, she found herself in better humor.

The men climbed out first and turned to offer their assistance to the ladies. Sarah accepted her husband's arm. Jasmine had to wait a moment before Mr. Hargrove reached inside for her hand, so by the time her feet touched the ground, the Cartiers were almost at the entrance.

Instead of releasing Jasmine's hand, Mr. Hargrove tucked it into the crook of his arm. He leaned over so that his mouth was close to her ear. "I trust you understand that I must appease your chaperones if I am to have access to your company."

She didn't know if she should be relieved or repelled by his explanation. "Sarah is very beautiful and accomplished."

"But she lacks a very special quality that you have in abundance." His eyes shone in the light of a nearby lantern.

Jasmine felt the blood rushing upward to stain her cheeks and hoped he could not see it. Prying her tongue from the roof of her mouth, she swallowed hard. "Wh–what is that?"

"Innocence." His smile made her heart stutter. She could hardly believe such a handsome, sophisticated man found anything interesting about her at all.

He found her lack of experience a good thing? Jasmine could hardly believe he wouldn't prefer a female who could match his own qualities. He was so suave, so comfortable in social situations. Perhaps he was teasing her? But a glance at his face showed nothing but admiration. She didn't know how to answer him.

The atmosphere inside was conducive to a romantic mood. Small round tables covered with white linen were scattered between vine-wrapped white columns of varying heights. Large potted ferns and tropical trees gave the illusion of privacy while kerosene lamps turned low made each table an intimate island. Jasmine felt as though she'd left America altogether and been magically transported to a romantic Greek ruin.

A waiter dressed in black formal wear led them to a table and gave menus to the gentlemen.

After glancing at the restaurant's offerings, Mr. Hargrove leaned toward her. "I don't know anything about your tastes, Miss Anderson.

Do you wish to order for yourself?"

Jasmine didn't much care what food was brought to the table as long as she was in his heady company. The only thing that would make the evening better would be if she and the actor were dining alone. "I trust you to make a proper selection, Mr. Hargrove."

"I don't know how proper my selection will be if you are involved." His heated look set butterflies loose in her stomach. "It would give me great pleasure if you would use my Christian name, Vance."

Kenneth cleared his throat and gave a tiny shake of his head before handing his menu back to the waiter. "I'm sure we'll all enjoy the braised lamb."

Taking the reprimand in stride, Vance smiled at his host. "I was telling your wife earlier that you're a very lucky gentleman."

"Why is that?" The frown on Kenneth's face did not bode well for the rest of the evening.

"Because you snatched up Mrs. Cartier before any of the other men in New Orleans could. I am sure you're the envy of everyone you know."

Sarah beamed at both men and put her hand over her husband's. "I'm the lucky one."

Kenneth sat back, his features easing a tad.

Jasmine was relieved. She listened to the two men discuss politics and the general state of the country, Sarah tossing in a witty comment now and then. The meal came, but she found herself unable to consume much. The butterflies still fluttering inside her stomach forbade her. She played with her fork, picked at a loose thread on her napkin, and managed to swallow a few sips of water. If tonight was a preview of what New Orleans had to offer, perhaps she should reconsider staying here.

❧

A black police officer studied David's badge, a furrow between his brows. "Didn't I see you here yesterday?"

David held out his right hand. "That's right. My name's David Foster. I'm investigating the Citizen's Bank robbery."

"Levi Campbell." The officer's grasp was firm. "The chief's down at the mayor's office, but Lieutenant Moreau might be able to see you."

It was a place to start. David knew he needed to enlist the support of the department if his plan was to succeed. Putting his badge into his coat pocket, he smiled at Officer Campbell. "Lead the way."

The constable who'd escorted him the day before sat at one of the wooden desks in the main room of the police station. A look of concern crossed his features as he recognized David. "Is something wrong?"

David wracked his memory for the man's name. French. Long. That was it! Longineaux. "Morning, Constable Longineaux."

A look of surprise and appreciation replaced his concern.

Before he could say anything, Officer Campbell blew out a breath to show his exasperation. "Pinkerton here wants to see the chief."

"Does it have something to do with the robbery?"

" 'A course it does." Campbell answered for him. "That's what he supposed to be investigating."

Longineaux sent a glare toward his fellow officer and turned back to his desk. "He's gone. I doubt he'll be back before dinner."

"I know that." The black man's answer was clipped and full of disdain. "I'm taking him to Lieutenant Moreau's office."

As they moved forward, David maintained an air of neutrality. He didn't want to get caught up in any local politics. He was supposed to work with local law enforcement, not take sides in their squabbles.

Turning into a hallway, they left the central office behind. David counted two doors on the left and one on the right before Officer Campbell stopped and rapped smartly on an unmarked entrance.

Someone on the other side barked out a command to enter.

Campbell glanced at him, his brown eyes cool. "Wait out here." He turned the knob and disappeared. After a moment the door opened again, and Campbell waved him inside.

Lieutenant Moreau was a short man with dark skin that hinted at mixed ancestry. His hair was as black as Jasmine's, and his eyes were a deep brown. He waved a hand toward a wooden chair and leaned back. "What brings you down to New Orleans?"

"The robbery two weeks ago at Citizen's Bank." David wondered how many times he would have to describe his mission. "We think it may be connected to a string of robberies that started in Chicago a couple of months ago."

Moreau moved a stack of papers to one side of his desk. "What makes you think the man we arrested has anything to do with your robberies?"

"In Chicago the thieves seemed to know the exact time to strike. They don't ever shoot anyone. They empty the safe, fire off a couple of shots into the air, and escape. Sound familiar?"

He could tell he had the lieutenant's attention. "Very."

"They've hit a couple of other locations on their way down here. My captain thinks they may be headed for Mexico next. We want to stop them before they get out of the country."

"And you think our prisoner can help you?" Moreau didn't sound convinced. "Do you want some of my men to interrogate him?"

David shook his head. "I don't think he's the type to be intimidated. But I think he'd do anything to save his own skin."

"I don't know why you think you could trust him to be honest with you." Moreau's eyes narrowed. "He's more likely to get you killed by giving you the wrong direction or sending a message to warn his friends."

Inspiration dawned on David with the other man's words. "That's it! He can send a message."

Moreau's eyebrows climbed toward his hairline. "You want him to warn his cohorts?"

David shook his head. "I want him to draw them out, get them to meet him. Didn't you catch him with a sizeable amount of money on him?"

"It's in the evidence room." Moreau rubbed his chin as he considered David's suggestion. "But I still don't see how you plan to work this."

"The one we're really after is not someone who actually carried out the robbery. The robbers are nothing more than puppets. Half an hour with Petrie convinced me he doesn't have the wit to execute one robbery with such precision, much less ten."

"Ten?" Moreau whistled. "They must be the luckiest group of men in existence."

"No one has that kind of luck. It takes careful planning and inside information to pull off that many crimes without a hitch. I believe a mastermind is behind them. He's the one I want."

"I see. But how do you plan to get Petrie to convince him to show his face?"

"Blackmail." David allowed a small smile on his lips. "I'll put a reward notice in the newspaper, and our friend can threaten that he's going to claim it if his boss doesn't take him back into the fold."

"What if the boss isn't the only one who shows up? I know Pinkertons are well trained, but I don't think you can take custody of the whole gang."

David knew he would need the support of the police department, but he wanted to lead the mission. "If you can supply me with a couple of men at the right time, I can manage."

Moreau frowned at him. "What about Petrie? Are you sure he won't betray you as soon as his friends show up?"

"I doubt he would want to get caught in the crossfire. He knows he'd be the first to die. And Mr. Petrie has a driving desire to live."

The lieutenant's face relaxed. "If you get Petrie to go along, I'll make sure you have what you need." He stood and held out his right hand.

David took it, his smile widening. "Thank you, sir."

He left the office and went to find the constable. He was anxious to set his plan in motion.

Petrie was less than enthusiastic about the plan. "I don't know who calls the shots. He sends us written instructions. I've never seen him, and I sure don't know how to send him a note."

"There has to be a way." David thought hard. "How do you get the money to him?"

"He tells us where to drop it off."

That wouldn't work. David considered a few schemes, each too unwieldy or unbelievable. Finally it came to him. "We're working at this too hard. All I have to do is tell the newspaper that you've turned over a new leaf since escaping the hangman's noose. You plan to tell us everything we'll need to arrest your leader. That will bring him out into the open."

"You're forgetting that I don't know what he looks like. I could walk past him on the street and never realize it. He could shoot me before I said a word."

"He'll want to know how much you've already told us before killing you. Once he shows himself, we'll take him down." David grew more excited as he talked. If he caught the man who was the head of the outfit, it wouldn't take long before they had all of the robbers in custody. He could practically hear Mr. Bastrup's accolades already.

Chapter Twelve

"I knew your plan for saving Les Fleurs was liable to get us all murdered in our beds." Aunt Dahlia glanced across the dining room table at her husband for support.

Uncle Phillip's grimace was exaggerated by a singed mark on his forehead. Proof of his efforts to save Les Fleurs. "All's well that ends well, Dahlia."

Although her husband's defection must have been a blow to Aunt Dahlia's esteem, she was not likely to be silenced by it. Like the other women in the family, she had a strong personality and boundless self-assurance.

With a sniff, she turned from Uncle Phillip to glare at Jonah. "Before you married Camellia, she was a good girl who understood how things should be."

"Aunt Dahlia, don't try to blame Jonah." Camellia kept her voice low even though she wanted to spring to her husband's defense. "If we hadn't done something, we would have lost Les Fleurs for taxes. The sharecropping system Jonah put in place saved us. We rent the land, and our tenants help us with the work. Everyone prospers."

"I don't understand why we couldn't keep selling our cotton to those Europeans who have always been so eager for it. You can't convince me that the Yankees aren't putting a great deal of profit into their own pockets."

Camellia refused to be baited. Conspiratorial Yankees, greedy tax collectors, and uppity former slaves—these were the things that vexed Aunt Dahlia the most. As well as what she viewed as Camellia's foolish decision to marry a Yankee sympathizer at the end of the war.

"Jasper Calhoun went to Natchez Under-the-Hill last night to celebrate the demise of Les Fleurs." Jonah continued the story he'd already begun. "He bragged about the fire to anyone who would listen."

"Why would he do such a thing?" Nausea threatened to overwhelm Camellia as she considered how narrowly they had avoided disaster. "Jasper brought his family here for the Christmas celebration last year like all the other workers. He's worked here for most of the past five years. Did he hate us all that time?"

Jonah's dark gaze showed empathy for her pain. "Apparently, he's felt ill-used for quite some time. Then everything came to a head with our decision to appoint a new overseer to replace Mr. Smithson."

"But Nahum got that job." Camellia had agreed with her husband's choice of the hardworking, honest man. Like the Bible parable of the men given talents, Nahum had taken what he had and increased its worth. Both he and Jasper had been among their first sharecroppers but the differences between them were marked.

Nahum's home was one of the prettiest on the grounds—the yard was always well-kept, and his house received a fresh coat of whitewash every year. His pride was obvious in the way he took care of his home.

The windows at Jasper's cabin were stuffed with rags, his yard had more weeds than grass, and his field had one of the lowest yields, if not the lowest, each year. Furthermore, he never allowed his children to attend classes at her school, showing his lack of concern for their futures. With all that, why would he think he could handle more responsibility?

"Some people refuse to see the facts before them." Jonah sighed. "He seems to have gotten it into his head that he would receive the promotion based solely on the fact that Nahum is black and he's white."

"I have no patience for that kind of attitude." Camellia straightened her back and glanced at her aunt, whose gaze dropped to the table between them. "The true worth of a person has nothing to do with the color of his or her skin."

Jonah cleared his throat. "I spoke with the sheriff earlier this morning. He rode out here to find out what happened, and he's promised to locate Jasper and take him in for questioning."

"Do you really think he'll tell the sheriff the truth?" She was unable to keep the skepticism out of her voice. Bragging about his misdeeds under the influence of alcohol was one thing. Confessing to the law in the cold, sober light of day would be different.

Jonah's mouth quirked upward. "I think the sheriff has the expertise to separate truth from lies. I imagine Jasper will have to answer for what he's done."

"I'm sure your husband is right." Uncle Phillip exchanged a glance with Jonah. "Jasper Calhoun will be going to jail for a long time."

Camellia was glad to see evidence of the affection between the two men. Of course, men seemed to rub along better in most circumstances than women. If only she could convince Aunt Dahlia to let go of her prejudices long enough to give Jonah a chance. . . . What would it take for the older woman to do so? Prayer was the only option. She prayed for their family every day. And for everyone on the plantation, including the treacherous Jasper Calhoun. Camellia's mind wandered in another direction. "What about his poor wife and children? How will they manage without him?"

"With a little help from us, they may be better off than when he was living there." Jonah pulled out his pocket watch and flipped it open. "I'd better get back to work. We still have a lot of cleanup to do from the fire."

Putting down her napkin, Camellia rose at the same time as her husband. "I've moved the classroom to the back porch for the time being."

"That's probably a good idea." Jonah kissed her on the cheek. "It may take us a week or more to rebuild your schoolhouse. But when we do, it should be better than before."

"Which wouldn't take much." Camellia thought back to their decision to use the old cabin and shuddered. Imagining a large room with generous windows and a separate desk for each of her students, she shooed her husband out of the room and headed to the back of the plantation home.

She was so thankful to be married to Jonah Thornton, a man with an abiding love for Christ and a shared vision for what their life should be. No matter what men like Jasper Calhoun tried to do to stop them, they would always rise again, secure in God's promises for their future.

Jasmine's heart felt like it was going to burst. . .into blooming flowers or flocks of songbirds. She'd never been happier in her life. The butterflies that had taken wing last night danced about every time she thought of Vance. Was this love? If so, she never wanted it to end.

A giggle escaped her lips. She was happier than she'd ever been. . . all because of Vance Hargrove. He was handsome and interesting and knew everything there was to know about the world of acting. Had a girl ever been more blessed than she?

Everything was perfect. The sun was bright outside, and she and Sarah had entertained a steady stream of morning visitors. Vance had not been one of them, but he'd probably been involved in rehearsals. He would come see her this afternoon. And he was going to take her to Lake Pontchartrain tonight. Her life was perfect.

"I can't wait to tell Maman and Lily about your new beau." Sarah appeared at the parlor door in a dark brown riding dress cut to resemble a military uniform. The matching hat was smaller than the one she'd worn to the park the day before. Perched at a jaunty angle, it had a curled brim and a veil. "Once we've told them all about Mr. Hargrove, we'll all go shopping together. I've heard of a charming new dress shop in the French Quarter I'm dying to visit."

Jasmine's eyes grew rounder. She wondered how many trunks

of clothing Sarah owned. She had always thought of Camellia as a clotheshorse, but her sister practically dressed as a Quaker in comparison to her wealthy hostess. "What about your afternoon visitors?"

Sarah fixed her with a knowing look. "Never fear, cher. We will be back in plenty of time to see your beau. Now get your parasol and let's go."

The journey to the Thorntons' home was a repeat of the drive to the park. Staid. Jasmine was beginning to grow inured to the yells of the other drivers as they sought to pass the cabriolet. At least the roof had not been let down, and therefore she could lean back and avoid their angry glares. By the time they arrived, her excitement had dwindled some. But she was sure it would return once she saw Vance again.

She could hear the excited voices of Noah and Magnolia as they entered the townhouse. After surrendering hat and gloves to the Thorntons' butler, she followed Sarah to the front parlor. Blake rose from his seat, and the conversation between Lily and Tante Charlotte halted in the wake of their arrival.

Magnolia, who had been playing with her brother, stood and ran to them, throwing her arms around Jasmine's skirts. "I'm so glad you found us."

Blake chuckled. "We may have another actress in the family."

"I hope not." Lily's mouth straightened into a tight line. "One is more than enough."

The words were like a stab wound to her abdomen. Jasmine hid her pain by dropping a kiss on Magnolia's head, focusing her attention on her beautiful niece. "I'm glad I did, too."

Magnolia let go of her legs and rejoined Noah on the floor.

Why was her sister so critical of the one thing she wanted to do? Why couldn't she be a little more understanding and supportive of Jasmine's dreams? Her life on a riverboat had not followed a traditional path. Why did she have to be so judgmental when it came to what Jasmine wanted?

"Lily tells me you had a wonderful time at the performance last night." Tante Charlotte rose and moved toward her. "Let's go to the dining room and you can tell us all about it over luncheon."

Lily stood and beckoned to Noah and Magnolia. "I'll get the children settled upstairs, check on Benjamin to make sure he is still napping, and join you in a minute."

Jasmine counted only five place settings as they entered the dining room. "Where is everyone?"

"Oncle Lloyd has taken your papa and Miss Matthews on a tour of the shipping office." Tante Charlotte took her place at the table. "They are not supposed to return until later."

Blake pulled out both Sarah's and Jasmine's chairs. "I couldn't convince Jensen and Tamar to remain, either. He insists the *Water Lily* is not secure if he isn't there."

Sarah reached for her napkin as Blake went to the opposite side of the table. "He is a good friend."

"So tell us about your evening." Tante Charlotte reached for a large bowl of fresh fruit in front of her plate.

Jasmine took a deep breath, thankful for Sarah's encouraging glance. "It was magical, stupendous, better than I have ever enjoyed in my life."

"Our Jasmine has caught the eye of a very distinguished gentleman."

Lily walked into the room at that moment. "Whom did you meet?"

"His name is Vance Hargrove." Jasmine saw the glance her sister and brother-in-law exchanged. Her chin went up.

"I see." Lily's disapproval was back in full measure. But then it had probably never gone away.

Sarah handed her the bowl of fruit, and Jasmine spooned some berries onto her plate before passing the food to Blake. Had anyone ever been so misused? So poorly understood? The only sympathetic expressions she saw in the room did not come from her family.

"Mr. Hargrove joined us for dinner." Sarah's glance was warm and reassuring. "Kenneth and I were both impressed with his wit and charm."

"Where did you meet this debonair gentleman?" Suspicion filled Lily's words. "At the restaurant? Is he a friend of the family?"

Jasmine's stomach tensed. She knew her sister would not like the answer to her questions. "At the theater."

Sarah waved a hand in the air. "We met him when I took Jasmine backstage. A crush of visitors prevented us from meeting Miss Barlow, but Mr. Hargrove came to our rescue. I believe he is above reproach."

"I see." Lily didn't sound reassured by Sarah's recommendation.

Sarah turned her gaze on Jasmine. "Now is the time to ask your sister for permission."

Jasmine could feel the concerted stare of everyone at the table. She lifted her chin. "We've made plans to visit Lake Pontchartrain this evening."

Now Blake looked as stern as his wife. "Alone?"

"I don't like the sound of that, Jasmine." Lily put her fork down. "You cannot go to dinner alone with him. . .at least not until I've met him."

She should have known her sister would be this way. Lily didn't want her to have any tiny bit of freedom. She wanted to make Jasmine into a replica of herself. Anger boiled through her blood. "I'm a grown woman, and I can decide how to spend my evening."

"You may be, Jasmine, but you're far from mature." Lily pushed back from the table. "I blame myself for coddling you too much over the years. Perhaps I should have sent you to a finishing school like the one Camellia attended."

"I don't need a school. I need to be treated like an adult." Jasmine could see the frozen expressions on Tante Charlotte's and Sarah's faces. She regretted airing her grievances in front of them, but Lily had started this. She would not back down.

Tears stung her eyes, but Jasmine refused to give in to them. Her sister would use them as an example of her naïveté. Gritting her teeth, she glared across the table. "I'm practically a prisoner in my own home. My desires don't matter at all. I don't know why I'm even surprised by you, Lily. You never want me to have any fun or to experience true freedom."

"Be that as it may, I am still your sister. As long as you live with me, you will do as I say." Lily's voice was shaking. "I forbid you to go out with this Vance Hargrove tonight."

Thrusting her chair away from the table, Jasmine stood.

"Where do you think you're going?"

Jasmine directed her words toward Tante Charlotte. "Please excuse me, I don't feel well." Without waiting for a reply, she spun and marched from the room, her head high and her shoulders back. She had no idea where to go, but she knew she couldn't remain in the dining room. Not until Lily could be more reasonable.

"Was I wrong?" Lily folded her French silk scarf and laid it in the trunk she shared with Blake. She'd worn it last night to the theater and wouldn't need to use it again while they were in New Orleans. "Am I being unreasonable to want to meet this strange man before I trust my sister with him?"

Blake sighed. "No, not wrong. . .but you might have waited until you were alone with Jasmine before you told her how you felt."

Lily's first reaction to his words was betrayal, but her conscience prodded her to listen to him. Blake was right. She should have pinned a smile on her face while Jasmine described her evening. Telling her sister her concerns could have come later. While she considered the Thorntons to be family, they were not actually relatives. She should not have aired her concerns in front of them. Would she ever learn to control her tongue?

"I've ruined everything."

Her husband's blue gaze chided her for the passionate statement. "This is not the first or the last argument you'll have with Jasmine. The two of you want very different things out of life. You want her to settle down close to you and raise a family with someone like David Foster. Jasmine wants to see something of the world. She craves excitement and adventure—the very things you are denying her. She feels trapped here."

"Trapped? She can rant all she wants about freedom. Her family makes fewer demands on her than most young ladies."

"That doesn't matter." Blake pushed away from the mantel and moved toward her. "All your sister can see is the restrictions we've placed on her. I think I understand some of Jasmine's actions better than you do. I felt much like she does when I was young."

Lily put a hand to her forehead. "She *is* young. And naive. She understands so little about the ways of the world. I don't think I was ever as young as she is. Dealing with her sometimes makes me feel like I'm a hundred years old."

"I don't know about that." Catching her hand, Blake raised it to his lips. "You're well preserved for a centenarian."

She appreciated her husband's attempt to make her smile, but she couldn't make room for his levity. Not when she was so upset over the argument with Jasmine. "Why can't Jasmine understand that I have her best interests at heart? Can't she see that we're trying to protect her?"

"I doubt it." Blake's face sobered. "How did you feel when your relatives told you what to do?"

"That was different. They wanted me to marry a man twice my age." Lily ignored the petulant tone of her own words. Couldn't Blake see the truth? "I'm not trying to push her out into the world before she's ready."

"Maybe she's ready."

The world seemed to move under Lily's feet. She sat down hard on the edge of the bed, reaching for the headboard to keep from falling over. Jasmine was not ready. At the rate she was going, she wouldn't be ready for several years yet. What did Blake expect her to do? Stand by silently and watch her sister ruin her life? That's exactly what would happen if she let Jasmine have her way. Her plans for the evening were a perfect example. She spared not a thought for her own safety, blithely planning to go to some unnamed location with a man she had just met.

Blake took her hands and chafed them. "Are you okay?"

"Do you really think she's ready?" Lily searched his eyes for the truth.

"I only know that everyone in the family—from your father to Camellia—has given Jasmine the foundation she needs to succeed. And we'll be here to love her no matter what else happens to her." He placed a soft kiss on her cheek. "Once she's tested her wings, she'll have a better perspective."

"I don't want her to get hurt."

"Everyone gets hurt, Lily. That's the way of this world. You can't be there for her at every turn. You're going to have to trust God to watch out for her."

Peace slipped into the room with his words, giving her a little protection from the fear that nipped her. Blake pulled her up from the bed and drew her into his embrace. His heartbeat sounded beneath her ear, its rhythmic beating as slow and steady as the thrum of a paddlewheel. Lily felt the prickles of worry ebbing even further as she stood within the circle of his arms. She closed her eyes and thanked God silently for linking their lives.

Blake was right. What had happened to her faith in the Lord's provision? She would give Jasmine the freedom she craved. She would even let her sister go out with Vance Hargrove once she made sure he understood the consequences of stepping out of line.

A knock at the door separated them. Blake sent her a reassuring smile before he went to answer it. Lily took a deep breath and prayed for the right words to use with Jasmine. She would have to apologize first. And no matter how hard it was, she would have to allow Jasmine to make her own mistakes. She would be a support to her sister's dreams instead of an obstacle.

Lily's heart fell as she realized Jasmine was not their visitor.

Sarah was the one standing in the doorway, a guilty expression on her face. "I'm so sorry for causing this trouble."

Blake performed a shallow bow. "I believe I'll check on the children and allow the two of you a little privacy."

He disappeared into the hallway as Sarah advanced into the room. Lily felt some of the peace leave with him.

Putting on a polite expression, she focused on Sarah. "It's not your fault. Jasmine and I have been feuding with great regularity over the past months."

Unshed tears moistened Sarah's eyes. "But this latest argument is my fault, and I've come to see how I can mend it."

"I'm the one who will have to do that." Lily perched on the edge of the bed again. "But you can tell me about this Hargrove character. Do you trust him? Is he from New Orleans? Do you know his family?"

"Yes. No. And no." Sarah sat beside her and sniffed. "His manners are exquisite. I would trust my own daughter with him."

Lily was still uncertain, despite Sarah's assurances. She needed to know more than what kind of manners he had learned. What sort of man was he? Could he be trusted to treat her sister with respect?

"I believe he said that he came from New York." Sarah's eyes narrowed as she thought. "At least he said he performed in New York. He's even spent some time in Europe. I remember your sister asking if he had ever met the divine Sarah Bernhardt. . ."

A woman of dubious reputation herself. Lily kept her opinion to herself as Sarah continued prattling on about Hargrove's exploits. If the man had done half the things he claimed, he would have to be more than thirty years old. What interest would a man of that age see in her sister? Lily shuddered as she considered the possible answers.

"Wouldn't that fix everything?" Sarah's question hung in the air between them.

Lily scrambled to recall what suggestion the other woman had made. Something about dinner tonight. Comprehension dawned. Sarah had suggested they go out to dinner together and invite Mr. Hargrove to join them. That way she could meet the man and judge for herself if he was an appropriate escort for her sister. "You're right." Lily smiled at her. "At least, I'm not sure that it will fix *everything* between Jasmine and me, but it will go a long way toward healing this latest breach."

Sarah's hug was scented with a floral fragrance that made Lily's nose itch. "I had hoped we could go shopping, but this is more important. I'll collect your sister right away. We'll go back home and word an invitation to him." She stood and swept toward the door. "I'm sure he'll agree. And then you can see for yourself what a nice man he is."

Lily sneezed twice in swift succession.

The sound turned Sarah around. "I hope you're not catching a cold. That would unravel all of our plans."

Holding a finger under her nose to avoid another sneeze, Lily shook her head. "Don't worry. I'm sure it's only temporary. I never get sick."

She went to the trunk and drew out her silk scarf. It seemed she would need it again after all.

Chapter Thirteen

Vance Hargrove was standing in the Cartiers' foyer when Jasmine and Sarah returned. Jasmine's breath caught when she saw the large bouquet he had in his hand. Blood red roses and parchment-hued lilies nodded as he swept a bow. "I was so cast down to learn that you were out, Miss Anderson. I had thought to leave this little token with your butler, but now I do not have to deny myself the pleasure of giving them to you myself."

Jasmine thought she might swoon with the pleasure of the moment. The recent scene at the Thorntons' house faded as she once again looked into Mr. Hargrove's coffee-colored gaze.

He offered the flowers to her.

"They're beautiful." Jasmine buried her nose in them, enjoying the sweet aroma.

Mr. Hargrove put a hand on his chest. "They're not half as lovely as you are. But alas, they were the prettiest blooms in the shop."

Sarah sighed. "Will you give us a moment, Mr. Hargrove? Jasmine and I need to freshen up a bit. You can make yourself comfortable in the music room while you wait."

"Of course." He kept his hand on his chest. "I would wait twice—no thrice—as long for your company."

Jasmine floated up the stairs behind Sarah. She put the flowers in her water pitcher for the time being, pulled off her hat and gloves, and sat down in front of her mirror. Her mouth was slightly parted, and her eyes glowed with pleasure. At least her coiffure was not windblown from the drive. She pinched her cheeks and checked her collar to make certain it was still pristine. The dress she had worn to lunch would have to suffice as she had not brought an extensive wardrobe with her.

Putting a hand on her stomach to still the fluttery feelings that had returned, she rose and walked to the bureau that held her pitcher and basin. Should she take the flowers with her so one of Sarah's maids could put them in a vase? Already the heady fragrance filled her bedroom. Deciding to leave the flowers where they were for the moment, she went in search of a fan. If Mr. Hargrove continued his compliments she was sure to need it.

Wondering why Sarah had instructed their guest to go to the music room instead of the parlor where she usually entertained visitors, Jasmine slipped down the stairs. She could hear the *plink* of a piano chord and wished she knew how to play. Perhaps Mr. Hargrove did. Of course singing was another accomplishment she lacked. Which meant she would never get any parts in operettas or other productions requiring singing.

She peeked into the room to see if Sarah had arrived before her, but the room was empty except for the tall man towering over the keyboard. With a deep breath, she swept into the room, her skirts rustling around her. "Thank you for waiting, Mr. Hargrove."

He spun around, and a wide smile broke out on his face. "That didn't take long. Dare I hope you are as anxious for my company as I am for yours?"

Why had she pinched her cheeks? They were bound to be flaming at the moment.

Sarah swept into the room before Jasmine could come up with an answer to his daring question. "Mr. Hargrove, I know you and Jasmine made plans to visit the beach at Pontchartrain this evening, but I have an alternative invitation for you."

Jasmine could not have been more surprised if Sarah had pulled out a pistol and aimed it at her heart. This was the first she'd heard of a new arrangement. Lily might have forbidden her outing, but as an adult Jasmine could arrange her time according to her own desires.

"Jasmine's sister was so upset she didn't get a chance to meet you last night." Sarah's laugh tinkled. "She saw you on the stage, and I believe she was a bit jealous that we got to share a meal with you while she was stuck at dinner with my parents."

At least Sarah had come up with a good excuse to give the man. But Jasmine knew the real reason for the suggestion. Lily was determined to control her life.

"I. . .of course I would be delighted." Vance looked confused. And why not? He was probably not familiar with meddling relatives.

She wouldn't have thought it was possible for anyone to extract the pleasure from her visit with Vance. Her lips thinned. If she got a chance to talk to Vance alone before he left, she would tell him that they need not change their plans. Or maybe she could send a note to the theater. She would make some excuse to Sarah and Kenneth and send them off to dinner with her sister. As long as Vance didn't arrive before they departed, the two of them could still go to Pontchartrain together. Alone.

"Excellent." Sarah looked pleased with herself. Her smile encompassed both Jasmine and Vance. "And now, if you don't mind, I am going to the parlor. I'm expecting a few of my friends to drop by for tea."

Masking her surprise, Jasmine nodded. She had never thought the opportunity to talk to Vance alone would be so easy.

Sarah paused at the doorway. "Make sure you don't close this door. I would hate for Lily to think I wasn't being careful of your reputation."

Jasmine's cheeks flushed again. She opened her fan and used it to cool her face. Her gaze met Vance's. Was he laughing at her? Her family?

The room was furnished with half-a-dozen straight-backed chairs, arranged in rows for musical evenings. Choosing one on the front row, she sank into it, her fan fluttering fast enough to lift her collar. "I. . .I'm sorry about—"

"Don't apologize." He sat next to her, his voice pitched low. "I think you've seen that I know how to make myself popular with chaperones."

Jasmine doubted her sister would be won over by a few compliments. Besides, she didn't intend to remain under Lily's thumb any longer. She would be free no matter what it took. "You don't have to do that. I'd much rather spend the evening alone with you."

Vance took her hands in his own, pulling her fan away and placing it on the chair behind him. "I would like that, too, but I don't want to cause you any trouble."

"What is going on in here?" David's voice caused Jasmine to jump.

Vance dropped his grip on her hands and stood to face the man at the door, the man whose eyes blazed green lightning.

Something must be wrong with Jasmine's heart. It felt like a frightened bird trying to escape a hunter's noose. She lifted her chin and willed it to slow down. She had done nothing wrong. Her eyes narrowed. Was Lily behind David's appearance, too? It would make sense as she had seen nothing of him for the past day and a half. Her chin went up another notch. Would she ever be free of chaperones?

❧

David could hardly believe he'd walked in on Jasmine making eyes at some stranger. Had she lost her mind? She glared at him like he was the one in the wrong, but he refused to accept any blame. He had not closeted himself with an unmarried lady. Which led him to another question. Where was Sarah Cartier?

"I suppose this is another of your swains?" The stranger's question interrupted their staring match.

"What?" Jasmine looked as though she'd forgotten he was in the room.

"Not at all." It was one of those moments when David knew exactly what to say. He smiled at Jasmine, causing her eyes to narrow in suspicion. But she need not worry. She was the one who had suggested their relationship after all. "Jasmine is my sister."

He felt the twin pricks of their stares. Jasmine looked as though he had slapped her. Then guilt entered her expression. It was too late for that. And posing as her brother would scare off the man he'd found her with. The man who shouldn't be alone with her.

"Indeed?" The stranger infused a large measure of disbelief into the two syllables.

Jasmine briefly closed her eyes. All the color had drained from her cheeks. For a moment David almost recanted. But then she opened her eyes. The deep purple in them seemed sad, mournful even.

"David, this is Mr. Hargrove. Mr. Vance Hargrove." The way she said the man's name made it obvious she thought David should know him.

Unable to put any significance on the name, David gave a brief nod.

"It's a pleasure to make your acquaintance, Mr. Anderson." Hargrove offered his hand, and David shook it, barely managing to suppress the urge to wipe his hand on his trousers afterward.

"Mr. Hargrove is a famous actor here in New Orleans." Jasmine recovered her composure and cast an admiring glance in his direction. "He is the star of a current production."

Which explained Jasmine's fascination with the man. David ignored Hargrove. "Where is your chaperone?"

Another wave of red darkened her cheeks. "Sarah is in the parlor."

"Does she know you're in here with. . .him?" David couldn't bring himself to repeat the man's name. He didn't like Vance Hargrove. He didn't like the shiftiness in his eyes or the wet gleam of his pomaded hair. He didn't like his voice or his clothes. But the thing he didn't like the most was the admiring glances he was exchanging with Jasmine. Something was not right. It made David itch to pull Jasmine out of the music room—get her to a safe place and convince her to avoid any future dealings with the actor.

"Of course she does." Jasmine sniffed. "Not that it's any of your business, but Sarah left a few moments ago and told us to leave the door open."

"I see." David walked to the piano and sat on the stool, resting his arm across the keys. Sarah might trust Hargrove to act the gentleman, but he didn't. Looking at the man put him in mind of a snake. A snake on the hunt for prey.

"Are you enjoying your visit to New Orleans?" Hargrove directed the question toward him.

"David is working." Jasmine answered the question for him.

"Yes," he interrupted her. "I'm working my way through every bar and card game in town."

"I suppose that's why you didn't join your sister at the theater last night."

David hid a yawn behind his hand. "I had more than one reason to choose other entertainment."

An understanding smile curved Hargrove's lips. "Have you enjoyed much success?"

"Not yet." He winked at the man. "But I'm sure my luck is about to change."

Jasmine was wearing a frown as her gaze bounced between him and Hargrove. At least she didn't challenge him. She had enough sense to know he had a reason for his falsehood.

Hargrove bowed to Jasmine. "I do have an appointment this afternoon, but I'll see you this evening."

David felt the hair on the back of his neck rising. He didn't like the idea of the two of them spending any time together.

The actor turned to David. "It was a pleasure to meet another member of Jasmine's family. I'm looking forward to meeting your other sister this evening."

This sounded much better. David allowed a little smile to relax the muscles of his face. Lily and Blake would put an end to the man's pretensions. "I'm sure you'll have a wonderful time."

Jasmine stood. "Let me show you the way to the front door."

Having risen when his "sister" did, David made as if to accompany them. Jasmine's warning glare stopped him, however. "I need to talk to you after you see Mr. Hargrove out."

She nodded and reached for the arm the actor presented. "I'll be right back."

David returned to the stool and tapped an impatient rhythm on the wooden top of the piano as he waited for her.

It took several long moments, but she finally reappeared, her cheeks suspiciously red. "Why did you lie to Vance about who you are?"

"Because you were about to tell him I'm a Pinkerton detective."

"At least it's the truth." She lifted that chin of hers again.

He pushed a hand through his hair. "I don't need everyone in town to know my business."

"But the Thorntons and Cartiers know. And Papa. And Aunt Tessie. Jensen and Tamar, too." She ticked off the names on her fingers as she listed them.

"They are all either family or close friends."

"Well, Vance is a close friend of mine."

"A close friend? How well do you even know him? Where is he from? How long has he been in New Orleans? Does he have family here? You don't know anything about him except that he's an actor."

"I can tell what kind of man Vance is by looking in his eyes and listening to him."

David couldn't believe how foolish she was being. Jasmine couldn't really think she knew Vance well enough to consider him a trusted friend. "We aren't children anymore. You seem to think life is nothing but a game, a theatrical production that will end after all the lines are spoken. But it's not. People aren't always what they seem."

"Vance Hargrove is." She turned on her heel and stomped toward the door.

"Be careful with that man." David raised his voice so she could hear him even in the hallway. "I don't want to have to pull you out of any scrapes."

"Don't worry." Her voice floated back to him. "You're the last one I would call on, dear brother."

His elbow slipped off the piano, hitting several keys and producing a discordant noise that made him wince. He supposed he would have to allow her the last word. His threat had been an empty one, and she probably knew it. David would always come to her rescue. Whether she returned his affection or not, he would always be there for her.

Chapter Fourteen

Lily winced as her amethyst earbob clamped down on the tender portion of her earlobe. She didn't like having to wear jewelry. It pinched and poked. But the jewelry was a gift from her husband. And they matched her lavender dress. She settled the matching piece on her other ear. She would make the sacrifice for his sake.

"What do you think I should say to Jasmine?" She glanced at his reflection in the mirror above the bureau.

Blake pulled his suspenders over his shoulders and attached them to the high waist of his trousers. "Dwell on the things you have in common instead of your differences. Let love guide you instead of your mothering instinct."

She leaned her head to one side as she considered the advice. "I want her to have a good time this evening."

"Then we should be taking her back to the theater instead of to dinner."

Lily walked to the bed and picked up her husband's black frock coat. "But we went to the theater last night."

He slid one arm into a sleeve before turning slightly to reach for the other one. As soon as the material was on his shoulders, Lily reached up and smoothed it. "I doubt Jasmine would complain if we returned every night while we're in New Orleans. Your sister loves the theater. She has ever since she was a child, and I don't look for her to change anytime soon."

A part of Lily dreaded the evening. But she needed to talk to Jasmine and reassure her that she would be more reasonable. She didn't want to drive her sister away. She wanted to avoid the type of division that Blake and his father had experienced. Spending the afternoon praying had helped, but Lily wondered if she would be able to maintain her calm.

"It's going to be okay, Lily." Blake put his hands on her shoulders and leaned over to kiss her.

Lily melted into his embrace, letting her fears go. She clung to him, wanting to remain in his arms a little longer before facing the people waiting for them in the parlor.

Blake hugged her tight before letting go and offering his arm. "You are looking very lovely this evening, Mrs. Matthews."

"Thank you, Mr. Matthews." Lily accepted his compliment with a smile. "You look very handsome yourself."

His tender look buoyed her. Blake believed in her. She sent a silent plea to heaven that his faith was not misplaced. And for patience and wisdom in dealing with Jasmine.

They negotiated the stairs side by side and entered the parlor together. Kenneth stood, and Sarah looked up as they entered. Lily glanced around the room, her face tightening into a frown. "Where is Jasmine?"

"Don't worry, dearest." Sarah stood and rushed across the room, her satin dress rustling in the quiet room. "Your sister wasn't feeling well this evening. I'm sure it had nothing to do with that little tiff between you. She had several visitors this morning and then again this afternoon."

Lily wanted to forget their plans for the evening and rush over to the Cartiers' home to check on her sister. She turned to Sarah's husband. "Did you see her? Is she coming down with something?"

Kenneth shook his head. "She had no fever, only a few nebulous complaints. I'm sure it's nothing that a restful night's sleep won't cure."

"I shouldn't have forbidden her to see that man." Despair laced her words. No matter what Sarah thought, it had to be the argument that had prevented Jasmine from coming. Her sister didn't want to be around her. The thought pained her. Where had she gone wrong? And how could she make it right?

Sarah put an arm around her waist and drew her toward the sofa. "That's not it at all, Lily."

"It has to be." Lily sat down and put her face in her hands.

"No." Sarah touched her arm. "Mr. Hargrove was coming to dinner with us until I sent him a message that your sister was not feeling well."

Lily lifted her head.

"He was at my home when we returned this afternoon. He's such a gentleman. I can understand why Jasmine would find him attractive. He presented her with a beautiful bouquet. And he is so handsome, so polished. When I invited him to dinner as you and I discussed, he accepted most graciously. Both he and Jasmine seemed pleased by the idea."

The information from Sarah set her head spinning. "Then I wonder why Jasmine decided not to come?"

"It is evident that you don't need to worry so." Blake offered his reassurance from the other side of the sofa. "If Jasmine was as smitten with him as you thought, she would have joined us, no matter how she felt."

Her husband's thoughts matched hers. Jasmine was as determined as any member of the Anderson family. No headache would have prevented her if she really wanted to see this Hargrove fellow.

Was Kenneth wrong? Was Jasmine sicker than he realized? That made no sense. Sarah's husband was a renowned doctor. He would recognize any symptoms.

The temptation to excuse herself and go across town to check on her sister was strong. Lily glanced around the room, her mind considering and discarding half-a-dozen excuses. But in the end, she realized she had only one course to follow. She couldn't wreck all their plans to go and check on Jasmine tonight. Holding onto an image of Jasmine sitting in bed, a cap on her head and a book leaned against her knees, Lily stood. "Shall we get going?"

Blake's gaze met hers, and he sent her an approving smile. The dread that had been building in her chest eased some. Jasmine was safe. And the two of them might do better with a little more breathing time.

This was a first step in allowing her sister to make her own decisions, an olive branch of good intentions. Perhaps it would help heal the breach between them.

The *Smoky Mary* was well named. Thick billows of gray smoke blew past them as the train picked up speed. But Jasmine could endure a little discomfort on her adventure. The *Water Lily*'s twin smokestacks were almost as obnoxious at times.

She still couldn't believe how easy it had been to slip away from the Cartiers' home. When Vance had called for her, after the departure of her host and hostess, Jasmine had blithely told the servants that she was going out.

The butler had not looked pleased, but he had not said anything. What could he say? He was not her father or any other relative. She was free. Finally free.

"I'm glad you managed to keep our assignation." Vance shared the narrow bench with her, his knee a bare inch from hers.

She giggled and fluttered her lashes at him. She'd practiced the move in front of her mirror all afternoon while she pretended illness. Apparently her hard work paid off. His scorching glance made her feel heady. And powerful. Maybe he wouldn't think her so innocent now.

When he put his arm on the bench behind her head, however, Jasmine gulped. She didn't want him to think she had no morals. Leaning forward, she pretended interest in the passing scenery. "How long before we arrive?"

He must have understood the message because Vance withdrew his arm. "Our destination is less than five miles away."

Relief coursed through her. He was too much a gentleman to make her uncomfortable. "How did you come to be in New Orleans?"

"I suppose you could say it is Tabitha Barlow's fault." He rubbed his hand on his pants leg. "She and I were performing in Dickens's play *No Thoroughfare*. Are you familiar with it?"

"Yes. I've read it, anyway. But I've never seen it performed."

"We were receiving wonderful reviews, but then the theater owner closed us down three months ago." Vance sent a winning smile in her direction. "So we came here. Tabitha has performed in the city in the past, so she had plenty of contacts."

A pang of jealousy drowned Jasmine's butterflies. Did Vance love Miss Barlow? He had been waiting in the hallway outside her door when she first met him. "Are you m—married to her?"

His laughter rang out, turning heads of some of the other passengers. "No, dearest Jasmine. We are friends, of course, and business associates. Once you begin working in the arts, you will understand how it works."

She opened her fan with a snap and used it to cool her cheeks. Jasmine felt like an adolescent schoolgirl. Vance must think her ignorant. She was afraid to say anything else and reveal to him her lack of knowledge.

Vance leaned forward to get her attention. "I believe I should be offended. Do you really think me such a scoundrel that I would pursue a lady while my wife pined for me at home?"

Jasmine's hand redoubled the speed of her fan. "No, that's not. . . I mean I just thought. . . I—"

"Don't." His dark eyes sparkled in the fading light. "I was only teasing you a little. I'm sorry. I didn't mean to upset you, Jasmine."

She let her fan drift to her lap as she stared into Vance's eyes, noticing for the first time the dark band of black that outlined his pupils. His smile disappeared. Why would his serious face cause her heart to stutter? Jasmine swallowed hard as she lost all sense of her surroundings. Vance Hargrove was the most exciting, most mature man she'd ever known. He made her feel both desirable and gauche at the same time.

The train lurched to a stop, breaking the spell between them. Vance stood and offered her his hand. "For the rest of the evening I'll do better, Jasmine. I promise not to tease or scare you anymore."

She managed a smile and put her hand in his. But she was beginning to wonder if she was completely out of her depth. They disembarked from the train, and she looked around. The town of Milneburg was not what she'd expected. In a way it reminded her of river towns. The waterfront was crowded with boats and rickety buildings. Even the water seemed filled with houses, suspended on long lines of piers. One two-story house had a wide porch on all four sides and a smaller guesthouse behind it.

Even though the sun had set, dozens of people walked on the lantern-strewn paths, some showing the effects of alcohol. Somewhere in the distance, a horn played a lively tune she didn't recognize.

The spirit of adventure which had begun their evening together returned to Jasmine. She intercepted an appreciative glance from one of the women walking past, and a secret sparkle coursed through her. She knew jealousy when she saw it.

"Do you like seafood?"

Jasmine wrinkled her nose. "We eat a lot of fish on my sister's boat."

"Ah." He changed direction, guiding her away from a huge white gazebo with exotic-looking parapets on top. "Then I believe we'll need to avoid the music pavilion."

As they left the crowds behind, the sound of frogs and crickets filled the air. Jasmine's footsteps slowed. "Where are we going?"

"Don't you trust me, little Jasmine?" He stopped and looked down at her. "I would tell you that I'm taking you to a pirate's hidden treasure, but I promised not to tease you. I know of an intimate little café I think you'll like."

Jasmine studied his face and tried to decide if he was being serious. Taking a deep breath, she nodded. " 'Lay on, Macduff.' "

His chuckle was so attractive. Unpretentious and open. Exactly like Vance's personality. " 'Hold! Enough!' "

She was pleased that he recognized her quote from Macbeth. It was something no one in her family would have done. No matter how many times she read to them from the classic plays of Shakespeare, they didn't understand. She was finally in the company of someone who did. And it felt like coming home.

Chapter Fifteen

Andrew Jackson held his seat on the rearing bronze horse, one of his hands loose on the reins, while the military hero held a "fore and aft" hat aloft in the other. When he had looked at the statue earlier in the day, David had thought Andrew looked calm and in control. The way David wanted to feel. But he knew many things could go wrong with his plan to discover who controlled the ring of successful bank robbers. Like the Union general who had added an inscription during the occupation of New Orleans, he believed he had a responsibility to uphold the law of the land. The words General Benjamin Butler had ordered were simple but profound—The Union Must and Shall be Preserved.

A hissing sound made him look at the constable crouched a few feet away behind a palm tree. "What time is it?"

"Five minutes later than the last time you asked." David kept his voice low. If the informant heard them, he would realize what was happening and disappear. They would not get the information they needed or an additional arrest. "He'll be here soon."

Gas lamps cast a sickly glow on Petrie's face as he leaned against the cast-iron fence surrounding the statue. David hoped he would remember their instructions. He would tell the man he was meeting that the police were about to close in on the ringleader because their group harbored a traitor. He would claim to know the informant's name but refuse to give it to his cohort in case the man was working with the snitch. Once he had the leader's name, Petrie would raise his right hand and place it on his head as a signal for David and the constable to rush in and make their arrest.

David shifted his position and let his mind wander to earlier, more pleasant visits to Jackson Square. He and Jasmine had explored the area many times during visits to the city. They had chased each other around the palm trees and bushes on the outside borders of the square. Tonight that same greenery was providing cover for himself and Constable Longineaux as they waited for Charlie Petrie's contact to arrive.

A shadow separated from the alley between St. Louis Cathedral and the Cabildo. David's heart rate increased. This might be it. He put a finger over his lips to warn Longineaux and bent his head in the direction of the cathedral.

Petrie must have heard footsteps even though the statue blocked his view of the man approaching. He glanced over his shoulder once toward the position where David and the constable waited, pushed away from the fence, and stood with his feet planted wide.

Filtering out the sounds of gaiety coming from the Café du Monde on the river side of the square, David stretched his hearing as far as he could manage. They were too far away. He couldn't hear a single word.

He raised his hand to tell Longineaux to stay here and slowly rose to avoid making any noise. The lawn between him and the two men didn't offer any hiding places, but it was dark enough that he should be able to avoid detection. David took a step onto the grass, moving with deliberate, quiet precision. He listened intently, but the men were whispering. Was Petrie betraying them?

It was a risk he'd convinced Lieutenant Moreau to take. Petrie could run, but he had to know he would be caught. Too many people knew what he looked like. During the trial, someone had taken a photograph of him that had appeared in the *Picayune*. He wouldn't get far.

He hoped Petrie would remember what he'd been told. The only way for him to avoid the noose was to give them the leader of his gang—not just the other members.

A carriage drove down the street, and David dropped to the ground. He didn't want the coachman's lamp to expose his position. Dirt clogged his mouth and nose, making him want to sneeze. He rolled over on his back and clamped a hand across his face until the need passed.

"You'd better be telling me the truth—" The phrase caught his attention. It sounded like their plan was working.

Petrie was talking now, his mumbled words defying translation. David turned over again and crawled forward. Just a few more feet and he should be able to hear everything.

A sound made him look back over his shoulder. What he saw brought his heart up into his throat. Longineaux had left his hiding place. Wanting to blister the man's ears for not following orders, David waited as he crept forward in a crouch.

Disaster struck with the suddenness of a lightning bolt. Longineaux tripped over some unseen obstacle and fell forward. With a loud *thud*.

"Who is that?" The shadowy figure shouted the question as he lunged toward Petrie. "What have you done? You're the filthy traitor."

Petrie staggered backward two steps as David got to his feet and made a dash toward them, his focus on the unknown crook. Out of the corner of his eye, he saw Petrie grab his stomach and fall to his knees, but he kept his attention on the other man.

David pulled his Smith and Wesson revolver and aimed it. The chance of hitting the man at this distance was slim, but he had to try. He planted his feet and held the weapon in both hands, drawing the hammer back and squeezing the trigger in one fluid motion. The loud report was followed by a grunt. His target staggered but kept moving forward. Before David could fire again, he was gone, swallowed up by the shadows of Orleans Alley.

"Foster, come back." The constable's voice sounded frightened. "You can't go into that alley alone."

He took a couple of strides forward before stopping. Longineaux was right. He trotted back to the center of the square, his jaw clenched. Petrie was on his back, groaning. A dark shadow spread over his shirt and onto the ground. Blood. A lot of blood.

David breathed a prayer for the man's soul as he dropped to his knees and pulled Petrie's hand away from his stomach. It was bad. He stripped off his coat and used it to try and staunch the blood.

"I'm sorry." Longineaux stood over them, wringing his hands. "It's my fault."

"We'll deal with that later." David bit out the words as he applied pressure on the wound. "For now you need to get help before he dies."

He didn't look up as Longineaux ran toward Levee Street. Even as he prayed for God to spare Petrie's life, he had the feeling the stab wounds were fatal. Even if a surgeon of Kenneth Cartier's caliber were kneeling next to him, it might be too late to save Charlie Petrie's life.

"How bad?" Petrie choked out the question between painful gasps.

David ignored his intuition and summoned a smile. "You're doing fine. Save your strength for when the doctor arrives."

Seconds ticked by and still no one came. Blood oozed around the fabric of his coat, filling the air with the scent of copper. David pushed harder, trying to stem the flow.

Petrie groaned and put a hand over David's. "O–O. . .fee—" A dry cough cut off his groan.

David's sympathy rose. He wished he could ease the dying man's pain. "I'm sorry, I didn't bring a canteen."

Petrie shook his head, coughed again. His eyes opened wide, and he reached up with one blood-smeared hand, his fingers catching David's shirt collar and dragging him closer. "Ophelia."

"What?" David could make no sense of the word. Why would Petrie mention a woman's name? He leaned an inch closer, hoping for more details. . .a last name. . .anything.

The hand on his collar went slack, and David sat back. Looking down he realized his question was futile. Petrie's eyes stared sightlessly at the sky. He was dead.

❧

Jasmine wondered if Vance would try to kiss her before returning her to the Cartiers' home. And would she allow him such liberties or risk being considered too provincial? But she couldn't allow him to kiss her. Yet the thought of his lips pressing against hers made her stomach attempt a somersault.

Pirate's Cove, the cozy restaurant he had chosen for their dinner, was conducive to a romantic rendezvous. Most of the couples sat next to each other instead of on opposite sides of their tables. This arrangement led them to all sorts of risqué behavior, from eating off of their partner's forks to nuzzling each other's necks. She was glad Vance sat across from her, even though his dark gaze had more than once made her breath catch.

Vance picked up the wine bottle he'd ordered and poured an additional amount in his goblet. "Would you care for some more?"

Jasmine shook her head. She had tried a sip but could not imagine why someone would choose to drink such a nasty-tasting beverage. "No thank you."

He leaned back and raised a hand to summon a waiter. "We are finished with our meal."

"I hate for the evening to end." Jasmine watched as their plates were whisked away.

A burning gaze from Vance threatened to consume her. "Perhaps we can return on Friday. I could rent a camp and let you experience the coolness of a bath in the lake."

Jasmine tried to hide her shock. Sharing a meal with him was risky enough for her reputation. What he was proposing now sounded scandalous. If any members of her family heard him, they would definitely forbid any further contact.

"I—my sister is planning to return to Natchez soon."

His facial muscles drooped. "So soon? I thought you would remain in New Orleans for a while."

The disappointment in his voice resettled her composure. She must have misunderstood Vance's intent. He cared for her. Was he falling in love with her? The idea took root in her mind. They would share the limelight and fame, acting together as they traveled all over the United States and perhaps to Europe. They could even form their own troupe.

"I wish I could stay here, but I doubt Lily will allow it." She grimaced at the memory of the angry words she had tossed at her sister earlier in the day. Jasmine raised her chin. It was really Lily's fault. Lily was not her mother. She needed to realize that Jasmine was a grown woman and could make her own decisions.

Vance dropped several bills on the table and stood. "When will you leave?"

"Far too soon." She pushed back her chair and headed for the entrance.

Instead of offering his arm, Vance placed his hand at the small of her back. "Even if you could remain several weeks, it wouldn't be enough time to suit me."

Gooseflesh erupted on Jasmine's arms. She was simultaneously freezing and burning. If this was what love felt like, she understood why her sisters had married. She wanted to spend all of her time with Vance. The thought of being separated from him was like a dagger to the heart.

They walked back to the train station and waited. "Thank you for bringing me here, Vance. It's been a wonderful evening."

"It is my pleasure." His gaze spoke volumes to her, promising constancy and passion, a love to last for all of eternity. "I've been the envy of every man within the resort."

Perhaps she would let him kiss her after all.

They boarded the train, sitting even closer than they had on the trip to the lake. His knee pressed against hers. His arm, warm and muscular, slipped across the back of the seat. This time she didn't lean forward.

He leaned close and whispered in her ear. "Jasmine, I have a confession to make."

Her breath caught. Was he about to declare his love?

"I cannot bear the thought of separation."

Jasmine shivered when he pulled his arm from the back of the seat.

But then he took possession of her hands, capturing them with his long fingers. "I wasn't going to tell you this, but I, too, am leaving New Orleans, although not as quickly as you."

Her heart fell, and she began to breathe again.

"Then why did you suggest we spend more time together?" Jasmine tried to pull her hands free, but Vance tightened his grasp.

"Please let me explain. I am not hiding anything from you, Jasmine. I didn't tell you my plans earlier because I thought we would have more time together. I know how young and innocent you are, and I don't want to frighten you."

She lifted her chin. "I'm not a child."

He smiled at her words. "And I am most grateful for that fact. What I feel toward you would not be appropriate if you were."

Jasmine stopped trying to pull away. "Oh!" A fleeting memory of Sarah's round mouth occurred to her. She hoped she looked as graceful.

"Tabitha. . .Miss Barlow. . .and I have received contracts to join a troupe on one of the showboats. I have not decided for sure, but I think it would be fun to cruise up and down the river for a while. The crowds every night would be different, and we would get to see so much more of the countryside than the view from the windows of a stagecoach."

"So you are going to join this troupe?" Her mind whirled. A showboat. What she would give to accompany him. It would be such a wonderful experience.

He nodded. "I think there might be room for one more."

The meaning of his words burst upon her like an explosion of fireworks on the Fourth of July. He wanted her to come with him. He didn't want to be separated from her any more than she did from him. No meddling family to chastise her. No rules to follow. Just her and Vance and crowds of adoring theatergoers. "Do you really mean it?"

He squeezed her hands and lifted them to shower kisses on her knuckles. "Of course I mean it. You would be perfect. Your fresh face and knowledge of the classics would be perfect."

Jasmine's toes curled in her shoes. She would do it. She would talk to Lily and Blake, tell them about this wonderful opportunity, and— A door slammed in her mind. When had Lily ever understood her dreams? "I can't."

Vance raised his head and stared into her eyes. "What do you mean?" He dropped her hands and shifted away from her. "Have I misread your feelings? Are you toying with me?"

She reached for his hand. "No, of course not. I. . .I think I may be falling in love with you."

He turned back to her, confusion bringing a frown to his handsome face. "Then why?"

"It's my family. They don't understand me. Lily is determined to ruin my life."

"I see." Vance's sorrowful tones wrung her heart. "Your feelings for them are stronger than your feelings for me."

Jasmine put a hand on his arm. "That's not it at all. Please believe me when I say I want to join you more than anything."

"Then you must change your mind." He ran a finger down the side of her face. "You must find a way to join me on the showboat. It would break my heart to think of never seeing you again."

The train lurched to a stop before she could answer him. Jasmine gathered her things and tried to keep the tears out of her eyes. She had to find a way to convince Lily to let her follow her heart.

"Didn't you say that your family is returning to Natchez?"

Jasmine nodded, her throat too clogged to allow speech.

Vance snapped his fingers. "That is the answer then. The *Ophelia* won't leave New Orleans for a week or so, but I know we'll be stopping in Vicksburg by the end of the month. That is not far from Natchez. You can convince your family and join us there."

She didn't want to tell him she doubted Lily would ever change her mind.

They walked back to the Cartiers' home in silence as she tried to imagine a future without Vance Hargrove. It was inconceivable. And yet no less so than getting Lily's blessing on her becoming Mrs. Vance Hargrove.

Chapter Sixteen

David kicked the leg of a chair, sending it tumbling to the floor. "Think, man. Petrie used his dying breath to give us that name. It had to be important to him."

Constable Longineaux jumped in response, making David feel like a jerk. He shouldn't take out his frustration on the police officer, but it was hard not to. The man who had escaped would certainly warn the others. They would lose any chance of catching them. The ringleader might even go into hiding or flee to Europe. It wouldn't be the first time a criminal escaped the arm of the law by leaving the United States.

"Let's start again." David took a deep breath, righted the chair, and dropped into it. "Ophelia is a woman's name. She could be a mother or sister or even a girlfriend."

"I'll make the rounds in the French Quarter and ask if anyone has heard of Ophelia Petrie." Longineaux rubbed the stubble on his cheeks.

Neither of them had found time to return to their homes and shave. Or sleep. David had spent several hours making out reports—one for the local lieutenant and a second for Mr. Bastrup in Chicago. They had been difficult to finish. He placed the blame for the failure on himself. It didn't matter what had spooked the man Petrie was meeting. When the mission failed, it was his responsibility.

Longineaux had spent his time taking care of Petrie's body, making sure it got to the morgue and was scheduled for quick burial at Pauper's Graveyard. Maybe they should put an advertisement about the burial in the *Picayune* and watch to see if anyone showed up to mourn Charlie Petrie.

"Charlie wasn't a local boy. His family probably doesn't live here, either. But it's worth making further inquiries." David looked at the next item on their list. "Shakespeare. The play *Hamlet* has a character named Ophelia. Maybe the ringleader is an actor."

"I didn't get the idea Petrie was an educated man. Do you think he would even know who Shakespeare was?"

Longineaux's question was valid, but David didn't want to make any hasty assumptions. The best police work came from following every possible avenue until it either ended or led to the culprits.

His mind conjured an image of Vance Hargrove. Wouldn't it be great if he was somehow involved? That would get the man away from Jasmine. He shook his head. Just because he didn't like Vance or the way he looked at Jasmine didn't mean the man was a criminal. David had to stay focused on this case if he was going to catch a killer. "I still think I'll check the local theaters and see if anyone is showing *Hamlet*. Petrie might have been trying to tell us to look for someone involved in the production."

"We could put an advertisement in the paper. Offer a reward for information leading to Ophelia Petrie."

"That's a good idea." David yawned, shaking his head to clear it of the cobwebs spun by his lack of sleep. "But we'd better send it to more than the local papers."

"I don't think Petrie was from back East." Longineaux stared out the window.

David followed his gaze. The sun was up. What had happened to the night? "Agreed. He had a drawl, just not the extra twang to indicate a lifetime here."

Longineaux looked down at the paper on his desk and started writing. "So Mississippi, Alabama, Georgia."

"Yes, and you may as well include Tennessee and Kentucky, too."

"Florida?"

David shook his head. "Let's see what we get first."

"I hope our luck changes." Longineaux drummed his pencil on his desk, an indication of either exhaustion or nervousness. "I'm sorry about last night. I should have remembered how clumsy I am."

The taps of the pencil threatened to get under David's skin. But he had to hold onto his temper. "It wasn't your fault. We both wanted to hear what was being said. Jackson Square simply doesn't offer enough cover closer to the statue. That's probably why the man chose it in the first place." He hesitated, choosing his words carefully. "You may have saved my life last night when you told me not to chase him. I made a note of it in my reports."

The praise brought a look of wonder to the other man's face. He cleared his throat. "Thank you."

"Let's get to work." David stood.

Longineaux's jaw dropped. "You can't go onto the street looking like that. People will either think you're a victim or a murderer."

David looked down and realized the man was right. Splatters of blood smeared across his shirt. He'd already tossed out his coat. He knew the blood would never come out of it. "I'll run by my apartment and pick up some fresh clothes."

"You need more than clean shirts." Lieutenant Moreau leaned against the office doorjamb. "Both of you need a couple of hours of sleep."

Longineaux jumped out of his chair and saluted. "But they could get aw—"

"Do you really think you could hold your own if you ran into those men right now?" Moreau shook his head. "All you'd manage to do is get yourselves killed."

Another yawn threatened to crack David's jaw. Maybe the lieutenant was right. While he wanted desperately to catch the gang, they needed to be smart about it. Deliberate action would win out over speed. "What time is it now?"

Moreau pulled out his watch. "Seven thirty."

David glanced out the window again. "Let's meet at the Café du Monde at noon. We can start there and work our way into the surrounding neighborhood."

Longineaux's red-rimmed eyes showed relief. "If you think that would be best."

"Don't forget to leave that report on my desk on your way out." Moreau sauntered down the hall.

Picking up the sheets of paper, David glanced through them once more. He wished he could give a better description of the man who had murdered Petrie. Or something else to prove that he hadn't completely botched this job. But nothing came to his mind.

With a sigh he followed Longineaux down the hall. Maybe this afternoon they would turn up a new lead to follow. If he could only figure out who Ophelia was. And what the name had to do with bank robberies.

❧

For once Lily found her father alone in the library. Since their arrival in New Orleans, he'd been spending a lot of his free time with Aunt Tessie. Practically living in her apron pocket.

He glanced up as she entered and put down the newspaper he'd been reading.

"Am I disturbing you, Papa?"

"Of course not." He rose to give her a tight hug. "You know I'm always available to talk to my daughters."

Lily clung to him for several long minutes, burying her face into his shoulder and breathing in the scent of river that always clung to him.

"Is something wrong?"

She forced herself to let go of him. "I don't know." Tears welled up at the corners of her eyes. "It's just. . .I'm worried about Jasmine."

The words were hard to utter, especially to this man whom she had once blamed for walking away from his parental responsibilities. What irony to once again admit that she needed his help. Since returning to their lives, Papa had allowed her to continue mothering his younger daughters. He had always been ready to dispense advice, however. Advice that had been valuable and effective in the spiritual, social, and educational development of both of her sisters.

He perched on the arm of Mr. Thornton's leather sofa. "I heard the two of you had an argument."

"I said some awful things to her—embarrassed her in front of everyone here." Lily paced across the room, her hands locked behind her back. When Jasmine had not come with the Cartiers last night, she had wanted to go talk with her sister. Apologize for her thoughtlessness if not for her decision. Maybe she should have.

"You've done an excellent job with both of your sisters, Lily. One thing you may not have thought about is how she's feeling. I'm sure Jasmine is as upset as you."

She didn't feel like she deserved Papa's praise or his sympathy. She was a failure. How had she ever thought she was up to the task of setting her sister's feet on the right path? Hadn't she learned yet that she didn't have all the answers? A little voice inside Lily's head whispered that she had more answers than Jasmine.

"Why don't you send her a note and explain how you feel and why you said what you did?" Papa's voice drowned out the internal voice. "You could invite her to go shopping. Jasmine may not love new clothing as much as Camellia, but she'd probably love to pick out some new gewgaw that she can't find at home."

Lily considered his advice. "It might work."

"But?"

She stopped pacing and looked at him. "I told her not to go on an outing alone with this actor that she met at the theater. At least not until after Blake and I meet him. Do you think I'm being unreasonable? I know she's an adult, Papa. But you know how naive Jasmine can be. She always believes the best of everyone. He could be a scoundrel, and she wouldn't see it until it's too late."

"You can't protect your sister forever. All you can do is give her the moral foundation to make the best decisions possible. Give her the tools she needs. God will handle the rest."

Lily began pacing again. "But what if she ruins her life? Who will I blame if she's carried off by some Lothario with a suave manner and a lack of morals?"

Papa's chuckle should have soothed her raw nerves. "I can't help but think of Jesus' parable of the prodigal son. Sometimes our children have to be allowed to fail. They have to be freed even if the result is disastrous."

"You think I shouldn't give her advice?"

"If she's not willing to hear it, what good will your advice do her?"

Lily chewed on the inside of her cheek. But she had to try, didn't she? She loved Jasmine. Who better to advise her?

"When everyone told you not to purchase a riverboat, did you listen? Did you follow the counsel of those who were older and wiser? They probably thought you were being naive."

"But I was—"

The shake of his head stopped her words. "You were younger than Jasmine is now. And you knew next to nothing about moving cargo on the river. You were naive. If not for God's provision, you would have failed. You might have even died on the river."

She stared at him, knowing how much the words must have cost him. He was right. Her own mother had died on the river in spite of everything. Looking back at those days, she saw her family in a new light.

Papa stood, putting a hand on her shoulder. "I know how much it must frighten you to think that your sister may be hurt. It's a fear every parent must face."

"So I should let her go her own way? Give her the freedom to fail?"

He squeezed her shoulder and nodded. "God has given us that same freedom. Think of how He must feel when He knows that we will yield to temptation. Some of us will pay the highest price for that—an eternity separated from His presence. Yet He knows how important it is not to compel us. He stands ready like the father in the parable to welcome us home. But He'll never stop us from leaving."

A tear slipped down Lily's cheek, and she flicked it away with an impatient finger. She didn't know if she was strong enough to let Jasmine go. Everything in her cried out against the idea. "Isn't there another way?"

He shook his head, his own eyes moist.

Before he could say anything else, the library door opened, and Aunt Tessie stepped inside, her attention focused on the glove she was putting on. "Henrick, are you—" Her question came to an abrupt halt as she looked up and realized Lily was in the library. "I'm sorry. I'm interrupting."

"No, don't go." Lily sniffed to keep her tears at bay. "Papa and I are finished talking."

Aunt Tessie looked from her to her father, an unspoken question apparent in the arch of her eyebrows.

Papa cleared his throat and nodded. "I'll be ready in a few moments."

The unspoken conversation between the two of them made Lily want to giggle. It was a relief from the heavy burden of guilt she'd been carrying.

"I'll just go see if Charlotte has—um—has finished that list." Aunt Tessie disappeared into the hallway, her discomfort obvious.

Lily turned to her father. Was he blushing? She knew she was grinning. "Papa, I'm so happy for you. Tessie is a wonderful lady."

His eyes opened wide, and he blew out a relieved sigh. "You don't need to send out invitations yet, but I have to admit being in her company does my heart good. I wasn't sure if you girls would be upset."

"Upset?" Laughter filled her, lifting Lily's spirits. "I think this is the most exciting thing that's happened to us in a long time."

"You don't think I'm being foolish?" His brown gaze begged for reassurance.

"Not at all." Lily put her arms around him and hugged him hard. "I think Tessie is one lucky lady to have snagged the attention of such a fine Christian man."

"And I think I'm blessed to have the love of such an understanding daughter." He dropped a kiss on her cheek before taking a step back. "Now you quit worrying so much about making Jasmine's decisions for her. You and she are alike in many ways. She's going to be all right in spite of what you may think."

Lily watched him walk toward the door, his step jaunty. Wondering how the father of the prodigal son had managed for all those years that his child was away from home, she shivered. She hoped she would never have to find out for herself.

❧

Jasmine stood at the rail as the *Water Lily* pulled away from the dock. How could the day be so beautiful when her heart was being torn in two?

She hadn't been at home with Sarah yesterday when Vance called on her, because Lily had shown up and insisted they go shopping together. It made no sense at all. Unless Lily had some ulterior motive. But she couldn't have known when Vance would come. It was all too confusing.

When Lily first showed up unannounced at Sarah's house, Jasmine had been afraid her deception had been uncovered. Certain that Lily had somehow found out about her evening with Vance, Jasmine had braced herself for a homily on deceit and ruination. What she'd gotten instead was an invitation to go shopping. Shopping? Something Lily abhorred. It made no sense.

"Are you looking forward to seeing Eli and Renée's boys again?"

Caught off guard by Lily's unexpected presence on the deck, Jasmine shrugged. Her sister was usually far too busy taking care of passengers during departure. She kept her gaze on the muddy surface of the river. Now was not the time to tell Lily she wasn't going to Memphis. "Remington is nice enough when he's not plotting some prank. As for Brandon and Cameron, they've never shown much interest in me."

Lily smiled. "They have matured greatly since they last saw you. I predict that they'll buzz around you like honeybees gathering nectar when they realize what a beautiful young lady you are."

Flattery was not something Lily excelled at. She sounded too bright.

The forced cheerfulness didn't sound at all convincing. Jasmine suspected she was trying to make amends because of the way she'd embarrassed her at the Thorntons' earlier in the week. Jasmine was ready to forgive her sister's boorish behavior. . .*if* Lily vowed to be more circumspect.

The horn sounded above them as Papa guided the paddlewheeler around a sharp curve.

Jasmine cast about for a different topic—one that would not concern her or her plans. She didn't want Lily to figure out what she planned to do.

"Did you give the children the toys we found yesterday?"

"Yes. They were excited. Benjamin loved the silver rattle you picked out."

Besides the toys for all of the children, they had purchased a lovely straw hat for Camellia, a magnifying glass to help Uncle Phillip read his newspaper, and a lacy shawl in shades of brown and coral for Aunt Dahlia. Jonah was getting a fancy stereoscope and several stereographic images of boats and trains.

"I'm sorry I didn't get to meet your friend Mr. Hargrove." Lily seemed determined to bring up uncomfortable topics.

Jasmine didn't know if she was sorry or not. If Lily had actually met him, she might have agreed that he was everything both she and Sarah had claimed. But then again, she might just as well have taken an instant dislike to him. This way Jasmine didn't have to defend her interest in him. "Perhaps he'll come to Natchez someday, and you can meet him then."

Lily's gaze swept her. "Did he tell you he was coming to visit?"

"No." Jasmine could not meet her sister's gaze. "You're probably right. I'll never see him again."

Silence enveloped them. Jasmine wanted to look up, but she didn't dare. Lily might not know everything, but she had an uncanny knack for discerning untruths. Not that Jasmine believed Vance would come to Les Fleurs without an invitation. He didn't need to. She was going to go to him, get a job on the *Ophelia*, and reach for her dreams.

"I'm sorry." Lily's hand covered her own. "I've been thinking about that trip to Chicago. The one you and I discussed back at Les Fleurs."

"You don't have to worry about that." Jasmine pulled her hand free. "I don't know if I even want to go to Chicago anymore."

"Really? I thought that was your heart's desire. What's happened to change your mind?"

Jasmine wished her sister would go away. "Nothing. I just realized that the big city is not as romantic as I'd once thought."

"Is it that man?" Lily grabbed her shoulders and pulled Jasmine around to face her. Her brown eyes were full of fire. "Did he hurt you?"

"Of course not." Exasperation lent sincerity to her words. At least she could be truthful about this. "Vance was a perfect gentleman."

Lily continued to search her face. "Something happened. You've been pining for the chance to move to Chicago for more than a year. You couldn't have changed so completely in less than a week." An odd look entered her eyes, driving out the anger and replacing it with sympathy. "Is it David? I know that you care about him, Jasmine, in spite of what you tell me. It's written all over your face."

David? Lily thought she was heartbroken because David was not returning with them? She opened her mouth to correct her sister's misunderstanding but snapped it closed again as she realized this might be the perfect way to avoid Lily's interference. Drawing on her experience playing the misunderstood daughter of King Lear, she hung her head. "I—he is nothing to me at all."

"Oh, dear." Lily drew her close and rubbed her back. "I'm so sorry, Jasmine."

As she stood within the circle of her sister's arms, Jasmine ignored the prick of her conscience. It was Lily's fault that she was driven to deception. If she told her sister the truth, Lily would drag her off to Memphis or some other bleak, depressing location and never let her out of her sight.

Her way would be better for both of them. For everyone in the family. She would disappear from their lives until one day when they would learn of her stunning success in the theatrical world. Then they would understand why she had left home in the first place.

Chapter Seventeen

The hired carriage rocked as it hit a rough spot on the dirt road leading out of Natchez. With practiced ease, Jasmine grabbed the hand loop above her head to keep from being jostled about.

Lily swayed with the movement, her arm around her drowsy youngest son. "I'm glad Papa took Aunt Tessie home."

"Mommy, Noah's touching me." Magnolia pushed at her brother's arm as she made the complaint.

Jasmine hid a grin as she listened to Lily dispensing justice to her nephew and niece. Had she ever been that young? She didn't remember arguing with David in the same way. Of course, Lily wasn't her mother... and he certainly wasn't her brother.

She felt a greater kinship with Benjamin, wondering if he would chafe against being the youngest. Jasmine knew firsthand how it felt. She was ready to be treated like a grown woman, receiving respect from her family even if they couldn't give her enthusiastic support. If everything proceeded according to plan, they would have to respect her. They wouldn't have any other choice. She would be out in the world, making her own way and excelling in her chosen profession.

A thrill of anticipation swelled within her. Maybe she would marry the handsome Vance Hargrove. . .if no one better came along. After all, once she became a famous actress, dozens of men would want her by their sides. . .maybe hundreds. She could choose a husband from among them.

The carriage slowed and turned off the road.

Jasmine leaned forward for a glimpse of Les Fleurs, her breath catching at the unexpected sight. "Look, there's been a fire!"

Her exclamation stopped the children's squabbling, and they leaned forward to see the blackened field. She heard hoofbeats as Blake, who was escorting them on horseback, spurred his mount forward.

Lily held Benjamin's head as she surveyed the damage. "I wonder what happened. Can you see the house?"

"Not yet." Out of the corner of her eye, Jasmine saw Magnolia reach for her brother's hand. The sight warmed her heart, reminding her once again of the close relationship she, Lily, and Camellia had once enjoyed. A part of her missed those days. They rarely—if ever—saw eye to eye anymore.

Blake returned, leaning down to report what he'd seen. "It looks like the only damage was to a couple of the cabins on the other side of the fields."

Benjamin woke and pulled on his mother's shoulder. Lily returned her attention to him.

Jasmine, along with Noah and Magnolia, continued peering out of the window. She hoped no one had been hurt.

Camellia and Aunt Dahlia stood on the front porch, waving their handkerchiefs. They must have heard the carriage coming.

Blake dismounted to open the door for them. Noah and Magnolia tumbled out first and went running up the steps to be welcomed by the two ladies as Blake took Benjamin. He set his youngest child on the ground and watched him run, as only a toddler can, toward the steps before helping Lily and Jasmine alight.

As she climbed the stairs ahead of Lily and Blake, Jasmine looked for any signs of strain in Camellia's face, breathing a sigh of relief when she saw none. In spite of the damage they had seen on the drive to the plantation, everything must be under control.

"Why don't you go inside and see if the cook has any treats left from our tea this morning?" Camellia held the door open and watched as Noah, Magnolia, and Benjamin ran to do her bidding.

"What happened?" Blake asked the question as soon as the children were out of sight.

"We were all nearly burned alive." Aunt Dahlia dabbed at her eyes with her handkerchief, even though Jasmine couldn't see any evidence of tears. "I thank the good Lord we weren't killed while we slept."

"Aunt Dahlia, you know the fire started well after we were up and about." Camellia hugged Jasmine first and then Lily. "Besides, the house was never in any danger."

Aunt Dahlia heaved a loud sigh. "I blame Jonah for bringing this on us."

Jasmine could not believe what her aunt was saying. Aunt Dahlia had never liked Jonah because he fought with the North during the war, but surely she could not believe he would purposely try to burn down their home.

"Aunt Dahlia," Lily and Camellia admonished in unison.

"Well, I do." Aunt Dahlia sniffed and turned to go inside. "You young people don't know as much as you think. Whenever someone tries to change the natural order of things, we all have to suffer the consequences."

Blake shook his head and turned to face Camellia. "Tell us what happened."

"I know you remember Jasper Calhoun." She waited for Blake's nod. "He set fire to the woods out of spite when Jonah didn't choose him as overseer."

"Why don't you sit down and tell us all about it? Don't leave out any details." Lily moved to one of three rockers to the right of the front door, arranging her skirts as she settled against the wooden seat.

Blake glanced toward the front door. "Where's Jonah?"

Camellia waved her hand toward the burned woods. "He and a few of the others are finishing up the repairs to the schoolhouse. It received the most damage, but I hope to hold class there again tomorrow."

Camellia and Jasmine sat in the empty rockers as Blake went in search of his brother-in-law. As succinctly as she could, Camellia described the fire and how narrowly she and the children had avoided the danger. "Besides minor scrapes and cuts, only one man was seriously injured. The doctor came to help treat him, and I'm thankful to say he is already back on his feet."

"Praise God no one was killed." Reverence filled Lily's words.

Camellia nodded. "Yes, He was definitely watching out for our welfare."

Jasmine was thankful to hear that the damage had been no worse, but she thought her sisters should also recognize the hard work of the men, women, and children who had risked their lives to fight the flames. Not that God had not been with them, but without the others, the plantation might have burned to the ground. But now was not the time to express her thoughts. She forced her lips into an agreeable smile.

"Let's talk about something else." Camellia looked at her. "Did you and David settle your differences, or are you still spatting?"

Lily cleared her throat and shook her head. "Blake and I were planning to make a trip up to Memphis right away, but I think we'd better stick around a few days to help you out."

While she was thankful to Lily for intervening, irritation pressed Jasmine's lips into a straight line. Why was everyone so interested in her relationship with David? He was her past. The theater was her future.

"Don't be ridiculous. I won't hear of such a thing. Jonah and I have everything in hand. Please don't change your plans. As you pointed out, we have so much to be thankful for."

Jasmine thought it would be good to add a little reinforcement. If Lily and Blake didn't leave, it might wreck her plans. Besides that, Lily needed to get past the idea that her sisters were helpless. Jasmine had no doubt Jonah and Camellia would do fine without Lily directing the repairs. "Didn't you say you need to talk to Eli Thornton about the railroad business?"

"That's true. He and Renée will know all the pitfalls of changing over from river to rail transportation. Now that so many people are moving westward, it seems we're going to have to consider the possibility of leaving the river." Lily stopped and frowned. "But family is more important than business."

"I agree, Sister. And if it were necessary, I would beg you and Blake to remain here a few days. But we're coping. You should go."

Jasmine held her breath as she watched the emotions crossing Lily's face.

"Are you going, too, Jasmine?"

Grateful for the chance to put her plans in motion, Jasmine stretched out her arms and yawned. "I don't think so." She looked at Lily, summoning all the pathos she could manage. "I'm really tired. Would you mind if I stayed here with Camellia?"

Lily shot her a concerned look. "Are you sick?"

"Not at all. Sarah was such a whirlwind of activity. I need a little time to recover from all that gadding about. I love staying with her, but it does wear me out."

"I know what you mean." Lily's expression turned to one of sympathy.

"So it's settled." Camellia headed for the door. "Jasmine is staying, and everyone else is leaving in the morning."

"I suppose so." Lily's nod eased the tension in Jasmine's shoulders. "Did you leave anything on the *Water Lily* that we need to send back before we leave?"

Without hesitation, Jasmine shook her head. "I have plenty of clothes here."

Camellia stopped and turned to her sister. "Are you planning to stop in Vicksburg?"

Jasmine's heartbeat tripled. Why would Camellia ask about Vicksburg?

"No, why? Do you need something from there?"

"Oh no. It's nothing. I was going to send a reply to a letter from Jane Baxter, but it can wait."

Jasmine's shoulders tensed again. She didn't want Lily and Blake to stop in the port that was her destination. If they saw her in Vicksburg, her bid for freedom would end before it began.

"It wouldn't be any trouble to stop." Lily stood. "We could send it by messenger to that bank where her husband works."

"Don't worry about it, Lily. I probably need more than one evening to write the letter anyway. I want to tell her all about the fire and that wicked Jasper Calhoun." Camellia shook her head. "Now that I think about it, I'm sure it wouldn't work."

Jasmine breathed a sigh of relief as she followed her sisters inside. For a moment she'd thought she would have to wait another day to avoid running into her oldest sister on the dock at Vicksburg. She also didn't want Lily to see either the *Ophelia* or Vance. Her sister didn't need any clues about her possible whereabouts.

❧

Camellia was leaving for the schoolhouse when Jasmine finally made her appearance in the front parlor. "You really must be exhausted. Do you feel all right?"

"Yes." The dark circles under Jasmine's eyes belied her answer.

"Are you sure you're not sick?"

"I—am—certain," Jasmine stated emphatically. "Don't try to act like Lily. One of the main reasons I didn't want to go with them to Memphis is because she's always hovering. I'm a grown woman. I can take care of myself."

"I'm sorry." Camellia could hear the exasperation in her own voice and knew some of it was directed at herself. It wasn't that long ago she'd felt the same way Jasmine did. Was she becoming as domineering as their older sister was at times? "I'll try to do better."

Jasmine looked contrite. "I'm sorry, too. I didn't sleep well."

"I was going to ask if you wanted to go with me to the schoolhouse, but maybe it would be better if you stay here and try to get some rest instead." Did she still sound like she was trying to manage Jasmine's life? "Or whatever you want to do."

Camellia's mouth dropped open as her sister darted across the parlor and threw her arms around her. She wanted to ask what was wrong now, but she was afraid to. Afraid she'd be accused of hovering. She returned Jasmine's hug. "I love you."

Was that a sniff? Was Jasmine crying? When Camellia pulled back, her sister's violet eyes were dry, so she decided it must have been her imagination. She searched Jasmine's face for some hint of what had her acting so oddly. "I got a new copy of *Godey's* last week. Would you like to read it?" It was the only thing she could think of to offer.

"No, thank you. I think I'm going to visit Miss Deborah at the orphanage, and I also plan to stop by to see Jean Luc and Anna." Jasmine's smile didn't seem as perky as usual, but Camellia put it down to her sleepless night.

"I could hardly believe it when Lily told me about Tessie and Papa."

"Are you upset?"

Camellia shook her head. "Of course not. Tessie's a wonderful woman. She taught me everything I know about medicine and healing. If not for her, I might never have learned how to be a proper nurse. If Papa's happy, I am, too."

"It seems a little odd to me." Jasmine wrinkled her nose. "They're so old."

Laughter bubbled up from Camellia. "Did you think romance was limited to the young?"

"Of course not. I was just surprised because it's Papa. I guess I thought he was still in love with Mama."

Camellia picked up her bonnet and walked to the window. "Mama will always have a special place in Papa's heart. But he has a right to seize happiness if he can find it with Aunt Tessie."

"I suppose."

Tying a large bow under her chin, Camellia glanced in the window to check her appearance. "Maybe we'll have a wedding for Christmas."

Jasmine shrugged.

Camellia supposed her sister was still trying to get used to the idea of "old people" falling in love. "I have to go, dearest. I'm taking a lunch to share with the children since it's going to be a long day." She turned to find

Jasmine studying the newspaper. "I'll see you sometime this afternoon."

"Don't worry if I'm not back when you return." Jasmine glanced up. "I may stay in town for a while."

Camellia pointed a finger at her. "If you go shopping without me, my feelings are going to be hurt." The laugh her comment brought eased Camellia's concern. She breezed out of the room with a kiss and a wave.

She enjoyed the walk to the schoolhouse in spite of the scorched ground from last week's fire. Wondering which of the children would be in attendance this morning, she opened the front door and sniffed. The mint she'd gathered yesterday morning and left inside had done the trick, replacing the pungent smells with freshness. No hint of smoke remained inside the room. Thanking God once more that Jasper Calhoun had not done any more damage, she checked the children's slates while she waited for her students to arrive.

The morning was a busy one as always. Camellia loved the bright eyes and eager minds of her pupils. Their week-long separation made the day even more special than normal. The hours flew by, and by the time she sent them to their homes, the shadows outside were beginning to lengthen.

Arriving home, Camellia pulled off her bonnet and let it dangle from one hand as she went in search of her aunt and her sister. Because it was the first room off the main entrance, she stopped to see if they were in the library. "Jasmine? Aunt Dahlia?" No one answered, which was not surprising. Jasmine had already read most everything inside, and their aunt probably never would. Moving to the parlor, she checked for the two women, growing a little concerned when she found the room empty.

They weren't on the porch or she would have seen them coming in. Had they gone to the dining room? Concern prickled across her skin when they didn't turn up there either. Before she could descend into a full panic, however, footsteps descending the main stairwell brought her into the foyer.

Aunt Dahlia steadied herself on the handrail as she negotiated the stairs. "Did you call me?"

Nodding, Camellia smiled. "Is Jasmine upstairs?" Her sister must have returned to her bedroom for a nap before dinner.

"I haven't seen her at all today." Aunt Dahlia reached the bottom step before continuing. "Didn't she leave with Lily and Blake?"

Camellia's heart clenched before she remembered that Jasmine had warned her she might not be back on time. She glanced out the window. It would grow dark soon. "No, she didn't go with them. She had some errands to run. I'm sure she'll be back soon."

"Someone needs to put a rein on that girl. She's allowed far too much freedom."

"According to what Lily told me, Jasmine would definitely not agree with you." Camellia gave her aunt a peck on the cheek. "I've got to go meet with the cook about the menu before I go upstairs, change for dinner, and check on Amaryllis."

"I'll send Jasmine up to you if I see her before you're done." Aunt Dahlia's sigh was filled with disapproval.

She opened her mouth to continue, but Camellia cut off her words with another kiss. "Thank you."

Aunt Dahlia entered the parlor as Camellia headed to the back of the house, her mind full of all that needed to be done prior to dinner.

When she finally made it back to the parlor, the lanterns had been lit. She entered the room and looked around expectantly.

Aunt Dahlia put down her needlework. "If you're looking for your sister, you're going to be disappointed. She's not returned."

A frisson skittered down Camellia's back. She was going to talk to Jasmine about being more considerate. It was fine to stay for dinner with friends, but she should at least send a message so her family wouldn't worry.

Jonah walked into the parlor, already dressed for dinner. "You look worried."

"I'm more irritated than anything." Camellia told him about Jasmine's absence. "Would you mind taking me over to the Champney's? I know she must have decided to have dinner with them, but I'd feel better if I knew for certain she's okay."

Jonah rubbed his chin with one hand. "Do you really think that's necessary?"

"Probably not, but I hate to think of her riding her horse back home in the dark."

He dropped his hand and nodded. "Okay."

Camellia hadn't realized how tense she was until her husband agreed. "Thank you."

His smile warmed her heart. "Go get your cloak. I'll have the carriage brought around."

Aunt Dahlia was shaking her head, but Camellia knew she had the most wonderful husband in the world.

Chapter Eighteen

Jasmine was ready to get off the *Evangeline* long before it docked at Vicksburg. She had purchased the cheapest ticket she could manage—an outside ride on the hurricane deck between the paddlewheel and the pilothouse. Several immigrant families huddled together and watched her with suspicion in their eyes. She tried smiling at some of the children, but their mothers gathered them closer and chided them in a guttural language she had never heard, apparently reminding them to steer clear of strangers.

Someone stepped into the pilothouse, and she caught her breath as a desire to see her father overwhelmed her. But that was silly. If Papa were here she wouldn't be on her way to meet Vance.

Wishing she had brought more than a shawl as protection from the damp wind, Jasmine set her chin and focused on the future. They should reach Vicksburg within the hour. She hoped it wouldn't be too hard to find Vance. Jasmine couldn't wait to see him. Would he be as thrilled as she? What role did he have in mind for her? She knew she would excel even if she only got to appear in a minor part for now.

It wouldn't take her long to rise to the rank of someone like Miss

Barlow. She might not have much experience as a professional actress, but Jasmine had been performing for family and friends since she was old enough to memorize lines. Everyone raved about her acting abilities. And it was due to her efforts that the orphanage could hire workers to replace the roof.

In spite of his parents' warnings, one of the immigrant children moved cautiously closer. Jasmine wished the little boy wasn't afraid of her. She would love to talk to him, find out where his family was headed and maybe even offer some pointers to his parents about dangers on the river. It would be so nice to help them like she had the orphanage. One day perhaps she would have enough money to fund an organization to help those in need. The idea warmed Jasmine better than her thickest shawl would have done. She would do it. . .as soon as she was famous enough.

They docked with little trouble, and she disembarked with her bag held firmly in one hand. As soon as she reached the other end of the gangplank, she began looking for the *Ophelia*. Her heart pounded when she spotted the long, two-story barge floating in front of a shorter tugboat called the *Miss Polly*. This was it. The beginning of the rest of her life. Raising her chin and tightening her hold on her portmanteau, Jasmine marched across the gangplank and stepped onto the *Ophelia*'s deck.

"Sorry, ma'am." A wiry man with a narrow face stopped her. "The next show won't start until seven o'clock. You can come back around five to purchase a ticket, but the doors won't open until a quarter to seven."

"I'm not—" Unhappy with the shaky sound of her voice, Jasmine halted her words and took a deep breath. "I'm here to see Mr. Vance Hargrove."

His face grew thoughtful. "You'll find him inside, but if you don't mind my saying so, you ought to turn yourself around and go home before he ruins your life."

"That's enough, Arnold. Are you already finished with the repairs to the backdrop?"

Jasmine recognized Vance's voice before he finished speaking. She turned, and there he was, as tall and handsome as she remembered. And his attractive smile made her knees weak. She thought she might die of happiness then and there. "Vance."

He swept her a deep bow, every inch the gentleman she remembered. "I wasn't sure you would come."

"I couldn't stay away." She blushed at the confession.

"Here, let me help you with that bag." He reached for her portmanteau. "How did you convince your family to let you come?"

Should she tell him the truth? She couldn't. He would think her a baby. And he might balk at accepting a runaway on board. "It wasn't hard. They accepted my decision and let me go." The lies tripped off her tongue without effort—almost like she was already playing a role.

His dark gaze searched her face for a moment as though testing her veracity.

Jasmine lifted her chin and stared back. Let him think what he might. She could be as imperious as Cleopatra.

He nodded and held the door open for her. "Come inside."

Jasmine stepped past him and came to a halt, her mouth dropping open. She had never seen anything so beautiful in her life. The main cabin was long, with a stage taking up the back third of the space. In front of the stage was seating for at least a hundred people. A red rope cordoned off the long padded benches. She supposed its purpose was to prevent anyone from sneaking in without purchasing a ticket. "It's beautiful."

"Wait until they light the candles this evening." He pointed out the numerous gold leaf sconces, each holding three candles. "Do you see the mirrors they're mounted on? They magnify the light until it's nearly as bright as noon inside."

The boat had been appointed to cater to rich customers. Thick carpet cradled her feet, the seating was softened by deep cushions, and an ornate chandelier hung above her head, holding what appeared to be hundreds more lights. "You must love performing in here."

"As will you." He held the red rope high so she could pass under it. Taking the lead, he stepped past her and walked up a set of steps onto the stage, waving to two men who were painting a backdrop off to one side of the stage. "I want you to meet someone special."

The rich red velvet curtain moved, and a beautiful woman stepped onto the stage.

Jasmine caught her breath. She had never dreamed she might be near enough to touch someone she so deeply admired.

"Vance? Are you ready to go over that scene now?" Tabitha Barlow asked.

"In a moment." He set down Jasmine's bag and reached for her hand. "We have a new recruit. A young lady I know you'll enjoy meeting."

The actress's gaze narrowed as Jasmine dropped a curtsy. "Really, Vance. Are you up to your old tricks again?"

Jasmine didn't pay much attention to Miss Barlow's words. She was too intent on trying to think of what to say to her. Why hadn't she thought of this? Her mind scrambled through reams of lines and came up empty. Only three words came to her. "I know you."

Miss Barlow's face lost its bored expression. She smiled at Jasmine and beckoned for her to come closer. "You do?"

"Yes, ma'am. You were playing the part of Laurette in *Richard Coeur-de-lion* in New Orleans. I remember it like yesterday. I was only nine at the time, but you inspired me to become an actress."

The smile drooped, and her eyes iced over as at least one of the workmen snickered. Miss Barlow looked past her to Vance. "Get her out of here this instant."

Before she could quite understand what she had said to upset the actress, Vance had grabbed her arm and dragged Jasmine off the stage. He hustled her into a narrow corridor and looked around. "Clem, come here."

She was surprised when the person who answered his summons was a slender girl not much older than she with a line of brown bangs across her forehead and a distracted look in her hazel eyes. "Clem?"

"Clem McCoy." The girl held a pincushion in one hand and a measuring tape in the other. "My real name is Clementine—it means 'merciful.' But everyone here calls me Clem."

"See that Jasmine gets settled." Vance turned to her, taking her hand to drop a kiss on her wrist. "I'll be in rehearsal this afternoon, but we'll talk after the play is over."

Jasmine's skin tingled where his lips had touched it. She wanted to ask him about the confrontation with Miss Barlow. Did the older woman misunderstand her intent to offer a compliment or was she simply too shy to appreciate such adoration?

"Come along." Clem walked down the hall, her gown swaying with each step.

Picking up her bag, Jasmine followed.

"You can share my room for now." Clem pushed a door open. "But I can't stand a mess, so make sure you pick up after yourself."

The room was barely large enough for the pair of single beds inside. A small dressing table took up one corner of the windowless space, its mirror the only brightness in the room.

"Thank you." Jasmine dropped the portmanteau on the floor and sank onto the mattress. So far, life in the theater was more confusing than exciting.

❧

Jonah turned into the Champneys' drive, and the warm light spilling from the windows encouraged Camellia to believe they would find Jasmine inside. But if Jean Luc and Anna had invited her to dinner, why hadn't they sent a note to Les Fleurs? The question pricked her concern, making Camellia more anxious than she should have been. Something wasn't right. She tapped her foot on the floor of the carriage as Jonah came around to help her down. His hand at her waist steadied her as they climbed the steps to the front door.

Leaning past her, Jonah lifted the knocker and rapped it smartly. The seconds crept by as she waited for someone to answer her husband's summons.

The door finally creaked open, and Camellia summoned a shaky smile, knowing how odd their presence must seem to the butler at this hour.

Jonah inclined his head. "We need to speak to Mr. or Mrs. Champney."

Camellia was right on his heels as the butler announced them. "Is Jasmine here with you?"

Aunt Tessie, Anna, and Mrs. Champney were sitting in the parlor. Anna and Aunt Tessie came to their feet.

Aunt Tessie spoke first. "I haven't seen Jasmine since the *Water Lily* landed yesterday."

Was it only yesterday? That carefree time seemed an eon ago. Camellia's knees turned to water. She was more frightened than when she'd been leading the children away from the fire at Les Fleurs. More frightened than when the Yankee army surrounded Vicksburg and shelled the city.

"What's happened?" Anna stepped forward, a concerned look on her face.

Camellia turned away to control her tears while Jonah filled them in briefly.

"What can we do to help?" The question came from Mrs. Champney, still seated on the sofa.

Camellia gave her the only answer she could. "Pray."

They were out of the house and back into the carriage with a minimum of fuss. Jonah whipped up the horses, and she followed her own advice as they headed to town.

"What if she's not here?" Camellia looked at her husband's profile. She wanted him to tell her everything was going to be okay, but not unless he really thought it would be. Empty promises would be worse than silence. She didn't need false hope.

"Don't borrow trouble." He put his free arm around her. "We'll find her in town, Camellia."

Why was it getting so dark? They needed light to check the byways for signs of an accident. She searched her memory for the time of the month and came up empty. "Will the moon be full tonight?"

Jonah spared her a glance. "No, but we'll be able to see well enough."

As he drove the carriage, she looked for any evidence of an accident.

Fear, dark as midnight, stalked her. She had managed to hold onto hope that nothing was wrong until learning that Jasmine had not visited the Champneys. Now that hope was gone. Something had happened to her sister.

What if she'd been abducted? They hadn't seen any bushwhackers in the area for more than a year, but what if one had been crossing their land this morning? Tears sprang to her eyes as fear swelled.

The hooves of the horses barely touched the ground as they rushed toward the orphanage. The rhythm normally soothed her, but this evening the sound only increased her anxiety.

Hope burst on her with the force of a lightning bolt when she saw Jasmine's horse tethered in front of the orphanage. "That's Juliet, isn't it?"

Jonah grinned at her. "I told you we'd find her."

Camellia climbed down before the carriage came to a full standstill, running toward the orphanage without a thought for her dress or her dignity. She pushed the front door open before Jonah caught up with her. "Jasmine!" She shouted the name as loudly as she could manage.

Jonah came through the front door as Miss Deborah entered the foyer from the back of the house. "Camellia, Jonah, welcome."

"Where is Jasmine?" Jonah sounded as impatient as she felt.

"Jasmine?" The confusion on Miss Deborah's face frightened Camellia, brought the fear roaring back. Miss Deborah had to know where Jasmine was. Anything else was impossible.

"Her horse is out front. Where is she?"

The puzzlement on the other lady's face deepened into a frown. "What horse?"

Jonah stepped aside so she could look down the walk through the open doorway.

Miss Deborah shook her head. "I'm sorry, Camellia. It may be Jasmine's horse, but she hasn't been here all day."

"Are you certain?"

"I saw her." Marguerite appeared from the same area of the house where Miss Deborah had been. "I thought she was acting a bit strange. She told me she was leaving her horse here and would send someone to retrieve it tomorrow. I assumed she had gotten a ride back to Les Fleurs."

What was her sister doing? Camellia wracked her brain for an answer that made sense but came up with nothing. "Is that all she said?"

Marguerite nodded. "I'm sorry."

"It's not your fault." Jonah put an arm around Camellia.

Miss Deborah wrung her hands. "What can we do? Do you want me to send someone to make inquiries downtown?"

This couldn't be happening. Camellia wanted to wake up and discover she'd been having a nightmare. But the rough texture of her husband's coat against her cheek told her this was no dream.

As Jonah explained what little they knew, she thought back to the morning. Had Jasmine been planning to disappear then? Or had she been forced to leave her horse behind by some heartless kidnapper?

Camellia couldn't feel her legs beneath her as Jonah half-carried her back to the gate. She sat with her hands in her lap, her gaze locked on nothing, as he tethered Juliet to the carriage.

"What do we do now?" She asked the question as he climbed onto the bench and turned their vehicle back the way they had come.

His jaw was tight as Jonah shook his head. "It's beginning to look like your sister has run away."

"Why would she do such a thing?"

"I have no idea. But then again I don't understand why ladies act the way they do more than half the time." He blew out a long sigh. "Think, Camellia. Did Jasmine say anything odd this morning? A hint of what she was planning?"

"We talked about Papa and Aunt Tessie." Camellia remembered her sister's reaction to the affection between them. "And she said she didn't sleep well last night. I remember thinking that she looked tired."

"Was she upset?"

Camellia didn't want to admit that Jasmine had been angry with her, but she knew she had to put her own feelings aside. She gave him a reluctant nod. "She thought I was being too controlling. She even accused me of being too much like Lily."

"None of you can be called mealy-mouthed."

A sob caught in her throat. "It's my fault, Jonah. All my fault. Lily is never going to forgive me for not taking better care of Jasmine. And I don't blame her."

"Shhh." His arm tightened around her once more. "It's not your fault, Camellia."

Hot tears bathed her cheeks. She wished his reassurances didn't sound so hollow. She had failed both of her sisters. Camellia had known Jasmine was acting strange this morning, but she'd been too focused on her schedule for the day. Instead of rushing off to teach the children, she should have stayed with Jasmine. She had made a terrible, thoughtless mistake. A mistake she would regret for the rest of her life. "What are we going to do, Jonah?"

"If she's run away, we need to try to find her." Jonah's voice sounded determined. "But even if we know where she is, we may not be able to compel her to return to Les Fleurs. She is twenty years old."

His warning brought her no relief. She wished for Lily's calm presence. Then the responsibility wouldn't be all on her shoulders. The thought was a revelation. Even in the midst of her fear, she gained a new respect for her older sister. Who could Lily turn to when life—in the form of her younger sisters—threatened to overwhelm her? Camellia felt shame at the knowledge that she had been as hard to handle at eighteen as Jasmine was now.

"What about asking David Foster to look for her?"

She sat up straighter and considered Jonah's question. David was the perfect answer. In spite of the differences that had sprung up between him and Jasmine, he would be concerned for her welfare. And he was a detective. If anyone could find her, it would be a Pinkerton man. Perhaps he could reason with her once he found Jasmine and convince her to come home. "Is he still in New Orleans?"

"I think so." Jonah turned the carriage onto their private drive. "We need to make sure Uncle Phillip didn't find her hiding out somewhere on the grounds first. But if she really is missing, we can send a telegram to David the first thing in the morning."

Uncle Phillip stood at the front door as they pulled up, his face drawn. One glance told the story. The last vestige of hope drained from Camellia. Feeling older than her aunt and uncle, she dragged herself out of the carriage.

"Mommy, Mommy." Amaryllis ran onto the porch, her sweet face puckered with worry.

"It's okay, Amaryllis. Mommy's here." Camellia held out her hands to her daughter, gathering her close and burying her face against Amaryllis's soft neck. Even though she felt unworthy of the love flowing from the little girl, it buoyed her spirits a little.

She felt Jonah's arms encircling both of them. "We'll get through this, Camellia." His whispered words were another pinprick of light piercing the darkness of her fear. "God is watching out for Jasmine tonight even though we cannot."

She prayed he was right.

Chapter Nineteen

David held out his left hand to the young constable who'd been such a help in his search for leads. "It's been a pleasure working with you, Constable Longineaux."

Longineaux grabbed his hand and pumped it once. "I'm sorry the leads didn't pan out, but I know you'll catch the thieves soon. I only wish I could be there when you do."

"If you get any response from those advertisements—"

"You'll be the first to know." The constable scraped his foot on the floor. "Who knows, maybe one of these days I'll come up to Chicago and see your Pinkerton operation."

"I'd like that." David left the busy police office, squinting at the sunlight as he considered what to do next. He could rent a horse from the nearby livery stable, but it wasn't that far to the docks. A walk might clear his head.

The sights around him faded as David once again went through the events at Jackson Square. What had Petrie been trying to tell him? He shook his head in frustration. He had run into an impenetrable wall here. It was time to leave.

The New Orleans Police Department had shelved their case when no new robberies occurred. As Lieutenant Moreau had told him earlier that morning, they didn't have time or the manpower to chase all over the country looking for a needle in a haystack.

It didn't take David long to find a riverboat heading north. After purchasing a ticket, he walked to the Cartiers' home. Packing his belongings, he descended the staircase that was his private entrance and walked across the porch to the main entrance of the house. The Cartiers' butler answered his knock and led him to the parlor.

Sarah had been reading a novel but put it down to greet him. "I'm so glad to see you, David. How is your work progressing?"

He sat in a dainty whitewashed chair and shook his head. "I've exhausted every avenue I can think of. It's time to admit defeat. I came by to thank you and Dr. Cartier for your hospitality. You've been very gracious hosts, never complaining about my odd hours or the amount of time I dedicate to my work."

"That reminds me." She snapped her fingers and jumped up from the sofa. "You received two telegrams this morning."

David stood when she did and waited while she went through a stack of invitations on the Queen Anne desk in one corner of the parlor.

"Here they are." Sarah turned with a triumphant smile and handed him the envelopes.

He opened the top one and read the message inside.

> ROBBERY PLANTER'S BANK VICKSBURG *Stop* INVESTIGATE CONNECTION
> PINKERTON DETECTIVE AGENCY

The information galvanized him. "It's from my headquarters. There's been another robbery, this time in Vicksburg." He would have to make sure the riverboat captain was planning to make a stop in that city. "Maybe I'll catch them there."

Sarah's head nodded, but her concerned gaze studied him. "You're so brave, David. I cannot imagine facing such danger. But open the other telegram. Maybe it says that the thieves were already arrested."

Even though he doubted such an eventuality, David nodded. His eyes widened as he saw the name on the envelope. "It's from Camellia and Jonah."

As he read the note, irritation and disbelief filled him. "Jasmine has done it now. It seems she's run away from home. Your brother and Camellia want me to help find her."

"That poor child." Sarah grabbed his arm. "You must help look for her."

"She's not a child." He looked down at Sarah's troubled expression. What did they think he could do? And what about his job? What about the people who suffered loss and hardship because their money had been stolen? Was he supposed to ignore their needs to go running after a spoiled brat? "Besides, I have no idea where she would go."

"But you know Jasmine better than anyone." Sarah loosened her grip and stepped back as though she could read his thoughts. "You cannot ignore her family's plea."

She had hit on the real problem. He owed a debt to Lily and both of her sisters. "If the boat I'm on stops over in Natchez, I'll make a quick trip to the plantation and find out exactly what's happened. Maybe I can suggest another detective they can hire to look for her."

Even though Sarah didn't say it, he could tell she wasn't happy with his answer. David didn't know what else to do, though. He couldn't—wouldn't—ignore his employer's instructions.

Besides, he'd already wasted enough time trying to curb Jasmine's headstrong personality. Perhaps if she found out what life was really like away from the protection of her family, Jasmine would grow up. Maybe she would finally learn to listen to others who knew more about the world. It wasn't all kittens and compliments. After a week or two of battling greed and disinterest, she would probably be eager to return to her family.

He bowed to Sarah. "Thank you again for your hospitality, Mrs. Cartier. I'll mention to Jonah your concern over Jasmine's welfare and ask him to send you a note once she returns to Les Fleurs."

"Thank you." She pulled herself to her full height and nodded regally. "I hope we'll see you again soon."

David left her standing in the center of the parlor, her chin high and her eyes moist with unshed tears. He could strangle Jasmine himself for causing so much worry. The girl never thought of anyone but herself.

He passed the music room and remembered the way she'd made sheep eyes at that self-absorbed actor. Jasmine had less sense than the sheep she imitated. She had no business leaving the shelter of her home and family.

But then he imagined her scared and alone, adrift in a sea of cruelty and violence. A fierce protectiveness smothered his irritation. Where could she be? Had she gone to Chicago or New York or somewhere else in her search for fame and glory? She needed a keeper, someone who would control her wild tendencies. He wished he had the time to expend on finding her. He would make sure Jasmine was okay. Then he would drag her back home and dare her to ever leave again.

❧

Working aboard the showboat was not as glamorous as Jasmine had imagined. Clem was sweet, and it was exciting to watch from the wings as Vance and the other actors performed *Romeo and Juliet* the night before. Talking to the male lead was another matter entirely. With two performances daily, the whole crew was busy with their various chores.

"Aren't you done polishing those sconces?"

Miss Barlow's querulous voice startled her, and Jasmine nearly fell from the ladder she was perched on.

"Be careful." The actress stepped back, entangled her shoe in the hem of her dress, and cried out. Before she could fall, however, Vance rushed forward and caught her.

"I'm sorry." Jasmine gritted her teeth as jealousy washed through her. Miss Barlow seemed to command all of Vance's time.

Standing with an arm around his co-star, Vance sent her a wink. "Leave the girl alone, Tabitha. She'll finish the sconces as soon as she can."

"Well, I don't know how we're supposed to practice when I can hardly see my hand in front of my face."

Jasmine had to agree with her that it was difficult to see without the candlelight. That must be why Miss Barlow's titian-colored hair seemed to be a different shade than she remembered.

The outer door opened, and sunlight spilled into the room. Angelica Fenwick, the second female lead and understudy for Miss Barlow, strolled in.

The older actress rounded on her. "I'm glad you found time to join us this morning. Your portrayal of Juliet's nurse was lackluster yesterday evening."

Miss Fenwick was as blond as Camellia but much more rounded. Her dimpled elbows and generous chest almost made her seem plump. Jasmine knew from talking to Clem that Miss Fenwick played the secondary parts, the parts that often had the better lines. She'd also warned Jasmine about the constant tension between the two actresses.

"That's not what Rafe said." Miss Fenwick's New England accent was evident in her clipped syllables. "And the audience didn't seem to mind."

"Rafe's opinion doesn't count for anything. Everybody knows he's in love with you." Miss Barlow pouted at Vance. "I don't know why I put up with this trumpery, two-bit operation."

Vance chuckled and released Miss Barlow. "Our generous salaries might be one of the reasons."

She swept down the central aisle, her irritation evident in the swish of her skirts.

"I don't know what you're looking at." Miss Fenwick sniffed as she looked toward Jasmine. "You may be new here, but that's no excuse for inefficiency."

Jasmine returned to her task with renewed energy. Miss Fenwick and Miss Barlow were still squabbling as she removed the last nub and replaced it with a fresh candle. Taking the tinderbox, she started lighting the central candle in each sconce as the manager had instructed.

Rafe Griffin, dressed in a purple doublet, made an appearance a few minutes later. Jasmine supposed he was handsome. His eyes were large and dark, his brow wide, and a pair of dimples bracketed his mouth when he smiled. But he wasn't nearly as handsome as Vance, at least to her. Standing close to her ladder, he showed his dimples. "You must be the new girl Clem was telling me about."

"I was about to send someone out looking for you, Rafe." Miss Fenwick addressed the actor, but her pale eyes shot daggers at Jasmine.

Jasmine wanted to sigh. She had not been here for two full days, and she'd already managed to earn the dislike of both the female leads. What had she done wrong?

Rafe pointed at a spot on his doublet sleeve. "Clem was mending my costume."

Harmon Easley, the owner and manager of the *Ophelia*, entered the stage from the wings. He was a burly man with beefy arms, a round belly, and bowed legs. "What's going on out here? Why aren't y'all practicing? Do I need to advertise for new actors?" He smoothed his mustache with a finger. "Or maybe I should turn this into a circus boat. I don't imagine animals would give me any more trouble than the lot of you."

Properly chastised, the foursome took their places on stage. Jasmine could tell the other members of the cast were waiting backstage from the occasional movements of the curtain. They were the stock company, the actors who filled in the minor parts for much lower pay.

"We'll begin with this week's farce, *Fish Out of Water*." Mr. Easley crossed his arms over his chest. "Places everyone."

As the one-act play began, Jasmine slipped into one of the empty seats, her heart thumping as they began. How she wished to join them onstage.

Someone sat down beside her, and she turned to see Clem's brown hair and plain garb. "If Mr. Easley finds you sitting here doing nothing, he'll sack you for sure."

Jasmine nodded, and the two of them slipped out.

"Here." Clem led her downstairs to the area where the props were stored. "I have to make some alterations to Lady Montague's dress. The girl playing that part was tripping all over the hem last night. It's a wonder she didn't fall and break her neck."

"Do you ever act?"

"No." Clem folded the material at the bottom of the skirt and pinned it in place. "Not for a long time. I tried it when I first started working in this business, but I didn't want to deal with the petty quarrels and backbiting. And the men who see you on stage get funny ideas about a girl's morals."

Jasmine remembered that the first night she'd met Vance the men had crowded around Miss Barlow's door, wanting to take her to dinner. That didn't sound bad to her. Bickering with her coactors, though, was not a pleasant idea. Perhaps she could find ways to accommodate the needs of the other actors by giving them sufficient respect. In her experience it was the best way to avoid confrontation. She sighed at the realization that she had not made a promising start. "I seem to have a talent for making people angry. Both Miss Barlow and Miss Fenwick have given me tongue-lashings."

"Miss Barlow isn't so bad. I've learned as long as you don't get in her way she's happy to ignore you."

Clem's advice didn't make much sense. She'd only been trying to compliment Miss Barlow when they were first introduced. For her troubles, she'd received a sharp word and been sent to her room like a young child. Even Lily hadn't done that to her in years. "I'm beginning to think you only see the good in people."

Clem shook out the skirt and eyed it carefully. "You need to give Miss Fenwick a wide berth. She'll scratch your eyes out if she thinks you'll get in her way, especially with Rafe. She doesn't like it if he even looks at another girl. Give him a wide berth, and she'll leave you alone."

"What about Mr. Hargrove?" Jasmine's heartbeat increased, and a blush darkened her cheeks. Even thinking about him made her quiver.

"He's a ladies' man." Clem put away her supplies before turning back to Jasmine. "But I can see you already know that."

"He's the one who first told me about the *Ophelia* and said I should meet the boat here."

"So he got you a job. I wondered about that. Mr. Hargrove must be sweet on you. But be careful. He and Miss Barlow have been friends forever."

"They're not. . .in love?"

"I don't think so. Maybe once a long time ago. They're mostly friends now, although she does like to keep him close by."

Jasmine clasped her hands in front of her, her worries easing. Vance must be in love with her. He'd spoken to the manager about her, made sure she would have a job on board. And to think she'd been miffed because he had not sought her company after the performance last night. He'd been doing something much more important—making sure she would have a reason to stay near. She was certain he'd seek her out as soon as he could.

Chapter Twenty

David lost a whole day because the boat he'd been planning to take north was not making a stop in Natchez. He cashed in his ticket and went looking for another berth. The docks were full of steamers, but many of them did not want to stop before getting farther north on the river. Finally he found a captain who agreed to make a short stop in Natchez before continuing. The only catch was that he would not leave that afternoon. He purchased the ticket, stowed his gear, and settled in for a long night. By the time the sun rose, he was more than ready to be active again.

Pent-up energy had him threading his way around the cargo of barrels and boxes as the side-wheeler pushed its way against the strong current. Memories of trips on the *Water Lily* clamored for David's attention, growing more distinct with each mile traveled.

A flock of pelicans turned the sky pink above the boat, reminding him of the time Jasmine had decided to capture one for a pet. He'd had to rescue her from the swamp and drag her back to the *Water Lily* before she became a tasty meal for a passing alligator. She had pouted for days until her father helped him carve one from a piece of walnut. He still remembered the look on her face when he presented it to her. He'd felt like he was ten feet tall.

That was the day he'd known his heart belonged to Jasmine Anderson. He had hidden the knowledge from her, feeling he didn't deserve her love. She was from a wealthy family while he had no family to speak of—only a downtrodden ma and a gold-hungry pa. Jasmine and her sisters had taken him in, given him a glimpse of what life could be like. He probably wouldn't be a Christian if he hadn't spent so many afternoons talking to Jasmine's father about Jesus and the Bible.

But even now he felt separated from them, his face pressed against an impenetrable window. Like the rich man in the Bible who could only see heaven from across a chasm, he was doomed to live out his life yearning for what could never be his. The kindness Jasmine's family offered him was more akin to affection for a pet. And now, even though he had a good job and an honorable purpose, if one of the Anderson sisters called, he came running like an obedient puppy.

They sailed past Dead Man's Curve and docked next to a timber barge at Natchez Under-the-Hill.

"Be back by three or we'll leave you." The captain's warning rang in his ears as he left the boat.

David waved at the man. "I'll be back." Finding a horse to rent, he headed for Les Fleurs. He noticed the charred ground on his way in and wondered if Jasmine had caused that disaster before running away.

Camellia met him at the front door, her hair an uncontrolled mass of curls around her face. The frightened look in her blue eyes told him how concerned she was about Jasmine. "Thank you for coming." She sat in one of the rockers and motioned for him to sit next to her.

David shook his head. He would rather stand. "I don't have long, so why don't you tell me what happened." David braced himself. As Camellia told him about the day Jasmine disappeared, he asked a few pertinent questions. The more he heard, the more his exasperation overcame his concern for Jasmine's safety. She didn't take time to think how her selfish actions would affect others. When would she ever grow up? He paced the length of the front porch. "Have you had any word since she left?"

Camellia shook her head. "I feel so guilty for what I said to her. If only I'd been more understanding or less caught up in my own needs..."

David didn't hide his snort of disgust. "You didn't do anything wrong, Camellia. Jasmine has no excuse for causing you all this worry. What did Lily say?"

"She doesn't know." The confession was a bare whisper.

"You have to tell her." David sat next to Camellia and took her hands in his own. "Don't worry about her response. Lily isn't unreasonable. She'll understand you had no control over your little sister. Besides, she loves both of you. She won't blame you any more than I do, but she may have an idea of where Jasmine would go. And she can check for any word of her up and down the river. A lot of people know Lily and Blake. Contacting all of them and warning them to watch for Jasmine may be the easiest way of locating her."

Camellia nodded. "I—I just don't know what to say to her."

"I know it's hard, but you can do it."

She surprised him when she pulled her hands free and stood. Even more so when she wrapped her arms around him in a fierce hug. "I'm glad you came. I know you'll find her if anyone can."

Her words caged him as securely as a prison cell. Before the door could lock him in, he pulled away from her. He was determined to keep his wits about him in spite of the warring desires in his heart. "I don't have much time to devote to the search, Camellia. As soon as I leave here, I'm going to investigate a robbery at Planter's Bank in Vicksburg."

She gasped, and the blood drained from her face. "Oh no. My friend Jane is married to an officer of that bank, Harold Baxter. Please tell me no one was hurt."

"I wish I could." David hoped her connection to the man at the bank would help Camellia understand why he couldn't devote all his time to finding Jasmine. He had to keep his priorities in order. "I don't know any details yet. But I'll make it a point to visit your friend and ask her to send you a note telling you more about the robbery."

Camellia nodded slowly. Her blue eyes shone like glass. "I'm so proud of you, David. I wish you and Jas—"

"I really have to get going." David cut her off before she could finish what she'd been about to say. No one wished for a match more than he. But Jasmine had other ideas about what to do with her life, and he had to respect her decision. . .no matter how ridiculous it was. "Either Mrs. Baxter or I will be in touch soon."

"I'll pray for both of you."

David returned to his rented nag and rode back to Natchez Under-the-Hill, relieved to see that the captain had honored their agreement. He'd already lost enough time. He wanted to find and arrest the bank robbers and return to Chicago. He would refuse any new assignment in the lower Mississippi Valley. Spending time close to the Anderson girls was tearing his world apart. He felt like a ship foundering among the hidden snags of loyalty and devotion. One day he was liable to wash up on a sandbar—broken and abandoned by both the job he felt called to do and the woman he adored.

❧

"You're going to play the part of Lady Montague." Vance Hargrove acted as though he offered her the moon.

Jasmine balanced on a stool, the gold skirt of Miss Barlow's ballroom costume spread around her. She had been reattaching the flounce when Vance found her, a tedious task that Clem said was needed on a daily basis.

She put down the needle and tried to summon a gracious smile for his sake. But it was beyond her acting ability to hide her disappointment. Her first appearance on a real stage would be as Vance's mother. And she knew *Romeo and Juliet* well enough to know that she would only have a line or two.

"Aren't you excited?" The light in his dark eyes dimmed. He glanced around the prop room, his gaze searching for an ally. "Clem, tell Jasmine what a big break this is. She'll be onstage."

"This is a big break, Jasmine. You'll be onstage." Clem parroted the words from the other side of the costume trunk.

Jasmine hid a grin at her friend's lack of intonation.

"I see how it is." A frown marred Vance's handsome face. "You think you're above such a small part. I suppose you think you should take Miss Barlow's place as Juliet."

"I'm excited, Vance." She tried to convey an enthusiasm for the breadcrumb he offered.

"I worked hard to get Mr. and Mrs. Easley to give you this chance." His mouth turned down.

Her heart sank at the disappointment on his face. Vance was being sweet and thoughtful. She had no right to trample on his kindness. "I'm sorry. I suppose it's a little overwhelming to think of going onstage so soon."

She ignored Clem's grunt. Clem had little respect for any of the actors. She was constantly pointing out to Jasmine the advantages of working with the production instead of reaching for fame as an actress. She might be right, but Jasmine wanted the adulation of the audience. She wanted to be sought after. She wanted her name on the playbills passed out in the town as advertisement.

Vance took her arm and pulled her off the stool. "Come with me."

"What happened to the actress who was supposed to be playing Lady Montague?" Jasmine asked the question as they left the lower floor of the barge.

Vance led the way, his long legs taking the steps two at a time. "She's too drunk to stand up. Mrs. Easley told her to get off the boat. So see, this is the perfect chance for you to be able to perform regularly."

Jasmine tried to hide her surprise. A drunk actress? She'd never dreamed of rubbing elbows with women who drank alcohol. Maybe that's why Lily had been so worried about her. But her oldest sister should know she would never do such a thing.

Vance halted suddenly and turned to face her. "Things have been hectic, but I want you to know how often I think of you, Jasmine. This is your chance, you know. Once you get on that stage, I know you'll be on your way to stardom."

Her bruised heart healed a little from the warmth of his words. "Thank you." She could swallow her disappointment. Vance was doing what he could. Maybe when they left Vicksburg, he would be able to spare some time for her. Maybe then—

Her thoughts ended abruptly when Vance gripped her arms and yanked her off balance. She fell against his chest with an audible *oomph*, and before she realized what was happening, his lips covered hers. Shock kept her still for an instant, and he took full advantage, slathering her face with his wet, soft mouth. It was like being kissed by a fish. Her mind and her body reacted violently to his assault. Twisting and pushing, she forced her elbow into his stomach, gaining her freedom when he stepped back.

"Mr. Hargrove." Jasmine put all the disdain she could manage into the two words, raising her hand to wipe the disgusting wetness from her mouth.

"I thought you felt the same for me as I do for you, Jasmine." He tried once again to pull her close.

This time she was prepared. She stiffened her arms and shook her head. "I hold you in high esteem. . .but I'm not some fancy woman you met in a tavern."

"Of course not." He dropped his grip on her and hung his head. "Don't you know how I feel about you? Don't you know how your beauty—your radiant innocence—drives me mad? 'Come live with me and be my love, And we will all the pleasures prove.'"

Christopher Marlowe's poem was one she had loved as a young girl, thinking it the height of romance. But he needed to understand that she wasn't about to let him ruin her.

Borrowing from the same poem, she answered him. " 'I don't need beds of roses or a cap and kirtle.' " With her nose in the air, she pushed past him to the stage door. Fame was awaiting her.

"Take your place upstage, Lady Montague." Mr. Easley's words were accompanied with a lift of his chin.

She scampered toward the back of the stage, thankful that she knew enough to understand his direction. Two other actors were center stage after the fight scene between the two families. Listening intently, she stepped forward as Benvolio ended his speech. Her heart pounded. "O, where is Romeo? Saw you him today? Right glad I am he was not at this fray." The words flowed out of her mouth with exactly the right emphasis and tone.

As Benvolio answered her question, a movement to her right caught her attention. Vance blew her a kiss just before he stepped onto the stage.

A moment more, and it was over. Lord Montague called her away, and they walked off the stage. "Well done." The older man, Stan Mitchum, one of the stock actors who played the smaller parts, sent her a smile. "You're a natural, honey."

The praise made her glow. Clem found her and dragged her back to the prop room so her costume could be altered. Then it was time to grab a bite to eat and get dressed for the performance.

As soon as the farce ended, Jasmine took her place behind the curtain. The chorus—two women—were already on stage and would soon introduce the audience to the blood feud between the Montagues and the Capulets. Miss Barlow, dressed in the resplendent gold ball gown with its newly attached flounce, stood nearby.

Between them, the men rushed forward, their swords raised. It seemed only a moment later that Lord Montague whisked her onto the stage. She faltered for a moment when she saw the number of people in the audience. It seemed every seat was taken. Mesmerized by the reality, she missed her cue and silence filled the stage.

"Hold me not," Lord Montague shook the arm that she had barely managed to retain her hold on. "Let me go."

Jasmine's gasp was loud as she realized what had happened. "Thou shalt not stir a foot to seek a foe." At least her gasp fit the part of a distressed Lady Montague concerned for her husband's welfare.

The scene played out without further incident. Vance, looking handsome in a crimson doublet and hose, winked at her as he returned to the stage.

She was in heaven as she exited and took the opportunity to glance once more toward the audience. What she saw made her heart drop to her toes. Jane Baxter, Camellia's best friend from the finishing school in New Orleans, was seated in the front row.

Had Camellia's friend recognized her? Jasmine tried to tell herself it wasn't possible. The heavy stage paint they wore disguised her features. And Jane wouldn't expect to see her here. As Jasmine stripped off her costume and returned to helping Clem with the other actors' costume changes, she decided Jane could not have recognized her. She was safe for now.

"What did you think?" Clem's curious voice gave Jasmine something else to concentrate on besides her fears.

"It was wonderful. I was born to be an actress. It was a small part, but the audience liked me."

"I heard you flubbed your first line." Miss Fenwick appeared in the doorway. "Do you have my green dress ready?"

Clem shook her head. "It'll be in your room by the third act."

"I'll not be pushed aside for Vance's latest trinket." Miss Fenwick glared in Jasmine's direction. "If she can't have my clothes ready on time, she'll have to give up acting. She wasn't hired for that purpose anyway."

"If you would stay away from those French pastries, we wouldn't have to keep letting out your dress." Clem shook a finger at the actress. "Go away before I tell Mrs. Easley that Jasmine should study for your role."

Miss Fenwick's mouth opened and closed several times, but apparently she didn't know what to say unless the words were scripted for her. Her face turned an ugly shade of red, and she turned on her heel.

Jasmine met Clem's gaze, and a giggle forced its way past her throat. Soon they were both laughing, tears streaming from their eyes.

Clem sobered first. "We'd better get back to work, or Miss Angelica Fenwick will have a real reason to complain. I don't want to lose the best friend I've had in years."

Grabbing her needle and scissors, Jasmine nodded and looked around at the pile of material. "How long will we stay in Vicksburg?"

"We have to perform in Memphis on Thursday, so we'll probably leave tomorrow after the early show."

Jasmine was relieved. Perhaps Jane had not recognized her tonight, but if she ran into the woman in town or if Jane attended another performance, she would be caught. The sooner the *Ophelia* left Vicksburg, the more likely she could remain hidden.

Chapter Twenty-one

"Did you see any of their faces, Mr. Baxter?" David asked the bank manager, even though he thought he already knew the answer.

A slight man with hair as white as a field of ripe cotton, Mr. Harold Baxter exuded an air of quiet competence. His hair must have grayed prematurely, because he looked only a few years older than David. He carried himself well in spite of the empty sleeve of his jacket. David wondered if he had lost his arm during the war and which side he might have fought for.

"Please call me Harry. That's what everyone around here calls me. Some of my fellow employees don't even know that my given name is Harold."

"All right, Harry. Now, about their faces?"

"The lower parts were hidden behind handkerchiefs." Harry frowned. "But they seemed to know exactly where to go, as if they already knew the layout of the bank."

"We think they spend some time in town, slipping in and out of the area while they learn what they need to know. Hours of operation, security, and the number of employees to name a few."

"You think I've seen them before?"

"It's quite likely." It was the only theory David could imagine. The bank robberies were too smooth. He had first believed they might have inside help from someone who worked for the bank, but these robbers had struck banks from Chicago to New Orleans. No one could have acquaintances associated with that many banks. What was the connection? The elusive "Ophelia" was the most obvious answer. He closed his notebook and stood. "Please think about the past few days carefully. Any new customers? Or perhaps your tellers might remember someone who has been hanging out in your lobby for the last week or so. Any little detail to help me catch these men."

"I'll be glad to, Detective."The other man stood and walked around his desk. "I want you to catch those scoundrels as much as you do."

"Thank you." He hesitated before going to the door. "I do have something else I wanted to mention to you, Harry. It's about your wife, Jane, and a friend of hers."

"Oh?"

David cleared his throat. "Yes. Camellia Thornton is a close friend of mine, and she was concerned about you and Jane when she learned of the bank robbery. I wish you would ask your wife to send her a note. I would send word, but I know she'll want to hear confirmation directly from Mrs. Baxter."

"You're a friend of Camellia's?" Baxter's face was warmer than it had been during their interview. "I insist you join us for dinner this evening. Jane will skin me alive if she discovers a friend of her old schoolmate is eating alone."

"Thank you, but I'm afraid I have work to do."

"I understand that, but you must find time to eat. . .if not tonight then another evening." Harry clapped him on the shoulder.

Realizing he couldn't refuse without sounding churlish, David inclined his head. "Thank you, another night would be better."

"Good. How about this Thursday? That should give you time to wrap up the most pressing of your business."

After receiving directions to the Baxters' home, David left. He had a lot of ground to cover.

Over the next several days, David met with the police, who had no additional information, and spent hours interviewing the proprietors and patrons of businesses close to the bank. No one had heard of Ophelia, and no one had noticed any strangers hanging about. How did these men manage to hide in plain sight? What magic did they use to pass freely through the town and escape notice? It was frustrating to find no evidence. . .again.

David was beginning to doubt his ability as a detective. He should be able to pick up the trail of at least one of them. So far, the only mistake they'd made was letting Charlie Petrie get caught. And they'd remedied that by killing him.

On Thursday evening, he returned to the hotel, pulling his extra coat from his bag and smoothing it with a damp cloth. He hoped it would pass muster tonight. Jane and her husband were obviously as wealthy as Jasmine's family.

Since the address was not too far from the hotel, he decided to walk. David wanted to turn away when he arrived at the Baxters' home, a graceful three-story mansion that was the largest house on the street. But it was too late. David stiffened his shoulders and climbed the front steps. The porch provided a panoramic view of the Mississippi River, and a cool, steady breeze teased his coattails as he waited at the front door.

A butler ushered him inside, took his card, and guided him to the main parlor. "Detective David Foster."

After the announcement, the man stood aside, and David entered the parlor. The room looked like a garden brought indoors. Images of roses graced the wallpaper, the curtains, and the rug at his feet. A large vase on the table in the center of the room was filled with fresh roses, their fragrance filling the air.

He saw Harry first, and then his wife—a tall, slender woman with hair as red as the roses she apparently loved. She walked toward him, a welcoming smile on her face. "Detective Foster, it's a pleasure to meet you."

David tried to imagine this beauty and Camellia as friends. They must have turned every male head in New Orleans. He bowed over her hand. "The pleasure is mine, Mrs. Baxter."

"Please, call me Jane." She smiled up at him. "I'm anxious to hear news of Camellia. How is her little girl doing? And Jonah? You must tell me everything."

They moved into the dining room, and David found himself comfortable with his gracious hosts. After regaling the couple with news from Les Fleurs, their conversation turned to the dismal economy and President Grant's latest scandal.

"Speaking of scandals, I suppose Camellia and Lily are quite upset that Jasmine is working as an actress."

David leaned forward, his gaze sharpening at Jane's comment. He couldn't believe news of the runaway had fallen into his lap like an overripe plum. "You've seen Jasmine here in Vicksburg?"

Jane sipped from her glass of lemonade before answering. "I didn't recognize her at first, but I know it was Jasmine. Those eyes of hers are so distinctive, almost purple in color. I always told Camellia her name should be Violet or maybe Iris."

"Where did you see her?"

Jane looked a little surprised at his intensity. "She was on one of those showboats."

He should have known. If not for his concern over the bank robberies, he might have even thought of looking for her on a showboat. It was an easy way for her to reach her destination, earn some money, and gain experience. Jasmine might be selfish and stubborn, but no one could accuse her of being dimwitted. "Camellia's been frantic since she disappeared from Les Fleurs a few days ago. I'd like to find her and send her back home. What was the name of the showboat?"

"It had one of those Greek-sounding names. Do you remember, Harry? Was it Portia?"

"That doesn't sound quite right." Her husband pushed back from the table. "I think I kept a playbill. Would you like to see it?"

"Yes." David could hardly believe he had found Jasmine. At least once he sent her home he could concentrate on his real job.

Harry returned with the gaudy advertisement in his hand.

As soon as David saw the name at the top, his heart clenched. He took the paper in his hand and stared down at it, his mind spinning. He couldn't believe it. Jasmine had taken a job on a ship called the *Ophelia*. Another name in bold typeface drew his attention, and the final piece of the puzzle fell in place. *Vance Hargrove.* He was the reason Jasmine had gotten a position on the showboat. And he was the common link for all of the bank robberies as well. "May I keep this?"

Both Baxters nodded.

David knew he had to find the boat right away. Explaining the gravity of the situation, he took his leave of them and half-ran, half-walked back to the waterfront. A city of boats rested there, some tied to the piers while others were roped together, forming floating islands. Dogged determination pushed him from deck to deck, posing as the concerned brother of a runaway as he made his inquiries. Finally he found a captain who knew the *Ophelia*.

"She left outa' here a few days back." The swarthy man scratched his beard. "I heard tell they was going to Memphis for a week or so, and then on to St. Louis, mebbe all the way to Chicago."

David's jaw clenched so hard he thought his teeth might break. "You're sure?"

The captain nodded. "I hope you find your sister."

"I will." He stomped away, his mind boiling. Should he send a message to Camellia and Jonah? What if Jasmine was no longer with the *Ophelia* by the time he caught up with the boat? He didn't want to raise their hopes at this point and have to disappoint them later. It would be better to wait. By this time tomorrow night he would have his hands on her. He would read her the riot act. . .as soon as he was certain she was okay. Then he would send her home and concentrate on his real job of collaring criminals.

❧

David wasted no time in locating the *Ophelia* as soon as he arrived in Memphis. A performance was about to begin, so he decided the easiest way to gain entry was as a theatergoer. He smiled at the lady who sold him a ticket and entered the room that held the theater. Impressed by the number of people in the audience, he chose a seat toward the back and looked at the new playbill in his hand.

Her name jumped out at him. The part of the nurse was being played by none other than Jasmine Anderson. She hadn't even had the sense to choose a pseudonym. Jane Baxter had said Jasmine was playing a minor part, but that must have changed. Was her rapid rise due to her talent? He hoped that was the reason. He ground his teeth at the idea that Vance Hargrove might use his influence on her behalf for his own dissolute purposes.

He ought to march himself to the crew quarters and confront Jasmine right now. But something held him back. What was it? He couldn't be reluctant to end her foolishness—her attempt to earn fame and fortune. Jasmine should be back at Les Fleurs dancing with men from her social circle, not consorting with philanderers and loose women. She should be surrounded by the protection of her sisters and extended family. Jasmine might not—would not—agree, but only because the little minx was as blind to the dangers around her as a field mouse being stalked by an owl.

Fish Out of Water, the first offering, was an uncomplicated farce about a series of misunderstandings between a couple that led to all sorts of trouble, including infidelity.

David found himself embarrassed by the sexual innuendos. This was exactly why working in the theater was not something an innocent girl should do. Jasmine probably didn't even understand the worst of the bawdy jokes, but it wouldn't be long before some helpful soul explained them to her.

He crossed his arms over his chest when the farce ended with much laughter and applause. David was growing increasingly anxious for the entertainment to end so he could get to Jasmine and get her out of here.

After the stage was reset, the curtain rose once more, and the two-woman chorus began telling the audience of the tragic events about to unfold in front of them. He recognized Jasmine the moment she stepped on the stage, even though she was playing the part of a much older woman. It was ludicrous. Tabitha Barlow might have been hired to play the part of Juliet, but she was much too mature. The drama would be more believable if she and Jasmine switched parts.

He had to admit, though, that Jasmine had talent. She played the part with understanding and energy. Shakespeare had written the role as comic relief, and Jasmine brought laughter to the audience with her facial expressions and gestures, even during heartrending scenes of the tragedy.

At the end of the play, David leaped to his feet, adding his applause to that of the rest of the crowd around him. A part of him wished it was possible for Jasmine to be an actress on the scale she dreamed of. God had obviously showered her with talent. But she needed a way to use her abilities in an uplifting, moral manner. If she remained a part of this world, she would lose the very spark that made her stand out from the other actors in the production.

He fought his way against the crowd and managed to reach the edge of the stage. Where would Jasmine be? Eating? Sleeping? Flirting with Hargrove? He thrust the curtains out of his way and found a door leading to a different part of the barge. As he reached for the handle, the door opened toward him, and two young women carrying mops stepped through. The first was a brunette, a girl he didn't recognize.

David forgot all about her when the second female gasped and let her mop fall. Jasmine looked like a startled fawn. He reached out and caught her arm before she could bolt. "What a surprise to find you here."

"Let go of my friend." The other girl rapped his knuckles with the handle of her mop. "I'll scream for help."

He winced but kept his grip on Jasmine. She would not escape so easily.

"Camellia must have sent you to track me down."

The other girl's mouth snapped shut at Jasmine's accusation.

David couldn't let her reveal his true identity. "Who better than your brother?"

"Well, you can just go back home to Natchez and tell Camellia—and Lily, too—that I'm fine. In fact, I'm more than fine. I've found a job and several friends. People who understand me and share the same interests. None of you needs to worry about me anymore."

"He's your brother?" The other girl picked up Jasmine's mop and handed it back to her.

His glare warned Jasmine to agree. She was the one who had first claimed he was a brother to her, after all. And it gave him the perfect cover story.

After a moment she nodded. "Would you give us a few minutes, Clem?"

"Ummm, o–kay." Clem emphasized the last syllable, infusing it with a great deal of curiosity. She must be an actress, too.

David dropped his hold on Jasmine's arm as soon as they were alone. "How soon can you be packed?"

"Packed?" She tossed her head like a restive horse. "Why should I pack? I'm not leaving. You are."

"Don't be ridiculous. You can't stay here."

"Yes, I can."

David gave her another warning glare. "I don't intend to argue with you. This boat is at best inappropriate for a lady with even the barest of morals; at worst it's dangerous."

"What on earth are you talking about?"

He glanced around to make sure no one lurked in the large room. "I have reason to believe that this showboat is involved in the bank robberies I'm investigating."

"That's ridiculous."

"No, it's not. In fact, it makes a great deal of sense. Before he was murdered, one of the robbers I was working with managed to tell me one word—*Ophelia*."

He saw the gooseflesh prickling her arms. Good. Jasmine needed to realize how much danger she was in.

"What makes you think he was referring to this *Ophelia*? There must be dozens of other reasons he would mention a woman's name. Or you might have misunderstood him." Her eyes widened. "Or maybe he lied to you. He was a thief, wasn't he?"

"He wouldn't have any reason to lie when he knew he was dying, and I've looked for any other connection. The *Ophelia* was in New Orleans during the robbery there, and in Vicksburg. It wouldn't surprise me at all if a bank in Memphis was the next target."

"So were dozens of other boats."

He should have known Jasmine would argue. She had never seen him as someone deserving respect.

The stage door creaked open behind them. "Jasmine? Clem sent me to check on—" Vance Hargrove stopped short as he stepped onto the stage. "Mr. Anderson. What brings you to Memphis?"

"I'm retrieving my sister."

Hargrove frowned at Jasmine. "I thought you said your family agreed for you to come."

David would have laughed if he hadn't been so exasperated at this further evidence of Jasmine's duplicity. "She didn't bother to ask permission."

"I didn't need to." Jasmine moved toward the other man. "I'm an adult. In spite of my brother's threats, I have every right to stay with you."

David wanted to step between them. He wouldn't be surprised if steam started pouring from his ears. Jasmine was not going to stay on the *Ophelia*, no matter what she thought. "You can't prevent my putting you on the next boat heading to Natchez with instructions to deliver you to Les Fleurs."

"Maybe not, but it won't matter. I'll run away again as soon as Camellia's back is turned. I've tasted freedom now, and I refuse to accept a life of bondage any longer."

He wanted to remove Vance's smirk by fastening a set of handcuffs around his wrists. But he couldn't let himself be distracted by pleasant fantasies. "Jasmine, I don't care if you have to spend the rest of your days locked in your bedroom, you're not staying here."

"The thing I don't understand is how your brother figured out you're on the *Ophelia* if your family didn't know."

Feeling like he'd been doused with a bucket of cold water, David shut his mouth at the suspicious words.

"I think I know what must have happened." Jasmine stepped into the uneasy silence. "Do you remember my hesitation the first time I took the stage?"

Hargrove turned his suspicious gaze toward her.

"Jane Baxter was in the audience. She lives in Vicksburg, but she's my—our—sister Camellia's best friend."

"Yes, she's the one who put me on your trail." Perhaps Jasmine would make a better detective than he did. Her story was convincing and stayed close enough to the truth that neither of them would be tripped up by contradictory details. He allowed a tight smile to loosen his mouth. "I promised Camellia I'd stop you from ruining your life, and I'm going to keep my promise."

"Wait, wait, wait." Vance took a step away from Jasmine and snapped his fingers.

David raised an eyebrow, wondering what Vance was going to say next. Was the man going to accuse him of an ulterior motive?

"I have the perfect answer to satisfy both of you. Your brother is worried about your reputation, and you're determined to stay on board because this is your dream, right?" Hargrove turned to him. "Do you have to return to Mississippi right away?"

David shook his head. He thought he might be getting an inkling of the other man's train of thought. "The rest of the family will get along fine without me for a while."

"Our tugboat captain is always losing his hands to more lucrative jobs, and you're bound to have some experience since you come from a riverboat family. You can work there and keep an eye on your sister until you're convinced she's safe with us." Hargrove beamed at both of them, expecting compliments on his brilliance.

"I don't think that's a good idea." Jasmine glared at David. "Having my *brother* close by is bound to inhibit my performances."

"Perfect. I'll do it." David grinned at her stormy expression. He offered a hand to the actor. "You've solved everything."

Jasmine stomped away from them, her outrage plain in every step. But David was pleased. He could nose around and gather more evidence before making arrests, starting with the self-satisfied Hargrove. And he could make sure Jasmine was safe. . .even if he had to threaten her with an arrest for conspiracy.

Chapter Twenty-two

Clem pushed Jasmine's arm up until it was parallel to the floor. "Be still or I won't be able to get your measurements right."

Jasmine didn't mean to drop her arm, but she was having a hard time with her concentration. David had sent a telegram to Camellia this morning and returned after breakfast with the information that they would be having dinner with Eli and Renée Thornton this evening. Had a man ever been more high-handed? If he hadn't been a longtime family friend, she wouldn't put up with his arrogance.

"I'm glad your brother got a job on the *Miss Polly*." Clem shoved a pin through the navy-blue material of the dress.

"Why?" Jasmine couldn't believe her friend was taking his side over hers. Did Clem want her to be bundled back to Mississippi?

"He's. . .he's single, isn't he?"

Jasmine's arm dropped, and a dozen pins pricked her side. "Ow."

"I told you to stand still."

"I know." She raised her arm again. "Please don't tell me you're developing an interest in David."

"He is handsome." Clem's face suffused with color. "And you can tell he's honorable by the way he treats all the women on board, even Miss Barlow and Miss Fenwick."

"He's not honorable. He's overbearing and egotistical. And a stick in the mud."

"He is not. You don't know how lucky you are to have a brother who loves you enough to come looking for you." Clem's sigh lingered in the quiet room. "It's so romantic."

David's popularity on the *Ophelia* amazed her. What did these women see in him? He had been here only a little more than twelve hours, and he was already the darling of every woman from Miss Barlow to the cook. He was David—solid, practical, bossy David. "Believe me, Clem. He doesn't have a romantic bone in his body."

Clem snorted her disbelief. "You can get down now."

Jasmine stepped off the stool.

"You only think he's romantic because you don't know my. . .brother." She couldn't help the waspish tone. Everything had gotten so mixed up. Convincing the others to ignore him was not getting her anywhere. Even the men seemed drawn to him. Mr. Easley had better watch out, or he might find himself replaced by her "brother."

She could only think of one way to get rid of him—tell everyone that he was a Pinkerton detective. But she couldn't betray him. She couldn't expose his real reason for taking the position on their tugboat, even though she knew David was wrong about the *Ophelia*'s connection to the bank robberies. She was as certain of that as she was her own name. Absolutely, positively certain.

The actors on board the showboat had their weaknesses, but not a one of them was evil. Last night and again at breakfast this morning, she found herself looking for something sinister in the people around her. But it was ridiculous. From the gruff Mr. Easley to sweet Clem, each and every one of the people on this boat was focused on providing quality entertainment. Besides, the *Ophelia* was making good money. Why would someone want to risk a lucrative income on a hanging offense?

Clem helped her pull the dress over her head. "I know I'm being foolish. No one as kind and handsome as your brother would ever look at someone like me."

Jasmine emerged from the dress with a gasp. "Don't you ever say anything like that again. Don't even think it. You're talented and beautiful and very special. You're worth a dozen Davids."

"Me? I'm just a farm girl who didn't want to spend her life plucking chickens and milking cows." Clem smoothed her hand over the material of the dress. "I once got a switching because I cut up Ma's curtains to make a dress for wearing to church on Easter Sunday."

Jasmine had been in trouble plenty of times, but Lily had never spanked her. "She must have been very upset."

"Especially when it turned out the dress I made ended about halfway between my knees and my ankles."

The picture that formed in her mind made Jasmine giggle. "What did you wear to church?"

"The same old dress I'd been wearing all year long. Ma made me cut my curtain dress into squares for making a quilt. It was pretty, but not nearly as pretty as the dress I'd dreamed of wearing." Clem's giggle joined hers.

Their shared laughter restored the camaraderie between them. Jasmine began picking up the scraps from the floor when an idea came to her. David had once told her he conducted interviews to get information. An interview was nothing but a bunch of questions, wasn't it? Maybe she could conduct her own interviews and prove to him that his suspicions were unfounded.

"Where was your parents' farm?"

"A small town in Ohio. The name wouldn't mean anything to you."

Jasmine nodded. This interview stuff was easy. "How long have you been on the *Ophelia*?"

"Only a year."

"What made you look for a job here?"

Clem got out her thread and picked up the dress. "You sure are curious this afternoon. Are you checking to see if I would be an acceptable wife for your brother?"

Feeling like she'd fetched upon a hidden snag, Jasmine blinked. "Of course not. I just thought I'd find out more about you. . .since we're friends and all."

The needle flashed up and down in quick motions. "I guess that makes sense. But sometimes people don't want to be asked about their pasts. Some might think you were being nosy or that you were trying to figure out their weaknesses."

So much for her future as a detective. Jasmine wondered how David managed to avoid raising people's suspicions. Especially people who had a reason to hide something from a lawman.

"I'm sorry. I was just interested in you, Clem. Will you forgive me for being a bother?"

"You're not a bother." Clem pulled on a seam to check its strength. "I just don't want you to make enemies here. You're pretty and talented, which is sure to make all the women jealous. Miss Fenwick in particular. Didn't I tell you earlier that she's the type to scratch your eyes out? If you go asking her questions, she may push you overboard."

"I'll remember that." Jasmine checked her appearance in the full-length mirror attached to one of the walls in the dressing room. "Mr. Easley called a rehearsal this morning. If you're done with me for now, I'll go read over my lines."

"Don't leave right away." Clem looked up. "Tell me more about your brother."

"I. . .I can't." She escaped before Clem could continue asking her about things she didn't want to answer. Her interrogation skills would have to improve if she was going to help solve David's case and get him out of her way.

❧

"Your garden is so beautiful, Renée." Jasmine smiled at the petite woman. "I don't know how you have time to tend it while taking care of your houseful of men."

She glanced up at the crescent moon and starlit sky above them, glad Renée had offered to walk through her flower garden instead of sitting in the drawing room while the men finished their dinner. Iona, Brandon's fiancée, had remained inside, concerned that the night air and pollen would give her a headache.

Renée settled her shawl around her shoulders. "It does take some time in the spring, but I think it's worth the effort."

"I never enjoyed the work, but the result you've achieved is breathtaking." Yellow daisies, pink and lavender dahlias, and lacy purple carnations swayed gently in the evening breeze. Jasmine breathed deeply, enjoying the fragrances almost as much as the carpet of blooms surrounding them.

"Your namesake is growing over here." Renée led her to a trellis in one corner of the garden. Delicate white blossoms peeked out from between velvety green leaves. She plucked a couple of blooms and tucked them into Jasmine's hair.

The sweet scent of the flowers brought a smile to her lips. "Thank you."

"It's my pleasure." Renée put her arm around Jasmine's waist. "I've been praying for your safe return ever since Lily and Blake told us you went missing."

Why did she have to bring that up? Jasmine pulled away from Renée's arm. She didn't want another homily about setting out on her own. Why didn't anyone understand her? All during dinner, Renée and Eli's sons had peppered her with questions about the showboat. She had enjoyed the attention and the admiration.

"I know you think you're a grown woman, Jasmine, but in Lily's mind you'll always be a little girl who needs her guidance. I feel the same way about my boys. My eyes can see that they're young men, but my heart knows how vulnerable they are, how much they still have to learn."

"Brandon's about to get married and start a family of his own." Jasmine liked Iona—a pretty girl from Memphis with a tinkling laugh and big brown eyes that seemed locked on her fiancé. "Surely you don't still see him as a child."

Renée pinched a dead bloom from the top of a rose bush. "But I do, dear. I know how quickly he can forget the lessons his father and I have tried to instill in him. Whenever I look at my sons, I think of

Jesus' parable of the sower. The dangers of this world are so pervasive."

Jasmine wanted to scoff, but the serious expression on the other woman's face warned her to remain quiet.

Renée swept her hand out to indicate the plants around them. "I've seen firsthand how easily seeds can be destroyed. Birds, heat, weeds, all three of the examples Jesus talked about have threatened my flowers."

The problem with Renée's comparison was evident to Jasmine. She might be named after a flower, but she was a person. She had the sense to stay out of the sunlight in the heat of summer, and neither birds nor weeds were a threat to her.

"It's only through watchful tending and God's provision that these plants reach maturity. Even then they can be destroyed if some insect or blight gains entry. That's how Satan operates. He's always quick to attack unwary souls. Lily wants you to thrive in the garden of life, but even more than that, she wants to make sure you follow the path God set out for you."

That's what Jasmine was trying to do. If everyone would leave her be. Their problem was not being able to see that her path was not a traditional one. She had so much to offer the world, much more than the women who were tied down with husbands and households.

Remington opened the door and ran to them, his impulsiveness propelling him forward. "Can I come to the showboat to see you acting?"

Renée shook her head. "I don't know if that's a good idea. We don't want to make Jasmine nervous."

"Don't worry. I've had a lot of practice performing for people I know. It will probably make things even easier."

Remington begged his mother to attend as they walked back to the house. Cameron was talking to David and his father in one corner of the parlor while Brandon and Iona had their heads together, intent on the magazine she held.

"We'll ask your father what he thinks." Renée pulled off her shawl and laid it on the back of the sofa.

"Pa, can we go see Jasmine tomorrow?" Remington was as tenacious as a bull terrier.

Following in his wake, Jasmine wondered if the Thorntons' youngest son would choose a path his parents approved of. Both Brandon and Cameron seemed more serious, more interested in working in the family business. But Remington was different. Perhaps he would like to join her in the theater. He was only sixteen now. By the time he was old enough to leave home, she would be established enough to give him a helping hand.

"What did your mother say?" Eli queried.

"To ask you."

Jasmine couldn't help smiling at Remington's hopeful expression. "I wish you would. I can speak to the manager about holding five seats for you."

"Make it six." Eli pointed his chin toward his oldest son. "They're inseparable these days."

The engaged couple were too engrossed in each other to realize they were being discussed.

As she nodded agreement, David cleared his throat. "I imagine we need to get back. You need a good night's sleep, and I am supposed to tend the boiler in a little while."

Renée's mouth turned down. "Must you go so soon?"

"I'm afraid so."

Jasmine would have disagreed, but she had to admit she was tired. Rehearsals, fittings, and two performances had made the day long. She wasn't sleeping well, either, worried about David dragging her back to Les Fleurs. The idea of resting her head on a soft pillow was so appealing that the sudden need to yawn made her eyes water. "I suppose we should." She had the satisfaction of seeing surprise in David's green gaze. Maybe that would teach him that he didn't know her as well as he thought.

They thanked the family for inviting them, even managing to pull Brandon away from his love long enough to say good-bye.

Eli walked them to the front door. "Are you sure you don't want to take our carriage back to the boat?"

Of course David answered for both of them, claiming the evening too perfect for being cooped up in a carriage. It was a good thing she didn't mind the walk. Raising her chin, Jasmine marched down the stairs without waiting for his escort.

He caught up with her in a few steps, of course, reaching for her arm. Jasmine tried to pull free of him, but his grip was too strong. Fine. He might be able to compel her to walk beside him, but he couldn't make her talk to him.

"It's a nice evening."

She ignored his puny attempt at conversation.

"I thought Brandon's fiancée was a sweet girl."

Jasmine kept her lips pressed tight. A nearby street lamp showed her the frown on his face.

"Do you hate me that much?"

His question hit her with the power of a lightning bolt. "I don't hate you."

"That's a relief." David pushed back his hat and wiped his brow.

He could be so silly at times. And his highhandedness, his failure to consult her most of the time, proved that he lied. "You don't really care what I think."

David stopped walking, forcing her to halt or risk straining her arm. "I care far too much about your feelings."

"You have hidden talents, Mr. Foster. You may earn a role in our next production."

"Don't call me that. Remember that everyone on the *Ophelia* thinks we're siblings."

She wrinkled her nose at him. "That wasn't my idea. I still don't understand why you introduced yourself as my brother back in New Orleans."

His laugh was closer to a dog's bark than a sound of amusement. Shaking his head, he resumed walking. "Did you enjoy dinner?"

"Yes, more than I thought I would. And she is a sweet girl."

It seemed to take him a minute before realizing she was referring to his earlier statement. "What was her name again?"

"Iona Woods." She choked back a giggle. What had possessed her parents to choose such a name for their daughter?

David's laugh sounded more natural this time. "I suppose it's better than naming her Piney."

Piney Woods. She doubled over with laughter. The sound of their merriment blended together like a harmonious chord, and suddenly she was once again the barefoot girl who loved running across the deck of the *Water Lily*. Jasmine turned toward him like she would have done back then, putting her hands on his shoulders as she allowed free rein to her mirth.

It felt natural when his arms went around her, held her close to his chest. For a moment no warning bells sounded in her mind, and when they did she found them easy to ignore. This was David after all, not some stranger.

His heartbeat thumped against her cheek even as his laughter began to lessen. She knew she should straighten, but it felt so good to be this near to him. David wasn't as tall as Vance, and he didn't wear a cologne to compete with the earthy, masculine scent that was uniquely his.

"Jasmine?" David's tentative voice made her tilt her head back.

The walls between them fell with the suddenness of Jericho's fortifications. The yearning look in his face touched her heart in a place so deep that it almost hurt. She caught her breath and watched as his eyelids drooped low, hiding half of his serious green gaze. On some level she knew he was going to kiss her. She wanted it, wanted to feel his lips on hers, wanted to draw even closer.

Her blood thickened, slowing her heart and making her ears ring. When his hooded gaze dropped to her mouth, she thought she might die. Yet how could she die when every inch of her was alive in a way it never had been before.

One of her hands reached up and pulled his head lower, throwing caution and sense to the wind. His lips captured hers, and she felt the earth shake below her feet. Joy filled her as they clung together. It was heady, exciting. . .and absolutely impossible.

The warning bells clanged loud and deep. What was she doing? This would never work. It was all wrong. Her hands pushed against his shoulders. "Stop."

"Jasmine."

"Don't ever touch me again." She spat the words at him, picked up her skirts, and started running. She didn't stop until she reached the *Ophelia*. But even when she found her room and readied for bed, her mind still ran in directions she dared not follow.

Chapter Twenty-three

David wasn't at breakfast the next morning. After the third female asked her where he was, Jasmine threw up her hands and left the dining hall. *Am I my brother's keeper?*

Vance followed her into the hallway. "I missed seeing you after the performance last night."

Jasmine stopped walking and pinned a smile to her face. At least Vance wouldn't want to know where David was. "I had to go to dinner with some family friends."

"Should I be jealous?" Vance put his hand on the wall above her right shoulder.

She raised her left shoulder in a shrug. "They're coming to the boat this afternoon. You can see for yourself."

"Something's different about you today." He put a finger under her chin and tilted it upward, studying her face.

Jasmine pulled her head back, banging it on the wall behind her. "I don't know what you're talking about."

"Vance, leave the girl alone and take this money to the bank. You know what we need." Mr. Easley's voice brought scalding hot blood into Jasmine's cheeks.

"I have to go." She ducked under Vance's arm and ran to her room. Closing the door with a snap, she leaned against it and concentrated on breathing deeply. Rubbing the back of her head, she wondered what Vance had seen in her. Something had changed inside her, but was it obvious on the outside, too?

The question that had burned in her mind last night returned. Why had David's kiss been so devastating? The difference between his kiss and Vance's attempt was like the difference between the painting inside the Sistine Chapel and the scribbles of a child. Vance's touch had been repugnant, nasty, and wet. With David she had felt as though their souls touched, as though their hearts had been soldered together.

Was this one of the assaults Renée had tried to warn her about last night? Would her attraction to David destroy the seed of her talent? Her chin hardened. She wouldn't allow it. With a nod of her head, she straightened and opened the door. She would not be distracted.

After the third time she had to be cued for her next line, Jasmine realized it would take more than determination to overcome the effect of the previous night. Tears of hopelessness threatened to spill from her eyes.

"We need a break." Miss Barlow's voice rang out across the theater.

The manager checked his pocket watch. "Be back in thirty minutes."

Miss Barlow grabbed her hand. "Come with me."

Long nails dug into her arm, but Jasmine was too downhearted to complain. She didn't even pay any attention when the older woman led her down a separate passage. But when Miss Barlow dropped her hand and opened the door to her dressing suite, Jasmine balked.

"Get in here."

Jasmine crossed the threshold, her eyes wide. The large room was filled with open trunks overhung by skirts, blouses, dressing gowns, and silk chemises. Feather boas in one corner of the room looked like a litter of kittens, and shoes in all colors of the rainbow were scattered across the floor like autumn leaves.

Miss Barlow ignored the chaos, picking her way to a slipper chair and sitting. "What's wrong with you?"

"I don't. . . I—"

A snort interrupted her. "I thought you were made of stronger stuff than this. You've only been acting for a few weeks, but everyone who sees you knows you're talented. You have something special, something few people—even fewer ladies—have."

The color rushed upward again. "Thank you."

"I invited you to my room so we can talk frankly, just the two of us." Miss Barlow settled back against her chair. "You and I have many things in common. I was about the same age as you when I first started."

Jasmine wished she could sit down, but she didn't want to appear too forward by either perching on the edge of Tabitha's bed or sitting at her dressing table.

"In some ways those days seem like yesterday. But then I look in the mirror and I realize how long it's been—almost two decades. I wanted to be rich and famous. I wanted to read about my performances in the newspaper. I dreamed of the whole world knowing my name, of my photograph being the most recognizable in this country, in the whole world."

"But you *are* famous." Jasmine glanced at all the clothes around them. "And rich."

"Pah, this is nothing. And yet it's all I have." The other woman stood up and kicked a shoe out of her way. Reaching inside one of the trunks, she grabbed up a skirt. "I wore this on a stage in Virginia the day before the war began. Those were hard days. Never knowing when one army or the other might lock us away as spies." A harsh laugh came from her throat, and she tossed the skirt down. "Of course I did my fair share of passing along information on troops and plans. All for naught."

Jasmine didn't know what to say. Miss Barlow had been a spy? The very thought of doing something so dangerous made her heart trip.

"That's all ancient history now." Miss Barlow uncovered a wooden chair and pointed her finger at it. "Sit."

As soon as Jasmine settled down, the actress returned to her slipper chair. "Even though you're talented, you'll need help to see your dreams come true. Someone who has contacts in the world of the theater. Someone who can get you noticed by the right people. Someone like me."

Shock held her still. Of all the things she thought Miss Barlow might offer her, sponsorship was not one of them. "I don't know what to say."

"Thank you is sufficient."

When Jasmine hesitated, Miss Barlow's eyes narrowed. "Oh, I see how it is. Vance Hargrove has turned your head. You think he's all you need to get ahead."

"I—"

"Do you think you're the first pretty girl he's gotten a job for?" A harsh laugh came from the older woman. "Has he already kissed you?"

Jasmine put her hands to her burning cheeks. How did Miss Barlow know? Was it true that Vance didn't care about her? What about his words this morning?

"No need to answer, I can see it on your face. You're lucky I've decided to take an interest in you. After he is through using you, he'll be on to his next conquest."

She wanted to cover her ears to shut out Miss Barlow's words. Could they be true? Was Vance using her for his own purposes? And what about Miss Barlow? "Why do you want to help me?"

"Good. I knew you were a quick study." Miss Barlow's laugh sounded harsh to Jasmine's ears. "Everyone has their reasons, even me. If you become as famous as I think you will, you'll soon leave this country and become a sensation abroad. That's when I'll want your help. But in all honesty, if I really wanted to help you, Jasmine, I'd tell you to go to your handsome brother and beg him to take you home. Leave before you're as washed up as I am."

"You're not washed up."

Another callous laugh answered her statement. "I'm a long way from the theaters in New York. It's too late for me, but you can still get out."

"I don't want out. I want to see the world."

The other woman leaned forward, her chin propped on her hand.

"The world is not the exciting place you're imagining. It's mostly unwashed farmers, empty promises, and mud."

Jasmine pushed herself up from her chair. She'd heard enough.

"You can run if you want, but I'm trying to give you the benefit of my experience. I've been snubbed by ladies who think they're better than me. I've been pelted with rotten vegetables when the audience decides they're not getting their money's worth. I've had to run for my life with nothing but the clothes on my back."

Picking her way through the mess, Jasmine finally reached the door and jerked it open.

Before she could get out, though, Miss Barlow added her parting shot. "If you don't take my advice to escape, come back to see me. I can help you more than you realize."

The words reverberated in her mind as Jasmine went back to her room. She was embarrassed and upset by the interview with Miss Barlow. It was all too much for her. Everyone wanted something from her, each one demanding something different. She didn't know which way to turn anymore. Feeling dazed and confused, Jasmine threw herself across the bed and let the tears flow. How had everything gone so wrong?

❧

David wondered what he was going to say to Jasmine the next time he saw her. Guilt scoured him every time he thought of the way she'd run from him. He was an idiot. All these years he'd remained silent. And for what? So he could frighten her away when she realized he didn't think of her as a sister?

He saw the Thornton family from a distance as they boarded the showboat. He wished he could visit with them again, but the only time he could search the *Ophelia* was during the two hours that the performance had everyone occupied.

Judicious questioning of the unsuspecting Titus Ross, the tugboat captain, supplied him with the location of the actors' rooms. He started with Vance Hargrove's. A large bed covered with crimson silk sheets made his stomach churn. He had no doubt the actor was a master seducer, although what women saw in him was a mystery to David.

A thorough search of the nooks and crannies turned up no notes or incriminating evidence. David found a strongbox concealed in one of the man's trunks and wished he could open it without alerting Hargrove to the fact that it had been discovered. But the box was too small to hold much. He would have to find a more blatant connection before he risked showing his hand.

Someone walking down the hallway had him diving for cover, but the footsteps passed Hargrove's room. David knew it was time to get out before he had to explain his presence in the actor's quarters.

After listening for other activity, he opened the door an inch. The hall looked empty so he crept out of the room, closed the door without making a noise, and tiptoed back to the room where the props were stored. He could always feign some excuse if he was found there.

"There you are." Clem's voice made him jump. "I wondered if we would see you at all today."

He turned to her and smiled. Of all the people on the *Ophelia*, he prayed Clem was not involved. "I had some business to do in town this morning. Do you ever get off the boat to see some of the countryside?"

Her round face turned pink, and David wished he'd kept his mouth shut. He hadn't meant to give her the idea that he wanted to pursue her. All he wanted to do was eliminate her as a suspect.

"I'd love to see Memphis." Her smile made Clem's face transform from average to pretty.

How was he supposed to ignore such a blatant invitation? He didn't want to hurt her feelings. Maybe she would be satisfied with a quick walk through downtown to see the shops. "We'll have to do something about that."

A sound at the door made David look over his shoulder. His heart dropped to his toes as he recognized coal black hair and dark eyes the color of violets. He'd imagined many scenarios during the long hours of the night, but none of the meetings he'd dreamed of included Jasmine overhearing him making plans with another girl.

"Excuse me, Clem, but I need to talk to my brother before the two of you leave on your outing." Jasmine's voice was cool and calm.

David ran a finger around the collar of his shirt.

"If you can tear yourself away, of course." Her tone suggested he'd be sorry if he didn't.

Clem looked at both of them, muttered some excuse, and left them alone.

Jasmine's eyes burned his skin. "What do you think you're doing?"

Was she jealous? The thought was ludicrous. Wasn't it? Now that he really looked at Jasmine, he realized something he had not before. The skin around her eyes looked bruised. "Have you been crying?"

She shook her head. "I— of course not. It's just been a trying few days. Everything'll be better once you leave."

Here was the condemnation he'd expected. "I'm sorry, Jasmine. I never meant to—"

"Hush." She put a hand to her lips and glanced around. "I don't want to talk about it. We were both carried away by the moment. The sooner we move past what happened, the sooner things can go back to normal."

"If you didn't come to talk about. . .last night, then what?"

"I think I might have a clue."

Fear stole into his veins, pushed his heart all the way up his throat. "You're supposed to leave that to me. I don't want you putting yourself at risk."

Her eyes widened.

He wanted to shake some sense into her. "Don't you realize that some of these people are killers? One of them, maybe someone who works on this boat, stabbed a man in cold blood. Charles Petrie died in front of my eyes. I couldn't bear it if something happened to you."

One of the minor actors stuck his head in the door but backed away when David sent him a warning glare. "Hurry up and tell me what you learned before someone else comes in."

"Mr. Easley sent someone to the bank today."

David waited a minute for her to continue. When she didn't, he sighed, the urge to shake her growing stronger with each passing second. Jasmine couldn't still think this was all play. She had to grasp the gravity of the situation. "What else?"

"Nothing." She closed her mouth, but he could tell she was holding something back.

"Does it have something to do with Vance Hargrove?"

"Yes—well—maybe. But I'm certain he's innocent."

"Tell me, Jasmine, and let me decide who's innocent and who's guilty. That's what I'm trained to do."

She huffed. "It wasn't much really. Only that Mr. Easley gave Vance a huge pile of money and told him to go to the bank. Then he said, 'You know what to do.'"

The way she dropped her voice an octave and thrust out her chest was so cute. Jasmine might be an actress, but no one would confuse her with the two-hundred-pound manager. He wanted to laugh but knew he couldn't. That's what had gotten them in trouble last night. He needed to keep his focus on the case.

"Thanks for keeping your ears open, but I don't want to tell you again to keep your nose out of my business. I don't need your help."

She rolled her eyes, obviously not heeding his warning at all. "Have you made any progress?"

"A little." David didn't want to go into detail. He could imagine her outrage if he told her he'd searched Hargrove's room. "Look, there's something else I want you to think about."

She crossed her hands over her chest, a sure sign she wasn't in a receptive mood.

He had to tell her anyway. "I'm not asking you to ignore Hargrove, but don't let him talk you into doing anything. . .well. . .anything you're uncomfortable with."

Her face hardened. "You mean like letting him kiss me? I hate to tell you, David, but you're too late with your warning. Vance has already kissed me, and it was. . . Well, it was more pleasant than some experiences I've had."

When the import of her words percolated through his brain, jealousy shut out all other emotions. He wanted to tear Hargrove limb from limb. He wanted to stalk back to the man's room and rip that strongbox open with his bare hands. "If you let him touch you again, I don't care what you say, you're going back to Les Fleurs."

She stepped back a pace. "Are you threatening me? After last night?"

"I'm not the same kind of man as Vance Hargrove."

"No. No, you're not." Her whisper was as sharp as a knife. "You're the kind who'll kiss one girl at night and romance a different one the next day."

"I don't care about your opinion of me, Jasmine Anderson. I've seen enough to know he's the worst kind of hardened rake. If you don't stay away from him and quit asking questions of the actors, I will stop you."

"You don't get to make those kinds of decisions, David Fos—Anderson. And the sooner you figure that out, the better things will be between us." A slow, dangerous smile appeared on her face. "Whether you like it or not, I'm going to help you solve this mystery. You can either work with me or ignore me. But I'm going to do everything I can to get you off of this boat, hopefully before we leave Memphis."

He watched as she spun on her heel and marched toward the door, her nose leading the way. He stomped on the floor once and had the satisfaction of seeing her scamper several feet forward before she realized he was not actually chasing her.

David decided he could keep an eye out for her safety, even though he would rather work alone. Something about the idea of working with her eased the pain in his heart, reminded him of happier times when they'd been as close as his next breath. They had enjoyed each other so much back then. Why had adulthood gotten in their way?

Chapter Twenty-Four

"Another bank was robbed yesterday afternoon."

Jasmine caught her breath. "It can't be a coincidence."

David shook his head. He had singled her out right after breakfast, telling her to meet him outside. They left the boat together and walked uphill toward the center of town.

"When did it happen?"

"During the matinee." He pounded a fist against his pants leg. "I can't quite make the connection to the showboat, but I know there has to be one. I know it."

"Don't worry, we'll find it."

"I've searched your boat from stem to stern. Hargrove is the only one with the means and opportunity. He's got to be the one."

Jasmine couldn't help but feel that David was prejudiced against poor Vance because of his relationship with her. "I don't see how he can be. He was right here all afternoon."

"Are you sure he was there the whole time?"

A fresh breeze grazed her neck, and Jasmine wished she could loosen the bun at the back of her head and let her hair fly around her face like she'd done when she was a child. "He's the star, remember? Vance has lines in most of the scenes. He couldn't have left in the middle of the play without it being noticed. It has to be someone else."

"I don't believe it's a coincidence that every town he's been in for the past year has been robbed while he was there. Unless he's some kind of albatross."

She knew better than to believe David was superstitious. He had a stronger relationship with God than she did. He must really be desperate to catch the robbers. "We're supposed to leave for Cairo tomorrow."

He looked off into the distance.

"David, are you listening to me?"

His green gaze lost its faraway look and focused on her. "Yes, of course. But I need to do a couple of things before we leave Memphis."

"What things?"

He shook his head and flicked her nose with a finger. "Nothing that needs to concern you."

She wanted to stomp her foot. When would David learn to treat her like an adult? As she watched him walk away, she gave in to the impulse to stick out her tongue at his retreating back. Maybe if she solved his mystery, David would finally admit she was a grown woman.

❧

Lily moved across the parlor as Aunt Dahlia stood, and she kissed the air next to the older woman's cheek. "You sleep well. We'll see you in the morning."

Aunt Dahlia's nose wrinkled. "Unless the Good Lord sees fit to take me home tonight."

"We're not going to worry about that, dear." Uncle Phillip put an arm around his wife's shoulders. He winked toward Lily and the others. "According to what I remember of my classical studies, Herodotus said, 'Whom the gods love dies young; Best go first.'"

Aunt Dahlia's face turned suspicious. "Are you making fun of me?"

"Of course not." He led her out of the room, bending toward Aunt Dahlia, and placating her with tender words.

Lily put a hand over her mouth to keep from laughing out loud as she, Blake, Camellia, and Jonah waited for the pair to get out of earshot.

"When did your uncle Phillip develop such a sense of humor?" Blake kept a straight face, but the twinkle in his blue eyes told her he shared her amusement.

Camellia, sitting on one of the pair of sofas, smiled at him. "He's been much happier since he realized Jonah and I are not going to let the plantation go to rack and ruin."

"I think he enjoys teasing your aunt." Jonah walked to the window and opened the drapes to let a breeze into the room.

Lily shook her head and settled on the sofa opposite her sister. "Every time we come home, things seem a little more comfortable than the time before. I'm so glad the fire didn't slow you down."

"When will you ever get over your wanderlust and come back home to stay?" Camellia opened her fan and waved it in front of her face.

"Not for another century or so." Blake took a seat next to his wife.

Lily thanked God for a husband who understood her so well. She tilted her head to look at him. "Don't let Blake fool you by blaming our absence on me. He would like for us to go even farther afield than we do presently."

"Tell us what you found out in Memphis." Jonah lounged against the open window.

"Eli and Renée are certain we need to make an investment right away, while the opportunities are wide open." Lily turned toward him. "Your brother is even considering leaving Memphis and moving out West to take better advantage of the situation."

Blake stretched out his legs and crossed them at the ankles. "I'm trying to convince Lily that we need to take a trip out there to see for ourselves."

"Where would you go?" asked Camellia.

"I'd like to travel all the way to California on the Pacific Railroad." Blake glanced toward her.

Lily nodded. She understood her husband's reasoning, but she wasn't quite ready to commit to spending a month or more away from the river. Especially now that Jasmine was running about on her own, getting into who knew what kind of trouble.

"What towns are you planning to visit?" Jonah straightened and moved toward the sofas.

Blake uncrossed his legs and stood. "Let's go look at that map in the library. I'll show you the exact route we'll take."

Before the two men could leave, the parlor door opened. Lily looked up, smiling when she saw her father's familiar visage. His smile sent her back to the distant past, the days of her childhood. A pang of sadness settled in her heart. Papa hadn't looked this happy since before Mama died. While she didn't want him to live the rest of his life mourning his first wife, his interest signaled the end of an era. . .at least in her mind.

"Where are the two of you going?"

"Blake's going to show me where he's taking your eldest daughter." Jonah moved toward the door. "Why don't you come with us?"

"Hold on just a minute." Camellia closed her fan and pointed it at Papa. "You're not going to leave until we hear a report about your evening with Aunt Tessie."

Papa's face was ruddy from years sailing the river, but Lily could still see a blush darken his cheeks. Her eyebrows rose. "I have to agree with Camellia. We want to hear every salacious detail."

When he rolled his eyes at her sally, Lily couldn't help thinking of her youngest sister. Jasmine had followed Papa's every footstep for years, picking up so many of his mannerisms. How she wished Jasmine would walk in that door right now. But when Jonah opened it, the hallway was empty.

"Can I not count on my own daughters to respect my privacy?"

Camellia shook her head. "Not when Aunt Tessie's heart may be at risk."

Papa sat on a chair, his hands hanging between his knees. "I guess you girls have noticed that Tessie and I have been spending some time together."

Lily exchanged a glance with her sister.

"She's a nice woman." He cleared his throat and looked up at the ceiling. "I may be asking her to marry me soon."

"Papa, that's wonderful." Camellia jumped up and ran to him, catching him in an enthusiastic hug. "She's the smartest, most thoughtful, kindest woman I know."

"I don't know how to take that." Lily used irony to cover her surprise. Love? Although she had known Papa had spent some time with Tessie during their recent trip to New Orleans, she hadn't realized how serious their relationship had become in just a few short weeks.

Camellia shot a laughing glance at her over one shoulder. "Present company excepted, of course."

"I hope you girls understand." Papa trained his gaze on Lily's face. "It's just that when you get as old as I am, you begin to realize your time on earth may be very limited. Tessie and I have no time to waste."

"Now Papa, don't talk like that." Lily's heart swelled with love for her father. "We want you around for many more years, and we want you to be happy. Tessie is a very lucky lady. She's going to make a welcome addition to our family."

Papa had stood when Camellia came to him. Now he gestured for Lily to join them. She rose and walked to where they stood, putting her arms around both her father and her sister. Lily was reminded of the verse that promised God's presence whenever two or more of His followers came together. The Holy Spirit was here.

Finally they separated. Lily felt the healing in her heart, relieved that the poignancy she had felt was only a fleeting echo of the past. As Lily returned to her seat on the sofa, she pulled her father along with her. Camellia also sat down once more.

Papa sighed. "I only wish Jasmine were here with us."

"She would be as happy for you and Aunt Tessie as Lily and I are." Camellia's voice was a little shaky.

Lily wished Camellia could let go of her guilt over Jasmine's disappearance. She'd been adamant in telling her middle sister that she was not at fault. Jasmine's decision to leave had been made long before she actually walked out the door. Any blame for their youngest sister's actions would be more properly placed at Lily's feet. She was the one who had tried to curtail Jasmine in New Orleans. If she had been a little less inflexible, Jasmine might still be here at Les Fleurs.

"I know you're right." The smile on his face was not as bright as it had been moments earlier. "I just miss the little minx."

"I do, too, Papa." Lily's throat constricted. It was hard to push the words out without letting go of her emotions. "I do, too."

Camellia's wobbly smile also hinted at unstable emotions. "At least we know she's safe, thanks to David."

"That's true." Papa gave a gentle smile. "But let's not forget that God is the One watching over both of them."

Lily lifted her chin. Why were they all sitting here moaning about the situation? It was time for action. "I think I'll go get Jasmine."

Camellia's gaze locked on her face. "What do you mean?"

"I know she's on a boat called the *Ophelia*. It shouldn't be that hard to find it. As Blake is fond of pointing out to me, river traffic is much reduced. We can go up to Cape Girardeau and farther if necessary. Even if I have to go all the way to Chicago, I'll find her."

"Do you think that's a good idea?" Camellia's cornflower blue eyes mirrored the doubt in her voice.

Lily nodded, growing more certain as she considered her plan. "I think it's a wonderful idea. Much better than doing nothing."

Papa cleared his throat and waited until she looked in his direction. "I disagree."

What could he possibly mean? What was wrong with going to look for Jasmine?

Her father looked like he was trying to marshal his thoughts. "Lily, Jasmine is twenty years old."

"But she's still—"

"I know." He interrupted her protest with a raised hand. "You are my oldest child, and I've always been proud of the way you've shouldered the responsibility for raising both of your sisters. In a way, they are your children."

Lily could feel the frown on her face. What did he mean? Yes, she loved Camellia and Jasmine in the same way she loved her children.

Wasn't that the way it was supposed to be? Shouldn't she want the best for them the way she did for Noah, Magnolia, and Benjamin? Of course, Camellia was settled. She had a husband and a home—a family of her own to raise. But Jasmine was different. Jasmine still needed her.

"I'm speaking to you now as a parent, Lily. Don't you remember the first time Noah scraped his knee on your gangplank?"

A picture formed in her mind of that day almost five years ago. Noah had been barely able to walk, but he had pulled away from her hand, insisting he could cross to the *Water Lily* by himself. Papa's voice described the scene exactly the way she remembered it. A bright spring day, the river overflowing its banks as it often did. "Noah fell and scraped his knee." She felt Papa had vindicated her concern. "But he could have fallen into the river. He might have drowned."

"That's true, Lily. Isn't that why you and Blake taught him how to swim? In case he ever did fall overboard? You didn't try to stop him from exploring the world. You gave him the tools he needed to conquer it. You have to trust that you and your sister have outfitted Jasmine so she can face whatever obstacles life throws at her. You won't always be there for her, Lily."

"I can be there for her now, though." Lily wasn't ready to give up the argument. She glanced at Camellia for support. "What would you do if we were talking about Amaryllis?"

Instead of taking her side, Camellia laughed. "I don't think comparing the needs of my three-year-old is quite fair. Like Papa said, Jasmine is twenty years old. Remind me again how old you were when you purchased the *Hattie Belle*, your first boat?"

"That's different." Lily voiced the objection, but it didn't ring true, even to her own ears.

Camellia raised her hand and held up one finger. "When you were even younger than Jasmine is right now, you bought a boat"—a second finger went up—"moved Jasmine and me onto it"—three fingers—"took off for New Orleans without any idea of what we would find there"—a fourth finger—"and failed to tell us the true identity of our captain." She dropped her hand back into her lap.

Lily felt misused and misunderstood. Everything she'd done had been for them, after all. To make sure both Camellia and Jasmine had choices. "It didn't turn out too badly, though, did it?"

"Of course not." Papa's emphatic answer made her feel a little less betrayed. "That's exactly the point, Lily. All three of my daughters have a bit of the Anderson stubbornness, and you are determined to make your own way in life."

Comprehension dawned. Unshed tears made her eyes sting. The tip of her nose was probably crimson.

"I know we all wish Jasmine had chosen a more proper vocation." Camellia sighed. "But we cannot force her into the mold we would choose."

"Do you think she's safe?" Lily felt one of her tears escape. She swiped it away with an impatient finger. "I'm so scared she'll make a mistake she can't recover from."

Camellia's eyes widened. "She's got a Pinkerton detective with her. David will make sure she's not swept away. And I predict he'll bring her back to us as soon as he thinks she's had enough of freedom."

"Why don't we take our fears to Jesus?" Papa's face rediscovered its smile. "He has promised to listen to our hearts' desires."

Lily nodded. "I'm sorry, Papa."

He patted her shoulder. "You don't have anything to be sorry about, Lily. You love your sisters. I know that. Sometimes you just get a little eager to solve all their problems for them."

Camellia moved from the sofa she'd been using and plopped down between Lily and Papa. Reaching for both their hands, she squeezed her eyes shut. "Thank You, Lord, for watching over Jasmine. We know You love her even more than we do, and we are putting our trust in You to call her back into Your fold."

As her sister spoke, Lily felt peace soak into her heart. When Camellia stopped, she took a deep breath. "God, please help me to lean on You instead of my own strengths, which are puny beyond belief. Thank You for my family, for a father and a sister who have my best interests at heart, even if they are a little harsh at times."

Camellia's choked laughter made her grin.

"Lord, our Father, the One who loves us beyond all understanding, we give thanks to You for sending Your Son to die on the cross for our sins. Sometimes we forget who is in control. Please forgive us for that. Be with my wondrous daughters in all their endeavors. Strengthen them, be with them, and help us all remember Your promises. You've created us for Your pleasure and called us for Your purpose. We rest in You, Lord. . . Amen."

The parlor door opened as her father ended their prayer. Lily could tell by the looks on Blake's and Jonah's faces that they had heard at least some of the conversation.

"Have you solved all the problems of the world?" Blake's question made Camellia giggle once more.

"I may wring Lily's neck. Would you believe she complained to God because Papa and I were giving her a little advice?"

Except for Lily, everyone in the parlor laughed. Camellia patted her knee before returning to her former seat on the other side of the tea table.

Blake took her place between Lily and her father, his concern plain on his features.

Lily fished in the waist of her skirt for her handkerchief, wiping away the telltale tears that had slipped down her cheeks during their prayer. "Everything's fine, honey. They were just setting me straight."

Her husband's dark eyebrows climbed toward his hairline. "They're braver than I am."

This time Lily was able to join in the laughter, even though she swatted her husband's shoulder. "Don't you start on me, too."

As Papa told his sons-in-law about his intentions with regard to Tessie, Lily mused about the advice she had received from him and Camellia. If she wasn't going to look for Jasmine—and she was beginning to agree that it would be a poor idea—maybe it was time for her to take that trip Blake had his heart set on. At least she would have something new to focus on. Something that would have nothing to do with the paths her sisters chose.

Chapter Twenty-five

The *Ophelia* remained in Memphis for longer than planned because of the number of people attending each performance. Jasmine realized the Easleys wanted to rake in all the money possible, but she was ready to head north. She didn't want to look out into the audience and realize Lily had caught up with them. And she was anxious to begin rehearsing for their Fourth of July production, a series of one-act vignettes on the highlights of America's founding. Clem had told her it would end with everyone on stage singing patriotic numbers. Jasmine hoped she could fake her part in the singing since she couldn't carry a tune in a bushel basket.

Jasmine was still excited about the production because Mr. Easley had slated her for the part of Princess Pocahontas. She would finally be the star on stage instead of second fiddle for Tabitha. If only they would leave Memphis.

Over the past week, life had fallen into a humdrum rhythm. The manager gave the actors mornings off unless they flubbed their lines the night before. She had visited Renée and Eli Thornton once but usually spent her mornings with Clem, helping the other girl with the never-ending work of keeping the costumes mended and altered.

The only times she saw David were immediately after each evening performance and before the dinner meal, when he escorted her and Clem back and forth from their room. She suspected it was his way of covering his real goal of hanging about to look for evidence. The more time that passed, the more she became convinced he was on the wrong trail. But she'd given up trying to convince him.

A part of her was anxious for him to stay with them. She'd grown accustomed to his protective presence. Besides, he needed to remain on board for as long as it took for him to agree with her staying when he did leave.

"I don't believe it." Clem's voice held more than a trace of irritation.

Jasmine put down the chemise she was stitching. "What's wrong?"

"Angelica has pulled another seam apart." Clem dug into a large bag that held scraps. "I don't have the right color to make a patch."

"What color do you need?"

"Magenta."

Jasmine snapped her fingers. "When I was in Tabitha's room last week, a torn scarf was lying on her chair. I wonder if she would donate it to the cause."

"You and Tabitha sure have gotten close lately."

"She's writing to some of her theater friends about me." Jasmine didn't know why she felt defensive. It wasn't like she was betraying their friendship. Clem had no wish to become a famous actress.

"Humph." Clem took out her scissors and started removing the stitches on Angelica's dress. "I hope you don't wake up one day and find her knife planted in your back. Women like Miss Barlow never do something unless it will benefit them."

"Maybe she wants to relive her glory days through me."

"Perhaps."

Jasmine blew out an irritated breath. "Do you want me to ask her about the scarf or not?"

"Yes, go ahead." Clem kept her gaze on the cloth in her lap.

Making her way to the other corridor that housed the first-billed actors, Jasmine wondered what Clem would say if she knew Jasmine's plans for the future included her. Once she was making enough money to support herself in style, she would need a talented dressmaker. Clem had an eye for the right color and style. If she was given free rein to create what she wanted, the result would probably be stunning.

Jasmine was surprised to see Tabitha's door ajar when she reached it. The actress was usually very particular about her privacy. Her heart thumped as she knocked on the door.

A scuffling sound from the room made her think the actress might be in trouble.

"Tabitha?" She pushed at the door but found she could not open it. "Tabitha, are you okay?"

"Who's there?" The voice that answered did not belong to Tabitha. Not unless she had learned how to mimic a man.

"David?"

The door stopped resisting her pressure and swung open, revealing David's blazing green gaze. "What are you doing here?"

Quashing the uncomfortable idea that he might have an assignation with the actress, she put her hands on her hips. "I have an irreproachable errand. What excuse do you have for being in a woman's boudoir?"

He pulled her inside the room by one elbow. "I'm looking for evidence, of course."

"In Tabitha's room? You've lost your mind. Do you really think a female can be your culprit?" She noticed he was wearing a workman's apron. Was he supposed to be on duty on the *Miss Polly*?

David dropped her elbow and stepped back. "No one's above suspicion, even though I agree that a female is not the probable culprit."

"If Tabitha catches you in here, she'll make sure you get sacked. Then what will you do?"

"I suppose I could depend on you to get me the information I need."

For a moment she thought he was serious. Then she saw the gleam in his gaze. He was about as serious as a clown.

Before she could counter with a biting remark, he raised a hand to signify his capitulation. "She's gone on another of her shopping expeditions." He picked up a feather boa from the floor and draped it over the back of Tabitha's slipper chair. "I saw her leave half an hour ago, so I have at least that much more time before I have to worry about her return."

"Have you found anything?" She winced at the derision in her voice. The inflection was uncomfortably close to Tabitha's.

"She spends more on jewelry and geegaws than she can afford on her current salary."

Jasmine glanced over his shoulder at a large bouquet of fresh flowers. "She has a lot of male admirers. Did you stop to think some of them might be giving her gifts of jewelry and geegaws?"

His shoulders drooped, and David nodded. "I know. But it's getting frustrating. I have to find something soon or admit defeat." When David spoke the words out loud, dismay filled her. Not that she needed him, of course. But his presence was reassuring. She even found herself looking forward to meeting him each evening after she had removed her makeup and changed back into her regular clothes. She would miss telling him about her impressions of the other actors and giggling with him over the odd world of the theater. "What about Mr. Easley? Did you find out what he sends Vance to do?"

A half-grin appeared on David's face. "He's a passable director, but your Mr. Easley is not much of a businessman. At least not when it comes to mathematics. Vance counts the money for him and takes it to the bank where he gets change. I'm sure that's what he was talking about."

"Will you finally admit Vance is innocent?"

"Of bank robbery, maybe. But that man doesn't have an innocent bone in his body."

Jasmine found herself unable to argue the point. Vance was much more circumspect whenever her "brother" was around. If David was working on the *Miss Polly*, Vance was becoming more and more insistent toward her. He made personal remarks and touched her with increasing frequency, brushing back a strand of her hair or running a finger along the back of her arm. Jasmine didn't want to offend him. Vance was the reason she was here, after all. But if he didn't tone down his gestures and words, she was going to have to tell him in no uncertain terms that she was not a woman of ill repute.

She wasn't ready to share that side of Vance with David. He was already too suspicious of the man. She turned her attention to the part of the room where she'd last seen the scarf she wanted, her cheeks heating as she caught sight of a pair of Tabitha's lacy pantaloons. "You really shouldn't be in here."

"I've seen lady's undergarments before." David's grin widened.

Grabbing up the brightly colored material she'd come for, Jasmine tucked it into her pocket. "We need to leave."

David's smile disappeared. He raised both hands this time, a mock surrender.

With a huff, she opened the door. "Come on." Stepping into the hallway, she waited for him to close the door.

"What are you two doing down here?" Vance's accusing voice startled Jasmine.

She whirled to face him, wishing she'd looked to make sure they were alone before leaving Tabitha's room. "I. . .I. . ."

"Miss Barlow's hinges weren't working properly. She complained that they squeaked like a herd of pigs whenever she opened or closed her door. Jasmine brought me down to see what I could do about them."

"Where are your tools?" Vance's suspicious gaze looked like it might bore a hole into David's head.

Reaching into his pocket, David produced an oil can, a wrench, and a hammer. "Any other questions, Mr. Hargrove?"

Jasmine breathed a sigh of relief. David was prepared as always. She glanced up at him. "Thanks."

He leaned over and kissed her cheek. "Anything for you, Sis." Whistling a merry tune, he walked away.

After putting her hand to the cheek he'd kissed, Jasmine shot a glance at Hargrove. "Excuse me, I have to get back to Clem."

By the time she'd negotiated the separate hallways, her heart had slowed its furious pace. She slipped through the door to the costume room and pulled out the scarf. "Will this do?"

Clem studied the material and pursed her lips. "I think so. What did Tabitha say about donating something for Angelica?"

"She doesn't know."

Clem reached for the scarf. "What do you mean?"

"She wasn't there." Surrendering the cloth, Jasmine giggled. "I helped myself."

"Are you saying you stole something from our star?" Clem's smile teased her. "I knew you weren't as sweet as you pretend to be."

"She did offer it to me." Jasmine resumed her seat. "All I did was wait a day or two before accepting her gift."

"As soon as I finish this, we'll talk about your costume. I have some ideas I want to try." Clem stitched as she talked, her fingers seeming to fly. "How daring are you feeling?"

Excitement curled in Jasmine's stomach. The Fourth of July pageant might be her ticket to stardom. She would do almost anything to ensure her success.

Chapter Twenty-six

The blue waters of the Ohio River mingled with the chocolate waters of the Mississippi at the town of Cairo, ensuring its importance both during and after the war. Fort Defiance still guarded the port, and plans had begun to build a customs house because of the volume of goods passing through the area.

Jasmine wrinkled her nose as she picked her way across the mushy ground between the ship landing and the open area where the Fourth of July celebration would be held. On one side of the field, a group of men worked with saws and hammers, building a raised platform for the stage. As she drew near, they stopped their work, one by one, elbowing each other and grinning.

One would think they had never seen a lady before. Cairo might be little more than a swamp, but it was not the very end of the earth. She lifted her chin and turned her back on them. Where was everyone? Mr. Easley had said they would begin rehearsals precisely at 10:00 a.m.

The buildings of the town were huddled against the clearer waters of the Ohio. She put her hand above her eyes and looked in that direction to see if she could spy any of the others. Had they gone to the fort instead of meeting here? Had she misunderstood the directions?

After several moments, she saw Clem walking in her direction and waved a greeting. At least the two of them could talk while they waited for the rest of the actors to appear.

The clanging and banging of the workers began again as Clem reached her. "What is all of that clatter?"

"Progress." Jasmine had to shout over the noise. "Shall we try to find a quieter spot?"

They strolled in the opposite direction of the workers until the sound diminished a bit.

Clem scuffed at the dirt with the toe of her slipper. "Have you been here before?"

"Yes, although we didn't land here often. My brother-in-law has family and several friends in Cape Girardeau, so that's where we usually stop." Jasmine looked back toward the tree-lined bank that hid the Mississippi from their view. "What about you?"

"Yes, many times. Did you know three states come together here?"

Jasmine pointed to the Ohio River's blue water, busy with small flatboats ferrying goods from the riverboats and railroad to destinations on its far side. "Kentucky. And the mud beneath our feet is in the state of Illinois."

Clem nodded. "The Mississippi River separates Illinois from Missouri. The first time we stopped here, I didn't believe the person who told me."

Trust Clem to find something romantic about Cairo. "Even if ten states met in this same space, Cairo is still so flood-prone that it's little more than a mud hole at times."

"True." Clem laughed. "I like to think that one day it will be a beautiful town with wide streets and stunning vistas."

"I don't know how you do it, Clem."

"What's that?"

"You always look for the best in life." Jasmine linked arms with her friend, and they walked along in silence for a moment.

"Has anyone seen your costume yet?"

Jasmine looked down toward her knees. Her dark brown skirt was narrower than what she was used to, but that was not its most noticeable feature. It was short, ending right below her knees. Below its hem her limbs were encased in brown leggings. The outfit was daring, making her feel bold, brave, and intrepid. "I don't know yet, but I think I was the topic of conversation over by the stage."

Both of them giggled.

"Not everyone could carry it off." Clem stepped back and looked at her.

Jasmine held out her hands and turned around to model her dashing clothing. "What do you think?"

"You'll turn every head in the town. The women may hate you, but the men will flock to see you from all over."

"Do you really think so?" Jasmine turned back in the other direction.

"I guarantee it."

They reached a lane of sorts and turned to follow it. Jasmine looked over her shoulder and realized the workmen had stopped their labor once more. "If they take this many breaks, we won't have a stage to perform on until August."

Clem didn't look back. Her gaze focused on a man walking toward them. "Here comes David."

Jasmine smoothed the skirt of her gown. What would he think?

She didn't have long to wonder as he pointed at her knees. "What on earth are you wearing, Jasmine?"

"It's my Princess Pocahontas outfit." She twirled once more. "Do you like it?" When she stopped moving, she looked to gauge his reaction.

If a thundercloud had landed on his brow, it could not be any darker. "I don't know why I expect you to behave with any decorum. If Lily could see you right now, she would be ashamed."

His words tore at her like the bite of a rabid animal, but she raised her chin and glared back at him. "You obviously need to build a house and raise a family in Cairo. We all know what it's like here when it floods. What better location for someone who is a stick in the mud."

David's jaw tightened. "Get back to the *Ophelia* and put on something less shocking, or I'm going to put you over my shoulder and throw you on the next boat to Natchez."

"I'm tired of your threats, David Foster. You're not going to intimidate me any longer."

Clem's eyes widened. "But I thought you were Jasmine's brother."

Jasmine bit her lip. She should not have let her anger loose. Now she'd ruined everything.

"I am." David took off his coat and wrapped it around Jasmine. "My full name is David Foster Anderson."

Jasmine was grateful he had managed to cover her gaffe, but it still didn't excuse her stupidity.

"Oh, I see. I misunderstood." Clem's wrinkled brow smoothed out. "I have an idea that may resolve your problem with your sister's outfit."

His hands squeezed Jasmine's shoulders, a warning to keep silent. "What is that?"

She leaned forward and turned up the edge of Jasmine's skirt. "I made a wide hem because I wasn't certain how short the dress should be. I can let it out and add a layer of lace to the bottom of her leggings so they look more like a flounce than. . .well, you understand."

"But I—" Another squeeze stopped her protest. Jasmine fumed but acquiesced. . .for the moment.

"Don't you realize you're asking for the wrong kind of attention from men? Is that the kind of reputation you want? Can't you understand yet there's a reason for rules? A reason to guard your reputation? I know you don't want to shame our whole family with your actions, so I have to wonder if the reason you do these kinds of things is a lack of confidence in your acting ability. Do you think you have to stoop to sensationalism to draw attention?"

Shame and anger mingled in her blood. Was David right? Had she gone from daring to scandalous? Or was he being too old-fashioned?

"Let out the hem." David's hands relaxed, kneading the taut muscles of her shoulders. "We'll see if the change will allow her sufficient modesty."

David pulled her up close to his body, shielding her from the glances of the workers as the three of them started back toward the showboat. Clem chattered nonstop about the weather, the town, and the patriotic celebration in an attempt to fill the silence.

Jasmine thought back to the day Tabitha had first offered to help her. She'd mentioned being snubbed. Was that what David was trying to protect her from? Should she care? Jasmine had her morals, her boundaries. For all he knew, the ill will of others might spring from jealousy rather than moral indignation. It might be part of the payment for the notoriety she craved.

They crossed the gangplank, and David removed his coat. "Don't forget to show me the outfit first."

Jasmine rolled her eyes. She would not let him see how ambivalent she felt. Reaching their bedroom, she unbuttoned the shirtwaist and jerked it off.

"I'm sorry." Clem sat on the edge of her bed.

"It's not your fault." Jasmine summoned a smile for her friend. "I wanted to wear it."

"It would be acceptable on the stage in a big city, but David may be right in thinking that the people here won't be as progressive in their attitudes."

Jasmine snorted. David didn't know everything. He wasn't an arbiter of decorum or fashion.

"He only has your best interests at heart." Clem's face shone with admiration. "I wish he were my brother. I would love feeling so cherished."

"You can have him with my blessing." What Clem didn't understand, what she couldn't explain to her, was that the man posing as her brother had only one goal—to ruin her life. And he was doing a fair job of it.

Jasmine pulled on her most conservative dress. His condemnation had stung. She would show David Foster—Anderson—that she would do as she pleased.

Jasmine still refused to speak to him by the end of the week. At least her anger ensured she wouldn't try to help him with his investigation.

Not that he'd intended to make her angry, but that girl knew how to push every boundary to its utmost extent. He refused to stand aside and watch her self-destruct, and if her enmity was the price, he considered it worth the cost.

This morning he had finally gained entrance to Angelica Fenwick's bedroom, the last on his list. He glanced around the crowded room. Were all actresses clotheshorses? Although David could understand that they might need a few extra items to supplement the costumes they wore, he was amazed at the number of outfits both Miss Fenwick and Miss Barlow carried around with them.

Even Camellia wasn't this bad. At least he didn't think she was. Of course, Jonah had once claimed that his wife had enough outfits to avoid repeating any particular one for a year. At the time David had thought the man was exaggerating. Now he was less certain.

He picked up an armful of crinolines to search the bottom of one of her trunks, his eyes widening to find a child's doll dressed in a pink gown and matching bonnet hidden under the actress's undergarments. He would never have thought Miss Fenwick the nostalgic type, but the proof was before him. The doll must be a treasured reminder of her childhood.

Replacing the contents, he moved to the dressing table in one corner of the room. The drawers were filled with brushes, perfumes, and bottles of rouge. Nothing to indicate that Miss Fenwick was guilty. Not that he'd really thought she would be. He couldn't imagine a female working with a gang of hardened thieves and murderers. But that didn't mean she couldn't be involved in some way—as a go-between or accomplice of some sort. As hard as it was to invade a woman's privacy, he had to be thorough.

Mentally reviewing the list of suspects one more time, David slipped out of the actress's room. He was beginning to agree with Jasmine's assertions that no one on board was connected to the robberies. What was he missing? The *Ophelia* had to be the clue Charlie Petrie had tried to tell him about with his dying breath. David shook his head. It didn't make sense.

Everyone on board both the *Ophelia* and its tugboat was talking about the big race that would begin the Fourth of July festivities tomorrow morning. Some of the tugboat crew even wanted Captain Ross to enter the race. David was glad the man had refused. His intuition told him that if the robbers were nearby, they would use the distraction of the celebration to their advantage. He planned to set up watch outside the bank and catch them red-handed. Once he had arrested the culprits, he would wire the home office that he was taking some time off and redouble his efforts to get Jasmine away from this band of gypsy actors.

The sound of a distant bell brought his head up. It was time for church. Clem had asked him last night if he planned to attend, but if he didn't hurry, he was going to be late. He squinted in the bright sunlight as he reached the outside deck, surprise and pleasure filling him at the sight of both Clem and Jasmine apparently awaiting his escort.

"See, I told you he was coming." Clem pointed her finger at Jasmine. "You owe me a forfeit."

Holding out an elbow for each of them, he grinned. "No one's ever placed a bet on me before."

"Don't act so conceited." Jasmine ignored his arm, stepping onto the gangplank. "Clem wouldn't leave until you appeared, even though I told her you'd make all of us late."

"I suppose we'd better hurry then."

Clinging to his arm for support, Clem managed to keep up with his long strides. Rebellious Jasmine was having more trouble. He could hear her huffing and puffing, but he refused to be manipulated by the sound. She had refused his offer of support, so unless she asked for help, she could make her own way.

"Will you take part in the pageant?" Clem sounded breathless, so David slowed his pace a little.

"I doubt it. I'm not interested in racing. I'll probably just wander around town and visit the booths." He had no intention of letting Clem or anyone else know his real plans.

Disappointment made her smile droop. "I see."

Jasmine caught up with them as David and Clem reached the dirt lane on the edge of town. The deserted streets didn't surprise him. Shopkeepers were either attending church or sleeping late on their one day off. Even the ferries would not run until after midday in observance of the Lord's Day.

As they reached the street the church faced, a movement at the end of a nearby alley made David turn his head. He only caught a glimpse but thought he recognized the dark hair and tall frame of Rafe Griffin. Expecting to see the man as they turned the corner, he immediately grew suspicious when no one appeared. Why was Rafe skulking about?

The question continued bothering him as they entered the one-room church. The center aisle was flanked on both sides by rows of benches. David would have preferred finding an empty spot in the back of the sanctuary, but Clem tugged him forward until they reached the front.

The preacher, a gray-haired man with a weathered face, smiled at the three of them. "Welcome."

David shook the man's hand. "Thank you." He stood in the aisle, feeling the combined gazes of the good people of Cairo on his face, as first Clem and then Jasmine sat on the first pew. When he sat, Jasmine put her hand on her skirt and pulled it closer to her body as though she didn't want him to touch her at all. He crossed his hands over his chest and ignored her.

"I was going to talk to you about the importance of stewardship today, but God helped me come awake before the sun this morning. He filled my mind with another sermon, one that I feel compelled to share with you." The pastor opened his Bible. "For those of you who brought your Bibles, I'll be reading from the thirteenth chapter of the Gospel of Matthew. I'm always amazed when I read this chapter about the sower of seeds."

David heard the intake of Jasmine's breath. He was glad she was listening. She had not been showing him much sign that she still turned to God on a daily basis. Maybe this trip to church would help her renew her faith.

"I've often wondered about the man sowing the seeds in this parable.

Many of you are farmers, and I know you wouldn't bother to plant your precious seed out there on top of rocks, would you?"

A couple of the men answered in the negative.

"Would you plant them so shallowly that animals could eat them or fail to pull the weeds from your fields before you planted your seed?"

No one answered the question this time, but David could tell by the silence behind him that the pastor had everyone's attention.

"Of course you wouldn't. If you did, your families would starve. So why does Jesus tell us about someone being so foolish?" The pastor stopped to let the question settle in. "Because He knows that any one of us can have a stony heart. He knows that any of us can become shallow and self-absorbed. We can forget our faith when we become distracted by the pleasures of this world."

David sat a little straighter in the pew. He hoped Jasmine was paying close attention. He knew God must have meant for the pastor to choose these verses for her sake.

"But that's not the only point of this story. It's not the only lesson Jesus wants us to learn. So why didn't He tell us about only sowing seed in rich, prepared soil?" The pastor looked straight at David, the fire of his message lighting his eyes. "Friends, you and I need to remember that we as Christians are the sowers. We're not supposed to worry about the fruit of the Gospel. We can't make the seed we spread grow. All God wants us to do is sow His seed. He will take care of the rest."

David's mouth fell open. He forgot all about Jasmine and her lack of faith as the truth pierced his own heart. He had been so busy trying to correct Jasmine's behavior, trying to make her act like he thought a Christian sister should. That wasn't his job. All God wanted him to do was sow the seed. He was trying to change Jasmine, an impossible task for a human being. Only Jesus could change someone.

As God continued to speak to him through the preacher, David determined to be the witness God needed him to be. He sent a prayer heavenward for the strength he knew it would take.

Chapter Twenty-seven

Folding chairs lined the decks of the two larger steamboats for the addition of paying guests during the race. Vance purchased tickets for himself and Jasmine—and with a little prodding, Clem—on the *Marc Antony*. The sun had barely escaped the horizon as they took their seats on the spotless deck. Streamers hung limply from the rails in preparation for the extreme speeds the boat would attain during the contest.

"Do you think we'll win?" Clem wore a hat with a wide brim to shade her face. She had secured it to her head with a blue lawn scarf that matched the color of her dress.

Jasmine could imagine an artist capturing her friend's excited face and fashionable appearance for use in *Harper's Bazaar*. "It doesn't really matter. All we have to do is enjoy the scenery."

A white-coated server appeared with steaming cups of chocolate to warm them against the cool, damp air. Vance handed her a cup, and Jasmine held it close to her face, inhaling the sweet fragrance.

"It's a shame your brother couldn't join us." Clem sipped from her mug.

Vance's face showed his disagreement with the statement, although he made no comment. "I don't see how we can lose. In fact, I've wagered a large sum of money on it. The *Marc Antony* is a modern boat with the latest innovations. She's only been on the water for half a year."

Jasmine slid a glance in his direction. "I hope you're not disappointed. It's not always the date on the boiler that decides the victor. The *Davy Crockett* may be older, but she has a knowledgeable pilot and an experienced crew. She might have been a better choice."

His unsettled glance toward her made Jasmine wonder if Vance needed to win his bet. The idea took root in her mind like an evil weed. If he was having money problems, it would make him more likely to join himself with bank robbers. But that made no sense, either. The man who had been working with the robbers wouldn't have money troubles. He'd be flush with his ill-gotten gain.

The boat filled up with other passengers—twenty in all—and the gangplank was lifted away from the bank.

Jasmine turned to Vance. "How long will the race take?"

"We'll be traveling downriver ten miles to a small island. Each boat must circumnavigate the island before returning to Cairo. The captain estimates that it will take less than two hours total to get back to the finish line at that cottonwood." He pointed to a large tree overhanging the bank some yards away. Someone had plaited its thick limbs with wide lengths of red. "The first boat to capture a ribbon will be declared the winner."

"We won't miss anything while we're gone, will we?" Clem leaned forward, her gaze fixed on the people beginning to line up on the riverbank. "I noticed the fliers mentioned races and equestrian exhibitions."

"I doubt it." Jasmine put her free hand on the arm of Clem's chair. "Most everyone is going to be waiting to see who wins the race."

"Yoo-hoo." A feminine voice gained her attention. "Look, it's Angelica and Rafe. They're on the *Davy Crockett*."

"Too bad they chose the losing steamboat." Vance's smug words were as irritating as a swarm of gnats.

Jasmine gritted her teeth and waved at the other couple. "As long as everyone has a good time, it doesn't really matter."

They watched as a short, barrel-chested man climbed onto the stage that would be the central focus of the day's activities and addressed the crowd. "Good morning, ladies and gentlemen. I know everyone's eager to begin our patriotic celebration, but please bear with me for a few moments while I cover some of the rules we'll be observing."

A general groan or two from the crowd showed their disapproval, but the man continued anyway. He warned that no weapons were to be discharged except the starter gun and asked everyone to maintain polite and civil manners. He went on to point out the doctor's tent next to the stage and expressed his hope that no one would be in need of medical service. He reminded them of the various contests that would be going on during the day, the dramatic performance that would begin at dusk, and the fireworks spectacular that promised to end the day with a "bang." A louder groan answered his sally, and a grin split the man's face. Reaching into his pocket, he pulled out a small pistol and aimed it toward the sky.

Jasmine saw the puff of smoke before she heard the report of his weapon. The crowd cheered as the deck below her feet began to shudder. Thick, black plumes of smoke poured from the twin stacks above their heads, while behind them, the paddlewheel roared to life. The race had begun.

Clem jumped to her feet, leaning over the rail and waving at the people they swept past. Jasmine would have joined her, but Vance reached over and put a hand on her arm. "If this race goes like I expect, things are going to be different for me in the future, and I hope different for you, too."

The girl she'd been when she first ran away would have been ecstatic because of his words and the intense look he gave her. Jasmine found herself hoping she misunderstood his intent. The direction of her thoughts surprised her. She had never thought of herself as being fickle, but whatever feelings she'd had about Vance seemed to have disappeared.

Was it her or him? Had she ever really loved Vance? She wasn't sure anymore. Jasmine shook off his hand without an answer and stood next to Clem, looking to see whether they were still in the lead.

At the moment it was hard to tell who would win. Their boat rode the choppy waters of the confluence with steady purpose, as did the

Davy Crockett. The smaller boats were out in front for the moment, but she knew that would probably change on the way back to Cairo when they fought the strong currents of the swift water.

"Look, is that the island?" Clem pointed toward a small spot of green ahead.

Jasmine shook her head. "If it's that close, the race won't last fifteen minutes, much less two hours."

Vance made a space for himself between them, but his eyes focused on her face. "Would you like to take a tour of the boat?"

She looked past him to Clem, who nodded. "I don't think there will be much to see out here until we reach the halfway point."

The three of them picked their way between the seats of the other onlookers and headed for the main room on the lower deck. A large table in the center of the room was piled high with an array of breakfast foods. Biscuits, fresh fruit, bacon, scrambled eggs, jams, and jellies looked tempting. They were welcomed by the staff and offered delicate porcelain plates and gleaming silverware.

Jasmine's stomach growled. She looked at Vance. "How much did our tickets cost?"

He shrugged, a smile on his face. "You're worth the price, Jasmine."

Clem rolled her eyes, accepted a plate, and began heaping food onto it. "I, for one, am glad she is."

Jasmine chose a fluffy biscuit and a spoonful of eggs, glad she hadn't taken time to eat before leaving the *Ophelia*. The food was delicious, and Clem's enthusiasm was contagious. She hoped the rest of the day would be equally enjoyable.

They had barely finished when one of the passengers came running inside. "We're about to reach the island."

Jasmine looked around to see that all four boats were running very close. She had no idea who would reach the finish first.

❧

"I don't have any hard evidence." David blew out an exasperated breath. It was often difficult working with local law enforcement. He should know by now that patience was the best defense against suspicion and resistance.

"But you still want me to assign a deputy to stay at the bank in case it is robbed?" Sheriff Ambrose Cunningham wore his uniform well. Although not as tall as David, his thick chest and muscled arms would inspire fear in any criminal. "This is one of the busiest days of the year. I only have two men working for me, and they need to be visible, not hidden away waiting for someone who's probably not coming anyway."

"What better time to rob the bank than when everyone is focused on the celebration?"

"I thought you said these bank robbers know all the details about the inside of a bank before they strike. What gives you the idea they'll try to get into our bank while it's closed?"

David relaxed his shoulders with an effort. The sheriff was a nice man, and by all accounts honest, but he obviously didn't like to depart from his routine. "Because it's the easiest way to commit a robbery. Why take the chance that someone might surprise them during normal working hours, when the Fourth of July activities give them the perfect opportunity to slip in, help themselves to the cash inside, and disappear before anyone realizes they're here?"

"I'm spread too thin today anyway. I don't see how I can help you."

"I understand." At least he had tried to work with the authorities. "You don't mind if I keep watch over the bank, do you?"

"Go ahead, young man. I've heard a lot of stories about you Pinkertons. I'm sure you can handle yourself if your fellows do show up."

David left the jail and put his hat on his head as he considered his next step. A glance toward the sky told him it was going to be another warm day. The population of Cairo was swollen with strangers from nearby villages. It was the perfect time for strangers to mingle unnoticed. He knew the one bank in town was too easy a target for Hargrove and his gang to resist. That's where he would wait.

Brick with wide windows, the two-story building offered no place for him to hide. David walked around to the alley alongside the building. Shadows filled the area. He stretched his hearing to its limit. If the robbers planned ahead, they might already be here. His hand rested on the gun he had strapped on before leaving the *Miss Polly*.

A sound in the shadows at the back of the alley made him slip off the leather guard holding his weapon in its holster. A rat dashed out of the darkness, closely followed by a scrawny cat. David grimaced at his jumpiness and reholstered his gun. Taking a deep breath, he entered the alley, looking for a place to hide while he waited for the robbers to strike.

This had to be the day, the day he would finally catch the robbers and end this assignment. He would take great pleasure in fastening a pair of handcuffs on Vance Hargrove and dragging him off to prison. He knew the man was guilty, felt it in his heart. He knew Jasmine didn't agree, but she didn't have his experience.

He stopped the thought as the pastor's message from the day before returned to him. Was he making the same mistake again? Was his smug self-righteousness keeping him from seeing the truth? David sank to his knees at the edge of the alley, locked his hands in front of him, and closed his eyes.

Lord, thank You for showing me the error of my ways. I know I'm apt to act before I think. Help me to wait on Your leading. You're in control. Please help me stop these men before they hurt anyone else. And God, forgive me for ignoring the beam in my own eye while I was so concerned with the mote in Jasmine's. I'm going to leave that problem up to You. . .or at least I'm going to try.

Feeling much more calm, David got back to his feet. When he looked in the alley this time, he saw a stairwell that led to the bank's roof. With an additional thanks to God, he ran to the wooden steps and climbed up. The view from the roof showed him every entrance to the bank. The thieves would not be able to get away. All he had to do now was wait.

Cheers from the riverbank told him that the boats must be within sight once more. Was Jasmine down there somewhere? Or was she still asleep on the *Ophelia*? He hoped it was the latter. Maybe she would have a good time at the fair and forget about the robberies.

A couple of young boys ran down the street, their laughter bringing a smile to his face. They dashed past the bank and disappeared, leaving him alone once more. David lay back on the flat roof and put his hands behind his head. Was this what his future would be like? Would he always be so alone?

He reached for his shirt pocket and pulled out the letter from his father. Turning it over in his hands, he heard Marguerite Trahan's question once again. Who would it hurt if he forgave his pa? If he let go of the past, of the terrible choices his mother had made, of the way he'd had to rely on the charity of others to survive?

A laugh floated upward on the breeze, interrupting his thoughts. Jasmine? David raised his head over the edge of the roof and looked down into the street. A couple was strolling past the bank. It was hard to tell who the woman was because her large hat hid her features from him. But the man was certainly not Vance. His hair was a lighter brown, and he walked with a slight limp.

As David watched, the limping man stopped, pulled the female into his arms, and began kissing her. She didn't struggle, instead reaching a hand up to caress his cheek. The man pulled her even closer, deepening the kiss. Suddenly realizing that he was spying on a private moment, David drew back.

They moved on, and his thoughts turned back to his father. Blake had told him Christ would help him figure out how to forgive Pa. But how? A scripture from Psalms floated to the surface of his mind. *"Be still, and know that I am God."* Was that the answer? He had rushed from one goal to the next for so long now that he'd not taken much time to still his mind and listen for God's voice. He felt his lips turn up in a smile. Only God would use a time like this—while he was watching for criminals to appear—to speak to him in that still, small voice.

David closed his eyes. *God, I'm listening.* Warmth enveloped him, a warmth that had nothing to do with the roof beneath him or the sun above. This feeling came from his heart, from the depths of his soul. And he knew. Forgiveness flowed to him and through him, targeting the emotions he had clung to for so long. With God filling his heart, the bitterness lost its hold. No matter what his parents had done or not done, his heavenly Father would never abandon him. The sadness that had weighted his soul for so long was lost in the realization that God had plans for his future, good plans. The words of the prophet Jeremiah sounded in his mind. *"For I know the thoughts that I think toward you, saith the Lord, thoughts of peace, and not of evil, to give you an expected end."* He basked in the love and understanding of his Father as he continued his vigil.

Multiple blasts from steamboat whistles indicated that the race was over, and he wondered who had won. The thought disappeared as David heard someone approaching the bank. His heart doubled its speed. Had his hunch been right?

Peeking over the roof edge, he saw nothing at first. David was beginning to think he'd imagined the sounds when a pair of men moved out of a shadowed doorway across the street, guns drawn. A thump below him was followed by the sound of shattering glass. The bank's plate glass window. David drew back and stood, easing his way to the street as he drew his own weapon. He breathed a prayer for protection as he rounded the corner of the bank building.

Two men stood at the busted window, their attention centered on the interior of the building.

David raised his weapon. "Hold it right there."

A rain of bullets answered him as both the robbers swung in his direction.

David ducked back around the corner of the building.

"Did we kill him?" He heard one of the men ask the question.

The only answer was the sound of footsteps running away from David's position.

"What's going on?" Another voice sounded, this one from farther away, probably the man inside.

"Get out o' there." The man who had spoken first yelled the warning as he, too, ran in the opposite direction.

David came out from his hiding place as the third man dove through the window back onto the street, rolled to a standing position, and took off toward the busy street where the fair was going on. A few steps behind, David centered his attention on catching the robber before anyone else's life was endangered.

❧

"You should have consulted Jasmine before making your wager. She comes from a riverboat family, after all." Clem's voice sounded less helpful than her words indicated. "Or David would have been happy to advise you."

Jasmine knew her friend didn't trust Vance any more than David did, but she felt sorry for him. He looked so hurt because the *Marc Antony* had lost. "Let's go see the flea circus."

Vance shook his head. "That's nothing but a sham."

"I don't care." Jasmine tugged on his arm. "Sham or not, it'll still be fun to watch. I've never seen one before."

Rafe and Angelica walked toward them.

"Maybe next time you'll buy a ticket on the winning boat like we did." Angelica sounded giddy. "I really thought your boat would win until your captain got you caught in that snag."

Vance grimaced. "Come on."

Jasmine sent the pair an apologetic glance as they headed down the street. Her gaze met Clem's. Vance needn't be such a sorehead. It was his own fault for making a bet in the first place.

They walked past booths and stalls that had been set up all along the street, stopping to watch a man hide a seed under one of three walnut shells. He slid the shells around on the surface of his board, his hands moving so fast Jasmine's eyes couldn't follow his movements. Then he offered to double the money of anyone who could guess which shell hid the seed. When he tried to get her to guess, she laughingly declined, and the three of them walked on.

The flea circus was a fun novelty, with tiny swings that moved back and forth and balls that rotated under their own power. Vance said they were run by mechanical means, like a pocket watch. Jasmine and Clem refused to believe him, pointing out the tiny insects who were currently "resting" in a jar beside the exhibition.

Tabitha stood in front of a stall that displayed handmade jewelry, haggling with the owner. She smiled when she saw them. "Clem, I have found the most beautiful length of cloth. I just know you'll be able to make me a new outfit with it."

Clem's face brightened. "Let me see it."

Vance expressed an interest in competing in a three-legged race. Jasmine encouraged him with a smile but stayed behind with Clem.

Losing interest as the two other women discussed lengths and styles, she watched a juggler who was tossing some very sharp knives above his head. A group of boys followed close behind him, nudging each other and exclaiming over the juggler's skills. One of them was liable to be hurt if he got any closer.

Jasmine darted out into the street to warn them just as someone ran out from a nearby building, a gun in his hand. Distracted by whoever was chasing him, the man zigzagged at the last moment to avoid colliding with the juggler. Panting, he ran straight toward her, his head turned to judge the distance of his pursuer.

"Look out!" Clem called out the warning, but Jasmine ignored her.

The man was definitely not part of the Fourth of July celebration, so he must be up to no good. She stood her ground and put out her hands to stop him.

David rounded the corner, his eyes widening when he saw her. In an instant, she knew the fleeing man was one of the robbers David had been chasing since the trip to New Orleans. The robber still didn't realize she was there, so he crashed into her full tilt. Down they both went, raising a cloud of dust when they struck the ground.

The world went dark. When the light returned, the heavy weight pinning her was lifted. She heard David yelling her name as though he were a long way away. Jasmine tried to take a breath, but something was wrong with her chest. She couldn't draw air in. Was she going to die? Fear as deep and cold as the river clawed at her. Jasmine put a hand on her chest and tried again. Finally her mouth began working. Air rushed into her lungs.

Someone grabbed her shoulders and pulled her into a sitting

position. "Are you okay?" She recognized David's voice.

Jasmine managed a nod. Where was the man who had run her down? Before she could ask the question, David pulled her into a tight hug, burying his face into her shoulder. "Jasmine, Jasmine, what am I going to do with you?"

She wanted to push him away, but he was holding her tight, as though he would never let her go. Someone else was patting her on the back. Clem. While Jasmine appreciated the concern for her welfare, she was beginning to get irritated. Had they let the robber get away?

"Where is he?"

David lifted his head, the green of his eyes almost completely hidden by his irises. "I thought I'd lost you." He stood, grabbed her arm, and jerked her to her feet, his face hardening into exasperation. "I may shoot you myself."

"If you let that man get away, I may shoot you." Out of the corner of her eye, Jasmine could see Clem shaking her head.

David turned her around. Sprawled on the ground was a man with a long, skinny face and dirty blond hair. His hands were under him, his ankles tied together with a length of rope. She hoped his hands were similarly bound.

"Are you hurt?" David stepped around her, positioning himself between her and his prisoner.

"Don't be silly." She blocked out the memory of not being able to breathe. At least her sacrifice had been worthwhile. And she could breathe fine now.

"You should have seen your brother." Clem clasped her hands in front of her, adoration spilling from her eyes. "I've never seen anything like it. He jumped so high, it was like he flew across that street. I thought he would be shot for sure, but your brother kicked the weapon out of the man's hand and roped and tied him as fast as a flash of lightning. He ought to be in one of those cowboy rodeos. He would win for sure."

David looked sheepish, almost embarrassed by Clem's extravagant praise.

Jasmine's stomach quivered. She'd never thought about David

getting hurt. He was supposed to be invincible. Her knees buckled, and she met his gaze. Something happened in that moment. Her world shifted. Everything changed, like the landscape after a flood. It was all so clear to her now. Clear and yet muddled beyond comprehension. She bit her lip and turned away. What else could she do?

Chapter Twenty-eight

"Let's try this one more time." David sighed and leaned his elbows on the table between himself and the man he'd managed to capture. "I need the name of your boss."

"Jack Sprat."

"His real name."

"How 'bout Abraham Lincoln?"

Irritation rolled down his back along with a drop of perspiration. He hadn't planned to spend the whole afternoon in the stuffy jail, but Hiram Daniels was proving to be a hard nut to crack. "If you'll cooperate with me now, I'll put a word in with the judge. Who knows? He might not even hang you."

Hiram, if that was even his real name, didn't seem too impressed with the offer. He was leaning back in his chair, his legs sprawled out in front of him. "I don't plan to stay in here long enough to get hanged."

David shook his head. "Who said you'd be here?"

The other man straightened and scratched his ear. He had a face only a mother could love—small eyes, a long nose, and a weak chin. "So where you gonna take me?"

"I ought to drag you back to New Orleans. See if they can't charge you with Charlie Petrie's murder."

Hiram shook his head. "I wasn't part of that. Felix is the one who did in poor ol' Charlie."

"Where is he?"

"Dead."

David raised an eyebrow at that news. It sounded to him like the members of this gang weren't under much control. They seemed to prey on each other as much as they preyed on the innocent. "How did he die?"

Hiram relaxed, a smile on his thin lips. "Fell off his horse and hit his head. Weren't nothing we could do. Leastwise that's what my buddies said."

It sounded like his buddies might have murdered Felix and made it look like an accident. Had they been worried Felix was working with the police? "When was that?"

"Near about two weeks ago, I guess." Hiram looked off into the distance, counting the days.

"Yep." He nodded. "I remember it clear. It was right before we got our orders to come up here and wait."

"How long have you been in Cairo?"

"Not in Cairo." The thief corrected David. "We been living in the woods."

David gritted his teeth. He was ready to get this interrogation behind him and catch the real culprit. "All right, how long have you been living in the woods nearby?"

" 'Bout a week. We been sitting around doing nothing until we got our instructions last night."

"What did they say?"

"To rob the bank." Hiram looked at David, his eyes flat.

"So you and the rest of your gang sat around for a week. You didn't do anything at all until you got a note telling you to rob the bank."

"That's right."

David slammed a fist on the table. Although the action caused his hand to ache, Hiram sat up, and the distant look in his eyes disappeared.

"That's not right. I know you got more information than to 'rob a bank.' Someone is giving you specific information on the strengths and weaknesses of every bank you've hit. I want to know who that person is and how he gets his information."

Hiram shook his head. "Listen to me, lawman. I ain't scared of you. I ain't scared of your threats. In fact, there's only one thing I am scared of."

"What's that?"

"Getting stabbed in the back by the man you want to know the name of."

"I'll protect you."

"Like you protected poor ol' Charlie?"

David felt his cheeks flush. "That was an accident."

"Well, I don't want no accident happening to me." Hiram grinned at him. "I know how to keep my skin whole."

The jailhouse door opened, and Sheriff Cunningham strolled back in. "Did you find out what you need, Pinkerton?"

"Yes." David nodded. "Hiram has been very helpful."

"What?" Hiram sat up, a shocked look on his his face. "I didn't tell you nothing."

The sheriff chuckled. "Apparently you're wrong. I wonder if the fellow he arrests will think you're innocent."

"That's not fair." Hiram's whine made David grin. "You're gonna get me killed for sure."

"I don't think you need to worry about it." David held out a hand to indicate the sheriff. "I'm sure there's more than one cell here. You should be safe."

Sheriff Cunningham nodded his agreement as he walked toward Hiram. "Come on, let's get you settled in and comfortable before your friend arrives."

David wished he could've gotten Hiram to give up Vance's name, but it didn't really matter. It was obvious Vance had orchestrated the whole affair. Nothing would convince him the actor was innocent. All he had to do now was arrest Vance and put him in the jail next to Hiram. He was certain he could get a confession from one of them before the week was out.

Leaving the jail, David was surprised to see how dark the sky had become. Was a storm brewing? A glance upward told him otherwise. He'd wasted the whole afternoon inside the jail with his prisoner. All the booths that had earlier lined the street were either gone or deserted. The celebration had moved to the raised stage where the actors from the *Ophelia* would perform.

At least he knew where to find Vance. David strode down the street, considering his next move. Although he knew Vance was guilty, others might be working with him from the *Ophelia*. Rafe, for example, had been skulking about town in a guilty manner. Was he another conspirator? Until David knew for certain, he needed to continue protecting his real identity. He would have to claim he'd been looking for Jasmine when he came upon the bank robbery, and his instinct had kicked in when he realized his "sister" was in danger. Any man in town might have done the same to protect the women in his family.

Blending in with the audience, David watched as Jasmine, modestly attired in her altered costume, beseeched Rafe, resplendent in a feathered Indian headdress, to save Captain John Smith from a beheading.

The gallant captain—alias Vance Hargrove—knelt at center stage, his head bowed and his hands tied behind him as an Indian brave menaced him with a raised tomahawk. As she cried out and ran to stand between Hargrove and the brave, David found himself caught up in the drama along with the rest of the audience. The fear on Jasmine's face was so real, her every gesture so natural that she seemed to have become Pocahontas.

She put her arms around Captain Smith's shoulders and hugged him tight. "You will free him, great Powhatan, or I will die with him."

David blinked and fell out of the trance Jasmine had woven. Of course she could play the part of Pocahontas with convincing authenticity. She and the Indian girl shared the same strength of will and imperious bravery. If she had to play a different part, Katherine from *The Taming of the Shrew* for example, he doubted she would be nearly as credible.

Powhatan relented, the brave retreated, and Pocahontas helped

Captain Smith rise to his feet. He thanked her for saving him and pledged to reward her with endless wonders from his homeland in exchange for her bravery.

Jasmine smiled up at him. "You owe me nothing, good captain. You have been a kind and honorable man. How could I let others harm you? Return to your people and tell them they are welcome here. You will live in peace among us. We are thirsty for the knowledge you will share with us. Together we will become a great nation."

They bowed and walked off the stage to thunderous applause.

It was time for him to act. David slipped through the crowd as Rafe, now dressed in a gray Colonial suit and white wig, escorted Angelica onto the stage for their skit about George and Martha Washington. Four tents had been set up behind the stage so the actors could change costumes. All he had to do was find out which one belonged to Hargrove and wait. He hoped to get him away from the area with a minimum of fuss.

Clem rushed past him, a blue scarf trailing from a mountain of material in her arms.

He reached out a hand to stop her. "Have you seen Vance?"

"He's changing in that far tent. He ought to be out in a minute or two."

Tabitha Barlow appeared at the flap of a different tent. "Clem, are you coming? I have to be on stage next."

"I'm right here." Clem grimaced and hurried away.

Several minutes ticked by, and David's shoulders tensed. Did Vance suspect he'd been identified?

"Did you find out anything from that man?" Jasmine's voice behind him distracted David from his worried thoughts.

He turned and smiled at her. "You made a very convincing Pocahontas."

"Do you think so?"

"I would have freed John Smith myself."

For a moment the chaos surrounding them seemed to disappear. Jasmine's lips parted, and her eyes widened. Like a moth drawn to a candle's flame, David felt himself yearning to caress her beautiful face, feel its softness beneath his fingers.

"If I didn't know better, I would think the two of you weren't even related." The sound of Miss Barlow's voice stung him, making David jerk back.

"Of course they are." Vance finally made an appearance, a stovepipe hat tucked under one arm. "Can't you see the resemblance? They have the same strong chins and high cheekbones."

David didn't want this conversation to continue. "I need you to come with me, Vance."

The actor looked surprised for a moment, but then he nodded, his face showing comprehension. "You've figured it out, haven't you?"

❧

"Tell Mr. Easley I won't be able to deliver the Gettysburg Address after all." Vance reached for Jasmine's hand and pressed a swift kiss on it. "If only you had been wrong about that race, this evening would be turning out very differently."

Jasmine pulled her hand from his. "What are you talking about? What's going on?"

"Nothing." David sounded so cold, so different than he had only a moment earlier.

Tabitha looked as surprised as she felt. "I think I'll go find Mr. Easley. . .make sure he knows about the change in the program." She walked away from them, leaving Jasmine to stare after her.

"You should go with her." David's voice brought her attention back to him.

"Not until you tell me where you're taking Vance and why he won't be back in time for his performance."

"Someone else can recite the address." Vance's gaze was sad, defeated. Guilt poured from him like a spring flood.

Jasmine shook her head. "I don't believe it. I can't. He hasn't done anything wrong."

"Of course he has." David blew out an exasperated breath. "You're just blind to the truth, as always. When will you stop ignoring the evidence right in front of you?"

Was he still talking about Vance? Jasmine had the odd feeling that David's words had a completely different meaning. She snapped her mouth shut.

David held a hand out to Vance. "Why don't you show us what's in your pockets?"

"Do we have to do that out here?" Vance glanced around. "I don't want everybody to know what's going on."

"They'll have to know sooner or later." David's face was implacable.

"Not if you tell them I decided to leave the *Ophelia* on my own."

Jasmine watched the debate, unable to accept the implications of their words. Could Vance have fooled all of them for so long? It didn't seem possible. Vance had kissed her. A chill went down her spine. If he really was all that David said, he could just as easily have stabbed her.

The three of them moved a few feet away from the stage, standing behind one of the tents where no one could see them. Jasmine prayed David was wrong. But her heart dropped to her toes when Vance reached into his pocket and pulled out a handful of bills. He avoided meeting her gaze as he slapped the money into David's palm.

"Do you believe it now, Jasmine? Vance is the one who's been going to the banks at every stop your showboat makes. He trades on his notoriety as a successful actor and his dubious charms to ferret out information from the tellers and officers at the banks. They never realize what he's doing."

Jasmine couldn't think of anything to say in the face of Vance's silence.

"Didn't I hear you tell Clem earlier that he missed the rehearsal last night?" David continued reciting the evidence of the actor's guilt. "By a strange coincidence, that's when the rest of the gang got the instructions they were waiting for. He's their leader—the reason the bank robberies are so successful. If I hadn't been there when they struck this time, he would've gotten away with it again."

Vance's head jerked up. "What are you talking about?"

"It's too late for you to claim innocence now, Hargrove." David folded the money and put it into his own pocket. "I've got all the proof I need."

"Wait a minute. Do you think I'm a bank robber?"

The incredulity in Vance's voice could not be faked. Hope sprang anew in Jasmine's chest. Something was wrong. She put an arm through his. "You won't take him to jail unless I go, too."

David's glance speared her. "You're not Pocahontas, and he's not the noble Captain Smith. He's a bank robber at best and a murderer at worst. Stand back and let me get him out of here."

She lifted her chin, ready to mount a strong defense.

But Vance shook his head and pulled her arm away from his. "Don't worry, Jasmine. We'll get this all sorted out. I may not be as honest as I should be, but there's no way I can be convicted of robbery."

"That's where you're wrong, Hargrove." David gave a shallow bow and spread his hand out in the direction of the town. "We'll see what the prisoner has to say about it when he sees your face."

Jasmine wanted to go with them, but she knew neither of the men would agree. She turned away and went in search of Clem, finding her standing near the stage, a worried look on her face.

"Where have you been?" Clem's question came out in a squeak. "Do you know what's going on? Where's Mr. Hargrove? Is he hurt? Miss Barlow is telling everyone he won't be back for his skit or the final pageant. I know he missed rehearsal last night, but this is inexcusable. Mr. Easley will have his head."

"Clem, I need your help." Jasmine kept her voice low and even. "I need some advice from someone I can trust."

"What's wrong? Does it have to do with Mr. Hargrove?" Her eyes widened. "Are he and David going to have a duel?"

Now it was Jasmine's turn to gape. "Of course not. What gave you that idea?"

"David was asking for him earlier, and I know how protective he can be. I thought maybe he'd heard that. . ." Clem stuttered to a stop. "I mean, I heard that. . ." She stopped again.

"What have you heard, Clem?"

"The doctor in Cairo told someone that we'll soon have a baby traveling with us." Clem's face turned as red as a beet. "And I knew it wasn't me, so I just thought. . ."

Jasmine's head buzzed as she jumped to the conclusion Clem was so hesitant to voice. "You think I'm pregnant?"

Clem nodded. "Aren't you?"

"No!" Jasmine's shout carried out over the audience. She pulled Clem away from the stage. "As soon as the performance is over, we've got to get back to the boat."

It took another hour, but they finally entered their bedroom and closed the door. Clem helped her out of her Pocahontas costume, and they both clambered onto the bed. "Clem, before I can tell you what's really going on, I need you to promise you won't say a word to anyone."

Clem's gaze turned solemn. She raised her right hand. "I promise."

Jasmine took a deep breath. Where should she start? "The first thing you need to know is that David isn't my brother."

"He's not?"

"No, we grew up together on my sister's riverboat, but we're not related at all."

"Then why is he—"

"He's a Pinkerton detective, and he's been trying to catch a gang of bank robbers who seem to have some connection to the *Ophelia*."

"Mr. Hargrove?" The other girl drawled the name, making his last name three distinct syllables. She might be from Ohio, but her voice sounded like she'd been born and raised much further south.

Jasmine nodded. "At least that's what he thinks. But something isn't right. At first Vance acted guilty, but when David mentioned the bank robberies, he seemed surprised. I don't know what Vance may have done, but I'm sure he's not part of any gang."

"What do we need to do?" Clem whispered the question as if concerned that the walls might overhear them.

"We've got to find out who the real culprit is." Jasmine lifted her chin when she saw the dubious look from Clem. But what else could they do? They couldn't stand by and let an innocent man hang.

❧

"I am not a robber."

"That's right." Hiram leaned against the wall of his neighboring cell. "Didn't you hear him? He's just a thief."

Vance put his head in his hands and groaned. "I know how it must sound, but you have to believe me."

David wondered why Vance continued to insist on his innocence. It made no sense to him. When confronted several hours earlier, he'd immediately produced money that proved his guilt. Why claim now that he was skimming money from the *Ophelia*'s manager? Why not just go ahead and admit the whole truth? "If you'll steal from the people you work with, how do you expect me to believe that you wouldn't take part in robbing a bank? Especially once you figured out how to keep your own hands clean in the process."

Vance's bleary eyes focused on his face. "Because it's the truth."

A part of David wanted to believe the man in spite of all the evidence to the contrary. But he was an actor. He could be playing the part of the innocent victim.

"It's like I told you. This morning I put a rather large wager on the *Marc Antony* to win the race. I was sure I'd double my money. It was a safe bet. That boat should have won."

"But it didn't." David stated the obvious.

"That's right. I know you won't believe me, but I'd decided to stop taking money from the Easleys. As soon as I won the wager, I knew I'd have enough to keep myself comfortable. I wouldn't have to pad my salary anymore. If only that stupid boat captain hadn't run us into a snag."

"And you don't have anything to do with the bank robberies?"

"No." Vance stood up and walked to the door of his cell. "But if someone aboard the *Ophelia* is working with the robbers, I may know who it is."

Hiram's face lost its grin. He sat up. "You'd best stubble it."

Vance hunched the shoulder closest to Hiram and looked toward

David. "If nothing else does, his reaction just now should tell you that I'm not the man you're looking for."

"I was pulling your leg." Hiram settled back once more, assuming an uncaring expression. "Go on and tell him your idea. I need a good laugh anyway."

David wondered which of them made the better actor.

"Haven't you noticed how Rafe Griffin has been absent from rehearsals lately?"

The question was like the tiniest leak in a levee. David thought about seeing Rafe sneaking through town Sunday morning. The man had been acting strange lately, less jovial than when David had first joined the *Ophelia*. Was he the real culprit? Was he worried the authorities would catch him after the death of one—no two—of his men? The questions swirled in his mind, making it hard to think.

"I need to get some sleep." David pushed himself up from the seat that had grown hard over the past hour. "They ought to be wrapping up the pageant by now. Sheriff Cunningham said he'd be back as soon as it's over."

"You have to listen to me." Vance put his arms through the bars of his cell and rested his weight on them. "Go back to the *Ophelia* and at least talk to Rafe. You owe me that much."

"I don't owe you anything." He had to give it to Vance Hargrove. The man had an overrated sense of his own importance. Not only did he try to convince David that he was innocent, but now he was trying to throw suspicion on another man.

And what about his plans for Jasmine? The very idea of the two of them together made him physically ill. David still remembered how Jasmine had sounded when she told him that Vance's kiss was better than his. He'd wanted to drag her back into his arms right then and prove to her that he could make her swoon. Maybe he should have. And maybe he should have gotten her off the *Ophelia* back then. At least she wouldn't be in danger of falling in love with a felon. David hoped she hadn't lost her heart to Vance. He hated to think of her mourning the man while he served a life term in prison, or worse, ended up dangling from a noose.

The sky outside the jailhouse lit up, and David walked to the window. Spider webs of blue, yellow, and red sparkled against the black sky before fading away. He had missed a large part of the celebration, but at least he'd been able to watch Jasmine perform, and now he had a front row seat to the grand finale. It was a fitting end to his mission.

The Illinois Central Railroad ran between Cairo and Chicago. The territorial marshal shouldn't have any trouble getting the criminals back for a trial. All David had left to decide was what to do about Jasmine. He couldn't leave her on the *Ophelia*. And he knew her well enough to know she wouldn't go back to Les Fleurs if he didn't take her there. She was more likely to board the train to Chicago herself, eager to prove Vance's innocence to the authorities in that town.

For a moment he considered the attractive idea of Jasmine in Chicago. . .but then discarded it. Now that he no longer had to focus on the gang of bank robbers, David knew he needed to get her back to the people who loved her, the people who would protect her from her worst enemy—her own driving ambition.

He left Sheriff Cunningham at the jailhouse and trudged back to the *Ophelia*. His stomach was empty, his heart weary. He didn't even know what he was going to say to the other actors on the showboat. Should he tell them the truth about Vance? If the man was as guilty as he believed, he wouldn't be returning. But what if David had arrested the wrong man? What if it was Rafe? Or Mr. Easley? Or some other man he hadn't even considered? The questions in his mind were absurd, the product of an exhausted mind. Vance Hargrove wasn't innocent. He couldn't be. The man was playing some kind of game for his own purposes, maybe trying to muddy the water enough so he could swim away, free to continue his wicked enterprise somewhere new. David could never let that happen.

Chapter Twenty-nine

Clem's quiet snores weren't the reason Jasmine couldn't sleep. Like a beaver worrying the bark from a sapling, her mind kept working at the question of Vance's guilt or innocence. David was smart and knew how to do his job. He wouldn't have arrested Vance if he wasn't sure the actor was guilty.

But how could Vance be guilty? After spending weeks in his company, she had realized he was not the dashing hero she'd thought in New Orleans. But a bank robber? She refused to believe Vance Hargrove was that evil. And what about the man who had been murdered? Could Vance have ordered his death? How could she reconcile this image of a cold-blooded criminal with the man who had, for the most part, been kind to her?

No matter how she looked at it, Jasmine could only find two possible answers, each of which excluded the other—believe Vance was innocent or believe David was right. She hadn't known Vance for even a year, and she had known David all her life. The choice was simple. Jasmine wished it was easy, as well.

She threw off her sheet and blanket, unable to lie still any longer.

Claustrophobia clamped anxious fingers around her throat. If she stayed in this room, Jasmine was afraid she would lose her mind. Rising from her bed, she exchanged her gown for the clothes she'd draped across the end of her bed and slipped out of the room.

Candles flickered in the hallway as she picked her way upstairs. Relief eased the tension in her neck and shoulders when she opened the door and sucked the cool night air into her lungs. The only sound out here was the soft sigh of a midnight breeze and the gentle slap of the water against the edge of the barge. Above her head God had flung a giant saltshaker of stars into the blackness of the sky. The trees on the opposite shore stood shoulder to shoulder, an army of enemy soldiers intent on subduing the countryside. The river was a dark and mysterious highway, capturing a sliver of light from the moon above as it rushed ever southward. She breathed deeply of the pine-scented air, trying to calm the melee in her head.

Turning her back on the river, Jasmine leaned into the rail, her gaze combing the bleak landscape of this side of the river for answers. The town of Cairo was dark, its citizens resting from the exciting day. A movement startled her as a shadow separated from one of the spindly pine trees between the riverbank and the town. Someone was walking toward her. Thoughts of murder and robbery came roaring back into her head. Was the real culprit sneaking back to the *Ophelia*?

Her heart clenched in fear, but before she could decide whether to run or scream—or both—an errant beam from the moon illuminated his face. David. Her terror abated with the recognition, replaced by curiosity.

His head was down; his shoulders drooped. Something was wrong. David should be elated by his success. Putting aside her own confusion, Jasmine called his name.

His head jerked up. "Who's there?"

"It's me, Jasmine."

"What are you doing out here at this hour?" He changed direction, walking toward the gangplank that connected the barge to the riverbank.

"I could ask you the same thing."

"I had to wait for Sheriff Cunningham to return. I didn't want to leave the prisoners alone." David reached her side, and she could see the frown on his face. "Your turn."

"I couldn't sleep." Jasmine left out the part about the walls of the bedroom closing in on her. "I decided to come out for some fresh air."

"You know the rest of Vance's gang is camped out somewhere near. I don't like the idea of your standing out here all alone."

She should be upset at his complaint, but Jasmine could hear the concern in David's voice. It echoed the way she'd felt earlier in the day when she had come face-to-face with the idea that David could have been hurt trying to protect her. It was time to apologize for adding to his burdens. "I'm sorry for causing so much trouble."

David said nothing. His face, half in shadow, didn't betray his thoughts. As the silence lengthened, she began to wonder if he would accept her apology. Had she finally pushed him so hard that he no longer cared about their friendship?

Another minute passed, and she couldn't stand it any longer. "Aren't you going to say something?"

"I'm just trying to overcome my shock. What's changed? Is it because of Vance, or have you finally seen what kind of people you're living with?"

Jasmine blinked. Maybe she was sleepier than she'd realized. "What are you talking about, David?"

"I'm talking about the loose morals and decadent lifestyles of the theater."

"And you think that's why I want to be a famous actress? So I can lead a shameful life? Sometimes I think you don't understand me at all."

"I know you're doing this for all the wrong reasons, Jasmine. You've said yourself that you want to be famous. Can't you see how destructive such a goal can be?"

She straightened. "Fame and fortune are not bad things. I can hold onto my morals and still be a part of this world."

David's eyes closed, and he shook his head. "I wish that were true."

"What about you? Don't try to convince me that you don't enjoy the slaps on the back for a job well done."

Jasmine waited for his answer.

"You're right to an extent. When I foiled an attempt to rob the coach I was on last year, I was pretty proud of myself. The passengers were so complimentary. It felt good. I accepted a job offer with the Pinkerton Agency with the idea that I wanted to spend my life repeating that experience." He paused and swallowed. "One day God tapped me on the shoulder. I was riding along with a payroll train that was attacked. I killed one of the robbers and wounded one, a kid too young to shave. A pastor on the train stepped forward and shared the Gospel with that kid right there in the middle of nowhere. He was saved that day—I watched as he changed. God used that pastor, but He also used me and the talents He's given me to make a difference. I like to think that if I save a man's life, maybe he'll have time to repent and turn to God."

What made him think God wasn't using her talents, too?

As if he had read her mind, David shook his head. "Providing an hour or two of entertainment isn't a bad thing in itself. I was proud of you back in Natchez when you were helping the orphanage, but what you're doing now is for your own purposes."

Jasmine was beginning to wish she'd never come up on deck. But she couldn't let his condemnation go unchallenged. "How can you say I won't touch lives? When I get to be famous, I can use my resources to rebuild dozens of orphanages."

"Like you're doing right now?" He cocked his head.

"That's not fair. I'm just starting out. Once I become a star, everything will be different."

"No it won't, Jasmine. That's just the point. Jesus said if we are unjust in the least things, we'll be unjust in greater ones. You can't wait to become rich or famous. You can't expend all of your talent getting the things this world labels valuable and expect to hold onto what's really important."

The words rang with power and truth. For a moment Jasmine felt like a curtain had been lifted. Was she already growing calloused and hard? Immoral? *No.* She was still the same person she'd always been.

"What about my obligation to Mr. and Mrs. Easley? To the other actors on the *Ophelia*? I know it's not your fault that Vance is guilty." There. Maybe by admitting that he was right, David would see that she was not the selfish, heartless person he accused her of being. "But that doesn't change the fact that we can't hope to replace him before getting to St. Louis. And my part may not be as vital as his, but I'm filling in for Angelica. If I leave now, the whole company might fold."

"All right, Jasmine, have it your way." He sounded so defeated. So tired. "I'll stay on board the *Ophelia* until it reaches St. Louis, since that's the end of its current run. But that's it. I think you're trying to run from God. Be careful that you don't get too far away to call on Him."

She watched him cross the gangplank with a heavy heart. Had she thrown away something precious by refusing to listen to David? Had she forfeited his protection? Jasmine hugged her arms as a damp gust of air blew against her face. Why couldn't David see that she was the same person she'd always been?

She would show him the truth. She would reach her goals in spite of his doubts. And she would use her influence to make changes in the world that impressed even David Foster.

❧

Jasmine awoke to the low tone of a steam whistle very close by. What time was it? She rolled over in her bed and groaned when she realized Clem was already dressed and gone. She had overslept again, thanks to her sleeplessness during the night. Ever since her talk with David, slumber had eluded her each night until the wee hours of the morning.

The past few days had been difficult for everyone. Hot, long days that led to short tempers, outbursts, and arguments. Jasmine had gone to visit Vance once before the U.S. marshal arrived. It had been an uncomfortable experience, and she was relieved she wouldn't have to repeat it.

Angelica had talked the Easleys into letting her reassume her role as the second leading lady, reducing Jasmine to the status of an understudy. No matter which play they performed, the most she got to do was the bit parts, the same as the rest of the stock troupe who received no recognition.

So much for her determination to show David how she could use her talents. At least they were supposed to leave Cairo today. The residents had seen all the plays in the *Ophelia*'s repertoire, even a reprise of their patriotic vignettes. Last night, the audience even booed poor Rafe.

The barge shook under her feet as she considered whether or not to bury her head in her pillow again. Were they already underway? Deciding it was too late to fall back asleep, Jasmine got up, hurried through her toilette, and headed for the dining room. Maybe a cup of coffee would clear the cobwebs from her head.

"Here's Miss Johnny-Come-Lately to join us. Clem said you needed your beauty sleep, and I have to say I agree with her." Tabitha's words contained the sting of a wasp.

Jasmine felt like sticking her tongue out at the snippy female. "I didn't realize we were on a schedule."

The others in the room paused for a moment before returning to their meals, except for Mr. Easley, who looked at her from his seat at the head of the dining table, his eyes narrowed. "Are you ill?"

"No, sir." She picked up a plate and chose some crisp bacon and a piece of toast from the buffet before sliding into a vacant chair next to Clem and across from Rafe and Angelica.

Jasmine noticed that Angelica's face looked blotchy and swollen, like she had been crying. What was she so upset about? From her woebegone expression, anyone would think she'd lost her best friend. . . but Rafe was sitting next to her.

"I hope not." Mrs. Easley took a sip from her coffee cup. "We've had enough of bad luck lately."

It was the same thing Jasmine had heard again and again since Vance was arrested. At first everyone had been shocked and unbelieving, but as the days wore on, they adjusted. Rafe was not as convincing as the male lead, and Mr. Easley was beginning to lose patience. She glanced at the man across from her, wondering what was bothering him. Maybe she should try to get him alone and question him. Offer him a sympathetic ear and even give him helpful advice.

"Everything will be better once we reach St. Louis." Rafe glanced at Angelica, a question in his eyes.

Perhaps she should start with Angelica. Whatever was bothering him most likely involved her as well and might be the root of the blond actress's obvious distress.

"I doubt you'll be much better." Mr. Easley sent a dark frown his direction. "But that may not be my problem by then anyway."

Angelica pushed back from the table and ran from the room. Tabitha made a face but said nothing.

Jasmine exchanged a confused glance with Clem. Something she didn't understand was going on. Her stomach churned. Even though she'd grown up with two older sisters, she had never liked emotional scenes. Especially at breakfast.

Clem cleared her throat and glanced toward the door—a signal for Jasmine to follow as soon as possible—before excusing herself. She must know something that she couldn't discuss in front of the others.

Jasmine toyed with the food on her plate, sipped her coffee, and covertly watched the others. What had happened before she arrived? The Easleys exited next, leaving Tabitha, Rafe, and Jasmine in the dining room. Time to make her escape. She tossed her napkin over her plate and stood. "See you later."

Neither of the other two said anything as she exited. She looked for Clem on deck, in the theater, and in the prop room but found no sign of her friend until she returned to her room. "What's going on?"

"It's Angelica." Clem opened her eyes wide and twisted her mouth.

Jasmine understood she was supposed to infer something from Clem's expression, but she had no idea what. "What about Angelica? I saw she was upset. I don't understand why unless she's afraid I'm going to get her parts again."

"Angelica is the one." Again that odd twist to Clem's mouth.

Jasmine shook her head.

Finally Clem made a disgusted noise. "She's the one who is going to— She's going to be a mother."

"What?" Jasmine couldn't believe what her friend was saying. With all the extra drama lately, she had forgotten the rumor that someone was in the family way. Everything fell into place. The way Angelica had been gaining weight. Her moodiness.

"The truth was bound to come out sooner or later."

"Is Rafe the. . .the one who. . ." Her face colored. She couldn't get the words out.

Clem raised her shoulders in a shrug. "Who knows? But you still don't get it. Have you thought what this is going to mean for you?"

First Vance turned out to be a criminal. Now Angelica was—*Disgraced* was the only word she could assign to Angelica's scandalous condition. What was wrong with these people? At this point she wouldn't have been surprised to find out that Tabitha was an alcoholic or that the Easleys ran a gambling den. Now Clem wanted her to be happy about assuming Angelica's roles on a permanent basis? "I can't believe you said that."

Clem looked as though Jasmine had slapped her. "Why? Haven't you heard that 'It's an ill wind blows no good'?"

"Angelica is far from the most pleasant woman on board, but I can't take pleasure in such a thing. Her life is going to change dramatically. She needs our prayers."

"When did you turn into such a goody-goody?"

Jasmine caught her breath. Had she strayed so far from her beliefs that her best friend on the *Ophelia* didn't know where she stood on spiritual matters? Did she even know anymore? Although Clem's cutting words hurt, Jasmine found herself more disturbed by the realization that David had been right that night. She had strayed a long way from what she once held dear.

It was time to find her way back to the person she used to be, back to the important things in life, back to God and her faith. She would start by trying to help Angelica. "I'm sorry you're disappointed in me, but we'll sort things out when I get back."

"Where are you going?" Clem's voice followed her into the hallway.

Jasmine continued on her mission without answering. She would tell Clem later. Right now she needed to talk to Mr. and Mrs. Easley before they did anything rash.

She passed Angelica's room on her way to find the manager and his wife, coming to a halt as she realized she could hear sobs coming from within. Her heart ached for the actress. She couldn't ignore Angelica's distress. Jasmine knocked on the door, turning the knob when the weeping continued. "Angelica, may I come in?"

"Go away." The actress was lying face down across her bed, her hair loose.

Ignoring Angelica's order, Jasmine sat on the edge of the bed and rubbed the actress's back. "It's going to be okay, honey."

Angelica turned her head toward the wall. "No, it's not. My life is over."

"You do have some difficult days ahead of you." Jasmine knew that sugarcoating the situation would not help Angelica. She needed someone who would help her face her future and perhaps even appreciate the blessings in her life. "You also have a lot of things going for you."

"You don't know anything about it." Angelica sniffed and sat up. "If I don't do something, I'm going to have a baby. My life will be over if that happens."

"What do you mean. . .if?"

"Tabitha says she knows of a doctor in St. Louis who can take care of my problem."

Jasmine was horrified at the suggestion. "You cannot be serious, Angelica."

"What do you know about anything?" Angelica could be a pretty girl, but the sneer on her face distorted her features, making her look like she was wearing an evil mask. "You waltz in here all fresh and innocent like you aren't planning to step into my shoes the minute the Easleys dismiss me. I know you want to steal my career."

"I have to admit I've enjoyed playing larger roles, Angelica. I want to be a serious actress, too. But I've always been eager to give them back to you."

"Well, you can have them now, unless I decide to go see Tabitha's doctor."

"You can't do that, Angelica." Jasmine reached out and pushed Angelica's hair away from her face. "You're carrying a life inside you. A life God has given you."

Angelica didn't pull away from her touch. An encouraging sign. Jasmine decided to risk going a step further. "I can't say I approve of the way you went about this—and we both know God is not pleased when we go against His Word and choose our own pleasure over His will. But you can't change the situation now. What you have to consider at this moment is the precious baby you'll get to love and care for."

"But what about my career?"

"That has to come secondary to the precious life you will bring into this world. That's what any loving parent does: put what's best for the child before his or her own dreams and wishes." Jasmine felt an inward prick as Lily came to mind. She knew deep down her oldest sister always wanted what was best for her. She pushed aside her guilt for now, as she needed to concentrate on Angelica. "Who's the father?"

"Rafe, of course." Angelica frowned at her.

"What does he say about the baby?"

Angelica twisted her hair and pushed it behind her shoulders. "He says he'll marry me."

"See? There's your answer." Jasmine paused as another thought occurred to her. "Do you love him?"

"I suppose so. But even if we do get married, I still won't be able to continue acting."

"That's true. But you'll be busy with an even more important role. You'll be raising a beautiful son or daughter."

Angelica rubbed her nose with the heel of her hand. "Do you think I can do that?"

"I'm sure you can. God gave you this baby because He knows it, too. You and Rafe can make a good life for your child. God has a plan for all three of you. All you have to do is follow Him."

A tiny smile appeared on the other woman's mouth. "You remind me of a lady from my hometown. She was always telling me about God and Jesus, too. You know, you're not as bad as I thought you were."

Jasmine couldn't help laughing at the backhanded compliment. "I'm glad to hear that."

Angelica pushed herself up from the bed, a look of hope on her face. She moved to her dressing table and pinned her hair in a bun. "Thanks, Jasmine. I'm going to think about what you said. I may even go talk to Rafe."

Feeling better than she had since David arrested Vance, Jasmine left Angelica's room. She didn't know if the couple would turn to God, but she prayed they would.

❧

David heard the *Miss Polly*'s paddlewheel stall. He looked back to see if he could identify the problem. No sign of a snag or sandbar. What was wrong?

A hint of black smoke rising past the blades of the paddlewheel made him wonder if something had happened to the pistons under the deck. The engineer stuck his head out of the boiler room. "I've got pressure building up in here."

Several of the crew ran away from the engineer, but David moved toward him. Boiler explosions were the most common reasons for the loss of a riverboat. And for the deaths of passengers and crew. If the boiler exploded, the ship often sank. Those who survived the initial explosion were in danger of drowning. In his years with Jasmine and her family, he had seen the ghastly remains of more than one such incident.

David threw open the door and ran to help Sal Benson, the engineer. Outside the cramped room, men yelled, and he thought he heard a splash. Had someone decided to jump before knowing whether or not it was necessary?

Throwing his weight against the largest valve, David prayed for the safety of the tugboat, the showboat it was pushing, and the lives of everyone aboard both vessels.

Sal kept one eye on his gauges as he tackled the other valves. "I think we're getting ahead of the problem. The needles are beginning to drop."

"Thank You, Lord." David grabbed one of the coal shovels and used it to jam his valve open.

Sal pulled a filthy handkerchief from his pocket and staunched the beads of sweat from his broad forehead. A gray streak caused by the swipe of the dirty cloth stood out in stark relief to his parchment-hued face. "That was a close one."

"What do you think happened?"

"I have no idea. I had just added fresh coal to the boiler when I realized it was too quiet. Even tossing a bucket of water on them wasn't enough to stop the pressure from building up. If you hadn't come to help me. . ." His voice trailed off.

Captain Ross's face appeared at the boiler room door. "Is everything all right in here?"

Sal nodded. "Thanks to David. He was the only one who wasn't too scared to help me get the boiler shut down."

"Is the *Ophelia* okay?" David didn't want to dwell on his actions. He hadn't been any braver than the engineer standing beside him.

"Yes, but we're going to have to land and figure out what's happened to our paddlewheel. Luckily we're only a few miles north of Wittenberg, Missouri. I hope to negotiate a safe landing there." He tugged on his cap and left them alone.

When David left the engineer, he helped the others knot lengths of rope around several grappling hooks. The plan was to hurl the hooks toward trees or any other targets that could hold their boat against the current of the river. He was glad they were far enough north of Cairo that the rough water of the confluence wouldn't be a danger.

A glance toward the barge showed that most of the passengers were on deck watching the activity on the tug. He caught a glimpse of Jasmine's windblown dark hair. Even though David told himself that he was no longer responsible for her safety, he knew better. Just seeing her tentative wave brought a smile to his face and made the muscles of his stomach loosen. Who was he kidding? As long as he drew breath, he would love Jasmine. But if she didn't soon change her ways, he would have to sever their contact. Watching her destroy her life was something he couldn't do.

After some tense moments, they managed to get the *Miss Polly* secure against the riverbank at Wittenberg. The showboat suffered no visible damage, but he knew the ride had been rougher than the actors were used to as the river current tried to separate the two boats. Finally it was done.

He crossed to the showboat and began searching for Jasmine and Clem, finding them in the prop room picking up the costumes and props that had become jumbled up during the maneuvers. "Are the two of you okay?"

Clem picked up a bouquet of silk flowers. "What's wrong with the *Miss Polly*?"

"A piston rod splintered."

Jasmine looked at him. "That's serious. I wonder how long it will take to replace it."

David shrugged and shoved his hands into his pockets. He had been avoiding Jasmine for days in an attempt to give her time to think about what she wanted to do with her life. Had his tactic worked? Had she considered her future from a different point of view, or was she still clinging to the belief that she could serve two masters?

"I've got to go check on something in our room." Clem put the flowers on a table before leaving.

A backdrop painted to resemble *Macbeth*'s Great Birnam Wood leaned against a papier-mâché arch. David pushed the plywood stage set against the wall. "I heard you've been busy over the past week."

"I don't have that much to do." Jasmine folded the costume in her hands and put it in one of the open trunks. "I mostly spend my time helping Clem."

"That's not what I mean, and you know it."

He heard her soft laugh. "I didn't do anything worth mentioning."

David stopped trying to straighten the arch. It would need professional attention. "Rafe has been singing your praises to anyone who will listen. He says you intervened on his behalf with the Easleys. That you begged them to keep him on since he's about to be a father. That took a lot of pluck."

"I was worried about him and Angelica. They're going to be a family. I know they should have gotten married first, but Angelica told me they're going to see a pastor as soon as we get to St. Louis."

"Which is going to take several days longer than expected." David picked up a skull, shuddered, and set it on a table as Hamlet's soliloquy about death rang in his ears. "I just wanted you to know how proud I am of you."

"Will it take that long to replace the piston rod?"

"I can't believe Wittenberg will have the proper replacement parts. We'll probably have to order it from St. Louis."

"If that's not the definition of irony, I don't know what is. To get to St. Louis we need to purchase a part from St. Louis."

This time his laughter joined hers.

"Did I see someone jump off the *Miss Polly*?"

David sobered. "Yes. The idiot apparently decided he'd rather take his chances in the water. He was lucky to be fished out a mile or so downriver. It's a wonder he didn't drown."

Jasmine nodded.

Silence filled the room for several moments until Jasmine stopped working and tossed a glance at him.

"Is something wrong?"

A tentative smile appeared on her lips, making her look so sweet. . . so vulnerable. "I've been thinking about what you said."

His heart thumped. "And?"

"You made a lot of sense, David, but I'm not sure I want to leave the *Ophelia* when we reach St. Louis."

David put a hand to his forehead. Nothing had changed. All his prayers, all his heartfelt words had meant nothing to Jasmine. Disappointment weighted his shoulders. What could he say to her?

She forestalled his words. "Before you start in on me again, please let me explain."

He put his hand down, offering a silent plea to God for fortitude. "Go ahead."

"Angelica cannot continue acting for obvious reasons. Someone will have to replace her." She stopped and looked at him.

Was she waiting for his agreement? If so, she would have a long wait. He could already see where this was going.

When he said nothing, she sighed. "You remember how I took over for her on a temporary basis when the Easleys thought her problem was overeating. My name was even on the playbill. I saved a copy as a reminder. Even if I can't go on to Chicago or New York, at least I'll be able to say I was a serious actress. That playbill is a memento of the time I—we—have spent on the *Ophelia*."

He shook his head. "You're falling into a trap. Even though I've never received applause for what I do, the praise I get makes me feel good—it brings me pleasure. If I'm not careful, though, those good feelings begin to replace something important. I start thinking I deserve the praise. That it's because I'm special—smarter or faster or stronger. It's like an addictive drug. The more praise you receive, the more you want."

"You still don't get it, David. It's not so much the applause that I want to hold onto, although that is part of it. I want to remember making others happy, helping the Easleys and Tabitha, Angelica and Rafe, Clem and all the others who depend on the *Ophelia* for their livelihood. I want to remember spending this time with you, too."

David considered her words. He still thought she should go home, but he had to admire her spirit. Jasmine was maturing. She was beginning to sound like a woman he had always hoped she would become. Should he agree? If he insisted on her immediate return, would he risk destroying the bridge forming between them? A bridge that could bring them together?

She smiled, her eyes lighting with mischief, reminding him of the girl he'd grown up adoring. "There's something else I wanted to talk to you about. I've already mentioned it to Clem, and she thinks it's a great idea."

"What's that?" He let go of his concerns for the moment. He would have to pray about St. Louis.

"Since Rafe is having to take over for Vance, we've struggled to find someone who can do his parts."

"I find that hard to believe." David frowned. Why was she talking to him about acting problems? "Don't you have several men in the stock company?"

"Yes, but none of them seems quite right. Ever since the trouble in Cairo, we've been losing people. The ones who are left are either too inexperienced or too old. They're not convincing, and the Easleys are worried our performances will fall short if we don't find a strong second lead."

"You're beginning to sound more like a manager than an actress."

She tilted her head, her violet eyes serious. "Clem said the same thing."

"So what will you do?" David's heart seemed to grow wings. Perhaps he should not worry so about Jasmine's plans. He sensed the change in her was deeper than he'd first thought.

"I thought maybe you could join us on the barge."

"What?" His mouth fell open in shock. "Please tell me you're not serious."

"Come on. It'll be fun. Remember how we used to act for our friends and family back home? You already know the stories, and the lines will come back to you after a few rehearsals." She stood and walked to him, her eyes begging for his agreement.

When would he stop being an idiot for this woman? "What about my work on the tugboat?"

"Don't worry about that. The Easleys will explain to Captain Ross. He'll have to find someone else to take over your duties." Jasmine hugged him. "I can't wait to tell Clem."

Relishing the feel of her arms around his waist, David gave in. It couldn't be that bad, could it?

Chapter Thirty

Tabitha stood on a crate, only her upturned face and steepled hands showing above Juliet's balcony. "O Romeo, Romeo! Wherefore art thou Romeo? Deny thy father and refuse thy name! Or, if thou wilt not, be but sworn my love, and I'll no longer be a Capulet."

Standing in the wings in the nurse's costume, Jasmine mouthed the familiar lines, her heart wrung once again by Shakespeare's words. No matter how often they were repeated or who actually performed them, her imagination carried her to the Capulets' garden.

"You should be Juliet." The words in David's slow drawl sent a shiver down her spine.

She turned in the crowded space, her elbow grazing his arm. "I doubt Tabitha would agree with you."

His mouth was only a breath away. Her awareness shrank until all she could see was his mouth. The memory of the night in Memphis returned to her in full force. The thrill of their lips pressed together, the strength of his hands cupping her face, the love and devotion in his gaze. The aftermath of his touch returned to her, too. She'd pushed him away, left him standing all alone. And when he'd tried to do the honorable thing and apologize to her, she had scoffed at his words, even taunting him. . .lying to him about Vance's kiss.

When he took a step back, Jasmine remembered to breathe. Fiery coals burned her cheeks. Jasmine put her hands to them, her mind skittering.

"Are you ready for your scene?"

"All I have to do is shout, 'Madam!' from the edge of the stage." His question refocused her attention, giving her something to think about besides the past. She looked him up and down. "I never realized how long your legs were until tonight."

He laughed, the sound warming her heart. "Thanks. Now I feel less self-conscious about these ridiculous tights."

"They look fine on you, better than they did on Rafe." She bent her head toward the stage. "You would make a better Romeo than he does."

"I doubt he would agree with you." He winked at her as he paraphrased her previous answer. "Besides, Rafe seems to have grown into his new role. I think it's because he knows his position is secure on the *Ophelia*."

"I'll be happier once he and Angelica are safely married."

David glanced toward the curtain between them and the audience. "I'm sure she's sitting out there watching to make sure he doesn't stray."

"She doesn't have to worry about that. Rafe has made it abundantly clear he loves her. He is constantly hovering over her. It would drive me crazy."

"You've always been too independent for your own good."

Jasmine pretended indignation. "And here I was thinking we were beginning to understand each other. I see now that you're still clinging to your mistaken opinion of my obvious strengths."

"You're wrong about that. I've always admired your strengths, Jasmine, even when I disagreed with your use of them."

"You used to like playacting with me." She squeezed her lips into a pout. "Or at least you always went along."

His face sobered. "That's because I care about you. Why else would I let you talk me into donning this ridiculous costume and making a fool of myself?"

She didn't know what to think about his statement. Did he really still care? Even after all she'd done?

"Jasmine, that's your cue." Mr. Easley hissed the warning at her.

Already? She moved to the edge of the curtain and put a hand to her mouth. "Madam!"

Tabitha answered her, impatience in her voice.

"Madam!" She repeated the summons before moving back to where David stood. "That's it for me until after your next scene."

When he didn't answer, she searched his face. "You're not still nervous are you?"

A twist of his lips told her the truth. And she'd been teasing him. Contrite, she assumed a serious expression. "You're doing a wonderful job. Mercutio is one of the hardest characters to portray—"

"You're not helping me feel much better."

"If you'd let me finish without interrupting." She put her hands on her hips. "I was going to say that you've conveyed his scornful wit perfectly. The people out there are laughing at the right times and staying silent when they should. You have them in the palm of your hand."

"Don't worry, Jasmine. You don't have to exaggerate. I'm not about to run off and leave you in the lurch." He touched her nose with the tip of his finger. "I've really enjoyed parts of the past week. Especially getting to watch all of you so serious about your art. It's given me a new respect for the theater."

"It's about time." She was glad to hear that David was not still angry about lingering aboard the *Ophelia*. "Now get out there and make me proud."

He saluted before moving past her. "Where the devil should this Romeo be? Came he not home tonight?"

Jasmine's heart soared as she watched him. Was it any wonder Vance had been such a disappointment to her? Even before she found out he was a thief and a bank robber, Jasmine had known the man couldn't hold a candle to David. What Vance lacked had nothing to do with looks or occupation. Although she'd been blinded by both of those attributes when she first met him, she had eventually come to recognize the emptiness in Vance's soul where his faith should be.

She hadn't suspected him like David had, but at least she'd known enough to keep Vance at arm's length. Even when she was denying her connection to God, He had kept her heart safe.

David returned to her side of the wings, but Jasmine had no time to compliment him on his scene. It was her turn to take center stage. In front of the audience, she delivered her lines with all the right gestures and inflections. Odd that she could perform even though being on stage no longer triggered the same heady surge of pleasure.

The performance ended to thunderous applause, and Jasmine took her place on the stage. She went through the motions of curtsying and smiling, moving forward with the other principals for an additional curtsy before stepping back to let Tabitha and Rafe bask in their stardom. When the curtain calls ended, David was surrounded by the rest of the cast. He was the new actor in their midst and deserved their congratulations.

Why did she feel so odd to see him being hailed? She wasn't jealous of his success. She was happy for David. Happy to see him enjoying the moment. Jasmine pinned a smile on her lips and added her thanks to the rest of the cast and the Easleys before slipping back downstairs to help Clem with the cleanup.

"I can't believe it's over." Clem stood in the middle of an avalanche. "How did David do?"

"He was extraordinary. If he didn't already have another job, he could succeed in the theater."

"If anyone can change his mind, it's you."

"I doubt David would agree with you." Jasmine smiled as she recalled their offstage banter. She would treasure those silly moments no matter what their futures held. As for his words about his feelings, she had no doubt she would lie awake considering them once she sought her bed. "And I doubt I would want to even if he did."

Clem rolled her eyes. "We'll see if you change your mind once we get to St. Louis."

"Don't count on it." Jasmine began to sort the mountain of costumes into two piles—one for washing, the other for mending.

For a brief moment she had a vision of being married to David, traveling around the world with him at her side. But then it faded. She knew better. David had his priorities, priorities that had nothing to do with the theater. Besides, she was starting to lose the passion for that dream herself. Jasmine didn't know if her feelings were a temporary aberration or a more permanent change, but she was leaning toward the latter.

As each day passed, she found herself more content with the idea of returning to Les Fleurs. Wouldn't Lily and Camellia be surprised to hear her admit that they'd been right all along? Although Jasmine couldn't regret her time with the people on the *Ophelia*, her brief stint in the public eye had taught her that life was more than accolades and applause.

What Renée Thornton had tried to tell her all those months ago—that she was supposed to being sowing the seeds of faith in this world—made sense to her now. Jasmine hoped to one day tell the sweet woman how much she appreciated her advice.

Once all of the costumes were sorted, Clem put a hand on her back and stretched. "That's all we can do for tonight, but we'll have to get up early if we're going to get all of these things ready for our arrival in St. Louis."

Jasmine was grateful that Clem had turned her attention from speculation about the future. Tomorrow would take care of itself. All they had to do was deal with today.

"Where is my script?" Jasmine upturned the pile of clothes on her bed. "I wanted to read through that scene once more before dinner."

Clem's hand halted midstroke through her loose hair as she twisted on the stool in front of their dressing table. "Stop making a mess. It's obviously not here. Do you think it's upstairs?"

Jasmine considered the question. She had not had it when she went to visit Angelica in her room after rehearsal. "It must be. I wouldn't worry about it, but I need to read through those Latin words once more. I kept stumbling over them this afternoon."

"Are you sure you don't have another reason for going back upstairs? Perhaps you and David need more practice..."

With a shake of her head, Jasmine exited the room. Ever since they started rehearsing *The Taming of the Shrew* back in Wittenberg, Clem had teased her about playing the part of sweet-natured Bianca opposite David's portrayal of the love-stricken Lucentio. At least they weren't Katherine and Petruchio. She was sure she'd never manage to be convincing in submitting to Petruchio's unreasonable demands. Jasmine much preferred sweet-natured, discerning Bianca, the pretty younger sister who chose David—Lucentio—from her bevy of admirers.

It was only a performance, after all. That's what Clem didn't understand. Rafe, or even Vance if he was not in prison, could be playing the part of Lucentio. The fact that she was looking into David's velvety green gaze had nothing to do with the way she stumbled over the Latin words in her lines. It was a difficult scene. That was all. David was only playing a part when he told her of his love during the scene. The same was true for her.

Jasmine knew she could overcome the problem by studying—by embracing the character of Bianca and forgetting everything but the performance. She had to. The Easleys would expect her to perform flawlessly at the St. Louis premiere tomorrow evening, and she was determined not to let them down.

Stepping into the theater, Jasmine was surprised to find it shrouded in darkness. Had Mr. or Mrs. Easley decided they could save money by extinguishing all the candles now that rehearsals had ended? The vast room was like a cave. She would have a hard time finding her script now. She stood still wondering if she should return to her bedroom for a candle on her own or fumble around on the stage and risk running into something.

"I thought I heard someone." A male voice coming from the back of the theater made her heart attempt to escape from her chest.

She recognized Tabitha's answering voice. "You're just nervous. Why do you think I snuffed all the candles? If anyone wandered in here, we'd hear them stumbling about. It's an effective way to ensure privacy."

"Are you sure?"

"I am. Now tell me why you think we should get rid of Hiram Daniels."

The name sounded familiar to Jasmine, but she couldn't quite place him. She left the question for now and concentrated on identifying the man's voice.

"Because he could still testify I had something to do with Charlie Petrie's death."

Jasmine put a hand over her mouth to keep from making any noise as understanding dawned on her. Charlie Petrie was the man who had died in David's arms. He was one of the bank robbers. And Hiram was the man who had mowed her down in Cairo.

Tabitha's laugh made the hair on her arms stand up. "Vance Hargrove will take the blame for that, not you and certainly not me. Hiram is too smart to say anything that could come back on us. He knows what happens to snitches."

"I hope you're right." The unseen man sounded less certain than Tabitha. "If a lawman knocks on my door, it won't be long before he also knocks on yours."

Jasmine placed the man's voice. Adam. . .no, Arnold Garth, one of the stock cast she had never paid much attention to. He and Tabitha were the bank robbers! They were the connection with the *Ophelia*.

Her first inclination was to go find David and tell him what she'd heard. But she needed to get proof first. Undeniable, incontrovertible proof. But what proof was there? Tabitha and Arnold would deny their conversation, and it would be their word against hers. She needed to continue listening. Maybe they would say something she could use against them.

"Don't worry about Hiram. We need to focus on getting this job done here. Then you and I can put our plans into action. It's about time to cut our losses here anyway."

"What are you talking about?"

"Things haven't been the same since New Orleans. Since Petrie's arrest." Tabitha's voice carried clearly through the empty theater. "There's something odd about that David Foster, too. I'm not sure what he had to do with catching Hiram and Vance, but he was involved in it somehow. Make sure you stay clear of him."

"I will. I may look for work out West." Arnold's laugh raised the hair on Jasmine's arm. "Maybe we can hook up in the future for another lucrative venture."

"Maybe. But listen, I visited two banks this morning. The best target is going to be Boatmen's Savings Institution." Tabitha lowered her voice, and Jasmine strained her hearing to its limits. "I wrote out most of the instructions this afternoon, but I didn't quite finish. It won't take me long to get it done. I'll give it to you after dinner. And this time I want you to stay with the men until it's done. I don't want any more mistakes or arrests."

"That wasn't my fault. Someone was waiting for us in Cairo. I never saw him, but I heard the gunshots. I almost didn't escape in time."

"It was a mistake to rob a town as small as Cairo." Tabitha's voice sounded hesitant, reluctant. "I thought it would do because of the Fourth of July celebration, but I was wrong. The bank must have hired a guard. Here in St. Louis, it'll be like it was before. The men will walk in, help themselves, and walk out. And we'll all be rich."

Jasmine had heard enough. She knew what to do. She had to get to Tabitha's room, find the note, and take it to David.

Thankful the unexpected darkness had kept her from stepping past the edge of the curtain, Jasmine felt behind her for the doorknob. She had to hurry. Slipping through the door, she held her breath and closed it without a sound. Glad she'd not changed out of the slippers she wore to rehearsals, she tiptoed down the stairs and broke into a run as she reached the corridor.

She didn't see anyone as she turned to the left and headed for Tabitha's suite. Opening the door, she was surprised to find it much tidier than her last visit. Was Tabitha packing in preparation for her departure?

With a sense of urgency, she looked for a note on Tabitha's dresser, opening each drawer to nothing but jewelry and face paint. A quick look through two trunks yielded nothing, but when Jasmine opened the top drawer in the table beside Tabitha's bed, she found it. A note on thick vellum. Her hand shook so hard, she could barely read the words. But she knew she had the proof David needed.

"What do we have here?" Tabitha's voice brought her head up.

The piece of paper drifted from her hand as Jasmine realized she was in serious trouble. Both Tabitha and her henchman stood in the door.

Arnold pulled a gun from the waist of his pants and trained it on Jasmine. "I told you someone was upstairs."

"It looks like you were right for once."

Jasmine closed her eyes and prayed for a miracle.

Chapter Thirty-one

David knew he was a little early for escorting the girls to dinner, but he wanted them to see the boat about to dock next to the *Ophelia*. Elephants, lions, and a hippopotamus were sights one didn't see every day. He knocked on their door and waited.

"Who's there?"

He recognized Clem's voice. "It's me, David."

She opened the door a crack. "I'm almost ready. But I don't know about Jasmine. She left several minutes ago to retrieve her script."

"I just came through there and didn't see her." He frowned. "I don't know how I missed her."

"She wasn't sure where it was. Maybe she went to see if she left it in Angelica's room. I'm sure she'll be right back."

"I hope so. I've got a special treat for the two of you."

Clem opened the door an inch wider. "What is it?"

"You'll have to wait and see."

She made a face and snapped the door shut.

David tapped his foot on the floor and waited. Other actors passed and spoke, but Jasmine still had not appeared by the time

Clem came out of the room.

"Still no sign of her?" Clem looked down the hall as if she expected Jasmine to be hiding behind him in the corridor.

David took her arm. "Let's go to the dining hall and see if she went ahead of us."

"I doubt that." Clem's face wrinkled in a frown. "She hadn't changed out of her costume. I can't imagine where she's gotten to. You're sure she wasn't in the theater?"

"Unless she was hiding from me." David was beginning to grow worried. It wasn't like Jasmine to disappear. "Let's go up and make sure, though. If we don't find her there, at least I'll be able to show you the surprise."

The theater was dimly lit by a small number of sconces. Clem called out her name while David went to look behind the Padua backdrop. "Jasmine, are you back here?"

"Look, David, I found her script." Clem held up the booklet. "She must have gone somewhere else."

He tried to quiet the alarm bells in his head. Jasmine had to be somewhere near. She was no longer a child with a tendency to wander off. "Let's go on outside. Maybe she's already discovered the surprise."

Clem folded the booklet and tucked it under her arm before meeting David at center stage. "I'm sure she's fine."

They walked through the auditorium side by side. He could tell Clem's unease matched his own. They would find her outside. Anything else was unthinkable.

He couldn't see anyone on the deck when they emerged from the stage entrance, but he could hear voices from the far side of the *Ophelia*, the side where the circus boat would dock.

"What's going on?" Clem glanced up at him, her eyes clouded with worry.

David led her around the front of the barge to the other side without explaining anything. Several people were crowded together, pointing at the barge floating toward them, its paddlewheel tugboat slowly guiding it toward the dock.

"I see a tiger." Clem's concern was temporarily shelved as she stared at the boat.

"That's my surprise. A floating circus." He moved her to the rail so she could get a better view, still looking for Jasmine's dark hair and the flowing blue costume she'd worn during the rehearsal.

Clem pointed to the large signs ruffling in the breeze as the barge inched forward: AMAZING ANIMALS, ASTONISHING ACTS, AND ASTOUNDING ACROBATICS.

David nodded, but his attention was still on the group of people leaning against the rail. Where was Jasmine?

The caged tiger Clem had first noticed paced back and forth, its growls bringing shrieks and exclamations from the women on the *Ophelia* as well as from the onlookers who lined the dock. Had Jasmine gotten off the *Ophelia* for some reason? Was she watching the excitement from there? His gaze raked the crowd but could not pick her out.

As he was about to leave the deck and return to the lower level of the barge, a man in a three-piece suit appeared on the upper deck of the floating circus. A monkey sat on his shoulder, its tail wrapped around his neck. "Come closer and be amazed. Watch in horror as one of our most experienced entertainers places his own head in the mouth of a man-eater. Hold your breath as a beautiful Egyptian princess lays her tender tresses beneath the huge paw of a ten thousand pound African pachyderm. Watch vicious hippopotamuses battle against prehistoric armored crocodiles, brought directly to you from the bloody waters of the Zambezi River in the dangerous wilds of darkest Africa."

Clem backed up closer to David. At first he thought it was because of the horrific description of the barker. But then he realized she was pointing in a different direction. Had she spotted Jasmine? "What is it?"

She gave a little hop. "Isn't that boat coming too close to us?"

David centered his attention on the tugboat guiding the floating circus. Something was wrong. He could see the men running back and forth, pointing toward the dock.

When he realized the problem, David's breath caught. Nothing was holding the two vessels together. Without the guidance of the tug, the barge would be completely at the mercy of the river current.

When he looked back at the floating circus, his heart climbed into his throat. "Get back! It's going to ram us."

Screams and shouts erupted all around them. David grabbed Clem's arm, but before he could get her to safety, a horrific crash sounded and the deck beneath his feet lifted into the air. He felt himself falling, his body rolling toward the opposite rail. His fingers scrabbled for anything to stop his momentum. The door to the theater slammed open, and he grabbed for it, nearly tearing his arm out of its socket in the process.

The squeal of grinding metal hulls drowned out the screams of the others. David dragged himself to his feet and staggered toward Clem, who had fetched up against the rail. He squatted next to her and helped her sit up. "Are you okay?"

She put her hands over her ears to shut out the noise and nodded.

David stood. "Good girl. You're going to have to get up and help the rest of the people out here get off the *Ophelia*."

The squealing stopped, and the deck leveled out once more. But David could hear an ominous sound of rushing water. The other barge must have torn a hole in the side of the *Ophelia*. A sizeable hole by the sound of it.

Clem put her hands down, terror visible in her wide eyes. "What are you going to do?"

"I'm going to find Jasmine." He helped her stand and gave Clem a little push. "We'll be out in a few minutes."

"Why?" Jasmine asked the question uppermost in her mind. "Why would you do this when you have so much, Tabitha?"

Tabitha's right eyebrow rose. "You can ask me that? You, the sweet young ingenue who is already being groomed to take my place?"

"You're wrong about that." Jasmine shook her head. "I'm leaving the *Ophelia* after this stop."

"Don't argue with her." Arnold looked much more formidable with a gun in his hand. She'd not paid much attention to him since getting a position on the *Ophelia*. Arnold Garth was just one of the background actors—easily forgotten. Effortlessly overlooked. Making him the perfect criminal. He was a little taller than Tabitha, with a wiry build and a hard face. "We've got work to do."

"Whether it's you or someone else doesn't really matter." Tabitha's sneer distorted her features as she continued talking to Jasmine. "You weren't there the first time an oafish theater manager relegated me to a smaller part because a younger actress needed a chance to shine. I can read the handwriting on the wall. I knew what was happening. There's no work for washed-up actresses. At least no decent work."

Jasmine's heart thumped so loudly it sounded like a bass drum in her ears. She wondered if she might be having a fit of apoplexy. Wouldn't it be ironic if she fell dead at Arnold and Tabitha's feet?

Tabitha moved to her dressing table, sitting and gazing at her reflection in the mirror. "You know, it only seems like yesterday that I was the starry-eyed girl who dreamed of seeing her name featured on a marquee."

Arnold shifted his weight from one foot to the other, a longsuffering expression on his face. Had he heard her story before? How long had the two been working together? How had they managed to carry out their plans under everyone's noses? What would they do with her now that she knew their secret?

"Hand me that note." Arnold gestured with the gun in his hand.

Jasmine bent to pick it up and moved toward him. Could she hold the slip of paper out far enough that he would have to reach for it? Grab his weapon when his attention was diverted? Her heart stuttered before resuming its hard thumps, twice as fast this time. She wasn't a Pinkerton detective. It would take him only a second to shoot her. Jasmine sought a safer solution.

"You said it yourself when you first came aboard the *Ophelia*." Tabitha's gaze locked onto hers through the mirror. "I've been in the theater since you were a child. Do you have any idea what kind of things I had to do to get the parts you're so eager to perform?"

Wishing she had never been so thoughtless, Jasmine looked toward the older woman. She wanted to put her arms around Tabitha and reassure her. Tell her that God loved her no matter how old she was or what she had done. But she was already so lightheaded, she didn't know if she could say what was needed before losing consciousness.

Tabitha balled up her fist and shook it at Jasmine's reflection. "My fame and glory tarnish a little more with each sunset, while you or girls like you swarm the theater, eager to grab my triumphs for yourselves."

Jasmine couldn't believe she had ever wanted to be like the pitiful woman sitting amid her tawdry finery. She understood that all the store-bought goods crowded into the suite were Tabitha's attempts to bolster her self-confidence. David's warning about replacing God with the sound of applause returned to her as Jasmine realized Tabitha was using jewelry, clothing, and money to bolster her fear of failure. She thought material wealth could fill the void in her heart, stave off the emptiness threatening to consume her. "I never meant to hurt you."

"Hurt me?" Tabitha pushed herself up and turned to face Jasmine. "You can't hurt me. Your name may one day replace mine on a playbill, although that remains to be seen. But I've made provisions already. I'm smarter than all the people on this boat. While you memorized your lines and offered pat answers for every situation, I've put together a profitable business."

Arnold chuckled. "You mean *we* have."

"I hope you're not trying to imply that you could have set up all of this without me." Tabitha turned on the man, exposing him to a full measure of fury.

The mask that Tabitha wore every day melted away, leaving her exposed in that moment. Jasmine wondered if the woman had ever been an innocent, decent girl. If so, the choices she had made in pursuing her goals had changed her into a cold, vicious liar. Someone who had to be more important than anyone else around her. Someone who would sacrifice everything, every decent impulse, to her god of fame and success.

Driving, relentless ambition had engulfed her soul. It was a high price, one that Jasmine knew she could not pay. If she lived through this, she would quit. She closed her eyes. *Lord, I choose You. I'm sorry, and I hope it's not too late. If You're listening, please believe me. I never should have tried to serve both my ambition and You.*

"What should we do with her?" Arnold shifted the focus off himself, apparently realizing how unstable Tabitha was at this moment.

Tabitha tilted her head, her eyes dangerously empty. "I like you, Jasmine. You're a bright girl. I could use someone like you. What do you say to throwing in your lot with me? I can promise you furs and jewels, excitement and recognition. You could be the distraction we need to keep our little group together."

Jasmine shook her head. She had already made her choice. God was the only One she would follow. Her heart slowed down and peace filled her. No matter what happened now, she knew He was in control.

"No?" Tabitha's voice held a note of disappointment. "I suppose it was a bad idea."

The older woman returned her attention to Arnold. "It's almost time for dinner. You get her off the boat while I go make an excuse for Jasmine's absence. We don't want anyone to suspect what's going on. Once we finish this job, we'll decide what to do with her."

A look passed between them. Jasmine translated it without any trouble. She knew they were going to kill her. They couldn't afford to leave her alive. She needed help if she was going to escape. She needed David to come to her rescue. A laugh tried to erupt, making Jasmine wonder if she would give in to hysteria after all. David had told her she would need him someday and he wouldn't be there. How right he'd been.

Lord, I know I don't deserve it, but I'm asking You to save my life if that is Your will. Please send David to rescue me, or show me a way to get free. And if I'm to die here—

The feel of the cold muzzle in her back cut off her thoughts. "Have a seat, Jasmine." Arnold's voice whispered the command in her ear. "We've got a little time before we leave."

Tabitha's lips twisted into a tight smile as she grabbed a black lace shawl. "Make sure you don't forget to deliver the message to—" She stopped speaking as the boat rocked under their feet. "What's going on?"

Their barge was safely tied to the dock so it couldn't be a problem with the *Miss Polly* again. Maybe a paddlewheeler had come too close to their berth before slowing.

Tabitha opened her mouth to say something, but the words were drowned out by a tremendous crash—like a volley of cannon fire—followed by the unearthly squeal of metal against metal.

Jasmine covered her ears, looking around for the source of the terrible sound. The word formed in her mind. *Collision!* Something large had crashed into the *Ophelia*.

Chapter Thirty-two

David ran through the dark theater and pushed through the door leading to the living area of the barge. "Jasmine. Jasmine, are you down here?"

A cry answered him. Weak, terrified. His mind refused to consider what might have happened to her. He just knew he had to reach Jasmine. He had to get her off of the barge before it sank.

He stood still a moment and listened intently. Where had the cry come from? The only thing he could hear now was the hiss of water. Brown and muddy, an inch of water pooled at the base of the stairs. It didn't look too bad. Maybe the *Ophelia* wouldn't sink.

Down the hallway to his right, a door banged in time with the rocking motion of the barge. Without hesitation, David ran in that direction, entering the room without pause. At first glance he thought the room was empty, but then he heard a weeping sound and looked again at the bed. "Angelica."

The blond actress was huddled in the center of the bed. Pillows, cushions, and a blanket bunched around her. She put an arm around her stomach in a protective gesture.

David held out a hand to her. "Come on. You need to go upstairs."

"What's happened?" She shrank back against the headboard.

"A floating circus got loose and has run into the *Ophelia*. Water's coming in somewhere. Come on, I'll help you."

Angelica nodded and slid from the bed. She drew back when her feet touched the water puddled on the floor. "It's cold."

"I know. But we have to go anyway." He forced a calm smile onto his face and clung to his patience even though he knew time was slipping away. He couldn't leave poor Angelica cowering in her room.

Footsteps ran down the hall toward them. "Angelica?"

David recognized Rafe's voice. "She's in here."

The tall leading man ducked into the room and scooped Angelica from the bed, picking her up as though she weighed no more than a ragdoll. "Let's get out of here."

"You get her out. I've got to find Jasmine."

Rafe looked back over his shoulder. "Could she be outside?"

David shook his head and waved the actor toward the staircase.

"Be careful." The other man tossed the warning back as his long legs negotiated the stairs. "Some of the animals escaped the other barge."

Wondering if the cry he'd heard earlier was from a wounded animal, David set his jaw. It shouldn't take him too long to search the rooms. Heading back to the left corridor, he threw open the door to the stateroom Jasmine shared with Clem, praying he would find her huddled on her bed like Angelica had been. But this room really was empty.

"David, come on." Mr. Easley waded through the water in the hallway, a determined look on his face. David realized the water covered the man's ankles. "We've got to get out of here."

He shook his head. "I can't find Jasmine."

Easley thrust a thumb over his shoulder. "No one's back there. I'm the last one out. Could she be with Clem?"

"No. I think Tabitha's missing, too." David could hear the fear in his own voice. He took a deep breath. "They weren't in Angelica's room, but I haven't checked Tabitha's yet. Maybe they're both there."

"I'll go with you." Mr. Easley slipped and fell backward into the rising water.

"You get out of here." David helped him up and gave him a push toward the stairs. "I'll be better off by myself."

Easley hesitated a moment, weighing the truth of David's words. Then he nodded and turned toward the exit. "Hurry."

David could see the hole when he turned down the right corridor once more. Something swam past, sloshing even more water past the barge's hull. A hippopotamus in the Mississippi River?

He forgot what he'd seen in the next instant as the loud bark of a gun dumped an extra measure of terror into his blood. As he ran forward, David prayed he wasn't already too late to save Jasmine.

❧

Tabitha looked around, her eyes wild. As water began to trickle under the doorway, she grabbed an empty trunk and threw it onto her bed.

"What are you doing?" Arnold tried to catch hold of her arm, but Tabitha pulled free.

"I have to get my things." She picked up two pairs of shoes and threw them into the trunk. Then she ran to her dressing table, picked up her jewelry box, and added it to the luggage. "Help me!"

Arnold shook his head and tucked away his pistol. "You're crazy, Tabitha. We've got to get out of here now."

She didn't slow down. Gathering up armloads of clothes from all over the room, she shoved them into the trunk, quickly filling it up.

Jasmine edged toward the door. If the two of them wanted to stay here and argue, it was okay with her. She knew how quickly the barge would sink once the water weighed it down. If she could slip past Arnold, she would make a run for it. He might chase her, but she'd stand a better chance of getting away once she was out of Tabitha's suite.

"Don't move another step." Arnold stopped trying to reason with Tabitha and aimed his weapon at Jasmine's head.

Jasmine froze. It looked like she wouldn't make it out alive after all. Water slipped around her ankles, raising the hair on her arms as she waited for the blast of Arnold's pistol.

"Put down that gun and help me." Tabitha shouted. She slammed the lid on the overfilled trunk and jerked it off the bed. Something happened then. Either the bed moved or Tabitha's feet slipped, Jasmine wasn't exactly sure. But the effect was disastrous. The heavy trunk became a missile, slamming Tabitha into the wall beside her. With a loud thud, the woman's head struck the wall, and she slid to the floor, her eyes shut.

Instinct sent Jasmine plunging toward Tabitha as the pistol went off, the bullet whizzing harmlessly past her. She didn't have time for thought. All she knew was that Tabitha would drown if they couldn't rouse her. "Put that stupid gun down and come help me. We've got to get her out of here."

"Aren't you something?" The contempt in Arnold's voice coupled with the icy water that rose with every passing second sent a cold shiver down her back. "I promise she wouldn't waste any time saving you."

The door slammed open, David's blazing green gaze locking onto her face.

"Watch out!" Jasmine called out the warning as Arnold threw himself at David, a murderous glint in his eyes.

She watched helplessly as the two men struggled, wincing as Arnold managed to land several blows. But then David began to gain the upper hand, his fists punishing the other man until Arnold finally stopped fighting and threw up his hands in a defensive posture. David stepped back, breathing hard, and swiped away a trickle of blood from the edge of his mouth. "Get your hands behind your back."

Arnold's expression turned fearful. "What are you going to do?"

"I'm going to arrest you as soon as we get out of here." David glanced around, his gaze lighting on a scarf draped across Tabitha's dressing table. As he moved forward to get it, Arnold shoved him hard. David went down to one knee. Before he could recover his balance, the other man fled through the open door.

Jasmine looked down at Tabitha's pale face. A large lump had formed on the woman's forehead, probably the reason she was still out cold. "Help me with Tabitha."

David glanced toward the doorway, shook his head, and moved toward her. "You go on. I'll get her."

Screams from somewhere nearby made her catch her breath. It sounded like Arnold had met his match. Even if he had been ready to kill her, she could not find any pleasure in whatever caused his shrieks. "I'm not leaving you alone."

David's sigh was louder than the water rushing into the room. "You never do what I tell you to do."

Heedless of the danger surrounding them, she smiled at him. "I'm just trying to save her life so she'll have a chance to know the Lord. Someone once reminded me how important a job that is."

His eyes softened. "Come on." He put his hands under Tabitha's knees and back, lifting her with a grimace. "When Rafe picked up Angelica, he made it look effortless."

Jasmine was glad to hear the couple was safe. Time was running out. She stood and realized the water had risen to the height of her knees. Would they be able to get out before the barge was completely engulfed?

When she stepped into the hall, Jasmine could see the hole in the side of the barge. A movement close to the opening made her squint toward it. She raised a hand and pointed. "Is that a lion?" A growl answered her question.

"A floating circus hit us." David whispered the information. "Rafe said some of the animals got loose."

As Jasmine's eyesight adjusted to the dim corridor, she saw the snarl that revealed the animal's deadly teeth. She clutched David's arm. "Is that what happened to Arnold?"

He nodded and inclined his head toward the other end of the hallway. "We need to get back to the staircase now. I don't think the lion will attack us unless he feels cornered, but I don't really want to test that theory."

They pushed through the rising water, reaching the stairs after what seemed an eternity. As they climbed out of the water, Jasmine realized how tense her shoulders were. She had expected every moment to feel the lion's claws tear into her back. She held open the door to the theater, expecting to see further evidence of the devastation caused by the collision. The room was canted at an odd angle, but that was the only indication something was wrong. Jasmine picked up her wet skirts and hurried after David.

When they reached the door to the outside, she felt like she was walking into a maelstrom. Voices shouted, and people were running back and forth from the *Ophelia* to the floating circus. A pair of elephants stood on the bank, their giant ears moving back and forth like great gray wings. Monkeys chattered and ran between the legs of the circus performers like rambunctious children. A large tiger, thankfully still confined, paced the length of its cage and growled at anyone who dared approach.

"There they are!" Jasmine heard Clem's voice and saw her friend jumping up and down as though her feet were made of coils.

Rafe ran across the gangplank and took Tabitha from David. "Did the lion attack you?"

David shook his head. "Arnold Garth wasn't so lucky."

"I see." Rafe settled the unconscious woman against his shoulder before heading back to the riverbank.

"I didn't think you would come for me, David." A shudder shook Jasmine's aching shoulders as they followed a few steps behind Rafe. She let her skirts drop to keep from displaying her legs to the curious onlookers. "You said you were done pulling me out of scrapes."

He looked straight ahead, his stride long. "Old habits die hard."

"Thank you anyway." Jasmine's wet skirts made it impossible to keep up with him. When he realized she had fallen behind, David turned around, his green gaze seeing more than she wanted. With a roll of his eyes, he came back and lifted her into his arms. "Don't you know yet that I'll always come rescue you?"

She put an arm around his shoulders and let her head drop down to his chest. She might be wet and exhausted, but Jasmine had never felt quite so treasured in her whole life.

Chapter Thirty-three

"I still find it hard to believe Tabitha Barlow is a bank robber." Clem sat on the bright, dimity-covered window seat, her scissors and a large square of cloth in her hands.

"I know." Jasmine wandered over and sat next to her, looking down at a carriage traveling along First Street. She was glad their boardinghouse faced the river. It afforded them an ever-changing view of the traffic and people. "I was so shocked when I heard her and Arnold discussing their plans."

"You were very brave to go to her room for the evidence."

"That's not how David phrased it."

Clem giggled. "He was upset because he doesn't like the idea of you getting hurt. That man loves you."

"Do you really think so?" Jasmine could feel the heat burning her cheeks. "He hasn't been by but once since the accident."

"He's got a lot to do. Trust me, he'll be here as soon as he can."

"I still can't believe the *Ophelia* is gone."

Clem snipped at a corner of the cloth and sighed. "I know. All those lovely costumes."

"Now you sound like Tabitha."

"Heaven forbid. Did she really try to get all her clothes packed into trunks?"

"And her shoes and jewelry." Jasmine could hardly believe it either. She still cringed to think of Tabitha's compulsion to save her material belongings over her life. The poor woman really didn't understand what was important.

Anyone looking at the dock today would never realize the drama that had played out there three days earlier. She sighed and turned away from the window. "I suppose it's a blessing how few people actually died that afternoon."

"Poor Arnold." Clem pursed her lips as she studied the material. "Imagine running directly into the path of that dangerous beast."

"The newspaper said the animals are being kept in several warehouses while new cages are made to replace those that couldn't be salvaged from the wreck." Jasmine wandered to the writing desk in one corner of their room, looking at the note she had written to her sisters. She had spent all morning on that task, trying to apologize for her actions. It was difficult to explain the choices she had made over the past months. Looking back, she barely understood the reasons herself. At least the letter would let them know she was unhurt and that she was coming home.

Clem picked up a doll and measured the length of cloth against it. "Do you think Rafe and Angelica will be happy?"

Jasmine watched her friend work on her project. "Is that who the doll is for?"

"Oh, no. It's for Mrs. O'Hara's daughter."

"The lady who owns the boardinghouse?" Jasmine was surprised Clem would put so much effort into a dress for a stranger's child. "I hope she appreciates getting an original design by a seamstress as talented as you."

"Since Mr. and Mrs. Easley have decided not to buy another showboat, I need something to do." Clem took out her needle and a spool of white thread.

"You could get a job on a different showboat. I'm sure the Easleys would give you a good reference."

Clem stitched away with her usual speed. "I'm tired of living on the river."

Jasmine was surprised by her friend's statement. She thought Clem loved the theater, or at least the costume work she did. Did she share Jasmine's disillusionment because of the immorality and greed rampant among the *Ophelia*'s actors? "What will you do?"

"Mrs. O'Hara's sister owns a millinery shop. She thinks I can probably get a job there if I prove I have sufficient talent." Clem grinned at her. "So now you see that my charitable work will benefit me as well as our landlady's daughter."

"I'm glad you've decided not to return to the theater." Jasmine tapped the table with one finger. "It's so different from what I expected. So debauched. I expected a world of excitement and adulation, not lechers and bank robbers."

"So you're not going to be an actress anymore?" Clem's needle halted midstitch. "What will you do?"

"Go home, I guess." Jasmine sighed. "I'm not really sure."

Choked laughter answered her sigh. "Save your melodrama for somebody else. I know a certain handsome detective who's not going to let you get very far away."

"Perhaps." Jasmine remembered the way David had carried her across the gangplank. "All I know is I need to pray about what God wants me to do for the future."

"You really are serious about this God stuff, aren't you?" Clem put down the doll dress, her gaze sober.

"I know I haven't been a very good example to you and the others on the *Ophelia*." Jasmine found the words difficult to say out loud. "Being a Christian is a very serious matter, something I forgot for a while. Christ lives in my heart. He's the One I want to keep my eyes on, the One I want to follow, no matter what. In a way, Tabitha helped me see how silly I had been. When she started packing that trunk as the ship was sinking, it dawned on me that I was guilty of the same thing—putting emphasis on the things of this world, things that have no eternal value. Jesus said that our hearts would be in the same place as our treasures. I forgot that for a while."

"I can't tell you I'm ready to make a commitment today, but I have seen a difference in you. And I like it." Clem resumed her handwork. "I hope you'll pray for me."

"I always do." Jasmine found encouragement in Clem's words. "But don't delay too long. We never know when death may be lurking around a corner. Arnold's death was terrible, the circumstances of course. But the worst thing of all is that he may not have been saved when he left this world. The idea of anyone having to be separated from God forever is too horrifying to consider."

"I see what you mean." Clem's thoughtful gaze raked her face.

Deciding to leave the subject for now, Jasmine made a promise to herself to redouble her prayers for Clem's salvation. She knew God loved Clem as much as she did. And His business was calling people to Him.

"What will happen to Vance?"

David winced at Jasmine's question. Did she still care for the man, after all? He had hoped, dreamed even, that she returned his feelings. They had seemed to grow so close after leaving Cairo. Had it been nothing more than an act on her part? "The charges of murder and armed robbery were dropped, but he's pled guilty to theft. He'll have to serve time."

Standing on the deck of the *Coriander*, he watched as they once again reached the intersection of the Ohio and Mississippi Rivers. How appropriate. His feelings were as turbulent as the merging currents below their boat.

He angled a look at Jasmine. Her beauty had deepened to a new level, a realization that made his heart ache.

"I still can't believe he stole money from the Easleys. From all of us on the *Ophelia*." A strand of her coal-black hair escaped from Jasmine's coiffure and brushed her cheek.

David's fingers itched to smooth it back, let his fingers caress her soft skin. He gripped the rail tighter instead. "He proved unworthy of the trust you placed in him."

"Maybe he'll change while he's in prison."

He should be warmed by her obvious faith in the man, but he was too human to completely avoid a wave of resentment. He cleared his throat and searched for a different subject. "Tabitha's facing more serious charges. She was involved in two murders and more than a dozen robberies. I don't see how she'll avoid being hanged."

Jasmine brushed the hair away from her face. "I can't help but remember how she tried to warn me away from the theater when I first began to gain recognition aboard the *Ophelia*. I didn't realize at the time that she had my best interests at heart."

"I imagine her motives were more about self-protection than altruism." He didn't want to hurt Jasmine, but she needed to understand how evil Tabitha really was. He remembered the interview he'd conducted after she was placed under arrest. She had tried to place blame on everyone but herself, painting herself as victim rather than villain. First it was Arnold Garth who had led her astray, then Vance Hargrove. She had even accused Clem and Jasmine of trying to usurp her position on the *Ophelia*. "She was jealous of you."

The errant strand of hair returned to Jasmine's cheek, tempting his fingers once more. "She may never change, but at least we gave her time to consider eternity. I hope she'll listen to God's voice before it's too late."

David's pain receded a little. Even if they were not meant to be together, at least he could rejoice in Jasmine's resurgent faith. "You're really serious about all this now, aren't you?"

"I'm sorry for my rebellion." She sighed and pushed her hair back once more. "I see now what you and my sisters were trying to tell me. I thought life in the theater was a magical existence, but now I understand that it's nothing more than a dangerous illusion."

"I don't know if you should rush to the other extreme, Jasmine. Over the past weeks, I've seen you and the others work together to create something special. Who knows what lives you may have touched, what lessons your plays might teach about the hazards of making immoral choices?"

David hoped she understood his point. While he didn't like the loose lifestyles of the actors on the *Ophelia*, he could see that a troupe of actors who were Christians might be able to use the stage to advance sound principles and even plant the seeds of salvation.

Her violet eyes widened in surprise. "I can't believe you said that."

"Why not? The theater is not evil in itself."

"That may be true, but it's still not the life for me." Her chin jutted out.

David suppressed his smile. No matter what happened to Jasmine, she would always be headstrong. He loved that about her. "What do you plan to do once you return to Natchez?"

"Rest for a while, I guess. Maybe I'll help Camellia teach the local children. I'm not really sure what God wants me to do at this point."

"I have an idea." David wanted to bite his tongue off. When would he learn to keep his mouth shut? He hadn't planned to say anything to Jasmine about what she should do next. It wasn't any of his business. If he'd ever thought they might have a future together, she had made her choice abundantly clear when she'd sighed over Vance's fate.

Shivering, Jasmine pulled her shawl up over her shoulders. "Are you going to tell me what it is or leave me guessing?"

"Are you cold?"

Jasmine raised her eyebrows. "A little, but I'm not going in until you tell me your idea."

"I was thinking about your work with the cast." David decided he might as well take the plunge. The worst she could do was laugh at him. "You witnessed to Angelica, helped Rafe keep his job, and even talked me into joining the performance. You have a real talent for management. If you combine that with your love for all things theatrical, maybe you could have your own theatrical company."

He held his breath and refused to look at Jasmine while she considered the idea.

"I don't know. . . ."

He let out his breath, interrupting her attempt to let him down easy. "Forget it. It's a stupid idea."

"No, it's not. It's brilliant." She put a hand on his arm. "You're brilliant. I was going to say that I don't know why I didn't think of it myself. It doesn't have to be on a grand scale like the theater on the *Ophelia*. I could teach young men and women how to act while keeping their Christian values intact."

David nodded, glad to see her so excited.

Jasmine stared up at him, her violet gaze suddenly serious. "Would you come to see the productions?"

"I'm sure I could visit Natchez from time to time." Although he wasn't sure if he could stand seeing her married to anyone else.

"So you're going back to Chicago?" Her hand fell away from his arm. "I had hoped you might find—"

He waited for her to finish her sentence, sighing when she turned away and hid her face from him. "What did you hope I would find?"

"Oh, never mind. It was a silly idea, anyway." Her words were whipped away by the wind, their meaning unclear.

He would never understand her. David wanted to walk away, leave her standing on the deck by herself. But something. . .some One whispered that he should stay. "Please tell me what you were going to say."

Were her shoulders shaking? He hadn't meant to make her cry.

David locked his own emotions away and reached for Jasmine, pulling her into a brotherly embrace. "I'm sorry. I didn't mean to upset you. Of course I'll be there for you. At least until you have a husband to watch out over you. It's the least a brother can do."

Jasmine gasped and pulled away from his embrace. When she turned to face him, her beautiful eyes were filled with annoyance instead of tears. "I am not and never have been your sister, David Foster. Don't you know yet that you're the only man I could ever love?"

Her words broke down the barriers between them. But he didn't take her in his arms yet. He still had a matter that needed to be straightened out. "I thought you liked Vance's kisses more than mine."

She shook her head, a blush spreading across her cheeks. "I was upset when I told you that. Vance kissed me once, but it was nothing to compare to the way I feel in your arms."

His last reservation disappeared. David opened his arms to her, his mind full of thankfulness. Even the river seemed to sing with joy as their lips met in a kiss that warmed his blood and sealed the bond between them.

Epilogue

Natchez, Mississippi
December 10, 1870

Lily stood on tiptoe and draped a pine garland over the door to the dining room. "It seems like only a few weeks ago that you were the one getting married on the *Water Lily*."

Camellia's gaze looked past her shoulder, and a smile curved her lips upward. "Yes, but then again sometimes it seems like Jonah and I have been together for decades."

"In a way you have. Or at least you've known him for that long." Lily stepped back to assess their decorations.

The smell of pine permeated the room. Holly boughs festooned with red berries decorated the row of windows. Camellia had brought crystal vases from Les Fleurs and gossamer tulle swags for the tables that would hold Papa and Tessie's wedding dinner in a few short hours. They still needed to place the chairs for the families, but then everything would be ready.

Jasmine walked into the room, her cheeks as red as the holly berries. "I'm so glad it stopped raining."

"Is the change in temperature the reason for those roses in your cheeks?" Camellia bent a playful frown in her direction.

Lily couldn't hide her smile as Jasmine's cheeks darkened further. It was sweet to see their little sister so much in love. Especially since she had finally come to her senses and realized what everyone else had known for a while—she was deeply in love with David Foster. "I imagine it has more to do with her escort than the weather."

Jasmine blew out an impatient breath. "Stop it."

As her laughter blended with Camellia's, Lily opened her arms wide and caught Jasmine in a brief hug. "I'm sorry, honey. It's just that we're so happy for the two of you."

"That's right." Camellia nodded, her blond curls bobbing around her face. "But I don't understand why you're waiting until spring to marry. You and David should join Papa and Tessie at the altar today."

Jasmine emerged from the hug and shook her head. "Today's their day. We can wait. Besides, I've always wanted to be a June bride. The flowers are so abundant then. I can just imagine how beautiful the garden at Les Fleurs will be."

"I think Jasmine is saying she doesn't care for our decorations." Lily put her hands on her hips and pursed her lips.

Camellia gasped and pointed a finger in her direction. "You look so much like Aunt Dahlia when you do that."

"Please." Lily relaxed her mouth.

"No, it's true." Jasmine looked from her face to Camellia's. "And she also looks a little like Grandmother, don't you think?"

Now Lily's cheeks were redder than Jasmine's. Her sisters circled around her, their frowns nearly identical. "No matter what you say, I refuse to believe I'll ever be as sour as our aunt."

"Of course you won't." Camellia stopped in front of her. "I love Aunt Dahlia, but she's mired in the past. You've got your sights on the future with this new shipping venture."

Lily let a relieved breath escape. She'd always wanted to be as adventurous as their mother. "I'm glad you and Jonah decided to invest, too. Eli and Renée are going to handle getting river shipments onto the rails from their office in Memphis. The only ones we have left to get involved are Jasmine and David."

"Perhaps later." Jasmine started to pull off her cloak. "Once we get more settled."

Lily had news she could hardly wait to share with her younger sister. "Blake and Jean Luc were talking about hiring the Pinkerton Agency to protect our shipments from bandits and Indians. I'm hoping they can insist on having David oversee the operations."

Jasmine's motions halted. "Really? That would be exciting. Maybe he and I could even travel together."

Camellia stomped her foot to get their attention. "Why is everyone so interested in leaving Natchez?"

Lily put a comforting hand around Camellia's waist. "This will always be our home. You and Jonah are doing a wonderful job with the sharecroppers and the family's assets. You're the linchpin that holds us together."

Jasmine nodded, her beautiful violet eyes wide. "Besides, you know you're the only one who can reason with Aunt Dahlia."

Camellia's eyes were suspiciously moist, but she laughed at Jasmine's mischievous expression. "You're a minx."

"I know."

Lily was nearly overcome with her own tears, her heart threatening to explode with pride and joy over her sisters. "I love you."

Jasmine's face lost its playfulness. "One thing I realized while I was on the *Ophelia* is how much I owe to you, Lily. I'm ashamed of my blindness to all the sacrifices you've made over the years."

"They're not sacrifices to me." Emotion clogged Lily's throat, making it difficult to talk.

"Jasmine's right." Camellia put both arms around her. "You fought everyone to make sure we could live our lives in the ways we chose."

Lily tightened the muscles in her throat to keep from melting into a puddle of tears. She felt Jasmine's hug in addition to Camellia's. Had anyone ever been so blessed?

After a few minutes, peace settled over her. Lily returned the hugs from her sisters. "It's an honor to help you when I can. I just hate the times we've been at cross-purposes."

"We're together now." Jasmine's voice sounded as choked as her own. "And we'll always be sisters."

Lily closed her eyes. "Dear Lord, thank You for all the blessings. Thank You for wiping away our tears and giving us 'beauty for ashes, the oil of joy for mourning, the garment of praise for the spirit of heaviness; that they might be called trees of righteousness, the planting of the Lord, that He might be glorified.'"

A brief silence filled the room before Camellia picked up the prayer. "Lord, I want to say thanks for my sister. You're the One who describes a virtuous woman as having a price above rubies. Thank You for filling Lily with all the characteristics that have made her a virtuous woman and a wonderful sister."

Jasmine's voice took over when Camellia stopped. "Thanks, God, for my wonderful Christian sisters. And thank You for watching over all of us so well. Bless our Papa and Tessie as they begin this new chapter of their lives. Help us to be ever mindful of Your love and sovereignty. May we sow Your seeds at every opportunity as we live out our lives in Your service."

"Amen." As she ended the prayer, Lily knew this would be a moment she would always cherish. A moment in which every fear was quieted and only peace remained.

❧

Benjamin stood between Lily and Blake, each of his hands in one of theirs. Noah and Magnolia were immediately ahead of them, their high-pitched whispers betraying their excitement at attending the wedding.

"Shhh." Lily put her free hand across her lips. "You're supposed to be as quiet as little mice, remember?"

Noah looked over his shoulder, his blue eyes full of mischief. "Magnolia doesn't believe Grandpapa is going to be a broom."

Blake chuckled. "Son, I'm afraid I have to agree with your sister."

Magnolia stuck her tongue out at her brother.

Lily prayed for patience. "Magnolia, that is not a ladylike gesture. Noah, Grandpapa is going to be a *groom*. It means a husband."

Noah looked to his father for confirmation, grimacing at Blake's nod. "I was almost right."

"Jensen says, 'A miss is as good as a mile.'" Magnolia raised her chin, a familiar gesture that Lily knew her daughter had learned from her. At least she didn't stick out her tongue again.

Suddenly Lily wanted to gather her family close and try to stop anything from changing them. She could remember Jasmine being as young as Magnolia was now.

She looked into the room they were about to enter, her gaze skipping over the decorations, past the expectant gazes of the guests, and fastening on Anna standing in front of the altar as Tessie's bridesmaid. Her eyes, the same bright blue color as her brother Blake's, matched her silk dress. It was made up in the modern style, with narrowed skirts and a bustle at the back. Lily wasn't sure she liked the bustle, but Camellia had insisted that all of their gowns should reflect the newest fashion.

Jensen and Papa stood on the other side of the altar. Papa looked as nervous as she'd ever seen him. He wiped his hands on the black material of his slacks. It was hard to tell Jensen's mood. His scarred face rarely showed emotion. As she watched, he leaned over and said something to Papa. A smile broke out on Papa's face, and he nodded.

Lily knew it was time. She focused on Noah. "Escort your sister to her place like we practiced."

Her gaze met Blake's as their oldest son held out his arm and Magnolia put her small hand on it. Could anything be more adorable? As she and Blake followed, helping Benjamin between them, she passed Uncle Phillip and Aunt Dahlia, who wore identical smiles this afternoon.

As they reached the front row, she looked to her left and nodded to Mrs. Champney and Jean Luc. His son, Achille, fussed and fidgeted in Jean Luc's lap. Tamar, sitting next to the Champneys, fished in her reticule and produced a stick of candy that the little boy accepted and immediately popped into his mouth.

Jasmine, her hand in David's, grinned at Noah and Magnolia as they sat next to her. On David's far side, Camellia dabbed at her eyes with a lace-edged white handkerchief, the smile on her face indicating that her tears had nothing to do with grief. Seated next to Camellia, her daughter, Amaryllis, swung her legs back and forth. The motion lifted her velvet skirt up with each kick until her father, Jonah, shook his head at her. She subsided with a pout as Lily sat in one of the two remaining seats on this row. Blake sat beside her and put Benjamin in his lap.

A rustle from the back of the room indicated that Tessie had arrived at the doorway. Lily stood with the rest and watched as Anna and Blake's aunt stepped into the room. Dressed in a white dress with deep flounces, the older woman radiated joy. Her veil floated around her like a rising mist as she moved forward, her gaze fastened on Papa's face. For an instant Lily was transported back in time as she glanced toward her father. The smile on his face was one she'd forgotten. She hadn't seen it since her mother died. In that moment, she knew Papa and Tessie would be happy together.

Time collapsed and expanded. Past, present, and future seemed to come together in one confusing instant as intense longing swept Lily. Where had the years gone? It seemed she'd only blinked her eyes and her baby sister Jasmine was all grown up and ready to leave home. Would it be the same with Magnolia? The future seemed so uncertain at times. How would she ever cope? What would their lives be like in another fourteen or fifteen years? Tears burned at the corners of her eyes.

"Is everything okay?" Blake's gaze met hers, at once concerned and empathetic.

"Yes." Lily could feel the pain ebbing as God covered her confusion with His grace. "I'm just being silly."

A smile chased away her husband's frown. "I love you, Lily."

She lifted her chin and returned his smile. "I love you, too."

As they sat side by side and listened to Papa and Tessie repeat their vows, a verse from the last book of the Bible came to her. *"And God shall wipe away all tears from their eyes; and there shall be no more death, neither sorrow, nor crying, neither shall there be any more pain: for the former things are passed away."* She and Blake—all the members of her family—had endured trials and tears, from the ever-changing fortunes of life on the river to the deaths of loved ones. But no matter what happened, faith guided them like a beacon in the night. Whatever the future held, she could rejoice knowing that God's promises transcended all else.

Diane T. Ashley, a "town girl" born and raised in Mississippi, has worked more than twenty years for the House of Representatives. She rediscovered a thirst for writing, was led to a class taught by Aaron McCarver, and became a founding member of the Bards of Faith.

Aaron McCarver is a transplanted Mississippian who was raised in the mountains near Dunlap, Tennessee. He loves his jobs of teaching at Belhaven University and editing for Barbour Publishing and Summerside Press. A member of ACFW, he is coauthor with Gilbert Morris of the bestselling series, The Spirit of Appalachia. He now coauthors with Diane Ashley on several historical series.

If you enjoyed

The Song of the River Trilogy

be sure to read. . .

Mississippi

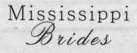

Brides

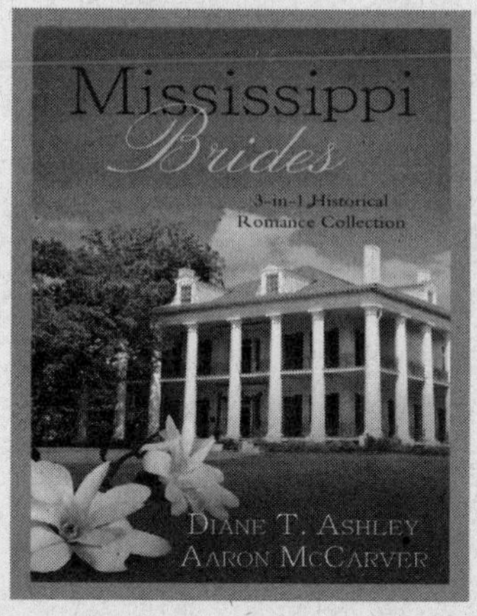

Three historical romances from writing duo

Diane T. Ashley and Aaron McCarver